The
Margarets

ALSO BY SHERI S. TEPPER

The Awakeners

After Long Silence

The Gate to Women's Country

Beauty

Grass

Raising the Stones

Sideshow

A Plague of Angels

Shadow's End

Gibbon's Decline and Fall

The Family Tree

Six Moon Dance

Singer from the Sea

The Fresco

The Visitor

The Companions

M A R G

An Imprint of HarperCollins*Publishers*

The Margarets

Sheri S.
Tepper

THE MARGARETS. Copyright © 2007 by Sheri S. Tepper. All rights reserved. Printed in the United States of America. No part of this book may be used or reproduced in any manner whatsoever without written permission except in the case of brief quotations embodied in critical articles and reviews. For information address HarperCollins Publishers, 10 East 53rd Street, New York, NY 10022.

HarperCollins books may be purchased for educational, business, or sales promotional use. For information please write: Special Markets Department, HarperCollins Publishers, 10 East 53rd Street, New York, NY 10022.

FIRST EDITION

Designed by Sunil Manchikanti

Library of Congress Cataloging-in-Publication Data

Tepper, Sheri S.
    The Margarets / Sheri S. Tepper.—1st ed.
        p. cm.
    ISBN: 978-0-06-117065-2
    ISBN-10: 0-06-117065-8
        1. Science fiction.

    PS3570.E673 M37 2007
    813'.54 22   2006047079

07   08   09   10   11   WBC/RRDH   10   9   8   7   6   5   4   3   2   1

In fond memory of
my friend of sixty-three years,
LAMBERT J. LARSON,
without whose encouragement
I would never have written a word

THE MARGARETS

Bargom, Adille's patron
Lady Ephedra, K'Famira, owner of House Mousselline
Progzo, Adille's father
Draug B'lango, Adille's clan leader
The Hill of Beelshi (site of unspeakable rites)

THAIRY (Human colony planet, also occupied by the Gibbekot)
Town of Bright
Naumi, [a Margaret] foster son of Rastarong
Mr. Wyncamp, school manager
Mr. Weathereye, elderly, odd personage with one eye
various citizens and louts
Fort Point Zibit (site of the academy)
Captain Orley, commandant
Sergeant Orson, in charge of first-year cadets
Grangel, cadet and lout
Jaker, Flek, Poul, Caspor and Ferni, cadets and Naumi's friends

TERCIS (Human colony planet, divided into "Walled-Offs")
Hostility (a Walled-Off)
Rueful (a Walled-Off)
Contrition City
Repentance (a large town)
Remorseful (a small town, site of the school, also a river)
Deep Shameful (a hamlet)
Crossroads (a village in The Valley)
Grandma Mackey [a Margaret]
Dr. Bryan Mackey, her husband
Maybelle and Mayleen, Margaret's daughters
James Joseph Judson (Jimmy Joe), Maybelle's husband
    Til and Jeff, their twin sons
    Gloriana, their daughter
    Falija, Glory's fosterling
Billy Ray Judson, Mayleen's husband
    Joe Bob and Billy Wayne (twin sons)
    Ella May and Janine Ruth (twin daughters)
    Benny Paul, son, twin died at birth
    Trish, daughter, twin died at birth
    Sue Elaine and Lou Ellen, twin daughters
    Orvie John, son, twin died at birth
    Little Emmaline, daughter, twin died at birth
        [At time of story, Billy Wayne has gone off to the army,
        Ella May has joined the Siblinghood of Silence, and Janine
        Ruth has moved to Contrition City.]

Pastor Grievy
Abe Johnson
Bamber Joy, Abe's foster son
Others mentioned in passing

FAJNARD (formerly Gentheran planet taken over by the Frossians)
The Fastness—where Gentherans still live
The Grasslands—occupied by
The umox farm
Medicines sans Limites. Volunteer doctors, human
Frossians
Mar-agern, [a Margaret] bondslave, herdewoman
Umoxen, wool-bearing animals, or perhaps not
Ghoss, humans, somewhat modified
Deen-agern, a Ghoss
Rei-agern, a Ghoss
Various Frossian slave drivers and overlords
Howkel and Mrs. Howkel, hayraiders
Mirabel and Maniacal, two of their children
Gizzardiles: inimical creatures

HELL (distant, little-known planet with a tragic history)
One buried Gentheran ship
Wilvia [a Margaret]

CRANESROOST (Human colony planet)

EDEN (Human colony planet)

B'YURNGRAD (Human colony planet)
The prairies, temperate zone
The Siblinghood
The Tribes, former bondslaves of violent disposition
Dark Runner, a tribal boy and man
Wolf Mother, a shamaness
M'urgi, [a Margaret] her apprentice
Fernwold, M'urgi's lover, a member of the Siblinghood
The icelands, an area of severe winters
B'Oag, an oasthouse keeper
Ojlin, his son
G'lil, a young woman rescued at the last moment
Ogric, a worker

AMBIGUOUS INDIVIDUALS OR THINGS OF VARIOUS OR UNCERTAIN LOCATION

Ghyrm, a deadly parasite

Mr. Weathereye

Lady Badness

The Gardener

Dweller in Pain

Flayed One-Drinker of Blood

Whirling Cloud of Darkness-Eater of the Dead

Sysarou, Gentheran Goddess of Abundance and Joy

Ohanja, Gentheran God of Honor, Duty, and Kindness

NONHUMAN RACES

Baswoidin: ancient, secretive, superior

Elos: Omniont race, graceful, sneery, arrogant

Frossian: Mercan race, boneheaded, vaguely humanoid, malign

Garrick: related to the Gentherans

Gentherans: mysterious, beneficent

Gibbekot: humanoid, furry, small

Hrass: Omniont race, tapirlike, unassuming, dirty, cringing

K'Famir: Mercan race, four-legged, four-armed, vicious

K'Vasti: Mercan race, distantly related to K'Famir, less vicious

Pthas: ancient, very wise, now presumed extinct or departed

Quaatar: Mercan race, ancient, prideful, arrogant, vengeful

Thongal: Mercans, hireling spies and killers

Trajians: a very ancient itinerant race, famous as entertainers

ORGANIZATIONS

Siblinghood of Silence: a secret organization including humans and
Gentherans

ISTO: Interstellar Trade Organization. A regulatory organization of all races
engaging in interstellar trade

IGC: Intergalactic Court. The final arbiter in conflicts among races

Mercan Combine: Confederation of vile races united by proximity, race,
language, commerce

Omniont Federation: Similar to the Mercan Combine, but less cutthroat
and more concerned with ethics

Dominion Central Authority: Oversight body set up by the Gentherans to
represent off-Earth humans

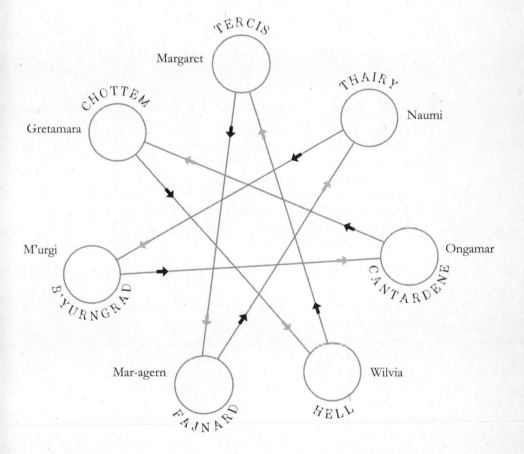

TERCIS

Margaret

CHOTTEM

THAIRY

Naumi

Gretamara

M'urgi

Ongamar

B'YURNGRAD

CANTARDENE

Mar-agern

Wilvia

FAJNARD

HELL

The
Margarets

What the Gardener Told Me
Might Have Happened

Once a very long time ago, between fifty and a hundred thousand years, a small group of humans fleeing from predators took refuge in a cave. Clinging to one another during the night, they heard a great roaring, louder and more fierce than the roars of the beasts they knew, and when they peeked out at dawn, they saw that a moon had fallen out of the sky. The sun was just rising, the changeable baby moon they were used to was with Mother Sun, so the fallen moon belonged to someone else.

The someone elses were walking here and there, clanking and creaking. Ahn, the leader of the people, noticed holes around the bottom of the moon, open holes as large as caves. The clanking things were frightening, but not so scary as the animals howling among the nearest trees. Ahn, the leader, had no memory of such things; neither did any of the other of his people. No clanking things. No falling moons.

Ahn nodded, thoughtfully. It was harder when it was a new thing. If they had a memory of the thing, it was easier to figure out what to do. Otherwise, they had to decide, then see what would happen. It did seem to Ahn, however, that hiding inside the moon was a good idea. When the moon went back up into the sky, the beasts couldn't follow. The holes smelled strange, so Ahn went first in case there were bad things inside.

2 Sheri S. Tepper

Just as there had been no memory of fallen moons, there had been no memory of those who owned the moon: the Quaatar, who disliked being fooled with, bothered by, or trespassed upon by anything. Even if Ahn had had such a memory, the immediacy of his people's situation might have made him risk it. Since he did not know it, he had no qualms about leading his people up the vent tubes and thence into a hydroponic oasis.

The ship's robots found nothing worth ravening upon the world; the ship departed. Inside, the stowaways lived rather pleasantly on the juicy bodies of small furry vermin that infested the ship and the garden produce that fed the noncarnivorous creatures aboard. When the ship finally landed, the people went out to find themselves not in the sky, as they had expected, but rather upon some other world, where their eager senses informed them there were no predators at all. The world was a paradise, and they fled into it.

Ahn's people never knew how they got there; the Quaatar were and are a little-known people. The females are said to be solitary, aquatic, and planet-bound. The males return to the water only to breed. It is said if one imagines a huge, multilegged lizard, hundreds of years old, who is able to talk and count from one to six, one has imagined a Quaatar. The race became starfaring only by accident. Early in their evolutionary history, they were approached by an advanced people who offered to trade for mining rights on the several lifeless, metal-rich planets of the system. Galactic Law required that they need deal only with the most numerous indigenous group. The Quaatar demanded first that three lesser tribes, the Thongal, Frossians, and K'Famir, who had long ago branched treacherously from the Quaatar genetic line, be wiped out. Since Galactic Law did not permit such a thing, the mining concessionaires offered many other inducements, finally agreeing, among other things, to move the other tribes or races far away. The Thongal, Frossians, and K'Famir, all of whom were more agile and far cleverer than the Quaatar, had no objection at all to being removed from the dismal swamps of Quaatar and given drier planets of their own. They were accordingly transported, leaving the Quaatar alone and unchallenged in their insistence that themselves, their world, and their language were sacred and inviolable.

For generations the Quaatar traded mining rights for fancy uniforms, medals, starships, and spare parts plus an endless supply of non Quaatar mechs, techs, and astrogators to keep the ships flying. Though Quaatar owned the ships and appropriated all the fancy titles (captain, chief science officer, and so on), they never learned how to go from point A to point B without relying on non-Quaatar crew members who could count much higher than six to take them there.

The Quaatar had not known they had stowaways until they saw Ahn's people leaving the ship and disappearing into the underbrush. The sight infuriated them. It should be mentioned that an infuriated Quaatar is something no reasonable individual wants to deal with. An aroused Quaatar is somewhat comparable to a tsunami engendered by an earthquake measuring eight or nine on the Richter scale while several supervolcanoes erupt simultaneously during a category five hurricane. The Quaatar ordered the ship to destroy the planet and were dissuaded only when the automatic system governor harshly reminded them the Galactic Court would not allow destruction of living planets.

Quaatar annoyance, once aroused, however, had to be slaked, not least because their vessel, sacred to the holy Quaatar race, had been defiled and would have to be resanctified. All non-Quaatar personnel were sequestered, for their own safety, while every deck was washed down with the blood of sacrificial victims (a supply of whom were always carried on Quaatar ships), who were first flayed to yield skins with which the entire exterior hull had to be scrubbed. Finally, skin, bones, and remaining tissue were ritually burned. This was time-consuming, yielding only mild amusement during the flaying part, and it was all the fault of the stowaways.

When the ritual was completed, the Quaatar turned their attention back to vengeance. Honor demanded that revenge be exacted upon those who had committed the trespass. Since the Quaatar could not find the beings who had fled the ship, they decided to maim them from a distance by using a recently and illicitly obtained brain block ray, which could be set to atrophy parts of the brain of any animal that had one. Since they had no sample stowaway to set the machine with (and would have been unlikely to do it correctly had they had one), they entered an arbitrary and random setting, trusting that their god, Dweller in Pain, who had been properly propitiated, would see to the seemliness of the punishment.

Accordingly, the stowaways' brains were fried. This left untouched the race from which they had come, which was equally guilty since it had produced the offenders. The Quaatar "captain" ordered the ship to be returned to the penultimate planet, where the brain block ray, still on the same setting, was set to cover the entire surface of the world during one complete revolution.

When the Quaatar departed, they left monitors behind to send images they later watched with great gratification as several generations of the creatures struggled to compensate for their new handicap. The ray had not made them completely mindless. It had merely wiped out the memory of certain things. This loss was a considerable handicap, however, and by the time several generations had passed, there were only fifteen or twenty thousand of them left.

"Can they ever get it back?" a junior Quaatar asked its elder. Very young Quaatar sometimes had ideas, before their brains solidified.

The senior drew itself up pompously. "There is no it! The it no longer exists!"

"Legend says everything exists, you know, where Keeper keeps everything."

"Tah. Is dirty K'Famir legend! If kept, is in a place these filth could never find, never!"

"Somebody says Pthas did."

"Tss," the senior sneered. "Dirty K'Famir legend says Pthas went many places nobody wanted them. K'Famir say Keeper much annoyed by visit of Pthas. K'Famir say Keeper changed rules, told Pthas only person walking seven roads at once can ever see Keeper. That is like saying nobody, never. That is good thing. Seven is unlucky for Quaatar. Six is enough number."

"If something had seven all-same-time universes, it could . . ."

"Enough!" roared the senior. "You are bad-lucking us with utterance? You want go in hold with sacrifices? You want skinning?"

The junior member tardily, wisely, kept silent.

Before continuing their journey, the Quaatar celebrated by torturing several of the non-Quaatar crew members, whose families later received the generous life insurance payments that had been guaranteed by the mining interests before the crew members could have been ordered onto the Quaatar vessel. Thereafter the Quaatar often talked about their vengeance with others of their kind, though always without mentioning the return to the planet of origin or the use to which certain crew members had been put. The return had not been approved by the chiefs of Quaatar, and both the torture of crew members and the use of the brain block was specifically forbidden by the Galactic Court, a body greatly feared though not at all respected by the Quaatar.

In time the Quaatar crew died, those with whom they had spoken died, and nothing about the happening was remembered except the prejudice that had been engendered against a race of bipedal, naked, rather ugly creatures, forever anathema to the Quaatar. The bipeds were Crnk-cha zibitzi, that is half-brained defilers, which was the worst thing they could have been. When humans finally made it off their home planet, the Quaatar greeted their appearance with revulsion, knowing immediately they were not fit for anything but killing, which was generally true of all other races except the Thongal, K'Famir, and Frossians, who were considered merely dirty and occasionally useful.

On the planet where the stowaways had left the ship, however, the people did go on living. They all knew that something was wrong, but they didn't know what it was. Something was missing, something they'd had before and didn't have anymore. Still, the growths were good to eat, with juicy roots, fruits, nuts, succulent leaves. The women had babies that grew very fast, for there was no hunger on this world. No hunger, no danger, no threats. A good place, this world, even though it had no moon at all. Very soon the word for moon was forgotten.

"Wake up little one," said Ahn's woman to the new baby. "Wake up, take milk, grow up fast." The older children played follow the leader, yelling to one another. "Up the tree, over the stump, down the bank, into the water, back again," they cried. "Right, left, right, left, right, left!"

"The fruit is ripe," the women called. "We should all pick it now, it's so juicy and good. We can dry what's left over." Lots of women were having babies.

Seasons were long in this new world, but eventually the winter came, not a cruel winter, just chilly and unpleasant. The people took mud from the riverbank and piled it into walls. They learned to make thick walls, let them dry, then tunnel through them to get from one room to another. When the rooms were nice and dry, they could build new rooms on top. They made baskets from tree roots and limber branches. "We're going out to get fruit," they cried. "We'll bring a basketful."

They cleared everything from around the mud houses, making a smooth, packed-down place where the women could sit making baskets and the children could play. If the children were too noisy, the men would cry, "Cross the ground! Go into the woods!" The woods were safe; there were no beasts. The words for beasts were forgotten.

Rooms piled on rooms until their dwelling was as high as they could build it. "We have to make room for more," they said. Some of them went a day's journey away and started another tower to house some of the children the women were having. Soon each tower had daughter towers out in the woods, many cleaned places for the women to work and the children to play. They had to go farther now to get fruit and roots, but it was still a very good place.

Time went by. Daughter towers had granddaughter towers and great-granddaughter towers. The people fought over picking grounds. "This is my picking ground, our people's ground! We've always picked here," the men cried, waving clubs. "Go away."

They went away. They had more and more babies. "We need a new place. We have to make room for more," they said. They followed rivers, they went along shores, all over the world. They had babies, and the babies had babies. The food was far less abundant. Each generation the babies were smaller.

Time went by. A plague spread among the people. Most of them died. The forest recovered. The plague stopped, the survivors went on living. Another plague; again the forest recovered. An asteroid struck. The people lived on.

"Wake up," the mothers said. "Wake up, drink."

"Follow," the children cried. "Right, left, right, left."

"Fruit now," the women said. "Now, hurry."

"Commin," cried the children. "We commin."

"My pick ground," the men said, clubbing one another.

Millennia went by. One night, when all the people were asleep, a Gentheran ship landed on a rocky outcropping where there were no towers. Gentherans in their silver suits came out of it and moved around looking at the towers and the cleared ground. They set tiny mobile recorders tunneling into the towers and tiny fliers hovering over the remaining forest. They talked among themselves and to the large ship in orbit.

"It looks like a total extinction coming!" said a Gentheran. "Can we get genetic samples?"

"Not without the permission of the people if they're intelligent."

"It's hard to tell whether they are or not."

"Leave it for now. We can always come back. You want to leave the monitor ship in place for a while?"

"We've never encountered an extinction in process before. It's certainly worth recording."

Accordingly, the large ship burned a deep, round hole in the rocky area, the monitor ship lowered itself into the hole and buried itself, with only a few well-camouflaged antennae and optical lenses exposed. A shuttle picked up the explorers.

On the planet, the people were so hungry they were eating the fungus that grew on the latrine grounds, down at the bottom of the towers. It was tasteless, but it kept them alive. When they couldn't find food, they would bring dead leaves or bark or bodies to put in the latrine grounds for the fungus to grow on.

Most of the women were no longer fat enough to have babies, so they picked special women to fatten and have babies for everyone. The fungus they were eating was full of their own hormones and enzymes; they became smaller and smaller yet. They no longer had teeth. They no longer had hair. Their ears were longer, their eyes smaller.

"Wakwak," woke the sleeping ones. "Rai lef rai lef rai lef," moved the food gatherers. "Krossagroun, krossagroun," they chanted as they went off into the remnants of the forest. "Mepik, mepik," as they searched for anything organic. They had no names. Each one was "me." At night all the "mes" lay curled against the tunnel walls, in the warm, in the safe. Gradually, words lost all meaning. They made sounds, as crickets do.

Time went by. Sometimes in the evenings a long, fat thing would come down right on top of several towers, squashing many of them. Shiny people came out of the ships to dig up several other towers. The shiny people made sounds.

"How many this time?"

"Whatever we can catch."

"What in hell does d'Lornschilde do with them?"

"How should I know. He pays well, that's all I care."

The shiny people pulled "mes" out of the wreckage one by one, discarding those who were injured or dead. They put the live ones in cages, the cages into the long fat thing, then squashed other towers and filled other cages before going away. In towers not yet squashed, the creatures slept curled against the walls, but the long fat thing soon came back, again and again and again . . .

The last time it came, some unsquashed mes ran away and hid at the edge of the sea in a little cave where they could stay warm. When day came, they stayed there, for they had no tower to return to, nothing to pick, no fungus to eat, and the forests were dead. They were very few, and very hungry. Eventually, hunger drove them to try eating the things that grew in the sea . . .

I Am Margaret/on Phobos

This account of the great task undertaken by the Third Order of the Siblinghood is written for my great-grandchildren. Even though they "know" what happened, children, as I know from experience, always want the details. "What happened next?" "What did he say?" "Did they live happily ever after?" The "I" doing the writing am . . . are Margaret. No matter what name I am given wherever I may be, "I" am always Margaret, for this is my story as well as the story of mankind, and the Gentherans, and, possibly, a good part of the galaxy.

When I was about five or six, I liked lying in the window of my bedroom watching the Martian desert move beneath me as the planet whirled. My didactibot taught me how to make a pinwheel out of paper and a pin, and told me to attach it to a railing by the ventilation duct. It whirled and whirled until the hole wore out, and it fell apart. It was the only thing I had ever made, and I wept over it, but my didactibot said in its usual mechanical, self-satisfied voice, that nothing whirls forever, not even planets and stars. At the moment, I thought it was just getting even with me for calling it a diddybot, which it didn't like at all.

That night, on the edge of sleep, however, I remembered that diddybots can't lie or mislead people because truth is built in, and therefore it was true that nothing whirled forever. The end of all whirling meant me, too. Terror grabbed me, and I cried out. Mother came in and comforted me, assuming I was having a bad dream. I didn't know how to tell her I was afraid of being a pinwheel, for she was a pinwheel, too, and someday whatever kept us spinning would wear out, and we would stop.

When I was older, I realized that all sane children come to this realization, but just then it was like a nightmare that I would wake up from. I didn't wake up. It stayed there, that dark hole in the future. Eventually I asked about it. Why did we exist? What were we for? Mother said hush don't think about it. Father said, take care of her, Louise. After a while I realized we never wake up from the nightmare, but we do learn not to think about it.

I watched the Mars surface, near Olympus Mons, where nests of snaky whirlwinds squirmed across the craters. The wind swept the surface all the time, erasing any marks the exploration robots made. Humans didn't do exploration. They stayed in the canyon depths of Valles Marineris except for maintenance trips to the wind generators on the rim. I couldn't see the towers with their huge, balanced vanes from my window, but I knew all about them. I knew about the water mines at the pole, too, where the coring machines chewed the ancient ice into slurry and sent it south, down long pipes to the canyons.

We were on Mars and Phobos because depopulating Earth was urgently important, and Mars was to be colonized as part of Project Compliance, to keep us from being classified as barbarians. I had no idea what that meant, and the didactibot refused to tell me. It didn't lie, but it only told me the things people thought I ought to know, so, obviously, I wasn't supposed to know about barbarians.

I was the only child on Phobos, and most of the things people said to me were politenesses. "Good morning, Margaret." "Too bad, Margaret." "Well done, Margaret." "How are you today, Margaret?" Each of these had an answer I had been taught to give: "Good morning to you, as well." "Yes, it is too bad." "Thank you for noticing." "Very well, thank you for asking." They never said anything different or strange or new.

Besides politenesses, people talked about work. Mother kept records in the hydroponic gardens, and she talked about sorting systems and constructive interfaces. Father worked in the lab, and he talked about new oxygen-creating bacteria and newly constituted biomic-clusters being sent down to the surface. Once I asked Father why they kept on doing it. He said it was to find out what would happen.

I asked if he didn't already know what would happen.

"Tell her," my mother said. "Tell her the way you told me."

Father flushed. "That was private," he said, leaving the room and shutting the door behind him.

Mother shook her head. "He told me about it when we were just getting to know one another. It was romantic and eloquent and non-scientific, so of course he doesn't like to repeat it."

"But you do," I said.

She smiled, a tiny secret smile I had never seen before. "It was a happy time for us, and he was eager about the work. He told me he dreams of creating a paradise down there in the ravines, a world in which all the living things work together to form a functioning mira-cle, something beautiful and marvelous and good. He never told anyone but me."

"But he doesn't know what will happen?"

"Not really, no. Sometimes experiments end up doing the oppo-site of what they intend; some tiny organism is wrong, and everything rots and dies. Other times, the project shows great promise, but it doesn't quite get there. Your father says no one will know for sure until it happens. That's how science works."

The other thing people talked about was the weather down on Mars. Sometimes there were storms that blew up so much sand they hid the planet behind a gray veil. When that happened, I pretended the storm had spun us off into nothingness, and when the dust cleared we'd have gone somewhere else. I didn't tell anyone this. They had been very upset with me when I cried about the pinwheel wear-ing out. I didn't want to upset them again.

The people down in Valles Marineris lived in the "green ravines." That's where the water came out of the polar pipes to be used and collected and used and collected, over and over. Green ravines had transparent roofs. Mirrors on the canyon walls reflected the pale sun-light down through the roofs, and the plants inside produced breath-able air. I thought when I grew up I'd get a job on the surface where

I could live in a green ravine and do something real: run a corer in the water mines or help maintain the wind power stations. Being a child on Phobos Station didn't seem real at all.

Grown-ups on Phobos had regular jobs, but my only job was to be schooled. Each year my didactibot added words to my vocabulary list, and that helped me explain things. I learned that the adults on Phobos were meticulous and painstaking and sedentary. Nobody ever went anywhere or did anything. Everybody had constipation and insomnia. Everyone talked about that, even in front of me. Politenesses, work, weather, constipation, insomnia, and ennui.

The consultants recommended more use of the gym for constipation and insomnia and more attention to hobbies to fight ennui. Phobian hobbies included playing in the orchestra, singing in the chorus, working with the theater group, or joining arts and craft exhibits. Everyone did things or made things fastidiously and meticulously, but not superlatively, so that nobody on station would think they were trying to show off. Showing off or "winning" caused ill feelings. So did criticism.

"But I think his painting is awful," I said once.

"It doesn't matter what you think," my father, Harry Bain, said. "You can find something pleasant to say about it."

"The colors were all muddled," I offered doubtfully.

"Then you say that you appreciate the earthy, organic tones," said Louise Bain, my mother.

One time, when the didactibot and I were getting along better than usual, we decided the wheels on Phobos were greased with meticulous, painstaking, fastidious, and scrupulous insincerity. The didactibot said it could find out if I was musical, or arty, or actorish if I wanted it to, but since no one ever suggested I might be, I assumed children weren't supposed to have ennui and left well enough alone. Diddybot said I was lazy. I don't think I really was.

My pastime was sewing. I did not enjoy it, but it was what Mother did, and Mother felt we should spend time together, "doing something." I actually learned to sew quite well. I made several sets of clothing for myself that were just as good as those brought from Earth on the *Ninja*, the *Piñata*, or the *Santa Claus*. Those were the three ships the Gentherans had given to Earthgov in 2062, shortly after they discovered Earth. The ships were given those names, the Gentherans said, because they had discovered a new world and appeared out of nowhere bearing goodies. It was supposed to be a pun, a kind of joke. I could understand the *Piñata* and *Santa Claus* part but not the *Ninja* part. Ninjas came out of nowhere, too, but they usually damaged people. Anyhow, people said it was nice to know the ETs had a sense of humor. Earthgov couldn't pay for the ships, but the Gentherans didn't mind. They were very helpful. Everyone said so.

Since very few children had ever been born on Phobos, and I was the only one who stayed, no one thought to make provision for entertaining a child, especially not one who was inquisitive or bored, which I was, by age six. By then I had experienced every variation of every possible human encounter—the public ones, at least—and I was tired of them all. I started hiding in corners and behind doors, listening, trying to learn new words and ideas. I became a sneak. My didactibot defined sneakiness as an antisocial adaptation to threat, mostly engaged in by solitary animals. I thought that was right. I was about as solitary as anybody could be. I didn't mean to be antisocial, but at least I learned that adults talked about other things when they thought they were alone.

They had many whispered words and phrases that were evidently not fit for saying out loud. I didn't know what they meant and didn't dare ask anyone, but I used them all the time. In my toy village, I staged plays with my dolls as the actors, assigning them forbidden words and phrases.

"If you don't behave, the proctor will get you," said a mother doll to a child doll as they walked down the tiny business street of the toy village, with its toy houses and toy church and toy trees, even though there were no trees on Earth, for no water could be spared for such things. "I'll tell him you're not two-three-four."

When I was about eight, the didactibot opened a library file for me that had whole books in it, some of it fiction, which is imaginary, and some of it real things I should know about, like history. At first, the fiction confused me. The characters mentioned things the other characters understood but I knew nothing about. The first few times I noticed this, I asked for explanations, only to find that whatever book I was reading immediately vanished from my library file. *Babies* was a bad word; *proliferate* was a bad word. Even my dictionary, though I didn't know it at the time, was carefully pruned to keep inappropriate subjects unthinkable.

All this did was make me determined to learn everything inappropriate in the whole universe, and I spent day after day digging into diddybot's files finding out what people didn't want me to know. That's where I learned about the six human colonies the Gentherans had secretly set up for us on other planets: B'yurngrad, Chottem, Cranesroost, Eden, Tercis, and Thairy. The settlement on Thairy was discovered by the Mercan Combine and the Omniont Federation in 2080, and they traced the people back to Earth, and they'd been going back and forth ever since. The Mercans and Omnionts were bunches of different races, almost all from carbon-based, free-water planets rather like Earth. There were other combines and federations of other kinds of life, too, but I didn't know anything about them.

Sometimes, when Earth was visible, I used my telescope to watch the Mercan and Omniont ships moving between the wormhole and Earth. They were huge ships, the size of little moons, but they might as well have been invisible. No one on Phobos ever mentioned them. The only explanation I could come up with was that all the adults had been on Phobos for so long that they had seen everything, knew what they thought about everything, and didn't need to discuss anything anymore. They were used to exchanging the same greetings many times each day and hearing the same jokes told over and over. I didn't think they realized there were no ideas in anything they said or that every single day they said the same words over and over, like birdcalls: chirrup, chirrup, tweet, tweet chirrup; caw caw cwaup, caw cwaup. Not that I had ever heard a live bird, but my didactibot was capable of vocalization!

Each year more books were added to the library list, and I was careful not to lose any of them. Years later I learned they had been bowdlerized, but the screeners hadn't been attentive or draconian enough to prevent a steady seepage of real information. Ideas oozed out of books like magma out of volcanoes. They solidified into whole, wonderful worlds, and I populated each one with beings and places I read of or invented: flora, fauna, forests, mountains, seascapes, all of them named, though no one knew those names but me, just as no one knew the names of the people I became in my various worlds: here a warrior who led the tribe through many dangers; there a shaman who could send her spirit to far places; here a healer who knew secret ways to cure sickness; there a telepath who could see into the hearts of others and communicate with animals; here a linguist who could understand all languages, ancient and new; there a queen who inspired her realm; here a spy who found out all the things the queen needed to know.

At the time it seemed perfectly normal to be six or seven other people. After all, I didn't have anyone else to play with. I knew, on one level, the different selves were imaginary, but at the same time they felt completely real. "I will be a queen," I told myself, repeating this until it became a mantra. I, a queen will be. Queen Willbea. No. That had an ugly sound to it. It should be softer. Wilvia. Queen Wilvia. That pleased me, and I bowed to myself in the mirror.

The spy evolved very naturally. She was the part of me who hid in corners, who was unobserved, who always listened and picked up information. Someone inoffensive that no one would ever suspect. Just like me. I didn't give her a name. Spies don't have names, just aliases.

"Others have been warriors, now me!" I cried to my mirrored self. I spelled it "Naumi." He was a quiet but very clever one. He wasn't huge and muscular, so he had to outthink other people. He became the warrior who guarded the borders, who protected the queen, and being him was fun because I liked being a boy sometimes. We had no animals on Phobos or Earth, but there were animals on many of my imagined worlds. Yaboons and gammerfrees and umoxen. I talked to them all the time in my guise as Mar, the telepath, who could talk to animals, and humans. I explored things as dark, smoky Margy, the shaman, the one who would travel in her mind. Traveling in my mind was something I did a lot of.

The linguist was going to be me, myself, I decided. I loved words. Learning words was the best part of learning anything, so plain Margaret was the linguist. The healer was young and very kind. She wasn't as clear as the others. I supposed she would come into being later, as I learned more about her particular talents, because a healer would be very useful.

Together, we were friends and companions. Wilvia the queen occupied a throne and meted out justice. Margy sent her mind to distant places to see what was happening, while the spy sneaked about and learned specific things about people. Naumi built barricades against the dreaded mind-worm, a creature I had run across in a footnote and could define only by implication. Deadly, certainly. Horrid in some unspecified way, and directed always by some malign and inhuman intelligence. This was enough to make me oppose it, or them, for all my people were on the side of good, always. As warrior, shaman, telepath, healer, spy, linguist, and queen we lived each day among wonders and marvels and were for the most part contented with our lives.

Shortly before my ninth birthday, one of those days came along that goes wrong from wakeup! My hair had horrid knots in it, my clothes wouldn't fasten, my head hurt, I spilled my breakfast on some of Father's papers, and he yelled at me. Halfway through the morning, I grew frustrated over something and heard, with dismay, my own mouth spewing a few of the words I had always kept secret! The result was worse than I had imagined. My mother washed out my mouth with Filth-away and told me I could not go down to the Mars surface on the birthday expedition I had been promised for over a year.

That trip had been my beacon, my lighthouse of hope, my only chance to see and do something new and interesting. I can't explain what happened then, though I suppose it was a tantrum. I had read of tantrums, I'd just never had one myself; but this time, I did. I screamed and threw myself on the floor and shrieked all my hatred and boredom, and I was so completely savage that both Mother and Father were frightened. They were no more frightened than I was, but at least they withdrew the punishment. When I got control of myself, more or less, I was servile in my thanks and fulsome in my promises of better behavior in the future.

Over the following days, however, my abject groveling gave way to an unfamiliar resentment, though only one of my people, Queen Wilvia, felt it deeply. My parents had forced Queen Wilvia to lower herself, to give in to them, and Queen Wilvia had done nothing to merit it. She didn't like them anymore.

Wilvia didn't hate them. Wilvia knew the word *hate* because I knew it, but experiencing it required a stomach-hurting, churning kind of feeling, the way I had felt during the tantrum. I labeled it carefully. It had been a very strong emotion, the first strong emotion I had ever felt except the arms-from-my-stomach feeling that I got sometimes at night, as though I had arms reaching out of my middle toward something I wanted terribly but had no name for.

Considering the matter calmly, over several days and wakeful nights, I decided what I wanted more than anything was simply to be somewhere other than Phobos Station. I didn't say any of this or even convey it by being sulky. I was docile. My "Yes, ma'am"s and "No, sir"s poured forth with honeyed smoothness. On the promised day, the excursion to Mars took place, beginning with a shuttle ride down into the great canyon, where my parents were welcomed by acquaintances of theirs who worked in the hydroponic gardens. In the gardens, I stood transfixed while a green leaf fell, lazily turning, spinning almost purposefully to land by my foot. I was allowed to take it, a souvenir of all that was alive and lovely-smelling. I saw the commissary, which had thick windows looking out over the dramatically shadowed canyon walls. The shadows moved entrancingly as luncheon and birthday cake were served. Then, while the adults talked (about nothing, using the same words, over and over), I excused myself politely and pressed close to the window. Farther down the canyon stood a magical building where Queen Wilvia might live, the ruby dome and golden towers of Dominion Central Authority, the governing body for all free humans who lived off Earth: us on Phobos and Mars, the people on Luna Station, and those in the six colonies.

One of the commissary workers happened by and took a few moments to point out several outstanding features in the landscape, including the dome.

"Who's in Dominion?" I asked.

The worker stopped, his brow furrowed. "What do you mean, who?"

"Is it humans?"

"Some," he said thoughtfully. "Some Gentheran, so I've heard."

"What are they like, Gentherans?"

He laughed shortly. "They're little, about your size, and that's all any-body knows. They wear full suits and helmets that cover their faces."

"But they're part of Dominion."

"Well, they found us, and they helped us . . ."

"Why did they help us?" I asked. I'd been wondering about this for a long time.

The worker shrugged. "They told us they owe us a debt, but they didn't go into any detail. Just said they owed us, take what they were offering and be grateful. That's what we're doing, I guess. We are grateful they've kept us out of the grip of ISTO, so far . . ."

"Isstow?" I had never heard it spoken.

"Interstellar Trade Organization," he whispered, with a glance over his shoulder to the table where the adults were sitting. "ISTO has given Earth a provisional membership because the Gentherans asked them to. So long as we have that, the Mercans can't cut up Earth for scrap."

"Margaret," my father called.

The worker hurried away. My brain spinning, I went back to the table to learn that one of the maintenance staff had offered to take me up onto the lip of Valles Marineris when she did her routine maintenance visit to a wind generator. It took a moment to take this in, because I was still lost in what the worker had told me.

"Well, Margaret?" said Mother impatiently.

"Oh, yes, ma'am, yes, please." I said, daring to say nothing more than that.

While my parents remained below with their acquaintances, I was outfitted for the excursion. I wore the helmet and air supply unit I had worn during the shuttle trip, an item owned by every person on Mars or Phobos, just in case, and I was inserted into a dust suit that was actually quite a good fit, as it was owned by a "little person" on the maintenance staff, one Chili Mech, who had been hired, so I was told, at least partly for her ability to get in and out of tight places. Thus clad, I rode beside the worker in the elevator that took us to the rim.

When we emerged, I followed the worker to the "stem tower," which is what the upright part of the windmill was called, and was told to stay there while the worker climbed the ladder to the rotor. I was not to wander away or go near the rim, even though there was a protective railing along it. Accordingly, I looped my arm through an upright of the ladder and stared ecstatically at the surroundings, relishing the differences from everything I had known before. There was a real horizon; there was distance and perspective; there was wind sound; there were dust storms moving about like whirling dancers. There were colors in the rocks and hills, new colors!

I turned to peer along the length of the canyon to the shining dome. There were Gentherans there, Gentherans who had helped Earth so the Mercans couldn't cut Earth up for scrap. Why would they want to cut up Earth for scrap?

This train of thought was interrupted by a metallic shriek from above, and I looked up to see that the worker had opened a large door into the rotor housing. The door closed behind her with another shriek, and for a little time, I watched the dust devils that formed out of nothing and engaged in wild dances that carried them halfway to the distant mountains before they vanished. The dance was accompanied by soft, barely heard wind song that subsided into a momentary and unusual calm.

Out of nowhere, silent as the dried leaf drifting down in the greenhouse, a whirling thing came out of the sky and landed in the dust not fifty feet from where I was standing.

It looked like a dragonfly, or rather, like the pictures of dragonflies I had seen in my book about the wetlands Earth once had. A hatch opened in the side of the golden thing. A woman came out, unhelmeted, unmasked, her movement stirring the flowing robes she wore into crimson billows.

"You, girl," she called in a glorious, glad voice. "Come with me!"

I felt . . . I felt something I had never felt before. Joy! Ecstasy! I felt . . . I felt the arms-reaching feeling, that this was it, the thing I'd needed, that I must go (that I must obey and stay where I was), that the woman was calling me (that I was probably imagining it). Standing there, with my arm thrust tightly through the stanchion,

I felt my legs pounding, I saw the back of myself running away, not wearing a helmet or a suit, just free as air. I reached the woman, saw myself seized up by the woman, was seized up, saw myself taken, was myself taken into the dragonfly, and felt it go.

Then I swayed with dizziness, my eyes fell shut, and everything slipped away.

I Am Wilvia

Aboard the dragonfly, I was seized with shyness. No one else was there but the red-robed woman and a boy about my age. He was the first young person I had ever seen, and he was looking at me just as curiously as I was at him. His hair was dark as the shadows on the canyon walls. His eyes glittered, as though they had lights in them. I liked the way his lips moved, the upper one curving and straightening, like a bow, I thought, one of those bows ancient desert horsemen had used, that same curve.

The woman lifted me into a seat, murmuring, "Girl, this is Prince Joziré. I am taking him to a place of safety. Joziré needs a companion, and we have chosen you to accompany him."

The boy reached out a brown hand to touch my paler one. I felt . . . I felt the arms-from-my-stomach reaching, and it was almost as though the boy had taken those invisible hands in his own and held them tight. "What's her name?" he asked the lady.

"What is your name, girl?" She smiled at me.

It took only a second before I realized who I was. "Prince Joziré, my name is Wilvia."

"Wilvia," said the boy, returning my smile with a companionable one of his own. "I like that very much." He turned to the pilot to ask, "And where is it we are going, again, ma'am?"

"Look there," said the woman, turning to the controls of her vessel. "Look there, Wilvia. See the road?"

I, Wilvia went to stand behind the woman, looking across her shoulder in the direction they were going. "It is a road," I gasped. There it was, stretching ahead of us in long, curving lines, translucent lines so the ones farther away could be seen through those nearer, the whole reaching on and on into unfathomable distance. "Where does it go?"

"This road goes to B'yurngrad, then on and on until it comes to the center of things and the edge of things. There's a little town on B'yurngrad, so buried in the grasslands that no one ever goes there. It doesn't even have a name. People just call it The Town. Some very wise people live there, and you'll both find friends among them. The two of you will be longtime friends and good companions."

I Am Margaret/on Mars

The next thing I knew, the worker was muttering to her-self as she carried me to the elevator: "Never checked the flow valve, stupid people, don't they teach their children that they have to check the flow valve every time they put the helmet on . . ."

When I fully wakened, they told me I had been briefly unconscious because of oxygen deprivation. Momen-tarily off my guard, I mentioned the dragonfly, only to be told quite firmly that I must have been delirious. I was quite, quite certain the dragonfly had not been the result of delirium, any more than the way my body felt was the result of delirium. I felt as though I had been split in two. I kept reaching in my mind for some other part of me. When I was well enough to stand, I searched the mirror for someone else standing behind or beside me, but there was no one there.

This episode, all of it, beginning with the tantrum and having my mouth washed out with soap, up to and includ-ing the departure of the dragonfly, began as simple confu-sion and ended by changing me forever. From that time on I was absolutely sure of two things: The first one was that somewhere else, there was another me named Wilvia. I knew this because she was no longer with me and be-cause I had seen her go; the second thing was that I had become a mutineer. Until then I had been a curious but customarily compliant child. From that time on, I became a con-firmed and silent rebel and simply refused to take part in chirrup tweet caw cwaup. I was determined to learn real language, many of them, all the ones there were! Didactibots were good at teaching people real things. I would get it to teach me the language of the an-cient Pthas, a language no one alive spoke anymore!

And that is what I did and it did, except during those times spent in my own worlds, with my other selves. I still had five of them as my companions, all of them but Wilvia, who had gone away and left me behind. Sometimes I thought she had been treacherous or faithless, but I knew that wasn't so. She hadn't forgotten me. Sometime . . . someday, I would find her again.

I was almost twelve in 2096, when the personnel of Mars and Phobos Stations were told the stations were to be closed. For several hours following this incredible announcement, people actually communi-cated with one another! They disagreed, yelled, orated, hectored, be-came variously rancorous, anxious, insulting, and grief-stricken. I learned more about them in that brief time than I had learned in the twelve years before. The focus on reality was brief, however. Very soon the Phobos habit of evasive reticence reasserted itself, and everyone turned to their assigned duties. Machinery was wrapped, lines were drained, equipment was secured, personal belongings were packed, and finally the entire staff was shuttled down to the green ravine that held the headquarters of Mars Surface Colony. There we awaited the ship that would take us to Earth.

Oh, how I loved Mars Surface Colony! There were new things everywhere. Despite Mother's sporadic attempts to keep an eye on me, there were simply too many people and too many things going on to keep me shut up. I met Chili Mech, the woman who had lent me her Mars suit for my trip to the rim, and I began to follow her about.

"You're like those old-timey pets," said Chili Mech. "Some little cat or dog. Every time I turn around, there you are. What's the attrac-tion?"

"You know things," I told her. "You talk about things."

"What things?"

"The Gentherans. Tell me about the Gentherans."

"Hasn't your didactibot taught you about the Gentherans?"

"Not really, no."

"Well, let's see. When the Gentherans discovered us, they told us the Earth biome was terminal, they told us how we could save it; but they didn't think we would, so they gave us some spaceships so Earth could set up a few colonies to preserve our species."

"Why?"

"What do you mean, why?"

"I mean, what was their reason for helping us? Did they just like us humans, or what?"

"The Keeper knows, kid, I don't."

"Who's the Keeper?"

"It's just a saying the Gentherans have. Anything nobody knows, they say, 'The Keeper knows.' Then you say, 'Well, ask the Keeper,' and they say, 'You can only reach the Keeper by walking seven roads at once.'

"Nobody can do that," I said.

"That's the point. It's like saying, when hell freezes over or when pigs fly. Pigs are extinct animals that didn't have wings . . ."

"I know that," I said, somewhat offended.

"Anyhow, the Gentherans insisted we set up one government for Earth, and one government for the off-Earth humans, because if some predatory race found us, all our political subdivisions would get eaten for lunch. ISTO only deals with one government per planet or group of planets, and if a planet doesn't have one government, the Combines just swallow all the local governments up. That threat scared people badly enough that Earthgov got voted in very quickly, and as soon as the colonies were running, they set up Dominion Central Authority. DCA has representatives from each of the six colonies plus one each from the little stations on Luna and Mars, plus a bunch of Gentherans, because they were responsible for helping set up the colonies."

"Someone told me you're the Mars delegate to Dominion."

"I am that. I've been here since the Gentherans picked Mars as the site for Dominion Central Authority and offered to build the DCA structure, around 2067."

"That's the same year my mother went to Phobos, with her parents.

She was ten years old. My father got to Phobos fifteen years later, and I was born in 2084."

Chili Mech shuddered. "Lucky man. He got out just in time. The eighties were bad years!"

"How do you mean?" I sat on the floor and crossed my legs, looking up at the little woman. "I never heard about that?"

"Well, 2080 was the year the Mercan Combine discovered the human colony on Thairy. They showed up in Earth orbit. You've seen the ships. Compared to the little Gentheran ships, they're enormous, like planetoids! They said they were from Interstellar Trade Organization. I can remember Earth people being all bug-eyed like kids at a carnival, here the splendid ETs were, come to solve our problems.

"Well, that didn't last long, just until the Combine and the Federation had a chance to examine Earth and decide it wouldn't be worth their while to negotiate a trade agreement because we had nothing to trade. Earth was falling apart, and it was too late to fix anything."

She pursed her lips, as though about to spit. "Then they dropped the bomb. Since we were out on the edge of nowhere, a very expensive destination to get to, they were planning to hang around in orbit until the imminent collapse occurred and mine the wreckage for scrap after everyone was dead."

My mouth was open, as it had been for some time. "They said it just like that?"

Chili Mech looked over my head into space, slowly nodding. "Just like that, with nine-tenths of Earth's population watching and listening. After we died, their retrieval robots would take the dead humans to make protein meal for their livestock, and their scavenger robots would take all metals."

"What happened?"

"What do you think happened with half a dozen huge ships, blocking off half the sky! Those prancing K'Famir with all the extra arms and legs! The dirty, hissing Hrass, the boneheaded Frossians, the sneery Elos? Arrogant as all hell, while Earthgov's people practically licked their feet! Nobody on Earth had done anything about Earth's situation for at least two centuries, but now everyone was scared spitless."

I waited, finally urging, "Then?"

"Earthgov sent a delegation to ask if there wasn't something, anything the Combine or Federation would do to help us. The Federation and the Combine just hung up there, acting totally uninterested for a while, but finally, when we were just about to give up hope, they offered to stave off our collapse by buying the only surplus produce Earth had: people. They said they'd buy healthy ten-to-fifty-year-old people from us on fifteen-year labor contracts, and they'd even transport them to human colonies once the contracts expired.

"By that time, everyone on Earth was so scared that any way out would have seemed like a good idea. Earthgov consulted with the Gentherans and accepted the offer." She stared at me, really looking at me. "By all that's holy, you've seen their ships going back and forth to Earth, girl. Didn't you ever wonder what the ships were carrying?"

I flushed. I hadn't. It was just about the only thing I had never wondered about. "No. I didn't. What did they buy people with? Money?"

"What good would that do? They buy humans with water."

I thought about that. "What happened then?"

Chili regarded me doubtfully, eyes half-lidded. "Well, that's a touchy subject. You better ask your mom about that."

"She doesn't talk to me."

"Ask her anyhow. You got a right to know."

Later, even though Chili wouldn't say anything more about the eighties, she did talk about other things. She said the Mars program was being phased out because there wasn't enough water on Mars to support a real colony, much less enough to relieve Earth's water shortage.

"Didn't people find out how much water there was when they first came up here?" I asked her.

Chili grinned. "Somehow the Gentherans 'made a mistake' in their calculations. They told us there was a lot more water than we've ever found. Some say the Gentherans always meant to have Dominion headquarter on Mars, so they phonied the data that supported the settlement effort until they got it built. We didn't find out the truth about the water until just recently. In fact, nobody else knows the truth about the water except Earthgov, so keep it quiet, huh, kid?"

Chili's com-link went off with a shrill whine, and that ended the conversation. After that, there were no opportunities for me to find out anything more. The arrival of the *Ninja* was announced, and everyone scrambled to be ready except those few who had volunteered to remain behind to maintain the water and power systems for Dominion Central Authority. I shut myself up in my bed cubicle and cried for hours because Chili was staying, but she'd told me I was too young to volunteer.

On Earth, during the six-month gravitational rehab program, I met quite a few Earthians. They were just like the people on Phobos. The words might be a little different: twitter twitter chirrup, chirrup twitter, perhaps, instead of caw, caw, cwaup, but otherwise, alike. No one said anything real. The daily information services spoke of a decrease in water rations, of the failure of certain algae crops, and the people said chirrup, chirrup, twitter. Or, for those of us in therapy: moan, moan, scream. Rehab was my first experience of real, sustained pain.

"What will we do if our water rations are decreased?" I asked the physical therapist who was helping me learn to walk in gravity.

"Oh, sweetheart, you don't want to talk about that. Let's not spoil the day. Left foot now, step, step, step . . ."

"How much water is a ration?" I asked the technician who was measuring my bone density.

"Honeybun, I just don't think about it," he said with a winning smile. "Measuring it doesn't help anything."

Twitter, twitter, I thought. Caw, caw cwaup. Moan, moan, scream.

The therapy was almost over when Father announced that a proctor would be making a family visit. I had almost lost my trip to Mars over the word *proctor*! I had had my mouth washed out over that word, a dirty word, one no nice child ever uttered. I felt myself flushing red with hostility and embarrassment. I shivered all over and stared at my toes.

"For goodness' sake, Louise," said Father. "That won't do."

"Of course not, Harry," Mother replied, her own cheeks red with chagrin. "It isn't a bad word, Margaret. It's just one we've avoided using until now. You'll have to say it to yourself. We'll have to use it in conversation. Otherwise, the proctor will wonder why his title makes us blush."

I considered rebellion. What had all that Filth-away business been about if *proctor* was not a dirty word? And now I was to use it in conversation? I, who had always been prevented from using any real words whatever? I felt moved to throw another tantrum (it had been over three years since the last one, after all), but I suppressed the inclination. Since I had no idea what this new freedom would entail, perhaps it would be wisest to know its limits before taking a stand.

Instead of a tantrum, I took part in conversations that were scheduled during family dinner so we could discuss the function of proctors and the circumstances which had brought us all back to Earth.

"Do you know what ISTO is, Margaret?" Father asked.

"ISTO is the Interstellar Trade Organization." That was the right answer, but I wanted more. "We have a provisional membership, but I don't know what it means. Provided what?"

It took Father a minute to switch from his usual frown to his recently invented fatherly look. "We have a membership provided the ISTO doesn't declare all Earthians a barbarian people."

"I don't know what that means," I persisted, even though this wasn't strictly part of the subject.

Father gritted his teeth. "ISTO recognizes four types of creatures: civilized, semicivilized, barbarians, and animals. Civilized people know about, care about, and protect their environments. Semicivilized people know and care, but can't do anything . . ."

"Why not?"

Mother said, "Because something prevents their acting in their own self-interest. Public apathy. Commercial interference. Religious opposition. Governmental corruption. The Gentherans say humans have a lot of that."

Father frowned at her and went on. "Barbarians know but don't care about their worlds, and animals don't even know. Animals or barbarians aren't treated like civilized people."

"But what does all that mean? What have we done about it?"

Mother's voice was dead and level. "Margaret, you know we had lakes and rivers once. We had forests once. We had animals on land and fish in the oceans. By the time the Gentherans came, all the freshwater on Earth was confined in pipes, the ice caps were gone, the rivers were gone along with hydroelectric power. All our food came from ocean algae because we had no water to irrigate plants. Our desalinization plants ran constantly, mostly on tidal and wind power. We had nuclear plants, but the Gentherans made us shut them down because the Intergalactic Court doesn't allow nuclear power on occupied planets. We already knew we were in trouble, and we told the Gentherans our problem was a lack of water . . ."

Father interrupted, "The Gentherans very politely told us we were mistaken, the problem wasn't water, the problem was us. The biome was collapsing, everything on Earth would soon die. The Gentherans said too many Earthians were in fact barbarians who didn't care what happened to Earth because they believed they'd be off in some lovely afterlife by that time."

"Would they be?" I asked, wonderstruck at this idea.

"I sincerely doubt it," Mother snapped.

"Didn't anyone listen?" I asked.

Father said, "The Gentherans weren't talking to the people, they were talking to our leaders. The Earth governments went as far as they could when they formed Earthgov and started the colonies, but they wouldn't do anything about depopulating Earth because they thought the public would start riots."

Mother added, "The government decided to break it to us slowly. They told us about the colonies, how colonists had been sent along with all the animals we had left in zoos . . ." Her voice trailed off.

Father sighed. "People were excited about that."

Mother said, "The news programs ran these lovely fantasies about all the people who were crowding us moving away . . ." Her mouth worked. Her eyes brimmed, and she shook her head impatiently. "A silly dream. Even if people shipped out every hour of every day and night, we couldn't keep up with the birthrate. We could never accomplish what the Gentherans said we had to do."

"What did we have to do?" I demanded.

She wiped her eyes and stared at her knotted hands, saying nothing. Father rose to his feet, face twisted in distaste.

"I can't deal with this, Louise. You tell her."

"Harry! Damn it. You're the one who . . . you're her father!"

"You're her mother, and you'll have to. She needs to know, and I can't." He left the room, closing the door behind him.

"What?" I said, thoroughly confused. "What should I know?"

Mother's cheeks were scarlet, and her mouth pursed, as though she had bitten into something sour. Her voice trembled as she said, "The Gentherans told us to apply a numerical rating to every person born on Earth. If a baby is its mother's first child, it gets one point. If the child is its father's second child, it gets two points and adding them together makes the child a three. Only those rated two, three, and four are allowed to have children or any scarce commodity. You're my first child and your father's third child, so you're a four . . ."

I cried, "Father has other children! I have a brother or sister?"

Mother choked. "No. When he was quite young, he had a relationship with a woman. She had twins who died as infants."

"But, if they died, then I'm his first child who lived . . ."

"It doesn't work that way," said Mother, nervously licking her lips. "Any child born alive is counted, whether the child lives or not. That isn't . . . isn't important. The Gentherans claimed it's the fairest way to reduce population. It doesn't cut off any genetic line and it leaves the gene pool as broad as possible." She paused, her hands knotted. "Finally, Earthgov passed the two-three-four laws, but they did it secretly."

Mother wiped moisture from the corners of her mouth with one knuckle of her clenched hands. "Earthgov was debating how to publicize the laws and begin enforcing them when the Mercans and the Omnionts showed up. You know what happened then! The Combine and the Federation said they'd salvage us. We begged for help. They offered to buy our people for water. Earthgov shilly-shallied, as usual. They thought they had a choice.

"They didn't have a choice! They couldn't get it through their stupid heads that there was no choice! ISTO says a living planet is more important than the members of any race on it, and if a race of barbarians or animals threatens a planet, the race has to be 'reduced,' and they were about to reduce us. It couldn't be kept a secret any longer. The story broke everywhere at once: the offer to buy our people, the threat from ISTO, the laws that had been secretly passed . . ." She fell silent, staring at nothing for a time. I waited. "And what they'd been afraid would happen, did happen! The anti–population control people started rioting. Those opposing them began rioting back! Some religious fanatics took advantage of the disorder to start a biowar. That was the Great Plague of 2082 that killed a billion people while those huge ships just hung up there, watching."

"They didn't help?"

"Gentherans help. Omnionts observe. Mercans profit," her mother snarled. "At least that's what the Gentherans tell us."

"That's why . . . it was the terrible eighties?"

Mother wiped her eyes. "That was the start of them. While the plague was going on, all the local wars joined into one big war among former nations and states and tribal areas. That was the so-called Eight-Week War that killed another billion people."

"I wasn't even born."

"No. The war happened right after your father arrived on Phobos. It's a good thing we were there. Otherwise, we might not be alive today." Her voice, already unfamiliarly shrill, went up another half tone. "We might have been just two more of the two billion people the plague and the war had killed, which still wasn't enough to suit ISTO, which started an inquiry . . ."

"Into what?"

"If the plague had been started purposely by Earthgov, ISTO would have regarded it as a good-faith effort to reduce population; if the plague was simply a crime or accident, it wouldn't have helped our rating at all. Everyone knew Earthgov hadn't started the plague, because the fanatics who did it had told the whole world their god had commanded they do it! However, the fanatics were all dead by that time, so they couldn't prove they'd done it, and that gave the Gentherans a loophole through which they *negotiated* with ISTO. They claimed that Earthgov had known the plague was going to start and had chosen not to stop it. That turned out to be 'reasonable grounds' for classifying us as semicivilized.

"ISTO agreed, but only if we immediately started enforcing our own laws by selling all our over-fours to the Combine and the Federation."

"They'd never been enforced."

Mother shrilled: "How could they have been! What with the plague and the war, nobody could enforce anything! ISTO said either comply at once, or the robot slaughterers would start arriving." Her voice rasped, she coughed, before going on in her piercing, unfamiliar voice:

"Earthgov declared martial law and began shipping people out, and that bought us provisional status as a semicivilized and threatened world. We've been shipping people ever since, and we're still provisional."

Mother's tone and expression were forbidding, but I wanted to know! I said, "I still don't understand why we can't talk about it!"

Tears pouring down her reddened face as she grated through clenched teeth, "Have you been listening to me, Margaret? I sound like a—a crazy person! I'm screaming! Even telling you about it makes me crazy! The war happened, and the plague happened, and even in the middle of all that, the proliferators just went on having child after child after child! Other people, those who called themselves the limiters, they blamed the others, the lifers, for destroying the world. If you want to know all the awful details, I'll remove the block on your didactibot and you can look up the Lifer-Limiter Uprising!

"Your father and I weren't here, but we've heard about it from people who were! The hostility was everywhere, in everything. Pregnant women were stoned! Obstetricians' offices were bombed. Hospitals were bombed. Mentioning babies in public could get you killed! We still can't talk about it!"

The door opened, and Father came back into the room, his face drawn. "I'm sorry, Louise. I just . . ."

"I know," she croaked. "I know."

The looks on their faces actually frightened me. I said placatingly, "I suppose if you were somebody with lots of children, it would be terrible to lose them."

Mother and Father exchanged a long look, and when Mother turned to look at me again, her face was gray. "It would be terrible, yes, even to lose one."

I Am Margaret/on Earth

As Mother pointed out, I was twelve years old, a grown-up young woman who would behave herself, who would not blush at the proctor's title when he arrived, for we needed the proctor's approval to get our permanent water ration cards.

"If the Omnionts are bringing water, and we're shipping out the over-fours, why do we need rations?" I wanted to know.

Father looked up from his desk. "Because until the sterilization laws were passed and enforced, every time we shipped someone away, we had two new ones popping up. That didn't stop until the Mercan Combine started buying toilet-trained toddlers as pets for the K'Famir."

Mother turned pale and left the room quickly.

In due time the proctor arrived, a narrow, sharp-edged sort of man who didn't even give us his name. He merely nodded once at each of us as he put his access-and-data console on the table. It clicked and flipped open in several directions, spreading itself across the entire surface before uttering an imperative beep. When the proctor hit a key, its purple screen fetched up a lengthy form.

"Now," the proctor said, drawing a chair up to the table and seating himself at the console. "Let's start with the simple things. Your names. Dates of birth. Identity numbers. Names of all siblings, living and dead. Parents' names and their dates of birth, and their identity numbers, and the names of all their siblings, living and dead. Places of birth, if known."

Mother took a deep breath and started out, "We are Louise and Harry Bain . . ."

Between them they came up with all the names and most of the dates, either from memory or from the family record book.

"Good," said the proctor. "Now, to your knowledge have you or have any of your siblings ever used a name other than the one they were given on their birth registry?"

"Mama's brother Hy," I offered, when no one said anything.

There was a pause. The proctor looked up, as did I. Mother's face was very still, as though she had been paralyzed.

Father said, "Hy wasn't her brother, though he was young enough to have been her sibling. He's Louise's uncle. Margaret's great-uncle."

Mother found her voice. "Hy was named for his father, Hyram, a name he hated. He . . . he doesn't live on Earth, however. Hy has always lived in the Lunar Colony."

The proctor, turning to Father, "And you, sir? Any aliases? Pseudonyms? Noms de guerre?" He winked, making a face, and for no discernible reason, a shiver ran up my back.

"Not that I know of, no," said Father with a frozen smile.

There were other questions, where people had lived, how long they had lived there. Mother and Father weren't always sure about the details, but the database filled in most of the gaps once it had people's identity numbers.

"Now your daughter," said the proctor. "Name, date of birth, identity number? Fine. Now we'll do your DNA."

He took sterile scrapers from a tube, scraped the insides of our cheeks, and dropped the samples into an analysis slot on the console. "All three of your DNA codes will be checked for familial consistency, that is assuming pregnancies were normal and unassisted?"

Father looked uncomfortable. "I don't know."

"You don't know, sir?"

"Twenty years ago my former partner had twins that died at birth. We were separated at the time, and I had no knowledge of them until later. I don't know the particulars."

The proctor said, "If you'll give me the woman's identity number."

Father shrugged. "I don't know. When I learned the children hadn't survived, I didn't even ask for genetic verification. It was a long time ago . . ."

The proctor nodded. "That's all right, we'll find the data on the previous reproductive history and we'll do the GV. Just tell me her name and where she lived at the time."

Father muttered, the proctor nodded and entered the data. "And your pregnancy, ma'am?"

Mother flushed. "Margaret's conception was unassisted."

"Very good. That's all we need. Your family will be filed as a unit. You'll be provided with the code at the time of filing, so you'll have it for reference if it's ever needed."

As his console refolded itself, the man turned to me to ask, "What were you studying on Phobos, Margaret?"

"I started learning ET languages," I murmured. "I know some Pthas, some Omniont, and quite a bit of Mercan Trade Tongue."

The proctor nodded. "I'm impressed. Fluency in ET languages is valuable, but few families are sensible enough to let their children learn them early, when it's easy for them."

I said, "Mother encouraged me. She says she wishes she'd learned languages when she was little."

The machine made a quiet sound, like a hiccup, and produced a screenful of figures. The proctor pressed a button, a machine voice said, "Clear."

"Very well," the proctor said, pressing a button. "We always compare, just to be sure. In your case, everything agrees with everything else. Provisionally, until we receive the information on your previous history, your registration rating, sir, is a two. You, ma'am, are a four. Your daughter a four."

"We're in good shape, then," said Father in a relieved voice.

"You are indeed, sir," said the proctor.

When the door closed behind the proctor, I whispered, "What did he mean, that we're in good shape."

Mother answered. "It means we can have a water ration. It also means anyone who's a five or higher can't."

Father cleared his throat and shook himself, as though to shed whatever mood he'd been in. "Margaret, I think we've had enough of this discussion. We need to take a family walk, get out of here. Right, Louise?"

Mother, looking very pale, nodded. "Yes. Oh, yes. Let's get out of here. Let's give ourselves a treat of some kind . . ."

I looked from one to the other, frightened at their tone. "Is something wrong?"

Her father said, "Everything's all right, Margaret. You can have water, you can even have a family when you've grown up."

"That is, if you pick the right husband," said Mother tartly. "One who hasn't used up all his quota sowing wild oats. No, no, Margaret, don't ask me to explain wild oats."

I felt something squeezing my stomach and farther down, in my belly. As the three of us took our rare, almost unprecedented walk, I looked into every store window we passed while my insides cramped and jumped as though I'd swallowed something alive that was trying to get out, split off from me. My skin felt damp. I thought I saw a shadowy presence moving around, reflected in the window, standing just behind me, but there was nothing there except my own white and frightened face staring back. After a time, I stopped looking and trudged along, eyes fixed on my feet.

Who Is Margaret?

It seemed to me I dreamed the proctor came, just as he had. I dreamed everything he had said and we had said, up until the point where the proctor turned to me to say, "Fluency in ET languages is valuable, but few families are sensible enough to let their children learn them early, when it's easy for them."

"It was Mother's idea," I said. "She says she wishes she'd learned languages when she was little, like her brother Hy."

"You mean her uncle, Hy?" said the proctor.

I stopped. Why had I said that?

Mother said, "My uncle Hy, yes . . ."

The machine interrupted with a harsh, buzzing sound. It spoke: "Duplicated reference to unverified identity, name Hy, maternal kinsperson. Possible data variance. Hold! Hold!"

The proctor sat back, his lips tightly compressed, as printed forms began to flow across the screen. He muttered, "We always compare with former records, just to be sure. There seems to be a record discrepancy."

"Discrepancy?" Mother faltered. Her hand shook on the arm of the chair. I had started toward her, but when I saw the fear in her eyes, I stayed frozen in place.

The flow of forms stopped, leaving only one on the screen.

"A medical record," said the proctor in a chill voice.

"Ma'am, your middle name is, I believe, Hazel? We have a record here of a perinatal death on Mars, specifically on the Phobos Station. Some twelve years ago. To Hazel Bannon, your maiden name, I believe?"

Mother tried to speak and couldn't.

Father said, "It wasn't on Earth. The emigration laws only pertain to Earth."

The proctor shook his head, nostrils pinched. "When the Mars projects were closed, their records were subsumed into ours. During this interview, your daughter twice mentioned an unverified identity. That triggered a universal search by the data system, all medical records and all identity banks."

Mother's eyes were so full of fear that I cried out, "Mother! What's wrong?"

"What's wrong," said the proctor, "is you, young lady. You are not a four. You're the second born of twins. You're a five."

"What does that mean?" I cried.

Mother sobbed, "Oh, Margaret!"

"You could be prosecuted for attempted falsification of records," said the proctor.

"We didn't know," Father cried. "Phobos never counted. We never thought we'd be coming back to Earth!"

"Well, sir. Earth is where you are. You and your wife may remain here, but your daughter, Margaret, will be required to report to the shipping point within the next ten days. The shipping officers will be in touch."

The dream was like watching a play. It was clear. The words were clear. In the dream, the proctor went away. When the door hissed shut behind him, Mother screamed, "I told you they'd find out, Harry!"

Father yelled at me for mentioning Hy's name.

I cowered, wept, then howled, halfway between fear and fury, "You're sending me away!"

Mother shouted, "They're taking you away!"

"You knew about this," I yelled. "You told Daddy they'd find out, so you knew I wasn't a four! Why did you go ahead and have me if you were just going to let them do this . . ."

It was as though they hadn't really thought of me until that moment. Mother fell to her knees and put her arms around me. Father stooped above us both, tears flowing.

I felt something squeezing my stomach and farther down, in my belly. I cried out with the pain, scrambled away from between them, and fled to the bathroom, where I stood, looking into the mirror while my insides cramped and jumped as though I had swallowed something alive that was trying to get out and split off from me. My skin felt damp. I thought I saw a shadowy presence moving around. For a moment I thought I could see it in the mirror, standing behind me, but there was nothing there except my own chalky white, scared face staring back at me.

From somewhere outside myself I heard something, or someone, saying very firmly, slowly, in a commanding voice: "It's all right, Margaret. Just take a deep breath, it's going to be all right."

I don't remember the subway trip to the South American elevator center, I just remember being there. It was huge, surrounded by sprawling dormitory and office buildings and centered on the immense reinforced and raised platform that anchored the elevators, some dozens of them, their transport ribbons virtually invisible, their translucent cargo pods making dotted lines that faded into invisibility, interminate fingers pointed at the silver shimmer of the staging platforms and the geosynchronous shipping station orbiting far above.

The authorities tried to discourage my parents from making the trip, but they insisted. They got no farther than one of the huge intake lobbies thronged with families saying good-bye.

"I'd have thought there'd be almost no one here," Mother murmured. "Surely people can't still be having children that are fives and over!"

"It's the backlog," Father murmured in return. "They're limited by the capacity of the elevators and the availability of transport ships. There are only four elevator terminals, one each in Sumatra and South America, two in Africa. There's been some talk about building more of them as ocean-based platforms, but the last time that was tried, a tsunami took it out. The problem is, building more would be expensive, and Earth can't afford it."

"I thought people would be flowing out," Mother insisted. "This is more of an ooze . . ."

"I'm not in any hurry," I interrupted. My voice didn't sound like me. It was a firm, solid voice, like a shield. Someone else had given it to me. I couldn't have contrived it on my own.

"That's the spirit," Father said, falsely cheerful. "You'll probably be here quite a while. We'll find a room nearby and visit you . . ."

The outposting officer, a tall woman with a shaved head and sharp, black eyes, immediately made the question of visitation irrelevant. "I'm a specialist in colony assignments, Margaret. You've studied ET languages."

"Some," I acknowledged.

"Some is better than nothing. If you ask for a colony posting, we can send you there rather than into bondage. Colony planets are in need of linguists."

Mother ventured, "Would it be . . . someplace where my husband and I could go with her? So we could be together?"

The officer gave her a brief smile, almost a grimace. "Sorry, ma'am. The ships aren't ours, they're Omniont and Mercan ships. Earthgov has negotiated for a few colonist slots on each one; it's the only way we can afford to send additional colonists, and we send no one over twenty-five. Anyone older than that doesn't pay back the shipping costs."

Father said, "A colony would be better, wouldn't it?"

The officer replied, "Most people think so, yes."

"What . . . where is the colony?" I asked. "I mean, what do people do there?"

"All colonies start out as agricultural," the officer explained. "Then we recapitulate the history of civilization, from the ground up, though we cut a few millennia off the process. We go in as agriculturists, build livestock herds, then start prospecting for natural resources. We reinforce the population with additional colonists as soon as the food supply is adequate, then begin extraction of natural resources and get some wind and hydro power plants going. Except for Eden and Cranesroost, we're well beyond that point in our colonies."

"So, why do they want linguists?"

"Trade. As soon as a colony has something to sell, usually agricultural or mining products, somebody has to sell it. The income helps support the inflow of former bondspeople from the nearby Omniont and Mercan worlds."

I found this puzzling. "But, if the colonists have been on Omniont worlds, haven't they learned the languages?"

"Races who buy bondspeople do not teach them the local language. They communicate through interpreters. They find the idea of conversing with their workers repulsive."

"I'd like to use the languages I learned," I said, surprised at a feeling of sudden warmth. I'd felt frozen for days, but this felt . . . it felt right. "Which colony would you send me to?"

"You'll be randomly assigned by a ship assignment computer. It separates bondspersons and colonists, then divides the colonists up by age, sex, skills, and the like, and assigns them singly or in small groups by chance. It avoids favoritism."

Mother cried, "But how will we know where she is?"

The officer started to speak, then looked down and shook her head slightly. I knew she was about to tell a lie. When the officer looked up, smiling, she said, "Your daughter will be able to send you a message after she's settled, but you don't need to worry about her. People her age are always adopted by adults. She won't be struggling on her own."

The words felt like truth, including the encouraging smile the officer sent my way. Something about it had been misleading, however. True, but misleading. I almost asked, "What is it you're not telling us?" but stopped myself. There was no point in drawing out my departure.

The officer had obviously dealt with this situation before. The moment the interview was completed, an usher took me by the arm and led me away as the sounds of Mother's farewells faded into the background. I didn't look back. It was all I could do to stay on my feet.

The first stop was a cavernous dormitory with numbered beds, where I was told to wait. I waited. Within the hour, someone found me there and told me where the toilets were and where the commissary was while attaching an elevator number tag around my wrist and a numbered identity disk around my neck. The fasteners of both items, I was told, were unbreakable.

"These are your coveralls, put them on. These are your shoes. Put what you're wearing into your baggage, put the shoes on just before you move to the pods. These are your baggage tags, attach them carefully. Bags are shipped separately."

I changed into the overalls and packed my clothes. I set the shoes on the foot of my bed, where I wouldn't forget to put them on. I tagged my baggage. Time passed while I sat in a cocoon of fog, too deadened to be afraid. Eventually, a loudspeaker summoned everyone to the adjacent commissary for a meal. The food was like all food, tasteless. No one seemed to be hungry. Back in the dormitory, after slow hours of nothing, I fell asleep, only to be wakened by another usher with a list.

"Ship change," the woman said. "You'll be going up this morning."

I fought down a surge of panic, telling myself it was better to be going anywhere than staying where I was. "Going up" meant putting on the required shoes, making a required trip to the toilets, then joining a queue that wound in a snakelike curve toward the elevator pods. As each one filled, it shifted sideways, locked on to the rising nanotube-reinforced ribbon, and departed, as did the one I was in, packed among hundreds of others, each with an oxygen mask, each in an identical coverall, each with number tags on wrist and around neck.

A voice said: "This stage of your journey will last approximately three days. When we reach the staging platforms at nine thousand miles out, you will have a brief recess while your pod is shifted to the higher-velocity elevators that will take you on the next lap, another twenty thousand miles to the export station. That journey will also take about three days. The officers passing among you will give you a dose of tranquilizers and one of time-release Halt, to shut down excretory function."

There were no windows. There was no wasted space. Rows of heads stretched in every direction. No one spoke. When the pod clamped on to the belt, a few people gasped, but only momentarily. Evidently it didn't clamp on all at once; it slid a little at first, then gradually firmed up so we didn't get jerked around. The feeling of being crushed eased, and after about three hours, I noticed that I felt lighter, though I didn't care greatly. Endless hours passed in a kind of dim nothingness. Orderlies came through, checking pulses. One or two of the people in seats nearby went limp, were unbelted and taken away. I was just starting to feel nausea when the pod abruptly unlocked from the belt and slid off to one side. The doors opened. People stumbled to their feet, out onto the domed, transparent-floored platform where we all stared disbelievingly downward at the Earth, a large blue ball, floating in blackness.

I had to go. So did everyone. As we filed toward the toilets, we were given premoistened cloths to wash hands and faces. There were no mirrors. I noticed men rubbing their hands over their stubbly faces. We were given something tasteless to drink before going into the next pod. The same announcement. The same shots. The same dimness and detachment.

At thirty thousand miles, the doors opened, we filed out. This time the drink they gave us was slightly larger, the time in the toilets was a bit longer.

"Pick up your baggage to your left," we were commanded. Our line shuffled forward, picked up our baggage, joined a new queue.

"Colonist number seven-seven-zero-five-nine-zero-two," said the checker, rubbing his eyes. "That way, to your left . . . To your right . . ."

I was so drugged and distant that when I felt myself split, it didn't seem to matter. One of me turned left, one right, into areas seemingly open to space. Half a dozen ships hung high above, tethered to the station by swaying skeins of boarding umbilici. Five of the ships were immense. The sixth ship hanging above the transparent dome was small in comparison to the others. The access lane leading to it stretched empty across the wide lobby space, while those of the larger vessels held seemingly endless lines of boarders.

"Margaret Bain," said a uniformed officer, glancing from my forehead to his list. "Number seven-seven-zero-five-nine-zero-two." He stepped to the lane divider and opened a gate. "Through there," he said, pointing at the empty access lane leading to the smaller ship.

"But, am I the only one going there?" I asked.

"Your number is the only number going there right now." The officer glowered. "Get over there and stop asking questions . . ."

I stared at the empty lane doubtfully. "Is that a colony ship?"

"Look, little girl. That's the ship you're supposed to be on. Now get over there before I have to call security."

I opened my mouth to say, no, it's wrong, but the officer was red in the face, angry enough to let me know it would do no good to argue. Cowed, I turned into the empty access lane, meeting the glances of those occupying the crowded lanes far to my right, a few staring at me curiously. Among those crowded bodies was another me, walking away, just the way Wilvia had walked away years ago, going somewhere else. I opened my mouth to yell at her . . . me . . . but couldn't think what I would say, even if she, I, looked back.

Before I could make up my mind to do anything, someone put a hand on my shoulder, a tall, robed woman. Her face looked familiar, as though I had seen it somewhere before. Not on Phobos. Not here on Earth. Where?

The woman smiled. "Are you hearing contentious voices, child? It's the place, don't you think? Or the situation? Almost guaranteed to make one question every move. Well, don't let voices bother you. This is where you belong." She took my hand and led me into the boarding tube. "Before leaving Earth, you had begun the study of nonterrestrial languages, isn't that so?"

Perhaps I answered, perhaps not, I don't remember. I do remember turning at the ship's door and looking across the huge lobby. If I was over there, I was lost in the crowd.

In the lock of the ship, the woman turned. "You're extremely young to leave home like this. All I can promise you is that you will not be unhappy where you are going."

"I was told it would be a colony planet."

"Oh, yes. The planet you're going to is called Chottem. It is a colony planet and my home. I know it very well."

"I've heard your voice before," I said, suddenly recalling. "The day the proctor came. Was that you? Telling me it would be all right."

"Did someone tell you that?" the woman asked. "Perhaps it was a friend of mine. We're all inescapable busybodies."

"May I ask your name, ma'am?"

The woman smiled briefly, somewhat ruefully. "Why don't you call me what everyone else calls me. I'm just the Gardener. And since you need a new name to go with your new life, let us call you Gretamara."

New Margarets/Who Are We?

"Bain, Margaret," said the checker, rubbing his eyes. "Number seven-seven-zero-five-nine-eight-two. That way, to your right."

The hallway to the right was crowded, traffic in it made more difficult by the baggage everyone carried. As I moved forward, I heard loud and emphatic voices ahead: "Enter your number, take your chances." "That way." "That way, move it. Wait, you dropped this." "Enter your number." "That way." "Another that way." "Okay, go with your friend there." "Now, you can go this way."

The boarding-tube ports were at a lower level. As those ahead of me moved down the slope, I could see over their heads to the tube ports. Two uniformed men operated a device and called out the results. As I approached, I saw it, some kind of number pad and a lever. Numbers were entered, and arrows lit up, right or left. The line ahead of me shortened, and soon there were only half a dozen left.

"You two together? Okay. Enter one number. Either one." "That way." "You two together?"

"No," a woman cried passionately. "We are absolutely not together."

"Okay," said the bored official from somewhere ahead of me. "Enter your number, sweetheart. Go that way." "Watch it, Bondy! She says you're not together, let her alone. Besides, your number comes up the other way."

I was next. The lever snapped. The arrow pointed right.

"That way, colony girl. Down to your right."

"Where is the ship going," I asked, without any real hope of receiving an answer.

"The colonists end up on Thairy, love. Run on now."

As I turned to my right, I looked back. Another me was standing there, looking at the arrow that had lit.

"That way, bondy girly. Down to your left."

I saw myself turn left, heard myself ask, "Where is the ship going?"

"It's off to Cantardene. Get moving."

Cantardene. What had someone told me about Cantardene? The K'Famir. The dreadful, evil K'Famir . . . somehow, she'd been mixed up. It wasn't a colony planet at all . . .

Margaret/on Earth

So, I, Margaret, dreamed I had been sent away from Earth, split off from myself, not once, but three times! When I woke, it was perfectly clear in my mind, and I wrote it down in my journal, just to remember it. Gradually, as the day passed, the dream faded. I forgot all about it until a long time later, a day when I felt terrible and lay in my bed full of fever and aching. To comfort myself, I did what I had not done for a year or more: I went among my people. The little shy one, the healer, she was gone. The one who had been my spy was gone. My warrior was gone. I took out my journal and read what I had written about the dream. Which one had gone to Chottem? Which one to Cantardene? Which one to Thairy? And where was Wilvia now?

I Am Gretamara/on Chottem

The Gardener called me Gretamara. She took me to Chottem, a blue-and-green planet. We flew across enormous, rolling grasslands into high, splintered mountains near the western sea. We dropped down a valley into a little village, a hamlet called Swylet. We alit near her house and walked to it through her garden, surrounded by a fence with a gate in it. A bell hung by the gate, and she said that people rang it when they needed her help. She was a physician, or perhaps something more than a physician, and she told me my task was to learn from her, to be a healer.

She told me about herself. Everyone in Swylet who had ever ailed knew the Gardener, and even the indomitably healthy had seen her moving about in the shade of the moss-draped trees beyond the fence. Gardener told me about the people, about generations of them, for she seemed to know everything they had ever thought, or wanted, or dreamed of. Gardener said there was always a Grandmother Sage, a Grandmother or Grandfather Vinegar, an Uncle Salt, an Aunt Pepper. The current Grandmother Sage, who was young when she had first sought help from the Gardener, was fond of saying that the Gardener's appearance had not changed over the years, that she was still as young-looking as in Grandmother's youth. Grandfather Vinegar—the current one—claimed that Grandmother Sage had probably dealt with three generations of Gardeners, the current one being the granddaughter of the one Grandma had known in her youth.

"But she's the same, the very same!"

"Ah, no, Granny," said the vinegary one. "It's just the appearance of this latest one has rubbed up against the memories of those others, wearing against one another like coins in a pocket until all the little differences are worn away."

Since the Gardener never left the garden by a route any of them could see, not so much as to step outside the gate, even Grandfather Vinegar could not venture a guess as to how she might have come by a child or a grandchild. Only women and children were invited inside her gate, and they only rarely, and a dreadful penalty was exacted from trespassers. Some of the grandmothers claimed to remember David Highnose opening the gate and walking two steps inside, two steps back out, and falling dead on the path, shriveled as an old leaf.

Aunty Pepper gave it as her opinion that the Gardener was married to the moon, though Uncle Salt said it had to be the sun, for what garden burgeoned by moonlight? Grandma Sage said if she was married to anything natural, likely she was married to the rain, for it was true that sweet rain came to the Gardener's place, even in droughtful times when the rest of Swylet got only the shout and splatter of a thunderstorm traveling through, much noise and little help. Those near the Gardener's fence sometimes heard rain falling, and if a person put a hand on the top rail, that hand would be wet with rain, though not a single drop fell on the dusty road outside.

All Swylet knew how she looked as well as I did: lithe and strongly built, with hard brown hands and a face that seemed to be all bones and eyes until one looked carefully and saw the curve of the lips, the flare of the nostrils, the way color came and went in her cheeks. I thought her very beautiful, though in a quiet way, the way a great tree is beautiful or a mountain. Between the straps of her summer sandals, her feet were brown as her hands. She wore a leather apron with many pockets over ankle-length dresses that were green in spring, gold in summer, red in fall, and blue in winter. Her hair was usually covered by a fine linen wimple topped by a wide-brimmed and battered leather hat. I never saw her wash herself, but she was always clean, and she smelled of flowers.

The people of Swylet also knew the Gardener's cats, very large, round-headed ones who came to the gate whenever a supplicant rang the bell. They were mostly tabby cats, a few black ones, and always at least one with slanting blue eyes in a narrow, speculative face. Each had a name, and the Gardener spoke to them in baby talk as she walked: "There, Bounce, beneath that borage a burrow. See to it tonight. Lightfoot, linger by the lilies. Someone starlit has left them in tangles. Tell me what creature is dancing there, do . . ." Then she would laugh, and so would the cats, in strange high voices, as though they were playing a game. The villagers stated as absolute fact that the cats sometimes danced on their hind legs and spoke among themselves.

I could not tell whether the villagers believed this was truth or had merely invented it for amusement, though Grandpa Vinegar and his ilk never allowed themselves to be amused. Grandpa Vinegar had grown old and sour from loneliness, for his marriage had ended long ago when his wife hanged herself by her neck from the barn loft, despairing over his having brought calamity home to taint her blood and kill the babe in her womb. This calamity came from his chasing after women in the sea cities before he came back to his betrothed in Swylet, barely in time for the marriage feast. So said the Gardener when the woman brought the stillborn to her, begging to know why. The Gardener took the baby to lie among her lilacs. She always took dead babies to lie in her gardens, and certain mothers claimed they could hear their children laughing as they danced upon the Gardener's meadows in the moonlight.

So, they talked about the Gardener, and when they first met me, they talked about me, but no more than they talked about the weather or the crops or the latest scrape the children were into. Generation after generation, the Gardener came down the path among her cats, talking to them as she came, and no matter what the supplicant asked for, the Gardener always gave something that would help. Babies were born and named and taken in their mother's arms to the Gardener's gate to receive her traditional gift of honeycomb on their lips. "That his life may be sweet," the Gardener always said, her voice humming softly among the droning of the bees. "That her life may be sweet."

And there I lived, and I worked hard learning what she taught me. I learned to plant and gather what I had planted and make elixirs from it and to mix them with others to treat specific conditions. I slept well at night because I was tired, and my hands grew callused and hard, like hers. Still, my life was sweet, and she took me on many journeys, including one that was unusual but very important for mankind.

You will need to imagine this:

A volume of amorphous, immeasurable space scattered with stars, singly or in clusters; some bright, some dull; each surrounded by a halo of luminescent mist that swims and wavers, sometimes penetrating the cloud that surrounds another star, sometimes separating from it; everything shifting, neither spiraling nor whirling as a whole but separately erratic, as though each point of light has a different destination.

Or this:

A forest. Here a tree immense past reckoning, its saplings gathered at its feet; there a huge, moss-hung hulk looming lonely at the edge of things; here a copse of fluttering leaves or a brushy labyrinth of old trees, branches intertwined. Imagine the whole underlain with shrubs and ferns over liverworts and fungi, while in the soil below little worms and bacteria writhe and multiply; everything moving slowly, undetectably, chaotically, one part going there, another coming here, all without apparent direction.

Or this:

An ocean inhabited by a thousand life-forms, some solitary, some in schools, some reef dwellers living by twos and threes, here a fanged eel, there a sinuous serpent, here a cloud of clown fishes, striped like a carnival, and over them all the colossal bulks of great basking sharks or whales, they, too, surrounded by clouds of diatoms and krill and bits of floating weed, all moving in separate routes toward indiscernible ends.

Imagine watching any of these for a million years or so as new stars come and old ones die, as old trees rot away and saplings grow tall, as whale bones litter the abyss and young fry hatch, as all the parts within each scene shift in relationship to one another, some touching, some separate, sometimes so remote that the individual seems undetectable by any perception save its own. Imagine that they speak, that space hums and bellows with their voices:

Star calls to star: "Here I am, who is like me?" Tree calls to tree: "I am I, who knows me?" Submarine dweller calls to other dwellers, innumerable calls: some subsonic, some deep, rhythmic pulses, some shrill eeps and squeals. When a response is detected, the thing that uttered moves separately but implacably toward its responder, as by gravity. So equivalence is drawn to equivalence until they are within touching distance.

Gardener took me to this place. She called it the "Gathering," and those assembled there were "Members of the Gathering." She said the place could as well be called Heaven, Valhalla, Olympus, or Glaspfifel, and those assembled could be called gods, spirits, essences. Regardless of title or size, she said each one of them, arose from a mortal source: Human, Gentheran, Quaatar, K'Famir, or any of a thousand others. Large gods arose from numerous sources, and small gods arose from few, size having nothing to do with potency. Any race of mortal beings may give rise to one god or many, and if, by chance or intention, an entire world is struck by a giant comet wiping out an entire living race, the Members associated with that race wink out like blown candles, at once both absent and unremembered.

Each Member, the Gardener said, can think only what its mortal source thinks, and each source visualizes its Member(s) differently. Earthians speaking of their gods: "Him" or "Her" or "Them," visualize very large persons, perhaps of great age, to denote wisdom, or strength, or power. Gentherans visualize kindly uncles and keen-minded aunts. K'Famir and Frossians and Quaatar visualize huge, fanged creatures with curved knives in each of their several manipulators, squatting above bloody altars. Though many mortals speak with authority concerning what their Members want—"Our Father wants us to sacrifice a bullock," "Kali demands we garrote a passerby"—the desires and demands of the gods are always determined by the desires and demands of the people. Whatever the prophet or priesthood comes up with, the gods parrot. The Members of the Gathering think only what their source thinks: bloody, painful, happy, kindly, arbitrary, logical, sadistic, nurturing—every god is always what the people suppose it to be.

Gardener says few mortals have ever seen the Gathering, and those who have seen any of it have seen only a tiny fraction of the whole. Even if mortals could gain access to the place and observe its continuous and eternally erratic movements as it sorts and re-sorts itself, they would be no wiser, for the Gathering is a spiritual mirror of the whole universe in which all mortal races are reflected through their deities.

Whenever a previously planet-bound race achieves space travel, they carry some or all of their gods with them into space. As soon as those deities emerge through the gravitic barrier around their home planet they are drawn inexorably to the Gathering. So when the Gentherans left their original home world, Gentheran Members appeared in the Gathering. So when the Earthians left their world to set up their little colonies, Earthian Members appeared. The Gentheran Members were few, very strong, and mostly cheerful, so said Gardener. The Earthian Members, on the other hand, covered the entire spectrum from horrid to happy, from bloodthirsty to benevolent, from sadistic to solicitous, and were, counting all the little saints of this and that, so very numerous that some of the oldest Members of the Gathering considered the arrival to be more an invasion than an advent.

The Gardener told me that a Quaatar Member, known to his inventors and worshippers as Dweller in Pain, was one of the most annoyed. DIP took an instant dislike to each and every Earthian Member, though it could give no reason for doing so. Members know only what their sources know, and no mortal Quaatarian knew why it disliked humans. It was a received aversion, passed down from generation to generation. Even if no prior reason had existed, the dislike might have arisen anew from the fact that many of the Earthian Members were rather jolly, and the Quaatar, being sadomasochists of the most elemental sort, did not approve of jolly. Pain, honor, blood, and death were the components of their ethos. Agony was their meat and drink, beginning in infancy when baby Quaatar, moving swiftly to avoid being eaten by their elders, often lost body parts in the process; continuing in youth through an endless series of rite-of-passage battles and on to the precedence trials of adulthood, events of ever-increasing excruciation until death intervened. In Quaatar male society, abhorrence of strangers and infliction of pain was the norm. Loathing the foreign or inferior and torturing the loathed was considered the usual thing. So Gardener told me, pointing out, as she did so, a few little Earthian gods with similar tendencies. "That is the god of jihad," she said. "That is the god of crusades. They are identical except for their names."

She explained that the Gathering is a sloshing sea of fluctuating factions, each wavelet betraying an ephemeral or lasting association. By the time mortal races leave their home planets, many of their gods have already amalgamated with one another. Small tribal godlets are often thrust together through shared execrations. All Death-Honor-and-War gods, for example, are identical. The people may fly different flags, but their gods are happy to drink blood from both sides of the battle. All Sun, Harvest, or Forest divinities are analogous. Even when similar mortal races arise on planets remote from one another, similar gods find one another easily.

The oldest deities of the Gathering, those originated by the Pthas, a source billions of years old and wise past belief, had set boundaries for the Gathering: Whatever the mortal races might do among themselves, their gods might not interfere with the sources of other Members. When detected, the penalty for such an attempt was instant eradication.

That "when detected" was a narrow but advantageous loophole, for, as the Gardener said, the right-hand tentacles, palps, or scravelators of the Members of the Gathering were only rarely aware of what the countersegmental organs were up to. Further, no part of the Gathering, including the oldest and wisest, was diligent in finding such things out. Even though the gods of the Pthas had instructed that neutrality or beneficence should govern the Gathering, there was no routine enforcement of that dictum. The Gardener says that mortals often pass laws they cannot enforce in order to be seen as "strong," or "determined," even though they know the laws will not solve the problem.

The Quaatar race was convinced that humans should be eradicated, but they did not wish to be wiped out in their turn, so they conspired in secret, drawing upon the skills of their planetary kinsfolk, the Thongal, the Frossians, the K'Famir.

These races, long separated from Quaatar, were still similar to the Quaatar in many ways. None of them had an emotion equivalent to gratitude, but all of them had a mercantile respect for debits and credits. The Quaatar were credited for having given the Thongal, the K'famir, and the Frossians planets of their own. Winnowed by circumstance, these races were now far superior to the Quaatar, but they greeted their elders with well-feigned respect and rejoiced at joining in vendetta against Earthians. They wished to conduct this massacre without implicating themselves, so, in the Gathering, a similar alliance with similar concerns occurred among Whirling Cloud of Darkness-Eater of the Dead of the K'Famir, Flayed One-Drinker of Blood of the Frossians, and the head of the Quaatar pantheon: Dweller in Pain. As reinforcement of their intentions, the leaders of the four races met on Cantardene, where they sacrificed to their bloodthirsty gods and swore to create a weapon that would seek out and kill humans wherever they were. Cantardene is the home world of the K'Famir, but the Gardener learned of it, and she told me, Gretamara, while I shuddered and wished . . . almost wished I could return to childhood, back on Phobos again.

I Am Ongamar/on Cantardene

During the seemingly endless trip from Earth to Cantardene, young as I was, I served as translator between the cargo and the Mercan crew—an assorted bunch of them: vicious K'Famir, cringing Hrass, sleek and superior Elos, and boisterous K'Vasti. Because I was in a state I can describe only as continuous fury, I did not cringe, and I did not bow. I knew at the beginning of the trip that they had misread my number, that I had been put on a bondage ship rather than a colony one. I had had time to get over it, I thought I had gotten over it, only to feel rage boiling up again the moment we, the humans, arrived and were marched off across a plaza. We were not chained. We had been warned in advance (or, I had been warned and told to warn the others) that acting up by any one of us would result in removing the whole group from sale as light laborers for household use and selling all of us to the mines.

When this warning seemed to have little effect, I then regaled my fellow bondies with stories of the mines. I'd heard a good deal about them during the trip. A few of the bondies had rebelled during the trip. They'd been dealt with publicly and fatally, and I hadn't been so stupid as to try to interfere. That memory and my description of the mines cowed the others into appropriate submission.

Trough-shaped fountains extended along the sides of

the plaza, most of them occupied by naked young K'Famir halfway between gill and lung stages of development. The young were of various colors: black, green, ocher, a few of dull red; all of them sleek and shining, exuberantly noisy, all eight limbs in motion at once as they sprawled and splashed, shrieking at one another in shrill, sibilant voices, conversations that I understood very well, having translated similar ones for what had seemed to be months. The K'Famir had a language of their own, but they used it only during religious observances and on very formal occasions. For commerce and daily life, they spoke Low Mercan, as did most of the vocal populations in the Combine. Though it was an ugly language, I was getting very, very fluent at gargling Low Mercan.

Up ahead of us we could see the bondage-block, a broad, low dais around which each servant offered for sale would be paraded. In a low voice, I reminded the group that we wanted to survive, and survival depended upon being servile. This was the intention I had started with: survive at all costs, do whatever was needful to get through the next fifteen years. I'd passed this intention on to the others. I'd told them, and myself, that anger could not help and might hurt our chances. We arrived at the block, and I breathed deeply, retreating into myself as I'd often done on Phobos.

My fellow servants were sold off, one by one, managing to do it without getting themselves whipped or beaten. By the time I was displayed, I'd managed to detach myself from the procedure. I walked about the dais while the auctioneer began the spiel I'd been hearing all morning: Young. Healthy. Strong. Almost immediately a heavily ornamented female thrust her way through the crowd of onlookers.

"I'll see her," the K'Famira called. "She may be what I want!"

"K'Famira Adille," murmured the pitchman. "You need a house servant?"

"I have house servants," she replied, throat pouch turning slightly pink in annoyance as she rearranged her voluminous scarves. "My housekeeper sees to them. I do not waste my time buying house servants. I want a pet."

"Most buyers prefer them younger."

"I don't want one I have to house-train. Humans look like a person cut in half, but they're said to be trainable. Walk it around again for me."

Obediently, I walked, impressions falling into place like coins into slots. When one studied language, one also studied its speakers. The skin around the K'Famira's eye sockets was not wrinkled: She was therefore young. A young K'Famira buying a pet was either a pleasure-female incapable of reproduction or a wife who had been warned not to attempt it. Infertility was a problem among city-dwelling K'Famir, exacerbated by the cultural prohibition against adoption. Male K'Famir accepted none but their own. Returning to the swamps for several seasons was usually an effective cure for the conditions, but that was not always possible.

I knew this in part because the Low Mercan vocabulary reflected the true situation: The word for city included the rootword for sterile; the word for swamp included the rootword for fecund. The word for a pleasure-female was made up of the words *urban* and *k'dawk*, a term for playful congress, indecent when used alone. *Playful* had been the word used in my glossary, but from what I now knew about the K'Famir, I doubted that any interchange between male and female could be playful. I now knew things I had not known I knew, for until now I'd had no mental hooks to hang them on. After a long voyage of listening to K'Famir talk, I had acquired hooks in plenty.

Because many K'Famira were sterile, pets were common. Any small, biddable creature would serve. Pets could be brought up in the family and kept for an unlimited time, or, when they reached adulthood, the pet could be freed to a colony. If the family didn't free it, the pet could be sold again for fifteen years of labor. One of the more discouraging facts I had learned on the ship was that time spent as a pet did not count against the term of bondage unless the family wished it so. The one encouraging thing I had learned was that K'Famir males did not find Earthians sexually attractive or at all interesting.

So, I focused on these trivia, standing very still and ignoring the manipulators running over my body.

"What's your name, human-female-young," Adille asked in Mercan, waiting for the translator to convey this to me.

"Margaret," I said, without waiting for the translator. "And I'm twelve Earth-years old."

"You speak Mercan?" Adille sounded almost outraged.

"I do, Great Lady," I said, focusing all my attention upon Adille's speech in order to blank out her smell.

"Well, then. You would be a bargain, wouldn't you?"

"I would seek to please the Great Lady," I said.

The cargo manager on the ship had been kind enough to instruct me in what to say. Great Lady. Great Lord. My only desire is to give good service. What does the Lord require? And so on. I had taught these same phrases to those in the cargo, though only a few of them had learned to say the words in Low Mercan. The cargo manager had told me he much regretted that he could not buy me for himself, as an assistant during future voyages.

"And your name, again?" Adille demanded.

"Margaret."

"Margaret. What a strange name, and yet, I suppose you're used to it. We'll keep some of it for you, wouldn't that be nice? My last pet's name was Onga. Suppose we call you Ongamar?"

And Ongamar I became. Ongamar who found her role not unfamiliar, for she fetched and carried, grateful to be frequently ignored, reconciled to being occasionally petted and fussed over, meantime listening to every word spoken in her presence and, when possible, those uttered behind closed doors. Thus I, she, expanded my Mercan vocabulary while learning a great deal about the K'Famir race and the Combine of which it was a member.

In general, I, as Ongamar, found the situation tolerable. The Mercan people were uniformly disagreeable, but simple pleasure-females—as distinguished from the breeding consorts of males in the hierarchy—had no dynastic ambitions and shared few of the more deadly K'Famir attributes. Though vicious if provoked, females were not routinely cruel; their interests were narrow and restricted to their own comfort; their servants and pets did not find them hard to please.

The males, however, were uniformly sly and vicious, even before they were sent to their male-only religious schools. By the time they left those schools, they were sufficiently menacing that pets, servants, and children stayed out of their way, and even consorts and pleasure-women were careful of their demeanor. There was no K'Famir law against the negligent or purposeful slaying of children or wives by male K'Famir, or the slaying of male K'Famir by male K'Famir, though penalties were exacted for slaying the mates or children of other males, which was considered to be theft.

As Ongamar, I was allowed to take my own exercise unsupervised in the walled gardens, which were extensive. My usual food was a tasteless kibble, made especially for pets of several humanoid races, but I was also fed scraps from the table, many of them delicious, though some were revolting. Adille's previous pet had been of an other race, but Adille learned which foods were acceptable while I invented ways to avoid being stuffed with foods that made me ill. Vomiting on the carpets resulted in a beating with one of the special slave whips made of flemp hide. The skins had microscopic, hook-shaped scales on them that tore the flesh and prevented the wounds from healing. Pets were beaten for any "dirty" behavior such as track-ing in soil or leaves or failing to put clothing away, or spotting any-thing with blood, which occurred when I began to menstruate, some little time after arrival.

The first bleeding upset Adille, and I was taken to a K'Famir veteri-narian, who explained the biological function to Adille, not to Ongamar, and gave a kit of supplies to Adille, not to Ongamar, that Ongamar was to be trained to use. Thereafter Adille speculated from time to time whether it might not be fun to breed Ongamar and raise a litter of little ones. When she mentioned this in her current patron's presence, how-ever, his throat sac bulged to its fullest as he bellowed that one animal in the house was barely tolerable and there were to be no more.

The semiaquatic K'Famir wore clothing as protection when out-doors, or as adornment. While at home they were constantly in and out of the fountains with which most of the rooms were furnished. Clothing for pets was allowed. When my own clothing began to wear out, I begged Adille for fabric to make simple, long-sleeved shifts. In public, K'Famir and pets without fur or scales wore voluminous scarves to prevent sunburn.

During the first year of captivity, I accompanied Adille and her current patron, Bargom, to the pleasure quarter to meet some old friends. They stopped at various stalls, including one tiny one where

Adille saw a kind of bib lying under a glass bell. Made of many tiny beads, it created pictures.

"Bargom!" Adille cried. "Look at this! Doesn't that look like you?" As it did, the bead colors shifting suddenly to create the very likeness of Bargom when he was startled, side-eyes very wide and angry.

"Nonsense," he said. "It looks like your mother."

I stepped a little to one side and saw what he meant. It did resemble Adille's female parent, who from time to time cohabited with Adille.

"How does it do that?" cried Adille. "Oh, Bargom, look at the tag. It's only twenty mantrim. You promised me something fun to amuse me during my molting. Buy it for me."

"Surely it's only a trick," he said.

"Not at all," murmured the stall owner, who had appeared from behind a curtain as they stared. "It portrays memories, which it captures from the minds of those who confront it. Each owner helps it develop more complexity. Here on Cantardene, K'Famir images mostly, though on occasion it will portray events."

I recognized him as a Thongal, a serpentine, periodically sexless race that was occasionally seen in the Cantardene markets. I had been told of this race at school. This particular Thongal had tattered ears and abraded hollows below his eyes where his heat sensors and rudimentary sex organs should have been, routine punishment on the home planet. It lifted the glass bell so Adille could see the necklace more closely while she stroked the shining surface of the minute beads.

"A strange thing to be so cheaply priced," said Bargom, peering at it but coming no nearer.

"A strange thing is not always much desired," the Thongal said, with a deprecating snarl. "K'famir prefer the familiar."

"Is it a necklace?" cried Adille.

"It could be, if one wished to wear it, though I am told it may become too heavy to be worn comfortably."

Adille reached forward and picked it up from the velvet pad, hefting it between her palps, laughing. "Not heavy at all! Oh, Bargom, do get it for me."

I reached up to stroke the glowing beads, running the tip of one finger over them, looking up to catch the Thongal's eyes fixed upon me.

"Pretty pet the lady has," said the Thongal. "May one ask its name?"

"Ongamar," said Adille, casually. "Though it had another one. What was it, human?"

"Margaret," I murmured, catching a peculiar expression in the Thongal's eyes. Amusement? Glee? Satisfaction?

"Margaret," it purred. "From Earth, no doubt."

Bargom had found a forty-mantrim note in his pouch, and the Thongal took it with a gloved hand, passing the necklace and the change back to Adille in those same gloved hands. Adille waited while I fastened the clasp around her neck, then we went on to the evening entertainment: dinner at a restaurant, where I stood beside Adille's place to cut her food, meantime watching her necklace shifting and changing, sometimes somber, sometimes violent in color and action.

After the meal, Adille and Bargom had front-row seats at a pouch-howling concert, while I waited in the "servant races" section, just far enough off the lobby to be spared the worst of the cacophony. When we reached home, the necklace was taken off and laid upon the ledge of Adille's grooming trough.

"You know," said Adille, rubbing her throat pouch, "it really is heavier than it feels. My neck is quite weary from it."

I stood beside the trough, examining the necklace without touching it, for when I had touched it before, I had felt a threatening emanation, tangible as a smell, as though something dangerous had wakened and looked at me with recognition. As the Thongal stall owner had done. As though he knew of me, which was an unpleasant thought.

"Great Lady," I murmured, "perhaps it might be best not to wear it very often."

"Nonsense, Ongamar," said the K'Famira. "It's just that we've had a long day, and I'm a bit tired."

I was unconvinced. To all the regrets I had brought from Earth,

I now added one more: a deep regret at having touched the thing at all. Somehow, though Adille had received the gift, I felt it had been intended for Margaret-by-any-name, as a trap intended for a particular victim might allow someone else to fall into it first. So Adille had been caught, but the trap was not dissatisfied, for it had caught me as well.

I Am Naumi/on Thairy

The ship bringing me from Earth landed on the colony world of Thairy. A door opened from the ship into a somewhere outside, a place full of mist, an impenetrable nothingness. Voices echoed, but they made no sense. Words were meaningless. I was moved here and there. I had a sense of motion but not a sense of being, as though it happened, had happened, was happening to someone else. I was aware, but not sensible of. I laughed quietly to myself, finding this all most amusing.

Then suddenly, not. Something reached inside me and pulled. It wasn't pain, one couldn't call it pain, but it was not something one wanted to happen, it was a strangeness one wanted desperately to stop happening. I cried out. There was an abrupt sound, as though someone spoke angrily in an unknown language, and a dark curtain came down.

When I, Naumi, wakened, I found myself in a narrow bed in a small, very clean room. Very clean, I thought, and empty, for it held only the bed, a stool beside the bed, and a few pegs with clothing hanging on them on the far wall. Above the pegs was a label: Naumi's clothes. Below the peg, a shelf, a label: Naumi's shoes. I read this with some concern. Who was Naumi?

The sound of feet outside somewhere, then a white door opened through a white wall and someone came in.

It was the very nice old man who only had one eye. His name. His name was . . .

"Mr. Weathereye," I said.

"You remembered," the man chuckled. "Very good! You see, I told you it would all come back to you. What else?"

"My . . . my ma. She was killed."

"That's right. And your father, also. But that was a long time ago. Since then, you've been living . . . where?"

"With . . . Pa Rastarong. He took me in."

"Exactly. You see, you knew all this. It's just that bump on your head that made you forget for a little while. You live near the town called Bright on the colony world of Thairy. You live with your pa, and your name is . . . ?"

"Naumi Rastarong," I said.

"Exactly. What else?"

I frowned.

"Reach for it!" demanded Mr. Weathereye.

I reached. There was something there, just out of reach. Ah. Well. What was it?

"Some other language," I said. "I know some other language!"

"You do indeed. Several, as a matter of fact."

We fell silent, the man smiling, humming quietly to himself while I was preoccupied with something else. "Mr. Weathereye," I said at last, "I don't feel like my skin fits!"

"That's natural," the old man said. "Any time you get a good bump on the head, that's natural. You'll feel a little strange for a while, but you'll get used to it."

We fell silent again, and this time I drifted into what was almost sleep. An elderly lady and a lanky, lazy-looking fellow came into the room and sat on chairs near Mr. Weathereye.

"Rastarong," he said. "Lady Badness."

They nodded. The woman asked, "How is he?"

"Ah," replied Mr. Weathereye, "feeling a little strange, as who wouldn't. All that long journey."

"Does he know his name?" asked the other man.

"Naumi," said Mr. Weathereye. "I asked him, the way we do, when he was half asleep, 'Hey, boy, what's your name,' and he said Naumi."

"What does it mean?" asked Lady Badness.

"How in galactic parlance should I know?" Mr. Weathereye said in a testy voice, running his finger around the edge of his eye patch, as though it itched him. "It's his name. I asked, and he told me."

"When can I take him home," asked Rastarong.

"Soon. Just don't hurry him."

"I have fostered before," said the other, slightly peeved.

"Of course," soothed Mr. Weathereye. "Haven't we all."

They rose and departed. Behind them, I was surprised to find my face wet with tears, my heart swallowed up in a sorrow I couldn't or identify or connect. Mama and Papa, dead and gone? No, not that. That was long ago. This injury they said I'd had. I couldn't even remember that. No, it was some word, some label that lay within reach of my tongue but not within reach of my mind. Who was that? And why was I grieving for her?

I Am Wilvia/on B'yurngrad

Joziré and I sat on a haystack above a town with no name, the remains of our picnic luncheon scattered around us. I was chewing on a straw and making pictures out of clouds when Joziré asked, "Willy, do you know when your birthday is?"

I thought a moment. "I don't even know how long a year is, here. I'm not even sure how long we've been here."

"Here is somewhere on B'yurngrad, and we've been here about three school years," he said. "I know because I'm working on volume three of the history of governance."

"I'm still reading about laws." I sighed. "The sisters at the temple say I have to learn all about laws before I can study justice. I think it ought to be the other way around, but they say not."

"It's the same with the brothers at the abbey. I have to learn all the stuff that didn't work before I can study the things that did. They say if a ruler doesn't know what didn't work, and why, he'll waste time, treasure, and lives learning it the hard way." He stared at the sky, cleared his throat, chewed his lip.

I made a face at him. "What are you so twitchy about?"

"Lady Badness says I have to go away to school next year."

I sat up, horrified. "Just you? Not me? Where?"

"Just me. Maybe it's only for boys. She didn't say where."

"I guess that's how Lady Badness got her name," I said angrily. "She's all the time bringing bad news."

"It's not bad, exactly. It's just . . . troubling. Lady Badness says I can't come into my full powers until I'm well schooled, and I can't be king until I come into my full power. . . ."

"What powers?"

"I have no idea. Something Ghossy, I guess. She says when I'm well schooled, I'll know, and if I don't get well schooled, it won't make any difference. I'm sure she's right, but . . . I don't want to leave you, Wilvia. Four years is a long time." He turned his head to stare sightlessly at the two nameless hills that rose gently above rolling grasslands, each bearing a school on its crest: the gray-towered abbey for boys, the white-domed temple for girls. His school; my school. Between the two, the town straggled down into the valley on both sides of a boisterous, nameless river crossed by half a dozen old stone bridges. From the hayfield where we sat, we could see the whole town: gardens, farmlands, orchards. For all we knew, it could be the only town on B'yurngrad.

"It'll probably be just as remote as this is," he said. "My mother sends me letters by couriers, telling me I have to stay hidden."

"Because of the Frossians trying to kill you."

"Well, they killed my father, they've tried three times to kill my mother, they've been hunting for us ever since we left Fajnard. Mother's spies on Fajnard say the Frossians want to wipe out the royal house before they invade, so our family won't be a center of rebellion."

I whispered, "The sisters told me about it, and I've studied all your mother's writings. I know she was the one who established the Court of Equity on Fajnard. Think of that, Joziré! A court dedicated to pure justice, one that can overrule the law! They didn't even have one of those back on old Earth!"

"I know." He fidgeted. "Willy . . . ?"

"What, Jos? Don't fidget."

"When I go away, will you wait for me until I come back?"

"Unless they send me somewhere else. Of course."

"I don't mean that. I mean, will you not get too friendly with any other boy until I come back."

I felt myself turning red. "You mean wait for you . . . that way."

He sighed deeply, running his fingers through his dark, curly hair. "You're really too young to make a promise like that. You're probably about thirteen, developmentally speaking, and I'm probably about sixteen. I know I have to go to this school, but I don't want us to be separated. That sounds soppy, but I don't want us to forget one another . . ."

I took his hand. "Jos, I'll wait for you forever. My stomach won't let me forget. No one else in the world can make a fried garlwog sandwich the way you can."

He aimed a blow at me. I blocked it and aimed one at him. I didn't dare let him go on talking that way, or I'd start to cry, and I didn't want to cry. We tumbled into the hay and came to rest, me with arms pinned at my sides, him above me, nose to nose.

"Promise!" he demanded. "Or I'll leave you here for the big wild garlwogs to make dinner of."

"They don't eat meat." I tried to laugh.

"You," he said, fixing me with his eyes. "You, they'd eat. Now promise."

"I promise Prince Joziré, heir to the throne of the Ghoss, that I, Wilvia, will not . . . get friendly with any male person until said prince returns."

He let me go suddenly and turned away to hide his face before he got up to gather the remnants of our picnic lunch into the basket. I had promised, but I could see it hadn't helped much.

"Jos," I whispered from behind him. "I really mean it. I will wait."

He forced himself to grin. "I know you will."

We walked back along the farm road, each of us thinking of all the wrong things we could say and do. At least I was. I was having other thoughts, too. Old ones. As we came near the town, we saw Lady Badness sitting on a waystone.

"There you are," she cackled. "I'd about given up on you. If you don't mind, Highness, I must speak with Wilvia."

He was Highness instead of Majesty because he hadn't been

crowned king, yet. And he did mind, but he gritted his teeth and plodded on.

"He told you he's going away," said Lady Badness, after he had gone halfway to the town. "You've promised to wait for him, but . . ."

I felt the words leave me like a gush of water. "I've promised. But is it because I really want to wait for him, or is it because I'm supposed to be a queen, and the only way I'll ever be a queen is if I marry Jos." I put my hands to my face, which was burning, wishing to call the words back. They had been true, the words, but I hadn't meant to speak them out loud.

"Ah," said Lady Badness in a satisfied tone, "that's the true question, isn't it. One you have to answer, Wilvia. Do you want to be queen?"

I stared at my feet, unable to answer.

"You see yourself with a crown. I know you do. You see yourself being gracious and wise. Isn't that true."

"Yes," I said grudgingly.

"Are you gracious and wise?"

I desperately wanted to lie, knowing it would do no good. "I . . . I don't . . . No. I'm not."

"Well, no matter how much Joziré loves you, he will not marry you unless you are gracious and wise, for the Queen of the Ghoss must be both. Becoming a queen is extremely hard work, and why would you want to do it? To be queen? Or to be with Joziré? Or because it is a worthy thing to be? If Joziré were gone, dead, would you go to all that work, just to be queen?"

We went up the hill together with the questions unanswered. I couldn't answer them. Not then. Not for a very long time.

I Am Gretamara/on Chottem

The Gardener told me that Swylet had been founded by several wagonloads of malcontents who, tired of being told what they might and might not do by the Lords of Manland, had set off westward in search of a place where they might do as they pleased. They left the coastal cities of Manland, Chottem's only human-occupied continent, and turned west, through the surrounding orchards and vegetable plantations, the dairy farms, the estancias with their horses and herds of cattle and haylands and grainfields, then left settled people behind as they moved into endless plains, where flocks of purple-feathered jibbernek bruised the sky at midday and whole villages of skritchers pranced on their rock-mounds, screaming alarm in the voices of old women. They climbed slowly into rolling hills, thence to a high tableland from which people could see for the first time retreating ranges of mist-valleyed mountains: indigo on azure on sapphire on ice.

Moving into those mountains they had arrived at last—and purely by fortune, so they thought—at a well-watered valley, hidden and protected by ramparts of immemorial stone. There at the end of nowhere they found an area fenced off, grown up in shrubberies and trees, and occupied by the Gardener. She welcomed them and told them to build beside the flowing river and to name their hamlet for the small, swift birds that nested there, the swylets.

Every now and then, a man or two from the village might back-track into the world on an urgent errand, to obtain breeding stock, or seed, or certain tools the settlers could not make for themselves. Sometimes they brought new settlers with them when they returned, though, as time went on, such additions became extremely rare. No one ever found the place by accident, though Swylet-born folk who went adventuring could always find their way home.

One such adventurer was the young artist Benjamin Finesilver. He had wandered the land with hunters, climbed the mountains with miners, sailed across the great freshwater seas of the north with fishermen. He had spent a season following the herds across the grasslands with the nomadic Skellar people, humans drawn from an ancient itinerant culture on Earth to inhabit the endless northern plains. From the black city of Bray he had sailed eastward toward the sunrise land of Perepume. The ship had anchored far out and discharged its trade goods into small boats crewed by little people no taller than his waist, who wore veils and talked a strange language in the high, sweet voices of children. They did not show themselves to strangers, the ship's captain told him, nor did they allow visitors.

To Benjamin, this was a great disappointment, but he was not long downcast. Since he had no way to see the farther side of the world, he would forget about Perepume and concentrate upon Manland. Though the eastern half of the human continent was flat, fertile, and relatively boring, the west and north held innumerable wonders in their broken, mysterious lands. Blue butterflies the size of a man's two hands. Beetles with gemmed carapaces that fought battles with the spears on their noses. A little fox the size of a kitten, which crept about the houses at night, crying like a baby, then laughing as it ran away when people came out. And the k'yur, which were rather like large cats but more like very thin bears, who stood atop the hills on three-moon nights and sang with the voices of angels.

Benjamin Finesilver talked with printers and booksellers and found them eager to help him. The people of the sea cities had plenty of time on their hands and plenty of money in their pockets, and though they were far too complacent and indolent to seek the marvelous for themselves, they were mightily amused by seeing or reading of anything wonderful and strange. The printers introduced him to people who published books, and the people who published books introduced him to people who financed such things, and thus Benjamin was brought to the attention of Stentor d'Lorn and his daughter, Mariah.

It followed that after ten years absence from Swylet, Benjamin returned with Mariah d'Lornschilde as his wife. She was lean and disdainful, with hair black as a traveling tinker's pot and blue eyes that silvered like swift fish in shallow water. She was taken aback some by Swylet, for it was smaller and slower than she had imagined. Still, she thought she loved Benjamin Finesilver, both because he adored her and because he had given her a way out of a sore predicament, and she was willing to spend a year or two in a dull, bucolic place if it pleased him.

Gardener knew this, as she knew everything about everyone in the place. She told me that even as a boy, Benjamin had been so eager to leave Swylet that he had paid very little attention to the place. Even had Mariah been interested in the hamlet, he could not have told her anything important about it, and he would never have thought to mention the Gardener to his new wife, even if he had remembered that the Gardener existed.

So, when the Grandmas came to welcome the bride, she was astonished when the first thing they said was, "You must go along to the gate and speak with the Gardener."

"And why must I do that?" she cried, laughing and shaking the ribbons in her hair so they danced on her head like butterflies. "In my home, my father speaks to the gardeners, and that is quite enough attention paid to them."

The Grandmas shared swift glances, some puzzled, some amused, a few even angry. "It's a custom," said Grandma Vine. "One we have. You might like to share our customs."

The others nodded, making light of it, saying yes, yes. Do share our customs.

"Well then, I will," said Mariah. "When I have time."

When they talked with her after that, time and again they would bring the Gardener into the conversation, for more than one had noticed the bride's waist was thickening and her steps had slowed. "A good time, now," said Grandma Bergamot. "Especially with your first."

Mariah, who felt nauseous most mornings and out of temper most afternoons, turned the talk to something else: the carpenter's newly built shop on the green, the plethora of lambs in the meadows, the way the cats kept on crying so strangely outside her window, keeping her from sleeping.

"Those are the Gardener's cats," they said. "Inviting you to visit."

"Nonsense," she said. "If the woman wishes to meet me, let her pay me a call." Indeed, she regretted mentioning the cats at all, for when she had peeped out the window to see what cried there, the moonlight had disclosed a crowd of furry, prick-eared animals dancing a gavotte. Mariah had a strong appreciation of her noble lineage and costly education. She was quite sure that if dancing cats existed anywhere in Chottem, her highly regarded professors would have told her of them. Therefore, she had simply been dreaming.

What could the women say? They had said no less than they had said to any of their own. They had suggested, invited, encouraged. If she had been of Swylet, they might have surrounded her, swept her away, and not let her go until they were outside the Gardener's gates, but she was not of Swylet. Who knew what family she came from, or what power it might have to upset their lives? Who knew what she thought or meant or intended with that easy, scornful laughter and superior mien that just missed being contemptuous. All very mannered, nothing to complain of, but very much as though they were *merely* a group of well-meaning ewe sheep while she . . . she was something else.

"Let her be," said the newest Grandma Vinegar. "She'll come to us soon enough when she needs to."

"No," said Grandma Bergamot. "I'll plead some tea for her. That much I can do, at least."

It was soon after my arrival on Chottem that Grandma Bergamot came to our gate and rang the bell. The Gardener and I went to the gate, the cats trailing around us.

"This is my ward, Gretamara," said the Gardener. "She has come to live with me while she learns to be a healer."

Grandmother Bergamot bobbed a curtsy, said a how-dya-do, and I greeted her with a smile. She glanced from me to the Gardener and back again, and I knew she was thinking we were kin, for we had the same tawny hair and green eyes, the same golden skin. Only our eyes were different. The Gardener's eyes were full of wisdom, but mine could have held only an endless list of the questions I had been asking since I arrived.

Grandma Bergamot recalled her errand and pled some tea for the new woman, who had come from far away.

"What is she like," the Gardener asked.

"Tall and dark, with silver eyes and a proud walk," said Grandma Bergamot. "She was Mariah d'Lornschilde in a sea city called Bray, and our Benjamin brought her home as a bride. She does not nest well here. It's as though she's counting the days until she can . . ."

I could see Grandma Bergamot hadn't known this until she said it, but it was right. We had seen the proud, dark woman. To us, too, it had seemed she was counting the days until she could . . . what?

"See my proud cock, there," said the Gardener, pointing at a pea-cock beneath a willow, tail and wings spread wide, quills rattling an accompaniment as he pranced before three inattentive hens. "See how he dances. He would dance to the cabbages if there were no hens about, but his joy would not be in it. Perhaps the people of Swylet are only cabbages to Mariah d'Lornschilde, and though she dances, joy is not in it for her."

"If her heart does not dance for Benjamin, then for what?" whispered Grandma Bergamot.

The Gardener shook her head. "Who knows. Gretamara will give you tea for her, Grandmother Bergamot, but I do not think she will drink it. Come back just before sunset."

I made the tea myself. The brew, heal-all, was the first brew I had learned, and when Grandma Bergamot came, I was waiting at the gate for her.

"I thank thee, Gretamara," said Grandma Bergamot.

"I will take your thanks to Gardener," I responded.

"Do you plan to visit long?"

"So long as the Gardener wishes," I said. "I am learning a great deal from her."

"And do you like it here in Swylet?"

"I have heard the history of Swylet and its people," I admitted. "And I like it very much where I am."

Grandma Bergamot took the tea. Gardener told me she had probably spent the day devising some way to get Mariah to drink it, and so she had. Grandma's own house was on the street where Benjamin Finesilver lived, and Mariah walked down that street each afternoon with a market basket in her hand and a parasol over her shoulder. So, next afternoon, when Mariah went by, Grandma Bergamot was sitting beneath her grape arbor, tea things set ready on a little table, and she invited Mariah in. "Do come. Have a cup of tea. I'm feeling lonely today."

Such a plea could not be politely refused, so Mariah came in and drank a cup of tea, while Grandma Bergamot only pretended to join her, for everyone knew the Gardener's gifts were for the intended ones alone.

"Odd," said Mariah. "An odd taste. Lovely, rather . . . what? Like rose petals but with something else. Where did you get it?"

"It's a brew gathered hereabout," Grandma replied. "If you like it, it would please me to make you a present of the packet."

Mariah started to refuse, then realized it would be rude to do so, and while she was often thoughtlessly haughty, she was never wilfully rude. She accepted the ribbon-tied packet with gracious words, picked up her basket and her parasol, and went off down the street. Though it had all worked just as Grandma Bergamot had planned, something about it had not been satisfying.

The Gardener stood on the stoop of her house, eyes fixed on the treetops as she spoke to me. "I see the packet of tea is going home in the marketing basket. It is sliding down as Mariah walks, and there it is beneath the apples and potatoes, the honey and the flour, the fresh eggs and the cut of lamb for Benjamin's supper. With most women, this would not matter, for she would see it when she put away the foodstuffs. However, Mariah is no cook, so Benjamin has hired one. There is Mariah, giving the basket to the cook, ah, yes. And the cook is putting the packet away in the cupboard."

"Won't Mariah ask for it?" I asked.

"No." The Gardener shook her head. "Tomorrow she will feel

well, very well. She will not think that it has anything to do with the tea she drank. In a day or two, the effect of the tea will wear away, but she will never think of it again."

Benjamin Finesilver, meantime, was getting on with his work. He had finished a good many paintings of places he had been. He had a comfortable study in which to work and sufficient funds to live decently for a year or so; he had written a good deal about the areas he had traveled through. He had not bothered to write anything about Swylet; he seemed scarcely to have noticed it since returning there. I saw him go by, several times. He did not even glance across the fence.

It was not long thereafter that Mariah considered it best to stay at home. She told Benjamin that the village women might show themselves swollen as melons as, indeed, most of the younger ones did at intervals, but Mariah's people did not do that. When one became ungainly, one stayed home with the front curtains drawn. One sunned in the garden and read books and sewed clothing for the baby, or so Mariah's aunts had instructed her. Mariah obeyed faithfully, though her days were so boring that she prayed for the baby to come quickly so her visit to this provincial backwater could be over.

Grandma Bergamot tried once again. She called on Mariah and was admitted if only because she broke the boredom of an endless afternoon.

"Our Gardener is a healer, you know," Grandma Bergamot said. "I know you've had the midwife here, and she's skillful, but when one has one's first, it does no harm to have a little something extra. Wouldn't you visit her, Mariah? In your carriage, just to her gate?"

"What is all this nonsense about the Gardener," cried Mariah in a temper. "I have written to my father in Bray. He has sent word that his doctor is coming to tend me, all the way from Bray, where my father is Lord Governor. When the baby comes, I'll be well enough provided for."

And that was that. The Gardener knew this as she knew everything that went on. She could stand in thought for a moment, staring into nothingness, then be able to tell me what everyone in Swylet was thinking or doing. This time, she stood outside the door, and her mouth was sad, for she pitied Mariah.

"Can you go to her?" I asked.

"I can do nothing out there. Only in here, which is why those in need come to the gate."

"I could go for you," I suggested.

She shook her head sadly, and I knew I could not do anything out there either.

Not long after, on a dismal morning with rain beating from a sullen sky, the baby announced its desire to be born weeks early, long before the doctor was expected to be there. The midwife was fetched. The labor went on. The midwife, in some agitation, suggested that someone go to the Gardener for Mariah, who was having a very difficult time. Benjamin Finesilver, who knew no more about childbirth than he did about Perepume, said nonsense, send for the village healer. This was done without improving the situation. The midwife again said someone should go to the Gardener, and this time Mariah screamed from her bed, yes, yes, go get someone, someone to help me . . .

Benjamin came himself, feeling a fool. Few men ever presented themselves at the gate, but he vaguely remembered having been taken there a time or two as a child, so it held no fears for him. He rang the bell, as the Gardener had said he would, and we went down to the gate. Benjamin begged something to ease his wife's pain. The Gardener asked him to put his hand over the gate, which he did, and she took it in her own while looking into his eyes. With a gesture, she summoned me to look at him also, and I saw what she had told me I would see.

After a long moment, she nodded and told him to wait. We went back into the house, and shortly she sent me to the gate. I told him, "Make a tea of this and have her drink a cup every hour. It will ease her pain."

"Will the child . . . will the child be all right?" he begged.

"You must bring your daughter here," I said, as I had been told to say. "To receive the Gardener's honey on her lips."

Thus somewhat comforted, he went back the way he had come, to brew the tea and make Mariah drink it and to see the pain leave her eyes, though the labor went on. After several more cups of tea and as many hours had passed, the baby girl was born.

"All's well, then," cried Benjamin.

"All's well with your daughter," said the village healer, turning back to the room where Mariah lay amid the crimson flood neither he nor the midwife had any way of stanching. "And your wife is in no pain."

All night Benjamin sat at the bedside holding Mariah's body in his arms. He would not look at the child the midwife brought to him, not until dawn came—clear, cloudless, hymned by birds— when he took the sleeping baby wrapped in its blankets and came down the street to the Gardener's gate. He rang the bell and waited, the tears still flowing down his face. By the time we reached the gate, Grandma Bergamot had come up from her house, for she had heard the bell.

"I've brought you the child," Benjamin cried, tears flowing down his face again. "Her mother is dead. You did not save her!"

"You did not ask me to save her," said the Gardener in a stern voice that cut through the fog of grief he was in. "You asked me to ease her pain. I did so. Grandma Bergamot asked me to save her some months ago, and I sent a medicine for her then."

Grandma Bergamot called, "Oh, she's right, Benjamin, she did, indeed. I sent her home with the tea myself. We tried to get Mariah to come here herself, but she wouldn't hear of talking with the Gardener . . ."

Benjamin gasped, recalling how Mariah had laughed about the Gardener. And he, he himself had not asked the Gardener to save her. Why? Why had he not? Sobbing, he thrust the child across the gate and into the Gardener's arms. "She's yours. Take her. I must take Mariah's body back to her people. I do not know how I will face them, and it is likely I will never in this life return to Swylet." He turned away, stumbling off toward his home, and by nightfall he was gone. The people of Swylet never saw him again.

Grandma Bergamot came to the gate, whispering, "Do you want me to take her, Gardener? I've raised five and helped with as many more." She peered at the baby, crying out a little. "Oh, but the wee thing, born far too soon!"

The Gardener shook her head, the silken folds of the wimple moving like grass in a wind, reflecting glimmers of light to play across her face. "Her father was one who looked so far he could not see a treasure lying at his feet. Her mother was one who looked so close, she could not see anything outside herself. The child was given to me. I will keep her and teach her how to see."

"But she's so tiny, so frail. Have you . . . I mean, do you know . . ."

The Gardener turned her eyes on the old woman and smiled until Grandma Bergamot flushed in confusion. "Do I know how to raise up a child, even one born too soon? Why, Grandma Bergamot, I knew you when you were Dora Shingle, a red, wrinkled squaller. I put honey on your lips. I gave your mother a galenical to cure your diaper rash. I fed you herbs for the summer fever and strong tea for the winter chills. I cured your earache and your sore throats and your belly cramps when the womanlies came upon you. Why would I not know how to raise one small babe who cannot be as troublesome as you were? Come in a moment and see for yourself."

Grandma looked around. No one else was about except two small red dogs chasing one another down the street. The gate was opened, and Grandma walked in, following us down the path, around the corner, through the shrubs, across the little lawn kept grazed short by fat ewe sheep, and through the door of the Gardener's House. The kettle was already hanging over the fire, and the cradle had been set beside it to warm, for we had known what was to happen. There was honeycomb on a plate, some of which went on the child's lips and some on Grandma Bergamot's and some of which was given to me.

"What will you name the baby?' Grandma asked, licking the sweetness from her mouth and wishing she were a child again, with no manners to keep her from begging more.

The Gardener smiled. "There's much thinking to do about that. Too small a name makes a person smaller than need be. Too large a name makes life a struggle to live up to. A name should fit, you know. It should be the size of the life it will signify."

Grandma wondered briefly how large a name Dora Shingle had been, before it occurred to her that now would be a good time to ask the Gardener some of the things she had long wanted to know.

"Gardener," she said, "since you're being so kind, would you tell me please where the cats come from?"

"Ah," said the Gardener, "well, where do cats come from? From kittens, no doubt."

Grandma Bergamot chuckled. "Oh, mayhap they do, or mayhap not. These cats of yours are no ordinary cats, Gardener."

"True," she replied. "Well, there's no reason not to tell you, Grandmother Bergamot, for your heart is good and you mean no ill to them. My cats come from the far side of Chottem, far east from the sea cities, where lies the blessed land of Perepume. There the cliffs rise from the sea to prevent invasion by ship, and great ragged continents of perpetual cloud prevent invasion from the air. Now that men have come to Chottem, however, it will not take them forever to find a way past these barriers. That means the people who live there may need to find a new world, though it will be a time before it becomes necessary for them to go." Then she turned to the cat at her side and said, "Isn't that true, lovely one."

"Oh, very true," said the cat, with a wide yawn as it stretched itself into a bow from tail-tip to tongue-flip. "As far as it goes."

Grandma put her hand on the cradle, which felt silky smooth under her hand. "This cradle is old," she murmured.

"Many children have used my cradle," the Gardener agreed. "Including some even smaller than this one." Then the Gardener said something else, then something else again, and before long, while I watched from the gate, Grandma was walking out and the busy dogs were in the exact same place they had been when she entered that gate. Though she felt she had been inside for a very long time, the sun still stood in the eastern sky as it had when she had entered.

She resolved to tell her friends about the cats from Perepume, and about the time standing still, for it explained so much that they had wondered about. The Gardener stayed young forever, because . . . because . . . Why was that?

Wonderingly, still licking the honey from her lips, she went off home, unable to remember anything except that Mariah d'Lornschilde had died in childbirth and Benjamin Finesilver had given his girl baby away to the Gardener and she herself had seen the child being rocked in its cradle by a girl called Gretamara.

Inside the Gardener's House, we sat sharing fragrant tea, the steam wreathing our faces and moistening our cheeks.

"Was there anything in what just happened that you did not understand?" the Gardener asked.

"I understood very little of it," I said. "I know you could have saved the woman's life but did not do so . . . I don't understand that. I know you are keeping the baby here, even though several of the women out there would care for it well enough for it to grow fat and healthy, and I don't understand that, either."

"This child," said the Gardener, laying her hand on the cradle, "is now the heiress of Bray. The previous heiress of Bray, her mother, was a foolish woman, a self-centered woman, family-proud and accustomed to the servitude of others. What reason might one have for wishing her daughter to grow up here instead of in the House of Bray?"

I thought that over. "Perhaps to let her learn of other things than she would learn there?"

"See, you do understand the answer, both to your first question and your second."

This was a troubling thought. "Then this child must learn to value things other than those Mariah valued."

"Yes," said the Gardener. "You and I must make sure of that. She will be high-spirited, I know, but she has no taint of evil. She will accept tutelage if both she and we are wise. We will court wisdom on her behalf by naming her Sophia. Sophia is the spirit of wisdom." She sipped her tea. "Are you happy here, Gretamara?"

I thought about this for some time, for I wished to say nothing to the Gardener that was not the truth. "I am often very happy here, Gardener. Your gardens fill me with such joy that it sometimes hurts. I value the ways of healing that you teach. Still, I think there is pain in much of what you do, and I do not understand why you changed my name or why we stay here, behind the fence, always alone."

The Gardener sighed, rising to look out the low, many-paned window that gave upon the garden. "As a young child, you had several people you enjoyed being, a queen and a warrior and a spy, this one then that one. Many children have such selves, harboring all kinds of possibilities within themselves. Each person contains the seeds of several persons. I have named one such person Gretamara to distinguish her from the rest. Gretamara is a healer.

"As for being alone, I am accustomed to solitude. My friends and I have a job of work to do. If it is to be done well, we must reduce distractions and interruptions . . ."

I interrupted, "But you're always being distracted and interrupted."

The Gardener laughed, "As you have just done! Not always interrupted, Gretamara, as you will learn. And, as I was saying, distractions and interruptions must be reduced without cutting ourselves off from one another or the daily lives of the people who have chosen and created us to care for and defend them. Our task must be accomplished without anyone noticing what we are doing. So, my friends and I live a compromise, sometimes meeting, sometimes separately, but always near a gate and a bell to summon us into ordinary life."

I asked, "Am I . . . one of your friends?"

A shadow crossed the Gardener's face. I thought it might be an expression of sorrow, but if so, it soon passed. The Gardener said, "Unlike ordinary people, Gretamara, we cannot choose what or who we will become: We are as we are made to be. You cannot choose to be one of us, but you can choose to be of inestimable value to our work. That choice is not to be made today, however, not even very soon. For the time being, your task is only to stay contentedly here, learning to heal those in need and whatever else I can teach you."

"May I learn another thing, then?"

"What thing is that?"

"Your stories, Gardener. Please, may I learn all of your stories."

"My stories?" The Gardener smiled. Outside the garden grew, the cats strolled, the sky paled, pinked, darkened. It wasn't a bad time for stories. "I will tell you a very old story about the angry man and the fish . . ."

Which she told me. A story that I heard again and again, later, many times, in many places.

I Am Margaret/on Earth

It did not take long to find out that Earth was no different from Phobos. People on Earth engaged in ritual repetition; most of them thought as little as possible; most of them occupied themselves with things and events that were not very important. Amusement stage dramas were the same as the ones I had seen on Phobos. All music had been so extensively filtered, corrected, and augmented by technology that it all sounded alike. Singing voices were improved by electronic means, as were the faces, the bodies, and the dramatic ability of actors and actresses. No one was plain; no one was allowed to be ugly; no one was very different from anyone else. In school, the stupid students got the same grades as the smart ones except for the tiny secret marks the educational archivists made in their records—in case a VIP needed a truthful reference.

I took my usual refuge in books, finding escape easier now that I had books written in other languages. No one had the time to sanitize books in Omniont or Mercan tongues, so Omniont peoples were allowed to be weird and eccentric, Mercans were unremittingly repulsive and violent. That most ancient of people, the Pthas, were enigmatic and profound. Their language was one of the most beautiful to hear, but the Pthas themselves were gone. They had ruled our galaxy for a billion years, fostering young races, helping people rise from barbarity to civility, but in the end, they had left our galaxy to explore the mysteries of the universe. The Pthas had taught that merely speaking their language would mold the mind toward truth. For that reason, so much as any human could learn to speak their language, I learned to speak Pthas.

The Quaatar were another story. They considered their language too holy for anyone except a Quaatar to speak, but I (along with two others in my class) learned to read and speak it. Out of bravado, I suppose. Showing off.

Each of the races whose languages we learned had different notions of good, bad, honor, dishonor, truth, or justice, a bewildering but marvelous array: more fruit for supposition and interpretation in one volume than in everything I had read until then. The K'Famir had no word for truth or justice; they had over fifty for degrees of torment and at least that many for honor, divided into classes, depending upon whose honor had been defiled, how grossly, and by whom. The Frossians had no words for good or bad: things were either edible or nonedible, profitable or unprofitable. The Quaatar had no words for equality, fairness, or impartiality. To each of them, every other Quaatar was either above or below them, while every thing or trait was either Quaatar or filth. The Quaatar word for filth was the same as their word for food: it applied to all non-Quaatar races except the K'Famir and the Frossians, who were called *gvoiup*, a collective noun meaning "morsels saved to be eaten later." Of course, as the didactibots never tired of reminding me, books were only books. Only long experience could truly teach translators how to interpret and explain these exotic beings.

When I was eighteen, I was admitted to the Advanced College of Linguistics and Policy from among whose graduates most of Earth's diplomats and ambassadors were selected—that is, those persons that Earthgov titled ambassadors or diplomats. What they were called by the other races involved was known only to a few, who thought it wisest not to publicize the matter.

ACoLaP, as the school was called, was one of the few educational institutions with a permanent exemption from the nondiscrimination rules. In all Earthian, nondidactibot schools, exceptionally bright students could move no faster than the slowest in the class in order that no lazy or inept student be left behind. It had proven easier to slow down everyone than to speed up the laggards. Earthgov, how-ever, felt this rule should not apply when Earth's planetary security was involved, which gave my admission a definite éclat. Both my par-ents basked in the glow generated by this accomplishment, and I was trotted out on various occasions to meet my parents' friends, rather as a prize cow might once have been.

Since neither Mother nor Father had been at all helpful in my achievement, I rather resented their gloating. I had to give myself a good talking-to in order to let it go. They were not bad people; they were as they were. If they had been different, probably so would I, and I rather liked the way my own life was tending, for I had met someone.

Sybil, one of my classmates, was the daughter of a largish clan of professional people, and Sybil invited several of her classmates, in-cluding me, to dinner at her family's home. I liked Sybil far better than the other students she had invited, for they were among a small elitist group at the college, about a dozen sons and daughters of extreme wealth and power. Though two of the young men had condescended to honor me with their attentions a time or two, I had not been interested, but my indifference did not extend to Sybil's brother. He was Bryan Mackey, young Dr. Mackey, currently established in the extended residency program of a premier and re-spected hospital.

Young Dr. Mackey had a mop of sandy hair, amber brown eyes, a wide mouth, and a disconcertingly penetrating look, which he fo-cused on me the moment we met. We sat next to each other at dinner. He asked me out. I agreed, somewhat nervous at having an actual date, and even more nervous on finding the experience enjoyable.

Thereafter, whenever he had a few hours off duty, he asked to see me, usually for dinner, where he very shortly fell into the pat-tern of complaining throughout the meal about problems in his professional life.

"The man doesn't know medicine?" he said of a superior.

"He's an administrator," I said, in what I hoped was a soothing voice.

"Yes, but he's a *medical* administrator. How in heaven's name can a man administer a program he knows nothing about?"

A week or so later it was something else, and something yet again the week after that, a whole chain of somethings I could identify very readily as "annoyances": directors who knew little but directed much; decisions that favored ease over idealism; rulings that frustrated his skill; orders that wounded his pride. I had seen it all on Phobos, where it had been decently hidden by custom. Here, his bleeding resentment was ripped out and laid before me in all its blatant gore.

"There's a better way to do that procedure! The damned rules were written twenty years ago! Mortality is a lot higher than it needs to be, if they'd just let us treat people the way we've been taught to . . ."

Slightly irritated, I said something I'd thought of many times but had heretofore refrained from saying. "Have you considered that they may want to keep the mortality as high as possible?"

He turned, eyes blazing, only to pale as though he had been slapped in the face by an icy wind. "You mean . . ."

"My father says population numbers aren't dropping fast enough. Desertification has eaten too much cropland there's no way of replacing. Look at how hard they're pushing emigration."

"Emigration! Call it what it is: providing slave labor for the Omniont Federation and the Mercan Combine."

I said, "It's not really slavery. It's bonded labor for only fifteen years. It's better than dying, Bryan."

"Have you ever seen a settlement planet?"

I shook my head, worried at his tone, which was more hostile and furious than usual, even for Bryan.

"Well then, don't be so damned sure it's better than dying."

I felt myself getting angry. "Do you enjoy being with me?"

"Margaret! You know I do!"

"Most times when we're together, I go home feeling . . . as though someone had been beating on me." Actually, I usually went home full of such vicarious anger on his behalf, such overriding animosity against those who were frustrating him, that I lay awake most of the night explaining to them what stupid people they were. I had little experience with violent emotion, and that little had been troublesome. Even on Earth, I had seen little or no emotion displayed until I met Bryan, who was looking at me now with wrathful exasperation. I spoke through gritted teeth:

"Could we . . . could we just have dinner together sometimes without your being . . . so furious about everything?"

He gaped, then closed his mouth with a snap, turning red, breathing heavily. I was about to get up and leave him there when he said through his teeth, "You're right! Father tells me the same thing. He says I mustn't take the day's frustrations home with me. Good heavens, Margaret, you must think I'm a . . . well, I don't know what. Rude, certainly."

I smiled in relief, demurred, insisted it wasn't all that important, just that I thought we would digest our meals far better (tasteless though they were) if we were less overwrought.

Once in a great while thereafter, he would begin a tirade, only to shake his head at himself, and say, "Forget it, it isn't important." Instead we talked about books, about an experimental theater movement, about music. One night, I went home with him for an hour or so, leaving him breathlessly to return to my parent's apartment. The next time I told Mother I was spending the night with friends. Neither parent questioned this. Both of them had fallen back into the Phobos habit, speaking constantly of work or speaking of nothing at all.

When Bryan and I could take a panting moment from our lovemaking, we decided, quite independently, that we were perfect for one another. Preoccupied by sensations that were completely new to us both (since early youth, Bryan had been kept far too busy to get sexually involved with anyone), fearful of saying, feeling, or doing anything that might threaten our delight, we played with one another very carefully, avoiding anything that might be in the least annoying. With Bryan, I felt complete. Those strange splittings-off that I had imagined happening on Mars when I was nine and here on Earth when I was twelve seemed to have healed. I didn't have that arms-reaching-out feeling with Bryan. My arms were delightfully full.

The fact that we didn't speak much about our relationship seemed natural to me. It was the way things had been on Phobos, it was in keeping with my upbringing. To Bryan, I realized it was purposeful, the result of continuing resolution, his perseverant gift to me, not to involve me in his rages, disappointments, frustrations. For this honeymoon of time, we rejoiced in one another, avoiding all irritating subjects, each of us remaining blissfully unaware of the other's true desires or plans or hopes for the future.

I Am Naumi/on Thairy

On Thairy, during dry-time's height, I spent a lot of time at the swimming hole by the river. Every year the wet-time runoff dug the hole anew; each year a deep spring welled a fresh coolness from beneath it; each year it stayed icily fresh, even when the sun-scorched riverbed mummified under its wandering wrappings of sand. I swam by myself sometimes, and sometimes Mr. Weathereye or Lady Badness went with me. Mr. Weathereye was forty at least, maybe older, and Lady Badness was variable, depending on how she felt: sixty-two on a good day and a hundred-two on a bad one. I called her Lady Badness because Mr. Weathereye called her that, and because whenever she talked about her life, she always said, "Ah, but there was so much badness then."

A school of tiny snout fish lived in the pool, along with a tangle of slimy green noomis and every wet-time a silver-scaled gammerfree spawned a litter of pups in a hollow at the bottom of the tree. The mother gammerfree sat on a protruding root and talked to me, or so I thought, at least, and it occurred to me that since I knew several languages, I should be able to decipher what the gammerfree was telling me.

She greeted me with a lilting whistle. Pursing my lips, I did my best to copy the sound. "Pheeeew," said the mother gammerfree before repeating the whistle again.

This time I did it better. "Pheeet," said the gammerfree, going on to another whistle. By the time the gammerfree was tired, I had several words I was sure of. *Pheeew* meant no good. *Pheeet* meant all right, or passable. Another whistle meant something to do with food, and that first whistley bit meant "Good day." Or maybe "Hello."

Lady Badness and Mr. Weathereye wandered by, she to soak her shins from the diving rock and Mr. Weathereye to study the botany of the area. Not long after, looking for trouble, here came wandering an ineradicable lout—which is what Mr. Weathereye called the type. He saw me sharing my sandwich with the gammerfree pups and promptly shied a stone at them while demanding I get out of the way so he could kill them. I jumped up when I first saw the lout, putting myself between stone and gammerfree pups and receiving a nasty cut on my chest for my efforts. When I said the lout should go away, he threatened to beat me flat. I braced himself for battle, but just then Mr. Weathereye came tripping up behind the lout and hit him across the butt with his walking staff. It was a long walking staff, and the far end of it achieved a considerable velocity during the swing.

"Why'd you do that?" screamed the lout.

"Why'd you threaten to beat my friend?" asked Mr. Weathereye. "Why'd you throw a stone at those little creatures?"

"They're vermin, stonin's all they're good for," cried the lout. "And he wouldn't get out of my way."

"What if I think you're vermin, and beating's all you're good for and you're in my way?" asked Mr. Weathereye, advancing as the lout withdrew in some confusion.

I settled back on the stone, and shared out what was left of my lunch with the frightened pups, all huddled together in fear. The mother gammerfree nuzzled me and gave me a quick lick with her rough tongue while I stroked her from her scaly nose to the tip of her scaly tail.

"Will the lout change his ways?" I asked around a mouthful of egg salad.

"They seldom do," said Mr. Weathereye, adjusting the patch over his bad eye, caused by an accident in the long, long ago when he was a mere youth. "By the way, Naumi, the schoolmaster's looking for you. I meant to tell you earlier."

School was out for the dry season, and since I had concluded the term satisfactorily, the schoolmaster had to be looking for me for some other reason than schoolwork. I put my clothes on and set out to find the schoolmaster, Mr. Wyncamp, knowing he kept office hours even during summer when school was out.

"Naumi Rastarong," he said by way of greeting when I entered his office, staring at nothing and pushing the papers on his desk around. Looking uncomfortable, he pushed his glasses up on his nose. "I have here a communication from the Dominion. It says that you have been selected to provide life-duty to the Dominion, and your escort will arrive on Valstat's Day with all the paperwork your pa will have to sign." Mr. Wyncamp chewed his lower lip and put the paper down as though it had burned him.

I didn't notice, for my brain had gone dead at the words *life-duty*. No one from the town of Bright had ever been selected for life-duty, at least not in the lifetime of anyone still living there. I knew about duty, of course. In school, everyone learned that submission to the Dominion brought with it the onus of taxes paid by everyone, and short service paid by some. Being picked for short service wouldn't have surprised me at all, for lots of young people were chosen to spend two years as child minders, cooks, builders, or crop harvesters. When somebody got selected for short service, well-wishers always said, "Two years is short stay for no more tax pay!" Two years of service did bring a ten-year exemption from taxes and interest-free loans for education, so it wasn't that rare or fearsome.

But life-duty, that was another thing altogether. It meant forty years in the service of the Dominion itself. The things people said when they heard about life-duty were usually of the very small comfort variety: "Well, look at it this way. It's better than dying from the pergal pox." Which was true, but so what? Though I had no way of knowing it, most youngsters, when advised they had been chosen for life-service, did exactly as I was doing: They sat with their mouths open, too stunned to object even if there'd been anyone to object to. The notice came from Dominion Central Authority; there was no mechanism for appeal.

After a while I looked up to see Mr. Weathereye standing in the hallway, leaning on his cane. When he saw me looking at him, he beckoned. I took the letter that Mr. Wyncamp had given me and trudged out into the hall.

"Life-service?" whispered Mr. Weathereye.

I could only nod. I was trying to recite the words of the Thankfulness Pledge that we said every morning at school, the one that went, "We thank those in the service of the Dominion at the sacrifice of their own ambitions . . ."

"I didn't even have any ambitions yet," I confessed.

"I think they try to catch candidates before they have many," opined Mr. Weathereye. "But I thought you wanted to be a warrior?"

"Well, I did, do. Mr. Wyncamp said I'm so good at battle games, it was likely I'd become a warrior. But, you know, I thought Thairy Guard is where I'd serve, at the very most." Thairy Guard was what Mr. Weathereye called Men Minus Mission. There wasn't much use for warriors on Thairy.

"Do you want me to help tell your pa?" asked Mr. Weathereye.

I said, "Y'know he's not really my pa."

"Yes, I know that."

". . . 'F I go alone, he'll think I'm making it up," said I. "He usually does, if it's anything out of the ordinary."

"That's what I thought," said Mr. Weathereye.

Outside, we met Lady Badness, who fell in beside us without even asking what had happened, so I figured she and Mr. Weathereye had had their suspicions all along.

Pa Rastarong's house was outside the town of Bright, a smallish place, set at the eastern feet of the Lowering Hills.

"Why'd they choose me?" I mumbled to himself.

Lady Badness said, "Some professorial type did a study, long time gone, trying to determine similarities of character among those chosen for life-service. Only thing similar among 'em all was nobody wanted to go."

"That's me, right enough," said I. What was I good at? Nothing much except school and battle games. Didn't much like team sports, though I was very quick on my feet and agile in getting up perpendicular sides of things when pursued by one or more ineradicable louts.

Mr. Weathereye had always advised that getting away from a lout was in most cases preferable to killing the lout, which I was perfectly capable of doing, because I was really *very* good at battle games, including the art of unarmed combat, though none of the louts knew it.

"They don't even know I could hurt them," I'd said.

"How would they know?" asked Mr. Weathereye. "Louts don't study battle games, and your teachers don't make a habit of talking about it."

"My name has been on the battle game roll of honor in the hallway at school," said I. "Four years running."

"The only thing rarer than louts who think is louts who read," said Mr. Weathereye.

"I'll miss people," said I. I'd always thought the people in Bright compensated for the fact my foster pa was kind of strange. The citizens of Bright considered friendliness toward children a duty, even when it wasn't a pleasure. Amiability was part of the effort good citizens put forth to get all seven-year-olds through their dozen-years, that period beginning at literacy and culminating (when it did at all) in passing the adulthood examination and receiving a citizen's ID. It took about twelve years to get there, starting between age five and seven, though some took more or less, and a few never reached it at all.

On entering the dozen-years, people gave up baby clothes and baby behavior. They put on the bright red tunic of students, which I had just set aside, and they behaved appropriately, or at least tried to give that appearance. It was appropriate to be willing to learn and to be respectful of elders; but whether one did or not, one had to achieve mastery of the essentials. Once that was done, and the adulthood examination was passed—I had passed—one took the oath of citizenship and became a member of society. One could then wear adult clothing and engage in adult behavior. One could marry, beget children, drive a flier, operate heavy machinery, or conduct business. One could even stay out all night and engage in lechery and sottishness, with no one to forbid it.

No one knew anyone who had failed the adulthood exam, though everyone remembered certain people who hadn't taken it but had been called to life-service and were not heard from thereafter. Their fate, whatever it may have been, was Dominion business and nobody else's, though family members had been known to kick up a fuss when Sonny or Honey disappeared, at least right at first. Fuss always resulted in a visit from a Dominion agent, who came to remind the family of their own oaths of citizenship, and after that, the families always settled down or pretended to. It was rumored that certain people might have been transported to Tercis, but no one knew for sure.

All this was on my mind as we turned from the cobblestone thoroughfare onto the graveled stretch of road that led to Pa Rastarong's house, an overgrown and ramshackle dwelling standing amid a clutter of what Lady Badness called lost opportunities and ill-starred innovations: the rusted model of a grebble thresher that had worked quite well until actually tried on grebble; the remnants of an all-sense information grabber with the unfortunate penchant for grabbing everything except the item desired; and the automatic power legs for fruit pickers that had on at least two occasions lifted their wearers into near-Thairy orbits.

"Pa's got a new invention," I offered.

"Ah," said Mr. Weathereye unencouragingly.

Undaunted, I continued. "He says it'll make our fortunes, mine'n his both. It's a kind of all-round rain deflector. If somebody wants to play ball at night, for example, or if somebody's having a wedding or a parade . . ."

"They rent a rain deflector," said Mr. Weathereye tonelessly. "Before I buy shares in it, I'd like to have one question answered. Where does the deflected rain go?"

"Pa's working on that," said I. "What he wants to do is just send it back up and back up, bouncing around up there, until people are finished with their party, then it can come down."

"The result could be a deluge," said Mr. Weathereye. "Perhaps an inundation."

"There's that," admitted I, kicking the front door, which opened with a protest of moisture-swollen wood and the crack of an already split frame.

Pa Rastarong was fast asleep on the living room window seat, the only place in the room sufficiently upholstered with pillows and padding to make a comfortable resting place. Mr. Weathereye sat down on the nearest stool and waited patiently while I shook Pa awake. When he was sitting upright, bleary eyes fastened on his unexpected guest, Mr. Weathereye told him about the letter.

"They can't do that!" spluttered Pa. "He's the only one I've got here at home!"

"It doesn't matter," said Mr. Weathereye. "Think about it. You learned the rules in school, just as we all did, now think about it."

Pa probably had learned the rules, but I doubt he'd thought about them since. He screwed up his face, trying to think. "Three categories of service," he said finally. "That's all I remember. And nothin' was said about life-duty when I took him on!"

He glared at Mr. Weathereye, who cocked his head and said soothingly, "You're right, of course. That's why I came along to tell you about the letter, because it sounds so unbelievable that Naumi could have been selected. It is true, though, and if you have questions about it, you can talk to Mr. Wyncamp."

"The teacher," said Pa in disgust.

"He sometimes is, yes," agreed Mr. Weathereye. "The Escort will be here on Valstat's Day with the papers for you to sign."

"'Nif I don't?" Pa said, working up a semblance of mule-headedness, as he sometimes did.

"I suppose they'll disappear you," said Mr. Weathereye without emotion. "That's what usually happens to people who forget the oath of citizenship." He stood up, bowed briefly over his cane, then stumped to the front door, where I let him out.

"What do I need to do?" I asked, as I followed him down the path. "Like, pack things up? Or not?"

"Not," said Mr. Weathereye, examining the far horizon as though something very important might happen there at any minute. "Everything you need will be provided. You may take memorabilia that will fit into a box no longer, wider, or taller than the length of your hand from tip of middle finger to wrist, not counting fingernail if it protrudes."

The days went by all in a rush. The Escort came to the house.

Mr. Weathereye and Mr. Wyncamp attended as witnesses. The Escort
paid over a lump sum to Pa, to compensate for the loss of my company, and Pa signed the papers saying he'd been properly informed of
the legality of the selection. He even wept a bit, surprising himself
almost as much as it surprised me and Mr. Weathereye. Crying wasn't
Pa's kind of thing at all.

The Escort had a flier waiting outside the door, and as soon as the
papers were signed, I took my box and my jacket and left, leaving the
two witnesses to comfort Pa. I thought Mr. Weathereye would probably comfort him in no time by investing in the rain deflector. He'd
invested in the information grabber, the elevator legs, and the grebble
thresher before, so it was likely he'd stay in character.

I Am Margaret/on Earth

One morning I arrived at the college to find a note saying the Provost wanted to see me. Though I had no reason whatsoever to think this boded anything but good, I confess to an attack of the frets, and I took an extra five minutes to comb my hair and put on a face that wasn't apprehensive. The Provost's name was Dione Esedre, and I had met her at gatherings of the college: a very cool person, very efficient.

"Margaret Bain," she said when I entered, just a tiny hint of question in her voice, as though to make sure she had the right person.

"Yes, Provost," I said.

She gave a little sigh and riffled through several papers on her desk. It was one of the conceits of ACoLaP that the people there, both teachers and students, still read words from paper; it was a truism that very few other people did.

"Four members of your class have been selected to attend a meeting that's being held at the local Dominion Offices. It's a meeting of diplomats, high officers in Earthgov, plus a few Gentherans. They want a few advanced students to sit in, on the theory that you'll all be working for them in the next few years and will do a better job if you know what's going on. Not sure that I agree, but it's not my place to argue." She emitted a smile brief enough to indicate she might be jesting, not long enough to indicate real humor.

"I'm very flattered," I said.

"Don't be, not yet. Here's the secrecy oath you'll be required to sign. Don't think it's just a matter of routine. It's deadly serious, and unless you're absolutely sure you can abide by it, don't sign it."

I remember clearly only one phrase from the document, which was "... on penalty of death," but that one was enough to make me look up, startled.

"I said it was serious," she remarked with another of those lightning smiles, a mere lip-writhe of amusement.

"I ... I'm pretty good at keeping my mouth shut," I said, thinking twenty-some years of perfecting the trait had succeeded remarkably well.

"If you're sure you can, go ahead and sign it. I confess, I'd love to attend myself. I've never seen a Gentheran."

"You probably wouldn't," I said without thinking. "They wear suits and helmets. Nobody ever sees them."

She looked momentarily offended, then relaxed. "Of course. I'd forgotten that you were on Mars."

The upshot was, I signed, and she gave me an identity card that had a password under a seal and told me where to go on the following day and not to mention it to anyone, not my parents, not my boyfriend, if I had one, or anyone else. I really would have loved to tell Bryan, but he was working that evening, so I was saved from temptation.

The following day, I went as directed, presented my card, seal intact, and was fed through a whole series of identification procedures involving eyes, fingers, biometric, physiometric, how I smelled, and the like. Finally, I was shown to a seat at the back of a windowless room containing a large conference table and chairs plus the usual side table holding drinks: nova-coffee, nova-tea, bottled Swish in three flavors that differed only in color. Each chair was equipped with a full-sense viewer, very advanced technology that I'd been exposed to only a time or two. I was gawking at the viewers when three of my fellow students came in, we nodded to one another without speaking, and they sat down at some distance. At first I was surprised to see them, for these very elite students were not particularly good at their studies. They made error after error in class (many of which our teachers simply ignored); on written tests they always scored incredibly well (adjective chosen for precision, in that no one believed the scores were real). They had a sneering attitude toward students from less exalted backgrounds than their own very moneyed ones. All of them had family members among the Directors of the College, and that probably explained why they were here. I had bested all of them scholastically, which had led more than one of them to advise me, sneeringly, that my test scores didn't matter, for the "way things were," they would succeed, and I would fail. So far as I could tell, none of them had any experience whatsoever with the way things really were, having been untouched by reality since birth.

Within moments, doors at the other side of the room opened, and several humans and Gentherans (small, as I'd been told, and in suits and helmets) filed in and were seated. I was so amused to see that the Gentherans were seated in elevator chairs, permitting them to rise to the level of the table, that for a moment I did not recognize that one of the ascending chairs held someone I knew: Chili Mech! She was staring at me.

I grinned and waved. She said something to her neighbor, lowered her chair, and came over to me. "Margaret, is that you?"

"Chili. It's so good to see you! I had no idea you'd be here."

"You must be one of the ACoLaP students! Good for you. You always said you were going to learn every language in the universe."

"If I said anything that egotistical, I was very young and foolish."

Chili said, "I must get back. They're going to convene. In case you didn't know it, Margaret, this is a meeting of both Dominion Central Authority and Earthgov Executive Council. You'll understand why when you hear what's going on. Can we get together during the break?"

"Certainly," I said. "I'd love to."

When the roll was called, I noted there were representatives present from the colonies, Chili being the one from Mars. The Gentheran names were real tongue twisters, the first speaker being named Sister someone. It sounded a little like Lorpa, if one accepted that there was something subtly wrong with both the L and the R. We were not allowed to record or take notes, but nothing had been said about not remembering, and I have a very good memory.

Sister Lorpa spoke Earthian very clearly, in a high, sweet voice, starting without preamble to describe something called the "ghyrm." I recognized this as a Cantardene word meaning "eater." She said Gentherans and Earthians had become aware of these creatures when several hundred human bondslave miners on Cantardene were killed by them.

"At the time," she said, "we considered this to be some kind of plague that would affect only people on Cantardene. We were shortly disabused of this idea when several humans in transit to Chottem from bondslave planets farther into Mercan space were also slain by the ghyrm. Since that time we have bent all our resources toward discovering what the ghyrm are and where they come from. Thus far, we have had virtually no success in answering the latter question."

She went on to tell us what her people had learned about the ghyrm. It was not a bacterium or virus, it was an organism that could take various shapes or appear to do so. Genetically, it was all one creature, and perhaps it had been cloned, though it appeared and acted differently in different circumstances or, possibly, when directed by some outside agency. It could take over a person or invade a small area and move rapidly from person to person to wipe out all human life as it had done on Cranesroost, where Settlements Two, Five, and Six were wiped out.

We students were not the only ones who exclaimed at this. Evidently, almost no one in the room had known about Cranesroost. The speaker asked us to put on the viewers, which we did. Silence fell. Someone, somewhere, turned them on.

The technology was beyond anything I had experienced. I actually became the person on Cranesroost. I was a settlement captain who knew all about the place. The settlement lay just within a hillside grove of miraculous trees, huge as cathedral towers and as bulky, effective barriers to wind and the worst of weather. Just outside the grove, the glittering sand of the lakeside sloped toward silver water, placid in moonlight, riffling recurrently as though from something breathing on the farther shore, perhaps something very large, one titanic arm pillowing its head as relaxed lips puffed, and puffed, and puffed, touching the quivering surface with the gentlest of exhalations.

I was the captain of the settlement, standing at the edge of the lake near a roost of cranes that appeared almost real in this quiet light. I knew the children had built them out of bits of wood and pipe, an evocation of times long gone, a time when cranes really lived, danced, mated, hatched, brought forth young. Seeing them in the moonlight, I, the captain, almost believed in them, or something like them. The Cranesroost settlement had seen birds, or things like birds. They didn't fly, but they ran very fast, and they ate the fishy things in lakes as cranes no doubt had done. We settlers called them fishers and hadn't learned much about them yet, for winter was pressing, and shelter had to come first. Observing birds would no doubt be a pleasant pastime in later years.

Unknown things were worrisome, the captain thought, even though the Gentherans gave the planet a good bill of health. There were native creatures, yes, some of them poisonous but none of them ferocious or sneaky or particularly intelligent, being more of the "I'll leave you alone, you leave me alone" variety. The captain relied on this when he had sent the scouting team out early that morning, but if there was nothing dangerous out there, they should have been back.

So he stood watch, waiting for three men and one woman who trekked around the lake to the north. Their orders had been to go as far as they could go by noon, then turn around and come back by suppertime. Suppertime was over hours ago. Suppertime was a dimming memory.

"Captain?"

"Who?"

"Me, sir. Gruder."

"I haven't seen a thing, Gruder."

"This isn't like Kath."

The captain snorted. "It isn't like any of them. You should be getting some sleep."

"The little one keeps waking, asking for his ma. I keep telling him she'll be home in the morning. Do we send out a search party, or not?"

"I don't know. I thought four of them was enough to be safe, you know. Four pairs of eyes. Eight strong legs and arms."

"What are you thinking?"

"I don't know what to think. Maybe they saw something a little farther off and kept going after noon. Then, coming back, the dark caught up to them. Maybe they're lying up there along the bank, just waiting for light."

"Let's hope so."

"Let's, and if they did, damn 'em, they can stand watch for the next hundred nights. Worrying us like this . . . what's that?"

"Where?"

"Down there, north. Along the lakeside. I saw light, fire. Like a torch. See it, there it goes again!"

We watched, nearly hypnotized as the one spark was repeatedly occluded by trees, then steadied, became two, then four, moving slowly in a line along the shore. The captain sighed. "I guess they got tired. Decided to rest before they made the trip back. Or maybe they're carrying something. Go on back to bed, Gruder. She won't be here for another hour, at least."

The other man yawned widely, took a deep, relieved breath, and returned to his cabin, one of the first ones built, the nearest to being finished. In the little paddock alongside the house a goat bleated, briefly disturbed in her rest. The captain stayed where he was, though he sat down on a stump to rest his legs. The sparks continued their arc around the edge of the lake, growing in brightness, then disappearing behind the nearer trees and emerging again, four of them, bright as stars.

"Welcome," he said at last, when the missing four stumble up from the shore.

"Captain?" said Kath.

"Yes. And Gruder's been up, too, waiting for you. Where in the hell did you all get to?"

"Brought you a present," said Kath. "Something we found." She approached, holding something out in one hand. We all peered at it.

"What's that? Beads? On a thong or a thread? Now who in heaven's name put that together on this world?"

Kath shrugged as I took it from her. "It was just lying there, on the bank, on top of a rock. Like it had been put there for us to find. Red bead, yellow one, blue one, a couple black ones. Funny, huh?"

"So, what kept you?"

She rolled her head on her neck as though it hurt. "We just . . . I guess we lay down for a while. Must have fallen asleep. We're really tired." She yawned, her eyes rolling away from me in the torchlight, whites showing all around like a frightened animal.

"Kath?" I said urgently. "You all right."

"Oh, sure, Captain. Sure. Just tired. See you in the morning."

I, we, the captain, glanced once more at the thing in our hands. A mere thread, like a bit of string, with half a dozen beads on it. Now who in heaven's name . . . Well, it didn't matter. Let it go. We could talk about it in the morning . . .

We felt only a few moments of what followed before someone, blessedly, shut off the viewer. There were exclamations, cries of distress, a general murmur that slowly quieted.

Sister Lorpa was still on her feet. "The beads were actually a ghyrm, perhaps more than one. We have established that the ghyrm take over the minds of the persons who carry it or them. We infer the ghyrm are directed by a reasoning force that may be a part of the ghyrm race or something quite outside it. This is pure speculation. We don't know."

Someone asked how the Cranesroost infestation had been discovered.

"In settlement Six, the last person infested woke to find every one dead and the thing around her throat. Though close to death, she was able to com the neighboring village, to describe the thing, to say she could not get it off her and that it was killing her. The person she reached followed standard emergency procedure: That is, he made no effort at rescue and informed Dominion immediately. Dominion personnel in noncontact suits found everyone in the three villages dead. They scouted the areas around the surviving villages and found nothing like the necklace of small beads mentioned in the com. From the captains of the destroyed villages, they retrieved the sensory recorders, one of which you have just experienced."

Someone said indignantly, "Cranesroost was off the wormtrails!

Its location was known only to the settlers and to Dominion! How did the ghyrm find it?"

This led to charges and countercharges, back and forth, much heat, little light, and the Chairman put an end to the discussion.

Sister Lorpa concluded, "We have had some breakthroughs. We have succeeded in capturing ghyrm, caging them so they cannot escape, and habituating some of our members to their presence. These captive ghyrm are infallible locators of others of their kind. Certain members of the Siblinghood have been trained to hunt ghyrm, using a captive ghyrm as 'finders.' They are very successful on a planetary surface, though all efforts to use them in space have failed."

That item disposed of, the Chairman introduced an elderly woman as "a member of the Siblinghood, Lady Badness." I saw one of my fellow students silently convulsed at this introduction, though from the look of the lady's face, amusement was not appropriate.

She introduced herself as the chairman of a biracial committee of Gentherans and Humans that had spent some forty-odd Earth-years trying to devise a nontraumatic method of depopulating Earth in order to prevent the final collapse of the biome on the one hand and a visit by ISTO slaughterers on the other. She spoke of the colonies as "emergency, last-ditch attempts to guarantee human survival and the survival of thousands of species of Earth organisms in case the slaughterers could not be forestalled."

She said she had several points to make. I set myself to remember them.

Firstly, she said Earth's governments had been warned that depopulation was an absolute necessity for Earth's survival. Secondly, she said the government had justified its inaction by quoting the standard statistical projections indicating that population growth was slowing, that as soon as all parts of the world had equal economic opportunities, population growth would stop, and total population might even drop. Thirdly, she admitted the standard projections were irrefutable but totally irrelevant, as human population had exceeded the number Earth could support over a century ago. Even while ice caps melted, while prehistoric aquifers dried up and the lands over those aquifers began to subside, governments had refused to acknowledge that humans were responsible. Only when aliens arrived in starships to tell them the end had come did governments try to deal with the situation, and by then, it was too late.

She said, "Outshipment, as you know, has slightly slowed but failed to stop the process."

Several people around the table uttered angry variations on "We know all that," rather loudly and, I thought, rudely.

Lady Badness merely stared at them until they subsided. "Of course you do. So do I, but we're putting it into the record one more time, just in case at some future time someone questions what we've said and thought and decided. This brings us to the fourth and final point. We must choose between two repellent futures:

"A, we do nothing, and the ISTO slaughterers will kill over ninety percent of all of the people now alive on Earth. I have seen records of that process. The best one can say for it is that it doesn't take long. It is both quicker and bloodier than the demise of Cranesroost. It is not a process I wish on any population, however, no matter how pig-headed that population may be.

"B, we impose the solution Dominion and the Siblinghood have been working on since Dominion was formed: the sterilization of ninety-nine point something-or-other percent of Earth's population."

I happened to be looking across the table at Chili. I saw her shoulders heave as she took a deep breath. I glanced at my fellow students. They looked outraged. I had been numb since the Cranesroost experience, and I stayed that way.

Lady Badness went on:

"Gentheran Research Laboratories has completed testing of the planetary sterilant. It will kill no one. It will simply make ninety-nine-plus percent of the fertile persons on Earth live out their lives without progeny. A small, random fraction of human beings has a genetic resistance to the sterilant. This genetic resistance is found among all subgroups of the population. There will be no genocide of any cult, culture, or coloration."

I sat with my mouth open, unable to believe what I was hearing. Around the table were murmurs and outcries. My fellow students were now whispering to one another.

"Those affected by the sterilant will produce a pheromonic by-product attractive only to other sterilized persons. There will be no other changes. People will continue to 'fall,' as they say, in love, but it will be the sterile with the sterile, the fertile with the fertile. Natural life cycles will go on, but very few people will have children.

"Today our only decision is to choose: A or B."

The Chairman spoke: "We will have no more discussion today. We act, or ISTO acts. Suffering is minimized if we act. Slaughter is certain if we do not. Will someone move the question? . . . I recognize Maintainer Chili Mech."

Chili moved that the Gentherans be directed to go ahead with the sterilant. The Chairman called for a second and got it. The vote was yes. Someone asked when it would take place. Sister Lorpa said within the year. Then nobody said anything for what seemed to be a very long time, and the Chairman announced a break for refreshment.

Chili came over and led me to a little table against the wall. All three of my fellow students had Lady Badness trapped in a far corner and were talking at her, too volubly, I thought, too disrespectfully. Chili followed my line of sight and shook her head, very slightly. "That's not a good idea," she said.

"I know," I murmured. "But it's very much in character for them. Usually, if they don't like something, the something ceases to exist."

"Really," she said. "Wait for me, Margaret. I'll get us something to drink."

I saw her speaking briefly to a couple of guards, who went to Lady Badness's rescue. Chili returned with the Gentheran, Sister Lorpa, whom I recognized by the insignia on her helmet. I rose and gave the half bow that is considered polite among Gentherans, saying, "It is rude of us to drink when you are denied refreshment."

"Not at all," she said, in that high, sweet voice. "Our suits provide whatever hydration we need. I understand you are here as an observer, under a vow of silence. You were much surprised by what you heard?"

I said, yes, I was, though I understood the reasons. What I was actually thinking at that moment was whether it had ever been important to me to have children.

She sat down with us, and Chili asked her what the next step would be.

"It's all been planned," she replied. "First, we'll mount a saturation publicity campaign announcing that population stasis has been reached. Since this has been forecast by politicians and proliferators for the past century, it will surprise no one and mollify many. We will announce that the population has crested and is now beginning to decline, very slowly. Newssheets will cover this event. There will be interviews with prominent pronatalist officials and religious leaders telling us how gratified they are. Our polls indicate that virtually all humans will be delighted with the news.

"At the end of the first year, population will indeed have declined by between one and two percent. We will issue frequent glowing reports on how well this is going. We do not plan any outreach effort among those who are infertile, but every childbirth will serve to identify those who are immune. The immunes must be provided with intensive reeducation. Meantime, the two-three-four rule will continue to be observed. Outshipment will continue."

"Must it?" I asked, a little fretfully, I'm afraid.

Sister Lorpa's faceplate turned toward me. "Your government has contracts with the Federation and the Combine. Unless you want a war of retribution, those contracts must be honored . . ."

"Well then, if outshipment is to proceed, will intensive education really be necessary?" I wondered aloud.

She did not answer, for we were being approached by a tall, dark man dressed in velvets, brocades, and gems.

"Sister Lorpa," he said, half bowing.

"Delegate from Chottem, Von Goldcreau d'Lornschilde," she said, turning toward me as if to introduce me.

He did not wait for this. "May I once again plead with your people to find my kinswoman, the heiress of Bray! She would be an adult woman now, some twenty Earth-years old! She is needed in Bray, and if she no longer lives, then evidence of that is needed in Bray! Our economic future depends upon it!"

Sister Lorpa said expressionlessly, "We are aware of your concerns, Delegate. Be assured, if we can assist in finding your kinswoman, we will do so."

He half bowed again and nodded to Chili, totally ignoring me.

"You asked about the need for education," Sister Lorpa said, when he had departed. "Delegate d'Lornschilde is from Chottem. He is a descendent of the founders of that colony, and he is claimant to the estate of Stentor d'Lorn, which, in truth, represents a large part of the gross planetary wealth. He pretends he doesn't care about the estate. At every meeting he urges us to find Stentor's grand-daughter and return her to Bray! It is all pretence and bluster; his real interest is in finding evidence of her death so he can claim the estate, for, like the rest of his family, he is interested in nothing but money and power. Despite the fact that he and all his kinfolk had to leave Earth because Earth had been destroyed by money and power, he has already asked the Dominion Central Authority for permission to exceed the population limits set for Chottem, excusing this on the basis that construction creates many of their jobs, which means more profit for him.

"Earth listened to that 'we have to make room' kind of nonsense for hundreds of years, and look where Earth is now! That man has taken no lesson from it. Human beings are incapable of learning any-thing outside their own lifetimes! We fight against this disability con-stantly! Oh, if only . . ." She sighed. "Well, 'if only' butters no beans, as you humans used to say."

"Sister, you're not going to tell the people of Earth about the ster-ilant, are you?" I asked, unthinking. I put my hand over my mouth. "Oh, forgive me . . ."

"There is nothing to forgive. No. We will not tell them. Sibling-hood has a definition of evil that our group has tried to keep in mind during our deliberations. *'To cause any creature willful pain is evil; to pretend that another sentient creature cannot feel pain is evil; to enjoy the pain of another, sentient or insentient, is ultimate evil.'* We would be causing willful pain if we told them; we would be committing evil if we allowed the slaugh-ter of mankind through our own inaction. The population drop will not be sudden. Those who die will be those one would expect to die, the aged, victims of accidents, the chronically ill. The human popula-tion will dwindle gradually over the next century, slightly over one percent of the original population per year, with only a tiny fraction of that number being born. At some point, when living conditions have improved, we will set the record straight for future genera-tions."

I asked, "What about those who want to have children and can't?"

The mirrored hood turned in my direction, showing me my own troubled face. "Some couples may be disappointed not to have children, but in most cases they will not speak of it, and neither will anyone else. It has been a long time since any pregnant woman showed herself in public on Earth. Since the plague, the war, and the Lifer-Limiter uprising of '81 and '82, people on Earth have not spoken of reproductive matters except behind closed doors, and very rarely even then."

She was perfectly right. People would not speak of it. They would be glad to have a little more water in their ration, a little different food to eat. Perhaps two "admit-to-the-park" permission slips each year instead of only one.

Sister Lorpa left us, and I asked Chili something that had been on my mind since the session. "What is this Siblinghood everyone refers to?"

She frowned, shaking her head. "They don't define it. One gets the impression it's a kind of lodge or secret society that does very technical, scientifically advanced work. It has both humans and Gentherans as members, and it is alleged to have members from other races as well. Their financing is secret. Their work is secret. When they have something to offer, they offer it. They're the ones who found out why mankind always destroys his environment . . ."

"What?" I demanded in astonishment. "There's a known cause?"

Chili gritted her teeth. "Margaret, forget I mentioned it! Remember, you're under a vow of silence. Yes, there is a reason, but it's not to be mentioned. You may learn of in time."

She returned to the table as the group reconvened, and several Gentherans spoke of the plans for rehabilitation of Earth. Much of it would be done by the Gentheran-Human Rehabilitation Corps, a body organized by the Siblinghood (here they were again). As soon as five percent of housing space opened up in any city, people would be moved into that space from suburbs of that city. The suburbs, when emptied, would be razed, highways leading to them would be removed, the land would be reseeded and reforested. These would be enormous jobs, so we were told, that would offer full employment to anyone wishing to work. Merely replanting desert provinces such as those formerly known as Brazil, Canada, Central Africa, and Indonesia would occupy several centuries' worth of effort.

Since cities were more efficient and easier to maintain as habitat than extensive, land-consuming suburbs, they would continue to absorb smaller urbs until all of them were gone. As space opened up in the cities, dwellings would be consolidated, and buildings would be razed to create parklands within the cities themselves, so that no dwelling would be far from open, green space. Outside the cities, reclaimed land would not be farmed until the population had dropped to the point that some or all of the algae factories could be closed.

Eventually, dairy animals would be returned to Earth, they said, and the seas would be restocked with fish and other living things. "It is possible even whales may be restored in time," a Gentheran said, visibly moved by the idea. "We have the genetic information, and it is not beyond our capabilities. When natural space is restored, human people will be allowed to wander through it at will, so long as they do so on foot or on muscle-powered vehicles, taking with them only what they can carry. The use of destructive, noisy machinery for recreational purposes must become anathema to humans, as unthinkable as eating one's young."

We were referred to the reports and studies supporting the plan, and to the specifications for each separate area, available in the document department together with a timeline of the expected stages of rehabilitation. I was not allowed to see or receive the documents, of course, just as I was not allowed to take notes or speak with anyone about what I had learned. All very strange and frightening.

The most frightening part, however, came the following day. The other three students who had attended the meeting were not in class. It took me only a split second to decide it would be inappropriate to ask where they were. Later that day, the Provost sent for me, and I found her sitting at her desk, looking rather pale.

"You wanted to see me, Provost?"

"We have had a . . . great loss," she said. "I wanted you, particularly, to know of it. It seems the others of your class who attended yesterday's meeting announced to one of the participants that they intended to tell the media what had occurred there."

I started to exclaim, and she put up her hand. "Please do not inadvertently mention anything that did occur."

I swallowed. "I would not do so, Provost. Perhaps my classmates thought the secrecy agreement did not . . . apply to them."

"No rule or standard has applied to them since birth," she said. "Great wealth breeds great arrogance, Margaret. Some months ago, each of the three was handpicked by the Directors to take junior but very important posts at Earthgov after graduation. If I were of a suspicious nature, I might guess that those three were picked to attend yesterday's meeting in order that their arrogance could be assessed under . . . controlled conditions."

"But . . . surely I wasn't picked for that reason."

"No," she said. "Someone else picked you, and before you ask, I am not to say who it was."

Though I had imagined Bryan's face if I told him what had happened, I was not about to commit suicide. I would, however, have given a great deal to have been enlightened. The thought that I, Margaret, had been picked by someone(s) to attend a meeting I couldn't talk about, that I, Margaret, knew what was going to happen to Earth, a secret known only to a handful of other people, was terrifying, and not the least of the terror was that there was no possible, ascribable reason why I should be involved at all!

I Am Ongamar/on Cantardene

Adille, the K'Famira, had said she would not wear the necklace again, yet it hung across her throat pouch the next day, seeming rather larger than before. She wore it the day after that, also, moving restlessly about the house as though something troubled her.

"Let's go for a walk," she demanded. We went out into the city, and I followed Adille's restless feet here and there, without direction, pausing wherever voices were raised or threatening gestures were made. A few days later, Adille dragged me to a public execution, which Adille had always sworn was only for rabble. I hid my face in my lap, winding my arms around my head to keep from hearing the accused screaming as his lower arms and legs were lopped off. It was not mere horror I was hiding from, it was the pain itself that I felt, no matter how I hid my eyes. The day after that we attended the baiting of a dozen traitors' families by wild klazaks, the sand of the arena running green and a dozen or more young K'Famira ululating from quivering pouches as the klazaks tore first the traitorous parents, then the young . . .

"Please don't make me go," I begged her the following day. "It hurts me, Great Lady. It hurts me to see people killed." I was taking a risk in saying it wasn't mere dislike, that it was torment? "I feel it . . . it hurts . . ."

"I know, I know," Adille said distractedly. "Of course,

yes, but I must . . . I must see it. Or something. Something different. Something new. I must . . ."

"You always said the executions were for the rabble," I cried. "Are we not rabble if we watch?"

"I don't know," Adille said, her mouths set in ugly lines. "But I must. I must. And it wants you with me."

Bargom disapproved of her wearing the necklace. He told Adille it was ruining her appearance, making her look old and tired. Several times he tried to take the necklace away, but he could not approach it. Each time he tried, he found himself headed out the door, away from it. In the end, he went out the door and simply kept going. During all this time, Adille complained that the beads grew heavier, until they achieved such a weight they could no longer be worn.

Then the sharing began. Adille explained it. She had to go out and find the things the necklace wanted to see, always in my company, then she had to return and lay hands upon the necklace to let it see the horrors through her memory. Mornings we went, and nights. Adille grew too weak to force me to go with her, but still she went alone, returning to lay hands upon the necklace, to which I was now inexorably drawn so that I, too, heard, saw, smelled everything. Years went by as Adille wandered, coming home each night to fall exhausted into bed, eating little, growing thinner with each day, while I eked out our existence by selling the ornaments of the house, then the furniture. The time came that Adille was seen watching something that should not have been watched by anyone. She had warned me that this might happen.

"It sends me places people aren't supposed to be. It makes me hide and watch, when no one is supposed to watch. It makes me climb walls, hide outside windows. I saw what my clan leader, Draug B'lanjo, did to the Omniont Ambassador. They sent his body to the Federation, claiming it had been done by the Hrass. I heard them talking. They want to stir trouble between the Omniont and the Hrass so they can take over the Hrass shipping routes."

"Doesn't that disturb you, Great Lady?" I asked. "The thing that happened to the Ambassador?"

"Him. Oh. I suppose it might have disturbed me if I hadn't been so worried about being seen."

I had always wondered if Adille felt anything at all for the victims she saw tortured and slain. Seemingly not.

She went on, "Someday, they will see me. Someday, I won't come home . . ."

And one day, she did not. Counting over the seasons I had been with Adille, I estimated it at somewhere between three and four Cantardene years. I myself was then seventeen, or eighteen.

The K'Famir who came to the house some days later told me to clean the house before Adille's father, Progzo, arrived to dispose of Adille's belongings. The necklace box lay on the dressing trough, and when I reached out to close the lid, the thing inside lashed out at me like a whip, wrapping itself around my arm. Frantically, I tried to pull it loose, to no avail, as it crawled across my body to plaster itself against my breast, seemingly rooted into the flesh. I could not escape the thing that had killed Adille. Because I had touched it, because I had lived in proximity to it, it had the same power over me it had had over her.

I was young and strong, however, which was lucky, for it took all my strength to bear the thing. Adille had made no provision for me, and her family did not want me. When the bondservant agency reclaimed me, the thing was wrapped against my skin, under my clothes, a bead or two showing at the throat or poking through a buttonhole. I wore a high-collared dress to hide it, and for a wonder, the bondage merchant did not require me to strip. I soon learned why. I had already been sold to House Mousselline as a seamstress, a creature to alter lingerie, a fitter who could work quietly and virtually unnoticed. I had had much experience at being unnoticed. Afterward I gained more.

The fitters, mostly Earthian, wore wigs of short gray hair that covered the lobes of their ears. The thinner of us had our bodies padded, and we were clad in sensible dark dresses, high-necked, ankle-length, and long-sleeved. Our feet were shod in shapeless shoes. We carried pincushions on our wrists and a measuring rod in one hand. It was claimed by House Mousselline that we were the heirs of an ancient Earth guild that had borne these symbols of craftsmanship through the centuries. Though rough and callused hands would have matched the rest of the image, our hands were, in fact, kept as soft as the fabrics we touched, for House Mouselline dealt in ultrasilk and vivilon and mazatec, all produced, so the labels said, on the Isles of Delight. At 250 credits or more a span, no one, not even Ephedra Mouselline herself, could afford their being snagged by some fitter's abraded knuckle.

Those Mercans who saw us, or more likely looked across us, saw human bolsters with lowered eyes and mouths full of pins: Miss This; Miss That; Miss Ongamar. The "Miss" was a courtesy title, a calculated oddity. Titles were not usually given to bondspeople, but in the intimacy of the fitting room, one did not want to disturb the mood of serene luxury by kicking or hitting a servant or even commanding them in the ugly lingua Mercan of the plantation. Fitters, therefore, were selected from among the few bondservants who were skilled at sewing and understood the language. They were spoken to with condescending politeness.

"Miss Ongamar, the Lady Mirabel wants three of the vivilon chemises, in violet and puce, and they need just a tuck under the lower arms." "Oh, Miss Ongamar, Princess Delibia has ordered the gold-mesh games gown by Verdul, and it needs an underdress by tomorrow afternoon. The Princess is green-fleshed, about a number four shade, so be sure you pick fabric to match." "Oh, Miss Ongamar, the Baron's plaything has ordered twelve pair of vivilon pantaloons, and they must be monogrammed with the Baron's crest over all four orifices."

Miss Ongamar's fingers nipped and pinned and basted. Her, my, hands darted. This to be seamed invisibly. That to be embroidered, very visibly. This to be let out just a bit, to drape a touch better over Dowager Queen Dagabon's ever-enlarging pouch; that to be taken in to fit the young neuter the Baron was currently amusing himself with. And when the showroom was closed and the workroom silent, even then I might be there, finishing up this little task or that one before going home.

Home. I actually had one.

One of the few privileges of being employed by House Mouselline was the housing allowance, actual money, to pay rent, to buy food. House Mouselline had no interest in maintaining a bondslave dormitory and kitchen. Those who worked for the house were expected to fend for themselves. The allowance was small; for the innovative, it was sufficient. So it was I went out the back service door into the Baka Narak, which I translated to myself, "Allee Sensual," and turned left to the corner. Another left would take me into the turmoil and clutter of Bak-Zandig-g'Shadup, "Street of Many Worlds," which was thronged with people of many races at all hours of the day and night. If I turned right, however, the way led down a short block to the service tunnel, and down the tunnel to the Crafter's and Seamer's Residential Compound for Bond and Free, where most of the employees lived. I, however, did not enter the compound. Instead, I went along the narrow service walk that ran beside it and into the cobbled courtyard at the rear, where the refuse bins were kept. Past their lidded bulks, next to the rear wall and the alley gate, a narrow door opened into home.

This had been space no one else wanted: unrentable, unusable, exactly the kind of space I had searched for since my bondage to House Mouselline. I had heard two fitters speaking of it, regretting that it would not do, for it had no heat, it had no light. I had made a modest offer for it, and the offer had been accepted. Within the limits imposed by my circumstances, the place was perfect. Inside were stone walls worn smooth by centuries and a stone floor old as time. Huge, ancient pillars supported the crushing weight of the upper floors. This had been the stable of a castle once, a monstrous fortification that had guarded the coast of a planet-bound people in the days of the last Regency, before the K'Famir had conquered the Welbeck people, slaughtered them (when they proved to be reluctant and untrustworthy as slaves), and taken over their world. Now the ocean had receded some distance, and the stable was almost a cellar, though it had kept a tiny window overlooking the enclosed garden. The grille allowed only an obstructed view of fruit tree branches, but the fresh, flower-scented air was welcome.

I shook my lantern to be sure there was fuel in it before lighting it. The place had at one time had water piped in for the animals. I had found the pipes, had worked away at them for a season with twists of wire, dragging out the rust and scale, making them workable again. I had found an old coal stove in an alley, had taken it apart with chisel and hammer, had carried it to my lair piece by piece and put it together again. It sat under the round hole where the flue of one just like it had no doubt inserted itself a hundred years before. Best of all, the place had a little, low, windowless room, no more than a closet, with a door that locked. The closet room was where I left it in the evenings, when I had to go out. If I carried it all day, I could not carry it all night, and the thing seemed to realize that. This evening I went to that room first, took off my outer clothing and detached it from me, shutting my mind against the sound, half growl, half sucking whine, when I pulled it away. It writhed into the darkest corner and did not move, even when I fetched water for it, for if it grew dry, it chafed me, and the abrasions burned like acid.

I poked up the fire in the stove, filled the kettle and set it over the flame, dragged the washtub into the middle of the floor, and took off my daily disguise. The gray wig first, then the padding around my body. As soon as the water was hot, I poured a sufficiency into the tub, stepped in, and gave myself the nightly sponge bath that washed away its residue, a slight stickiness that smelled of mold. When I had emptied that tub down the floor drain, I heated the kettle again, and yet again to give me enough water to sit in, legs over one towel-padded side, head leaning against the other. It was the best time of day: the feeling that time had stopped, the warmth of the stove on my skin, the softness of the perfumed water. House Mousselline sold essences to put in bathwater; Miss Ongamar had become an expert petty thief.

Bathtime was also time to review what I had heard during the day:

A neuter talking to another as it tried on ribbon trousers, discussing its patron's purchase, from the Omnionts, of new technology that detected ship-shields. "They're giving him an award for inventing it?" Crow of laughter.

A sterile female speaking of the breeding wife of her consort. "The stupid plassawokit can't do a thing but lay eggs! It's a wonder she doesn't drop them in the public street."

A trader's wife telling the delightful story about her husband completely fooling buyers and charging them triple for merchandise. "Ridiculous Gentherans in their shiny little suits. No more brains than a glabbitch."

I remembered everything, making cryptic notes so I would not forget. The cracked mirror I had taken from a trash bin let me examine my face, running my fingers along the pain lines, noting the dark circles that surrounded my eyes. I bore no scars, but there were other signs of the burden I had carried all these years. Even now, while I sat here in the comfortable warmth of my own place, it could reach out to touch me, its touch like fire.

When I was ready to leave my lair, I appeared much thinner. My hair was now curled at the sides of my head, like a mane. I had sprayed my legs in one of the currently fashionable colors, and they peeked seductively from the slits in the long, full trousers, topped with a multicolored, sparkling jacket discarded by a humanoid patron, expertly mended by myself. My face was entirely different, the eyes wider and brighter, the green-painted lips much fuller, while across my forehead and back across the center of my skull extended the bony protrusion of the K'vasti people, a humanoid race akin to the Frossians, who frequented the pleasure quarter both as buyers and bought. House Mouselline sold clothing, but it also sold cosmetic prostheses, and I had acquired an armamentarium of parts: noses, ears, forehead and jaw growths, mouthfuls of various teeth, as well as mittens and gloves that counterfeited the hands of a dozen races. I could make myself up to be a K'vasti, a Frossian, a Hrass. I had been all of these and a dozen others. I had found it necessary to be each and every one of them to find the things it wanted.

Sometimes I became virtually invisible, a nonentity clad in gray robes, my gray skin marred by oozing eruptions caused by exposure to the charbic root used to fumigate dwellings. Sometimes I emerged as a creature anatomically unlike myself, the effects managed by prostheses and skillful dressing. Sometimes I went out as myself, or almost myself, a humanoid that got itself up to appear attractive in order to be an acceptable client in the places I sometimes had to go. Or, as tonight, a K'Vasti who would be welcome in the secret quarter, where creatures with certain tastes congregated, where tonight, as every night, something quite dreadful would likely happen within my sight and hearing.

From the courtyard the alley gate gave access to one of the twisting, narrow streets that tunneled toward the pleasure quarter. I walked freely, as might any one of the various races who thronged the area, four or five different sexes, some who had no gender at all, some bond, some free. Half a hundred eating houses were scattered on the near edge of the quarter, serving the foods of a hundred planets, several of them not only edible by humans and K'Vasti but deliciously so. Eating was my first intention. I would enter the quarter after I had eaten, but only as a last resort, if I could not come up with something to share with it in any other way.

Ahead of me, back against the wall, a Hrass huddled, the way they did, always appearing frightened to death. Possibly with good reason. Moved by an inexplicable urge, I went to stand behind it.

"You are Hrass," I said in the creature's own tongue.

"Soooo," it replied, noncommittal.

I shifted to the K'Vasti dialect. "Can you understand me?"

"Soooo!" An affirmative.

"I have something to tell the Hrass. Earlier this year, Draug B'lanjo of the K'famir killed the Omniont Ambassador. He sent the body to the Omnionts, saying the Hrass had done the killing. Draug B'lanjo did this because he wants to take over the Hrass shipping routes."

I turned on my heel and left him. If he talked to the wrong people, they would be looking for a K'vasti. Therefore, I must remember to burn the K'vasti prosthesis as soon as I got home, but not before, for the sharing had to be done every night before midnight, and today had produced nothing usable: no new scandals murmured across my bowed head, no crimes of violence or passion described while I stitched. No corruption uncovered or pretenses betrayed while I listened. So far as Bak-Zandig-g'Shadup was concerned, today might almost have been Eden, and therefore useless to me. Any daytime Eden had to be followed by a nighttime hell, with me doing as Adille had once done: walking the pain path, the horror road, the tortuous routes toward the terrible.

The thing fed on blood, pain, and death. If it knew where these things were, or would be, it would send me there. Sometimes, in the middle of the day, it would squeeze me, tighter and tighter, until I could not breathe, bringing me to the very edge of suffocation, in order to relish my panic.

"Miss Ongamar, are you quite all right?" Lady Ephedra would ask.

"Oh, quite, Lady Ephedra. A spasm of indigestion, I think. Nothing severe."

"You looked quite ashen there for a moment. Would you like to go home?"

I could not afford to lose a day's allowance, as Ephedra Mouselline knew very well. The words seemed kind, but the intent was unmistakably minatory, and the thing relished this as well.

In those short times, each day when I was not at the command of it or Lady Ephedra, I sometimes thought of my own life and future. The time would come when my years of bondage were completed. Release from the thing was probably not possible after so long a time, but as my time of release approached, if I could encounter someone human or Gentheran, I could warn them. I had seen humans and Gentherans in the pleasure quarter. They were always closely watched by steel-helmeted security officers. I could not legitimately speak to a human as a bondslave, but I could, perhaps, as a K'Vasti, assuming my disguise would fool the officers.

If such an opportunity ever came, I would not ask for help for myself. I was as guilty as the worst of those I had observed. I knew that purposeful watching was in every respect as evil as the torture itself. Peering into the darkness of pain was the equivalent of inflicting pain. Watching torture was the equivalent of agreeing to torment. Making a spectacle of it was equivalent to doing the torture oneself. Yes. Whether the torture was real or only apparent, the watcher was guilty, for the watcher chose to see it, thereby creating an appetite. My pursuit of agony made me as heinous and depraved as those who committed it. No matter that I did it to save my life, or perhaps only continue what passed for my life, it was evil.

It would be better for me to kill myself than to continue as I was. Of all the choices I might make, that was the only good one, and I was determined to take the thing with me when I did it. I did not have the right to leave life with this duty unperformed, but I would hang on only until I could warn someone.

I Am Gretamara/on Chottem

One evening, as we sat on the porch of the Gardener's house, watching the Gibbekot playing with Sophia, I wondered aloud what had happened to Benjamin Finesilver, her father.

The Gardener shook her head slowly and sadly. "You know that Mariah expected her father to send a doctor from the city of Bray. D'Lorn had hired a guide, a man named Bogge, who actually knew the way here, but shortly before the doctor was due to leave Bray, Benjamin Finesilver arrived at Stentor d'Lorn's door. His carriage contained Mariah's body, wrapped in cerements.

"Benjamin was sobbing, Stentor was blind with fury. Had Benjamin not been so obviously torn by grief, Stentor would likely have killed him on the spot.

"'Was there no help for her?' Stentor cried out.

"'Only the Gardener,' said Benjamin.

"'The WHAT?' demanded Stentor.

"'The . . . local wisewoman, midwife kind of person,' Benjamin said. 'Everyone told Mariah to go to her, but Mariah wouldn't go. She said you were sending a doctor from Bray . . .'

"'And what had this woman to say?'

"Benjamin looked up, confused. 'To say? Nothing. Mariah never went to her.'

" 'Wasn't she summoned when Mariah was giving birth?' "

" 'The Gardener can't be summoned, sir. She is not . . . not a mere person. One has to go to the Gardener, not the other way round.' " The Gardener fell silent, her eyes following Sophia.

"I am surprised Benjamin knew that much," I said.

"I doubt that Benjamin did know it until after Mariah was dead. Certainly it was more than Stentor could accept," said the Gardener. "Benjamin tried to explain that the women of the town had tried their best, but Mariah would not take their advice. Then Stentor asked about the child. Benjamin had no more wit than to say, 'I did not wish to endanger a newborn upon the road, so I left her in safety with the Gardener, sir . . .'

"And that was the end of Benjamin Finesilver, Gretamara. His departure from life went unnoticed save by several faithful and tongueless servants of Stentor d'Lorn who were ordered to see him on his way. The following day, while Stentor was locked in his chambers, raging with grief, Bogge, the wanderer he had hired to take the doctor to Swylet, came to the palace and was turned away by the gateman. 'He doesn't need you to take the doctor. It's too late for the doctor. His daughter's body has already been placed in the tomb of her family.'

"Bogge was uncertain what propriety demanded of him in such a case. 'Should I speak with the Lord? I have already spent some of the money he paid me . . .'

" 'If I were you, I'd stay away for a time,' said the gateman. 'Likely the Lord doesn't want to be reminded of it. As for the money, it was probably little enough. I'll tell him you came and offered.'

"And so the gateman did, sometime later, after Bogge had departed for some other place. Only then did Stentor d'Lorn realize the consequences of his haste in disposing of his daughter's husband. Benjamin would have known the way to Swylet. Bogge had claimed to know the way, but the gateman knew neither where Bogge had gone nor when he would return. None of the wanderers currently in Bray knew of Swylet or Bogge.

"Since that time, Stentor has sent his agents here and there in fruitless searches for a mountain place known as Swylet. The name does not appear on any map known to the archivists; it is not mentioned in any account cited by explorers-cum-amateur-geographers."

"How do you know this?" I asked.

"I was there," said the Gardener. "I needed to know, for Sophia's sake, and I could not know truly unless I was there."

"You could not know what he was thinking?" I asked.

The Gardener shook her head. "Except as his actions betrayed his thought, no. Almost all humans are at least partly my people, but not he. He is as dark to me as a K'Famir or a Frossian. I do not know what he thinks or feels, but I know he has not given up the search. He has willed everything to his granddaughter, setting aside only a sizable reward for whatever person shall return her to Bray."

I shivered at the fate of Sophia's father and the darkness that dwelt within her grandfather, and I thought it was as well that only the Gardener and I knew where the heiress of Bray might be found.

I Am Naumi/on Thairy

When I was taken for life-service, the Escort helped me aboard a small flier and directed me to take the seat nearest the single window.

"Flown before, boy?"

"No, sir."

"Well, first time is always memorable. From that seat you'll get a good long look at Thairy from the route we're going."

"Where are we going?" I wondered, as the words left my lips, if I was even allowed to ask questions.

"Academy," the Escort replied. "You're being taken directly to the academy at Point Zibit. That's across Gentheren country from here. You ever met a Gentheren?"

"No, sir."

The man laughed. "Well, of course not, and neither have I, nor are we likely to. You just settle yourself back there. If you start to feel sick to your stomach, tell me right away."

"Yes, sir."

The flier went gently upward, the Escort glancing back occasionally to see whether I was going to be all right or not. Not that he'd hold it against me if I wasn't, but I supposed washing out the flier wasn't one of his favorite ways to end the working day.

I amazed myself by feeling exhilarated. Excited, in a nice way, and eager to look down on Bright, so tiny, like the little toy village I remembered having . . . no, seeing somewhere. No, it was one I'd imagined, when I was a child. Strange. I didn't really remember having it, just . . . knowing about it. The toy village moved away from beneath us as we followed the road, the one I had never followed farther than the quick route to the swimming hole. It wound over little hills, past tiny farms with toy barns, and as we climbed higher, whitish dots appeared in the fields. Cows, maybe, though they seemed too large. After a while the road began to twist back and forth like a serpent, we went steeply upward, and I was looking down on mountains. Every now and then a house roof winked sun in my eye or a stretch of narrow river glinted silver amid the endless carpet of trees.

We went higher yet, crossing a great cracked slab of red cliffs onto a tableland even more thickly forested than below. There the trees were interrupted by wide streams, sizable lakes and towns where piers thrust out into the water. Suddenly there was only water. What I'd seen earlier hadn't been lakes at all. They'd been . . . inlets, that's all, inlets. This was the lake. Or maybe it was a sea. Only seas weren't high up, like this. Seas were down in bottomlands.

"The Upland Sea," said the Escort. "Impressive, isn't it. This mesa is huge, the size of a continent, and it's higher at the edges than in the middle. They say it's what's left of a caldera, the edges are the rim-rock, the middle had a lot of ashes in it. Water filled it up, then ate waterfalls down the edges, washed out some of the ash after every rain, every snow, gradually wore it down to where it is now. Gentheren country. There's the city."

He turned the flier on its side, so I could look down. A city made of glass and trees, a wide grove of trees, monumentally tall and joined together with spider silk bridges and canopies.

"It's beautiful," I said. "Can we go closer?"

The Escort laughed. "If you want to be shot out of the sky, maybe. We're as low as we're allowed to be."

"They don't let you land there?"

"I told you, it's Gentheren country. Humankind stay off. Entry by invitation only."

"I thought Thairy was a human colony," I protested. "They told me in school it was."

"It's a human colony, down below, off the mesa. Plenty of room down there. The Gentherens don't bother us, and we don't need to bother the Gentherens."

Soon the city was behind us, though the forested height went on for hours. I yawned, stretched, yawned again, fell into a doze. Later I woke and looked down to see the far edge of the continental mesa approaching. On this side it ended abruptly in a sheer cascade of black stone that flowed all the way down to the sea.

There, on the narrow shore between precipice and beach, was a town, a ribbon city only two or three streets wide but endlessly long. Directly below us, a hook of land extended into the sea, a curving extrusion covered with walls, squared-off fields, streets, structures, all of them as rigidly angled and paralleled as ruled lines.

The Escort pointed down. "Fort Point Zibit."

"The academy?"

"Right. Now, Naumi, that's your name, right? Naumi, I'm going to let you in on a secret. When you get there, some snotty cadet is going to ask you your name. You say, 'Naumi on X, sir.' The joke is, while you're on Academy grounds, you're 'on X-zibit.' That's because the upperclassmen watch everything the younger ones do and the officers watch the upperclassmen. Every cadet is somebody on exhibit."

"That's silly," said I, flushing.

"Well, do it or don't do it," said the Escort. "But if you don't, you'll wish you had. Weathereye said you had louts back there in Bright."

"Yes, sir."

"Well, Naumi, there's louts here, too. The difference is, these louts have to play by rules, but sometimes they make the rules, and they can lout you to death if you don't play by the same rules they do, silly and otherwise. I'm telling you this because that friend of yours, Weathereye, asked me to."

The flier landed on a strip of paving by the sea, and when I stepped down onto it, the sun made a glittering road of light stretching from the sea edge at my feet to the great orange orb hanging only a finger's width above the ruled rim of the horizon. I had left in the morning, without breakfast. I had come all the way west to the sea, and now I was hungry. It had been a long day.

"You Noomi?" called a voice from beyond the fence.

I started to say yes, then stopped. The person there had an unmistakably loutish look to him. I picked up my light pack and plodded across the yard until I was only an arm's length away.

"Nah-ow-me on Ex," I said very quietly.

"What kinna name's that?" the stranger asked.

"Any kind at all," said I.

"Well, I don't like it," said the other. "I think I'll rename you noomi. That's a kind of worm."

"That could work both ways," I offered, with a level stare into the other's eyes. "Them as names, get named."

"Grangel!" someone yelled. "Quit slopping about and bring the new cadet over here."

Grangel turned slightly red and spun on his heel. "Yes, sir," he called, then, over his shoulder, "This way, noomi."

I followed him at a sufficient distance to avoid being either tripped or elbowed. As we approached, the uniformed officer at the controls of the hovercar got out and stood erect. Though I was untutored in what might be expected, Mr. Weathereye had always said that civility could not possibly be resented by any civilized person; that if resentment were offered, it was a sure sign of loutdom.

"Naumi Rastarong, sir," I said, bowing slightly.

"Welcome, cadet," said the officer. "I'm Captain Orley. Pile yourself in the back there. You've had a long trip, and I imagine you're hungry."

"Yes, sir," I replied, salivating. "Very."

"Then we'll leave the civilities for another time. Grangel, you have post duty this shift."

"Yes, sir."

"Well then, I'll let you go on over to the gate. No need to go all the way back into the Point, then turn around and come back. You did have early mess?"

"Yes, sir," grudgingly.

Grangel was left to plodding while I was whisked, the captain giving a running commentary as we went. "These are the main gates. Post duty is guard duty, standing watch at the gates. All cadets do it sometimes, but most of the time it's done by what we call black-checkers, those who accumulate black checks on their record for fighting, harassing, disobeying orders, or showing disrespect to officers."

The gates fled by, huge stone pillars flanking metal grilles on wheels—open—and half a dozen statue-stiff cadets standing guard. "Sometimes the black-checkers get tired of being idiots and shape up. Sometimes they get tired of being punished for being idiots and quit. We don't care which, quite frankly. Too many cadets are children of privilege who think we're here to serve them instead of the other way round. I know you're not, so I can say this without fear you'll quote me to your parents." The vehicle turned into a wide street that ran straight toward the sea. "This street is called The Parade. That's the armory to your right, to your left is the officers' residence, then the officers' dining room. Right is the cadet mess. That means dining room, too, but officers get to use fancier words. Same food, both places. Now, that's First Cadet Row going off to the right, men's and women's houses on the left, classrooms on the right. Four streets, First Row for first years, Second Row for second years, and so on."

By the time we reached the fourth street, I could see that it was shorter by far. "Not as many fourth-year cadets, sir?"

"Not so many, no. The big break comes at the end of years one and two. Most everyone who gets into third year goes on to finish, including some of those children of privilege I mentioned earlier. People send their children here because they can't do anything with them, then they act surprised when we can't either—though not as surprised as we are when we can do something with them. Off to the left are the sports fields. You like sports."

"Not much, sir. I'm better at other things."

"What things would those be?"

"Battle games, sir. And academics." This was Mr. Weathereye's word. Mr. Wyncamp just called it schooling, but this place seemed to call for Weathereye kind of language.

"That's interesting," said the captain. "A word of advice, if I may."

"Of course, sir."

"Pick some sport, don't care what. Something you hate the least, maybe. Claim it. Make that yours. It's useful to have while you're here. Something you can do in the games for your Row or your House, whether it does you any good or not. Understand?"

"Swimming, sir?"

"Of course, swimming. You like that?"

"I'm fairly good at it, sir. And mountain climbing."

"When you say mountain climbing . . ."

"Cliffs, sir. Straight-up places. Places other people don't usually go."

"Hmmm," said the captain, swerving the vehicle to head back the way we had come. Outside the cadets' mess, he beckoned to a tall, bearded fellow who was lounging by the steps and called, "Sergeant Orson. Here's the one you've been expecting." Then, to me, "Sergeant Orson is a good man. Pay attention to him. Tell him your troubles, if you have any. If you don't, tell him you don't. Understand?"

"Yes, sir, Captain Orley."

Then I was standing on the roadside, smelling food as the man approaching me grew larger with every step until he loomed like a tree. "Cadet Naumi," he purred from a truly overwhelming loftiness. "Welcome to Point Zibit."

The seventh morning after my arrival, the sixty male and female residents of Houses 4A and 4B ran up the side of a mountain. I was accustomed to running, though not on an uphill track. Still, I acquitted myself fairly well, coming over the last rise and down into the final clearing slightly ahead of the middle of the pack. Stamina, Mr. Weathereye had always told me, is half attitude and half practice. I had the attitude, and the practice would no doubt come.

Sergeant Orson stood at the entrance to the clearing, pointing across it to the large commissary wagon, already thronged by earlier arrivals. I joined them, noting the wide choice of foods, including several things I would eat only if I were starving. I took a modest plateful of the tastier stuff and wandered about the clearing as I ate it.

East of the wagon, a section of cliff had fallen to create a vast pile of scree. Behind the wagon, north, the road continued upward along the cliffs, separated only by a narrow strip of sloped woodland from the seaward precipice to the west. The south side of the clearing held the road we'd come in by, as well as a picket line where eight huge horses were tied. As I passed, I stroked all eight enormous soft noses and leaned my head against one or two huge, silver-maned shoulders. The horses' feet were feathered with brushes of silver hair above hooves as big as dinner plates.

Grangel, the cadet who had renamed me Noomi and whose cronies had helped in making it a universal term of ridicule, dragged in close to last. He was loud in his outcries of displeasure at the food choices left for the laggards until Sergeant Orson silenced him and climbed into the wagon bed, calling for attention. Reading from a prepared list, he divided our group into teams of six and told us we could take a short rest, after which we were to collect stones from the scree along the base of the cliffs and use them to construct drystone walls "this long . . ." displaying lengths of cord, ". . . and this high . . ." displaying shorter ones, ". . . in the areas already staked out west of the road.

"I'm going back to Zibit with the wagon," he cried. "We'll return with your supper about sunset. Have the walls done by then."

The hostler and the sergeant busied themselves stowing the mess wagon and hitching the team. I, who had decided it would do no harm to get a good look at everything, picked up two measuring cords from where they'd been dropped, strolled over to the staked area, and looked it over, then walked over to the edge of the scree and looked carefully at the stones there. What seemed at first glance to be a mountain of raw material would actually yield a much smaller volume of usefully flat and stackable rock. A much better selection of flattish stones lay above my head to the left, where a narrow shelf extended above and along the upward road. What stones had collapsed there had not fallen as far, and less stone had fallen on top of them, making them less splintered than most, though the shelf would take some climbing to get to. On my way back, I saw the hostler remove a number of shovels from the wagon and lay them under the thorny growth at the foot of the trees, where they were easily visible to anyone who was using his or her eyes.

I returned my plate to the wagon and sat for a few minutes, taking deep breaths. Sergeant Orson bellowed at us to start work, and the horse-drawn vehicle rolled slowly away down the hill. I stared after it, feeling the rumble of those wheels up through my feet and legs. We had flown over the high mesa to Zibit in a flier. The officer who met me had used a floater. The obviously heavy commissary wagon was drawn, however, by eight huge horses. All very interesting.

My team was number six. The other five members of it, two girls and three boys, immediately began rushing or staggering back and forth as they fetched stones to the assigned site. I went a bit farther up the road, thrust my fingers into a few narrow slots, found a few almost invisible footholds, and worked my way up to the shelf where the flat stones had piled. I began dropping the stones onto the roadway beneath, taking care not to drop them upon one another. When the largest one of my teammates came near, I said over my shoulder, "Hey, Ferni. I'm picking flat ones for the bottom row. If I drop them down there, can you help me carry them over? It'll go faster if somebody picks and the other people carry, you or me, one or the other?"

Ferni, a generally affable cadet, took a look at the wall I had ascended and said, "Go ahead. It's easier to take them from here than dig them up out from under all the little ones anyhow."

Within a very short time, Ferni was joined by the other two boys, Caspor and Poul, and the girls, Jaker and Flek, who also found it easier to take the stones I dropped down than to dig them out of the general rockfall, especially with all the squabbling over territory that was going on. Meantime, I mentioned quietly to Ferni that one of them should always stay by our stone pile to prevent it being borrowed from by neighboring teams, and Ferni quietly passed the word to the others.

I, meantime, was counting to myself: so many stones to the row, so many rows to the layer, so many layers to make the wall. Midafternoon came, and team six had not built a foot of wall while some of the others had sizable structures. Grangel, working with one of the fastest teams, was loud in his mockery and direct in his abuse.

"Look at the noomi bunch!" he cackled. "Buncha real slow worms!"

"We better build something," complained the smallest of the group, Poul. "Everybody's ahead of us, and they're calling us names."

"Good enough," I conceded. "I think we have almost enough stone to complete the job. We'll start with the largest flat ones we have, but let's grab a couple of those shovels over there to level the soil first."

We leveled, to cackles of derision, particularly when I poured a thin stream from my water bottle at various spots on the leveled area to see if it went anywhere.

"They think old Orley told them to dig a latrine!"

"Ho, Noomi, you puttin' in a swim pool?"

The leveling process uncovered several jutting stones, the smaller of which I insisted we remove. We bridged the larger ones when we set flat base stones around them. The big, flat stones were laid up quickly into courses one and two. As we were midway through the third course, cries of dismay erupted from the neighboring group five, whose quickly built wall suddenly collapsed in a cloud of dust when one hasty rock carrier tripped and fell into it.

"Slowly," said I in a low voice. "Don't look at them, look at what we're doing, starting on course four. Make sure every stone is level and wedged to the next one. If it teeters, it's in wrong!" With no comment, the other five went on building while I fished my coil of twine from my pocket, one of the things I'd brought in my memorabilia box, tied one end of it around a small stone, and heaved it over a low branch that jutted just above where we were working, lowering the stone until it hung just above the earth alongside their wall.

"What are you doing?" demanded Ferni.

"We did our best to level the bottom," I replied. "Now we have to be sure it's rising straight, otherwise it'll topple over like that other one. Point your fingers, lay your palm where it just touches the string and your middle finger just touches the wall, move it up and down and you can tell whether the wall's going straight up. If we had some really straight sticks, we could put in some stakes, but there aren't any."

"There's shovels," said Ferni. "Nobody's using them."

I grinned at him, and together we brought over the shovels and made a line of them, each handle adjusted by plumb line to be straight up and down. No one had watched us doing this because all eyes were on group two, where Grangel was summoning attention by showing off what heavy stones he could lay in place. As he heaved an especially large one atop their structure, I clenched my teeth and held my breath. The rock immediately below the space Grangel was attempting to fill was roughly spherical, wedged into position with small, also rounded pebbles. When Grangel's burden hit the wall, the round rock slipped sideways, the smaller pebbles shot out of place, and half the wall collapsed as the spherical stone bounded across the space between walls two and three, hit wall three a resounding blow and destroyed a large part of it.

Groups two and three began to direct their scorn at Grangel instead of at me.

"Pay no attention," said I. "Caspor and Ferni, we're going to need more middle-sized and small flat rocks to finish off. You'll find the best ones right under where I was getting them. The four of us will go on building if you'll gather more stones for us, and don't waste a trip. Pick them carefully."

The wall went on growing. Almost flat, it rose regularly equidistant from the vertical shovels, needing only a final layer to reach the required height. Each layer contained stones of varying thickness, but all were leveled and interlocked, with no rounded ones used at all. While Jaker, Poul, Flek, and I leveled the course for the last layer, Caspor and Ferni moved back and forth with the smaller flat stones I had asked for.

Only four teams were still building. Teams two and three were madly piling rock, making up for lost time; five had not yet totally recovered from its collapse, and six was still leveling its last course while the teams that had finished amused themselves by insulting those who had not. "Noomi" had become a favorite word, and I noticed our team looking sideways at me. "Don't expect me to notice that nonsense," I said quietly. "We're all too busy doing what we're supposed to do: build wall." When team six laid the last few stones securely on the layer beneath and took the shovels back where they'd been found, the sun was sinking beneath the sea, its rays penetrating the western fringe of trees, turning our work into sharply contrasted shapes of shadow and brilliance. Around the clearing, the teams were lying about, their backs against convenient tree trunks.

Ferni murmured to me, "The more even the walls are, the fewer shadows on them, did you notice that?"

"Enough to decide where I want to sit down," said I, leading the way to a large tree, well away from the building area. The others assembled around us, sprawling around the tree's roots. Lying as I was, my eyes fixed on a shadow above the shelf I'd climbed earlier. "Ferni, Jaker," I said. "What's that up there on the rock wall?"

"It's a bush," said Ferni.

"Above the bush," I said.

"A shadow," said Jaker. "But see the way the light goes into it. It could be a cave."

I started to stand up, so I could get a better look, when I felt a premonitory shiver in my feet. "Listen," I murmured to the group. "When the wagon gets here, no matter what happens, just don't say anything. No yelling or jeering."

"But I'm hungry," whispered Caspor.

"We all are, but we're not going to yell about it."

"Wagon coming," called someone from team two.

The team nearest the road got to their feet and began cheering.

Our team six remained where we were, sprawled around the tree as the horses came into view at the top of the rise sloping down into the clearing. By now, most of the cadets were on their feet. The driver clucked to the team, the horses bent to their collars, jerking the wagon over the top, and down they came at a gallop, thundering, the stones echoing the noise. The ground shook. The walls shivered. Small stones popped out here and there; minor avalanches began. The horses kept coming. One by one the walls slumped, tottered, fell.

"Ours stood up," whispered Caspor, sitting up. Then more loudly, "Ours stood up!"

"Shhh," said I, loudly enough that all five of them could hear me. "Don't you dare cheer or yell or anything."

There was a good deal of shouting going on as blame was assigned and denied, resulting in several bloody knuckles and at least one split lip.

The wagon came to a halt. Sergeant Orson jumped from the wagon seat and moved among the collapsed heaps.

Our group got up, everyone yawning and stretching, making good theater of it, as Lady Badness used to say back home in Bright. The other five were giving me little looks, grinning.

The side of the wagon went down. Food smells drifted out.

"Well," said the sergeant. "You bunch, team six, there by the tree. Come get your plates while I walk around and inspect the others."

We were back under the tree with highly piled plates on our laps by the time group four, with two-thirds of their wall still standing, went to eat. Teams one, eight, and nine each had half a wall standing, and they ate next. Five, seven, and ten had some wall standing, though not much, but still, they got to eat before groups two and three, who were sullenly watching others enjoying their supper.

When all had been fed, the officer strolled over to our tree. We put our almost empty plates aside and stood up.

"Good job, cadets. Who's the leader here?"

"It was a group task, sir," said I. "I think we all worked equally hard."

"Built rock wall before, have you?" the officer asked, moving his gaze across us, receiving several no sirs, including one from me.

"Hmmm," he said, turning to look at the newly built wall behind him. "You leveled the soil?"

"Yes, Sergeant," said three or four voices.

"I don't see a large pile of unused stone. Selected the stones carefully before you hauled them over here, did you?"

"Oh yes, Sergeant," said Caspor and Ferni.

The sergeant turned to Caspor. "I'd have to swear somebody knew what he was doing. What is it you're best at?"

"Not much, Sergeant, except numbers. I do real well with them."

"And you?" to Ferni.

"I'm good with animals, Sergeant. Like those big horses."

Jaker, Poul, and Flek disclaimed any abilities whatsoever. Sergeant Orson frowned.

"And you," he said to me.

"Battle games," said I without expression. "I'm very, very good at battle games, Sergeant."

"You mean strategy, Cadet?"

"Of course, sir. What else is there?"

One day, just for exercise, I decided to run up the track along the cliff to the clearing where we had built the walls. I had some free time, and though the shadow on the cliff side was only a tiny mystery, I never did like mysteries, especially ones that might be solvable in an hour or so of free time.

Getting up the wall was only a minor problem. There were a number of grips and good places to put one's feet if one had the wits to see them and remember where they were when the time came to climb down. The shadow was indeed the very narrow entrance to a cave, one that would show up only when the sunlight hit it at a particular time of day. I climbed onto the lip of it with some elation. Since it was morning, there was no sunlight to fall inside the west-facing entrance, but I'd brought a torch, just in case. It lit a level floor that went straight in, past a dark recess to the left, then bent around a corner to the right. I walked it quietly, just in case there was something in residence, though it didn't seem likely. Unless it was something with wings.

I had no sooner had the thought than the torch was knocked from my hand by a flurry of wings, headed out. Birds! Rather large birds. They circled over the clearing, complaining loudly at my intrusion. I looked up to see nests stuck tight to the walls, visible even without the torch in a flickering blue light that came from farther in.

The light was just around the corner in a section of tunnel that looked just like any section of tunnel except for the light itself, a whatever that I couldn't really see. It was more a blue shivering in the air, an evocation of some other . . . what? Without thinking about it, I took two steps into it and found myself somewhere else. Though I couldn't see where, not clearly, it was very definitely somewhere else.

I held very still for a long moment. This was not something I wanted to do right at that moment. Some other time, maybe, but not right now. Carefully, I stepped back, one step, and two, and was back in the tunnel once more, with the very strong feeling I had just avoided some very great danger.

Watching my feet carefully to be sure I didn't stumble into some other unsuspected threat, I climbed carefully down the rock face and jogged back to Zibit, all the while reviewing what I'd seen and felt in the cave, saving it, as it were, in my mental memorabilia box. Something to take out and look at from time to time. Something to keep for the future.

• • •

Occasionally, as time went on, and only when I was out of sorts, I regretted having been so successful in that first cadet exercise, for it had an unanticipated result. I had ended up with Caspor, Ferni, and Poul as constant companions in the dormitory, and with Jaker and Flek tightly attached to the group during field exercises. Ferni, I really, genuinely liked. It was a feeling I couldn't really identify, one I'd never had before, an internal heat, a wanting feeling. It wasn't an appropriate feeling. Or maybe it was an appropriate feeling but not . . . not for an appropriate person, even though something inside me felt Ferni was . . . completely appropriate. More likely I felt this way because he and I were so much alike. We were both orphans. Both reared by foster parents. Both, surprisingly, with vacant spaces in our memories, and both of us ending up at the academy without warning or provocation. After some thought, I decided it would be best for me just to set the feeling aside and enjoy working with him.

As for the others . . . Jaker and Flek could have been sisters, both quiet, both unexpectedly strong and very determined in everything they did. Caspor and Poul had been sent by their parents. None of them seemed to have particular skills except for Caspor's uncanny mathematical abilities and Flek's mysterious affinity for armaments—she could break down and reassemble the model RB27 faster than the rest of us could decide how to start.

"What they're like doesn't matter," I told myself sternly. "It's just like building rock wall. You don't complain about what you have to work with, you just make it work!"

I set out to learn everything I could about each of the five, so we could knit together to stand strong and indivisible. It turned out, the best way to do this was by involving the whole group in solving problems. It let us see everything from as many points of view as possible. Even though Jaker didn't usually solve problems on her own, she always saw something in them the others had not seen, and the same was true of each of them. I began to see things differently myself. Here was the problem, and there was the way it went, and it swerved around Caspor and fled toward Ferni, then Flek, then went on, touching each of them, sometimes circling back, until suddenly, one of us saw it! There it was, the route laid out as if in flashing lights, an avenue so well marked that we could not possibly mistake it. A high road, paved and guttered. We had only to point it out to the others, lead them down it, and at the end, there was the solution, right where it should be.

"The talk road," Ferni called it. "Let's help old Naumi find the talk road." And help they did, to their own benefit no less than mine. It was a new experience, this having friends and working together. I hadn't realized until then how lonely my life had been before.

Neither Sergeant Orson nor Captain Orley seemed to take any notice of this. Several dormitory mates did take notice of this to their dismay, for we had become so tight that bullying any one of us brought a quick and unpleasant retaliation.

A plump, gray-haired woman who worked in the kitchen had taken a bit of liking to me. She thought I looked like her son, long since grown and gone away, so she sneaked me extra cookies that I shared with the others, and she kept me up-to-date on the local news, like who was dropping out and who wasn't. So, one evening I went to see if she had anything for us. She told me to go through into the kitchen next to the officers' dining room and wait for her while she finished putting tomorrow's loaves in the oven.

I went where she told me, quietly, as was my habit, though not with any idea of sneakiness. I heard people talking in the dining room. One of my professors said, "Cadet Poul. You know the boy, Captain Orley."

"Of course I know the boy, the son of . . ."

"Very much the son of the largest import-export firm on Thairy, right! I didn't think he'd last out the year."

"You mean he will?" asked the captain in amazement.

"He will. It seems a trio of his dormitory mates plus a couple from the women's dorm have a study group led by young what's-his-name, the foundling boy from Bright? Ah, Naumi."

"A study group?" in a tone of slight dismay.

"It's not unheard of, Captain. We even suggest it."

"I wasn't saying it's a bad idea. I was just surprised. Poul's actually learning something? He'll pass?"

"Better than merely pass, by a good bit. So will the others. It seems Caspor is in charge of things mathematical. Ferni is in charge

of things biological. Flek, it turns out, has a family interest in armaments . . ."

"I didn't know that!"

Well, neither had I known it, and I found it very interesting indeed, so I went nearer the hatch between kitchen and dining room
and sat down quietly on the floor.

"Surely you know of Flexen Armor. Flexen Magma Canon, FMC?
Her grandfather is Gorlan Flekkson Bray. Originally from Chottem."

"She's that family? I had no idea."

"Cadet's the offspring of one of the daughters, her surname isn't
the same, and the mother didn't make anything out of it when her
daughter was registered. She's been wandering around the factories
with her maternal grandfather since she was old enough to walk.
She chose to come here, and her grandfather recommended her to
the academy. She's packed to the gills with engineering information she has no idea she knows, or knows the usefulness of."

"I suppose the rest of them have hidden qualities as well?"

"Not that we know of. Jaker is a quiet, self-contained young
woman from another extremely wealthy import-export family. The
Jakers and the Pouls are linked, matrimonially, with cousins in common. She has no outstanding abilities, but she, too, is learning. And
Naumi . . . well, he doesn't shine in any particular class. He doesn't
attract attention. That pack that follows Grangel—all of whom will
be dropping out any day now, one fondly hopes—harassed him a bit
when he first arrived, but that's dwindled off to nothing . . ."

"But he leads this group?"

"Oh yes, sir. He wouldn't say that, of course, but he does. That's
his outstanding quality, I guess. That and something else . . ."

"Which is?"

"You know we give the cadets problems to solve. Tactical problems. You know. We're looking for optimum, seventieth, eightieth
percentile answers. Most cadets are lucky to rate over fifty percent
with a solution. Naumi and his group come up with the optimum
answer nine times out of ten. The tenth time, they come up with an
answer we've never received before, and when we give it to the battle
simulator, it comes back as an even more highly rated response, one
that the simulator hadn't thought of. He always says it's a group

effort, what he calls a talk-road effort, and from what we can learn, it is, but he's always the one that pulls the group together."

This was news. I knew we'd been doing well, but not that well.

"It seemed to us," said a professor, "that is . . . we all thought he should be recommended to the war college, at once. Why wait four or five years with ability like that?"

There was a long pause, then Captain Orley said, "I objected to the boy being admitted, nobody that he was, late in the year as it was. I thought it would be a handicap both for the boy and for his house. However, I'm a man who can eat my earlier opinions for breakfast without choking on them, which is a good thing. This boy got in because he was recommended."

Mr. Weathereye. I knew it!

Someone said "Every cadet who comes to Point Zibit is recommended by somebody!"

The captain said ruefully. "Oh, he had that sort of recommendation from his schoolmaster and friends back in Bright. That's not what I'm talking about. Naumi was recommended by the Third Order of the Siblinghood."

Someone, I think it was Professor Hilbert, the mathematics man, said something in a harsh voice. "The Order. I find a great deal wrong with that, Captain Orley. First, though I know the Siblinghood is real enough, I find some difficulty in believing the Third Order actually exists. Secondly, if it exists, why is this supposedly all-powerful, all-knowing group interested in a schoolboy? And finally, assuming such an organization does exist, how does one verify that any information comes from that organization and not merely some clever-cock who wants to pull strings?"

Captain Orley murmured a reply while I was wishing I could have seen his face, to know how he felt about it. "It's a bit like discussing God, isn't it? Is there one? If there is one, how do we know it is speaking? How do we know what it wants?"

"Exactly," snapped Hilbert.

"The eternal questions," the captain went on. "Which always come down to the same answer. One has to trust the interface between oneself and it. The prophet. The sacred writing. The beatific visions. Then the second prophet who clarifies the issues. Then the new writing, and the new visions. Then a declaration of heresy and a reformation. Then a schism. Then a sect. Except that with the Third Order there is no writing, no visions, no prophet that we know of . . ."

"Then how in the name of all good sense . . . ?" yelled Hilbert, while two or three other people said, "Shhh, shhh."

Captain Orley raised his voice. ". . . how does the lowliest member of the selection committee, myself, wake up one morning to find the message pinned to my shirt, which was in my locker, which was locked, which was inside my room, which was locked, which was in the officers' quarters, which are guarded. A real message, which I read half a dozen times before it disintegrated into shiny dust."

Hilbert huffed. "Ascribe it to whatever you ate and drank the night before, Captain. You were seeing things."

"I could tell myself that. There are five of us on the committee, however, and we had not dined together for a long time. Nonetheless, it happened to all five of us. Same message, same location, more or less, all in places protected against intrusion, all signed, 'The Third Order.' I'll be glad to give you the names of the other four if you'd like to hear it directly from them."

I noticed I could see them reflected in the side of one of the big pots hanging on the wall. I saw them glancing at one another. I wondered if they were reviewing everything they had said, wondering if maybe this Third Order might be listening.

"Tread carefully, gentlemen. If what you tell me is true, if what I have told you is believable, it is likely Naumi will come to us, or someone will come on his behalf, if and when he, or they, consider the war college is a good idea. If Naumi chooses not to stand out, then I would suggest you let him . . . stand in, just where he is, where the Third Order recommended he be."

I told Ferni about it, back at the dorm. He asked what the Third Order was.

"I never heard of it," I said. "Honest, I never. But I was called for life-duty, so maybe . . . maybe it's just something they want me for."

"That makes you out to be pretty important," Ferni said with a lofty look. I swear, sometimes the way he drew himself up that way you'd swear he thought he was king of the world.

I said, "Not necessarily, Ferni! A squirt of axle grease can be important if that's what you need. That's probably all I'm supposed to be. Something to help turn a wheel."

We left it at that. I think Ferni forgot all about it. I put it away among my mental memorabilia and tried not to think about it, though sometimes I did, wondering what it all meant.

I Am Margaret/on Earth

Except for the rumors and whispers that followed the disappearance of our three classmates, college life was undisturbed for a time. I was fully focused on the final section of my "lateral studies," those intended to broaden understanding of linguistic development. Everything known about the Pthas and their linguistic survivors had been reviewed; the aeon-long changes in the Quaatar language likewise; along with the accepted works on dialect development among Mercan and Omniont planets. The last thing on the list was to consider a speaking race that had lost its use of language, as recorded by a Gentheran exploration ship. My friend Sybil, Bryan's sister, had made a vomit face when mentioning it, so I'd been putting it off.

Still, it was a required thing, so I settled my earpieces, keyed my didactibot, and faced a barren planet dotted with tall, irregular lumps. With a hiccup and purr, the lecture began in the same sweet, high voice I had heard at the meeting, Sister Lorpa's voice. Or one of her kin.

"While on a routine journey of exploration, the Gentheran ship *Pendaris Kuo* happened upon an uncharted system with one live planet. Since the planet was occupied by a previously unknown race, a monitoring shuttle was implanted into a rocky area to provide a longitudinal recording of the inhabitants.

"The earthen towers you see are the homes of the only

land animal living on this world. These clay mounds are analogous to the termite mounds found on Earth during the multispecies ages. Since there is no evidence of a precursor race on the planet, Gentheran historians researched the archives to determine how these creatures may have arrived there. An ancient Quaatar logbook entry may have described the ancestors of this population stowing away on a Quaatar ship, then fleeing the ship on this planet, 'Into the thick vegetation that covered the world.'"

The point of view receded. "Assuming that one tower was built initially, and extrapolating from the growth rate observed by the buried ship, we see here how the towers spread, resulting in the complete deforestation of the planet. There is evidence of several natural disasters that virtually eliminated these creatures on this world, but each time forest growth returned, they also returned to destroy it.

"Gentheran researchers picked a tower at random and fed audio-optical leads and chemical sensors into it, using the ordinary micro-burrowers used by xenoarchaeologists. These fibers provide sufficient light to permit a pictorial record of life inside. Only the various types are distinguishable from one another. Members of each caste or type are identical.

"The first recording begins at dawn. The creatures you see before you are curled against a tunnel wall, sleeping. To give human students some sense of scale, each creature could easily be held in your cupped hands."

I could see why Sybil had been disgusted by the creatures. So was I. They were naked and gray. They had large ears that were folded against the head, each head pillowed on one skinny arm. The legs were short and almost as thin as the arms. They had no noticeable sexual organs. The faces had a common bilateral pattern, one shared by many races: sight and scent organs grouped at the upper end above the ingestion aperture. These mouths were toothless, the creatures had no chins and no appreciable necks.

A second type of individual appeared, slightly larger, with a larger mouth. As it passed along the line, it uttered a sound, *wakwak wakwak,* as it kicked the feet of each sleeper. Those kicked stood up, each in sequence, as room was made by the previous riser. Uttering this continuous *wakwak wakwak,* the kicker went up the tunnel, while behind it the wakened creatures made a half turn to face the direction it had gone, moving their two legs in a steady rhythm while making a continuous sound: *railev railev railev.* The line began to move, slowly at first, then more quickly as space opened up between the awakened ones.

I yawned. Bryan and I had been together the night before, and I was sleepy. Covertly, with a guilty glance at the monitor, I keyed the lecture to fast-forward, stopping shortly before the end. ". . . the protolanguage these creatures may once have spoken has not been identified. The Gentheran expedition did not take genetic samples, since sampling of speaking races is forbidden by IGC rulings without the consent of the individuals. The Gentheran research team was unsure whether this population was or was not a speaking race, though their opinion was that language had once existed but had been lost, and the current sounds made by the creatures were mere flock-murmur, the sort of recognition noises made by birds. The researchers chose not to presume what the IG might rule on the matter, and as yet, no researcher has been sufficiently interested in this oddity to return to the world in question. The buried Gentheran survey shuttle is still there, however, recording the passing of the race and the probable reforestation of the planet, which has been labeled in Gentheran, 'Drdpls,' or, in Earthian, 'Hell.'

"For students, the importance of this report lies less in what it tells us about this race than in what it tells us about language. We believe that at one time, this creature had language formed and ramified by experience. Brought to a world with no inimical organisms and plentiful food, it expanded endlessly until it occupied the entire land surface of the planet. As food became scarce, the creatures became progressively smaller, eventually reaching the stage we see now.

"Along the way, all meaning was lost except for verbal signals, the kind of signals any animal species develops in order to stay in touch with its own kind, call others to a feeding spot, or alert others to danger. Every linguist should know that language must be used to be retained, and the compilers of this report have warned that human language on Earth is also being reduced. As humans become more crowded, they become less tolerant of variety. To fit into a crowd, people must be similar, and Earth's population today is a vat of homogeneity with only a pretense of choice remaining. One may pick model x with one curlicue or model y with three, the tasteless brown cracker or the tasteless yellow cracker, the actual difference in either case being nil. Any real choice among things of unlike value might lead to disparity, which leads to conflict. Ideas also contribute to disparity, and therefore in crowded populations, ideas must be restricted to the least controversial, the least interesting. Children all receive the same grades in school. Workers all receive the same pay. Clothing is similar; foods are identical; and with the passage of all distinctions, the words for them also pass. Who now knows of oranges, whale blubber, corsets, chopsticks, panty hose, nutmeg? What is a cable knit? Where might one find a T-bone? . . ."

I pushed the stop and reversed, listening to this last bit again. What was a cable knit? Or a T-bone? I had known for years that people didn't say anything, but I had never considered that they might actually be losing language! Suddenly interested in this, avid to learn more, I keyed the machine to play it over. My intention was interrupted by a crash as the rear door of the classroom was banged open.

Around me the whispers fell into silence. The man in the door was a black-clad proctor. During the last ten years, proctors had become both ubiquitous and universally dreaded. He spent only a moment scanning the room before striding directly toward me. He leaned down, spoke quietly, waited while I stood and started to gather up my study materials.

"Leave them," he said. "You won't need them."

I saw a dozen pairs of eyes on me, some of them curious. I shrugged, hands out, obviously as ignorant as they were, trying desperately to look nonchalant. What had I done? Or more likely, what did they think I had done? Did this have anything to do with that meeting? Did they think I was involved in what my fellow students had said . . .

The monitor spoke from the front of the room. "Settle down. Get on with your lessons, please."

Outside in the hall, I asked, "Where are we going."

"To the Provost's office," the proctor replied, not breaking his lengthy stride. "Stupid woman insists on seeing you." I trotted to keep up with him, readying myself for a considerable walk, only to be surprised that a car driven by one of the security staff awaited us at the main corridor.

Cars were silent and fast. The driver, an expressionless woman with her clearance code tattooed on her forehead, left us at the Provost's office, where I stood just inside the anteroom door, watching the car dwindle down the hallway, trying not to huddle under the watchful eyes of the proctor.

"Do you know what she wants me for?" I asked.

"I don't answer questions," said the proctor.

It was a threat. There was just time to realize that before the Provost's aide came for me and took me to into her office.

The Provost looked up. "Margaret."

"Yes, Provost."

She rose. "Margaret, I'm sorry about this. If you were not a party to this deception, you will be shocked at this news." She walked around the desk.

"A party to what? I have no idea . . ."

"You are seemingly a student here under false pretenses." She shut the door between us and the proctor.

My mouth dropped open momentarily, before shame and anger snapped it shut. "I am a four, Provost. I am my mother's first and my father's third child."

The Provost nodded, saying more softly, "That was thought to be true ten years ago when you received citizen's approval at age twelve. Two years ago, however, as you are no doubt aware, it became apparent the planned population cuts had not been deep enough, and the selection criterion was moved back another generation. Only twos to fours from two to four parents are now approved."

"Yes, ma'am. Of course I know that."

"All over-fours were instructed to report to the local emigration office?"

"Yes, ma'am."

"Interesting, because it appears that your mother's older brother was born as a twin. Your mother is, therefore, at least the third child of both her mother and her father, a six."

"I don't understand! My mother didn't have an older brother. She had an uncle almost as young as she was, but . . ."

"The medical records establish that your mother had two older brothers. Twin boys were born to your maternal grandparents."

"Uncle Hy?" I murmured, completely lost. "He's Mother's uncle, and he lives on Luna!"

She shook her head. "He may well live on the moon, if he chooses, but he and his brother were born on Earth, and they were your mother's siblings, not her uncles." With a sorrowful expression she reached across the desk and took my hand. "I have seen the records, and this is true, Margaret! You must accept that it is true."

"But . . . but, Provost, that would have been recorded! It would have been in the . . . in the files . . . I would have known . . . Mother would have known . . ."

She shook her head, patted my hand, and said compassionately, "You really didn't know. I'm so sorry."

"Mother thought Hy was her uncle!"

"She may have been told he was. The record of your family's enrollment session is in the permanent files. This year, when the emigration rule was moved back a generation, all the modules were instructed to fact-check and recompute. The module noticed an anomaly, a person named Hyram living on Luna. Original records established that Hyram was a twin of George, who died at birth. Your mother was a six, therefore neither you nor your mother may be registered among two-fours any longer."

"But . . . I'm still a four."

"Though it makes no difference, you really aren't. You were also a twin, whose sister died at birth. It is very rare to have twins in successive generations on both sides of the family, and your father begot twins, which means you're a three on your father's side, a two on your mother's, so you yourself are a five, the child of a two and a six." She looked at the papers in front of her. "Strange. If you hadn't mentioned the name of Hyram during your registration session, no one might have caught that part of it."

I had mentioned it? I sagged, catching myself on the edge of her desk. She rose, put her hand on my shoulder, whispered, "There's nothing I can do, Margaret. There is no appeal. But I insisted they bring you here because I want you to know something. I said you were selected to be at that meeting, and you were, by the Third Order of the Siblinghood. I doubt you've heard of it, and I know nothing more than the name, but that very fact may be important to you in the future. Say it?"

I gaped. "The Third Order of . . . the Siblinghood?"

She opened the door, saying brusquely, "Proctor? Take this woman to the Resources Office for outprocessing."

I was driven home in a Resources floater, black, with the gold symbol on the doors: a stream running down a hill, a tree on the hill, above that a cloud, a sun, the words ENOUGH FOR ALL. That symbol always reminded me of that historic educational effort called "No child left behind," which actually meant "No child gets ahead," for compliance meant dumbing everything down so no one would learn more than the least capable. "Enough for all" really meant "Too little for everybody." As we went, the false windows displayed pictures of tree-lined streets, the vents emitted the smells and sounds of summer: flowers and cut grass, birds singing, children playing. All false. All mere pretense. There was no water for trees, grass, flowers, and solar radiation would kill any child who played outside.

Halfway home, I suddenly thought of Bryan. Bryan! What could I say to Bryan! Sybil was in the class the proctor had just taken me from, and she would tell him! Bryan was a third generation two, a first child of first children, so he might feel that I was too shameful to . . . He might even think it best not to tell me good-bye . . .

In that, I misjudged him, for he arrived at my home almost immediately after I did.

"Margaret, I just heard. Sybil told me. Where's your mother? Did you have any idea about this?"

"No," I had said, tears streaming down my face. "I hadn't. Mother is already gone. She left me a note."

"What did they tell you?"

"Seventy-two hours to prepare for shipment out."

"I had no idea it would happen that fast! Listen to me, get your things together, but don't sign any bondage agreement or do anything until I get back to you . . ."

He was abruptly gone. What did he mean, until he got back to me? What on earth did he think he could do? The agreements were pro forma. They would take me regardless. Still, it was typical of him to try fixing things. He had become a doctor because he had always wanted to fix things. Well, this wasn't something he could fix, and I wished he had stayed with me, held me close, pretended for a little while this wasn't happening.

In the meantime, I stood in the middle of the room, tears streaming down my face as I told myself what I had to do. I had to pack. I couldn't go off without anything to wear. At least I was strong and healthy. At my age I would live through the fifteen years. Mother, though. Mother had never done a day's hard labor in her life, and she was . . . what? Fifty. I moved witlessly around the apartment, into my cubicle and out of it. I opened the closet door, took things out of drawers, put them back, thinking distractedly that Bryan needn't have ordered me to do nothing, for nothing seemed to be all I was capable of. I focused on what I was doing for all of thirty seconds, then forgot whatever it was. I found myself sitting, unable to react in any way to the chaos going on inside me.

In early evening my father came home and fell crying upon my shoulder.

"She told them I didn't know," he said. "I did know, Margaret. I just never thought it would make any difference. On Phobos it didn't make any difference, and we never planned to come back here . . ."

I put my fingers over his mouth. "Don't tell them that, Father. If Mother told them you didn't know, she did it for you. Let her do it. Let her at least feel good about that."

"I should be with her!" he cried.

"You're thirteen years older than Mother is. They won't take you on a labor contract, you're too old. Concentrate on what you can do to help her. Send packages, maybe . . ."

He seized upon this idea and fell abruptly into the old Phobos habit of saying the same things over and over with minor variations. He would do this, she would do that, they would stay in touch, he would provide, she would reply, he would find out, perhaps he could visit . . . then, starting over, he would do this, she would do that. I nodded, responded with monosyllables, let him talk until exhaustion took over and we both slept.

On the second day, Father left to say good-bye to Mother at the assembly point where she was being held.

"Do you want to come, Margaret?"

"I'm not allowed to leave the house."

"But surely . . . not even to say good-bye?"

"Not even that." It was true, but also, I preferred not to go. I had no idea what I could say that would not be hurtful or accusatory, and neither of them deserved that. They'd raised me with all the affection and care Phobos thought proper. The rules were made by whom? Dominion? Earthgov? ISTO? Certainly my parents had had no control over that. But still . . . still . . . Father said they had known! If they had known, why hadn't they at least warned me? Let me get used to the idea . . .

I resolved once more to focus on packing. Sturdy clothes, shoes, warm things in case my destination would be cold. One could always strip down to almost nothing if it were hot. I caught myself folding and unfolding, taking out and putting away, accomplishing little.

And then, unexpectedly, Bryan arrived. He tugged me toward a chair, made me sit down, and took my hands in his.

"I've been finding out about a colony planet called Tercis. It has a subdivision, rather like a state or province, called Rueful . . ."

"Rueful!" I cried.

"Don't interrupt with questions, Margaret. We haven't that much time. Rueful has very few doctors. Doctors and some other professions are allowed to volunteer for places like that." He gazed at me expectantly.

What did he want me to say?

"Why would you volunteer, Bryan? You're in your last year of the specialized training you've always planned on. If there are few doctors, it must be primitive! You wouldn't want to go there! How could you practice medicine there?"

"We've talked about how I feel about practicing medicine here, Margaret. Over and over . . ."

Well, of course we had at one time, before we had agreed not to, but why bring that up again now? "Yes. So?"

He took a deep breath, and blurted, "And if I volunteer, I can take my wife with me . . ."

I stared at him, unbelieving. "You would never volunteer for something like this on your own, Bryan, and if you're doing it for me, I can't . . . can't accept it."

He drew me into his arms, spoke into my ear, urgently, roughly. I must accept it. He loved me, he had loved me since his sister had first introduced us. He had always intended to marry me. No, of course he hadn't spoken of marriage, it hadn't been the right time, but that didn't make it less true. He couldn't, absolutely wouldn't, lose me!

I tried to reason with him, without success. He wouldn't let up. He went on arguing, demanding. Over and over, becoming more intense with every repetition.

Finally, in acute misery, I cried, "Oh, Bryan, if you really do love me, then leave me alone for a little while and let me think about it. I can't stand any more of this."

Bryan went away. When Father returned to the house, I did not mention Bryan's visit. I hoped Bryan would have second thoughts and give it up. I was shamed enough. I couldn't bear to carry any more humiliation than I already felt, and if Bryan made such a sacrifice, he would hate me, and I would spend my life regretting it. It was absurd, preposterous.

I went on packing and repacking, finally achieving the best arrangement anyone could achieve who had no idea where she was going. Bryan did not return, and as I wiped tears from my face, I gave silent thanks for that. In the morning, however, as we were about to leave for the assembly point, he came back, a pack on his back, traveling cases in both hands.

Father blurted, "Bryan, what are you doing here?"

"Came to get Margaret, sir."

"To get . . . you've volunteered for bondage?" It wasn't unheard of, but it was exceptionally rare.

Bryan turned and grasped my hand. "You didn't tell him what I've decided?"

I cried, "I wanted . . . I hoped you'd change your mind."

"I haven't." Without releasing his grip, he turned to face my father. "I love Margaret. I've volunteered to provide medical service on Tercis. Margaret and I will be there together. It's not a high-tech civilization, but it's far from bondservice. I have the authorization papers with me. All Margaret and I have to do is com the Bureau of Volunteer Services to record a contractual union, then she can go with me."

I stood dumb, incapable of words or feeling.

Father broke from his astonishment to ask, "What colony, Bryan? Do you know anything about it?"

"It's a good-sized planet, one the Dominion has divided into sections for human populations of various types. The place that most needs a doctor is called Rueful." He laughed briefly. "It's also inhabited by the Rueful, who practice a religion called Ruc."

"Who are 'they'?"

"Just an ordinary human population, rural, needless to say. Rueful has a few small towns, half a dozen middle-sized ones, one small city, a lot of open country. Almost entirely agricultural. Fewer than a million people in the whole place. The Dominion Settlement Board provided the original supplies: seeds, domestic animals, the usual settlement stuff. According to the Board it's very natural, trees, rivers, some local wildlife, birds, that kind of thing."

"What technological level?" Father asked.

"Three," Bryan said, flushing a little.

"Three! So they have electricity."

"That's about it. Horses for transportation. Actually, you can go all the way across the settled area in a couple of days on a horse. It never gets really cold on Rueful, and they heat the houses with stoves burning wood or coal. There's a coal mine and a lot of forests."

"What language do they speak?" I asked.

"Regular Earthian standard plus some Mercan or Omniont jargon the ex-bondspeople have picked up. We'll understand one another. The area we'll go to is called The Valley. It has no doctor. No hospital. Not much of anything in the way of health care." Bryan's brows pulled together, making a deep furrow between his eyes. "We'll have to build something, a clinic, a small hospital. But I can practice medicine the way I need to, without all this damned bureaucratic red tape! And Margaret will make a good nurse . . ."

Which would have been the last thing I would ever have considered being! Even as a child, I, Margaret, hadn't played at being a nurse . . . a healer. The healer part of me had been totally . . . separate. I wasn't interested in people's bodies. The very idea was appalling!

I tried not to let my dismay show on my face. The whole universe was conspiring to make my education useless.

He pleaded, "Margaret, we don't have much time!"

"Margaret?" urged Father.

I cried frantically, "Father, I tried to talk him out of it. This isn't fair to him . . ."

I was talking to his back. He was leaving, saying, "I can't offer anything to this discussion!" The door shut behind him.

Bryan stared after him.

"My father . . . often . . . departs when things are difficult."

Bryan took my hand. "Margaret, we'll be together, you'll have a job to do that needs doing, your life expectancy ought to be the same as on Earth or better, you won't be eaten by some ET monster or worked to death in the fields by some ET slave driver."

I drew away from him. "But you were so enthusiastic about your new residency . . ."

He almost snarled at me, face darkened with passion. "Damn it, listen to me, Margaret! I've given it up. No matter what you say, yes or no, I can't get it back. It's gone!"

The words clanged at me as though I were inside a huge bell! Something inside me snapped. If I had to be dragged away against my will, at least let it be by someone who cared about me.

"All right, all right! I suppose it's for the best. I'll go with you."

Bryan seized me in his arms, laid his cheek against mine, then released me. There was no time for talk, he said. No time for anything but continuing the process, getting to the assembly point. It took only moments to make the com contact with the Bureau of Volunteer Services, to give my identity number to the authorization clerk, and the whole thing was done.

Rather than drag my father back into the situation, I did what I knew he would prefer. I added a postscript to the note I had already written, saying Bryan and I were going together. I was numb, in the grip of that same, weird vacancy I had felt on the day the first proctor came, as though I had been split in two, as though some monstrous cleaver had irrevocably sliced me apart from myself.

And yet, when I turned to Bryan, ready to argue once more, I saw on his face an expression of exaltation. He clasped my hand between his and smiled gloriously at me. I bit my lips, choking back what I'd meant to say. If this was how he felt, it had to be all right. It would turn out to be the best thing I could do. He had given up . . . whatever he had given up, but I would make it up to him. No matter what it took. I told myself this, over and over again. A mantra. I will make it up to Bryan.

At the assembly point, we were taken aside by a young usher who led us to a smaller area set aside for volunteers. There our papers were processed by an efficient woman who, when she saw we were headed to Tercis, shook her head and bit her lip.

"Are you leaving anyone here on Earth that you hope to communicate with in the future?" she asked.

"My father," I said haltingly. "Bryan's family," turning to him, only to find him staring, red-faced, at his feet.

"You weren't told that will be impossible?" she asked.

I shook my head.

"There's a time anomaly on the Tercis route. The way around it is too expensive to consider. You'll arrive on Tercis . . . sometime before you leave here."

I thought of the international date line on Earth and nodded, showing I understood. I thought I did.

"The difference is about fifteen to twenty years," she said. "Any message you sent might arrive before you were born."

"You knew this?" I asked Bryan.

He confessed that he did. For a moment I was furious, then I wondered what difference it actually made. The Gentherans were the only ones who could travel among the stars without losing their lives to time. Bryan and I had known we would not see our families again. In fact, it made no difference at all.

"You should have told me," I said. "But it doesn't matter."

In the dormitory we sat for most of a day and a night, silently holding hands. I repeated the mantra to myself whenever I began to get edgy, echoing it again as we queued for the subway. Once we were seated, exhaustion took both of us, and we slept all the way to pre-shipping.

Anxiety didn't return until we actually boarded the elevator. We stood at the mouth of the pod, confronting all those heads, like beads, like bubbles, a pavement of heads, all going away, to where? To what? Was it even certain there was a destination at the other end? Then we were seated; officers came through with their calming sprays; and all my concerns were temporarily put to rest.

I remember turning to Bryan, and saying dreamily, "Bryan, do you know anything about the Third Order of the Siblinghood?" His eyes were shut. He didn't answer. I went back to the mantra. We were going up to the shipping station, to Departure. We would be put aboard a ship. We would go to Tercis. Bryan and I would live on Tercis, together. All I had to do was just . . . do what I was told to do, go where I was told to go. Everything . . . everything would be all right. I would make it up to Bryan.

I Am M'urgi/on My Way
to B'yurngrad

... I drew away from him. "But you were so enthusiastic about your new residency!"

Bryan almost snarled at me, face darkened with passion. "Damn it, Margaret, listen to me, I've given it up. It doesn't matter what you say, yes or no, I can't get it back. It's gone!"

The world clanged at me as though I were inside a huge bell! Something inside me snapped. If I had to be dragged away against my will, let it be by Earthgov, by the Dominion, by someone I could hate. Let me not be eternally burdened with someone else's sacrifice! "No, Bryan. No," I screamed at him. "You had no right to do this without my agreement. I will not."

Brian turned white, stared at me in disbelief, then turned on his heel and left me without another word. Numbly, I took up my pack, waiting only a moment to be sure he was gone. I would leave now, while Father was out of the room. I would find my own way to the assembly point and avoid his reproaches for not accepting Bryan's offer. During the previous sleepless night I had written a farewell note. Let that suffice.

At the assembly point, the usher led me through vaults sonorous with regret. "What do they call this place?"

"We just call it the separation lobby. People from their kin. Earth people from their planet. The optimistic from their hopes, and the pessimistic from their estimations of how bad it can be. The answers are always *none* and *worse*."

I was stunned. "You don't try to be comforting, do you?"

"If we're honest, there's nothing comforting we can say. Some of us lie. Some of us don't, like me. I have to put it into words I can handle or the scope of it swallows me. We see millions go through here, and damn few of them go smiling. Today it'll be a bit easier on you. Several ships have come in for immediate loading, so we're sending people directly to the subways. Here's your check-in pass, follow the red line down that way. It takes almost a day to get there, use the toilet before you go, don't drink anything after."

I stumbled away amid others, to join the long queue of émigrés lined up to board the continental subway that would move us a day-long journey to the elevators. Away. Going away, and I couldn't feel anything.

When I arrived at preshipping, one of the ubiquitous ushers saw me standing alone, and said, "Down that hallway, that's your dormitory. Lately we've sped up the process. You shouldn't be here more than a day."

"And then where?"

"You'll probably be in the third or fourth ship out. Either way, you'll be going to B'yurngrad in the Omniont Federation. Actually B'yurngrad is an Earth-colony planet in Omniont Fed space, but it's also a transshipment point for the Omniont worlds in the area. You'll probably change ships there."

"Probably?"

"To smaller ships that'll take the cargo to various Omniont planets. You should be glad it's Omniont space, by the way."

"Why is that?"

"Omniont Federation is marginally better than Mercan Combine."

"How do you know that?"

"We know how many ships go to bondslave worlds, and how many go from those worlds to the colonies. Omniont and Mercan get about equal numbers of bondspeople to start with, but more of those from Omniont worlds survive to go on to the colonies later.

"Don't let it get you down. You look strong. You'll make it. And don't think about sending messages. Travel through space is also through time. Bondspeople are always asking us how they send messages back to their people here on Earth. We tell them, don't bother. More likely it will get here after your people are all dead."

"But ... representatives from our colonies have meetings every year, on Mars!"

"Sure, and the Gentherans provide the travel on little ships that go point to point with a technology no one else has. No one knows how they do it but them. They say it wouldn't help the trading races, because trading ships are too huge to use it, though the time problem is one reason the ET long-distance ships are so huge. They carry whole families aboard. Toward galactic center, among the crowded worlds, time is less of an issue. You can actually travel among them without losing all your friends every time you leave one world to go to another."

I gaped at him. No one had ever mentioned this.

"You probably haven't slept much lately. Go that way, then right to section ninety-seven, row eighty-eight's at the back, bed five-A will be extreme left, here's your bed ticket. Get some rest."

Wondering how the usher expected anyone to rest, I plodded into the cavernous dormitory. Though almost every bed had an occupant, it was almost frighteningly quiet. I found the row and section without difficulty, thrust my bags under bed 97-88-5A, and fell onto it. I was exhausted, I was frightened. I admitted to myself that I should have gone with Bryan. Finally, I told myself I had the choice to cry about it or throw a tantrum or to go to sleep. Of the three, only one would do me any good, so I turned on my side, shut my eyes, and concentrated my whole attention on not screaming. Eventually, I actually did sleep.

Later, how much later I have no idea, I was awakened by a loudspeaker. "Any outshippers able to speak any Omniont or Mercan languages, please report to your dormitory office at once."

I heard it perfectly well, but decided it was part of the frustrating dream I'd been having. They damn well had my records, and if my language skills had been any use to them, they should have let me know before now. Without opening my eyes, I turned over and kept on dreaming.

I Am Mar-agern, Going to Fajnard

"Outshippers, attention. If you speak any Omniont or Mercan languages, please report to your dormitory office at once."

I heard it perfectly well. I sat up, stood up, paused, looking at my bags for a moment, then collected them and trudged down the long aisle toward the distant office. The sleepy-looking officer inside looked up when I entered.

"I speak some of the Omniont and Mercan languages," I said.

"I'm sure that's a great comfort to you," snorted the officer. "Why tell me about it?"

Angrily, I snarled, "Because there's a loudspeaker announcement that anyone who speaks those languages is supposed to report to the dormitory office. Is that here, or somewhere else?"

He sat up, shook himself, and went to his com, where he spoke in muted tones for some little time. "Come with me," he said over his shoulder as he headed out the door. "They're sending transport to take you to the elevators. Oh, by the way, what's your number?"

"All I have is my bed number?"

"That'll do. Give me your bed ticket. We can crosscheck it to your identity. A Mercan ship was delayed here when their cargo translator for the voyage took sick. They can't wait any longer to leave."

"A Mercan ship?" I whispered. "Their cargo translator?"

"Mercan, right. When they say cargo translator, they mean the person who translates commands to the cargo, the bondslaves, the outshipped."

I could not reply. Seemingly, all the fates in the universe were stacked against me, and I was absolutely incapable of making a beneficial decision about anything at all. The choices that had seemed best to me, possibilities that had shone with hope and encouragement, if only slightly, always turned to shit. Perhaps it would be better simply to take what came, refuse to choose anything, leave the choosing to others who were not damned as I was to do the wrong thing at every opportunity.

I Am Ongamar/on Cantardene

I, Ongamar the spy, was kneeling between the left feet of a K'Famir pleasure-female, pinning up her skirt so the gold-plated graspers above the pads would show seductively, when I realized I could hear the chatter from an adjacent fitting booth through the floor-level ventilation duct. The pleasure-female had been drinking xshum all morning, provided by House Mousselline. She was barely able to stand and would not have heard an earthquake, so I had no need to ask many loud questions about the fitting to disguise the fact I had heard what was going on. Human hearing was far better than that of the K'Famir. To normal human ears, they always sounded as though they were shouting.

"Tonight there will be a midnight sacrifice on Beelshi," squealed the customer in the next booth. "I asked Wonbar to take me, but he said no females. I think they sacrifice females, that's why they don't want females watching."

"Surely not," said Lady Ephedra in a conciliatory tone. "We would hear of such a thing. People would disappear."

"Pocomfis disappear all the time," said the first voice. "They have no place to live, they work at ugly things, who cares if they disappear."

"What God would accept the sacrifice of a pocomfis?"

asked Lady Ephedra chidingly. "Sacrifices must be worthy, which means expensive. Half a flibit would buy a pocomfis. There now, move your upper arms, now the lower. Ah, it doesn't bind, does it. Good. If you'll take it off, I'll have it ready for you by closing time tonight."

Pocomfis were the maimed ones, those who had lost an arm, a leg, an eye, a sexual organ. If the lack could not be effectively disguised with a prosthesis, then one was an outcast. Being maimed was shameful, for it meant the gods had decided one was unnecessary, disposable, unimportant. What Lady Ephedra had said was quite true: pocomfis were cheap as dirt; cheap things were not a worthy sacrifice. A worthy sacrifice had to be expensive, very expensive: both vulnerable and without a family that would retaliate.

Beelshi was a low hill just outside the town, its slopes covered with the large earthenware jars in which the K'Famir dead were interred. Adille had attended a funerary ceremony there and described the place to me, her pet: a hilltop crowned by an ancient plaza, somewhat cracked and weedy, surrounded by temples and mausolea. A huge rounded boulder stood at its center and was stained, so Adille thought, with blood offerings people had made to Whirling Cloud of Darkness-Eater of the Dead, chief god of the K'Famir pantheon.

If true, such sacrifice would feed the thing for me! I could arrive at Beelshi early enough to hide among the funerary jars. Likely the sight would be enough to please *it* for some time. Though *it* had become too heavy for me to carry, *it* still insisted that I find something new every day, even as the number of unexplored sites and events grew smaller. I would go in the guise of a Hrass. I had the lengthened nose, a wrinkled protrusion that was almost hoselike. I could emulate the squinted eyes of a creature that avoided the light, the gray skin, the slightly scaly long-fingered hands. Add to this the voluminous dirty robes usually worn by Hrass, and I would be Hrass so far as the K'Famir were concerned.

Early that evening, I left my place through the alley gate, scurrying tight against the wall, the way Hrass usually moved. When they ate, walked, talked, bargained in the market, they always tried to have a solid wall behind them, and when they crossed open space, they moved as fast as possible. In general, the K'Famir disregarded them, for most of the Hrass on Cantardene were crew members of those disreputable ships that carried necessary but disgusting cargo: uncured flemp hides, for the making of slave whips; bathrop manure for the mushroom farms; dried charbic root to be ground into powder as a poison for vermin. The robes I had procured were authentic, both in fabric and in odor, thereby guaranteeing I would be overlooked and ignored.

I went through alleys, as Hrass would go; I muttered to myself, as Hrass invariably did. I gained the foot of Beelshi before it was totally dark and found, as I had hoped, that it was as yet unguarded. I climbed the hill, not by one of the main paths or the stairs, but by edging slowly among the jars until I reached one of the smaller mausolea surrounding the hilltop plaza. The building had a decorative lattice around it, one easy to climb, even burdened as I was by my garments, and the roof of the place was above the head level of any K'Famir.

Once atop the roof, I found it had a massive parapet penetrated in several places by rain spouts, wide metal troughs, the outer ends shaped into gape-jawed monsters. The troughs were large; one of them emptied into the plaza; the parapet was half my height thick, certainly wide enough to hide me from above. If I crawled into the trough, I could remain there, invisible to those below but able to see the altar area through the downsloping jaws of the spout.

When I had hidden myself, I examined the surroundings carefully while there was still enough light to do so. Many of the temples and mausolea shared common walls, and those that did not had only narrow spaces between them. They made a complete wall around the plaza, broken only by the wide flight of stairs that extended down the hill to my left. The plaza itself was made of large slabs of flat stone, cracked by age, with small, dusty plants growing in the cracks. At the center was the great stone Adille had spoken of, equipped with metal eyes around the upper surface, and beside it, another stone Adille had not mentioned: an irregular pillar, buried for part of its length in the soil. The pillar seemed to be uncut, and yet I had the strong impression that the upper end of it had a face. Perhaps it was only that the side nearest me was slightly hunched, like a shoulder, making the upper part appear headlike. A broken line of jaw. Two hollows that might be eyes. Altogether, a sinister-looking thing.

I turned my eyes back to the flight of stairs. At the very bottom, a company of guards was being posted around the hill. Within the next hour, two other rows of guards were posted, one midway up, one just outside the buildings that edged the plaza. If I had delayed my arrival, it would have been impossible. I curled into the smallest possible compass, cushioned my head on one arm, and actually dozed off, pillowed and warmed by the many folds of the heavy, malodorous robes.

I was wakened by the shriek of metal, the boom of a drum, the growling chant of many voices. Below me, lit by cressets, the metal door to the mausoleum shrieked against the stone of the threshold as it was drawn open. Peeking over the edge, I saw several K'Famir as they went in and returned carrying cages that were set at the edge of the plaza. In the flickering light, I could see they had small creatures in them, the size, so I thought, of a rat, perhaps. I had never seen a rat, but they had figured in the stories I had read as a child. Small enough to be held in two hands, large enough to be frightening if a lot of them came at you. These creatures were not coming at anyone. They were crouching in the cage, their large ears flared, their large noses quivering. No tails, I told myself. Not rats, because they have no tails. They looked like frog dolls, except for the ears. I concentrated on the chant, recognizing many of the words but not all. A hymn to their god, Whirling Cloud of Darkness-Eater of the Dead. The chant mentioned an offer of sacrifice, something, some quality that was to be . . . credited? The words fell into place. An offering would be made that was to be credited to the account of those who made it. This struck me as funny, and I almost forgot myself enough to laugh. What a strange mixture of worship and accounting. I amused myself with the idea until the first small creature was laid upon the round stone, tied to the metal eyes, and selected members of the group began applying blades and heated irons to its body. The creature screamed. Oh, by all that was holy, I heard words. It spoke words.

Not understandably, but unmistakably! I buried my head in my arms, pulling my robes over my ears, but nothing prevented the shrill screaming from going on, and on, and on . . .

When the torture ended at last, I looked up. A netted cage was being placed over the mutilated body. The chanting resumed, urgently. The tall pillar of stone wavered before me, actually seeming to look downward at the circling fog that had materialized inside the cage. The stone spoke. I heard it, not with my ears but with some deeper sense of recognition. The fog swirled. Solidified. I could not see what had materialized inside the cage, but whatever it was touched a deep well of revulsion. A knife was thrust into the small creature, which emitted one final shriek, then the cage was removed from over the corpse and carried away, down the hill while another victim was selected to receive the attentions of another group of K'Famir. After that, another, and another after that, and another. Each time the torture, each time the death, each time the stone looked down, something solidified inside a cage and was carried away. I lost count. I stayed curled tightly, head buried, until at last a silence came and dragged on and was finally broken by a familiar voice, someone I knew, someone I had met. I looked up, listened. It was Progzo. Adille's father!

"This was the last of the sacrifices we bought from the supplier who trades with us through the death-house. Some time gone the supplier warned us these sacrifices were becoming few; the place that bred them was empty of them. The supplier sent us a sample of another sacrifice, one that could be provided in unlimited numbers. Then that supplier ceased dealing with us.

"These new ones will work very well," he trumpeted. "We have found a new vendor to provide them through the death-house. We have the original sample here. Others will soon arrive from the new vendor. Bring it!"

From the temple beneath me a K'Famir emerged bearing a child in its arms, a human child of perhaps nine or ten. At the altar, the child was asked his name.

"Fessol," he said, shyly. "I am Fessol."

They were the last words the child uttered, but they were not the last sounds he made. He was larger than the small creatures, and the torture was done carefully. It went on until dawn. The cage was set in place, a larger thing materialized within. The tall pillar almost seemed to bend above it.

"Too much light to carry it into the city," Progzo said. "It might be seen. Put it into the place and lock the door."

The cage was put in the mausoleum below me. The K'Famir and their guards departed. Only Progzo and two other K'Famir lingered on the step.

"Will this kind work as well on humans as the others do?" one asked.

Progzo answered. "Our supplier sent me a few of these a long time ago. They were much more expensive than the other kind, the little ones, so I tested one myself. I arranged for it to fasten on my daughter's pet, a human. It was my daughter it fastened on, but she did not live long. Her pain was amusing."

"I, too, find females' pain most amusing," the other answered.

"Adille's pain was not worthy. She was sterile. A mere plaything. Of no value. The ghyrm feeds on the human pet now."

Some time after they had gone, when the plaza was completely empty, I struggled down from the temple roof and went into the plaza itself. A few torches still burned. The bodies of the victims were nowhere to be seen. Had they been taken away? Perhaps eaten by the K'Famir? Perhaps by Progzo, who had arranged for the death of his daughter, and for my continuing pain. Progzo, who had spoken of a human child as a new form of sacrifice?

I had thought I was past any anger, but what burned in me at that moment was too hot to be anything but rage. A torch burned beside the door of the mausoleum, which had been locked with a length of chain threaded loosely between the door handles, loosely enough that I could push one door open to make a sizable crack for the torchlight to fall through. The cage was just inside, and in the cage was a creature I knew all too well.

"Come," it whispered. "Come here. Feed me."

The crack was too small, and the cage that held it was of too small a mesh for it to escape. I was about to turn away when something behind the cage caught my eye. A pool of light held between the massive, uncut stones of the far wall. And not far from it, a pool of dark among the boulders of the adjoining wall. Between them, a machine of some sort. A very strange machine. I stared, stared, almost too long, for the thing had extended a tentacle and was feeling its way toward me through the crack. Only its little gasp of anticipation alerted me. I turned and struggled witlessly down the hill, through the alleys. I had seen nothing during the night that I had not seen the K'Famir do before. All male K'Famir seemed to be experts in torture; perhaps it was something they learned in their malehood school, but this was the first time I had seen it used against an absolutely helpless victim instead of against an adversary, or against a female consort or daughter they wished to be rid of.

I dreaded the fact that *it* was waiting for me, eager to make me relive it all, to drain me of everything I had seen, felt, heard, smelled. Well, *it* must not learn what I had heard! *It* must not know that I knew how its kind were made! Without at all understanding why, I knew without any reservation that the thing must not know of it.

Past experience helped. I had learned that if I concentrated on the pain and the blood, *it* would pass over the specifics of surroundings and torturers. Particularly . . . yes, particularly when *it* was very hungry. I delayed feeding *it,* therefore, until after I had eaten and had arranged my thoughts carefully. Then I fed *it,* concentrating on the little creatures, on how they had writhed and cried out and screamed, playing the scene over and over in an endless loop, until the thing drew away, satisfied.

As I dressed for work, my mind was busy sorting out what I had seen, putting together all the clues and sayings gathered during my time on Cantardene. On my walk to work, I fit everything into a scenario that was consistent with what I had learned and observed, not only last night, but all during my enslavement.

Male K'Famir prayed to Whirling Cloud of Darkness-Eater of the Dead, personified by the standing stone. The sacrifices acceptable to the Eater of the Dead were pain, terror, panic, horror. All these were bankable, and the aim was to build up a credit account with the god. If Adille's father, Progzo, had a large credit account with the Eater of the Dead, the god would not eat Progzo when he died. Perhaps the Eater would even allow Progzo to feast at the god's table. Moreover, the god was not a myth. There was actually something there, in that stone!

I had been only twelve when I had arrived on Cantardene. Things I had learned before that time were indistinct in my memory, but I recalled reading of a human tribe who had had such a god, such a worship, such an obsession with blood and pain. They had built high temples, they had torn out the hearts of their victims, cut off their hands and feet, let the blood flow until the temples were red with it. Even so late as the twenty-first century, only shortly before my own time, there were makers of films and plays who had rejoiced in gore, who had made suffering an object of prurient amusement for desensitized audiences. Some such were even produced in the name of religion, as though cruelty could ever elevate mankind! Viewing cruelty, religious or not, only did to the viewers what it had done to the K'Famir. It helped create new torturers.

The gods of the K'Famir, however, went further. They took pain and horror and created from it creatures like the one to which Adille had fallen prey. Every time the ritual was held—and this was just one city of Cantardene, there were many other cities, probably many other hills and rituals—living persons were tortured to death and *things* were produced. Did anything of the victim live on in the horror in the cage? I thought it unlikely. Only the pain and horror were embodied in something that lived to create more pain and horror.

And was the god really a god, or was it some other kind of life-form? Some other, unknown race of beings? Though, of course, such life-forms might be considered gods, of a kind . . .

And where had the strange sacrifices, those little rat-sized beings, come from? Where had the little boy come from? The pools of light and dark inside the mausoleum, how had they come there? A mausoleum was a death-house. Progzo had said he obtained it through the death-house. Traded for it? If the pools of light and dark were gates into other places, could trade pass through them, even of living things? Perhaps the strange machine was some kind of control . . .

I could do nothing about it. Not yet. All I could do was go back to work.

"Are you well, Miss Ongamar. You look quite pale."

"Quite well, thank you, Lady Ephedra."

"We have much work today."

Much work indeed. I took my place in the fitting room, my ears alert as I listened, listened, listened.

I Am Margaret/on Tercis

As I well knew from my eighteen years on Tercis, residents of the Rueful Walled-Off (officially listed as *Tercis, Expiatory Sect 909*) are expected to be at services each Rueday morning. In The Valley—as the southern, sloping, arable half of Rueful is called—Ruehouses are found even in small hamlets, such as Crossroads, Sorrowful, and Repentance. Contrition City, supporting its own notion of its importance, has a dozen or more, as does Deep Shameful, and others are found in every town in the northern, more mountainous half of Rueful, the Heights. In Rueful, on Rueday, one goes to services unless one is bedridden, witless, or dead.

Around Crossroads, attendance is expected even of the walking comatose, a chronic condition afflicting several local residents: Hen Kelly, for example, or the Johnson brothers. Bodily present, spiritually and cerebrally nowhere, they let their heads fall back onto the edge of the pew while their sagging mouths exhale vapors strong enough to stupefy any congregant within breathing distance. Ma Bastable from Ma's Kitchen and Ms. Barfinger from the Boardinghouse, both very high-chinned and solemn in their Rueday lace collars, always sit behind these miscreants, glaring at the back of their heads from opening prayer right up to the end of services when the pastor says, "It is time to rue."

Ceremoniously the two Keepers open the Ruehouse doors to let the penitence flow down the hill into River Remorseful while all of us stand perfectly still until the last person finishes ruing. However long it takes, no one moves or makes any kind of noise until the pastor speaks the words of forgiveness. When something really bad happens in Rueful, it will always be blamed on an interrupted ruing that's risen up to become a contumacious influence. Well, no. What they actually say is, "Damn rue-bug is loose amongst us!"

On this particular Rueday, Bryan and I and our twin daughters, Maybelle and Mayleen, were almost last to leave the Ruehouse, walking slowly and solemnly to give all that contrition time to get well away, so we wouldn't step in it and track it home. Truth be told, both of us were so weary we couldn't have walked any faster if we'd tried.

"Pastor," said Bryan on the front stoop, gravely nodding.

"Doctor," the pastor returned, with the same nod, and a slightly less formal one to me and to the children. "Missus Margaret. Miss Maybelle, Miss Mayleen."

The other congregants had scattered, some to the northern road, some to the road that led across the river bridge, some to the streets of the little town of Crossroads, at the south end of which stood the clinic and the doctor's house, our house.

"Well, even though I didn't get enough sleep last night, I still stayed awake," said Maybelle with a sigh.

"You were very good," I told my sixteen-year-old daughter unnecessarily. Maybelle was sometimes wakeful at night, possibly because of her heart condition, not immediately dangerous, Bryan said, but one he would keep an eye on. "Thank you for not snoring during services."

"She wasn't any better than I was," said Mayleen angrily. "I was just as good, better even."

"You were very good," I said wearily. "No one said you weren't, Mayleen."

"You and Maybelle are twins," said Bryan in his falsely jovial, 'speaking to Mayleen' voice. "Equally good, equally pretty, equally smart, in everything."

I found myself thinking desperately, Oh, dear God, if that could only be true! Some days I wished Mayleen had had the heart trouble so she'd have less energy to devote to dissension, dissatisfaction, or to discovering new injustices she had suffered. Some days I thought Mayleen was sixteen going on two, and Maybelle was sixteen going on fifty.

Bryan stopped and turned toward us, asking, "Who's that man staring this way, Margaret? Is he staring at the girls?"

"Billy Ray Judson," I said quietly. "You know his parents, Bryan. Judson owns that farmland north of the Conovers' place. We've met them and the younger half brother and sister several times. They were at the Ruehouse Festival last month."

Bryan nodded, forehead furrowed as he dredged up the memory. "Oh, yes. James Joseph is the boy, the girl's name is Hanna. James is a nice, polite boy, but even if we know the family, his brother shouldn't be directing that sort of stare at a schoolgirl."

"I'm not a schoolgirl," said Mayleen. "He likes me, that's all. You don't think people should like me?"

"Of course people should like you," I said with a degree of desperation, wagging my eyebrows at my husband, who ignored me in favor of returning the Judson boy's stare with a slightly censorious one of his own. "Your father just means you're a little young to get involved with someone Billy Ray Judson's age."

Maybelle started to say something, thought better of it, and tugged her sister by the hand. "Race you to the house," she said.

"I'll just walk," said Mayleen, sauntering slightly away from our family group to smile enticingly at the Judson boy.

Bryan started to say something, and I snarled, "Don't," in my firmest voice, locking my arm through his and speeding my footsteps to abbreviate the whole encounter. Maybelle moved along quickly at my side, asking her father a question about the clinic, thus deflecting him from saying, thinking, or doing anything about Mayleen. Meantime, I considered for the thousandth time the subject of twins. Twins should be similar, and identical twins should be identical; but Maybelle had all the goodness and good sense of any two normal people, and Mayleen had none at all. That fact was both frustrating and painful, for in any future I could imagine, Mayleen would carve out a hard and unrewarding life for herself.

This line of thought led inexorably to another: It was probably best

that my first babies, the twin boys born soon after Bryan and I arrived on Rueful, had died at birth. Mayleen and Maybelle had been
the second set, and we'd stopped there. I no longer grieved over the
two dead children. Though Maybelle was a kind, good girl, if the two
who had died had followed the girls' pattern, there might have been
at least one like Mayleen. Having even one more like Mayleen would
be insupportable. I simply could not have managed.

This little exchange had hooked me on one thorny link of an endless chain of interlocking memories, all of them embarrassing or
hurtful, all of them inappropriate for a woman who had just been to
the Ruehouse! I made myself look at the clinic up ahead, pure white,
shining like a beacon, without a spot on it. Wrong word. I derailed
again, wishing my life could be that spotless, gritting my teeth in fury
and ordering myself, STOP THINKING. Stop regretting. Stop chasing yourself around like a dog after its own tail! The memory chain
went only one place! Back to Earth on the day the proctor came,
never anywhere else!

During our first couple of years on Tercis, while Bryan was teaching me to help him in his work, he had told me I was a natural healer.
Since virtually all of what Bryan called "healing" I found intensely
embarrassing and distasteful, I'd choked on that accolade. Sometimes
I thought my repugnance was some failing in myself, other times I
wondered if any solitary child reared without intimacies on Phobos,
as I was, could grow up to be comfortable with the duties "healing"
required. Doing it for sixteen years hadn't made it any easier, but
the bargain I'd made with myself required that Bryan and the children never know how difficult and disgusting I found it. I'd kept
that bargain! They didn't know, but I did. I'd found no way to keep
myself from knowing it, hour by hour, rue it on Rueday though I
would. I sometimes felt it would have been easier to labor in a Cantardene mine with a whip at my back than to do the things Bryan
expected of me.

As we mounted the porch, I glanced back to see Mayleen flirting
and giggling with the Judson boy. The Judson man. He had to be at
least in his midtwenties. I stared, openly disapproving, until he shrugged
and turned away. Mayleen waved and called after him before unwillingly joining the rest of us.

"It's nice to have paint on the house," I remarked in the complacent, calm voice I'd practiced until it became second nature, the one that carried just the right message of *everything's lovely, everything's just fine* I ran my hand along the door molding. "It really looks wonderful."

"Never saved the life of a painter's son until this spring," said Bryan, with a wry twist to his lips. "So this is my first paint job as a fee. Pity the boy didn't get sick a decade or so ago."

"Better late than never, Daddy," said Maybelle. "You always say so."

He did always say so. He always said a good many things: that every day was a beautiful day, that our troubles had all been worth it; that each year would get easier; that we had a good, pleasurable life; that we'd done the right thing; that he was better off here than on Earth. Maybe he really believed it, but I'd been too busy atoning for Bryan's self-sacrifice to have entertained the notion it had been anything but a martyrdom for him. No matter what he said, I knew what he'd sacrificed.

"Where's Daddy, Mom?"

"Out back, Maybelle. Don't bother him."

"What's the matter?"

"Hen Kelly's mother died."

"She's been dying for years. Daddy shouldn't feel bad. It isn't his fault."

"He thinks . . . he knows he could have cured her back on Earth. It makes it hard for him."

It was hard for him, and what could I do to make it up?

He'd ask, "Where did you get this piece of equipment, Margaret?"

"I think someone brought it in from the next Walled-Off, Bryan. Is it something you can use?" He'd been grieving over not having it for two years, and it had taken me a year and a dozen broken regulations to get it smuggled in.

"Of course it's something I can use! But it's not a technology we're permitted to have yet. The Walled-Off Inspectors . . ."

"Let me worry about the Inspectors," not mentioning the valley grapevine I had tapped into, the informants I paid off with eggs or fruit or other barter that patients had offered to meet their bills.

"I didn't think we could afford a larger furnace for the clinic, Margaret."

"Bryan, it's one that was taken out of a building being remodeled up in Contrition City. It didn't cost anything." It really hadn't cost anything: except the time spent in cultivating Billy Ray Judson's father, who did a lot of remodeling in Contrition City; except for the pies I baked every few weeks for the wagoner who brought it down to Crossroads; except for the winter's worth of preserves I'd given Abe Johnson, who had put the boiler and pipes together. Most of the clinic improvements came about in similar ways: the windows, the added room, the shelves in what Bryan was pleased to call the pharmacy.

"I saw Daddy out back again, and I think he's crying!"

"I know, Maybelle. The little Benson boy died."

"I thought Daddy knew how to fix his back."

"Daddy did know, dear. Daddy just didn't have the special medical equipment he needed in order to do it."

Every day I told him that I loved him, though I'm afraid my love weighed light on the scales, particularly as lovemaking became infrequent, then rare, then extinct, killed off by unending exhaustion.

Still and all, I had seldom seen him lose his temper, and never as badly as he did a week or two later when Maybelle said to us quietly, privately, while Mayleen was somewhere else, "Daddy, Mom, I'm pretty sure Mayleen's pregnant by Billy Ray Judson."

As the words left Maybelle's mouth, Bryan turned as red as an apple, and his face swelled. "Get your father a glass of Hen Kelly's best," I demanded. Maybelle darted toward the kitchen, and I seized my husband's shoulders and pushed him into a chair.

"She's not going to marry that ne'er-do-well," he grated. "That . . ."

"Bryan, hush. Listen to me. I know you're angry. I'm angry. But I'm not surprised." He erupted under my hands, and I thrust him down, hard. "No, don't say anything, just listen. I'm not surprised. It's exactly what we could expect from Mayleen. She isn't Maybelle. She's another person entirely, and nothing I do or you do is going to make her grow up or become sensible. Now listen to me!"

He stared at me, amazed. In all the time we had been on Tercis, it was only the second time I had raised my voice to him, and it was definitely the first time I had openly acknowledged Mayleen's particular . . . difficulty. Maybelle came in with a glass of Hen Kelly's five-year-old best. I put it in his hand, and said, "Maybelle, close the door and watch out the window to be sure nobody's out there listening."

I leaned over Bryan once more: "Billy Ray's father has built up a good construction business in Contrition City. Judson was married twice. His first wife got herself killed in a drunken brawl in the tavern where she evidently spent most of her time, and it's doubtful whether Billy Ray is actually Judson's son, though he's always treated the boy as his own. It was the second wife who reared Billy Ray, along with Hanna and James Joseph . . ."

"I'm really not interested in their damned family history," snarled Bryan, lowering the glass.

I laid my fingers on his lips. "Bryan, the family history is important! Judson still has title to the land he was awarded when he first settled here, near Crossroads. He built a house on the piece across the river and lived there for a few years, but he never farmed it because by the time the population built up to the point market farms made sense, he already had his construction business well established. Now lately, Billy Ray's been talking about farming. His father told him it was a hard life, and he wouldn't advise it . . ."

"Advising Billy Ray not to do something is absolutely guaranteed to make him want to do exactly that!" opined Maybelle from the window. "Mr. Judson should have begged him to be a farmer and forbade his joining the army!"

I shook my head in reproof, but I was smiling a little, and Bryan was staring at both of us as though we'd lost our minds.

"How do you two know any of this?" he demanded.

"Maybelle and I go shopping, we listen. We have the quilters over, and we listen; we go to the Ruehouse, we listen. And Maybelle is right, it might have prevented a lot of misery if Judson had forbidden Billy Ray to join the army, because he'd have done it, just to upset his father, and that would have at least removed him from Rueful. Now listen to what I say, Bryan! Mayleen's exactly like him. If we say black, she says white. Our opposition would only make both of them that much more determined. That's by the by, however.

"What's relevant is that Mr. Judson has already given property to the three children. He's given Hanna some income property in Contrition City, and he's given half the farm to each one of the boys. Billy Ray is eldest, he picked the land across the river with the house on it. It's his, and the farm is big enough to support him and Mayleen."

"When did this happen?" Bryan demanded.

"Billy Ray getting the farm? Over the past few months. Mayleen wants to marry him—no, I haven't heard her say so, but I'll wager Maybelle has."

"She's right, Daddy. It's all Mayleen talks about."

I nodded. "And if she's pregnant, which I have no doubt she is, unless you're capable of forcibly aborting her, Bryan, then locking her up in the attic for the next ten years, she's going to manage being with Billy Ray, one way or another."

"And you accept this?" he asked angrily.

"Accept it?" I, sighed, at a loss. As I'd accepted Rueful? As I'd accepted becoming his nurse? As I'd finally accepted that one of my children was born to misery. "What are our choices, Bryan? Tell me if we have any. I'd love to know."

He mumbled and grumbled to himself, gradually losing steam as his kettle cooled.

I said, "There's one good thing, Bryan. Our family here, Maybelle, and you and I, will be much, much happier with Mayleen married and living somewhere else. Ninety-nine percent of our upsets and problems are Mayleen."

Bryan said plaintively, "God, Margaret, she's only sixteen!"

"After the number of years we've lived in The Valley, you should know every man here believes if a girl is big enough, she's old enough, and the ruing can come later!"

Bryan, deflated, rubbed his forehead. "I didn't foresee my own daughter being considered big enough."

"Well you can rue that come next Rueday. Maybelle and I'll stand right beside you and rue it double."

"No, I won't," whispered Maybelle. "Because you're right, Mama. We'll be so much happier if she's somewhere else. She just makes our lives a misery."

It was a mistake, of course. I had forecast Mayleen's life, but I had not considered Mayleen's children, all ten of them. Yet another mistake to add to the endless chain. Still, as I often tried to console myself years later, it was quite possible, given Mayleen's stupidity and Billy Ray's pigheadedness, nothing could have prevented it, even if I had known where it would lead.

I Am Wilvia/on B'yurngrad

On B'yurngrad, my years of study had come to an end. I was congratulated by my instructors and was honored by being summoned by the High Priestess for an interview concerning my future life. I had never been to the High Priestess's office, which was known to be high in the dome of the Temple, between the outer shell of stone and metal and the inner shell of plaster and gilded tiles. One of the novices offered to guide me up the endless stairs that spiraled through echoing spaces above the Temple vault.

"Does the High Priestess climb these stairs every day?" I asked, puffing slightly.

"Wilvia, we don't know," said the novice, a woman even younger than my twenty years or so. "When she summons us, we climb up, and she's there. If she doesn't summon us, we don't go, and we have no idea where she is."

We climbed farther. The stairs leveled into a ramp that curved gently upward to a wide door.

"In there," the novice said. "Knock first."

I knocked. A voice bade me enter, which I did, struggling with the weight of the door. The room was empty except for two chairs, one of them occupied by Lady Badness.

"Well, come in, Wilvia. Don't stand there gawking."

"I didn't know you . . . how long have you . . ."

"How long have I been head of this agglomeration? A very long time. Is it rewarding? Yes. Does it take a lot of my time? Not really. Your teachers are pleased with you."

I flushed. "They seem to be, yes. I'm surprised. The final examination was not at all as I expected it to be."

"The judging of cases. No. It's never as we expect it to be. That's why we train women judges here at Temple. It is the nature of men to make rules for everything and to play complicated games with them. For them, the game is more important than justice.

"Ordinary people prefer justice. They prefer that things be taken case by case, they prefer an attempt at justice over the rules of law, for they know that pure law is often used by the clever to victimize the innocent. Sit down, child."

I lowered myself into the other chair. In the center of the room was an open well surrounded by a railing. I could hear the shush of footsteps and the murmur of voices far below in the Temple. Above, a similar hole pierced the dome to show the sky, where white birds darted across an infinite blue.

Lady Badness spoke: "You have done what was required, learned what was necessary, and I have come to take you away."

"Away?" The word, leaving my mouth, sounded bruised and tentative. "But . . . Joziré will come here to find me . . ."

"Joziré is waiting for you on Fajnard. His mother, the queen, has died, not at the hands of Frossian assassins as was feared, but from sorrow, an illness we do not know how to cure. Joziré must now take the throne. He wishes to do so with you at his side, *if* that will be good for his people. Will it, do you suppose?"

"He never sent me word," I cried angrily. "Never once . . ."

"He could not have done so without risking his life and yours. Would you have wished him to do that?"

I bit my tongue. "Lady Badness, no. I didn't think."

"You will have to think if you marry Joziré, will your marrying him be good for his people?" repeated Lady Badness obdurately. "You marry them when you marry him."

Over the past five or so years, in those few moments when I had had time for reflection, I had asked myself this question many times.

"I believe I will be good for his people," I said firmly. "I will love them as I do him, and they will be my people."

She nodded, looking at me with what I thought might be sadness. Not joy, at any rate.

"Then I must tell you what is forecast for the lovely lands of the Ghoss. They may soon be threatened, probably by either the Frossians or the Thongal. If that happens, you may need to leave your people, your country. You may need to leave Joziré, for his sake. You may have a long, troubled time in your life. You may know sadness, and sorrow, and loneliness. You may have to work very hard just to stay alive. Or, you can forget Joziré. You can stay here. It will be safer. You will be among friends. I think it is only fair to give you warning before you put your foot on the path . . ."

She stared at me, into me. I know what she saw, a kind of whirlwind, doubts and sorrows and joys all spun together like the whirlwinds on Mars. Joziré's face, his eyes, the feel of his hands. The dragonfly ship. The woman in red. What I had left. What I had promised.

I heard myself say, "Even if all that is true, every word of it, I still choose Joziré. I still choose to be queen, to rule justly, to do what he would have me do."

And that seemed to be answer enough. She stood up and gestured. A ship edged its way over the window in the dome and dropped a ladder down. Old as she looked, Lady Badness went up the ladder like a tree rat, and I went after her. The ship was piloted by the same woman in red who had brought me here with Joziré all those years ago. She smiled at me, indicating the older, one-eyed man with her. "Mr. Weathereye, Wilvia." I bowed, he nodded, the ship moved away.

I was not conscious of time passing, which it must have done, before we saw an enormous highland centered upon a tall, white palace. We set down in the paved courtyard.

"These are the highlands of Fajnard," said the one-eyed man, turning toward me. "Much work awaits you here. Do you think you're up to it?"

I simply stared at him, my mouth open.

Lady Badness said, "I have seldom seen anyone work as hard as

Wilvia has done. I have faith in her." She leaned forward and pointed through the open door of the ship. "See, there!"

A man was approaching. I looked, and looked again. He was taller, and stronger-looking, and even more handsome, and . . .

"Joziré," I cried, and went running toward him.

Behind us, the ship left very quietly.

I Am M'urgi/on B'yurngrad

I found my first housing on B'yurngrad in a hostel kept by
the Siblinghood of Silence. The first person I met there
was a tall, dark-haired, lean-faced fellow named Fernwold,
who stared at me as though I was long-lost kin. He was, so
he said, the sorter-out, the questioner and annoyer who
fitted awkward pegs into weird-shaped holes wherever
that was possible.

"First thing," he said, looking me over from head to
toe, "is for us to learn how you came here to B'yurngrad?'

I gritted my teeth and prepared to be terse. "I was
twenty-two years old, on Earth, recently identified as an
over-four, being shipped out. I might have ended up on a
ship that went into Mercan space if I'd told them I speak
Omniont and Mercan languages, so I kept my mouth shut.
I was put on an Omniont ship that was scheduled to stop
here on B'yurngrad to transship its cargo to various Omniont worlds."

He cocked his head. "You stopped at this transshipment point, and . . ."

". . . And the ship unloaded the bondspeople onto
three smaller ships that had come to pick us up. Two ships
left. I was on the last one, and while it was still sitting in
the port it developed something called a core resonance.
Does that happen?"

He nodded. "Often killing a lot of people."

"The repairs were going to take a long time. The shipmaster was told to get rid of his cargo, as feeding us was expensive . . ."

"How did you know that? Did the shipmaster tell you?"

"Of course not. I heard him talking to his superiors, whomever. They said sell us if possible, but get rid of us. I inferred that meant kill us. It seemed logical."

"So when you said you spoke alien languages, you meant you really speak them, not just know a few words?"

"I really speak them, yes. That was to have been my lifework. Translation. Diplomacy. Understanding. And why are you staring at me, what did you say your name was?"

"Fernwold. Ferni, for short. A good friend at the academy called me that. I'm staring because you look like him."

I discounted this as unlikely. "Fernwold. Some person or group bought us or ransomed us—at least they paid something to get us released, or hosteled, whatever. The next person I met was you."

"The Siblinghood of Silence ransomed you," he said, looking thoughtful. "Thus moving you from bondservice into sibling service. What's that old saying, from the roasting spit into the fire?"

I stared at him, openmouthed. "The who?"

"The Siblinghood of Silence. You haven't heard of them?"

"I've heard of something called the Third Order . . ."

He put his finger to his lips, eyes conveying a definite message. "No. You haven't. No matter how well you remember it, you haven't heard of it, but you do remember the Siblinghood."

"A bi- or multigender fraternity of some kind?"

I thought his responsive smile rather wolfish, hearkening back to my childhood love of animal books. His eyebrows were dark and extremely mobile, two physiognomic punctuation marks that leapt about to mark each utterance, parenthetical or exclamatory. Just now they were tented, conveying amused disbelief at my ignorance.

"Rather more than that, Salvage. It is on behalf of the Siblinghood that I am here to find out what each member of the ransomed cargo may be fit for. Some of them will be easy. They'll be kitchen help. They'll go to the workshops of the building crew. The High-house of the Siblinghood here on B'yurngrad is always in a state of reconstruction. Its work changes minute by minute and hour by hour.

"They'll tell us to build a dormitory for fourteen Thrackians found floating, because maybe the Thrackians can give us some information about this, or that, or something else. Or they'll say they need a new kitchen for the Pfillians who have ritual requirements for their food. Or, as now, they'll tell me you Earthians habitually segregate by sex, so we need two temporary dormitories, please . . ."

He touched my shoulder lightly. "Of course, such segregation is fully voluntary. I have very nice quarters if you're not intent on that old Earth rule."

"I am quite intent on obeying all such rules," I said, resentfully intractable. "Who are they, the Siblinghood?"

"What do you care, Salvage? Fate has dropped you into kinder hands. No real bondage for you."

"My name is not Salvage. It's Margaret. And I love it, the way you say no real bondage?" I laughed. "I don't know what you call building walls and laying floors, Silencer, but bondage isn't far from it."

"So, give me a reason to assign you somewhere else, pretty one. I'm not hard to get around. Anyone with a warm heart can do it."

I took a moment to think. "I've already said I know languages, Sibling. Several. Even many. Surely among all this important work your Siblinghood is busy doing, there must be a position open for a translator."

"Hmmm." He stood, stretched thoughtfully, glanced at the barred windows and doors, said, "Don't go away," in an amused voice, and left.

I was there for several days while all those around me were assigned here and there. I sat. I borrowed a book on the language and customs of the Hrass and read it cover to cover. When he returned, it was with a different demeanor. "I have your assignment," he said. "Eventually, your language skills will be of great use. For the time being, however, you are to be trained by a shaman who has sent word you are to be renamed. This is necessary, I am told. You are to be called M'urgi." He wrote it down for me. "It means 'explorer' in a dialect spoken here about. Pronounced as I did, MAR-gee."

"Gee as in game," I said witlessly. Something in what he had said had rung a bell in my brain. The reverberations made me tremble. "As in gossip, gamble, garden, or even Mar-gar-et, which is what the

Mercan crewmen on the ship called me, with a giggle and a slither when they did so! Why must my name be changed?"

"Shamans on B'yurngrad always name their novices, and it's customary to do it in advance of training so the novice can get used to it. That's what we'll all call you from now on . . ."

When I started to speak, he shook his head at me. "Don't ask. I am as surprised as you are, and anything I might tell you could be wrong. You're to wait here until your . . . ah, 'mentor' gets to someplace where you can safely be handed over to her. Meantime, you're to learn your new name and report to the supplies officer to be fitted out with clothes."

"I have clothing with me," I said.

"Not the kind you'll be needing," he replied with a wry, sideways grin. "Yours don't smell right. Not smoky enough."

Before I could ask what he meant, he was gone.

A shaman. Shamaness. Shamana. What was the female version? Did it matter? Why did it sound so very, very familiar?

It wasn't until that night, when I was just falling asleep, that it came me with such force that I sat up, fully aware. A shaman. Of course. That was one of my people. Margy! M'urgi? Close enough. I lay down again in the quiet darkness, mind spinning with something weirdly like hope.

The next day, he came back.

"It will be a while, M'urgi," he said. "Your future teacher is off on the edge of nowhere, seeing what the tribes are up to . . ."

"Tribes?"

"Bondsmen from Mercan planets who arrived here in no mood to settle down. Wildmen. They kidnapped a few shiploads of females, and they live out in the grasses in skin-covered huts, taking their herds north and south with the seasons and practicing a strange, violent, blood-and-honor religion. They come into the towns maybe once a year to sell their wool and hair and cheese. They learn nothing, for they're convinced they know everything that matters. They're boring. Even hearing about them is boring, so why don't we relieve your boredom. And mine."

We did so, finding much to talk of, much enjoyment in the talk. When I asked him to tell me about the Siblinghood, Fernwold said:

"Since you're to be a shaman, I can tell you this, though we don't speak of it usually. The Siblinghood is an organization of humans and Gentherans and a very few persons of other races. Most of the humans are a different kind we call Ghoss, though some of them are ordinary people, like me. Along with the humans and Gentherans are some extraordinary members who have strange and wonderful capabilities, men and women who are . . . something else."

"And what does it do, this organization?"

"It helps out here and there, when the human race itself gets into trouble. Which we inevitably seem to do. And the Third Order is trying to achieve some other grand vision . . ."

"And you're a member of this group?"

"A very, very minor member, yes."

"If there's a Third Order, I suppose there's a first and second one."

"Not any longer. Both existed; both were destroyed. The only thing I know about the Orders is they're attempting to find a unique spacial configuration, some esoteric galactic connection. What they call a 'cluster.' The First Order found one, the Second Order found one, and both times it promptly broke apart and killed a lot of the Siblinghood people who were exploring it."

"Someone broke it?"

"Maybe, or it may have just happened. The configurations they're looking for are only temporary. Finding them is like finding dew on the grass. Just because it's there at dawn doesn't mean it's going to be there ten minutes later. The Second Order operated much more secretly, just in case the first configuration was purposefully destroyed. They found over fifty partial configurations, but some of them were traps and others were just blind alleys. They discovered who set the traps and removed them, but by that time, they'd been delayed too long, and the cluster was gone again. The Third Order is being extremely security conscious. No one outside the Siblinghood knows who's part of it, or what it's found out, or even what it's looking for, and even we insiders know almost nothing, and if you're smart, you'll keep your mouth shut about the nothing you know."

The few days turned into twenty. By the end of the twenty, Fern-wold and I were closer than friends. On the twenty-first day, I was sent away, to spend the journey time wondering who it was I had thought I loved, back on Earth, and why it was I thought I had loved him. Strangely enough, though I grieved to lose Ferni, I had gained a certain peace of mind. For Margaret, I had probably decided badly, but for M'urgi, the decision about Bryan had been the right one.

I Am Mar-agern/on Fajnard

When I arrived on Fajnard, in the Mercan Combine, I was still well shy of my twenty-third birthday. On arrival, our group of bondservants were chained together, though lightly, and escorted on foot across the port, which swarmed with races I had read of or heard about, and as many more I had never known existed. Our destination was a warehouse where a group of Bondsfolk Relief workers fed us and gave us bondservant clothing: trousers, shirts, long vests with pockets, a light jacket with pockets, a heavy, waterproof jacket with pockets, and a wide-brimmed waterproof hat, plus some softer material from which to make our own underwear.

Prior to our being sold, we were examined by two human doctors from Medecines Sans Limites who explained that they had volunteered to work on Mercan planets in order to care for those in bondage. Their existence in this far-off place brought Bryan vividly to my mind. Seeing my distress, the doctor asked me if I was injured or ill, I blurted out Bryan's name, and what had happened, while the doctor regarded me, unmoved.

"Though I can understand your reluctance, from my point of view, you were a fool," he said calmly. "None of us want to start a life from a position of indebtedness, even though everyone alive profits from the past. You're here now, however, and if you're to have any kind of life after you leave here, you must forget the past. Regret and nostalgia will result in depression, which is fatal on this planet. Pay attention to what I'm about to say: The most important rule is to repress how you feel about things and be supremely alert to what is happening around you. How you feel, what you think isn't important. What you do, how you act, is important! Don't act or speak until you have some inkling of what the result will be.

"I'm picking the first part of your own name, Mar, and I'm adding the suffix 'agern' to it. On Fajnard, long names are indicative of aristocracy or nobility. Bondsfolk are allowed the shortest possible names, and the suffix 'agern' means 'slave.' Your tag says Mar-agern! That's your label! Repeat it over and over to yourself, keep it in mind so you can be quick when some Frossian utters it. When a Frossian yells 'agern,' it means whatever bondsfolk are closest, so be alert for that, too.

"Sleep whenever you can, wherever you can. Try to stay as clean as possible. The purchase contract specifies bathing facilities, but that doesn't mean your buyers will have them, or that they'll be sanitary, or that they won't be frozen in winter. That means you sometimes use your drinking water to wash with, or the water that's used to water stock, usually umoxen. Since they produce the finest wool among the known worlds, the Frossians are careful of them, and their water is probably kept clean. If you have any difficulty staying clean, cut your hair off, all of it, everywhere on your body, as that will reduce infestation.

"Frossians are a three-sex race. All the queens are on one planet, elsewhere. Never ask where. That question can get you killed. There are a few hundred breeding males on Fajnard, the workers and soldiers are neuters, and they're the ones who'll be ordering you around. They're touchy, easy to anger, preoccupied with their own status in their own particular work crew. Anything you do wrong reflects on them, so don't do anything wrong.

"Eat sparingly and save the least perishable of what you're given in a pocket. If you don't have a pocket, use the materials we gave you to contrive one. You may be given three meals today and only one or none tomorrow. If you feel just slightly unwell, don't let it show. Even if you feel quite sick but can put on appearance of working, do so.

This marks you as a noncomplainer and builds a store of tolerance among the overseers. Then, if you think you're dying, kick up a real fuss, and if you're loud enough, they'll probably send for one of us, particularly before they've had their value out of you, that is, during the first ten to twelve years you're here."

"They send for one of you?"

"There are several MSL doctors here, male and female, and we've trained some helpers who've worked out their bondage. The Frossians tolerate us because they get more work out of healthy servants. We're certifying that you're healthy to start with. If you're careful, you may stay that way."

That was my last earth-human contact. On the following day, our shipload of émigrés was sold. I had dreaded the poking and prying that I expected to accompany this process, but seemingly the buyers were not interested in touching the merchandise. A scaled, bone-crested, tailed, four-legged, two-armed Frossian emerged from a crowd of similar beings, put a rope around my neck, and led me and two others to a weirdly ornamented wheeled vehicle that lurched as though it had no gyros. We went through the city into the country-side, grasslands on all sides, occasional copses of strange, bulbous-trunked trees with horizontal, cylindrical branches from which huge straplike leaves hung like shutters, turning as the sun moved. The end of each branch ended in something that looked very much like an eye, and the eyes followed the progress of our vehicle.

At the end of the journey, a cluster of shabby buildings in the midst of endless grass, another Frossian led me, still roped, to the barn. The ceilings were low enough that I knew I could touch them by reaching up. I did not reach up, for I had already learned that any voluntary motion on my part brought a choking jerk on the leash. A long aisle ran down the center of the building between open pens on either side, pens without fronts, just three walls dividing the structure into equal areas filled by huge animals.

They were furry . . . no, woolly. Enormous brown eyes peered at me with unmistakable intelligence. The ears were long enough to be amusing, even funny, and the horns were long enough to be danger-ous. And the tails! Curving upward and forward, each of them spread long, fine wool in a perfect parasol above each animal or, when lowered, a blanket, so evenly distributed it might have been spread by some domestic who had just changed the linens. I could not see their feet, for the hind legs were bent under their bodies and the front feet were curled against the ponderous chests. Four-legged. Not unfamiliar, as though I might have seen their like in a book, or more likely their attributes. Horns like cattle. Faces like buffalo. Coat and ears like poodle dogs. Those marvelous umbrella tails? Giant anteaters came to mind, though as I recalled, their tails had been more brushlike. Of course, I knew them only from books.

The Frossian spoke in his own language. "You are responsible for feeding them, and watering them, and cleaning up after them and taking them to pasture and bringing them back. Any one of them gets hurt or dies, you get hurt or die. You stupid humans don't understand anything Frossians say, but the whip will teach you."

"On the contrary," I said in only slightly halting Frossian, "I understand very well."

The Frossian's eyes widened momentarily, before his arm lashed out, clubbing me across the face as he hissed, "I explain! We don't talk to slaves, and we don't want them talking to us, especially if they contradict what we say!"

He left me lying in the straw, facedown, half-stunned, realizing suddenly that the word for *contradict* in Frossian was the same word as *insult*, that the word for *explain* was from the same root as the word *demean oneself*. From the umox nearest me, a strange, whistling call rose up. Still dazed, I looked at the creature and saw that it fluted the sound through its nose. Within moments, I was surrounded by a group of people who looked so like me, I would have sworn they were family. They were Ghoss, they said, speaking to me in Frossian.

"Oh, girl, umox say you spoke to overseer. Such a bad idea to speak where any overseer can hear you!"

"Why did you do such a thing?"

"Didn't they warn you. The doctors? Didn't they say not to speak? Not to move or speak? Surely they warned you!"

"Ummm? Here, let us see your eyes, let us see your arms."

"Not too bad. You'll have a strange-colored face for a few days."

"Now you can count on that one's enmity so long as you are here."

Finally, then, I remembered the doctor telling me not to speak, and I cursed myself silently. So proud of my ability to speak, I had to do it! Pride. Rotten pride. Obviously, pride was something to be forgotten.

"Who are you?" I asked.

One of the women spoke. "I am Deen. We are Ghoss, dear girl, as you no doubt are yourself."

"I'm not Ghoss, whatever. I'm human."

"Well, of course, Ghoss are human. Tsk. Here, let me put some salve on that. Don't worry, the doctors gave it to us. It won't harm you."

And so my servitude began with the first lesson: Do not speak unless among the Ghoss and where no Frossian could hear. With the Ghoss I spoke Frossian while I learned their own language, one with strangely familiar words in it, an old language, they said, dating back to the time they had been brought from Earth by the Gentherans and given to the Gibbekot, the indigenes of Fajnard.

"The indigenous race? You mean, this isn't a Frossian home planet?"

"The Frossians have no home planet except one place where the queens live. Frossians eat up planets as a plether of umoxen eat a field of hay." Deen snorted her derision.

"What's a plether?"

"So many as will fit into a pen, Mar-agern. A plether of umoxen is fewer than a plether of Gnar, but both take the same barn space. As I was saying, the Frossians take everything they can take without triggering action by ISTO, then they go ruin some other world. When they came here, our Gibbekot friends went into the mountains, but some of us . . . well, let us say we do not hide as well as they. The Frossians forced us to stay here and work for them."

I thought this last was less than truthful. The Ghoss had nothing about them of abasement or servitude. I conjectured that they might be here for some other reason. What that reason might be, I had no idea, and it wasn't explained, even though I became woven into the life of the Ghoss, almost one of them.

I would have been quite content to be Ghoss if I could have managed it, for they had invisible networks of solidarity and succor that prevented even the least among them from being trod upon and broken. If you were Ghoss, you just knew when help was needed, but I had no such connection. For me, help did not come unless some Ghoss actually saw my trouble or the umoxen let them know. Either way, they would arrive with salve for the welts, with painkiller, with soft words, with behind-the-scenes string-pulling to save me further punishment. They claimed me in kinship, even though I knew I was not kin.

"You always claim not to be Ghoss, but you obviously are!" said Rei-agern, a middling old one, with an interestingly ugly face.

"I am a bondservant from Earth. None of my family ever were Ghoss, there are no Ghoss on Earth."

"Well, there obviously were sometime, because that's where we came from originally, some thousands of years ago."

"Captured and enslaved," said I sympathetically. "I'm sorry."

"No such thing," cried the other. "We were never slaves of the Gibbekot! We were their friends, their coworkers. We stayed at their invitation, true, but it was not into slavery! Many of us went with them when the Frossians came, and those who did are still with the Gibbekot, back in the hills."

I thought the talent they had might have been a gift from the Gibbekot, for they were something other than merely human now. Perhaps they had mutated, or evolved.

I soon learned the routine. Rise early, go to the privy, wash in the bucket, go to the kitchen, take whatever food was offered, return to the barn, open the big door, and urge the plether to get up and move. The umoxen seemed to take a perverse pleasure in being difficult to rouse, and it was days before I realized they were playing with me. When I stopped chivvying them and took to leaning on the doorpost, chewing a straw, careless of whether they moved or not, they moved. The same ones always led, the others followed with one small, brown one at the rear, and I walked by that one, soon enough with my arm across the creature's shoulder, feeling through the wool for any sharp seed or spine that might fret an umox.

As I walked I watched everything, looked at everything, attentive to the presence of continuous miracle. There had been no grass, no fog on Earth. I had suppose these things to be of one kind. Grass was green. Fog was gray. Instead, neither was ever a single color, ever a single thing. The umoxen relished the fog, murmuring their way through it, the moisture condensing on their wool so that when the sun broke through, it lit a procession of jeweled chimeras, garbed in rainbow.

Sometimes an umox would come up behind me, so softly I did not hear it, then suddenly *whuff* at me from behind, frightening a yelp from my throat, and at that they laughed. I knew it was laughter, though silent, for their shoulders shook with it.

"You are naughty animals," I told them. "Shame on you." At which they laughed the harder. They had voices that ranged from that same high, fluting call I had heard the first time I met them to a low, satisfied rumble I could hear through the soles of my feet.

"Can you get me some brushes?" I asked the Ghoss. "Some brushes, a pair of pliers, maybe a large comb."

"We can," they said. "But the herdsman won't let you keep them."

"I'm going to hide them in the pasture," I confessed. "In a hollow fence post."

So equipped, I began grooming my charges. First the little brown one that I walked with to the pasture each day. I worked the comb through its wool, slowly, carefully. I brushed the long wool of its tail, strand by strand, not hurrying. It was a way to pass the time, not something I had been told to do. Soon the little umox began to rumble-hum, the sound of a deep-toned stringed instrument, stroked with an endless bow. The next umox added a tone, then the one next to it, and soon there were twenty humming, one vast, endless harmonic chord that sounded upward, through my bones.

When I had finished with the little brown one, I turned to find my next victim and was confronted by the leader of the plether, who looked at me significantly and turned, offering its tail. From that day on, I spent my days grooming the plether, two days per umox, strictly in rotation. I hid my implements in the hollow post each night. Before long, I was telling them stories of Queen Wilvia and the nazeemi and the yaboons while they rumble-hummed along, not only my own plether but all those within hearing, a vast harmonic sound that continued until my brain sang with them, and time went by without my noticing it.

The pliers the Ghoss had found for me were useful in reaching seeds that had worked their way back inside the long, sensitive ears or pulling thorns from their strange feet: an almost complete circle of hoof surrounding a soft center made up of four stubby fingers that curled up, out of the way. Usually they could pull thorns from one foot with the fingers of another, but sometimes, especially among the old ones, their ankles had stiffened, and they could no longer do it for themselves. They came to me from all the plethers around, flopping down on their sides with a great whoosh of expelled air, holding up the painful hooves. Sometimes, also, they caught something in their teeth that their long, flexible tongues could not retrieve: a piece of fencing wire or a short length of the cord used to bind the hay. I asked the Ghoss to get me scissors and pliers that were more pointed. Time went on as I told endless stories of my worlds, of Naumi the warrior, and Margy the shaman, of the nameless spy and of Queen Wilvia, who ruled a far and wondrous land.

It had been summer when I arrived, and I had slept on a pile of hay beneath the shelf where the water buckets were kept. When the nights grew colder, the overseer told me I was to sleep in the same place, though he knew it was exposed to every current of air from above and below, a place where it was impossible to stay warm.

"The better to keep her wakeful," the overseer laughed to his cronies. Since the Frossian knew well I was always wakeful from first light until the night bell, expecting me to remain wakeful through the night was mere persecution.

Deen-agern said so. "Mere persecution, Mar."

"What's mere about persecution, Deen? If you live under it, it's not mere, believe me."

"Well," the older woman huffed, "we *all* live under it. All us Ghoss."

"They don't treat you like this, and I'm not Ghoss." By this time, I spoke in the language of the Ghoss, not fluently, but understandably.

"The overseers think you are."

"Well, they're wrong, and so are you."

The Ghoss had been right, however, about the enmity of the Frossian herdsman. He remained implacably hostile. He began by stealing my clothes, piece by piece, until I had only one set of trousers and shirt to cover me. In the summer, it didn't matter, but now that it was winter, the absence of cover was long torture through every night. The Frossians didn't like the cold. According to the Ghoss, the Frossians preferred warm planets with high heat and humidity. In summertime, there were often only a few guards left on the place; their overlords were somewhere wet, basking in the sun.

The first wintry night below the bucket shelf, I stayed awake while cold breezes caressed my backside through the cracks and another ice-wind hand played its fingers over the rest of me. My second night, I dreamed of fire. Fire on hearths, fire in forges with hammers ringing, bonfire on the heath with people dancing, fire on eastern mountains glowing against the clouds in a false dawn more feverish than rosy. Fire anywhere, anytime, so long as it was warm.

During the day that followed, I decided to weave a thick blanket for myself from discarded rags, all wound about with tail wool from the umoxen themselves, tail wool I gathered from hedges and fences about the place. I would have to hide it somehow, so the overseer didn't take it. If I had been Ghoss, the overlords would have been more cautious with me, but evidently they knew I was not, even though I looked just like them. No true Ghoss would have been ordered to sleep below the bucket shelf, so someone, or some set of someones, obviously regarded me as neither one thing nor the other. I myself had heard the least overlord, him of the twisty mouth, with nasty words dropping from it like spit, describing me:

"She's an abomination, a *Mar*. The *frumdalt* want to get rid of Mar. We should get rid of it now."

"Merely an aberration," the middle overlord had replied on hearing this muck. "We haven't enough bodies to do the work, surely not enough to go about killing this one and that one until nearer their time. We can get rid of it later, but not now. It still has work years in it."

The word the least overlord had used, *frumdalt,* was unfamiliar to me. *Fruma* was the name of the carrion birds who frequented the river bottom. *Dalt* was one word used for a hilltop or tower. I asked the Ghoss.

"*Frumdalt?*" said Rei-agern. "I think it means 'god,' or perhaps something else to do with their religion, but we don't pay attention to their religion."

"A frumdalt might be something on high that eats dead things," I suggested.

"Ah," said Rei-agern with a puzzled look. "On Cantardene they have a god called Eater of the Dead."

Next night I lay down on my bucket shelf, curled into a tight ball, waiting for the herdsman to make his last inspection, which he did, coming in to poke me in the process, to be sure I wasn't asleep. Then, he went off to his warm bed in the snug quarters in the loft, leaving me to stand shivering by the shelf, pulling my scant wrappings around me. I dozed, fretfully, coming fully awake to find the little brown umox lying next to me, warm as a little furnace.

"Don't," I told it, looking into its eyes, deep and dark as those forest pools I had dreamed of as a child. "The herdsman will take it out on you. He wants me to suffer here. He mustn't see you here, he might do something dreadful to you."

The little one went back to the other umoxen where they lay tightly together in deep bedding, covered with their great, fluffy tails. It took a lot of cold to chill even one umox, much less a plether. I sat shivering as I heard the little one talking to the others, knowing its voice, slightly higher than the big ones, slightly sweeter.

"Mar-mar," said a large umox, one or several of them. "Come here."

"I'm dreaming," I thought to myself. "I've been frozen under the damned shelf and now I'm dreaming."

"Here," said a deeper voice, joined by several others to make a low, harmonic sound in my head, as though great chimes were ringing there. "Here, young one."

I rose like a puppet and staggered toward the plether bedded in the hay. As I came near, one shifted, then another, letting me fumble my way to the center of the plether, where a nest of hay was waiting, already warmed by the huge body that had lain there. "No need to go to the cold far," whispered the voices. "Warm is here. Lay self down . . ."

Which I did, though it was more a stumble-flop than a graceful recline. The warm tails of half a dozen umoxen moved slightly to cover me from head to toe, leaving only a little space around my nose and mouth so I could breathe. "I'm dreaming," I advised myself. "I'm in my own hay nest, and I'm dreaming."

"Dream then," whispered the umox. "Dream a thing we have meant for you and made for you. Dream what you will do when you wake."

For the first time since winter came, I was comfortable. The thick tails of the umox were blanket-warm though light as air, feathered from tip to rump with the finest wool in any world known to man or Ghoss.

"Why didn't you invite me before?" I murmured, half asleep.

"Why didn't you tell us you were cold before?" the umox murmured in return. "You tell us stories of Queen Wilvia, you tell us about the nazeemi, you tell us many things we already know very well, but you do not mention to us that you are cold. If you cannot tell the whole world simply by being, as the Ghoss do, then you must tell us. Little one saw you shivering and went to warm you. You feared for her. She came and told us. We do not let those who care for us come to harm."

"I'm sorry," I murmured drowsily. "I'm sorry I'm not Ghoss."

"Even if you are not Ghoss, you are quite likely our good friend."

I did not try to decipher this, for I was already asleep. In my dream, I wandered with umoxen, walking beside them as they trekked over vast green plains below ranges of snowcapped mountains, while high above us a golden bird cried strange words from the roof of the sky. I knew I was in an umox dream and had no wish to leave it.

Early in the morning, the herdsman came through with his staff, prepared to poke me again, but he found my space already empty. I, meantime, peered at the taskmaster through a fringe of tail wool that hung over my eyes. When the man moved away, gone to breakfast, the great bodies shifted again, making a way out. By the time he and I encountered one another, I was on my way back from the privies.

He stared at me with some suspicion, noting, perhaps, a certain unwarranted rosiness in my cheeks, a certain rested look around my eyes. "Cold last night," he muttered in an evil tone, obviously hoping I would answer.

I pretended not to hear him, merely standing where I was with my jaw sagging witlessly until he moved away.

He said nothing more, though I noted several questioning glances during breakfast lineup. When I had eaten, I returned to the barn and my winter chores, forking down the fragrant hay into the long troughs that lined the day barn before letting the umox into the day barn and starting the long job of cleaning out the night barn. Fine, rich hay for eating was the guarantee of high prices on the wool market, and there was plenty of it to be had on Fajnard. All the lowlands were grassland, all edible, sweet-smelling, and useful, and it never rained during haying season—so said the Ghoss.

As I had begun to do on my first day in the barns, I accompanied the rhythm of the pitchfork with a silent chant that kept my mind away from the past as the doctor had suggested. "Fif-teen" pitchfork into the haystack, "more" pitchfork raising hay, "years" pitchfork tossing hay, one step along the road to understanding how I had come here and what it all meant. One step, then another, and another, and another, three steps more along the road to discernment. Fifteen long, long years.

Eventually, it was spring. Fourteen . . . more . . . years, I chanted to the pitchfork. And then fall, winter, and spring again. Thirteen . . . more . . . years. And so on, and so on, and only a few more years.

I Am M'urgi/on B'yurngrad

Night on B'yurngrad. A steppe wide as an ocean, rustling with grass. Far in the night a broken horizon surmounted by a toenail of moon and a spear blade of dew-bright stars, pointing downward at the cleft between two hills.

"See," whispered the old woman, reaching to untie the long plait in which her hair was usually confined. "See," fingers moving upward through that hair, casting it forward, letting it move in the wind to blow like a veil before her eyes. "See, there, where the spear points downward, where the lance falls to reach the heart of water . . ."

"I see," I, who had been Margaret; I, M'urgi, whispered.

"This is the sign of the hunters, the skull-faced ones, who go wandering in the night. When this sign comes, they come eastward, running in the grasses. In this time when there are no wolves, they are the wolves of the night, they the tigers, the leopards, the swift-footed hunters. Prick your ears to the wind."

I listened. At first I heard nothing. The old woman's hand touched my ear, featherlight, and I heard. Through the wind-rustled grasses came the pant of breath, the fall of foot, the small rattle of bone beads strung on thong. One, at first, then several more.

"I hear," I murmured.

"How many?"

"Five, maybe six, but if six, the other is far off, following."

"If six, he is the one we want. Find him."

I closed my eyes, laid my hands palms upward on my knees, straightened my spine as though it were a cannon barrel, and shot my perception upward, through the top of my skull. Looking down, I saw myself, the old woman, the tiny fire before us, the circle of amber light that ended just beyond our haunches. I laid myself forward upon a dark pillow of air to follow the night road, the road of discovery, sending my thought in the direction of the sound, swooping along the dark air to meet it, even as it moved to meet me.

I came first upon the five skull-painted ones, panting down a narrow cleft between two hills, feet thudding on the soil, one well in advance of the others, a long pole carried over his shoulder with a pouch of something at its tip, then three more men, then a laggard. The sixth was farther back, nearer the place they had begun, and I flew toward him, sensing the old woman at my side.

Almost we missed the child. A boy, perhaps ten or eleven. Not yet come to strength, certainly, howsoever he burned with purpose, the hard red glow of it easily visible, even from our height.

"M'urgi, if this one lives," the old woman whispered, "over a thousand will die, for he will betray them and their good purpose. I have seen it."

"How many times?" I asked.

"Ten times watched, five times seen."

"Then it is equally likely he will not do the thing."

"I will be dead before the time comes," whispered the old woman. "I pass the burden to you, M'urgi. It lies before you."

I shivered in the chill dark, in fear of night, in grasp of bloodshed, in danger of being mistaken. A long moment went by before I said, "I accept the burden."

The night road retracted beneath us. The sky opened and dropped us beside the dim coals of our fire, which we covered with ashes before sitting down once more.

"What did the lead man carry," I asked, "at the end of that long pole?"

"Ghyrm," replied my teacher. "Ghyrm to use against another tribe, one he wants to do away with so he can take the women."

"Will the ghyrm take only men?"

"The ghyrm will take those they are purposed to take."

"Where did he get it?" I whispered.

"He bought it with pain, from someone who sells for pain. From Cantardene, most likely. Hush. They come."

Five runners approached, darting past not far from us, eyes set on their own road, sparing no glance that might have discovered two smoke-faced, black-garbed women hidden downwind in the dark. The air moved to me, and I smelled their sweat. When they had gone, I built up the fire once more. Much later, another footfall, this time interrupted.

"Hey, boy," I said. "Where you goin' in the night?"

He spun, frantic, relaxing when he saw us women sitting there, amber light reflecting from our faces. "Find m'dah," he said wearily. "I trail 'm this fah."

"And where's he gone, then?" I asked.

"Dunno. D'wanna be lef wit de women. No more."

"Ah! Fahr sure." I patted the ground beside the fire, inviting him. "He'll be mazed, he will, come back this way and find how far you come! That's a clevah idea."

"Is't?" he asked doubtfully. He had not considered whether it was clever or not. He had only thought of his shame, being left behind with the women, the babies. "Yeah," he claimed, inflating his chest as he approached the fire. "Is clevah. D'you hab watah?"

"Hab tea," I murmured, seating him by the flame, guiding his hands to wrap around the crude mug. "Y'know, some dahs don tell reasons propahly. You dah tell you his reasons, leavin' you?"

The boy spoke from inside the teacup. "Nah."

"Thot so. Prob'ly somethin goin on back in camp, your dah, he wants to know 'bout it. He wants to know do you keep you eyes open, you mouf shut. He can leave no mahn dere, for watchin. He can leave a son, though, son old enuf, smart enuf to watch. Thas prob'ly what he thinks."

The boy put the cup down, obviously in the grip of unaccustomed thought. "You spose? An I muck it all?"

I, M'urgi, shrugged. "You make it back in time, he nevah know. An, if he ast, did somethin happen, you say nothin happen or somethin happen, jus the way you see it."

I was speaking to the air. The cup lay empty and the boy was gone, back along the trail. The old woman said, "He may not make it back, tired as he is."

"He'll make it back," I said. "I've seen it."

"Ah. And when did that happen."

"Last night. You took us along the night road to the north. I saw the encampment there, saw the coming shadow cover it, heard the second wife buying poison from a traveler, saw the boy lying behind a bush, listening. Same boy."

The old woman smiled, though wearily. "I didn't see it."

"You were far ahead, scanning for whatever it is we're always looking for."

"It's ghyrm we're always seeking, and those who sell them," the old woman said with a touch of annoyance. "And you didn't mention the boy."

I nodded, familiar enough with her to be unmoved by her irritation. "It meant nothing, until tonight. Who are they, Wolf-mother?"

"The hunters? Followers of the ghyrm-way since the first bondsmen came from Cantardene. On that planet some evil creature taught them this way they follow: brother against brother, family against family, tribe against tribe, never a peace long enough for them to grow numerous, but with strong taboos on killing the women so they can always recover their strength. Faces painted like skulls to show they fear no death, for he who dies for honor goes to the place of Joy. Death and honor lovers. That's what moved the boy on the trail, honor."

"He will tell his father about the second wife. What will his father do?"

"Fly and see," the old woman whispered. "If you care enough to spend yourself on them. If you ask only for my guess, well then, the father will watch to see what she does. And she, she will try to poison him, so her own son can take that boy's place. And the man, he'll be so angry, instead of crying her crime aloud and sending her back to her family in shame, he will forget the taboos and will kill her. Her family will kill him for breaking the taboos. His brothers will kill her brothers. They will be much preoccupied with killing one another, and larger conflicts will pass them by. The boy will not be responsible for a thousand lives. Perhaps."

"To what purpose?"

The old woman shook her head. "We can see tomorrow, even next season or, for some things, a year. Farther than that, the road of discovery becomes a path of shadows, mere shades of portents of things uncertain. I saw that boy lead a raid a year from now, down from the hills into a village. I saw everyone in that village dead. Ten times I saw, five times I saw them dead. Perhaps in that possibility, the wife had killed her husband, the boy had laid blame and sought revenge. Whatever. It is your burden now, your duty to crouch over the fire and see."

"Is this why they sent me, Wolf-mother? Is this my life?"

"Only those who sent you know why, M'urgi. Only they know what your life will be, though I have seen a shadow on it . . .'"

"What sort of shadow?"

"One that kills. Someone wants you dead, M'urgi. Sometime. Not yet, but sometime. In the meantime, there are more chants for you to learn, and more herbs for you to pick, and many futures for you to see . . ."

I laughed, without rancor but without amusement, either. My hands and face were black with soot from the fire. My hair felt as though several generations of birds had been nesting in it, leaving their lice behind. The hides that warmed me stank to high heaven. I had been with the old shaman woman for almost ten years. Whatever my unknown benefactors might expect of me in the future, I sincerely hoped it involved bathing at more regular intervals.

And, ah, it would be nice to see Ferni again.

"You're thinking about him," said the old woman in a minatory tone.

"I have seen myself with him elsewhere, Wolf-mother. In a dream I saw myself among the tribes, many tribes, all gathered together. And he came out of darkness into light, carrying something mysterious. Then I blinked, and when I looked up, I saw my own face, three times. One me a lot like me. One me much older. And one me looking out of a man's face."

"Thinking of him, dreaming of him, that'll get you killed," said the old woman.

"How long since you've had to warn me of that, Mother."

"A year or two," she replied grudgingly. "Maybe more."

"Maybe many more. You speak of dying. I have sworn to fulfill your burdens. When I have done so, then, perhaps, I may think of him? Find him in that place I dreamed of, among the tribes."

"Then," came the reply, a whisper in the night. "Only then. Perhaps."

I Am Margaret/on Tercis

On Rueday, all the Judsons are present in the Ruehouse, from me, Dr. Bryan's widow, Grandma Mackey, right down to Mayleen's daughter, Emmaline, youngest of the fourteen who'd been born to Mayleen, the ten who had survived. Though I have been Ruing for close to forty years now, I am still unable to confine my ruing to Rueday. Ever since Bryan died, I have stood here each Rueday, between my daughter Maybelle and my granddaughter Gloriana, eyes tight shut, hands twisting at one another, body trembling like a branch of autumn leaves in a chill wind while I rue having let Bryan sacrifice himself for me. Not that Bryan is the only thing I rue. I rue the twins, oh, the twins, my two sets of them, Maybelle's one set, Mayleen's seven sets—not even including all the ones miscarried or born dead. Oh, for how many years have I rued, and still I wish I could go back and undo it all.

In the pew behind me, Mayleen was ruing having a sister and a sister's family who were so rotten to her. Marriage and motherhood had not changed Mayleen; they had merely confirmed her misery. Billy Ray Judson was probably ruing that his brother had ever been born, for Billy Ray was as Billy Ray had ever been, jealous and hateful.

The seven Billy Ray Judson children who still lived in Rueful would be spending their ruetime as they did most of the rest of their time. Each Rueday I told their names over to myself. The eldest, Joe Bob, had left home to work on the Conover Farm, down The Valley. Perhaps he was ruing the fact he had not joined his twin in volunteering for the army. The second oldest twins had left years ago. Ella May had applied for membership in the Siblinghood of Silence and been accepted. Janine Ruth, her sister, had also applied and been refused, so had moved up to Repentance, which had more scope for her talents, which I refused to think about. Only one of the third set of twins had lived, Benny Paul, who was probably spending ruetime planning how to get Jeff, Gloriana's brother, into trouble. Trish, the survivor of the fourth set, who was simple but not asexual, was probably thinking of whatever boy was currently making use of her. Sue Elaine and Lou Ellen had made up the fifth set, and Sue Elaine was without doubt ruing the existence of her cousin, Gloriana Judson; while little Orvie John and even littler Emmaline, each sole survivors, rued the fact they had been given no breakfast this morning and probably no supper last night and were so hungry it was very hard to be quiet. The moment I laid eyes on them this morning I knew the money I had most recently given their mother had not been spent on food! Poor babies.

I knew them so well. I did not know them at all.

Next to me, I knew that Maybelle was resolving to be more patient with her twin. James Joseph Judson, Billy Ray's half brother, Maybelle's husband and Gloriana's father, was probably ruing not chastising his son Til, who was becoming more and more like Benny Paul. Til's twin, Jeff, was conscientiously ruing whatever iniquities Til and Benny Paul had got him into most recently. He always rued saying yes; he always said yes because Til was his brother.

Maybelle's daughter, barely pubescent Gloriana, usually had a lengthy list to rue, I'd seen her look up attentively when Pastor Grievy asked us to rue ". . . the great failing of our people in the long ago . . ." and I wagered with myself she was trying to figure that out. Gloriana was a great one for figuring things out.

I knew them so well, and I really did, even Til. They were family, while Mayleen's husband and children seemed more foreign than a tribe of Frossians. Or yaboons.

The choir voices began a slow diminuendo.

In the next pew, Abe Johnson had his eyes tightly closed. He usually spent double the average time ruing his mail-order wife, who had vanished, leaving him with her son, Bamber Joy, an event Abe would never understand if he rued the whole matter for a hundred years. Even he, however, eventually felt Pastor Grievy's tightly focused gaze boring through his eyelids, and with a sigh, lifted his head. The words were spoken, and we slowly left the Ruehouse.

People walked to and from services on Rueday as a minor religious thing, only faintly colored by notions of expiation or propriety. Most people who felt reasonably well did it out of habit unless the weather was intolerable, which it rarely was. All Tercis's extremes, either icy or furnace-hot, had been reserved for the coldhearted and the hot-tempered; the Rueful had been granted a Walled-Off with a pleasant climate.

The Judson clan gathered briefly at the Ruehouse steps. I touched Mayleen's shoulder. "Have you heard from Ella Mae, Mayleen?"

"Of course not." She shrugged my arm away. "She's in the Siblinghood of Silence, so she's silent so far as her family is concerned."

"I thought she might have a furlough this summer."

"Not with us, she won't. Last time was enough." She stalked off after Billy Ray, while I furtively gave the two little ones the cookies I had brought in my pocket. As quickly as a squirrel hides nuts in his mouth, they hid the cookies in their raggedy clothes. As Billy Ray led his brood westward on the highway toward the bridge that would take them across to their farm on the west side of the river, I saw them breaking off little pieces and taking sneaky little mouthfuls.

"Oatmeal," whispered Maybelle. "And raisins, and eggs."

I nodded as I cast a glance southward where my old home stood, now an addition to Ms. Barfinger's Boardinghouse. "And sugar," I whispered. "And butter."

Jimmy Joe and Maybelle led us toward the road that wound down sloped meadows and northward on the river's near side, strolling hand in hand, as if they were courting instead of having been married practically forever. Til raced on ahead as though eager to fit a whole day's devilment in before sunset. Gloriana ambled along beside me, stopping when I stopped to admire a flower or a fluttering bee-bird, and Jeff trailed behind, probably still trying to think of a way to keep Til from getting him into any more trouble.

By the time our family neared the bottom of the hill, other people had turned off, and we were alone, moving north along the pasture road.

Gloriana whispered, "Grandma Meg, what did Aunt Mayleen mean about the Siblinghood of Silence?"

"It's a kind of organization," I said. "They don't accept just anyone as a member. Only men and women who really want to spend their lives doing good for people. They call it the Siblinghood of Silence because they're not allowed to talk about what they do."

"I hardly remember Ella May."

"She's strong, and has a rather plain, pleasant face, and she's a good person." Unlike, I didn't say, her twin sister.

"That's why she left, I guess. Daddy says the only way you can give Aunt Mayleen and Uncle Billy Ray anything without their being nasty about it, is drop it off after dark and hope the dogs don't drag it away before morning. Probably Ella May tried to do them some good."

Which was one of the more perspicacious things Glory had said recently. Mayleen and Billy Ray would definitely resent any effort to do them good. "I think Ella May tried very hard to help them the last time she was home," I said. "I think they told her not to come back."

I saw her tuck that away, probably to think about later.

"Grandma, what was the great failing Pastor Grievy always talks about?"

Aha, I'd been right. "Probably something that happened a long time ago, before your Grandpa Doc and I came to Tercis. It might have been something that happened to cause the Walling-Off, when all those bondslaves were being dumped here, ready to kill anyone who looked at them crosswise."

"You and Grandpa Doc came later."

"We came here directly from Earth without any bondage in between. I was twenty-two, he was thirty."

"And Grandpa Doc talked you into coming here."

I pinched my lips and clenched my hands. "In a manner of speaking I suppose he talked me into it, yes. It was come here or go elsewhere, and this seemed appropriate at the time."

"Tell me about him."

"Glory, for heaven's sake. You remember him!"

"Not really. He died six years ago, when I was only six or seven. I wasn't grown enough to . . . to know what he was really like. As a person, I mean, not as a grandpa."

"Well, when we get home, come on up to my house, and I'll show you some views of him and tell you about him."

I stared resolutely ahead, down the road, wondering when, if ever, I would be finished with trying to explain Bryan Mackey. How could I explain him to Gloriana when I couldn't explain him to myself after all our years together? And when, under heaven, was I going to be able to stop trying to make it up to him and let him go?

After he died and I decided to sell the big house in town to Mrs. Barfinger, Jimmy Joe built what was locally called an "old-mother house" for me, up the hill behind his own place. The house wasn't so far away as to be troublesome going back and forth, but it wasn't so close as to infringe upon my privacy, or his and Maybelle's. The house was surrounded by trees and set at the back of a wide, rocky ledge that gave a view across most of the valley. I had grown to love the place more than I had ever loved the house in town, perhaps because I could be alone there, and loneness was comforting to me. When we got there, Gloriana echoed my thoughts, saying as she usually did, "I like this better than your other house. The other one was too big."

"It needed to be big," I told her, as I rummaged through my desk to find the viewcubes of Bryan. "We had three children, and Grandpa Doc was always bringing home stray cats."

"I don't remember lots of cats," said Gloriana doubtfully.

"It's just a way of speaking, Glory. I mean stray people. People in need of a bed or a bath or a meal."

"So he was nice to people."

I found the viewstage and set it on the window seat while considering this. Yes, on the whole, he had been nice to people, sometimes even those he was furiously angry with. Glory came to stand beside me as I flicked through the views. Bryan, a sandy-haired young man smiling, his arm around a young, pregnant Margaret, who had drawn cheeks and dark circles around her eyes; Dr. Mackey, a man thinner and older, still smiling, with a strained-looking Margaret at his side and teenaged Maybelle and Mayleen at his feet. That was taken just a few weeks before Mayleen got married. Then Grandpa Doc, a gray-haired old man seated beside light-haired Grandma, smiling, always smiling.

"He doesn't look angry," Glory said. "You tell it like he was always angry." She sat in the old rocking chair and touched her toe to the brick floor to make it sway. "I don't remember Grandpa ever acting angry."

"He almost never let it show," I admitted. "When we lived in the big house in Crossroads, he used to go out back and chop wood until he calmed down. One of the Walled-Offs here on Tercis is called Hostility, you know? Grandpa claimed to be afraid he'd be sent there, and he said there was nothing better for getting rid of hostility than an hour with an axe and some very resistant wood." I put my handkerchief to my face, stood up, and walked to the window, where I stared out, my back to Gloriana.

Gloriana knew I was crying. She changed the subject. "Grandma, whose fault is it that Lou Ellen's family's so poor?"

I cleared my throat and dabbed at my eyes. Whose fault indeed? "Start with the fact Billy Ray never really worked his land. He was too busy chasing your Aunt Mayleen, who was sixteen at the time! They got married because she was pregnant. Your mother met your father at Mayleen's wedding, so some good came of it, even though that's where being poor started. Since we couldn't have stopped it without chaining Mayleen to the wall, it's nobody's fault."

"Aunt Mayleen and Mama are different."

"They have different lives. There's a difference between having a very large family starting when you are sixteen, or having a small family after you have both an education and a livelihood."

"Billy Ray always talks about being a farmer," said Gloriana. "But he doesn't even know what kind of a farmer he is. It's always something different that doesn't work out. But Mama and Dad are farmers, too. Sort of."

"Your mother and dad aim lower. A few chickens for eggs, a little garden for summer vegetables, a few fruit trees for preserves and jelly. And even if they had none of that, their jobs over in Remorseful would support you and Til and Jeff."

"So, if it weren't for the money you give Mayleen, they'd go hungry?"

"Even with it, they go hungry," I said angrily. "I give it for food, but they don't spend it on food! Did you see Emmaline's face this morning? That poor baby! I'm going to stop giving money and concentrate on cookies! Oatmeal cookies keep really well!"

"Couldn't Uncle Billy Ray get a job that would support the family?"

"He doesn't want a job; he wants to farm. He says he can support the family farming if things would just go right. If the universe would just cooperate, he'd make a living. Since it's the universe at fault, nobody should blame him."

Glory chewed on that for a while. "Anybody could say that about anything."

I murmured, "I give thanks every day that I ended up in such a cozy little house as this one in such a lovely place as The Valley, even if Ruers are mostly a little sad and not all that interesting."

"We've got some interesting people. Bamber Joy's stepfather is sort of interesting."

"Abe Johnson? Well, advertising for a wife isn't all that interesting, but getting one with a half-grown boy-child, a wife who pretty soon runs off, leaving the boy-child behind, that's rather interesting. And where in heaven's name did she go? Rueful isn't that big! She should have turned up somewhere."

"Bamber Joy says he's going to find her someday."

I shook my head at her, warningly. "Bamber Joy. The name alone is enough to guarantee he walks a hard road, Gloriana."

"He didn't pick his name. I like him."

"Your mother and I don't mind your liking him. We just object to your getting into fistfights on his behalf."

"He never starts them! Somebody needs to fight for him."

"Well, you're two of a kind."

"Objects of derision, you mean," Glory snapped.

"That wasn't what I had in mind, no. You're simply taller and a lot smarter than most of the local residents."

Gloriana flushed. She always flushed when someone said something complimentary about her. "I have to go," she said, getting to her feet and giving me a peck on the cheek. "I promised Lou Ellen a picnic down at the ferry pool."

"Oh, Glory . . ." I said.

"Well, I *promised,* and she's probably waiting for me."

She turned and fled, out the door and away down the hill before another word could be said. I went to the door, still blotting my eyes, watching the girl going away, always going away to something else, somewhere else, restless as a fleabit cat, just like me, restlessness chronic and exhausting to control, constantly throwing shovelfuls of activity over my wretchedness, trying to bury what wouldn't stay buried.

It had been a battle that took its toll on flesh and spirit, but I had not let Bryan see it. All my youthful dreams had been lost. The doubts had begun to circle almost as soon as we'd arrived, like those ancient carrion birds, scenting the rot that was setting in. And for what? If we could have made a real difference in Rueful, I would have been proud of our struggle, but all we really did was exhaust ourselves to keep a few pigheaded people alive a year or so past their time. Not a great achievement. If it hadn't been for the idyllic fantasy Bryan had woven for me during the few days before we left Earth, I wouldn't have been hypnotized by his exuberance, caught up in his certainty that love would see us through life, that it was a fair bargain for both of us, that it would all work out well.

"I've loved you since I first met you, Maggie. You were worth every year." He had told me that, time and again. I wish he hadn't said it. If he'd been angry with me, just a few times, I could have given myself some room. As it was, I had to be as faithful and helpful as was humanly possible. Even so, I never honestly felt the scales were balanced. All the good times we planned were things we would be doing now, and he was gone. There were more doctors in Rueful now, things would have been easier. We could have had time together. My fault. I shouldn't have let him bring me here. I should have taken my chances like everyone else.

Instead, here I was, grandma to a very troubled brood. What the proctor had said back on Earth was true: my family did indeed run to twins, lots of them, and of them all, only Maybelle, and Jeff and Gloriana seemed capable of love and joy. No, that wasn't fair. Probably Joe Bob, which is why he'd left, and Ella May's joining the Siblinghood of Silence meant she had it in her to be happy and good, or the Siblinghood wouldn't have taken her. And little Emmaline and Orvie

John? They might turn out all right, too, if they didn't starve to death first. The others though, well, they were fruit of a blasted tree, born because of bad choices I'd made, one after the other.

Likely, if I said any of that to Gloriana, the girl would say, "Well, Grandma, if that's so, here's right where you belong! You sound mighty rueful to me."

And, as Gloriana all too often was, she would be right.

All of which was fruitless and melancholy. I needed to get out of the house and do something. I knew the way to the ferry pool, where Gloriana was going, and I decided to join her there.

I Am Margaret/on Tercis

Sparkle in the noon-light, river running, road dust fluffing in a teasing wind, grass bending and swaying, Gloriana on her way to the ferry pool. From the road, I saw her running through the meadows down toward the river. Ahead of us, the Great Dike ran east to west, a wall of black stone, onetime southern edge of a mighty water that had covered a great part of south Rueful to a considerable depth. The water had worn its way through the top of the dike and begun chewing a channel all the way to the bottom. How many millennia it had taken to gnaw its way down, no one in The Valley knew, but we all gave thanks for the wide-cupped plain of loamy soil it had left behind. This was fat soil, coveted by anyone who knew how to farm.

The day had warmed, and my face was wet, though it would be cooler near the river. Something was pushing the season. Every weed patch had turned into a jungle, every garden was sprouting a thicket, and each day was already full of lazy stupefactions from noontime right up 'til supper. I watched as Gloriana crossed the grassy riverside, eaten into a lawn by the Birkin's geese, who honked at her querulously as she went by. "Glory, why such a hurry, have some nice grass."

"Thank you, no," she said. "I'm meeting Lou Ellen, and I'm already late." That's what it sounded like to me, at least. Not that I spoke Goose. Not that I spoke anything much anymore. Sometimes I lay in bed at night thinking in Earthian, then translating those thoughts into Gentheran, or Pthas, or one of the other tongues I'd taken so much trouble to learn. I grieved over that. I grieved over the possibility I was losing my mind, too. Sometimes lately I had thought something was being said when there wasn't a sound; sometimes I had known something had happened even though I hadn't seen it. Senility. The madness of the old. I had gone so far back in time getting to Tercis that I was probably older than my own father right now. And thinking that, madam, I said to myself, will drive you bonkers.

Gloriana climbed down into the river bottom to walk under the high arch of the bridge. Dominion had built the bridge to speed transport of materials quickly from Walled-Offs in the west to Walled-Offs in the east. Some nights we could hear the trucks roaring far across The Valley, growling and echoing as they crossed the bridge, then fading to a distant beelike hum among the mountains. They never came the other way, so we supposed they must return through other Walled-Offs, north or south, taking export stuff to the spaceport near the Western Sea.

I didn't follow Gloriana's route. Under the bridge, the river bottom was scattered with rounded black boulders separated by narrow lanes of sand. Gloriana could swivel her way through them, but I no longer had hips hinged like that. The pool where the old rope ferry had been, prebridge, was on the far side of the dike, a circle of dark water with green rushes all around it, quiet as a dream even on noisy days. That's where Glory said Sue Elaine's sister, Lou Ellen, was waiting.

When Lou Ellen was tiny, she had been very frail and had spent more time at Glory's house than she had at home. It was easier on her to be in a quiet place rather than in Mayleen's house with its cold drafts in winter and swarming flies in summer, where rackety, quarrelsome people were always going at it hammer and tongs. Besides, Mayleen didn't have the patience for helping Lou Ellen eat, and Sue Elaine had said right out loud it would be better if she just starved to death and got it over with. Lou Ellen ate very well if the food was mashed up soft, and Gloriana was good at doing that. The two of them had spent hours playing card games on Glory's bed, upstairs, where no one would bother them. Lou Ellen was a good player; there was nothing wrong with her mind even though her body had been fragile as a sooly leaf eaten away by worms until nothing was left but lace.

One day I heard Lou Ellen ask, "Glory, are you my friend? Sue Elaine says I don't have any friends."

"Of course I am, Lou Ellen. What you think I'm doin' here?"

"I thought maybe it was just you're my cousin."

"That too. If you'd rather have me for a sister, I could be your blood sister, just like the blood brothers in those stories Aunt Hanna tells us when she comes visiting."

"I'd like that," Lou Ellen whispered. "Oh, I'd like that."

Through the slit in the door I had watched while Glory got a darning needle and cooked it in the flame of the coal stove so it wouldn't have any germs on it, then pricked their fingers and pressed them together and swore to be blood sisters forever.

"Not just for this year or next year or the year after that, but blood sisters so long as I live," Glory said. Glory was only in first grade then, but she could already write pretty well. She and I had taught Lou Ellen to read and write. The two of them wrote the promise out together, very neatly, and put their names on it. Glory put the folded-up promise in an old lozenge box, wrapped the box in a piece of oil-cloth, and buried it at the foot of the tall, standing stone halfway up the hill toward my house. Glory had always said the stone looked like a huge, armored person, standing guard over the valley. I saw it all, and the place by the stone was a good place for a promise to be protected and safe. The whole thing was so dear it made me cry, but I never let on I'd seen them.

Instead of going below the bridge, I went up to the near end of it, toward town, crossed the road, and went down the other side on the steep path through the woods. When I got to the bottom, deep into the shadows of the trees, I saw Glory coming out from under the bridge, looking toward the old, splintery pier, gray as a goose feather. She smiled radiantly, raised her hands, and called, "Lou Ellen!"

I stopped. I was intruding on her. Everyone, even young people had a right to their private time. Still, I didn't feel like going home. I sat down with my back to a tree and thought about having a nap. I shut my eyes.

"How long you been here?" Glory called.

I think my eyes must have opened, just a slit. I saw Lou Ellen on the pier. She shrugged waveringly, almost like heat waves rising. Her voice came like a whisper of wind.

"Don't know," she murmured. "A while. You look all hot. You bothered by something?"

"Me? Not much." Glory felt her face. "Well, yes, I am. Here it is summer again, about time for me'n Sue Elaine's birthday party, and as per usual, nobody's invited you."

Lou Ellen smiled, then whispered in a soft little voice I could barely hear, "Do you want to go to the birthday party?"

"Ballygaggle no, Lou Ellen! I don't even want to *have* a birthday party unless I can have one of my own. I'm tired of sharing my birthday with somebody I don't even like just because we were born in midsummer. It's the same dumb thing every year. Grandma and Mama make a big fuss over it, and everybody gets their feelings hurt, and Grandma goes around all sad and doesn't talk to anybody for days and days afterward!"

"Then why should my feelings be hurt not being invited someplace I don't want to go anyhow? It's nice I don't have to."

At which point I should have picked myself up and gone home, but I didn't. I was asleep, so I couldn't.

Glory asked, "You going to help fish?"

Another of those wavering shrugs. "You do it, Glory. You like catching them."

Glory opened her pack and got out her fishing gear, a string tied to a piece of stinky meat, and lowered it into the shallows near some rocks. Within two minutes, a big crawdad grabbed it with his claws. Tercis crawdads weren't earth crawdads, but Earthians had given them the same name because they had pretty much the same look to them, claws in front, legs behind. She pulled it out and put it in the bucket.

"You're sure lazy," murmured Gloriana

"I know." Lou Ellen sighed. "I've been like this lately."

Lou Ellen went on dreaming, Glory caught crawdads, the sun slipped down from the top of the sky.

"I've got twenty-one," Glory said, yawning. "That's ten each. What do you think's better? Should we flip for the extra one, then maybe have hard feelings, or should we just toss the littlest one back?"

"Throw it."

"You pick which one."

Lou Ellen drifted over to the bucket and pointed, but as Glory tried to toss it, it nipped her, pinching like crazy. She danced around, waving her arm and yelling ow, ow, leggo, leggo, her eyes so scrunched up it took her a moment to notice the two people who came out of the reeds across the pool and walked across the deep pond toward her, their feet leaving not so much as a ripple in the mirror surface of the water. In my dream, I had seen them coming.

Glory's eyes flew wide, and she forgot about the crawdad, which hung twitching on her finger while she stared at the impossible people. To me they looked to be partly silver and partly blue, as though extremely cold people were contained inside coats of clear ice, but they didn't look at all frozen. Their eyes and arms and feet moved, their huge, furry ears twitched back and forward, and their little pink triangle noses wrinkled at the corners, just like cats. They had that same sort of upper lip, too, split just below the nose and curving up on either side to make a rounded W shape. If cats could smile ingratiatingly, that's what these people were doing.

Glory said something like How do you do, or Hello there.

Lou Ellen said, "Who you talking to?"

Glory looked down where Lou Ellen was sitting at the end of the pier and said, "Them."

Lou Ellen looked all around. "Who's them?"

Glory turned toward the smaller cat-person, and said angrily, "Now, that's not fair! You're going to get me locked up again, everybody thinking I'm crazy, and that's not a nice thing to do. You let Lou Ellen see you, too."

The bigger one remarked, "Of course. How thoughtless of us," and he cast his eyes over toward Lou Ellen, who immediately screeched and grabbed at Glory, getting the crawdad's other claw instead. It pinched her, and she howled.

"What is it your intention to do with these creatures?" asked the bigger one.

Glory said, "We'd planned on eating them."

"Are they edible?" the smaller one asked. "They seem to be quite barky and fibrous."

"The tail meat inside the shell is very nice," Glory said, self-consciously shifting herself into politeness mode. This meant doing what I had told her, over and over. Concentrate on good grammar, speak quietly, without expletives—even silly ones, like "Ballygaggle" instead of her daddy's "Balls!"

"Then you're carnivores," said the bigger cat-person.

"No, we're Judsons," Glory said. "Gloriana and Lou Ellen Judson."

"A judson is . . ." said the smaller one, leaving it hanging like it was something she didn't know what to do about.

"A family," Glory told them. "It's a family. Like, we're related. Lou Ellen and me, we're cousins. Her daddy and my daddy are half brothers, Billy Ray and Jimmy Joe Judson, and her mama and my mama are twin sisters, Mayleen and Maybelle Mackey."

"Sisters who are very like one another, perhaps?" asked the smaller one, her eyes glowing.

Glory took a long breath before she said, "Not all that much, no. Aunt Mayleen thinks my mama's cornered the market on selfishness, and my mama thinks Mayleen's too lazy to breathe on her own, but it makes no nevermind because Lou Ellen and I are best friends, no matter what."

"It's good to have friends," said the smaller one to the bigger one. "No matter what kind they are . . ."

"Besides," Glory interjected, "I didn't catch on to your asking about carnivores right at first, because I was thinking of the Conovers, the folks on one of the farms down the road. But I do know what a carnivore is, and we're not quite. There's another word for what we are . . ."

"Omnivores," said the smaller one in a satisfied voice, like she'd been planning a dinner and had been worrying what to serve. "No, we're omnivores, too, so I wasn't worried about our having a meal together. My companion's name is Prrr Prrrpm by the way. I am Mrrrw Lrrrpa, and since you have called your cousin Lou Ellen, you must be Glorrrr-iana."

In my dream I said their names, over and over, the *r*'s rolled like an engine running, and when they used Gloriana's name, her jaw dropped, and it took a minute before she could say, "I'm Gloriana, but how come you know that?"

"We were given directions," said the larger one. "We were told to find Gloriana Judson at this river, by this pier, early summer, period two, day ten, at twelve-forty-nine in the afternoon local time. We have a locator." He removed a gadget from his belt and held it out: an egg-shaped, translucent blue thing with a silver handle.

"What does it say?" she asked.

"It says you are . . . who you are."

"And why does it say that," Glory demanded.

"Because," said the littler one more softly, "you, no other person, are the optimum person to help us with our task."

Gloriana considered this. She looked baffled. They just stood there, as though they expected her to do something, and in the dream, I could see her considering what might be proper.

"We were about to have our lunch. You're welcome to share it, if you like. We've got enough crawdad tails for five each and enough potatoes and bacon and apples for everybody."

"What fun," said the smaller one. "What can we contribute?"

"There's that roast pleckle leg," he said. "And a whole basket of whalp berries. And those preserved grum stalks the trader gave us when we visited on . . . somewhere."

Or something similar. The two cat-people walked up onshore as if it was all decided, shedding their ice coats as they came, and almost immediately the two of them had a fire going, the groceries out of their bags, and water boiling a lot faster than water ever behaved for me when I was in a hurry!

Glory wrapped the potatoes. "We'll prob'ly have to have 'em for dessert," she said, as she buried them in the fire. "They'll take a lot longer to bake than the crawdads will to boil."

The food the cat-people had taken out of the bags seemed more voluminous than the bags themselves, but Glory didn't comment on that, which was dreamily appropriate. When the crawdads were cooked, the four of them took the shells off and ate a bit of them and a bit of grum stalk, which Glory said was spicy and tart and a little peppery, and then a whalp berry or two, very sweet, then a bite of apple, and then some more of this or that while the little wind sent wavelets clucking around the splintery lopsided pier and terci-crows cussed at each other in the trees.

The two cat-people were full of questions about the Judsons and the farms and what they raised and what did best, like turnips, and what didn't do so good, like anything fancy they might get more than fifty cents for. Glory waded out into the pool to get the jar of kinda-lemonade she kept there, where it stayed cool, and when she came back, they passed the drink around, and along about the third drink, the smaller one wiped her mouth on one paw—it did look like a paw, but it had fingers like a hand—and looked Glory straight in the face.

"Gloriana Judson, could you find the goodness in your heart to do us a favor?"

Glory looked suddenly skeptical, and I knew she was thinking of Bobby Duane Hansen's Crusade of Help. Bobby Duane lived over in Repentance, but he was always crisscrossing The Valley in a wagon, suggesting very strongly that people find it in their hearts to help him out. Pastor Grievy thought Preacher Hansen was a poor excuse for a Ruer since Ruers weren't allowed to connect their religion to money, and it was usually cash money Bobby Duane was asking people to help him out with.

"What's the catch?" Glory asked.

They looked confused, so she said, "Usually, when somebody asks you to find it in your heart to do something, it means the heart's going to find heartache right soon in the doing. At least that's what my daddy says."

"Heartache?" said the smaller one to the big one.

"Displeasure," he said, trying it out. "Pain, suffering. No, no. No suffering, no expense, no pain or adversity."

Lou Ellen was looking at Glory sadly, as though Glory had done something really unpleasant, slapped a baby, or kicked a puppy.

"It's no nevermind," Glory said, catching sight of Lou Ellen's face. "I'm just shooting off my mouth. Grandma says I give the wrong impression because I do that all the time, and it's a defense mechanism from being teased for being a mutant, and it's one I should grow out of. You go ahead and ask your favor, and I'll let you know can I do it."

The two cat-people exchanged looks, then the larger one asked, "Why are you suspected of being a mutant?"

"Oh, because I'm taller than any girl my age, and I've got this hair so black it sometimes looks blue, and my eyes are a weird color. I don't look like any of the Judsons, not any of 'em."

"I believe you are within the range of human variation," said the smaller person. "I, personally, know several people much like you, and it is unlikely you are a mutant."

The larger one was silent for a moment, nodding quietly, as though to affirm his companion's judgment. Then he stood up very straight and said, "We have a girl-child, very young. Though she is scarcely more than a baby, a great mission is foreordained for her, a duty to perform when she is a little older. Others, our enemies, will seek to prevent her doing this. Since our child must be old enough to walk and talk, at least, before she can undertake this great duty, she needs an unlikely place of safety and warmth in the care of an improbable custodian."

Glory looked at Lou Ellen, who whispered, "Why didn't they leave this baby with her grandma?"

Soft-spoken as she was, they heard her fine. "Our enemies would think first of that. She would not be safe anywhere our people are known to live or in any district where we are known to visit. This is a place we have never been before and may never come again, and this will assure she is well hidden."

"Isn't there anybody else to do this thing you're talking about her having to do?" asked Glory.

The little one reached out for the big one's hand and held it tightly. "When a task is unequivocally assigned by great wisdom, there is no point in complaint or argument. It will be done by our child, Falija, or it will not be done at all. We hope only that she will be staunch-hearted and that we can return to help her when the time has ripened."

This was said with terrible sadness.

"You're going away?" Glory asked. "You're leaving her?"

"We must. To protect her, by leading our enemies away," said the littler one, with a strange, choked sob.

Lou Ellen whispered: "How old's the baby? Is it weaned yet? Is it potty-trained?"

Her question made perfect sense. Glory's brothers, Till and Jeff, were sixteen, so she'd never had any experience with potty-training or baby feeding, but after Lou Ellen there'd been Orvie John and little Emmaline plus several babies in between who'd lived a little while before they died. Lou Ellen knew all about babies.

"Weaned?" said the smaller one. "Oh. Mammalian feeding of infants, yes, no, that is, Falija is old enough to eat food such as we have just eaten. She is also omnivorous. She can drink water from a cup. She can digest milk, but she prefers meat or vegetable things. She is still very little, not yet knowing how to . . . read? Write? Or speak very much. Our babies are . . . potty-trained almost from birth, and we use a low sandbox for the purpose."

"How long you figure you'll be gone?" Glory asked.

The bigger one shook his head. "We cannot see the future."

"And what if you don't come back?"

"What we can do, we will do, and if all goes well, we will return in time. Will you keep her for us?" The larger one sighed. In my dream, for it was a dream, the sound came to me half through my ears and half through my heart, like the grieving wind of late autumn that pulls the last leaves down, or the dark breath that gasps at the light when a deep old cellar is opened. The sigh fluttered wearily inside me, finding no rest, and Glory's face held an expression that must have been like my own. She couldn't say no.

"You know," she said, "some people don't like anything that's any different from what they're used to. I've got some personal experience with that, and I wouldn't want this little one to come to any harm . . ."

The smaller one whispered, "If you will love her, and keep her warm, and feed her, and clothe her and teach her as she grows, she will be able to keep from harm. Our people have their own ways."

"Feeding people isn't always easy," Lou Ellen commented. "Last winter, my folks didn't eat all that regular . . ."

The cat-people nodded, like they'd already figured that out. The bigger one took a little pouch from his pocket and handed it to Glory. She opened it and looked at what was inside. All I could see was a vagrant sparkle. "This is a connection to something like . . . a bank," said the big one. "When you need money for Falija, for her food, or clothing, or whatever she may need, you speak the need into the bag. Then set the bag down and leave it for a time, and when you come back, you will find what you need beside it."

"Well," said Gloriana. "That's something."

The smaller one whispered, "It will not provide forever. It is tied to us, and what happens to it, we feel. It can be broken, and we with it, so hide it away from anyone greedy or wicked or silly. It is better kept a secret thing."

Glory ducked her head. I knew she was thinking, of course it would have to be hidden away because Jeff couldn't keep anything from Til, and Til ruined everything he was a part of, and next thing I knew, they reached up into the air and pulled the baby out of nowhere as though she had been there the whole time, in an invisible crib, just floating along behind them.

She looked like the pictures I had loved in my children's books, so long ago on Phobos. She was definitely a kitten, but the size of a biggish cat, like the pictures of Earthian tiger or lion cubs, only more slender and delicate. She had big eyes, tall, tufted ears, and a triangular face pointed at the chin. She looked fragile, like something made of glass and covered with satiny golden fur, with the same curved mouth and the same pink nose as her parents. She yawned, showing elegant fangs in front and a line of chewing teeth at the sides.

Glory reached out to take her. The cat-baby looked up at her doubtfully, but when Glory cuddled her, one of the little paw hands came up to pat her nose, and Glory looked down at her in absolute adoration.

Lou Ellen said, "You're holding her wrong. You should support her head."

"It's all right," said the little cat-person. "Falija is already very strong. You don't need to worry about her neck or bones or muscles. Just . . . treat her gently and lovingly, will you, please?"

Evidently their kind of people didn't cry, because from all the sadness I could feel emanating from them, if the smaller cat-person could have cried, she'd have flooded the place.

"One more thing," the littler cat-person said, taking a little green book out of her pocket. "When Falija begins to speak, read this book to her aloud, several times. It is the key to her learning. Promise?"

"I promise," Glory said, reaching out for the book without taking her eyes from the baby.

"Good-bye," they said, and they were gone, just like that.

Later, I woke up, still under the tree, thinking what a lovely, silly dream that had been. I was stiff from sitting on the ground so long, but the remembered dream resonated happily all the way home.

Next morning I went down to get a few eggs from the chicken house, pick up my milk and paper, and maybe have a cup of tea with Maybelle while she got ready for work. I heard her moving around upstairs, and when she came down she was shaking her head the way she did when Gloriana did something weird.

"What now?" I asked

"That silly child has promised some woman she'd take care of the woman's cat while the woman is on some kind of pilgrimage to the Shrine of Sorrow over in Deep Shameful. Says the woman gave her money to do it."

I'm sure I looked at her witlessly. A cat. "When did you find this out?"

"Just now! I went in to wake her, and here in the bed is this cat. Big one, and not full-grown yet. She'd already made it a little sandbox by the door, so I can't get angry about it."

All I could think of was the strange dream I'd had the day before. "It wasn't dressed up, was it?"

"What wasn't?"

"The cat?"

"The cat was in its fur, like all cats are. What's the matter with you, Mother!"

"Sorry," I said. "I guess I'm not awake yet."

Glory came into the kitchen as her parents were getting into the carriage, plopped herself down across from me, and asked, "Anything interesting in the paper?"

"Some tragedy, some comedy, nothing that'll matter in a hundred years," I said. "I understand you've got a cat."

"It's not mine. I'm just taking care of it for somebody."

"So your mother said. Why don't you come on up to my house and be my company for breakfast?"

"I'll have to get the cat."

"Well, get it. Bring it with you."

Glory got the cat. Without clothes on it, I couldn't tell, really, whether it was like my dream cat or some other cat. We walked up the hill to my house. Billy Ray and Mayleen always fussed about my living where I did. I had told them, "Joseph built the little house for me, Billy Ray. You build a similar house over on your side of the river, I'll split my time fifty-fifty."

"I'm safe," I told Maybelle. "I told him that five years ago, and Billy Ray's still working on the plans."

When we got into my house, I got the kettle started on the wood cookstove. My little kitchen was squeezed in between the big cookstove and the sink, just big enough to turn around in, a one-person-only space. The rule was if I cooked, Glory cleaned up, and vice versa. The only other rooms were the bedroom and bathroom at the back, next to the warm closet behind the stove that held the big water tank. James pumped it full each morning, and the cookstove chimney went up through a smaller tank to make hot water.

When I put our forks and mugs on the table, I asked, "What's the cat's name?"

"Falija," Glory said.

I couldn't remember whether that name had been in my dream or not, and it didn't bear worrying about. I said, "It's time for strawberry jam. Are you going to pick for me this year?"

"Sure. Lou Ellen'll help." Glory set Falija on her lap and scratched her fur around her ears.

I continued my examination of Falija. "That's a very strange cat. Could be a Manx, since it doesn't have much of a tail."

"It's a new kind," Glory said.

I supposed she was right. It was a new kind to me, at any rate.

"It's more . . . omnivorous, like people," Glory said. "The . . . lady told me so."

Falija was standing on her hind legs with her front ones on the table, making the little prruup prruup noises. "She's hungry," Glory announced. "Can I fix a plate for her?"

I nodded, fascinated by this little animal. Glory found some left-over oatmeal in a pot on the stove, an apple in a bowl, and a chicken leg in the refrigerator. She cut everything up in pieces and put it on a plate. The moment Falija saw it, she jumped off the chair and cleaned the plate, including the pieces of apple, eating slowly and neatly, while I scrambled eggs and made toast.

When the cat had finished eating, Glory fetched a little bowl of water and Falija washed. First she took a little drink, then she dipped her paw in the water and washed her face, and dipped and washed down her neck and around her ears, and then she dried off the paw on the rug.

"That's not any ordinary cat," I said around a mouthful of scrambled eggs. "Gloriana, tell me truthfully, where did you get that creature?"

Glory looked out the window for a while, then she looked me in the eye. "A lady gave me some money to take care of her for a while and keep her safe. She's very smart, Grandma."

"She's a mutation of some sort," I half whispered, as though I were afraid someone would hear me.

"That's what everybody says I probably am, because I don't look anything like all the rest of the Judsons. Every single one of them has light hair and blue or green eyes but me, including you, and Aunt Mayleen and Mama, and they're only Judsons by marriage."

I stared out the window. "Oh, somewhere in the line, there's always a dark-haired ancestor."

"Well, it's nobody recent," said Gloriana. "And nobody else is my size, either."

Falija climbed onto my lap. She had claws, but when she climbed, she just barely caught the clothes. Her claws didn't touch the skin, and there she was on my lap, turning around and around, and settling down to have a nap, still going prruup prruup prruup and opening those huge eyes to stare at me. I stroked her, very softly, while her little pawlike hands pressed and released against my leg, kneading and kneading.

"She certainly acts like a mammal," I said. "That's what kittens do with their feet at the mother's mammaries, pressing and kneading that way. It's like baby goats and lambs and calves, butting at the udder. But, Glory, those paws, those eyes, she's not a real cat. Some kind of marsupial, maybe? Her hind legs and pelvis aren't built like a cat's, and neither is her head. She has a much higher skull than a cat . . ."

"Maybe she's just a newly discovered species."

"No species I ever learned about while I was at school. No kind I've ever read about, either. Of course, there's no special reason she should be terrestrial." I gave Glory a hard, searching look. "I'd be inclined to say she's neither Tercian nor Earthian."

"I've told you the truth," Glory said, turning red. "And you can see for yourself she's just a baby and needs taking care of. And that's what I'm going to do."

"All right," I said, "But Gloriana, you promise me something. If you need help with this little one, you come straight here to me! Promise, now."

Since I was already the one Gloriana went to when she was in trouble, I figured it would be an easy promise.

When Glory had finished with our dishes, Falija was asleep, so we sat out on my little porch while Gloriana went back to wondering why she was so different from all the other Judsons.

"And something else," she said. "How come my mama and Lou Ellen's mama don't look alike when they're identical twins?"

"They used to look alike," I said. I fetched the album from the bookshelves inside. "See there, that's when they were babies. You couldn't tell the difference between them." The picture was of Maybelle and Mayleen as babies, sitting back to back on a picnic bench, like a pair of bookends. "It wasn't that they were born looking different, Glory. It's how they've lived their lives."

"They have different personalities," Glory said. "You'd think that should be the same, too."

"One would expect so," I said, for hadn't I expected just that? Time to change the subject. "Your mother says you have a litter box for Falija."

"Yes. And she knows how to use it."

"She has a very short tail. Hardly as long as my thumb. She has a poophole." That's what we all called it. It isn't polite, but the more common words are abusive and contemptuous, and the correct terms occasion intense embarrassment among the Rueful, as though they referred to something esoteric and possibly blasphemous.

"Poophole is at least a specific vulgarity rather than generalized lewdness," said Glory, grinning at me. She sometimes quotes me word for word. She remembers a lot of things people say, whole paragraphs that seem to stick in her mind like a caramel on teeth. Funny child. I loved her very much.

"Lou Ellen was with me when the lady gave me Falija," Glory said, not looking at me. "I asked her to stay last night, but she wouldn't. Whenever I ask her to stay, she says, 'No, no, Glory. It's all right. It's a pretty path along the water and through the fields, and I keep looking for . . . things.'

"Grandma, what do you think she's looking for? It's a mile up to the notch where the bridge is and three miles from there, by the road, to Billy Ray's farm. Lou Ellen says it doesn't take her any time at all, so she has to have a secret way to cross the river. She never shared it with me, and we share everything, absolutely everything, but not that, and it hurts my feelings."

I didn't have to answer, because Falija had wakened. She reached up with a little paw and patted Glory's chin, wiping off a tear. Then she licked the paw, and that made Glory smile and forget about Lou Ellen.

I didn't forget, however, because I'd seen her in that weird dream yesterday. On the pier. Talking to the strange people, Falija's parents. I didn't believe that dream had been real, not at all, so perhaps I was going absolutely mad, instead of simply partially mad, an idea that for some time had seemed rather convincing.

I Am Naumi, with Fernwold

"I knew a woman, Naumi," said Fernwold, who was sitting in hot water up to his chin. "Years ago."

"Ah," I replied, opening one eye. "And you're just now remembering her? Why?"

"You just reminded me of her, somehow. Perhaps it's the way the steam curls your hair around your ears. Hers did that, too. Or maybe I was just thinking of hot pools, and it reminded me of B'yurngrad. That's where she was . . . is."

I gritted my teeth at the thought of Ferni and his woman, reminding myself sternly that this obsession was a private one, never mentioned, never to be shared. Ferni had every right to be attracted to some woman, damn her, whoever she should be. "Who is this woman?" I asked, managing to sound interested.

"Set out to be a translator for the Diplomatic Corps. Got detoured into being a bondslave. Freak accident marooned her on B'yurngrad. Siblinghood picked her up, sent her into the wastelands to learn shamanism."

"Did she have a name?" I asked, merely to show I was listening.

"M'urgi," Fernwold said. "That's what the shaman named her. I forget what it means."

"Something mythic, no doubt." I sat up a little so I could see the arrival and departure board by the door. I liked very much being with Ferni, but if he was going to talk about women, I would just as soon be somewhere else. Besides, nonplanetary transshipment points had a reputation for last-minute changes in boarding times.

In this case, it was no help. I still had entirely too much time. I let myself slip into the wet once again. This particular transshipment point, Gilfras Station, had been established by that ancient and honored race, the Pthas, only they knew how long ago. Its current crew mined comets for water and made a very good thing out of it, that is if everyone paid what Ferni and I had paid for a private bath, and why in heaven's name had I done that!

Ferni mused, "A name that's mythic? I suppose that's possible. Last time I was among other Siblings, I heard the shaman died, and M'urgi was called to active duty, still on B'yurngrad."

"How long since you've seen her?" I asked.

"Been with her? Oh, ten, eleven Earth-count years, I suppose. Maybe more."

"Not unusual for you. I didn't see you for a full five years after we left the academy."

His forehead furrowed as he said tentatively, "I was busy, running about. That whole time is hazy."

"And you're wanting to go see . . . what? If you remember her correctly? If she remembers you?"

With a great thrashing of water, Fernwold sat up.

"There was something about her, Naumi! When I first saw her, I felt I'd known her for years. When we talked, I could have been talking to you, she was so familiar. She could have been your identical twin."

"No she couldn't!" It sounded rude even to me. I amended, "That is, not if she was female."

"I don't mean biologically." Ferni subsided, letting the water flow over his chin once more, stopping just short of his lips. "Psychologically, maybe. Maybe nothing, just an addled mind seeking connections." He stared moodily into the water, seeking answers. "I applied for some leave to go find her a few years back. They said no. She was busy, too busy to be interrupted. The Siblinghood is worse than the

Omnions, I swear. At least the Omnionts let you go after fifteen years."

"Do you want to be let go?" And oh, wouldn't I bless and curse the day that happened. If Ferni were just . . . elsewhere, where he could be remembered with joy and without this constant internal battle not to get personally involved!

"That's not what I meant!"

Silence except for the soft plutter of wavelets against the sides of the tiled pool, the shlush of the water running away to the boiler, the gurgle as it returned.

"If you can get your shamanistic friend off your mind for a little while," I said. "I asked you to meet me here because I need your help,"

Ferni looked up, lips curving. "I have more to say about her, but I can give you a few minutes, Noomi."

Ignoring the slur, I explained. "The Siblinghood has given me a problem." I paused to think, rubbing my face with the back of my hand. I needed a shave. At age thirty-six, thirty-seven, maybe it was time to grow a beard. Which was simply a divagation, putting off the ridiculous, or the sublime, I had no idea which. I said as quickly as possible, "Somewhere within our reach there's a being no one has ever seen, and this being knows everything."

"What did you say?"

I repeated myself.

"The Siblinghood knows this?" Ferni, incredulous.

I sat up, removed the wet towel from around my head, and said, "I'm told the Siblinghood presumes this to be true."

"Why, in the name of Chamfalow's chief cook?"

"Well, this is the way it was explained to me: Mankind is in a very dangerous situation regarding survival as a race. Unlike every other presumably well-intentioned race, we do not have a racial memory . . ."

"You're joking! The Gentherans have a racial memory? The Pthas had a racial memory? And the Garrick?"

"According to what I've been told, all of them do or did, yes."

"Since one already knows a good deal of human history, one expects there must be a catch in there somewhere."

"Isn't there always? As I understand it, the memory in question would include everything back to the time our parental primate stepped down out of a tree. Maybe even farther back, to the first time we crawled out of the ooze. And, we must know it, not learn it. Know it so we feel it in our bones. Or membranes, if we didn't have bones at the time. We have to remember war, not merely think about it. We have to remember struggle, and pain, and having beasts eat our children. Presumably, this inner knowledge would halt our tendency to do the precipitous, silly, and often very dangerous things that people reared in relative safety often do for stupid or prideful leaders, like sheep running ahead of a purposeful, nipping dog.

"The only hope of finding such a memory lies in our finding someone or something who knows everything, including the true history of the human race. The solution also requires that this thing or creature exist within our reach, since if it doesn't, its mere existence is of no consequence to mankind."

"Ah," said Ferni, wiping steam out of his eyes. "And?"

"The problem they've given me is to find the being."

"To *presume* there's a being, then *find* it."

"More or less, yes."

"I presume there's a pot of universal elixir sitting on the bench in the changing room; I think I'll go find that." Ferni snorted, getting water up his nose.

I didn't reply.

Ferni said, "You're serious?"

"Deadly serious. They told me it is likely the penalty for not finding it will be our own extinction, sooner or later, and not much later at that. Have you ever . . . have you ever seen recordings of the planet they call Hell?"

"Ugh." Ferni ducked under the water, came up spluttering. "I'm a member of the Siblinghood, Naumi! I've never heard of any of this! Unless . . . could it be a Third Order thing?"

My eyebrows went up at this. "This plan or plot or whatever one may call it, is being implemented by a small secret group within your organization. Is there a secret group called the Third Order? If so, very interesting, because it's not the first time they've fiddled with my life. They had something to do with my being at the academy in the first place."

After a considerable silence, Ferni offered, "I know the name. Is it possible some kind of . . . spatial anomaly is involved in all this?"

"Well, if the thing exists, it has to exist somewhere. An anomalous location might explain why no one knows where."

"I wonder if the old talk road would come up with anything?"

"The other four are meeting me on Thairy. That's why I asked you to meet me here. There's a quick route from here to Thairy. And to B'yurngrad, if you're wanting to look up your shamaness. Just think, one day there from here, one day to Thairy from here. No lost time. Lucky Pthas to find the wormhole to end all wormholes . . ." I realized I was babbling and fell silent.

Fernwold steamed. "All this vapor is doing nothing for my powers of ratiocination. Assuming I have any. Do we know anything at all about this being?"

"The Siblinghood archives have several ancient stories that involve something or someone called the Keeper. Many of them were preserved by the Pthas, and that fact lends them additional credence. Some of the stories drop clues to the Keeper's approachability. The number seven figures prominently. There are a few phrases common to most of the stories. 'One person walking seven roads at once finds the Keeper.' Or, 'Seven roads are one road.' Most of the stories are about untangling a difficulty or solving a problem . . ."

"And we want this Keeper because it, or he, knows everything?"

"It, I think. Knows everything. Yes."

Ferni emerged gradually from the water, heaved himself out of the pool, and reached for a towel. "Tell me one of the stories."

I gawked at him, then averted my eyes.

"Come on, Noomi! Presumably they told you some of the stories. Tell me one!"

"I can tell you one about a man and a fish," I said.

Now it so happened that a man of Dabberding was walking along the River Rush one day when a fish spoke to him from the shallows along the bank.

"Hi there, you, man," said the fish. "How is the world treating you?"

"Not well," growled the man of Dabberding. "My wife is ill, my children need shoes, the cow went dry, my donkey is lame, my old dog is on her last legs, and a fox is eating my chickens, one after the other."

"Ah," said the fish. "That must make you very angry."

"It makes me boil," said the man of Dabberding. "My wife is sick because my neighbor dragged her out in a rainstorm to help him gather up his geese. My children need shoes because they went to help their mother and ruined the shoes I'd just bought them. The cow went dry because my neighbor said his bull would breed her for less then I usually pay. The bull was no good, but my neighbor wouldn't give me my money back. The donkey is lame because my wife had to ride her in the mud, into the village, to see the healer. My old dog is on her last legs because she caught cold for trying to bring the geese in, and the fox is eating my chickens because my neighbor's no-good bull bashed a hole in the coop, and I've no wire to fix it with."

"So you're angry," said the fish.

"Oh, if my neighbor were here in front of me, I'd bash him bloody," said the man of Dabberding. "This is all his fault."

"Is there anything you're angry about that the right information wouldn't fix?" asked the fish.

The man of Dabberding thought for a while, then he said, "I would know how I could heal my wife, how to make shoes for the children, where I could find a good bull, where I could find a little money to rent another donkey to let my donkey rest until his leg gets better, who's giving away a good pup so my old dog could lie contented in the sun, and how to keep the vermin out of my chicken coop."

"Then the problem is solved," said the fish. "I will tell you where to go."

So the fish told him to go down a certain forest road, and up a certain steep hill, and through a long thicket, and out onto a precipice where a little temple stood all by itself, and inside the temple was an altar, and on the altar was an image. "That little image has all the information in the universe," it said. "There's nothing it doesn't know."

So the man of Dabberding set off down the forest road. As he went, he thought about his encounter with the fish, and as he thought about that it gradually came to him that the little temple the fish spoke of might possibly belong to King Frum the Furious, and a bad-tempered, ill-natured king he was, too.

Still, the fish hadn't said anything about it, so the man from Dabberding went on until he came to the steep hill, which he climbed, and into the thicket, which he fought his way through, then out onto the precipice where the temple stood. Sure enough, inside was an altar stone, and on the stone was an image, a statue of a little old man with a long beard and a wrinkled face and squinched-up eyes, sitting cross-legged and peering at a golden book in his lap, a book with writing that flowed across the page like water.

Well, the man from Dabberding didn't even pause for thought. He took the image, wrapped it in his jacket, and went across the temple to look over the cliff edge to see where he was in relation to the river and the places he knew. He had just located the river when he heard loud voices coming from below. He looked around, and there was a path coming up the cliff from one side with men on it, and there was another path leading along the cliff with more men on it, both headed in his direction. He couldn't get back to the thicket without being seen. He couldn't even get into the temple without being seen. If they found him with the little image in his shirt, they would kill him for sure.

So the man sobbed silently, threw the image far out into the air, watched it fall partway, then he sat down on the precipice and waited.

The men arrived, among them King Frum the Furious, and they found the image missing at once. They surrounded the man of Dabberding and asked him where the little man with the golden book was. "I don't know," he said truthfully, for he hadn't seen it land. "Who was it an image of?" he asked, because he didn't know that either.

They knocked him down and searched him, but he had no statue. They searched the edges of the thicket, but there was no statue. And all the while the king lamented and lamented that his luck was gone, the pride of his lineage was gone, the image of the keeper was gone.

"Keeper?" asked the man from Dabberding. "What's a keeper?"

"It's a thing that knew all the king's secrets," whispered one of the men-at-arms. "That little statue knows everything that has ever happened in the whole world."

"In the whole universe," whispered another man-at-arms. "Where could it have gone?"

"An eagle, perhaps," said the man from Dabberding. "Or a large raven. Ravens like sparkly things."

"That's true," said the first man-at-arms, and he went to tell the king, who was still lamenting. After a time, the man-at-arms came back and told the man from Dabberding to get himself gone before the king remembered he was there, which the man did very quickly, fading himself into the thicket like a rabbit into a burrow.

The man got himself through the thicket, down the hill, back down the road, and again to the riverbank where he'd met the fish. "Fish, fish," he called. "I'm very angry. I barely escaped with my skin."

The fish came up to the bank, and when the man told him what had happened, the fish asked, "Is there anything making you angry that can't be solved with the right information?"

"Probably not," said the man.

"Well then, go get the information," said the fish. "It must be lying along one of the seven roads that lead to the bottom of the cliff."

"Seven roads," cried the man. "It's already getting along toward evening."

"Then you'd better hurry," said the fish.

Since the man had seen the riverbank from the top of the hill, he figured the roads must come from the river, so he walked along the bank in the proper direction until he came to a road that turned toward the cliff he could see through the trees. He ran very quickly along that road, stopping only once when the sun caught something shining in the undergrowth that turned out to be one of the legs of the image he had tossed from the top of the cliff. Well, one leg was one leg, but a leg wouldn't help him, so the man went on down the road until it came right to the foot of the cliff and turned back toward the river at an angle.

So he ran and ran along this road, stopping only once when he saw something lying on the path, which turned out to be the other leg of the image he had thrown from the cliff top. Well, two legs was two legs, but the whole statue was better, so he went on running toward the river, where the road suddenly turned back toward the cliff again. On that road he found an arm, and on the next turn, another arm. And on the next turn, which was number five, he found the body, and on the next turn toward the river again, he found the head, which was all very well, but the book with the letters running across it was still missing.

It was almost dark when the man started on the seventh road, going toward the cliffs for the fourth time, and he was actually at the cliffs when he saw it, shining at him in the last of the sunlight. So he sat down and put the statue together, and when he put the book into his lap, he saw words there.

"How to cure your wife's illness," he read. And this was followed by a recipe for a medicine made out of very common plants that the man found on his way home.

That night, after he had given his wife the medicine, he looked at the book again. This time it said, "How to cure lameness in a donkey," followed by a recipe for a poultice made out of very common things he happened to have around the house. And when he had done that, he looked at the book again, and saw the words "How to make ruined shoes like new again," followed by a simple procedure the man was able to manage before he went to bed.

In the morning, the book told him of a widow living just down the road who had a pup she was giving away and who also had a bull she would let him use in return for the resultant calf. Then the book told him where he could find some discarded fence to mend his chicken coop. And last of all, the book told him what to do in order to be rid of his neighbor, a few very simple words having to do with misdeeds discovered and forces of law on the way, whispered in the neighbor's ear.

The neighbor packed his cart and moved out before lunchtime. The man from Dabberding watched the cart go off down the road, the useless bull hitched to the back. Then the man from Dabberding remembered what the man-at-arms had said about the Keeper knowing everything in the whole world, so he knelt before the image and said, "Keeper, you have been very kind to me, and I'm not angry anymore, and I want to do for you whatever you most desire. Please tell me what that is."

Then he looked at the book, and the words ran across it, saying, "Roads out, roads back, seven roads was one road. Cow, donkey, dog, wife, shoes, fox, neighbor, seven cures was one cure. Two arms, two legs, body, head, book, seven parts was one Keeper. Let one person walk seven roads at once, go where they meet and find me there." And with that, the Keeper vanished, leaving only the story behind.

"That's the story," I concluded.
"Sorry, Naumi, but it doesn't tell me much."
"It didn't me, either," I replied.

"When did you say the others are getting to Thairy?" he asked after a few moments.

"They'll ostensibly come for the class reunion, but they'll arrive several days early."

"Well then." Ferni dried his legs, saying thoughtfully, "I wish M'urgi were here. She had a very good head on her shoulders."

I frowned, for the name teased at me. "M'urgi. Interesting name. Why don't you go find her, Ferni?" I took a deep breath, managing a casual tone. "We have quite a bit of time before the reunion. Bring her along."

Fernwold, wrapped in the towel, sat down on the stone bench beside the pool and fixed me with his "This is important" stare. "I was going to locate her anyhow, because of this other thing I wanted to tell you about. It happened a day or two ago. I was sitting in a tranship-tavern waiting for departure time, the way one does, not thinking about anything much, when I overheard someone saying, 'The word came down all the way from the top.' Someone else replied, 'That doesn't make sense.' The first voice said, 'Sometimes it doesn't make sense, but the orders are, she's got to be killed, and it has to be done soon.'

"That got my full attention. The second voice said, 'Why her? Why some smoke-flavored old shaman's hag from the steppes of B'yurngrad.' The first one said, 'No hag, she's young yet.'"

I frowned at him. "So, you put shaman, smoke-flavored, B'yurngrad, and suchlike together, assuming they meant your friend?"

"Exactly. I casually looked at the people around me. A dozen races at least, most of them speaking interlingua . . ."

"Any accent?"

"No lisping, so not K'Famir. They didn't curse one another, so probably not Frossian. There was no discernible stink, probably not Hrass." He paused. "There were a few elder races there, too, very strange old ones, the kind that make you go elsewhere when you see them coming, you know . . ."

"Quaatar? Baswoidin?"

"Quaatar? Yes, now you mention it. There were a couple of them." He sighed. "You're at least taking me seriously."

"It could be serious. Why, precisely, do you believe so?"

"Some time ago, the word filtered down through the Siblinghood that the leaders wanted to be informed if any of us caught wind of 'Top-down threats to specific and seemingly harmless humans . . . '"

"If you've quoted the conversation correctly, the threat was definitely top down. It may be be smart to check on her, my friend."

"She probably won't even remember me."

Oh, she'd remember him! "Come now. Unforgettable Ferni?"

My friend laughed ruefully. "Meantime, I'll keep your puzzle in mind. Will the others be with you for a while?" As he dressed himself, he seemed to forget whatever the strangeness had been. He looked more like himself.

I said, "All during reunion. I'll be there for even longer, because I've agreed to teach a course at Point Zibit."

"Professor Noomi," drawled Ferni. "Why, I knew him when he was only a worm."

I Am Mar-agern/on Fajnard

As the end of my years of bondage approached, the enmity of the Frossian overseer increased, and its verbal hostility toward me became more frequent. It had not forgotten I could speak and understand Frossian, so I knew these open threats were part of its general plan of harassment.

"We agree," said Deen-agern, the Ghoss, when I mentioned it to him. "Frossians do not forget much. They are completely ignorant of enormous areas of knowledge, but they don't forget things that happen to them. It's time we got you out of here, Mar-Mar."

"I have less than a year of bondage left!"

The Ghoss raised a nostril. "You have only as long as they want you to have. Fifteen years is enough for most slaves: the bones are weakened, the back is bent, the strength is exhausted, and the Frossians are willing to let them go. Only draining the last of a slave's strength at the end of its bondage proves they have gained their money's worth: a full fifteen years of labor, with the least possible strength left over to go elsewhere, often just enough for the ex-slave to totter across the landing field to the colony ship. This is so well known that we counsel bondspeople to pretend greater and greater weakness during their last several years."

"You've never told me that!"

"We had no reason to, even though you've stayed strong, and the Frossians have felt they weren't getting full value for their money. Now, however, something new has happened. We've heard the Frossians talking. Some very important breeding male has communicated with the planetary leader here on Fajnard. It, in turn, has informed the least overlord that a bondswoman who speaks Frossian is to be killed, quickly and without delay. The least overlord has told the overseer, the one who keeps threatening you."

"Why?" I cried. "The only Frossians I've ever seen are here, here on Fajnard. Why would some overlord care about me?"

"You don't know; we don't know. Certainly the least overlord doesn't know or care, and the overseer doesn't care because it was going to kill you anyhow. You'd be dead by now except for the umoxen. We know they warm you in winter, protect you at all times. They prevent the Frossians from stealing your clothes and food and from fouling your water. Is this not so?"

"You know it is."

"Well, depend upon it, the overseer also knows it's so. Very soon now, some Frossian or other will separate you from the umoxen, take you elsewhere, and you will not return."

"The overseer hasn't said this."

"Of course not. The overseer knows you understand what it says. It says only what it means you to hear. To make you look in the wrong direction."

I frowned, saying hesitantly, "Where am I to go? This is the only place on Fajnard that I know."

"There's a better place, and we'll take you there. It's the place we Ghoss go, when we are weary of serving the creatures."

"Why you serve them at all is more than I can understand!"

"True. It is more than you can understand, at least for now. After a time in the hills, you may understand it."

The next evening, when a plether of umoxen were pastured in the fields with only me to watch them, several of the huge creatures wandered over and began to hum at me. "Mar-Mar, time to go away."

"You've been talking to the Ghoss," I said.

"Ghoss been talking to us," they remarked. "Time. You stay until tomorrow, something bad will happen, so, we go tonight. Get on up." It knelt on its front legs, giving me a foreleg to step up on.

It was the first time one of them had offered to carry me, but I did not hesitate. The small group of them started for the fence between the pasture and the river bottom, all the rest of the plether following along. At the fence they simply leaned against the posts until they broke off, then amused themselves by trampling vast lengths of fence into the ground and crossing them with trodden umox-paths, back and forth, humming as they went, finally splitting in a dozen different ways, one of which led through the riparian woods and into the wide but shallow stream of late summer. Here the umox knelt again as I splashed into the water. I saw the umoxen distributing themselves widely among the stream-side woods. The umox I had ridden touched my cheek with its tongue and went to join them.

"Mar," said a familiar voice. "Over here."

Rei was standing in the stream, a pack on his back.

I went to join him. "I didn't bring anything with me."

"You didn't have anything you'll need," he said. "Come, we go upstream. Stay in the water."

The water was cool but not icy, coming only to our ankles. I put my head down and waded, occasionally turning aside from a large stone or dead tree that had been washed down during flood. The journey was hypnotic, the water gurgling around my feet, the plethers humming in the pastures we passed, the small creatures cheeping and chirping in scattered reed beds. I lost track of time and did not think of it again until I looked up through the branches of a shutter-leaf tree to see the sky growing light. The branches creaked, the leaves turned to face the sun, an eye at the end of a branch winked at me.

We had entered a low-walled canyon. Rei said, "Far enough! We will sleep through the daylight."

"Where?" I asked wearily.

"My customary wayhalt. Up there." He turned between two massive tree boles onto an almost invisible trail that led up the canyon wall to a small cave, well hidden behind a protruding outcropping of stone. We sat, Rei took food from his pack and handed it to me. We ate without speaking, and I fell into sleep the moment I lay down.

Rei's hand over my mouth wakened me. "Shhh," he whispered. "We have searchers down in the stream."

Together we crawled to the mouth of the cave and peeked around the outcropping that hid the entrance from below. I saw torches and smelled their smoke. I heard the angry jabber of irritated Frossians.

"There's no trail."

"If there was a trail, we couldn't see it in torchlight."

"Better go back, get some provisions, come back and try again in the light."

"The least overlord will kill us!"

The voices continued their jabber, becoming softer as they retreated, back the way we had come. Rei stood at the opening of the cave, reading the air as the Ghoss often did, for it was full of messages from their kinfolk, who might be anywhere on the planet at all.

"Deen says the Frossians are angry," he reported, with an air of satisfaction. "They had a great deal of trouble rounding up the umoxen. Some of them think you were probably killed in the stampede. The least overlord, however, insists that they find your body. He has to tell his overlord that he has seen you dead with his own eyes. Your enemy, the herd overseer, thinks you have slipped away in the confusion. He has sworn to hunt you down. We must hurry to reach the falunassa."

I puzzled at the word as I translated it into Frossian. *Those in the faraway*. "Is that their name?"

"It's a descriptive term for people in hiding. Here, they are the Gibbekot. If humans live on a planet, the Gibbekot become falunassa in faraway mountains perhaps, or deep deserts, or great canyons, always in the most secret places. They are not fearful. They simply prefer not to have the problems that result from unlike creatures housed too closely together."

I stared into the distance. "Won't the Gibbekot object to my coming?"

"No. You've been described to them. We told them the umoxen had adopted you. That was sufficient endorsement." He returned to the cave and picked up his pack. "Let's put space between us and this place before those Frossians return."

Luckily, we had a moon providing enough light to let us see our way on up the canyon, past confluences with other small streams, the wash growing narrower, shallower, and rockier the farther we went, at last dividing itself neatly into two tumbling brooks, left and right, both leading up stony channels.

"Here we go," said Rei, as he turned to the right and began climbing up the stream, from rock to rock.

I followed. There had been a time, I reflected, when this journey would have been impossible for me. On Earth I would have been too weak and too flabby to have walked any distance at all carrying a pack. My flesh had grown hard during the years of bondage. Perhaps I should thank the Frossians for that.

During the next few hours, as we passed several other places where streams or dry washes came in from the sides and as the stream we followed became a mere trickle, I became less sure I should thank anyone. "Rei, how much farther do we climb?"

"Not far. You're doing well."

It still seemed a great distance. The sky was growing light when a breeze from behind us carried a great uproar to our ears. Shouting. Something mechanical, roaring.

"Aircar," said Rei. "Hurry."

I managed to be close behind him as he climbed the last plunging stretch of piled stone and stood erect at the top. "There," he said, pointing. "Gibbekot country."

We stood on a natural dike. The source of the stream we had followed was a small lake stretching from the dike at our feet eastward toward green pastures sloping upward to gently rounded hills, these backed in their turn by receding ranges of blue mountains. Umoxen grazed in the valley, but there was no sign of other inhabitants.

Rei moved to one side, thrust his hand into a crevice in the rock, and pulled. Somewhere wheels turned and creaked. Somewhere a valve opened and the lake before us developed an eddy that spun itself into a vortex. Below and behind us, a spate of water boiled out of the rivulet to gush wildly over the rocks we had climbed, the soil where we might have left tracks, any surface where any trace of us might have remained. Rei stood for some time, watching the water wash away all traces of us, and when he was satisfied, he thrust his hand into the crevice once more and shut the water down. As it silenced, we heard the roaring again, nearer.

He plunged into the shallow water and began to wade around its edge. "There are a dozen sizable streams entering the river we walked in. After rain, any of them might be in spate. There are about fifty little canyons and washes on this upper stretch, where we climbed, and the same is true of the other forks. Even if the Frossians have the patience to search them all, they are unlikely to get this far, and if they get this far, they will get no farther. Frossians like dampness, but they're afraid of open water." He raised his head and called across the valley. The echoes returned, amplified. An umox, the nearest, turned ponderously from its grazing and came toward us, down the left side of the lake. Rei plowed through the shallows to intercept it, with me close behind. The umox waded out to meet us; Rei grabbed handfuls of the creature's long hair and pulled himself onto its back, then tugged me up beside him. The umox lumbered out onto the meadow and across the grasslands toward the nearest grove of trees. It did not speak to us, at least, not in any way I could hear.

"Scenters won't be able to smell us," I said.

"Not over the smell of the umoxen, no," Rei agreed. "Here. Pull the back of my cloak up over yourself. It's unlikely they will see us, and we will be under cover soon."

I covered myself. Rei lay flat on the broad umox back, and I lay on his back, both of us covered in a cloak very much the color of the umox's wool. The roaring came close, closer. The umox stopped, grazed, took a few steps, grazed again. I was about to panic when Rei murmured, "From above, the umox is one of a herd, all grazing. Hear them?"

I did hear them, all around us. Our own umox was working its way steadily through the herd toward the edge. Peeking from below the robe, I saw trees not far away. The herd leader snorted, and all of them moved into the trees, quite quickly, as the machine roared directly overhead, turning to return, even lower.

By that time, we were on the ground, lying in a hollow beneath a fallen tree, and the herd was moving into the open pasture once more. Rei said, "Anyone searching along the ground will find valleys full of umoxen on every side, streams everywhere, many little canyons and tricky places easy to get into and hard to get out of. Frossians have explored here from time to time, but none has ever left here to tell others what he may have found."

"Why did you bring me here?"

"We Ghoss were told to bring you, reason enough."

"Told by whom, Rei!"

He shrugged. "Those who have the authority to do so."

I gave up in frustration. Be thankful, I told myself. Be damned thankful you're here instead of down there. The words resonated, bringing a childhood memory. Be thankful we're up here, on Phobos, not in that windstorm down there on Mars. Be thankful you survived your bondage. Be thankful for your strength, your endurance. Be thankful you didn't go with Bryan, wherever he ended up going. Be thankful you didn't run off on the dragonfly, when you were a little girl. Be thankful the woods are all around us, for the aircar circled endlessly above us.

Be resentful about all those years of language study, however, for all they did was get you into trouble with the Frossians. Of course, I wasn't dead yet. Language might still have some use.

"Here," said Rei, pointing ahead once more. "Here is the Gate of the Gibbekot, and through it is the way to your freedom."

Our way led into a shallow valley grown up in forest. On both sides the trees marched up slopes that grew gradually steeper. This was a new thing for me. I had labored for fifteen years among the riverside woods that drained the pastures of the umoxen: a few large purple-leaf trees, widely separated, with thin saplings and brush between, and never any feeling of being cut off from the light. Here, the darkness was a palpable presence even at the edge of the forest, a deepening reality as we went farther to be surrounded by many kinds of trees: the shutter-leaf, which seemed ubiquitous; silver-leaf, columnar black-bolled trees with leaves that were silver on the bottom; parasol-trees, with huge, tall green-gray trunks culminating in a flat canopy well above the general forest, some dark green, some laden with brilliant red fringes. We could see perfectly well, it wasn't a question of being unable to see, but it was like seeing in late evening, bulks and masses of shadow, movement rather than form, a muffling of sound along with nose-filling, palate-touching smells, mostly resinous, occasionally threatening. I shuddered.

Rei patted my shoulder and pointed to a tree we were passing. "That's what's making you shiver. We call that Fros-bane. Take a good look at it. You don't want to touch it, ever."

The bole was a pale green, smooth as my own skin, with tiny beads of amber upon it, evenly spread as dew.

"See those drops? That's the bad stuff. Like an acid. Eats your skin, gets into your blood, you end curled up in a circle, screaming at the pain. The Gibbekot have planted them all through the woods, along here. They're immune to the stuff, but the Frossians aren't."

"The trees might work better if they didn't smell so bad," I opined. "I'd avoid them just because of the smell."

Rei grinned. "Frossians have no sense of smell. Didn't anyone ever tell you that?"

I glared at him. "They've been saying I stink for the better part of fifteen years!"

"They say it because we say it. If the hay is moldy, we say it stinks. The Frossians think it means rotten, evil, malign. They can see in the infrared, but they have no sense of smell. Ghoss do, however. Umoxen do, and the Gibbekot don't want to hurt Ghoss or umoxen."

I thought about this. "Is this tree natural? Or was it genetically created by the Gibbekot?"

"Why do you ask?"

"Because poisons and thorns and other defenses usually evolve against a particular life-form. The Frossians aren't native here, so it wasn't against them. What kind of thing threatened these trees to make them develop this defense?"

Rei said over his shoulder, "The Gibbekot got them from the world where the Frossian queens live. It's the only world that's truly Frossian, the great hatchery from which they all come, and there are deep valleys there full of trees that had already evolved defenses. The Gibbekot just sent for them."

"The Gibbekot are spacefaring?" I asked in amazement. "You never said they were spacefaring."

"I still haven't. I said sent, not went. Now hush. You're making too much noise. That aircar may be carrying listening devices, and we need to keep our eyes and ears open."

To me, whatever path we followed was indistinguishable from any other way among the trees. The forest floor was covered with a thick blanket of leaves, needles, mosses, all held together by the wiry stems of ubiquitous creeper that grew only a finger's width high but unendingly wide. When I turned to look back, the way we had come, I couldn't see a footprint anywhere. The creeper simply flattened beneath our feet and sprang back once we had passed.

I whispered, "How are you finding your way?"

"Ghossways," came the reply. "Now hush."

I hushed. We heard the aircar behind us, in the direction of the lake, I thought. It came a little closer, then turned back the way it had come. We walked for an hour or more, then began to climb as the floor of the valley climbed. By this time, evening had come, all aircar sounds had ceased, and the darkness beneath the trees had increased enough that I was eager to emerge from the gloom. Within a few hundred yards, we came from the shadow into the red light of sunset, the sky scattered with clouds ranging from gold to crimson to violet-gray. Before emerging, we scanned the sky carefully to be sure it was empty. When we were sure, we climbed a slanting ledge to an outcropping of stone that jutted from the hilltop, a narrow slot in it leading to another small, sheltered cave.

"How many of these places are there?" I asked.

"Enough to hide us, whatever direction we go. Tonight we stop here," said Rei, gesturing to include sandy floor, smooth walls, a store of firewood stacked high against one wall, a water jar, sacks of food. "They know we're here. When they're ready, they'll send for us."

"And until then?" I asked.

"We can build a fire, heat some food, talk about the weather, read a book—I brought one for you . . ."

"A book," I breathed. "I haven't read anything for . . ."

"I know," he said. "I brought you a book written by a Gibbekot. We'll read it together, and that will give you a taste of their language."

I warmed myself at the fire, ate the food Rei provided, drank the tea he gave me, something new, something with an oddly attractive taste. I started to look at the book, a simple collection of words, one to a page, but was too sleepy to go on. Yawning, I curled up beside the fire.

I was not asleep. It felt like a dream while asleep, but I knew it wasn't a dream. Rei watched me. When I was totally relaxed, he reached out to shake me. I tried to speak, couldn't speak, tried to move, couldn't move. I should have been afraid, but I wasn't. It was peaceful where I was, a firelit bubble of complete tranquillity.

"She's sleeping," he called.

The two beings who materialized at the entrance to the cave spoke to Rei with soft voices as they carefully unwrapped something they had brought with them. Rei turned me onto my stomach and applied whatever it was gently to the base of my skull. I felt something there, a kind of creepiness, as of something settling into place.

"How long will she be like that?" asked Rei.

One of the beings said, "Until it's completely absorbed. It grows up under the skull in back, very thin, very flat. Then it has to connect to the rest of the brain, and that takes a while."

The other said, "It takes a good while, actually. It could take as long as a season . . ."

"She'll go on sleeping all that time?" asked Rei, with a furtive look at the stack of supplies.

"Yes. She's profoundly asleep, though a dream state sometimes occurs, and she may be aware this is happening. Don't worry about the process, it's always successful. All her body functions are slowed down, as though she were hibernating. She won't need to eat or drink. Just send an emanation if you need more supplies, and someone will bring them. Keep her warm."

"We'll be safe here?"

"Completely," said the larger one, with a lick at his fangs and a twist of his furry ears. "You may depend upon it. When she wakes, there will be a period of confusion. Just ease her through it, and don't forget to read her the book."

"But she already knows her language."

"She doesn't know ours," said a visitor, departing.

Rei took the book from my hand and put it safely with our packs before covering me with a blanket. I remember thinking how thoughtful they had been, but then, they had known we would be coming.

I Am Wilvia/on Hell

On Shore, which is what the water people call their world, little towns have been built all up and down the sea's edge, many of them on stilts above the water, and waterside property is already filled. Some of the people have moved back into the forest and built mud houses there. It is warmer in the forest, where the trees break the sea winds at night, but the people come back to the shore in the day-times, to fish and gather seaweed, while the children race up and down the sandy beaches, in and out of the warm, rolling sea. Most of the females are pregnant most of the time, and there are many, many babies.

Through sensors planted here and there, I, Wilvia, watch, I, Wilvia, listen. Half insane in my solitude, I have memorized their faces and names, have learned their simple language. I understand when one tribe of the people talks of starting a new village. The old village is getting crowded, they say, and they think it would be good to go up the river a long way. The good food of the shore can be found up the river, too, where there is room to spread out. Also, the biggest trees grow along the river, the best ones for boats! They can build boats and trade the boats for things to eat.

"Maybe we should leave big trees," says one of the males. "Takes a long time to grow a big tree."

"There's more," says another one of the males. "There's plenty of big trees. They'll never run out."

"I guess you're right," replies the first one. "We do have to make room for more of us all the time."

"Oh, yes," the other replies. "We always have to make room for more."

"Fools," I say, thrusting my forehead against the screen I am watching, reaching out to turn off the sound. "Oh, fools, fools."

Perhaps I should go outside. Perhaps I should show myself to them. Become their queen, perhaps, if they don't kill me first. Rule them as Joziré and I ruled the Ghoss . . .

We had a Trajian juggler at the court. The Trajian are long-lived but few, inveterate wanderers, often abused and abased, seemingly unable to settle in any one place. Their females command a very high bride-price, as there is only one of them for every two or three males. My juggler, Yarov, was a solemn little long-armed fellow with no assistant, no mate, for he had been unable to raise the bride-price necessary. He had stayed with us for a surprisingly long time. When I knew we might have to flee, I gave him a box of gold and gems, things he could use to travel, to keep himself, to buy a wife, for I knew how lonely he was. He stood before me, his little mouth open, as though he could not understand kindness. I told him it was not half what I owed him for the pleasure he had given us.

I wonder about him often. He did a wonderful trick, tossing a little carved king into the air, which separated and came down, arms, legs, torso, head, crown, seven separate pieces that were miraculously reassembled and tossed skyward again. I took it as an omen. Though our reign might be broken, we would reassemble and reign again . . .

So, should I reign over these creatures?

No, and no, and no. Those who brought me here said both my life and the future of mankind depends upon Queen Wilvia staying hidden! Hidden on this virtually unvisited planet called Hell, buried in this ancient Gentheran ship, only its sensors connecting me to reality, only its maintenance system keeping me alive. Only this stale tragedy to occupy me: these fools . . .

So, I am in hell, Wilvia is in hell. But, oh, my children, where are they? Beloved! Where is he? Where are those I love while I cower here, of no use, no use to them at all.

Joziré and I ruled the Ghoss, and we did it well. I was pregnant, expecting our first child, when the Thongal came. Joziré was taken off in one direction, I was taken in another. For a while, I was hidden in a Walled-Off on Tercis. It was a strange place, but better than this. The hunters followed me there, so we went to Chottem, to live among the Gentherans. There, the Gardener visited us from time to time to reassure me that Joziré was well. That was far, far better than this. Then hunters came to Chottem, so we returned to Tercis, only for a little time, and my protectors brought me here. My guides said no one would find me, and they would be my companions.

But they had to leave. Just for a time, they said. They planned to return. Perhaps they were caught, killed . . .

Patience. Patience. I say the word over and over, accompanying each thud of my forehead against the steel. And how long will patience alone keep me relatively sane? Is it even important to be relatively sane? I wait, and weep, as I watch the little creatures outside begin the destruction of their world yet again.

I Am Gretamara/on Mars

Under the dome of Dominion Central Authority on Mars, Sophia and I sat among a scattering of people, Human and Gentheran, most of them chatting quietly among themselves. Later in the day most of them would attend a meeting of Dominion Central Authority. This earlier gathering was by invitation, in order to hear a report on the effect of the general sterilant, and on Earth's rehabilitation since its application. Sophia had come to Dominion headquarters to conduct certain business before she descended upon Bray, and the Gardener had thought I would be an inconspicuous companion.

"Sophia," I murmured. "Your business here on Mars is completed, and strictly speaking, we are not invited to this gathering."

"Let us stay until they throw us out," she said, her eyes bright. This was her first trip away from the Gardener, away from Chottem, and she was excited by everything. "Tell them that as the heiress of Bray, I am interested in the work of the Dominion."

"Actually, only a few members of Dominion were invited to be here," I whispered. "However, if we are very quiet, and if you keep your cloak around you and your hood shadowing your face, they may not notice us."

She giggled. If she removed the cloak, both of us knew very well they would notice her, whether they noticed me or not.

The Gentheran laboratory representative was as Gentherans always are, fully suited and helmed. He spoke Earthian, as any Gentheran did who had anything to do with humans. "Out of respect," the Gardener had said, though she had not explained respect for what.

He introduced himself as Prrr (rolled *r*'s) Tgrr (a great many more rolled *r*'s.) "Our cooperating contractors and researchers have asked us for an update on the Earth rehabilitation situation. You will recall that during the first Earth-year after the sterilant was applied, the population, exclusive of those outshipped, dropped by slightly over one-point-one-nine percent. It was predicted that between point-nine and one-point-two percent of the population would die naturally in that time, so we are well within the estimates.

"The task of consolidating the population into smaller areas met resistance only during the fifth and sixth year, when the first consolidations took place. There is still some complaint, but it is generally pro forma griping that precedes orderly acquiescence. We make no attempt to remove outlying population centers until the nearest city has lost at least five percent of its population. Only then are outlying populations moved into the vacated housing and the empty nonurban communities razed. Though the process is slow, it is happening everywhere, which makes it an enormous undertaking. We have enlisted all human construction industries to help us in rehabilitation, and all children over the age of ten are required to assist in restoration of grasslands and forests.

"We have replanted five percent of the Brazilian desert where at one time jungles grew in leaf mold containing thousands of microorganisms atop hard, infertile soil. When the trees were burned, so was the leaf mold, along with the microorganisms. The stony, sterile ground was barren. On these barrens we have planted hardy 'starvation'-type coverage: many thorns, few leaves. When these have had a few decades to accumulate organic detritus, we will plant slightly less hardy things at their roots. After another few decades, we can plant the next generation, and so on. It will take over two hundred years for each acre to achieve fifteen percent of the organic mass it once held. It will take a millennium or more for each acre to achieve any-thing approaching the fertile growth that was its glory as one of Earth's chief oxygenators."

The listeners murmured at this.

"I have said nothing about fauna. Earth fauna was almost totally destroyed long before the sterilant was applied. We have genetic ma-terials from the creatures that were typed before the forests were de-stroyed, but the typed ones were mostly larger animals that made up only a tiny percentage of the total life-forms. Many bacteria, for ex-ample, were never collected, never known to exist. The people of Earth did not understand that humans were part of a worldwide or-ganism, that something as tiny as a cluster of bacteria could mean the difference between life and death for every living thing, the differ-ence between a functioning, flourishing planet and a desolation. We Gentherans believe, as did the Pthas, that this is also true on a galac-tic scale: Very small things make very large differences, and we must be careful about destruction, even of things that seem useless or evil. We are experimenting with biotic clusters that are functionally paral-lel to the lost ones, but we cannot expect to achieve a total replication unless we find a pocket, somewhere, of the original forest. Such mi-raculous finds have happened during reconstructions of other plan-ets, in the mouths of caves or in narrow canyons. We might be lucky enough to find one.

"It is too early to discuss any rehabilitation of the oceans. Perhaps in three or four hundred years, that process may be begun. Are there any questions?"

We listened to the ensuing discussion, some of which reminded me quite a bit of conversations I'd heard on Phobos, as a child. It was concerned with rehabilitation contracts and with the imposi-tion of sustainable economic models. Earth had always operated on a continuous-growth model that requires a poverty class. Sustain-able models require productive work by all members and are quite different.

When all the talk was over, the Gentheran thanked them for their attention and the audience, chattering, rose and dispersed. In the doorway, Sophia and I lingered.

Sophia said, "Why didn't the Gardener tell us about planetary economics? I shall have to read up on it. To tell the truth, Gretamara, I'm a little frightened of going on to Bray."

"I know, dear. The unknown is frightening, but you have always known it was what you had to do."

"Yes, but it was always some time in the future. Now it's immediate, isn't it. If it were not to be today, surely I would not be here, arranging all the legalities."

I grinned at her. "Oh, that's true enough, Lady. If it were not today, you would not be here, nor would I. I hope you feel the Gardener has taught you well."

"Both of you have taught me to hold my tongue," said Sophia meaningfully. "I have given you my oath to do so."

Most of those who had attended the brief meeting had gone even as other delegates to Dominion began to arrive. Two Gentherans came toward us and introduced themselves as Mwrrr Lrrrpa and Prrr Prrrpm. I identified them to myself as smaller one and larger one.

Smaller one of them said, "Von Goldereau d'Lornschilde has just arrived. He's over there by the door. He's been badgering us for years to find the heiress of Bray, and we're told she is here." She turned her mirrored helmet toward Sophia. "We are told you have grown up in a little town on Chottem, in the care of our friend, the Gardener. Would you mind dreadfully if we made the introduction?"

Sophia turned to me with a slight, wicked grin. We had planned for her to meet Von Goldereau, either here or in Bray, so I said, very seriously, that the Gardener and I would both be delighted. The two Gentherans turned and went toward d'Lornschilde purposefully, while Sophia and I walked a less direct route that brought us up behind him just in time to hear the Gentheran crow, ". . . but now we have great news to impart, Delegate Von Goldereau d'Lornschilde! You may rejoice, Delegate. The heiress of Bray has been found!"

We could only see the back of Von Goldereau's neck, which turned a peculiar ashen shade. "Found?" he choked. "Where did you find her?"

"Precisely where she has been all along, in the little village of Swylet-Upon-Sea, on Chottem, in the care of the Gardener."

We had edged around a little so we were able to see that some color was returning into Von Goldereau's face. "In the care of a gardener!"

He sneered. "She'll be completely unschooled. She'll be a bumpkin, a rustic, a peasant! Totally unable to accept the great responsibilities she will have to shoulder. It's best that I take her in hand, I think. See that she's educated properly . . ."

"Oh," said the other Gentheran, the larger one, "we think that will be unnecessary, Delegate. She has been reared by a great friend of Genthera."

The delegate's skin fell back toward its former ashen shade. "Genthera? What had Gentherans to do with her?"

"Enough to assure she would be no bumpkin."

"But she was left with some herb grower? Some vendor of vegetables?"

"Yes. With a great friend of our people."

He could find nothing to say, not a word even when the smaller one nodded to us. Sophia threw back her cloak and hood and moved around in front of the man, so he could see the loveliest woman he had ever seen, the perfected image of Stentor d'Lorn's daughter. She was dressed in the most recent style adopted by the wealthiest class in Bray, her hair tumbled about her head in a black cloud set with diamond stars, and when she offered her hand, the sparkle of stones from her fingers and wrists almost blinded him. Quite perfect! Just as the Gardener and I had planned it.

"Delegate," she said in the cool, careless voice she had inherited from her mother and had long practiced to perfection, "I understand you have been looking for me."

Von Goldcreau found his voice, the upper register at any rate. "Only to offer any assistance I can." He bowed low over her hand and would have kissed it had she not withdrawn it quickly. "May I offer to escort you to your home?"

"Thank you, no," she replied. "Here at Dominion headquarters, I have been arranging for various things to be done in Bray. We have sent people there to attend to my business. They will see that the local legalities are taken care of, and they will offer proof of my identity. I will be returning there very shortly."

"The Great House has been largely untenanted," said Von Goldereau with a note of desperation. "Surely you will allow me to hire servants for you, to see to its being readied for your arrival."

"Kind of you, but unnecessary, Delegate. Workers have already been dispatched, people I know and trust. Even as we speak, they are opening the house my grandfather built."

He was at a loss, and I knew why. The Gentherans had been making unscheduled visits to Bray for some time, and it had become much harder for Von Goldereau d'Lornschilde to keep the family business operating in the way Von Goldereau, and Stentor d'Lorn before him, had preferred. There were things going on in Bray that he did not wish Dominion to learn of, that Dominion had not learned of, yet, however diligent its search. Certainly he didn't want the heiress to know of them until he was sure where her allegiance lay. With Stentor d'Lorn, he would have been on solid ground, but with my friend, he was at sea.

I could read his thoughts on his face. He was thinking it might be best to miss the meeting of Dominion and hurry back to Bray. He was also thinking that, on the other hand, something might occur at the meeting that was important, and the other delegates from Chottem might take advantage of his absence. His eyes, his hands betrayed his thought. So caught between two fires, he saw Sophia's amused expression, the look of one who read a clearly written book.

She said, "Von Goldereau, we are kinfolk. Please do not upset yourself over my return. Be assured that my friends throughout Dominion have the matter very well in hand. I am at the age of reason in Earth-years, the age we humans seem to feel appropriate for the acceptance of responsibility. At this age, we need no regents, no guardians, no overseers or protectors except those we have selected to oversee and to protect. Do not trouble yourself on my account."

And with that she turned and swept away, glittering like a fountain, with people bowing as she went and me hurrying after her, trying not to laugh. It wasn't funny. I knew that there was really nothing funny about it, and yet, for just a moment, I was delighted.

From behind me I heard the deeper-voiced Gentheran say: "Bumpkin, I think you said, Delegate d'Lornschilde. Or was it peasant?"

Von Goldereau did not reply. When we reached the door and looked back, we saw that he had gone. We both knew he was returning to Bray as quickly as possible.

Meantime, the heiress of Bray put her arm around me and said,

"That was interesting, don't you think, Gretamara? The man is up to something."

"If what the Gardener has told us is correct, Lady, we know the man is usually up to something, and something well beyond a bit of thievery or corruption. We will need to watch him."

"When do we leave?"

"Now," I said. "She's waiting for us now."

We went down to the smaller landing lock. There were several Gentherans standing about, staring in astonishment at the great golden dragonfly piloted by a woman in red robes, apparently a human woman. For many reasons, mere humanity seemed increasingly unlikely to me.

In the ship, the Gardener spoke softly. "The Gentherans back there are a bit confused. They have seen the ship; they have seen me. Among the cognoscenti I am rumored to be a member of the Third Order of the Siblinghood, as I was of the First and Second Orders. They saw me come to transport the heiress of Bray and her companion. Now they are retelling old tales in which my arrival always presaged great events. They are saying my arrival today cannot be coincidental."

I asked, "Are there to be great events, Gardener?"

She said, "It is time you knew: The Third Order of the Siblinghood, as did two Orders before them, has been trying to solve the 'human problem' for a very long time."

"The human problem?" I asked, somewhat offended.

She put her arm around me. "Forgive me, Gretamara, but your race as a whole has the unfailing habit of fouling its nest, ruining its environment, killing its original planet, and doing its best to kill any others to which it is moved. Because we love and admire the human race for its many good qualities, we call this not 'the human condition,' meaning an irrevocable state, but 'the human problem,' one we wish to solve. The effort has gone on for some millennia, without result, and some of those involved in the effort are beginning to believe it is a waste of time and treasure.

"In searching for the solution, the Siblinghood has relied heavily upon on its Gentheran members. The Gentherans have traditionally been supportive. Now, however, many Gentherans are questioning whether a solution is possible. Also, they complain that the Third Order has kept the work so secret, even from most of the Sibling-hood, that no one knows what's going on."

"I presume you kept it secret because some evil fate met the First and Second Orders," I said.

"Evil fate, yes. To our surprise, our plans were betrayed to unex-pected adversaries twenty thousand Earth-years ago, and again ten thousand years ago. After each of these failures, we waited until all memory of the events had been lost by the opposing races before we began again. This time we have worked in almost total secrecy, but secrecy loses friends. People are reluctant to trust that things known only to others are worth the effort, and also, they've begun wonder-ing if the antihuman feeling on the part of other races may not be well deserved."

"Weariness and lack of support I can understand," I said. "But why do they care what others think or feel?"

Gardener shook her head. "If a widespread, mercantile race feels intense enmity toward another, both trade and travel are affected. Those friendly with the enemy are also considered enemies, some-times to their loss. If humans were hated only by one or two races, as during the other episodes, it wouldn't be so troublesome, but this time at least three or four other races are involved. The Quaatar. The K'Famir. The Frossian. And the Thongal."

"Quaatar?" said Sophia. "From what you've taught me, they're not even in contact with humans! They don't buy bondspeople. Their territory is astronomically remote. How could they be bothered by humans?"

"The Quaatar bother easily. Some time in the remote past, they may have encountered humans under adverse circumstance. Perhaps a Quaatar tried to eat a human and got an upset stomach. That would have been enough. Every sentient race in our galaxy knows how easy it is to anger the Quaatar. We aren't sure what happened; we only know something happened, for the Quaatar hate humanity with all the viciousness of hundreds of generations, one piled upon another, and they have recently influenced others in the Mercan Combine, notably their congeneric races—Frossians, K'Famir, and Thongal—

to feel the same way. At a psychic level Quaatar, Frossian, and K'Famir interests and opinions have coalesced into a metaphysical force directed against mankind. If they are aware that the Third Order is trying to help humans, they will do whatever they can to thwart us, or kill us."

I said, "But they don't remember the last time."

"No. We waited until they had forgotten, until the records had fallen to dust."

"But you say 'if they know.' You aren't sure that they know."

Gardener almost whispered, "We are not sure if they know, or how much they may know. This time we have been diligent in spreading what is called 'disinformation.' If they are aware of false stories we have spread, they will intervene by destroying certain refuges and seeking for certain fictional agents. This will tell us that they suspect. If they are aware of the truth, they will pick a different set of targets. By their actions we will see what they know, but at what cost? Our plans will be in ruins. A dilemma, isn't it?"

Sophia stared at her. "The real refuges and the real people must go unnoticed."

"Exactly. If they are suspected, they may be harmed."

"But," I said, "if you seem to protect them, you draw notice to them."

"Yes. And that is why we are taking great pains to protect surrogates for both. But, are the vile races fooled, or not?"

I thought on this for a time. "You have taught me, Gardener, that elevated and powerful creatures usually do not carry their own garbage. They tell others to do it, and the word is passed down the chain to underlings. As the command travels farther from those on high, the less secret it becomes. Do we have people who listen for such things?"

Gardener nodded. "Oh yes, we have listeners, Gretamara. Disaffection is not so far advanced among the Gentherans that they have abandoned us. They listen, a great many of them, in many, many places." She laughed, something she did seldom. "And now, we three are about to be become listeners by doing something we do very rarely, lest we be discovered."

I looked out the front of the dragonfly ship and saw that it followed a shining road that seemed familiar to me.

"When we arrive at a particular place," said the Gardener, "I will take a shape that's not my own. You will hide inside my skirts. You won't make a sound, you won't ask a question. When we leave will be time enough for questions, but for now, you will listen. All the pieces of our puzzle are in motion, the time approaches, and we must know what our enemies are planning. We will risk ourselves to see if they will tell us."

Sophia had turned quite pale, and I took her hand in mind. "I was here once before with the Gardener," I said. "Years ago. We will be all right." She clutched my hand strongly. After a time the ship seemed to stop moving toward the space ahead that was cluttered, scattered, littered with blobs, clusters, clumps, bunches and sprinklings of . . . somethings.

Slowly we floated nearer, hearing as we did so a great murmur, as of waters washing endlessly against the edges of the galaxies.

The Gardener whispered, "This is the great tree where all mortal created deities roost, all the Gods from every-place, every-race, every-time. Look to your left and down. Those are the Earthian Members. Do you recognize any of them?"

When Sophia did not answer, I said, "I see an old man with an eye patch," I said. "I forget his name. One of the gods of the people of the north that I read about as a child. And that very strong one with the hammer. That might be Thor."

"Actually," the Gardener murmured, "he is Thor, Hercules, Apollo, Gilgamesh, Adonis, Osiris, Krishna, virtually every young male deity known for strength, beauty, and intrepidity, just as my colleague, Mr. Weathereye, is Odin, Jupiter, Jove, Allah, Jehovah, or any other ancient male deity known for wisdom, power, and prescience. And the old woman there, Lady Badness, is Erda, Norn, Moira, Sophia, the wisewoman who can detect the pattern in the weavings of happenstance before mankind hears the shuttle coming."

"I'm named for her?" asked Sophia.

"For her, yes. And I, Gardener, am also Demeter, Cybele, Freya, Earth Mother, Corn Goddess, a thousand names of female deities wise in the ways of growing things, solicitous of women and children, caretakers of the beasts of the field and the woods. Some of us Members are sizable, for many mortals, including humans, believe in strength, and power, and nurture, and wisdom."

"What are all those hunched-up things?" asked Sophia.

The Gardener shook her head. "Sophia, those are the gods many humans prefer. They are hunched from ages of sitting on people's shoulders, whispering encouragement."

"But they're *tiny!*" she said, in disbelief.

"Many humans prefer tiny gods," said the Gardener. "Tiny gods of limited preoccupations . . ."

"Limited to what?" I demanded.

"To mankind, of course. And to each believer, particularly. Each human wants god to be his or her best friend, and it's easier to imagine god being your best friend if he is a tiny little god interested only in a tiny world that's only a kind of vestibule to an exclusive little heaven."

"Some of them are yelling," said Sophia.

"Oh, yes. Those are hellfire gods. Since there is no supernatural hell, they never really send anyone there, but their sources get enormous pleasure, thinking about it."

"And those," murmured Sophia. "Off to the side, all together?"

"I know what those are," I said. "Gardener told me those are dead people whose spirits have been imprisoned here. Some group or other on Earth has deified them or sainted them and claimed they can do miracles, so instead of passing on, humans hold them here, at least until they're forgotten."

"Can they do miracles?" asked Sophia wonderingly.

Gardener murmured, "We only know what our Sources know, we can only do what they can do. Many times persons actually heal themselves, or their bodies do it for them, but they prefer to believe one of us did it."

"What do you mean, you can only do what men can do? Men cannot fly about the universe in dragonfly ships," said Sophia.

"The Gentherans can," said the Gardener. "And long ago I melded with Sysarou, Gentheran goddess of Abundance and Joy, just as Mr. Weathereye down there has melded with Ohanja, Gentheran god of Honor, Duty, and Kindness. Gentherans have much the same needs mankind has; they have created similar deities, and we of Earth have melded with all the more accepted ones."

"You can do that? Meld with the gods of other species?" I asked, astonished.

"If we are similar enough, yes, which is a good thing, for Gentherans remember far, far into the past, and since we have melded with them, we, too, remember far more than do the gods of mere Earthians."

In the little silence that followed, I thought to myself that even if these gods could do nothing their people couldn't do, the Gardener, no matter how she disclaimed it, had powers they did not have.

She whispered, "I am looking at that mob of little Earth gods, hoping to find among them a disguise I can use."

The dragonfly ship came closer. "There," Gardener said, pointing. "That little female one. Its name is Oh-pity-me. It cannot see the sun for the daylight nor the stars for the darkness, and it is worshipped by a surprising number of people. It is not fierce enough to be interesting to the K'Famirish Members, and they will find it utterly unthreatening. I choose that one. Now, come with me and be very, very still."

The ship moved and unbecame. The Gardener was a small, dark cloud that hid us within her robes of dripping sorrow. We could see, we could hear, and we could understand everything we saw and heard, including the conversation of the three dark shapes nearest us, each lit by sullen fire.

"These are Dweller, Darkness, and Drinker," the Gardener spoke without sound. "Dweller in Pain, of the Quaatar. Whirling Cloud of Darkness-Eater of the Dead, of the K'Famir. Flayed One-Drinker of Blood, of the Frossians. Listen!"

Dweller snarled, "Look who is near to us. An Earthian Member. This is not your locus, Member. Yours is over there, among that shabby pile of Earthian trash."

"I am where I am," the Gardener whispered. "I am weary of them. They are noisy sometimes. I like it better here."

"Why, it's a little weeper," sneered Darkness. "Not like the rest of them."

"Not like them, no," whispered the Gardener. "They want only to go on. I want to end."

"Soon you may have your wish," giggled Drinker.

"Oh, if only that could be," murmured the Gardener. "Can you make it happen?"

"Ah, yes," chuckled Dweller, emitting a belch of fire. "We intend to make it happen."

"But Earthians don't want to die," the Gardener persisted.

"They'll try to stop us," sniffed Darkness. "They and the Gentherans . . ."

"The Gentherans?"

"Dweller has seen Earthian Members mixing with Gentherans. This means they are plotting together," said Drinker.

"They're always plotting," breathed Gardener. "I want to destroy them, and myself . . ."

Drinker whirled slowly, a ragged spiral of torn skin, dark with bruises, wet with blood. "We have learned that Gentherans watch intently over certain people . . ."

"Our Sources hired Thongals," giggled Darkness. "Very sneaky Thongals to find out what people the Gentherans are watching over. The Thongals found two of them among our people: one feeding a ghyrm on Cantardene, one feeding the umoxen on Fajnard. They are dead, or will be soon. Perhaps you can find others for us . . ."

"What are the Earthians and Gentherans plotting to do?" moaned Gardener, in the little god's weary voice.

Drinker gaped hideously. "Whatever it is, we'll stop it."

The three turned toward one another, put their heads together, murmuring. Gardener drew apart. Soon we found ourselves a distance away, the dragonfly around us.

"They suspect," said the Gardener. "And it seems they have identified some very important people."

"Are those gods real?" I demanded.

"I am one of them, Gretamara. We exist, but we are not real in the sense that a tree is real or a rock is real. If all the people in the universe were gone, the rock or tree would still be there, but we deities exist only while our people do."

"My parents believed there is only one god," I insisted.

"Oh, I believe there is One," the Gardener agreed. "A being larger than any mortal god; a being that encompasses the universe without being dependent upon it, preexistent and postexistent, a being so vast only a fool could claim to know its purposes, One who sets all into motion, then waits . . ."

"Why did it create the K'Famir?" I interrupted angrily.

"I did not say 'create.' The K'Famir are not a creation, they are a consequence, as are we all, Gretamara. Health or disease, pleasure or pain, joy or grief, all are consequences of the creation of life: All are possible. If no room is left for the possible, it is not life, it is mere repetition. Within our race, we encompass the scale from great good to absolute evil; we have had great leaders and philanthropists, and we have had serial torturers and killers. These last, mankind has regarded with sick fascination, trying to understand them as human beings. They should not try, for they are not human beings. Body shapes are only that, a shape, but when evil inhabits us, it is the same evil that inhabits the K'Famir. If you believe all humans have a capacity for good, then you must identify those who have none as something other than human. Only death ends them.

"The One god does not meddle in its creation, but we mortal gods often pretend it is our business to do so. We cannot move a straw upon a mortal world, but we can move ourselves from place to place . . ."

I asked, "How did we get here if you cannot move a straw?"

The Gardener smiled. "Where is here? Did I move you? Or did I merely whisper in your ear to see what I see? Now I shall whisper again, and what wonder! You will somehow be moved to Chottem, to Bray, to the house of Stentor d'Lorn, to find whatever secrets it holds and whatever darkness it hides."

I Am Margaret, at a Birthday Party on Tercis

On the day of the birthday party, we loaded the food into the wagon and drove across the bridge toward Billy Ray's farm.

"How many of 'em this year?" Jimmy Joe asked me.

I sighed. "The only ones left at home are Benny Paul, Sue Elaine, Trish, and the two little ones, plus Mayleen and Billy Ray."

"Humph," said Jimmy Joe. "Seven of them and six of us. Thirteen. Suppose that's an omen? I suppose their contribution to the festivities is hamburgers? Someday I must taste one."

When Mayleen and Maybelle were little, I had mentioned that hamburgers were an old Earth tradition for summer gatherings. I had never tasted a hamburger on Earth, nor had I at Mayleen's, even though she provided "hamburgers" at every birthday party.

This year would be no different, I saw as we approached, for Billy Ray was lighting the fire, using lots of coal oil. Mayleen, standing among billows of ugly, smelly black smoke, slapped the meat patties on the grill. They both came over to help us unload the food we'd brought from home, leaving the smoke and the flames to sort it out between them. Later, we each took one of the resultant "hamburgers," covered it with a bun, then lost it over where Uncle Billy Ray's dogs waited with their tongues out.

Maybelle had made salads; I'd brought fried chicken and two birthday cakes. The two little ones ate like starving creatures and went to sleep under the picnic table, icing all over their faces. As soon as the food was gone, Benny Paul pulled Til away, and Jeff followed them, his feet dragging. Trish and Sue Elaine sneaked off after. I watched the departure with some anxiety. The hangdog look on Jeff's face did not bode at all well.

Billy Ray started his usual after-food tirade. It seemed Joe Bob, the oldest boy, had threatened to call the placement people and get Benny Paul sent to some other Walled-Off. "Got no right to do that," Billy Ray shouted. "There's nuthin wrong with Benny Paul!"

Except killing the Conovers' prize bull out of meanness. Except pimping his sister, Trish. Plus many other barbarisms I only suspected.

"You gotta go speak to Joe Bob," he said to me. "Get him to tell 'em there's nothing wrong with Benny Paul."

I said. "I wouldn't feel right getting involved in a family argument, Billy Ray. That's between you and him." I got up and went over to the picnic table to pour a glass of berryade.

I heard Maybelle say, "Please don't get Mother involved."

"I just said . . ."

"We know what you just said," James interrupted very quietly. "Just please don't fuss Grandma over it."

Billy Ray gave him a nasty look. "This is my place, and I'll fuss who I damned well please, Jimmy Joe. You all don't like it, you can leave." He got up and stamped off to the house before I got back with my glass full.

Glory was peeking through the branches, waiting for the usual sequence to play itself out. Since Billy Ray had stomped off mad as soon as he'd stuffed himself with food, it was about time for Mayleen to do likewise.

"Don't see why Mother ought to be left out of family things," said Mayleen in a nasty voice. "It's her fault, all these Mackey twins. It's bad enough being pregnant all the time without having two babies to bury or take care of at the end of it."

Maybelle said sharply, "Mayleen, I know Papa talked to you just like he did to me. You didn't have to get pregnant all the time."

"That's my business! And I don't thank you for butting in!" She got up and stamped back to the house.

James looked at his watch, the little muscles at the corners of his jaw jumping around like water on a hot skillet. He walked off and came back with Jeff, who looked relieved to be going.

"New record for the shortest time," said James, as we drove off. "Total elapsed time, arrival to departure, including the unpacking of and setting out of food and the collecting of leftovers, one and one-quarter hours, not counting travel. Half an hour shorter than last year. Keep workin' at it, we'll get it down to where we can just drop off the food and turn the wagon around in the driveway."

Since our teatime had been cut short, when we got to Maybelle's, I went into the kitchen to put the kettle on. Outside, Jeff was giving Glory the ringroot bracelet he'd carved for her birthday.

"What was Benny Paul up to?" Glory asked him when she gave him a thank-you hug.

"Him and Trish," he said, making a face. "They were going to do a sex show for us, and Til said we'd get to . . . take part."

"Jeff, you've got to stay away from him."

"We're brothers, Glory."

"You'll be roommates in another Walled-Off if you're not careful! Billy Ray said Joe Bob threatened to call the Placement Board about Benny Paul, and if Til's been part of his nastiness, Til may have to go, too."

The shock on Jeff's face as he went by the kitchen door told me he'd never thought of that. The look on my face, mirrored in the door, said I'd never thought of it, either. I stood there, dazed, wondering what other important things I'd missed.

I certainly wasn't missing anything about Falija, for by this time, she was staying at my house most of the time. Glory came up to see her and said her living with me was a good thing, to keep her away from the boys.

"But I like Jeff," said Falija.

Both of us froze. I thought I had misheard, or maybe Glory was playing a trick on me, but Glory was staring at Falija, as surprised as I.

She said, "You're talking!"

"Umm," said Falija. "Yes. But it's not quite right."

"It sounds perfectly fine to me. How long . . ."

"Oh, a while. I practice at night when everyone's asleep."

Well, there was no nonsense about my being asleep this time! Fully awake, I'd heard it with my own ears. I heard more of it after Glory left, so it was no trick of hers. I had to believe it. By late summer, Falija was talking a lot, though only to Glory and me, and she was walking on her hind legs whenever she couldn't be seen.

"It's a good thing nobody else sees her," Glory said. "It's getting harder and harder to believe she's just a cat." She looked up to find my eyes fixed on her, but I forbade myself to ask the question. Glory shrugged, as though to say, "Either you believe me or you don't, and so far, you haven't."

James came home from work one night, shaking his head. "Grandma, where'd you tell me Billy Ray's oldest girl went?"

"You mean Ella May? She joined the Siblinghood a long time ago, when she was only about fourteen. Why?"

"I just wondered if we ought to let her know . . ."

"Know what?"

"Her twin sister, the one who moved up to Repentance last year . . ."

"Janine Ruth." Somehow, I knew what was coming. Ella May's twin was Mayleen all over again. "She hurt somebody."

He nodded. "Placement Board sent her to Hostility. I thought somebody ought to tell the family . . ."

"James, if you don't want to be blamed for causing it, you forget you ever heard about it."

He thought about it for a moment. "You're right, Grandma. They'd figure someway it was my fault, or Maybelle's."

Falija talked more clearly every day. She was able to get out of sight very quickly, so I stopped worrying about her going places with Glory. Whenever Glory went fruit-picking, Falija helped her. There was scarcely a branch too thin for her to climb out on and scoop fruit off the tree quick as anything. Glory could spread out a blanket and Falija would drop the fruit onto it fast as Glory could put it into baskets.

One night the two of them wakened me in the middle of the night. Glory said, "Falija found something she thinks we ought to see, Grandma."

"Fine," I said. "We'll go see it in the morning."

"No," she said. "Falija says it has to be now."

I wavered between outrage and curiosity. Curiosity won. I put on shoes and a big sweater. Falija led the way down to the road, up the valley, until we got to the rise before the cemetery.

Glory said, "I don't go in there, Falija."

Falija said, "I'm not taking you in there. We're going up the hill."

So we clambered up the ridge of the rise, past the cemetery fence, and onto a big flat rock between two thimble-apple trees. Beside the rock was some deep grass where we could sit in the moon shadow of the trees, and the fiddlebugs were making a noise so much like a ringing in the ears you couldn't tell if it was inside or outside your head.

"There," whispered Falija.

Down the hill two little girls were running stark naked, hand in hand, along the meadow, and behind them some other children, all naked, some of them paired off and some alone. Along behind them came Lou Ellen.

That's when I realized I was dreaming again. I had that same, misty feeling I'd had down at the ferry pool. The naked children gathered around Lou Ellen. Glory started to get up, and Falija put a claw into her arm. "Don't," she said. "They'll run away if you go down there."

Some older, familiar-looking children came through the trees. They were as tall as grown-up people, but they had no breasts, and there was no hair on their bodies. I thought I should know them, but I couldn't remember who they were.

"They're all children," Glory said in confusion.

"Well," Falija said, "not so much children as just young, and they're all the same person, really. Some grown larger, some not."

"Why not?" Glory whispered.

"Oh," Falija whispered. "Where they are, they don't need to be old. They've already learned everything they can."

I was dreaming again. I had to be. A woman wearing red robes that billowed and flowed around her like a rosy cloud came out of the woods. She stood for a time, watching the children until they wandered into the trees on the far side. Lou Ellen was with them. I had never seen her with that expression of joy on her face. Bliss, I'd call it. Absolute bliss.

"Who is that woman in red, Grandma?"

"I can't quite remember," I said.

I remembered when I wakened in the morning, though. It was the woman who had taken Wilvia away, and it had all been a dream. Even after I found my big sweater there on the bed, I told myself I'd just been chilly in the night, that was all.

School started the next week. Glory, Bamber Joy, and I went down to Ms. McCollum's store to buy school supplies. I always went in first and paid Ms. McCollum for the children's supplies while he and Glory sat on the stoop enjoying a cold drink. This time, I heard heavy footsteps coming onto the front stoop, and two men came slamming in, walked up to the counter, and asked Ms. McCollum if there was anybody in town who had a new cat.

Ms. McCollum looked as though she didn't know whether to laugh or get angry. It was a silly question, but at the same time, it sounded threatening. She had to swallow before she answered, very slowly. "I guess everybody in the valley has a new cat at least once a year. There's kittens everywhere you look."

"Not a kitten, ma'am. This is a dangerous kind of cat from another world."

"There's a lady over in Remorseful who sort of collects cats, but they're just ordinary cats. I sure haven't heard about anything like that."

I knew she meant Dorothy Springer, a retired schoolteacher who had a barnful of cats and spent her whole pension feeding them and having the vet fix them. The two men didn't react; they just stood there for a minute, silent. They sounded so mechanical, I had the strange idea that maybe they were shifting gears, or waiting for instructions. Then, with not so much as a thank-you, they turned around and left.

When we got home we told Falija about it, and the hair on her neck rose until she looked like a lion.

"They didn't come from your people," Glory said to Falija. "Your people know where you are."

"Her *people*?" I asked, with lifted eyebrows.

"She means my parents," said Falija firmly. "Anyone sent by my people would know exactly where I am."

"We've got to be sure no one else in the family says anything," Glory said in a worried voice.

All this was extremely upsetting. I had spent months sorting out what I chose to believe was real from what I had dreamed from the fictional stuff that was left over. At least, I thought I had. Now this new thing! A threat from who knows what from who knows where against someone who shouldn't exist in the first place!

I cleared my throat, turned toward Glory, and said in my most portentous voice, "You had a cat earlier in the summer, but it went away some time ago, didn't it?"

Glory stared at me for a minute before she caught on. "Yes. Of course. The lady who left it with me came and got it."

I said, "The family hasn't seen it for some time."

Glory shook her head and grinned at me. "No, ma'am."

I was invited to supper that night, and at the table, Glory said, "I kind of miss the cat I was keeping for that lady. None of the barn cats are very friendly. Maybe Ma Bailey'll give me one of her kittens."

I said wonderingly, "The cat you were taking care of. Is it gone?"

"The lady came along the road when I was riding my bicycle. She told me thank you and let me keep the rest of the money."

"I thought it ran off," grunted Til.

"You gave it enough reason to," muttered Jeff.

After the dishes were done and the chickens shooed in, Glory walked back up the hill with me. We sat down on the porch, and I said what I'd been thinking about for days, "Glory, I've cultivated blindness as long as I can. I've always congratulated myself on being a realist, but it's getting so I can't tell the difference between what's real and half real and mostly supposition. I want you to tell me everything, whether you think I'll believe it or not."

Glory gave me a look.

"I won't doubt you," I said firmly. "Whatever you say."

She took a deep breath and started in. The cat-people. The money bag. I have never believed in telepathy, not really, even though one of my childhood imaginary people was supposed to be a telepath, and the only alternative to having seen it myself was to think I had read it from Glory's mind. Believing I had seen it was easier. It had not been a dream, it had been real, but I had suppressed the reality of it.

Surprisingly, to me at least, when I finally took it in, things made more sense than they had up until then. Falija was not just an anomaly. She really was a treasured creature of some other race, and we really had to keep her safe.

Glory said, "I never fed Falija cat food any more than the barn cats get cat food. They eat what they catch. Falija eats what I eat. There's no cat-food trail anybody can follow, and Falija doesn't even associate with other cats. She won't go into the barn at all. Whenever she sees a barn cat, she gets all strange."

"How do you mean, strange."

"All sad, upset, silent. So I don't take her in there."

"What about the money bag?" I asked her. "The one the people gave to you to pay for Falija's needs." Glory had given me the money so Sue Elaine couldn't borrow it without asking, which was one of Sue Elaine's many unattractive habits.

"It's in my boot," Glory said. "With some dirty socks shoved down on top of it."

I mused, "It has to have a power source. People use detectors to find metal and things like radioactivity."

We went down the hill together and up the back stairs to her room. She shook the bag out of her boot, and something else fell out with it: the little book Falija's mother had given Glory, which Glory had told me about. We had both forgotten what the person had told Glory to do with it. Glory stared at it with her face all knotted up. I felt absolutely idiotic. Here between the two of us we'd forgotten the one thing we were supposed to do for Falija, even though I hadn't really believed it until tonight!

We talked about a safe place for the little bag, and we eventually decided to bury it next to metal, not as easy as you'd think on Tercis, where metal was rare and expensive. We finally thought of the cemetery fence. Glory got a trowel out of Maybelle's gardening basket, and we hiked over to the cemetery to bury the bag next to a fence post. If anyone used a metal detector, they'd think it was reacting to the post, though I thought it likely that the bag was of a technology far, far beyond metal detectors. Chances were, whoever might look for it would be equally sophisticated. Nonetheless, we scattered the place with rocks, weathered side up, then we went up to the thimble-apple rock to be sure we hadn't left any sign of being there.

When we looked down the meadow, there they were, all Lou Ellen's friends with Lou Ellen among them, moving out into the moonlight on the meadow, dancing like leaves dance on the wind, almost weightless, floating up and down, free and glorious, as though they had forever to dance in. They sang, too, with Lou Ellen's voice among them, joyful and blithe.

I looked down at Glory. She was gazing down the hill with such longing that it almost broke my heart. She wanted to go down there with Lou Ellen. I started to say something, then stopped. Some things couldn't be fixed with words. She wiped her eyes on her sleeve, then stared, way across the meadow. I followed her gaze. There was the woman in red, looking straight at us from the edge of the trees. I could feel the woman's eyes on me, almost stroking. I lifted my hand; the woman smiled and waved and disappeared into the forest.

"Who is she?" Glory asked.

"A dream from my past," I said. "A woman who flies a dragonfly ship. Everything down there in the valley is a dream."

Falija wasn't around when we got back, but the next morning, Glory came up to apologize for forgetting about the book.

"I forgot what your mama told me to do, Falija. I was supposed to read it to you when you began to talk."

"I've been talking for a long time," Falija said, with a little frown between her eyes.

Glory flushed. "I know, Falija. It's my fault. I'd forgotten it until last night. Now listen." She opened the book. On each page there were only a few words. The first page started out: 'Our word for insight is ghoss.' Ghoss was spelled out as guh-HOSS, so the reader would know how to pronounce it. The next page had another few words, and so on, a few hundred of them altogether.

Then I took the book to look at it, and Falija stared at me in a funny way and said, "Please, read it to me again, Grandma." I did. When I'd finished, Falija went off in a corner by herself after putting the book on one of my bookshelves, hidden behind some other books.

That night, Falija came into my bedroom and climbed up onto my bed, digging her claws into my shoulder. I woke to see her frightened face inches from my own, eyes as big as moons. I held her while she curled up on my chest, shivering as though she'd been frightened half to death.

"What is it?" I whispered. "Falija, what is it? Tell me."

"In my head," she said. "There's a whole world in my head, and I can't shut the door in between . . ." Then she said something in another language that went on and on, and she shut her eyes and just lay there, shivering like an abused animal. At first I didn't realize what she'd said, but then it came to me. She was speaking Gentheran. I wrapped my arms around the little person, to comfort her, and we stayed that way for a long, long time. Falija would shiver, then she'd calm down, then she'd make this pitiful little noise and shiver all over again.

"My home," she whispered. "My home is the land of Perepume on the world of Chottem. I can see the cliffs of Perepume, where the spray from the green ocean smells like spicebush and pine. I see the forests, where the wind sings in the boughs. I hear the tongues of Perepume, lilting and laughing through the long nights. They were there, inside my head, in my mother-memory. The words you read to me opened the door to the mother-memory all at once, and it scared me. I didn't know where I was!"

I held her tight. "That must be how your people pass on information," I said, trying to sound very calm, as though it wasn't anything unusual or strange. "I wish our people could do it that easily. I'll bet you know all the history and geography now, without even having to read a book or study about it."

Falija looked confused for a moment, but then her ears came forward, and she did her cat smile. "I think I do. I really do."

"That would be wonderful," I said enthusiastically. "Gloriana will be so jealous! Just think, no homework."

"What's homework?" Falija asked.

I explained about school. It seemed to soothe her to hear me talk, so I went on about being in school myself, when I was younger, and how difficult some classes were. "But your way, you just have one sort of scary night—and that's our fault for forgetting the book until now. But, you have it! It's all right in there. Oh, Falija, I really envy you." And it was true, I did.

Falija curled a little tighter against my chest and seemed to doze off for a while. Then she woke up, and said, "Grandma, they have human people in my world."

I half opened one eye and said sleepily, "Do you suppose that's why your family left you with Gloriana? Because they already knew about human beings?"

Falija looked puzzled. "Maybe. They're in my world . . . no, a special few of them live among us. And there are bad creatures, Thongals. They were on Fajnard, too. They tried to capture the king and queen of the Ghoss, who barely escaped . . ." Her eyes got big, and she didn't say anything more for a long while. I slept.

"It's part of a story," said Falija loudly enough that my eyes snapped open. "It starts at the beginning, and it goes on to the end. Shall I tell it to you?"

"You can't just pick out the important parts?" I suggested sleepily.

"No. One tells it all, or one doesn't tell it. I think Glory should hear it, too. It's a long story . . ." She stood up. "I'll go get her. We'll come back here."

And she was out the door, silent as a shadow.

They came back up the hill together, Falija draped over Glory's shoulder. I turned on the light as they came near, the light scoring deep shadows into the ledge before the house and throwing an amber glow on the bottoms of the branches.

Glory opened the door and yawned. "Falija says you have something important going on here."

I was at the stove, putting on the kettle. Falija jumped up on the sofa while Glory came to set out the cups and get the sugar and tea out.

"What kind of tea, Grandma?" she asked.

"Oh, that strong one I use to wake up with," I said. "I'll never get back to sleep, after, but never mind."

Glory measured the tea. The kettle boiled, the tea was steeped, and we moved over to the sofa, where I put my nose in the steaming cup and felt better immediately.

"All right," I said to Falija. "What is it?"

Falija said, "I now have the memory I got from my mother before I was born. It just didn't open up until tonight."

"How did this mother-memory get into your head?" I asked.

Falija got wrinkles between her eyes, looked puzzled for a moment, then said, "In early pregnancy, our females duplicate a certain part of their brain, and the duplicate moves down what's called an epispinal duct to the womb, and this mother-brain part connects to the baby's mind before the skull grows around it. Then, after the baby is born, that mother-mind gradually makes connections with the baby's brain, and, when the child learns to speak our language, the words link up and open the way to all that information."

I chewed on this for a while. "Not until the child learns to speak?"

Falija said, "That's why the book was so important. Ideas are expressed in words, and even the ones that are thought of in pictures or feelings need words to decode them, so babies have to have words in our language to tie them to the mother-brain. If I'd grown up among my own people, I wouldn't have needed the book, because I'd have heard the words from the first. It's very interesting, isn't it? There's so much of it, it will take a long time to absorb it all."

I said, "You already know some things, though. You know where you're from."

"From Perepume, yes. I know there are humans on my world, and the humans call the planet Chottem. Perepume is a separate part, a . . . continent. I have memory of a world called Thairy and one called Fajnard. My people live on both of those as well, and so do humans. I know the names of a lot of other worlds, all of them occupied by different people, all spread out and joined together by . . . channels, ropes . . ."

"Wormholes?" I offered.

"Spcc'ci in my language," she crowed. "Yes, wormholes. The whole network is huge. Almost none of the people in it know about all the other people in it, but my people know secret ways to get from place to place very quickly. And I know the story, the one I said both you and your grandmother should hear."

"The one you woke me up about," I said.

"That one. Yes."

"Well, nighttime is a good time for storytelling. Let me turn out some of these lights. Open the stove door and bring the teapot over here, Glory. We'll sit in firelight."

And then, to Falija, "Tell the story."

"In the long, long ago, the Gentherans came to Earth the very first time . . ."

"Not that long," I said. "It was only a century or so."

"No." Falija's eyes glowed in the light of the stove. "You mustn't interrupt the story. The first time Gentherans decided to visit Earth thousands and thousands of years ago, they discovered your people living in caves and making crafty things with their hands and thinking crafty thoughts. Your people fought with each other quite a lot. The Gentherans are a curious people, very interested in other beings, and they thought your people were intriguing, so they took some of them to Fajnard, near where a lot of my people, the Gibbekot, live. They gave the humans a place with caves to live in, near good soil where they could plant crops. After that it seemed like no time at all, they were overcrowded and began to fight with one another.

"So, the Gentherans decided to change the humans a little, not so much as would make them unhuman, but enough to make them less likely to overcrowd and fight. Sometimes a Gibbekot baby dies before the mother-mind leaves the mother's head, and when that happens, our doctors can take the partial mind and give it to other creatures. So the Gentherans obtained an unfinished mother-mind from my people, one that had our language in it and some of our other talents, and the Gentherans cloned enough of these mother-minds to give them to all the humans.

"In the humans, it had an unforeseen side effect. Some Gibbekot are almost telepathic, and the partial mind that they cloned for humans had that quality, and in the humans it was stronger! Suddenly, the humans understood one another better, they stopped lying and cheating and fighting each other, their lives became much more contented, and remarkably, they passed the mother-mind on to their children! They named themselves the vabil ghoss, which is to say *those having insight,* in my language. 'Enlightened ones,' I guess you'd say.

"Both the Gibbekot and the vabil ghoss still share the highlands of

Fajnard very happily. In time, they dropped the vabil part of their name and were known just as the Ghoss. Ghoss do some things better than we do, and we do some things better than they do, and Ghoss went with my people when colonies were established on Thairy and Chottem."

I frowned in concentration. "Your people must have liked us a good deal!"

"The Gentherans had a special reason to be interested in humans. That's why they're so set on helping you. Gloriana, you know your cousin Trish? You've told me about her, and I've seen her because I was curious. She's not quite complete, and I've even heard you, Grandma, feeling sorry for her."

"So?" said Gloriana.

"In time long past, an armada of Gentheran ships was traveling near a variable star, and the radiation caused a mutation in all the unborn babies. They were born physically deformed and mentally limited. Their fingers never developed, they couldn't stand erect or learn to speak, and because of that they couldn't access their mother-minds and were forever trapped in babyhood. Even though they couldn't mature into true Gentherans, they did mature sexually and were able to have children. Because they were mute and crippled, our people called them, 'the afflicted.' Our people grieved over them just as you do over Trish, Grandma.

"When the Gentherans found your race, oh, many thousands of years ago, they had some of the afflicted ones with them. Your people were . . . silly about them. They just loved them. Your people, especially your children, were just delighted with these poor, handicapped Gentherans, and the poor, handicapped Gentherans liked them just as much.

"As soon as this was known, Gentherans began bringing their handicapped ones to Earth. Your people adopted them. Some of them lived with you, some moved out into the wild, some even evolved into other types, but they were all . . . happy, as they could never have been among Gentherans . . ."

Into the silence, I said, "She's talking about cats, Gloriana." I stared at Falija, trying to figure something out. "Falija, your people are the Gibbekot, right? Then who are the Gentherans?"

"The spacefaring moiety of us," she said. "Half of us are spacefarers, the other half are settlers, but we're all one people." She sighed. "The afflicted were no longer such a great sorrow to our people because they were happy. Everywhere there are humans, they're still happy, and we owe their happiness to you."

"Anyone would have loved them!" cried Gloriana.

Falija replied, "Not as you do. Gibbekot are not perfect. No creature is perfect. Gentherans expect their children to be like themselves, and they grieve when that is not so. Seeing the unfortunates still makes us uncomfortable. Ever since then, the Gentherans have felt a debt to humans, and they've kept in touch with Earthian people, even though they're not happy about the way humans behave.

"Up until meeting humans, our race believed that each intelligent race was either ethical or vile; either it had evolved a moral and ethical system or it hadn't. The K'Famir and the Frossians are vile races. They take what they want, they kill when they feel like it, they're amused by torture, and they never identify with their victims. Some humans are exactly like them.

"The Gentherans and the Gibbekot have an ethical system, along with rules of morality. They try to be fair to all thinking beings as well as some or all living beings that don't think. Some humans are exactly like them, too.

"Before that time, we thought every species had one kind of mind or the other, but not both. Except for you humans. Human politicians brag about the good they're pretending to do while they take bribes not to do it. Human commercial interests talked about helping people while they destroyed all the fish, trees, and clean water on Earth. The Gentherans know a lot of evil races and a lot of good races, but the human race is the only hypocritical race we've ever encountered.

"The only race that espouses virtue and can't practice it?" I murmured.

"Exactly, and our people wanted to know why. When they investigated, they found there was a physiological difference. They learned that every ethical race has a racial memory, and every vile race has none. Ethical races are fully aware of their own history. We Gibbekot have millions of years of increasingly intelligent, purposeful being in our minds along with all the happenings and all the consequences of those happenings along the way.

"But humans don't have a racial memory, and neither do the K'Famir or the Frossians, or the Quaatar, or the . . . well, a good many others."

I was dumbfounded. "You can remember everything?"

"Yes. We really can, though it's not so much remembering as it is just knowing. You don't have to remember which way is up or what green is, you just need to learn the word for it. Even though my people were very fond of the strange humans, they were upset that every generation of them made the same mistakes. Instead of knowing what war was by remembering their own children screaming as their entrails spilled out and their skins burned off, your people talk about patriotism and bravery. Which is more real to you? If it's been twenty years since your last war, humans don't recall the reality, so if some not very bright leader yells, 'If you're brave and patriotic, you must defend our cause,' off you march.

"Imagine that you remembered being the very first premammal, and remembered being various primates, and remembered being every kind of prehuman. My people thought humans needed that, in order to stop making the same mistakes over and over."

"Real do-gooders, the Gentherans," I muttered. "We have written histories, after all!"

"Oh, yes," said Falija, twitching her ears. "The smarter ones of you can read about the past, and you can record what you see, and you have retained enough information between generations for science to develop, but few people pay attention to history. If some powerful person wants to do something history says is foolish, he just claims what is written isn't true, or doesn't apply to the present, and since most of you haven't read it, you believe him. You have improved, that's true. You finally learned that human sacrifice didn't do any good. You finally learned that slavery was evil; that is, most of you did, for a while, but not all of you forever. Some races would have tried selective breeding at some point, but you cared more about being unique than you did about being good. My people think you'll go extinct soon if you don't have a racial memory. I guess that makes us do-gooders."

I stared at her a long time. "Perhaps your people were thinking of giving us the kind of minds you have."

Falija said slowly, "It would be logical, wouldn't it, but there's nothing about that in my mind, and I can't imagine how it would be done. Where would they get one? You don't remember your first ancestors. You have no memory of ninety-nine percent of what makes you what you are! Instead you have comfy baby-stories you tell yourselves to explain why you're not good people. What sin you committed or how you didn't do what this god or that god told you. Instead of learning how not to be bad, you learn how to be forgiven and carried off to heaven. Most of you find it easier to believe the baby-stories than to learn from history and science, because it takes brains and hard study to understand history and science, but the stories are simple and comfy. People who want things easy and comfy resent people who study things. They teach their children the comfy stories and tell them not to worry about studying, just buy a ticket to go to heaven, and gradually, everyone becomes as ignorant as everyone else. It's happened time after time on Earth."

From what I knew of Earth's history, she was right. "Yes, Falija, I know how that works. And I have never until this moment been envious of cats." I picked up my teacup, found it empty, and poured a bit more. "What else do you remember?"

Falija nodded. "There's another group, the Siblinghood . . ."

I snorted. "Even I know about that! You remember Ella May, don't you, Glory? Mayleen's second eldest, Janine Ruth's sister? She was accepted by the Siblinghood, and more power to her!"

Falija went on, "The Siblinghood helped the royal family when Thongals attacked on Fanjard."

I said, "If I remember my studies, Fajnard was overrun by the Frossians."

"That was later. The royal family was attacked by Thongals twice. The first time was thirty-six or -seven years ago when they killed King Joziré the First. His wife fled into hiding with the crown prince, who was only a baby. The Siblinghood helped hide Prince Joziré, while he grew up and was educated.

"Meantime, the Frossians stayed in the lowlands of Fajnard while the Gibbekot and most of the Ghoss fortified the highlands. A few of the Ghoss always pretend to be slaves on the lowlands in order to keep an eye on the Frossians. Peace was maintained, and after a number of years, the Gibbekot and Ghoss thought it would be safe for Prince Joziré to return to Fajnard.

"He was about twenty then. He married his childhood companion, and they were crowned as King Joziré the Just and Queen Wilvia the Wise . . ."

"Wilvia?" I faltered. "Queen Wilvia?"

"Why?" asked Glory. "Is there something wrong with that name?"

I shook my head. "No, child, it's just a case of imagination meeting reality head-on. I used to play dress-up as a child. Most children do, I suppose. I often played I was a queen, and that was her name, Queen Wilvia. I can't believe it."

"The young queen became pregnant," Falija said. "And then, suddenly, with almost no warning, a group of dissident Thongals invaded the highlands, and again tried to capture the king and queen. Well, the queen was taken into hiding at the first sign of trouble, and the king was smuggled off Fajnard in another direction."

"Does this have something to do with the great task your parents said you were to perform?" asked Glory.

"I believe so," said Falija, ears forward and eyes slitted. "I have a story in my head, about the man who talked to the fish. I remember a saying. 'Who knows? The Keeper knows. Well then, ask the Keeper. Where do I find it? All alone, walk seven roads at once to find the Keeper.' If my mother memorized all that and put it in my mother-mind, it had to be important, didn't it? And all that about young King Joziré and Queen Wilvia. The threat against them hasn't stopped! Some race or group is trying to kill them!"

I asked, "Do you have any other languages in your head?"

"P'shagluk khoseghu bahgh," said Falija. "Ephais durronola."

I gasped. "Quaatariis. Pr'thas!"

"What?" cried Gloriana.

"She speaks Quaatar," I cried. "And Pthas! Oh my blessed soul. We only studied Quaatar because it was a precursor to an obscure Mercan tongue. It's a foul language, full of nasty words, and only the Quaatar could consider it holy. As for Pthas, well, they were the ancient and revered ones, the only people, it is said, who knew the name of the Great Experimenter . . . don't ask. That's just what was said. We have much of their language preserved, but of course it's not spoken anymore. Oh, I wish I'd known about this earlier."

Glory's face went red, all the way back to her ears. "If I'd told you, you'd have accused me of making it up!"

I stared at my shoes, ashamed. "You're right. I would have. I humbly beg your pardon. You'll have to forgive me without holding a grudge, Gloriana, because you and I must share this secret cooperatively, to keep Falija safe."

I Am M'urgi/on B'yurngrad

I entered the oasthouse through the summer door, which would have been enough to make those inside dislike me even had I not brought sleet gusting in to make a brief fog above the hearthstones. Their thoughts were on their faces: icetime was hard enough on the men, offering few and seldom comforts, without having them sullied by some fool southlander woman who couldn't tell a summer door from an icelock.

High-booted and wrapped in heavy furs, burdened with a high basket securely strapped to my shoulder, I stood for a moment in seeming ignorance of their hostility, though the lack of any greeting confirmed I had set myself wrong with them. B'Oag, the oastkeeper, made the matter clear, snarling, "Dja ne'er see an icelock where'er in devil's keep yah come from?"

The chill voice that came from behind my thick scarf was well practiced to have all the power it needed. "The summer door was nearest, Oastkeeper, and I have come too far to consider niceties." I unwound the scarf from my mouth, then from my neck and shoulders, and finally from around my head to display the golden diadem banding my forehead. At once the oasthall was murmurous with contrived conversation, all the men staring intently into one another's faces, talking of the season, the temperature, the monotony of the winter diet, anything except me. Even

B'Oag's eyes darted toward his other guests, as though to anchor his intention elsewhere, before reminding himself that he was, after all, on home ground, his name on the oasthouse sign, and not, therefore, required to give way.

"I'll be needing a room," I said. "Supper, also. Wine if you have it, or cider, or tea, if that's all there is."

The oastkeeper's eyes roved quickly over the company in the room. That meant his rooms were all filled. I saw his assistant, perhaps his son (they resembled one another), nod covertly from his chair in the corner, indicating he would take care of it, and B'Oag nodded shortly in return. "M'boy Ojlin'll have a room made up, mistress."

"Envoy, Oastkeeper. My title is envoy. One who wears the circlet has that name and no other outside the Siblinghood. I am come for a reason you already know. Let us not fence with one another. The night is too long and cold for that."

He flushed and fumbled while I regarded him with level, amber eyes. He, like many others, was fascinated by my eyes. He considered them catlike. These people told stories of us. They said it was something we ate off there in the badlands that made our eyes glow. Or if not something we ate, some dreadful thing we did. They were only lenses of a particular kind, which anyone should have been able to figure out. Human worlds are always awash in superstition, only a stubborn elite proof against it.

"I'll also need a lockroom," I murmured, easing the straps over my shoulders and putting an end to his speculation.

At this he paled, his nostrils pinched shut, as though to shut the very smell of me out. "Ask Ogric there." He nodded toward a dwarfish man near the stair. "Ogric keeps the key. I'll be putting your supper on the table by the copper."

Ogric did indeed have the key, though we had to go out into the storm to use it, for the lockroom opened onto the oasthouse courtyard. Still, it was in a sheltered corner, so I did not bother rewrapping myself before opening the door and peering into the closetlike space, floored and walled with square stones, a handspan to a side. "Is it sound?" I asked, holding out my lantern to survey it.

"D'rocks tall as me, everone in wall, everone in floor. Top slab, d'tooken ten umoxes lif' it."

I nodded, half smiling to myself as I calculated mentally: each rock a handspan square, each one a man's height long, laid so that the walls were a man's height thick, the interior space two man's heights high, one wide, one long, the slab on top a veritable mountain. It had taken only fear to move these northerners to this prodigious labor and only stupidity to go to all that trouble, then put a wooden door on the place.

"Ah," I murmured. "So it's tight, is it?"

"Aye . . . ma'am, dad'is. Comes ere ragin' crazies mid ice, we drow'm in dere. Dey stay. Dairn'd nodin geddin ou'vit."

"I'll take the key," which I did, from a hand that trembled slightly before Ogric turned and fled back to warmth, leaving me alone in the dim light of the lantern. I stepped inside with my basket, shutting the door behind me. A short time later I stepped out without the basket, shut the door firmly, and locked it behind me, then put my ear to the heavy, ironbound planks to listen for what sound might come from within. Hearing none, I took a deep breath, and another, pushing all the stench of it from my lungs, gasping as I replaced foul air with clean. Finally, I picked up the lantern and made my way back to the oasthall, now bereft of the greater number of its former occupants.

"Ruinous on business, envoys," B'Oag was saying to his son when I entered. He looked up and flushed. "Meaning no disrespect, ma' . . . that is, Envoy."

"I take no offense, Oastkeeper. We are not good for business. We are not supposed to be. Comfort yourself with the knowledge that if I find what I seek, I will not be here long."

"And that would be . . . ?"

"Do not trifle with me, Oastkeeper. You know what I'm here for and probably where it is and who has it. It's likely everyone in the district knows, including the children in their cradles. I have no doubt the whispers began the day he or she brought it home, whoever that person may be."

B'Oag mimed innocence, widening his eyes and pursing his lips. "Envoy, I have no idea . . ."

I turned away from him impatiently. "I left my burden in your lockroom, Oastkeeper. When my task is done, I'll go my way, taking it with me. If my task is weary and long, it will grow tired of its imprisonment, and then . . . then you will wish you had made it easy for me."

Without waiting to judge the effect of this threat, I went to the table by the wide, bell-shaped copper that hung over the heat source: a hot spring, a little fumarole, maybe a boiling mud pot, though it didn't smell like a mud pot. The copper funneled the heat upward into coiled flues that ran first through the oasthall, then into the rest of the place, including the spaces for animals. The laundry probably had its own source, preferably a hot spring that provided hot wash-water for clothes and linens.

The cider was already on the table, along with a plate covered by an overturned bowl to keep warm a dish of stewed meat, legumes, grain, and herbs. I took off the scarf, then the coat, hanging them on the back of a nearby chair. I wore boots to my knee, and trousers above that, thick with padding to keep out the cold. I stripped off my gloves and my padded jacket, becoming smaller as each layer was removed. At last I sat down in my shirtsleeves. I knew what they saw. A slender woman not yet of middle years, pale brown hair in many tiny braids making up a complex pattern that ended in a beaded knot at the nape of the neck, golden eyes glittering in the firelight, skin reddened by the unaccustomed heat. I must have looked quite ordinary, except for the eyes and the gold Siblinghood diadem with its jewel blooming upon my forehead as though it carried fire within itself.

Something moved at my throat, and I took it from beneath my shirt, a tiny feathered thing that blinked in the firelight before settling itself on the table beside my plate. I beckoned, and B'Oag came to my side. "A pinch or two of raw grain, Oastkeeper. I found this little one in the snow, barely alive. Do you know what sort it is?"

"Chitterlain: one that waited too long to go south."

"Well, I am of no mind to let it freeze."

He fetched the grain, a small handful, and scattered it on the table where the chitterlain lay. It stirred itself to peck at the offering, at first doubtfully, but then with renewed energy, stretching its four wings, first one pair, then the other. I poured a bit of water into a saucer and put it where the creature could drink from it.

B'Oag whispered to his son while I ate, the others in the room kept their voices down. Several times, all speech stopped when sounds came in from outside, a ragged howling, a snuffling at the summer door, a low growl, almost like a purr, a shrill yap or two followed by shriller yips. Dire wolves and their pups. Ice cats and their kits. The great ape-bears had already gone deep into their dens. All feathered creatures except the thunder-buzzards had fled south long ago. Now there were only the winter beasts, the winter men (for their women-folk stayed home in snowtime), and one envoy from who knew where.

"What's in the basket?" the boy asked B'Oag, in a voice I could hear clearly, his curiosity overcoming his prudence.

I saw B'Oag go white again, lips pinched. "Ojlin, hush, or I'll hush you! We don't mention it! We don't question it! We don't know about it! It's not of us, it's of them!"

The opening of the icelock door went unnoticed among the howl-ing and growling outside until a chill draft announced the cracking of the inner door to admit a tall form, as thickly bundled as I had been. From the corner of my eye I saw him removing his gloves one finger at a time, slapping them against his thigh to remove the ice crystals, laying them on the nearest table while he unbuttoned the thick coat, furred outside with a shag woven of the long, curly winter locks of adult mountain gnar, furred inside with the soft woven fleece of the young. Beneath it were seemingly endless layers of other clothing, which he merely unbuttoned in series, all the while looking about himself, ceiling, floor, shuttered windows, the hot copper with its armspan wide coil of metal flue above it, both hood and flue radiating welcome heat.

I ignored him and went on with my meal.

"Oastkeeper?" he asked at last, through the scarves still hiding his face.

"B'Oag Thenterson," he said. "An 'ow may we serve you, sir?"

"Food. Whatever she's having smells good. And a pitcher of cider, if you have it."

"This early in the icetime, we've got it," said B'Oag, as the stranger paced slowly across the floor.

Before I realized what he was doing, he was at my shoulder, lean-ing above me. "Envoy?" he whispered, almost in my ear.

I turned, startled, looking up into a face I remembered as in a dream. "Fernwo . . ." I breathed. "Where did you . . . what are you . . . ?"

"Hush," he murmured. "There's a roomful of ears about us, don't you know? Ears ready to mishear, noses to smell conspiracy where none exists, mouths to twist good intentions into evil certainties. We know all about it, Envoy. We were told often enough."

"Sit down," I quavered, taking a deep breath. Then, more evenly, "You're being conspicuous."

"Thank you, yes. I'll sit here next to your friend. Chitterlain, isn't it? A bit far from its kindred. But then, so am I. It's been a long road, finding you."

I set my spoon down, lifted my glass to sip at the cider it contained, willing myself to appear impassive. Envoys were always impassive, facing life or death with the same quiet comportment, the same emotionless mien. This wasn't death. It was suddenly too much life, but appearance could be everything.

B'Oag arrived with plates, bowls, a pitcher of cider, another glass. He stood uncertainly nearby.

"Put it here," said the new arrival. "The envoy is an old acquaintance, and I'll sup with her."

The oastkeeper had only waited for the word. The plates came down with purposeful clatter, Fernwold pulled out a chair and sat facing me. I had again dipped my spoon.

"Good?" he asked.

"Passable," I said. "Anything made with smoked or salted meat is passable at best. This is dried in the smoke, not too salty, and the oastkeeper has traded for seasonings, too, which some of them up here don't bother to do. They figure people get hungry enough, they'll eat anything."

"Including envoys?"

"I doubt they consider envoys among the general run of people who frequent oasthouses."

"And you're here for . . . ?"

"In pursuit of duty, Fernwold . . ."

"Ferni," he suggested, smiling. "You called me Ferni."

"Fernwold," I said again firmly. "Why are you here?"

"I learned you were sent. I had some time and a reason or two. I decided to offer assistance to my old friend, Margaret."

I shuddered, only slightly. How long had it been since I had heard that name? "Say it as B'yurngrad says it, if you say it at all. I am M'urgi, shaman of B'yurngrad steppes. You are Fernwold, seeker and assessor. I am, from time to time, given the crown of an envoy—as are you, I've been told—and we're not allowed assistance."

"We're not allowed to ask for it. It can be given, and it often is."

"By whom?" I whispered. "I've never had help!"

He shrugged, took a great gulp of the steaming cider, belching slightly as it expanded the cold air in throat and belly. "Perhaps they never thought you needed it until now. No. Perhaps I knew you never really needed it until now. Don't go all proud on me, love. We know one another too well for that."

"Knew," I breathed. "Once."

"We need one another's help, whether you know it yet or not. And everything we knew of one another, we still know, Shaman, and it was a good deal more than can be dismissed as 'once.' I told you then what I tell you now. I knew you the moment I saw you. We are mates, M'urgi, whether we meet once a lifetime, once a decade, or every day. Nothing changes when we are apart."

My hand on the pitcher trembled only slightly. "Some of that is right."

"Which part?"

"Nothing changes when we're apart. It's when we're together things must change. Ferni, where have you been!"

He gritted his teeth. "My recent life has not been one I wanted to drag you into. Or thought I had the right to. I worry about the parts of my life I don't remember!"

I paled. "The Siblinghood wiped your mind?"

"Perhaps they. Or someone, something else that's left me missing a few years here and there. I remember everything since meeting you, however. And before that, the academy, I remember that." He drank again. "Are you carrying?"

I bared my wrist, letting him see the round sucker marks where it had drunk my blood, not much of it, just a little every day, enough to keep it from going dormant, but not enough to give it the power to overcome my will, so long trained and tried, like steel forged, folded, beaten, and hardened, over and over again. I pulled the sleeve back into place. "They have a lockroom. Built of stone, a maht thick."

He touched the marks gently with a fingertip, erasing them and the soreness that had accompanied them. "I'll never understand northerners. It's carried in a basket woven out of reeds or straw. Any latched closet would hold the crippled ones we carry, but they build a lockroom thick enough to hold the devil."

"They've never seen one, Fernwold. I have seldom seen one. We take some pains not to look at them until we have to, don't we? Fear and superstition always follow the unseen, the unknown, the whispered of." I sighed, wiggling my fingers, now free of pain. "I would have healed me after I'd eaten, when I felt warmer, but thank you." They taught us this healing of the ghyrm wounds. It took only concentration and a little strength. A little more than I had had when I came in.

"I know," he said, returning to his supper. The chitterlain moved over near his plate and regarded him with beady eyes, then began preening its feathers as though it had decided he was harmless. He smiled. "They talk, did you know that? The chitterlain?"

"I did not," I said. "You mean like a . . . what was it, a parrot? A mimic?"

"No, no. They talk. There's a one-eyed old fellow, a member of the Siblinghood, I think, hangs about from time to time. He says they're the last remaining of a race of creatures that once were starfarers, city builders."

"This little one?"

"Yes." He leaned down close. "You understand what I'm saying?"

"Sooor," it trilled. "Loor ti ellld."

"Which means?" I asked.

"Which means, 'Yes, I speak of old times.' They live in colonies, the chitterlain. They spend the winters in the south, getting fat and telling stories to their children. In the spring, they fly back to the northland."

His voice was weighted with sadness, and he turned back to his meal. When the soup and cider had warmed him somewhat, he turned to the more substantial and savory stuff. "Are you here on retrieval?" he asked between bites.

"I thought you were told where I was."

"I was. I didn't ask why, for my errand had reason enough."

"And what was that?"

"First to find you, then warn you, then to protect you. There's a threat against your life."

I shrugged. "That's been the case since I left Earth."

"This is specific, but I don't think anyone's followed you here. What's the situation?"

"The Siblinghood tells me they have a ghyrm here."

"Recent enough that nobody has . . . ?"

"We're never quick enough to prevent somebody from playing the fool!" I snapped. "Otherwise, this retrieval could have waited until the thaw."

"When are you going to find it?"

I shook my head, looked around the room, where this chair and that had been emptied since his arrival. "Not here. This isn't the place to discuss any such thing. Let's talk about something else."

"Very well. Have I told you it's a good thing you stayed out of Mercan space. I've been on a few of those worlds recently. Rinwall. Bonxar. Fajnard." He dropped his voice, almost to a whisper. "I've gone into the mountain fastnesses of Pcrepume a few times, visiting the Gibbekot, who say revolution's brewing on Fajnard: Gibbekot, Ghoss, and umoxen on one side, Frossian overlords on the other."

"You go spying for the Siblinghood?"

"The Siblinghood is merely keeping an eye on what's happening. They haven't offered the Gibbekot any help as yet. You'd have known if they had."

"I've been away from the news for some while," I said. "Are the Frossians involved in this supposed threat to me?"

"It's possible. Their nature is to be loyal supporters of whatever demagogue has the most power, and though there are no Frossians on B'yurngrad, the threat could come through them to someone local." He frowned. "You're thinner, M'urgi. You look well, but thin. It's strange, when I see you I think how well you've taken to the discipline of our calling. Most women don't like the solitude."

I considered this. "Most *people* don't, male or female, but people who grow up as solitary children already know the eremitic life. We find it more comforting than onerous. The work is easy enough, except when we're carrying, and that isn't often."

"True. This one you're hunting, any idea where it came from?"

"The wild tribes have been using them as weapons for as long as I can remember."

"None reported on Chottem," he murmured. "None on Thairy. Fajnard is suspect, of course. Frossian society would be meat and drink for the ghyrm-things."

"Except among the tribes, we've heard of few on B'yurngrad. Not here, not yet."

"Except for the ones in our keeping, no?"

I made a face. "Let's not talk about them. I have far more than enough of them. What's the news?"

So we talked: of the legal maneuvers in the city of Bray, on Chottem, to have the heiress of Bray declared dead so the ancillary branches of the family could claim the fortune; how the sudden arrival of the heiress had thrown all that into a heap; of the most recent results of the Great Walling-Off, Dominion's social experiment on Tercis; of rumors that the Queen of the Ghoss, Wilvia the Wise, who had disappeared from Fajnard long ago, had been seen on Tercis some years before; of the Reunion of Academy Alumni that was to take place at Point Zibit on Thairy and of Ferni's friends who would be there. Inconsequential talk, as the chitterlain ate and drank its fill; casual talk as the chitterlain flew to my collar and burrowed into the warmth of the scarf about my throat. All the time, Ferni's eyes never left my face.

When we had finished our meal, he asked, "Have you a room here?"

I slanted a sideways look at him, deciding whether to admit it or not, deciding I really had no choice.

"May I share it?" he whispered.

"Ah, Ferni," I murmured, half to myself. "After all this time. Over ten years! Sometimes I thought I'd only dreamed you, now here you are. Why now?"

"Couldn't help myself." He smiled as he started to reach for my hand but stopped, aware of the eyes and the ears still in the room. He stood and went to the counter where B'Oag stood. "We'd like another pitcher of cider, Oastkeeper. Is there a heating coil in the envoy's room? If so, we'll talk out our business there, rather than ruin your trade for the whole evening."

"I thank you for your consideration," said B'Oag, glancing around his nearly empty oasthall. He turned to his son. "Ojlin, be sure the steam coil is turned on full in the envoy's room, and take up a pitcher of cider."

"That's all right, Oastkeeper," Fernwold murmured. "Here's your pay for our dinner tonight and for the room. I'll carry the cider and set the coil myself."

B'Oag, bewildered at the largess on the counter before him, made no objection to this at all.

I Am Ongamar/on Cantardene

On Cantardene, years had passed since I, that is, Miss Ongamar, had witnessed the sacrifice on the funeral hill. I had fed the thing with parts of that happening, fed it to such satiety that it hadn't bothered me for several days. Then came rumors of the population crest on Earth and the accompanying restoration of the planet, fed day after day by statistics showing that Earth's population was actually and consistently falling. Within a century, so it was whispered, the population would be reduced from eighteen billion to the tenth of that advised by Dominion as a sensible maximum human population for the foreseeable future. On hearing of this, the K'Famir threatened to sue for damages in the Interstellar Trade Organization. If Earth's population fell, there would not be enough surplus humans to provide slave labor, and the K'Famir had contracted for slave labor!

Responding to the suit, the Dominion announced that humans would continue to be shipped as bondslaves into both Omniont and Mercan areas of influence for the term of the contract, which was fifty Earth years. The Mercan Combine, and its K'Famir representatives, immediately accused the Dominion of restraint of trade and threatened various unpleasant consequences, such as tariffs, raids on colony worlds, and the like if the downward trend were not immediately reversed. To all of these the

Dominion replied that Dominion business was Dominion business, not subject to Combine or Federation demands.

The matter had then been appealed to the ISTO, who referred it to the IG Court of Justice, where the Dominion view had recently been unanimously sustained, the court holding that habitable planets, being few and extremely valuable, were more in need of protection than was the provision of cheap labor on planets with an enormous population of an idle elite, and further, that the welfare of the planet must always take precedence over the greediness of its inhabitants or, in this case, their purchasers; and, yet further, that a decline in the population of a previously highly proliferative species, if indeed this had happened, was more a matter for celebration than harassment.

The most recently circulated rumor was that Dominion Central Authority had recently disappeared from its usual seat on Mars and left no word as to its whereabouts, thus forestalling forcible retaliation by the Combine. Dominion had, at least for the time being, vanished in the smoke.

"What will we do for fitters?" Lady Ephedra demanded. "All our fitters are Earthian slaves. Tell me, Miss Ongamar! You are Earthian! What will we do for fitters?"

"I suppose you will have to pay them, madam," I said, through a mouth full of pins. "There are always Earthians willing to work if the pay is good."

"Pay fitters?" Lady Ephedra was shocked into silence. "I've never heard of such a thing."

"Pay workers? Not for the next few lifetimes, at any rate," I heard a K'Famir crew boss telling his friend. "They're still bringing shiploads of them out from Earth. By the time we've used them all up, the Earth colonies will be overpopulating, just as Earthians always do, and we'll buy up the excess. Just wait and see!"

I acknowledged to myself that it was selfish to feel so, but I was grateful that Earth had been struck by salvation, despite itself! Not that Earthians appreciated that fact, according to the K'Famir, though that may have been wishful thinking. All this babble continued to feed *it*, day after day, and thankful as I was, I detected something worrisome in the thing's appetite, a nervous undercurrent that reminded me of a childhood time when I had stuffed myself with candy, each mouthful creating a need for another mouthful, so that no amount of the sweetness satisfied me. I had been very sick, very sorry, and so the thing in its stone closet seemed almost to sicken as it gorged on the talk about Earth.

Could one imagine that *it* felt anxiety? Or, more likely, that the creature or organism that directed the ghyrm and its appetites was feeling anxiety. Something I might turn to my advantage? Now that my contract as a fitter was drawing to a close, was there a way I could escape from *it*? Though the years on Cantardene were longer than Earth years, I believed that less than half a year remained before my official enslavement would be over. I could look forward to being taken to one of the colony planets, and I had applied to go to Chottem, with B'yurngrad as a second choice. Even Thairy or Tercis would be acceptable. I had been twelve when I arrived on Cantardene, twenty-two when Adille had died, I was almost thirty-seven now, actually older than that, if one figured in the relative length of the years. If I could leave the planet without the thing, distance would surely attenuate its influence on me, or so I prayed. If I could not escape *it*, would *it* expect transport to an Earthian colony? I had not, myself, committed any evil yet, and was determined to avoid doing so.

I tried not to think of the possibility that I would not be allowed to go at all. My hands busied themselves with a vivilon chemise, setting in a gusset without a moment's thought while my mind remained caught in its web of anxieties. I knew things about the K'Famir that I should not know. I knew things about the Mercan Combine that I should not know. Creatures of various kinds had talked back and forth over my stooped body, giggling over pillow talk, telling secrets. I knew that the Mercan Combine planned to take over Chottem, that the Omnionts intended to annex Thairy and Tercis. Oh, not right away. Not until all the servants on Earth had been pumped into the system. The thing had sucked up this information with groans of pleasure, but still I had felt its underlying dissatisfaction, its barely sensed agitation.

This morning I had told *it* I would not return until late, for I intended to go into the pleasure quarter to hear what other races thought of the news from Earth. It had hissed at me, as it always did, a threat, a certainty of death if I did not return timely. How *it* would accomplish this, I didn't know. Adille had simply died of weakness, for *it* had drained her dry. I felt no weakening as yet. My mirror showed no dissipation of strength or premature aging. The thing didn't want to weaken me. It wanted to go on using me.

I bent over to pick up a few spilled pins and once again heard conversation from the neighboring fitting room.

"I'll have Miss Ongamar take care of it. I never have any complaints about her work." It was Lady Ephedra's voice.

"She's been with you quite a while," said a languorous, uncaring voice. "Not cheating the decree, are we, dear?"

Shrill squeals of laughter. "Aren't you dreadful to say such a thing! She's been with me for a long time because she's very good. Quite the best I've had. A decree is a decree, but I confess I shall hate to turn her over to the males up there on the Hill of Beelshi."

I stopped breathing. Lady Ephedra's voice went on. "I don't know why they always want humans. They don't use any of the other slaves as sacrifices, only humans."

I gritted my teeth and breathed lightly, lightly, they mustn't know I was listening. In case someone peeked in, I had to keep my fingers busy, but that voice could only belong to one of the baron's neuters. Of all the K'Famir, I hated the neuters the worst. At least the others seemed to know they were being cruel, the neuters did not even realize it. They had no minds at all.

"How much longer does she have?" asked the languorous one.

"I may be able to stretch it to a year," said Lady Ephedra. "For some reason, they wanted her dead several years ago. Someone, somewhere ordered it. I misled them then, telling them she had died, and I have lied to them several times since, extending her term of bondage. Very soon, I shall not be able to lie to them anymore."

"Do you always obey the decree and let the males kill your fitters?" the neuter asked.

"Oh, yes," said the Lady Ephedra. "Stretch it out as one may, one must obey, eventually. One doesn't know what they may have picked up in the fitting rooms. They always die on the hill, shortly before their terms expire."

In the neighboring room, I straightened, my hands still working as I finished the chemise and set it aside, momentarily amazed at how easily I had done the task, created a piece of clothing for a creature more like a spider than a human, a creature with eight extremities, with two mouths, four eyes, no visible ears, and several sets of copulatory organs, some of them used only for pleasure.

So they did not intend to let me go. Though it was likely Lady Ephedra didn't know precisely how her fitter was to be killed, she knew it would happen. I was suddenly very warm, almost hot, the fury rising in me like a wave. I would kill them all, I would burn down House Mouselline. I would . . .

I would do nothing precipitant, I warned myself. I had been fortunate to overhear. It gave me time to make a plan. Time perhaps to get away. Time certainly to arrange that someone in Dominion would learn of all the things I knew.

"Are you finished, Miss Ongamar?" asked the Lady Ephedra from the doorway of the little room. "Everything completed."

"Oh, yes, Lady Ephedra," I said, bowing humbly. "Just straightening up before I leave."

I Am M'urgi/on B'yurngrad

Ferni rose early and quietly from the warm bed where I lay, still half asleep. He left the door ajar, and I heard him speaking to B'Oag in the oasthall below.

"You're putting a fine polish on that copper," he said.

"Been rumblin' at me," B'Oag complained. "In the night. D'ja hear it?"

"Once or twice," Ferni said. "It didn't sound like an imminent eruption."

"Yah, well, last time it went, it didn' give any warning atall. Never hurts to check, see all the seams're tight."

"You have a relief valve, don't you?"

"Be a fool not to, wun I?"

"Any chance of getting some breakfast? Do you have a henhouse here?"

"Oh, sure. Sev'ral nice little vents comin' off this spring, 'ere. Got one of 'em cased up through the henhouse 'fore it warms the barn. Keep a lantern out there, so eggs we got. Hens won't lay 'thout light, 'thout heat. I got jibber sausage, too, smoke or plain. The bread'll be baked another little while. Y'wanna take it up?"

"Good idea. The longer she rests, the quicker her job will be."

There was silence for a few moments before B'Oag remarked, all too casually, "I heard somethin' a few days back. Mebbe somebody's got one a those, like she has."

Ferni said, "I'm sorry to hear that. People who happen on those things usually don't live long after."

"Thing is, this person has a fambly person sick, like to die. This person knows the . . . the thing takes souls to Joy."

Ferni made a sound of rude derision. "Oh, again I'm sorry to hear that. That story is put about by the things themselves, so people will let them in, let them near. I've met with teachers, wisemen. The creatures don't take the soul to Joy. They just eat it until nothing's left. Envoys like her upstairs are sent to stop the soul-eating, to trap the evil thing and see it's put where it can do no harm."

"Y'mean there's no Joy? No bein' took up?"

"Who would say the good are not taken to Joy? They may well be, but not by these things. The person who found this one was worried because his dear one is near to dying?"

"She," B'Oag corrected. "Where's these things come from, then, these evils? Did a man make them?"

Ferni said, "They're parasites, Oastkeeper. Like a louse or a flea, only more deadly. We don't know who makes them, but we will find out!"

"You're one a them, then. Them silence people."

No sound. Ferni didn't agree or disagree. Perhaps he only waited, his nose full of the same wonderful smell that had opened my eyes wide. Someone had opened the oven door and filled the oasthouse with the aroma of new-baked bread.

"I'll see to breakfast," said B'Oag. "Ya'll wait?"

"I'll wait," Ferni said. "No need for you to make the trip upstairs."

I dozed, only a moment until I heard the thud of Ferni's step on the stair, and I grinned when he came in, unable to help it.

I sat upright, pulling the blanket around my shoulders. "By the Ghost of Joziré, that smells edible."

He set it on the foot of the bed, turning a troubled face toward me. "By the Ghost of Joziré? Why's he a ghost? I thought . . . I thought he was just hiding out somewhere."

I examined his face. "It bothers you to think he might be dead? Did you know him?"

"Of him, yes. A good man, so I've been told."

"It's just something people say, Ferni. What did you bring for breakfast?"

"Eggs," he said. "Sausage and fresh bread and tea and what looks like"—he uncapped the small stoneware jar to see what it held—"honey."

I made a lap and beckoned for the tray.

"I have news," he said.

"The oastkeeper decided to speak of it, eh? I thought he knew where it was."

"Well, he hasn't told me where, yet, but he's told me why. Somebody's on death watch."

"Then we'll hope we're not too late."

"After breakfast," he agreed. "And, by the by, what's this oath on King Joziré's ghost?"

Spooning honey onto fresh bread, I said, "I've seen it, the ghost."

His mouth fell open, and it took a moment for him to latch it up again. "Come now."

"You're the one sent me to that shaman, Ferni. What'd you think she'd teach me? How to make tea?"

Now it was his turn to think. "Quite frankly, I didn't think about it at all. At the time, I was just told to do it, send you, I mean, and I thought you'd be safe there."

"Safe I was for a time. Then safe I wasn't, but I was less fearful than previously. You say you've heard a threat. Well, I've seen one. Someone does want me dead."

"What did the shaman teach you?"

"She taught me ways to fly, to escape, to die, if necessary. To see spirits and converse with ghosts. To speak at a distance to someone receptive. Though she seemed to think I knew most of it already. It was in my bones, she said, else all her teaching would have done naught."

Ferni asked, "So what did the shade of King Joziré have to say for himself?"

Around a mouthful of egg, I said, "When I saw him on the night road, he said he was wandering, seeking Wilvia and his children . . ."

"His children?" Ferni gaped at me, forehead furrowed.

"Twins. A boy, a girl."

"What makes you think Wilvia and the children died?"

"I didn't say they did!" I snorted. "I didn't say he did."

He muttered, "Well then, what you saw wasn't a ghost. What you saw was a night wanderer, a spirit: alive, asleep, dreaming."

This was perfectly possible. "He seemed so familiar to me that I didn't even wonder. I didn't think of him being a spirit wanderer, though I do that myself."

After we had eaten and put on multiple layers of additional clothing, I put the chitterlain in a cage Ferni had borrowed from the oastmaster, set it in a warm place with food and water inside, and went to retrieve the basket from the lockroom. Then we heard B'Oag's reluctantly given directions, which concluded with: "She's only a lass, Envoy. Go easy with her."

"Easy as I can," I replied. "If it's not too late to go any way at all."

The ice storm had given way to frigid calm. The road was only a shadow-edged depression that curved around the snowy hillocks before us. Ice lay beneath the thin layer of new snow, too slippery to traverse until we strapped thorn-feet over our boots. The world was painted in shades of metallic gray, silver where weak light struck it, pewter where shadows fell, iron beneath the cover of ice-laden trees. When we had gone far enough to be out of sight of the oasthouse, I gave Ferni my tool kit to carry before opening the coin-sized window in the basket. It had to be held well away from me as the questing tentacle emerged hesitantly into the cold. It squirmed, then slowly flailed the air, up, down, right, left, suddenly becoming rigid as it pointed in the direction we were traveling.

We held our breaths as much as possible, for when the ghyrm were not well fed, they stank, sending out their smell to others of their kind, calling a gather of the hungry. Alone, ghyrm were weak, easily crushed, burned, poisoned if one had the right tools, and thus unlikely to survive long treks in dangerous country. A gather of them, on the other hand, stank with a feculent rot that made creatures emerge gasping from burrows or plunge unconscious from the skies. Both of us had seen records of tribal settlements ravaged by ghyrm in which nothing was left alive beneath, upon, or above the soil.

The tentacle began to swerve slightly to the right of our line of travel. Shortly, we came to the narrower lane that went in that direction, a barely shadowed trail around the breast of the hill. The tendril quivered.

"When will you basket it?" asked Ferni, observing the questing tentacle with disgust.

"As soon as I'm sure we have the right place," I replied.

The house lay just behind the hill, dug in for more than half its height, small, shuttered windows high upon its walls beneath the deep eaves of the high-pitched roof. The door was set at the inner end of a roofed tunnel that led through the hill to the house wall. The tentacle quivered its eagerness. Before we entered the tunnel, I took my tool kit from Ferni, opened it, and fastened it around my waist, where I could reach it easily. I slipped the killing knife from its sheath and put it near the tentacle, which shrieked as it lashed back into the basket. I shut the opening and set the basket on the snow.

"What makes them yell like that?" asked Ferni.

"I don't know any more than you do," I retorted. "The Siblinghood doesn't tell us. I've always supposed the blades are poisoned because they make ulcers on our skins if we touch them."

The latchstring was out. Ferni released the inside latch, letting us into a long, ice-cold room, ashes on the hearth, an inside door standing ajar. We peered through the crack: a bed, a body lying on it, another beside it, no movement in either. I stepped back.

"It's loose in that room," I said. "Probably on the girl."

We pushed the door open and went to the side of the young woman lying beside the bed, pale as the snow. The woman on the bed was long dead. Ghyrm-kill were often virtually mummified, making it impossible to learn when they had died. We did not see the thing itself.

The girl's chest moved in a shallow breath. I said, "She's still alive, so it's on her somewhere, under her clothes. They can sometimes move quickly. There are too many hiding places in here, including us. Take the girl's feet, I'll take the hands. We want her outside on a nice, empty, hard-packed snowbank."

We carried her out through the doors and the tunnel to lay her on the snow some distance from the house. I returned to the basket and opened the porthole once more, carrying the basket near to the girl, watching the tentacle as it quivered, quivered, stretched itself to the maximum length near the girl's breast. I set the basket a safe distance aside, took my killing knife in one hand and a cutting tool in the other, starting at the girl's throat and slitting her clothing as far as her waist.

"There," whispered Ferni, pointing with the tip of his knife at a pulsing red mole on the girl's breast, a mole with legs that trembled as it sucked her life into itself.

"How long does one of them take to kill a person?" he asked.

"If there's only one small one, half a day or more. Lend me your knife."

He held out the sheath, and I drew forth a twin to my own, a broad, curved blade with a slightly hooked end. With a knife in each hand, I bent forward, catching the thing between them like grist between grindstones, mashing and twisting the flat sides of the blades to pulverize what lay between.

A scream came from between the blades, impossibly shrill, barely within the limit of hearing, and was echoed by a howl of fury from the basket as the tentacle turned toward the house, quivering, quivering.

"More of them in there?" asked Ferni.

"If the tentacle stays rigid, yes," I said, scrubbing the blades in the snow to clean them. "When they kill someone, they sometimes split into buds. The buds don't always grow, but sometimes they do."

"The Order wants us to capture them . . ." he said doubtfully.

"I know," I said, returning his knife carefully. "Several times I've tried, but it's impossible to capture the tiny ones. There's no way to hold them securely outside a laboratory. We have to put everything that may be contaminated in that building, then we have to burn it."

"What about her?"

"We strip her bare, shave her head and body hair into her clothes, throw them into the house along with that spot on the snow, which could conceivably have buds in it, search her body, wrap her in one of our coats, and take her back to the oasthouse."

"She'll freeze!"

"It's partly the cold that's kept her alive so far. The things aren't as active in the cold. She won't freeze in the time it will take us to get her back. I've done this before, during even colder times. I'm quick at it."

Under the clippers from my tool kit, the girl's clothes and hair fell away like wool from a shorn sheep. I scanned every intimate part of her, an inspection that Ferni regarded with discomfiture.

"I violate her no more than needed," I explained. "I look only in the creases. The creatures do not enter the body orifices. They have gills, and they need air. Here, wrap her in my coat, I have four or five layers on besides it. They'll keep me warm enough until we get back."

"How do we fire the house?" he asked.

"An incendiary in the pocket of the coat. Pull the lever and toss it inside."

I checked to see that the tentacle still pointed rigidly at the house, forced the tentacle into the basket, and closed it, then put the bundled girl over my shoulder and started back the way we had come, leaving the basket for Ferni. From behind me came a sudden whoosh, then the crackle of flames and the sound of curses. He caught up to me where the lane joined the road.

"Let me take her."

"When we get halfway, you can have her."

We went on trudging toward the steam plume above the oast-house, sun breaking through the clouds above us in momentary encouragement. At the halfway mark, we traded burdens, arriving finally at the oasthouse under B'Oag's accusatory frown.

"We committed no violence on her," I snapped from behind my colleague. "The thing was killing her. It already took the woman. Was that her mother?"

He looked down guiltily. "Her ma, yes."

"Well, she didn't get to Joy, Oastkeeper. She's simply gone, erased from existence. That's what the creatures do. You should talk to your neighbors and let them know the facts."

"What about her?" he grumped, pointing at the girl.

"I'm taking her to your baths, where I'll search her skin, to be sure there are no more." I would do it, though I was positive there were no more. My "finder" should have reached for her if there had been. However, I remembered too well finding a bead of a thing on my clothing one time when I undressed for bed, and I'd been positive that time, too.

"What about her ma's body?" B'Oag asked Ferni.

"We left it in the house, and we had to burn the house behind us, for there were more of the creatures inside."

The oastkeeper grumped, "Thought what you were for was to catch 'em, take 'em away. That all was a good house."

"You can't catch the tiny ones," Ferni told him sternly. "Some are too small to see. And, since you knew about all this, now we'll need to know who may have brought it here and who else knew about it besides you."

B'Oag scowled. Ferni scowled back at him, a look that transformed his normally genial face into one of threatening ferocity, threatening enough, at any rate, to result in a less overtly hostile conversation.

I left it to Ferni and lugged the girl off to the baths, where I stripped off even the silky shirt and trousers that served as a warm bodysuit by day and decent sleepwear at night. During a northern winter on Fajnard, one got bare only in the tight oasthouse baths with their deep tubs of steaming water, constantly draining back into the stone basin they came from, constantly renewed and reheated. I took the girl into the tub with me, held her nose, and submerged her for a long count of thirty. No ghyrmlets surfaced, gasping for air. I dragged, her out, wrapped her warmly, got myself dressed, and took her to a warmed bed. Her body was alive, but only time would tell if her mind still was.

It was some time before I returned to the oasthall to find B'Oag looking haggard and ill-used, ostentatiously avoiding my eyes as he attended to business. Ferni sat waiting by the copper, a steaming cup in his hand. Seeing me approach, he set out another and poured from the pot. "Well?" with raised eyebrows.

"She's clean." I took a grateful sip of the hot tea. It had honey in it. "The basket?"

"Back in the lockroom. B'Oag says the girl, G'lil, and her mother worked with the weavers' guild in the nearest town south, place called Vaccy. Summers, after shearing season, the local women weave at the mill; winters they weave with small looms at home, piecework, special commissions, fancy stuff they've no time for in summer. When the weather permits, they pick up supplies at the mill. Not long ago, the girl came in here, wanting to talk to B'Oag about Joy, how people got taken there when they died, what could be done to assure it happened.

"Finally, she admitted it was her mother who was dying. The doctors in Vaccy said there was nothing more they could do. B'Oag says he told her to take the doctors' word for it, just keep her mother warm and well fed. The girl asked him if that was true even if someone had found a Taker. That's what they call them around here. Takers. He told her all that was foolishness. This is what he tells me now, which may well be a lie. His excuse was that he didn't think she'd actually found one. Then you arrive, making him believe she might actually have done so. We discussed where she might have found it, and he said the only place the girl ever went was to the mills and provender stores in Vaccy."

"The mills import raw material and export fabric?"

"They do, yes." He turned back to his tea. "They buy wool and hair from the farms around here that were started when the colony was founded: sheep, camel, goat. The mills import down from Choubirds raised somewhere in Omniont space, and umox wool from Fajnard. The fiber for ultrasilk and vivilon comes in as cocoons, great sacks of them." He laughed. "According to B'Oag, the mills label the fine fabrics as coming from the Isles of Delight." He laughed. "Seemingly the K'Famir merchants don't want it known their underwear is woven by dirty humans."

I shook my head. "This girl didn't weave vivilon, her hands are hard as rocks. Nonetheless, she was there, at the mill. Your mentioning cocoons makes me wonder . . ."

He nodded. "When B'Oag mentioned it, it struck me that cocoons with something live inside could make an excellent hiding place for vast numbers of infant ghyrm."

I thought about this for a while. "It doesn't answer the question of how she knew what she'd found, or thought she knew. The things are repulsive in their own shape, but they usually pretend to be something else."

"I've heard that."

"This search-and-destroy business we accomplished today is new to you, isn't it."

He nodded again. "So?"

"So what have you been doing during your years with the Siblings? I thought all of us were out seeking ghyrm."

He shook his head at me. "There are more things than ghyrm threatening the Siblinghood. There's the question of the survival of the human race. There's exploration for new colony planets, and from time to time certain people need to be located, which we also do. That is, those of us who are not, like you, busy killing ghyrm as a full-time job."

"What people do you locate? And for whom?"

He merely smiled at me.

"Oh, right. You're a Sibling of Silence. Very well. We won't talk about that. What shall we talk about?"

He mused, "I was interested in your story last night, about how you got here to B'yurngrad. You said you could have gone on a ship into Mercan space. Any idea where it was going?"

I shook my head, still annoyed by the memory. "I found out later, yes. It was headed for Fajnard. Where the Frossians are. How about you? How did you get into the academy?"

"I don't know, and they don't say. They just tell you you've been recommended, and that's it. Many of the cadets were from well-to-do families, and heaven knows I wasn't. I got in with the group I told you about the other night, Naumi and the others, and we all did well through our fellowship, six of us, all of us helping each other when needful. When I graduated, I was sent on one of those 'can't remember' missions . . ."

"Which is . . . ?"

"One I literally can't remember. They take the memory away, so no matter what some inimical force might try, they can't get it out of me. I don't even know if I joined the Siblings before or after, but I've been with them ever since."

"At least you've traveled. Except for my youth on Phobos and ten years or so on Earth, I've spent my whole life here on B'yurngrad, and I spend too much time regretting all those years of school, learning languages I've never used. When the shaman died, I fulfilled her burdens, which I'll tell you about another time; and then I was briefly apprenticed to a full-time ghyrm-hunter. That's when the Siblinghood made me a member."

"B'yurngrad isn't a bad world. It has some really beautiful places on it."

"Unless ghyrm have been reported at one of them, I've never been there."

"No vacation?" he asked, seemingly astonished.

"I've never asked for one," I said, somewhat surprised at my own admission. "I didn't know it was allowed."

"It's a rule that we're allowed to have vacations. You're probably entitled to at least a year's off-time by now." He mused, staring at the still-steaming cup before him. "Tell you what. There's something happening, something I think you'd be helpful at. Let's arrange for some vacation, and we'll do some traveling together."

The idea was attractive. I could not remember being so taken with an idea for many years. Not since . . . not since childhood. Not since the visit to Mars.

"Mars," I murmured. "The dragonfly."

He looked at me wonderingly. "Is that where they are? On Mars?"

"Where what are?"

"The dragonfly ships. The ones the . . . person pilots. It was a kind of vision or dream Naumi had, at the Academy. I don't really remember what he said." He laughed ruefully. "Do you ever get these weird memories? As though you've been somewhere or done a particular thing before?"

I could only nod, yes, indeed, we all did.

In the morning, the sun came out, the day warmed. The girl, G'lil, who had spent the previous night bundled up next to the coil in my room, began to moan and quiver. At noon, she awoke, and I fed her soup, as much as she would swallow.

"Now," I demanded, "suppose you tell me where you got that thing that we stopped from killing you."

"What thing . . . you mean the Taker. Ma . . . where's Ma?"

I took several deep breaths and told myself to be patient. "G'lil. Your mother is dead. She was not taken to Joy, she was eaten, and you came very close to being eaten, because that is what the ghyrm do. They are parasites, like leeches, they live off other creatures' lives."

"But," she cried, "but Ma said, but the man said, they said she'd go to Joy, it would take her there."

"It didn't take her there! It didn't take her anywhere."

"I don't believe you," the girl cried. "I won't!"

From the doorway, Ferni spoke. "She has too much invested in pretty lies, M'urgi."

"I know," I said grimly. "So, we do this another way." I put both my hands on her shaved head, closed my eyes and chanted. The girl quivered, tried to squirm away, then went limp, eyes wide open, seeing something. She moaned, cried out, then began to scream.

Below us, in the oasthall, furniture tumbled, boots thundered up the stairs. B'Oag came down the corridor bearing a truncheon, his face red with anger.

Ferni held up his hand, stopping the big man as though he had run into a wall. When Ferni beckoned, B'Oag came to stand beside him in the door. The screams were subsiding into moans once more. I removed my hands and stood up, staggering a little. G'lil's eyes opened. "Aaaah," she cried. "Dead. All dead."

"Right," I snapped rather weakly. "All dead. As your mother is dead. As you would have been dead."

"What did you show her?" Ferni asked in an awed voice.

"I showed her that little colony from Earth, Cranesroost. I showed her in lengthy detail how that looked, before and during."

"What?" demanded B'Oag.

Ferni said, "The envoy showed the girl a memory of a human colony that was eaten by the ghyrm, Oastkeeper. When the ghyrm were through with them, nothing human lived in those places at all. Not a hair. Not a cell."

"He said . . ." The girl wept. "He said it would take her to Joy. The man said it would."

"Now we get to it," I growled. "What man?"

"The man at the mill. I was there to get supplies for the winter weaving, and he was delivering sacks of cocoons to the mill boss. He heard me telling my friend how bad off Mama was, and he said he had something that would help her. He said he couldn't give it for free, but he gave it to me for a half jig-bit, for almost nothing. He said it was a Taker."

"What did it look like?" asked Ferni.

"Like a few beads on a little string of vivilon. One red one, one blue one, two yellow ones. He held it to my ear so I could hear it sing. He said put it around her neck . . ." The girl shuddered. "Oh, Ma, Ma, what did I do to you?"

I sat down on the bed, suddenly exhausted. "Do we have to burn the mill, Ferni?"

B'Oag began to rumble threateningly, like his own heating system readying an eruption.

Ignoring him, I continued "It's within our authority, but I dread the upheaval that will cause. These people have little else to sustain them."

"There may be an easier way," Ferni replied. "Let the girl rest, and come with me. And you, Oastkeeper, don't get in an uproar over something that may not happen."

We went outside, some distance from the oasthouse, where I sat wearily on a wall.

"I've never seen that done before," said Ferni.

"It seems to be a talent I have," I said. "The ability to see other worlds, to take a spirit shape and go into other worlds. My shaman had it, too. It was she who taught me. Once I have seen something, I can show it to someone else . . ."

"How did you see that destruction?"

"I had seen a little of it before, on Earth. For the rest, I reached out to some creature that had seen it all: not with human eyes, but good enough for all that. It may have been a horse, or a dog, or even a goat. My shaman taught me to connect with the minds of animals. That's why the chitterlain is content to stay with me. She knows I'm taking her south, where her kindred are."

He muttered, "Since the mill is all that sustains these people, I believe we can ask our Siblings to exterminate any pests that may be sheltered there without harming the mill itself or the people thereabouts."

"They can do that?"

"I'm told so, yes, on a small scale. There's been some recent technological advance among my old academy friends that give them the capacity to disinfect one building, more or less, though not yet a city, and certainly not a planet. I can't make contact from here, however."

"How did you get here?" I asked, amazed that I hadn't wondered this before.

"There's a flier, hidden over behind one of those hills."

"Well, go then. Find out about it."

He gazed at me thoughtfully. "M'urgi. While I'm at headquarters, I'm going to arrange for some time off for both of us. Whether they approve the strike or not, I'll be back here within the next few days to get you . . ."

"You're taking a lot for granted," I half snarled.

"No. I'm not taking anything for granted, and you know it! This is important, and I can't even take time to explain it to you now. Just remember, I'll be back within a few days. Stay here. If they approve the strike, it will happen during the next few days. Tell B'Oag he has to get everyone out of the mill who may be working there or maintaining the place. If anyone lives close, they should go away for a few days. May I rely on you for that?"

"Of course."

"Then you may expect them to send the machine, unless I bring word they can't when I return."

"They, being who?"

"Dominion or the Siblinghood. One or both."

"Ah yes." I shrugged. "One or both. Or as we in the field say, one is both. Sometimes they seem joined at the heart."

We returned to the oasthouse. Ferni packed up his belongings and departed. I explained in some detail to B'Oag that he had to see to emptying the mill.

"They won't do as I say, Envoy!"

"Tell them they may do as you say in comfort, or I will come down there, and they will do as I say with pain. I will lay my hands on them and show them! You saw how that girl suffered. Do you want it for them as well?"

When he had grumbled his way onto the road, I returned to the girl, who grizzled at me lengthily about her bare skull before demanding sulkily to be taken to her home.

"No home there anymore, girl. The thing you brought into it multiplied like weeds in the spring. We had no way to get them out of your house, so your house had to be burned."

The lamentations started afresh. I hadn't time to wait them out, so I told her, "B'Oag will give you a job here for the rest of the winter. You will have company here, including B'Oag's son, Ojlin, a marriageable young man. By spring, I have no doubt you will have a new home of your own to worry over."

This seemed to be a new thought, and she perked up. "Ojlin, he wunt look at me, all bald like this."

"Tie a scarf around your head until it grows out."

The idea of having a future was interesting enough that she stopped crying. That evening B'Oag returned to report. "The envoy wanted the place empty, and I done that all, and what in billy-be-drat is that girl doin' behine my counter with my son?"

"Helping you, Oastkeeper. She needs a job, you need the help. Your son needs a wife."

"Now you just wait, woman . . ."

"Envoy," I corrected him with a steely voice. "I will not wait, B'Oag. I have come, I have found what I was sent to find, killed what I was sent to kill, sorted out the results of both finding and killing, and the job seems well done to me. I have thus far made no fuss about your part in the matter. Do not cause me to choose otherwise." I fastened my eyes on his, my hands slightly outstretched as though at any moment I might lay them on some part of him.

B'Oag gulped, breathed heavily, gulped again, and said no more. By evening's end, he was showing G'lil how to tally up the day's receipts.

I spent two more days at the oasthouse, feeding the chitterlain and sleeping, mostly. On the third day, a strange machine came out of the western sky, hovered over the mill at Vaccy for some time, then went away again. Those of us who ventured into the mill the next day found a great many dead mice, rats, spiders, and other vermin, along with a scattering of strange-looking creatures the others could not name. Like squid, I thought, recalling pictures I had seen as a child. A pulpy and bulbous thing with tentacles and suckers on it. I named them and kept talking until everyone knew the name and the danger.

The following morning, when I woke, I found Ferni waiting for me in the oasthall. Wordlessly, he took my pack and tool kit, tucked the chitterlain into the collar of my shirt, where it would stay warm, and led me out of the place to be half blinded by the sun on the snow.

"Where are we going?" I asked him, as I put on my goggles.

"Someplace south and safe," he replied, then, seeing my skeptical look, "Well, someplace safer than this, where your chitterlain will find its kindred. Then . . . a little later, we're going on to Thairy."

"To see your old friends at the academy?" I asked.

"To see old friends," he agreed. "And perhaps new ones."

I Am Margaret/on Tercis

Glory and I were sitting on my porch, mending under-wear.

She said, "Bamber told me his mama left a note when she went away. He couldn't read yet, but Abe read it to him."

"I didn't know that. I thought she just disappeared."

"His mother said she was in danger, and so was he, so don't attract attention."

"Could she have been an escaped bondswoman?" I asked.

"Bamber honestly doesn't know, but Abe kept the note, and when Bamber learned to read, he read it for himself."

"I remember you two helping one another learn to read in first grade. Does he know you tell me about him?"

"I wouldn't tell you unless he thought it was all right. Bamber doesn't mind your knowing, Grandma. He says he thinks you're a lot like his mother."

"I hope not," I snorted. "Leaving a child like that!"

"Bamber says she must have had reasons, and Abe isn't mean to him or anything." Glory knotted her thread and bit it off. "Bamber's funny about a lot of things. He's just as smart as I am. In school, he knows all the answers, but he just gives enough right ones to get by, then he puts down wrong answers for the rest."

"Why does he do that?"

"What the note said. He doesn't want to attract attention."

"I suppose his mother might have had reasons for wanting him to be unnoticed," I admitted grudgingly.

"Abe Johnson's still a peculiar choice. I wish we could adopt Bamber," Glory said.

"We've already half adopted him," I replied with some indignation. "We see that he has clothes, even if some of them are hand-me-downs. We pay for his school supplies. And between your mother and me, we feed him about five times a week. Considering everything, I think we're being very helpful."

The conversation stuck in my mind, though. There weren't many diversions in The Valley. Any little irregularity was food for surmise, so why had I ignored the mystery of Bamber Joy's abandonment? Whatever the reason, it wasn't the boy's fault!

A day or so later, I recruited the two of them to help me pick up chicken feed and groceries. At the store, I treated the young ones to the bottles of sweetberry drink they liked, and they sat down on the steps while I went inside. I was barely through the door when a car came booming across the bridge like a thunderstorm on wheels, more noise than you'd ever hear in Crossroads, and of a particularly irritating kind. The only vehicles we see in Rueful are driven by sedate officials on Dominion business, so the minute I heard the sound, I thought of the men who had asked about the cat.

The machine slid sideways into the turn, kicking up a cloud of dust as it kept right on coming, a danger to every child and chicken in the neighborhood. It didn't slow down until it was almost on top of the store. The two men got out, looking like they were headed to a hanging.

I got over by the potato bin just as they banged their way in. One of them said loudly to Ms. McCollum, "Have you found out anything about a new cat yet?"

Ms. McCollum came right back at them. "What's its scientific name? One of the people here in The Valley wanted to look it up. She wanted to know was it Earthian? Maybe an ocelot?"

The taller one said to the other, "Did the people at the office tell you the scientific name of the cat, Walter?"

Walter said, "No, Ned, they did not. We will have to get that information."

The taller one continued, "So, you have not heard of anybody with a strange sort of cat, ma'am?"

"Most everybody has one or two ordinary, everyday cats."

"Has anyone been buying unusual amounts of cat food, ma'am?"

"Only Ma Bailey, because her mama cat had kittens that're starting on solid food."

"You have seen those kittens yourself, ma'am?"

"Everbody in town has seen 'em. Just step down the street to Ma's Kitchen, and she'll try to give you one, and another to keep it company."

The two men turned to go out, and I followed them to the door. On the porch, Walter stopped and glared at Glory. "Little girl, do you know anyone around here who has a strange cat?"

"First off," Glory said, "I'm not a little girl. Little girls are younger than ten, and I'm considerable older than that. And no, I don't know anybody who has a strange cat."

The man stared through her as though she weren't even there. I shivered, for Bamber was looking up at the man with eyes so blank they could have been cut out of blackboard. He stood up slowly, getting himself between Glory and Walter.

"My steppa, he shoots cats. Can't abide 'em. Maybe he shot the one you're lookin for."

The two men blinked slowly, then got back in their car and went tearing back up to the bridge, where they turned east and kept going, raising more clouds of dust.

Bamber turned to me, and said, "Grandma, whoever sent those two sure didn't intend anybody to look at them close."

Glory said, "You mean the way they talk?"

"They talk like the machines talked in the place we were before my mom came here and left me with Abe."

She cried, "Bamber, you just remembered something. You had a memory!"

His mouth dropped open. "I guess I did. That's funny."

He took a slow swallow of his drink, then shook his head. "You know that stuffed turkalope the sheriff hangs out in the trees at our place? Every year he hangs it there?"

Turkalopes are large Tercisian birds that run quite fast and don't fly very well. Some people raise them for meat, though I've never cared for the taste.

"Why does he do that?" I asked through the screen door.

"Because it's illegal to bother or kill the wild ones, so the sheriff hangs up this stuffed one, then he hides until some idjit tries to kill it, then he arrests them."

"Why are we talking about stuffed birds?" asked Glory.

"Because those two guys are like that stuffed bird."

I realized what he meant. "You mean a decoy! Hold the thought while you load that chicken feed, Bamber. Let me get the groceries."

I picked up the few things we needed, paid Ms. McCollum for it and the sacks of feed the young ones were putting in the wagon, and we started for home. As soon as we were out of earshot, Bamber whispered, "If decoy's the right word, then there's somebody we can't see watching those two decoys to see if anybody's interested in what they're saying or doing."

That was more talk out of Bamber than I had heard if I had put his whole year's conversations end to end.

"Because . . ." Glory whispered.

"Because," he said, "if somebody takes an interest in those two men, that person may know something about the cat." He turned that blackboard gaze of his toward me, a tiny smile on his lips. "But we're onto them, aren't we, Grandma!"

Bamber unhitched for us at Maybelle's house. We left the chicken feed in the barn and carried the other stuff up the hill to my house. Falija wasn't there, though Glory and Bamber said hi to Lou Ellen.

I made chicken sandwiches with pickles for them while Glory and Bamber discussed what the men might really be up to. As usual, Lou Ellen didn't want all her sandwich, so Glory split what she didn't eat with Bamber.

"Should we do something about those men?" Glory asked. "Or would that just get us arrested for shooting at the decoy?"

"The safest thing to do with bait is pretend you don't notice it," I told them. "Sniffing at it might be even more dangerous than trying to eat it. Glory, I do wish mightily we knew what this is all about."

Bamber gave me a very straight look. "You can trust me to look out for Glory, ma'am." Then he ducked his head as though he'd scared himself, speaking up that way.

"Well." I grinned at Glory. "It seems we have an ally."

"I'm glad," said Falija, suddenly appearing on a chair nearby. "Allies are good things to have."

That startled Bamber, and he stood gaping as though he'd lost his wits.

"Falija, what do you think about those men?" Glory asked.

"Grandma's right. We should take no notice, not even if ten more of them arrive and dance across the bridge waving large tambourines."

"Tambourines?" I said.

"Isn't it a word? I learned it just this morning. A festive instrument to accompany dance. Can't you visualize those two men with tambourines?"

This set Glory and Bamber to snickering, and even I had to laugh. When the children left, they stood for a while on the porch. Glory said, "I really don't know that much about her, Bamber."

"Her suddenly showing up that way! I seem to remember something about cat-people who do that," he murmured. "They live on Thairy, and Chottem, and Fajnard, and they're called the Gibbekot."

They went on down the hill, their two dark heads almost level with one another, their long legs moving easily. Glory and Bamber Joy. Maybelle didn't encourage the friendship because she felt Gloriana shouldn't be particularly friendly with any boy until she was quite a bit older. Knowing what I knew about Gloriana, I thought friendship, boy, girl, or animal, was what she needed, and the two of them were good for one another.

A couple of days later The Valley grapevine spread the news that Dorothy Springer had been found murdered in her house. The sheriff had called the Rueful Public Safety officers for help, because there hadn't been a murder in Remorseful in anybody's memory. I wondered if this were another decoy. No one in Rueful would kill someone else to find out who cared or who didn't, and I had to remind myself that Ned and Walter weren't from anyplace as simple as Rueful.

"What are they saying at school?" I asked.

Glory stared at her feet. "Mary Beth Conover said it had to be a crazy person, but others said no, if the person was crazy they'd be in Schizo-ville, the Walled-Off for crazy people."

"You didn't take an unusual interest, did you?"

She shook her head no. "You think it's another decoy?"

I told her I didn't know. The presence of Ned and Walter here in Rueful, where they didn't belong, had mostly annoyed me, but now, I felt frightened.

That night Glory and I hiked over to the cemetery and pretended to pull weeds along the fence—just in case someone was watching us— while she dug up the little pouch the cat-people had given her. It was the only connection she had to them, and she'd told me if she needed something from them, she might need it in a hurry. Back at the house, we folded it flat, ripped a seam in the lining of her jacket, and put the bag inside. Then I restitched it, almost invisibly, so no matter what happened, she would have it nearby.

Half the town went to Dorothy Springer's funeral. Everyone was sorry she was gone, particularly the local folks who'd taken it upon themselves to feed her forty or fifty barn cats until they could find homes for them. School let out early in the afternoon, and the Remorseful Ruehouse was full of young people and their families. Bamber and Glory went with me, and we were just part of the crowd, which was a good thing because Ned and Walter were there, sitting in the back row, scanning the congregation.

We saw them on the way in. When we came out of the church, they were gone, but they were out at the cemetery when we arrived there. I had brought a bouquet, some wildflowers and some from my little garden. A lot of other people had done the same, and from under my lashes I watched the two men focusing on every person who laid flowers by the grave, trying to find something unusual. Glory started to cry, but by that time most of us were a little tearful.

"The Remorseful cemetery isn't as pretty as the one near Crossroads," I said when the burial was over. "But it does have a nice view of the mountains. Here, take my handkerchief, Gloriana. I didn't know you knew Dorothy."

"I just knew her to say hello to. It's just . . . just . . ."

"I know. The minister enjoyed himself, didn't he. Made a real three-hanky affair out of it."

"He did. Sort of."

"If it's any comfort to you, I have a friend in the sheriff's office, an old patient of your grandpa's. She told me Dorothy was dozing in her chair, the way she did of an evening, when someone hit her on the head with something heavy. It was very sudden, and she probably didn't even feel it. Also, she was well past ninety, and beginning to show signs of failing. She actually told me she wished she could just die quickly, in her sleep, and that's almost what happened."

"Was she a friend of yours?"

"Oh, for about forty years. She was one of Grandpa Doc's patients, too. Well then, most everybody around here was! You don't need to grieve over her, Glory."

"It wasn't grieving so much as thinking I could have caused her to die, Grandma! Even though it was Ms. McCollum who actually mentioned Ms. Springer to . . . you know who . . . it could just as easy have been me."

"Death usually makes us feel guilty," I told her. "As though those of us still living are part of a conspiracy. Let's not brood on it, Glory. Til and Jeff are spending the night with friends, and your mother suggested that she and your dad would relish an evening to themselves, so I'm inviting you and Bamber to have supper at my house."

I'd made a big pan of what farm folk called "all-in," meat, cheese, beans, grain, and spicy sauce. Different kinds of peppers grew well in Rueful; almost everybody used them, red, green, or yellow, plus the tiny purple ones that set your mouth on fire.

Bamber ate three helpings of all-in and two of dessert. He was apologetic about it until I told him he was a growing boy, and if I remembered rightly, they ate all the time. Bamber flushed and looked pleased, as though he'd received a compliment, as perhaps he had. He'd been told he was normal boyish, and Bamber probably didn't often get to think of himself that way. After dinner, Falija, Bamber and Glory did the dishes, and I sat on the porch, watching the battle-bats skydiving for bugs until the dishwashers joined me.

Glory asked Falija if her new brain had told her anything new and helpful.

Falija smiled a cat smile. "As a matter of fact . . . it's still light enough for us all to see. Let's take a walk in the woods. Maybe we'll find something interesting."

Since Bryan had died, I often went woods wandering in the dusk or moonlight. I knew Falija saw well even when it was quite dark, so we wouldn't get lost. She led us up the hill, past a huge chunk of black rock that went up like a steeple, then up a steep slope—me scrambling, with Bamber boosting me from behind—that ended against two huge boulders separated by a narrow slit. Following Falija, we squeezed inside. The opening split in two, and Falija led us to the right. Directly ahead of us was a screen of some kind, a wavering light, as though someone had turned a breeze-riffled pond on its side. I would have stopped right there, but when Falija plunged right through it, the children went after her, so, naturally, I went after them.

We stood in a tunnel of wavering light. To our right was a line of squared-off boulders that made a low barrier between us and the drop beyond. Bamber went to the gap between two of the stones and peered downward while I tried to figure out how we had possibly climbed this high! We were on a ledge, out in the clear, high above the nearby hills, with a view that went all the way to the next Walled-Off, but nothing looked familiar: no town, no pottery chimneys, no notch where the river flowed. On our left, the cliffs went up into the sky where the last lavender clouds of evening floated in front of a full moon, just rising over the mountains. I stared at it, and it at me, and its expression was completely different from any moons I knew.

I whispered, "What do you call this place, Falija?"

"I guess I'd call it a very good place from which to watch what goes on down there," Falija said, pointing through the gap in the stones. The ledge followed the half circle of the cliff; directly across from us water poured from the cliff top into a pool far below, where a wide green lawn was edged by young trees. The trees were horsing around in the wind, like boys at a school dance, pretending not to notice there were girls there—and there really were girls there, though it took me a little while to see them, for they were pale as moonlight, their skins shining firefly green and their eyes glowing like lamps.

If they had clothes on, they were transparent, but clothes or no clothes, they looked nothing like human schoolgirls. I wasn't sure they were girls at all. They could be . . . just themselves, not male or female.

"What are they?" I asked.

"They're nyzeemi," said Falija. "At least that's what they are in our language. I just found this place this morning, and when I got back, I looked in your encyclopedia to see if you had anything like them. You don't. Nyzeemi aren't human, or female, or mythical."

"Where did they come from?" Glory asked her. "I've lived here all my life, and I've never seen them."

"You've lived back there, but never here, in their world," Falija said. "Though we're not actually in their world. We're just inside a way-gate. It's something like the window above the cemetery, where we went to see the dancers. You get to that one by jumping off the rock between the thimble-apple trees."

Bamber shook his head. "Falija, how did you know about the gates?"

She said, "My people use way-gates to go back and forth. They're instantaneous. If you can see way-gates, you can move around the galaxy like moving around your house. My people came here through a way-gate. It was all in my mother-brain."

Glory blurted, "You didn't come in a spaceship?"

Falija laughed, a kind of purr-hiccup, a prrrit prrrit prrrit, with the pitch going up at the end of each syllable. "From Chottem, where my parents came from, it would take several years to get to Tercis in a spaceship. Spaceships go through wormholes to get from one planet to another, but not all places are connected by wormholes. Really big spaceships, with lots of power, can generate their own wormholes and the protective field that lets people go through without getting scrambled.

"Way-gates are different. There's no other kind of space involved, they just step across folds, if you know right where they are. My mother-mind remembers hundreds of them. Why did you think they came in a spaceship?"

"I just supposed it," Glory told her. "Your people sure didn't come from anyplace on Tercis that I'd ever heard about."

"No," Falija admitted. "And neither did those men who are hunting for me. They probably came through a wormhole, and something evil sent them after you three."

"Me!" Glory squealed like a snared gaboon.

"Glory?" I blurted, sounding just as surprised.

Falija nodded seriously. "I think so," she said. "Maybe it's more like a feeling because you and Glory and Bamber . . . all three of you are part of my duty."

I, of course, with my usual arrogance, had been assuming that Falija was part of mine, so this set me back on my heels.

"Why me or Bamber?" Glory asked.

"I don't know why," Falija said. "Do you know why, Grandma? I've seen you biting your lips a lot lately, as though you were thinking."

I shook my head. "I have no idea, Falija. And since I'm usually thinking something or other, lip-biting is more or less a constant."

She turned and pointed to the trees below. "It's selection time. The nyzeemi are picking their trees. They have to do it while the trees are still young, so they can grow old together . . ."

Behind the young trees, the forest stretched endlessly away in ranks of hills before jagged lines of mountains against blue distances. Some little way back from the clearing, at the end of a glade, a grove of huge old trees towered above the others, only their leaves shivering, for the branches were too huge to be moved by the wind. I happened be to be looking at them as several old nyzeemi melted out of the bark and wandered out into the clearing, followed by others. They weren't as thin as the young ones, they moved more stiffly, they were wrinkly and aged, with twisty arms and long, long fingers. The old ones spoke to the young ones, pointing at the trees, their clouded heads nodding.

"They're advising the young ones whom to pick," said Falija.

"All the trees I see are from old Earth," I said. "Earth sent tree seeds with our colonies, so it must be a colony planet down there."

Falija considered this. "I suppose that could be, but considering the size of those trees down below, it's more likely the seeds came from Earth thousands of years ago, when there were still forests on Earth."

"It's so beautiful," Glory whispered.

Falija whispered, "There's an ubioque down there who keeps the moss soft and the waterfall beautiful, just to attract nyzeemi for the trees."

"There's an ubi-thingy for every place?"

Falija shook her head. "Only beautiful, natural places. There were ubioques on Earth, but once their habitat was gone, they died . . ."

She stopped suddenly, her ears pricking. All the wind and murmur sounds from below had stopped. We heard something approaching: loud, inappropriate, a hideous clamor like rocks bashing together. Falija whispered, "It can't see us, but it might be able to hear us. Be still."

The nyzeemi vanished. The wind dropped. The trees drooped in absolute quiet. The soft purling of the waterfall was lost in the clamor as a long, gray thing like a huge, lumpy snake came bashing through the trees.

"The people here call it a gizzardile," whispered Falija. "This is a huge one, and those lumps are the stones inside it that it uses to mash up the creatures it swallows."

The gizzardile attempted to coil itself into a circle, a task made more difficult by the many unyielding lumps inside itself, which the gizzardile seemed to be working back toward its rear end. When the heavy rear end was bunched together, the more sinuous front part began to rise, much like the pictures I have seen of cobras rising out of snake charmers' baskets, except that this creature's rising seemed to have no upper limit. We held our breaths as it came ever higher, stopping with the top of its head no great distance below us, facing into the waterfall, where it dipped its huge, fanged mouth with loud slurping sounds.

I couldn't take my eyes from it, from the multiple pairs of bowed legs along its sides, the spiny extrusion that might be a dorsal fin, though just now it lay in a wrinkled pile along the creature's spine. I am not usually afraid of serpents, knowing as I do that most of them are harmless and useful in keeping vermin in check, but the look and smell of this thing could have been designed to instill fear.

It had a stink peculiar to itself. If malice smelled, it would smell like that.

After slurping at the falls for what seemed an interminable time, the creature lowered itself, redistributed its lumps, and moved away through the trees with the sound of a retreating avalanche. It left a slick gray-slimed trail on the ground. As the end of the tail disappeared, a crowd of tiny people came out of the woods pushing barrows and carrying shovels. They dug the grayness up and carried it away. Immediately, the green mosses moved back into the places the slime had been, and the little people followed the slime trail back into the trees.

"Where are they taking the stuff?" Glory asked.

"They probably know of a way-gate nearby, one that opens into a fire pit or a volcano or even into a little sun, and they'll dump it to be burned."

"And what are those little people?" Bamber demanded.

"I'm not sure," said Falija. "In your world, little people are mythical, and they're called different things. These are quite real. In their language they're called a word that means filth-carriers. They have no sense of smell and no aesthetic perceptions, they aren't bothered by nastiness, though they themselves are quite clean, so they make their living cleaning it up when it intrudes on special places."

"So that's a magical world down there?" asked Bamber

Falija replied in an astonished voice, "No, of course it's not magical. It's completely real. It simply has a lot of life-forms that you're unfamiliar with."

Glory asked, "What do you mean, it's not magical, it's real?"

"It's a real world. It has real qualities. Up is always up and down is always down. Fruit falls from a tree, it doesn't float to the sky. Creatures are born in this world, and grow up and eventually die. What's true today is also true tomorrow.

"If this were a magical world, all those things would be subject to change by anyone who had power or could command it by spell or enchantment. Magical worlds can't exist in our universe because their rules change constantly, and there's no difference between evil and good. Power is power, and everyone does whatever they can get away with."

"I always thought magic was sort of nice," said Glory.

Falija's ears drooped. "Humans are fascinated with magic. Your people like to believe in powers that will break all the laws of the universe, just for you." Falija shivered. "My bones feel it's getting really late back home. It's time to go."

So we went back through the shimmering gate, down to my house, all of us silent and full of wonder. Falija and I stopped off while the other two went on down the hill. For a moment I wondered if I should call them back, tell them not to mention what had happened tonight, not even to Maybelle or James. I decided they knew enough to keep their mouths shut, and in fact, they did.

The first day of the following week, I drove Bamber and Glory over to Remorseful to school. Some of the people who had been taking care of Dorothy Springer's cats were interested in setting up an animal refuge in her memory, a place for stray cats and dogs and whatever. They'd asked me if I would help, and I'd said I'd talk with them about it that morning. School hadn't started yet, and most of the students were out on the lawn when we arrived. The children got out of the buggy just as a series of unusual noises came from the main street, down the hill, where the stores and bank and offices were, like a huge door slamming repeatedly. Everyone jumped up, peering down the street and jabbering. Before anybody could move in that direction, the head teacher came out of the school and told everyone to get inside until we knew what had happened.

I hitched the horse and went inside with the children, thinking how ridiculous this was, in Rueful, of all places. Bamber went out the back door of the school before I had a chance to ask where he was going. Inside the doors, the head teacher was telling everyone the Dominion Alarm system had already summoned Dominion officers, and everyone was to stay inside with their belongings at hand, in case they needed to be sent home.

A moment later, a Dominion Police flier buzzed up over the hills and headed for the downtown, and only moments after that, Bamber Joy sneaked back into the school and came to find Glory and me. He said he'd sneaked over to Main Street where supposedly armed men had robbed the bank. He'd seen Ned and Walter in front of the bank, waving their arms and claiming to have seen the robbers running off into the woods. Since woods covered most of the mountains around town, the alleged robbers could be anywhere. That's the way Bamber said it, alleged robbers. The police had already sent for scent-hounds and fliers and heaven knows what else.

Not long after that, a Dominion Officer arrived to tell everyone to go home and lock themselves in. Bamber disappeared. Glory, Til, and Jeff got into the wagon with me, and we were just at the edge of town when we saw Billy Ray's wagon with him and Benny Paul in it, recruiting people for search parties. They yelled at Jeff and Til to get in the wagon, and Til was over there before I could say a word. Jeff said he'd wait and go with his dad, which was quite sensible of him.

We left Jeff unhitching the horse at Maybelle's, while Glory and I went up to my house to discuss the matter.

"I think this is another decoy," she said. "Even if the bank really did get robbed."

I said, "Real or not real, when a so-called robbery scatters every able-bodied man and boy from The Valley into the mountains, it makes me a little nervous, doesn't it you?"

Falija's eyes were as big as teacups, and her ears were back.

"There," Glory said, stroking Falija's head. "That's exactly what Bamber thought, especially since Ned and Walter were telling the sheriff where the robbers went. But, Jeff isn't gone, and neither is Bamber. His stepdaddy probably went with everyone else, but Bamber will show up here just as soon as he finds out what's happening."

And he did, a fairly short time later, sticking his head in the door, panting like he'd run five miles, which likely he had.

"Ned and Walter are back," he said. "They've got four or five other guys with them, and they're going house to house down the valley road, coming this way, waving fake badges and saying they're deputized by Dominion to search every house for the bank robbers."

"They'll find me," said Falija, sounding a little panicky. "They will. They'll sniff me out."

"Then we need to go somewhere else," Glory said in a determined tone. "Don't we, Falija?"

Falija looked at her, and the creases between her eyes went away. "Of course! Up the mountain! Where I took you the other evening!"

"Right," said Bamber Joy. "Through that gate! Maybe we could even close the gate behind us. Glory and I'll come along to keep you company."

"Glory, and you, and I," I said. "Unless Falija would be safer going alone."

"Grandma," said Falija, "there's no time to explain now. They're looking for me, yes, but they're also looking for anyone who helped me, and that includes all three of you. I wouldn't be safer alone, and I'd have failed my duty."

Glory said, "They were asking for scent-hounds to be brought in . . ."

Falija said, "In that case, they'll find me or anyone I've been with or anyplace I've been lately . . ."

"Should we take Lou Ellen?" Glory asked, sounding worried. I started to say something, then bit my lip.

Falija gave Glory a troubled look. "Glory, Lou Ellen will be all right. She'll either meet us on the way or she can visit her other friends, and they'll keep her safe."

A few more words bubbled up among us, and we confused each other for a few minutes with ifs and buts, but the upshot was that I wrote a note saying I had the notion to go camping up the river over the next few days, and I was taking Glory and Bamber Joy along to fetch and carry. Glory took the note down to her house, put it on the kitchen table, dumped her books and stowed a few things in her backpack, grabbed her bedroll and jacket, and rejoined Bamber and me, who were making up a couple of packs and bedrolls ourselves.

I said, "Spare socks? Underwear?"

Glory said, "I brought some of Til's clothes for Bamber, since he didn't have time to collect anything."

I locked my door behind us but left the curtains open so anybody could look in and see nobody was home. Just about that time, Bamber saw two cars coming along the road from the bridge. If they got to the Judson house, they'd see the note, but since we weren't really going where the note said we were going, it didn't matter much if Ned and Walter followed the false lead.

We went uphill, walking on rocks so as not to leave a visible trail. Bamber came last to be sure no one had made any marks or dropped anything. We reached the spire of black rock, and from there we could hear men yelling down the hill. Glory climbed halfway up the rock to get a better view and reported there were two cars in the driveway as well as her daddy's buggy, her parents, and Jeff, along with several other people.

When we got to the slit rock, Falija told us to help her make a rock pile right beside it. Bamber and Glory fetched some bigger ones while I gathered small ones. Glory went into the slit in the rock, took my hand, and helped me over the pile. Falija and Bamber came through and reached back to arrange the stones into a teetery heap that looked as if it had fallen that way, a perfect place to break a leg. They topped it off with a few broken, dried branches that pretty well filled the crack between the stones.

This time we went straight through the watery tunnel and out the other end onto the ledge. It was daytime, and the nyzeemi weren't there. When we looked back, a black pool filled the whole width of the ledge behind us.

Falija said, "Get up on top of the railing stones."

"On top?" I said, shocked. We were quite high enough already.

"It's the only way down," said Falija, climbing onto a stone herself.

Bamber and Glory climbed up, each took hold of one of my arms and pulled me up between them. Falija said to shut our eyes and jump, and that's what Bamber and Glory did, dragging me off the ledge with them. I thought of screaming, but by the time I'd decided on it, we were floating. We landed soft as featherweed floss. Bamber and Glory let go, and I stood there trembling. After I decided I was all in one piece I took a deep breath and asked Falija, "What was that?"

"My people put a kind of elevator there. It isn't magic. It's just a force field. They sometimes put them in places like this where the way-gates end up in difficult places. I knew the field was there. I could feel it."

"The people can't follow us?"

Falija shook her head. "Not unless they know precisely where this way-gate is, because if they are what we think they are, they can't smell it or see it, the way my people can. Each gate creates an aversion field so nonsensors walk on past it without even noticing."

"Well," I remarked, with a glance at the ledge we'd jumped from, "we probably shouldn't go too far. We might get lost, and we'll want to be able to go back . . ."

Falija was shaking her head. "Grandma, I'm sorry, I thought you understood that the gates go only one way. There are ways to get back to Tercis, but the closest is five worlds away from here."

I felt my face go dead. All my blood drained to someplace below my feet. For a moment I tottered there, feeling lost and out of place. I thought about fainting and decided not to. As I'd learned so long ago on Phobos, what was, was. All fainting did was delay dealing with the inevitable. "Well then, just in case you're not totally correct about their coming after us, let's get out of the foyer of this place and into some part that's not quite so exposed from above."

That seemed sensible to everyone, so we moved off quietly under the trees, hearing nothing at all from behind us or even around us. A few bird sounds. A tiny breeze. That was all. After a time we came to a trail and turned left along it, simply because leftward ran downhill and it seemed easier. I was breathing very hard.

"Are we moving too fast?" Falija asked, concerned.

"It's not the walk, it's the . . . what, Glory?" I asked her.

"The difference," Glory said. "The strangeness. The not knowing whether they'll catch up to us and what they'll do."

Falija said, "I'm certain they won't catch up to us. Not now. Not today. Not here." She took my hand and caressed it. "Nobody expected us to come here, so we don't need to worry about dangers coming after us, just the ones we may happen on."

"Which isn't likely," said Gloriana quickly. "Is it?"

Falija shook her head. "Not around here, no."

When we had gone about a mile down the trail, we heard voices coming in our direction, people singing, a clinking noise, a strange sound halfway between a whinny and a moo, then the crunch of wheels. We left the trail and went back into the trees to lie down and peek out without being seen. In a few minutes a wagon appeared, hitched to two large creatures covered with close, curly hair like a sheep's. Their tails arched forward over their backs and head, the long, silky hair making a parasol over the entire animal. They had horns like cows, single hooves like horses, plus long, silky ears that extended almost to the ground.

The people in the wagon looked rather human, if one could accept green humans somewhere between Falija size and human size. Those with ribbons tying up their dark green hair were on one side of the wagon, and those with kerchiefs around their necks were on the other.

"Let's try that last chorus again," said the right-hand animal, speaking perfectly intelligible Earthian. "One, two . . ." and they all began to sing, girls high, boys medium, the team of animals, baritone and bass.

> "The right time of day
> For raiding hay
> Is three o'clock in the mornin'.
> The world is asleep
> and the birds don't peep
> so the farmer has no warnin'.
> We can cut, we can bale
> with a sharp toenail
> and an energy that's unflaggin',
> And the entire crop
> fits under the top
> of our 'inside-out' hay wagon . . ."

"What are those people?" whispered Bamber.

"The team are umoxen," said Falija thoughtfully. "And the people are hayfolk. All winter they let their toenails grow. By summer they're as long as scythes, then they hitch up their wagons and go dance through the hayfields at night, cutting enough hay to get them through the winter."

"What do they do with it?" Gloriana asked.

"Eat it," she said. "That's why they're green. They call themselves hayraiders, but they only take the first cutting, so the farmer doesn't lose everything."

"Except the fruits of his labors," said I disapprovingly.

"Not exactly," Falija told me. "The farmer depends on the hayraiders to do the second and third cutting for him, and there's some other kind of arrangement as well. It's fair to both."

"Then why are they called raiders?" I asked, outraged.

"Because they like it. It makes them sound adventurous and bold. It's a lot more fun to dance in the moonlight than it is to work in the noonday sun, especially if it's illicit."

"What's an inside-out hay wagon?" asked Bamber.

"One that seems bigger on the inside than it seems on the outside."

Glory asked, "Why do they speak Earthian?"

Falija said, "A surprising number of worlds do, particularly worlds where Gentherans have been. Gentherans call human language one of the two great gifts from Earth. Earthian is a lot easier to read, write, and speak than most languages, as well as having an enormous vocabulary. So, whenever you find several races living together, chances are they'll speak Earthian. The hayfolk and the umoxen also have their own languages, of course. Shall we ask them for a ride?"

I shook my head doubtfully. The wagon did look filled to overflowing with creatures. Suddenly, however, the left-hand umox called, "Who's out there? I hear you thinking! Come out now, before they come slishing and slashing after you!"

Falija led us out onto the road as the hayfolk came down from the wagon. Their toenails were longer than my forearm, gently curving out to the sides. I supposed they had to curve that way, or they'd have to walk with their feet far apart. The biggest one came forward, stopping far enough away that he wasn't threatening to cut anyone off at the ankles.

"Well, Gibbekotkin, and where did you pop from?"

"Here and there," said Falija. "Is there room in the wagon for passengers?"

"Depends on who's asking," said the nigh umox.

"And where they're coming from," said the off umox.

"And where they're going," said the largest raider.

"Falija is asking," she said, "for her friends, who are coming from danger and going toward refuge, so far as is possible."

"Who's after you?" asked the nigh umox suspiciously.

"Don't know," she said. "Just know they are. Human-type men . . ."

"Who sound like robots," Glory offered.

"Lurking and lying," said Bamber.

"Up to no good," I supplied.

"The unmentionable's creatures," said the largest raider, nodding vigorously. "We've seen 'em here and there in their great, smelly wagons. Very good description. Climb up on the driver's seat, you two ladies. Gibbekotkin in lap, brother in back. My name's Howkel, by the by."

Glory and I climbed onto the seat, and Falija settled across both laps while Bamber Joy squeezed himself among the raiders. When the wagon started to move, I thought Bamber probably had the best of it, because the hay was soft but the seat certainly wasn't.

The banks of green moss on either side of the road were so clean they looked freshly vacuumed. The only fallen leaves in evidence were brightly colored, unbroken, and set out in artistic arrangements. Now and then the wagon passed a little pile of twigs and branches set by the trail, as though waiting to be picked up by something.

"Have you any new stories?" one of the girl hayraiders asked. "We usually tell stories on long rides."

"I have one you might like to hear," said Falija. "It's about a villager who talked to a fish."

"Oh, tell it please," said the Hayfolk.

And as we rolled along, Falija told a strange tale about a fish who helped a man out of his difficulties by directing him to the Keeper of all information. It was interesting, but rather complicated. I'm afraid I dozed a little, waking up just as Falija said, "And so, since that day, whenever the man has a difficulty, he has walked seven roads at once, for only in that way can he find the Keeper again . . ."

I said to Falija. "If that whole thing was in your memory, Falija, maybe it's important."

"Some stories are very important," said Howkel. "Specially in the summer grasslands of Fajnard."

"This is Fajnard?" I cried. "Fajnard is under the rule of the Frossians. This isn't a good place to be!"

Howkel snorted. "The Frossians think they run the world, but they actually only occupy about a tenth of it, around the lowland cities. They're used to rampaging onto a world, digging up the ore, cutting down the trees, moving on. They have a chant, 'Move in, dig up, cut down, move on.' No ore here. Trees are poisonous to 'em. The wealth here's in grass after it's fed to umoxen to make wool, but that's slow work, year after year. Frossians aren't used to patience. They're already getting itchy and neglectful. Pretty soon they'll decide they'd rather be somewhere else. While there's Frossians here, hayfolk have nothing to do with them! We stay far from the cities, up here in the highlands."

"Wind coming," said the off umox.

They stopped the wagon, all the hayfolk got off and went into the woods. The long-haired umoxen lay down and tied their ears under their chins with the four stubby fingers in the middle of their hooves. When the fingers were folded up, the hoof part hit the ground, but when they wanted to, the umoxen could use those fingers almost like hands.

Very shortly we heard the wind, and we all lay down as well. It came louder and closer, then it came down the trail, a whirlwind that went past us like a train going full speed, and when it was gone, so were all the little twig piles along the road.

So the moss beds had been vacuumed.

"What kind of world is this again?" Glory asked Falija, who was grooming her whiskers back into shape.

"A natural world," she said. "One where certain creatures are embodiments."

"Embodiments do vacuuming?" Glory asked.

"The embodiment of order might, or the embodiment of beauty."

"Is this where your people live?"

She shook her head. "Some of them, yes, but I don't know what direction they might be in. I do have an anticipatory feeling, though. As though enlightenment may be around the next corner."

Glory sneaked a look at me. I was chewing my lip.

"You know, Grandma," Glory said, "you might as well tell us now. There's something bothering you."

I shook my head, then looked at Falija, then looked up at the sky. Maybe I was asking God for a sign.

"She will," said Falija. "But not now, not with all these hayfolk about."

The hayfolk came out of the woods as the umoxen untied their ears and got to their feet, making harrumph, harrumph sounds. "Where are you headed?" Falija asked the nigh umox.

"The Howkel Farm. Just outside the woods. Dallydance is just down the road, if you're looking for a town."

"Are there humans there?" Glory asked the umox.

"Like you? No. A few of the ordinary sort, though. Like her," and he pointed at me with one leg.

Glory tried to sort that out. "She's my grandmother. We're the same kind of people."

"Humph," said the off umox. "Tell that to the gizzardile. You don't even smell alike."

"That's enough of that," said Falija in a commanding tone. "We don't discuss how people smell, and umoxen aren't the best judge of odors, anyhow."

It was true they had a decidedly barnyard smell, which all of us present were more or less used to, but the umoxen took it as an insult.

"Oh, isn't it a commanding Gibbekotkin! Doesn't it have qualities of leadership! Pardon us, your royal sagacity, but those two, the boy and the girl, are alike, and that one, the old woman, is something else again. And anyone who says different is blind as a battle-bat, smell or no smell."

"Here, here, what's this," said Howkel, who was the last to emerge from the woods. "Controversy? Argument? On such a lovely day? What are you umoxen up to?"

"Harrumph," said the nigh umox. "Nothing at all. Except having my intelligence insulted and my fragrance referred to in a tone of derogation."

"Tsk," said Howkel. "Well, folk, you've lost your ride for sure. I never ask the umoxen to haul anyone who's insulted them. If you get so far as our farm, though, do drop in for a meal and a bed. Dame Howkel is a fine cook, if I do say so myself."

And with that, he and his tribe leapt upon the wagon, dumped our backpacks onto the road, and trundled off, leaving us standing there with our mouths open. I felt I'd done nothing but gape for weeks.

"Now what?" I asked, simmering.

"Now," said Falija very softly, "now that our curious hayraiders have departed, it's time Gloriana knew the truth."

I could feel myself turning red, then white, then gray before my legs went out from under me and I was suddenly sitting on the grass, not knowing how I got there. Glory got her water bottle out of her pack and moistened a clean hanky to make a coolness for my forehead.

Finally, I murmured, "It was twins, Glory. All those twins."

"What was?" Glory asked. "What about it. I'm not one!"

"I know. I know. I married your Grandpa Doc, and I had twins. Conjoined twins. They died almost as soon as they were born. And we thought, well, it's probably for the best, it happens sometimes, next time will be normal. Then I had your mother and your aunt Mayleen, and they were joined, too. Grandpa Doc had to cut them apart because they were joined at the back of the head. That was the end of having babies, so far as I was concerned. We figured, it was just me, you know. Some mutation that happened on our way to Tercis. Years went by. Then Mayleen . . .

"Mayleen was only seventeen when she had Billy Wayne and Joe Bob, and they were joined, but Grandpa Doc separated them all right except for the terrible scars. After them, two or three sets died, then it was Ella May and Janice Ruth. Then Benny Paul and his brother who died. And more dead ones in between before Trish survived. Then Sue Elaine and Lou Ellen. We'd already realized, by then, that every time Grandpa separated twins, one of them was . . . wrong, somehow.

"Your mother, Maybelle, is sweetness itself, but Mayleen . . . And Joe Bob is a sensible, kind person, but it's good Billy Wayne went into the army, because he's as bad as Benny Paul. It was the same with Ella May and Janine Ruth. Ella May applied to the Siblinghood because she couldn't stand it that her sister was a really vicious person. It was as though only one out of each pair had any goodness. Trish is like an empty bottle. Nothing there at all but babble and bubbles. And it went on and on, sometimes one lived, sometimes neither, five times both. And you know what happened to poor Lou Ellen after she and Sue Elaine . . ."

I saw Glory's face change, saw it convulsed with fury, and suddenly she was screaming, "It wasn't fair letting Sue Elaine have legs and not letting Lou Ellen have any!" Then there was a vast quiet, as though the whole world was waiting for her answer.

I whispered, "The nerves to the legs were connected to Sue Elaine's brain, not to Lou Ellen's. There were only two legs, only one spine attached at the pelvis. Actually, Lou Ellen didn't have any legs, Glory. You know that. Grandpa Doc had to separate them. He waited until they were three. You used to play with her on the bed for hours, and you knew . . ."

"She got well. She does too have legs now," Glory said. "She does. She goes everywhere with me!"

Falija put her paw on Glory's hand and let the claws out, just a tiny bit. "Glory, Glory, Lou Ellen is dead. You know that. You saw her dancing with all her selves. You know she isn't really alive. In your heart you know that."

Glory's hands went to her throat, as though she were choking, but still she cried out, "Bamber's seen her! Tell them, Bamber!"

"Well," he said in a sad voice, "I've seen her ghost, Glory. But then, I can see people's ghosts, and I guess you can, too."

"She's buried in the cemetery," I said. "I know you wouldn't go to her funeral or even into the graveyard to see the stone, but her grave is there, Glory. Really."

Glory looked around, trying to find something else to prove Lou Ellen was still alive. "You make her sandwiches," she said frantically. "You say hello to her."

"Just to keep you contented, Glory, so you won't go back into the state you went into when she died. You end up eating the sandwiches yourself. And nobody says hello to Lou Ellen until you look at her and show us where you think she is. Except Falija says you really can see her, and now Bamber says he can, so you're not . . . you know, what we thought you were . . ."

"You all thought I was crazy. Mama and Daddy and you!"

"Well," I cried, "I beg your forgiveness for that, but there was just no end to the tragedy and the loss and the pain. And when your mama had Til and Jeff, it was the same thing. Jeff is a wonderful boy, but Til . . . Til's another one like Benny Paul. When your mother got pregnant the second time, Grandpa Doc knew the babies wouldn't live, because a friend of his had sneaked across the Walled-Off to lend him some other medical machine that The Valley doesn't have.

"I . . . I went up to Contrition City and I went to the refuge there, the one for pregnant women who want to give up their babies for adoption. Women sometimes come to Rueful just for that reason, you know. I asked for a woman who would have a baby about that same time Maybelle would; Grandpa arranged for a private place for the birthing. Maybelle's babies were born dead, all scrambled together. We never told her. When she woke up, you were there, and she and your daddy have always thought you were theirs. Nobody knew you weren't except Grandpa Doc and me and the real mother."

"And Mama got her tubes tied," Glory said in a dull voice. "But Aunt Mayleen didn't."

"Not right then. She and Billy Ray were dead set against it, but Grandpa did it the year before he died. He told her she had an infection he had to clear up, but what he really cleared up was her having any more babies. He just said it was the infection did it, and that's what he told Billy Ray."

"I can't understand how you kept all this quiet," said Bamber. "That many conjoined twins would have been on everyone's tongue."

I said, "If my husband hadn't been a very fine doctor, if he hadn't had a few advanced medical devices that he really shouldn't have had in Rueful, and if he hadn't had me to help out, it would have been a circus. But Billy Ray's farm is away from everyone, and so is Jimmy Joe's. We never allowed anyone to see the babies until they were apart. Later, when they went to school and played with other children who saw the scars, we had stories to explain what happened. With Til and Jeff, it was an accident in an old barn. With Maybelle and Mayleen, the scars were small anyhow, just at the back of their heads, mostly covered by their hair, and we just told them they were born that way . . ."

"How did you keep Mayleen quiet?" Glory cried. "When she started having twins, she'd have screamed about it."

"Not Mayleen. You know what the folks in Rueful would have thought about it and said about it. She didn't want that. She'd have died before she'd have admitted it, and Billy Ray likewise."

Everyone was still. I was watching Glory, thinking she'd break out any minute with tears, howls, accusations, but she seemed more . . . interested, or troubled than outraged.

"I don't know what this means," Glory complained. "I feel like

I'm lost. Not . . . not orphaned, exactly. I know that Mama and Daddy love me and that you do, too, Grandma. But I feel like there's part of me floating free, like a wood chip going down the river, turning around and around, with no idea where it's going . . ."

"Which means the umoxen were right," said Falija. "Glory and Bamber are a different sort. What did the woman look like, the one who gave up Glory?"

I wiped my eyes with the wet hanky. "I never saw her. She sent an old woman to bring Glory to us, a very old woman. Budness or Bodness, she said her name was. She said the mother was too broken up to do it. Well, I understand that. No woman gives up a child unless things are terrible for her. As for Glory, well, even as a baby she had dark, dark hair and brown skin, and when I commented on it, the old woman said the baby's father was very tall, and very dark. I asked her what had happened to the father, wondering, you know, why the mother was giving up her child, and the old woman said he had disappeared and the mother couldn't raise her little girl alone."

"Why didn't you just tell Mama the babies died?" Glory asked, still in that curious, almost uninvolved voice.

"Because your mama has a heart condition, Glory. You've heard us mention it. She almost died when Til and Jeff were born. And she almost died again when she saw them, and again when they were operated on. And she's fretted herself for years over the fact that they aren't . . . equally endowed. Grandpa Doc didn't realize how serious your mother's condition until after the Til and Jeff were born, but after that, he just couldn't let her go through all that again."

Glory turned to stare at Bamber, her eyes moving from his hair to his eyes to his height. Like hers, all of them. He had an arching nose and a wide mouth, like hers, one that always looked like it had too many teeth in it. Dark, vital, lean, and fit. I felt soft compared to both of them. I could have howled.

"I knew we were alike," Glory said very softly. "More like family. I never looked like the Mackeys or the Judsons. Do you think we have the same parents?"

He thought about this, troubled, as she was, but not angry. "It's possible," he said at last. "I don't remember what my mother looked like. I don't remember anybody before we came here to Rueful. It would explain her leaving me with Abe Johnson, because she might have wanted us to grow up near one another . . .”

I was listening to this with continuing amazement. I had known about Gloriana's birth mother! Why hadn't it occurred to me that Bamber might have had the same one?

“What about when Til, and Jeff, and Trish, and all of the rest of Mayleen's children start having babies?” Glory demanded.

“Grandpa Doc fixed them all, before he died, even Emmaline, when she was just a baby. We had quite a plague of appendicitis among the girls and hernias among the boys, but none of them will have children, not even the nice ones, and that's another reason why your cousin Ella May joined the Siblinghood. She and Joe Bob were old enough and sensible enough that Grandpa told them the truth. Oh, Glory, it was such a burden for your grandfather. I know he felt he'd been cursed. I felt I was a curse to him. . . .”

Glory murmured, “Then I'm glad I wasn't Mama's baby, really, but I'm glad I'm her child.”

I broke down then and cried, while Bamber and Glory tried to comfort me, though every now and then Glory would mutter that it would have made so much more sense if we'd just admitted it to one another instead of trying to keep it secret. Perhaps later I could explain that both Grandpa Doc and I had been from an older time on Earth, when things like that couldn't be talked about at all. Maybe he had been ashamed of it. I *had* been ashamed of it. Maybe he'd had dreams of his family going on, down the generations, and he just couldn't admit to the world that they wouldn't. And then, too, I knew Bryan hadn't struggled to keep life in some of those babies, when he'd seen how awful their lives would be. Like Lou Ellen. That poor baby had whispered to me that she prayed to die, so the pain could stop. Glory had just been so generously accepting that she'd never realized how dreadful Lou Ellen's life really was . . .

Glory stood up, her jaw set. “I think I've had about all the emotions I can take for one day.” She took a deep breath and helped me get to my feet. “If we're going to find someplace to sleep by sundown, we'd better get started.”

I Am Margaret, with Hayraiders on Fajnard

We reached the gate of the Howkel Farm at nightfall. While Falija and I waited at the gate, Glory and Bamber went to the door and knocked politely. Dame Howkel answered the knock.

"So you've arrived!" she said. "Good enough. I always say to Lafaniel, that's my husband, Lafaniel, that he truckles too much to them umoxen. Nice creature, true, polite in their habits, but set on having their way! Beckon your folk in, now, and we'll see about supper."

The two beckoned as instructed, I thinking meanwhile that I'd never imagined anyone quite so round, green, and cheerful as Dame Howkel. Once inside, however, I forgot about the probability of eating hay, for the aroma was of something very savory. Dame Howkel bobbed a curtsy toward Falija.

"Welcome, ma'am and Gibbekotkin. Howkel'l be along shortly. Our young have had their supper, us oldsters waited for you."

She showed us the way out back, where a washbowl sat on a table next to the well beside a stack of towels and a steaming kettle. Once back inside, we were given mugs of fragrant green tea, and by the time Lafaniel Howkel showed up, we were deep in conversation with the Dame concerning the plight of Fajnard.

"I was speaking of the Frossians," said the Dame to

her husband. "I was telling how the Gibbekot planted those acid trees all along the valleys to stop the Frossians coming."

"I would've warned you of the same," Howkel said, pouring himself a mug of tea. "They smell very pungent, so they're easy to avoid. You'd think the Frossians'd learn to look at the trees to see which ones do it to 'em, but they never do."

He turned toward me and said pointedly, with a sidelong glance at Falija, "Since you're Ghoss, you'll be going to the Gibbekot, won't you? They'll be wondering where that child is, wanderin' off and findin' the comp'ny of strangers."

"I'm not from Fajnard, and they're not Ghoss," said Falija, in a lofty tone. "We came through a way-gate from Tercis."

"Not Ghoss? Then what are they?" demanded Howkel.

"Same race," said Falija. "Not the same . . . talents."

"You say a way-gate," breathed the Dame. "I didn't know we had a way-gate anywhere near here."

"Never seen fit to mention it to you," Howkel said, fixing Falija with a doubtful eye. "We have a pair of 'em, one that comes in from Tercis, and one that goes out to Thairy. And right now, there's gizzardiles lyin' both ways like sentries!"

"We saw one," said Bamber. "Very ugly."

"Supper," said Dame Howkel in a peremptory tone. "Let's not upset ourselfs with gizzardiles right afore supper."

We sat down at the long, wide table, the Dame at one end, Howkel at the other, his feet neatly crossed so his toenails curved inward before him, making floor space for the feet of those at his sides. Each place held a large bowl of stew, which had a certain verdant leafiness about it, but also bits that crunched or melted. We talked about food, the Dame ticking off many kinds of nuts and roots and seeds that made up hayfolk meals. "Along with hay," she said, listing the kinds of hay, each with its own taste and texture.

"Have you always been hayraiders?" Gloriana asked.

"Hayfolk," said Howkel. "Not raiders 'til the umoxen came, and they was brought from the plains below by the Gibbekot. They was the ones started cuttin' hay from the grasslands, not knowin' we was countin' on it for winter food for ourselfs. Generally nice folk, the Gibbekot. We told 'em we needed it, and they worked it out right away. We get first cut. After that, we cut hay for the umoxen, and we get umox wool from the Gibbekot in return. Hayraidin's just doin' what we always did."

"You always cut the hay at night?" asked Bamber Joy.

"Oh, sure. Nicer, cooler at night, and there's usually a moon, since Fajnard has five of 'em."

"Did you always have those remarkable toenails?" I asked.

"Our people say we always did," said Dame Howkel. "Course, I cut mine, now I'm past dancin' the hay, and we all cut 'em off after the hay's in for the season and sell 'em in the market for sickle blades. No better edge nowhere than Hayfolk toenails. Besides, it's warmer in the winter if you can keep your feet under the blanket 'stead of lettin' 'em hang out the foot of the bed. Now, suppose you tell us where you're headed. We can tell you the safest roads, depending on where you're going."

Falija, who had been rather quiet since Grandma's revelations on the road, made a little annunciatory noise, then: "My duty is to guide these folk in walking the seven roads of the Keeper. It is a task I was given by my people."

All of us turned to her in amazement, Bamber and Glory with their eyes wide, the Howkels with their mouths wide, me with both eyes and lips shut tight, afraid to say the wrong thing.

"When did you decide that?" cried Glory.

"It came to me while I was thinking of the fish story," Falija said. "You remember what I told you about my language and my mother-mind. I said you sometimes have to hear a word in context before you can understand what it really means. I had the seven roads in my mother-memory. It's my job to help the walker walk the seven roads. I knew the story of the fish, but it didn't connect to anything in my mind until just a few hours ago. All seven roads are one, and they must be walked simultaneously by one person." Her voice faltered. "There's nothing in my mind about how that's to be done."

"What is it, a riddle?" asked Bamber.

Falija shook her head. "All I know is, we just have to keep going."

"On this road?" I demanded. "In front of the house?"

Falija dropped her head, shaking it slightly, saying in a sorrowful voice, "I don't know."

"Road you came by was a way-gate road," said Howkel, pushing his chair back and honing his toenails together with a sound like steel on whetstone. "That road out front just goes to Gibbekotika by way of the mountains, that's all. So, likely it's a way-gate road that's meant."

"And there's one that goes on to Thairy," murmured Bamber Joy. "You said."

"Well, yes," mused Howkel. "A way-gate road as well."

"That's two roads that are one road," said Glory.

I took a deep breath. "Are all the way-gates one-way roads?"

"One way," Falija murmured. "I remember that someone long ago invented a machine to reverse them; but when they're let alone, they're always one way."

"My oh my," the Dame said, shaking her head. "That's a lot of confusion and supposition, that is. Seems to me you'd be better off finishing your supper, having a good night's sleep, then deciding what you're going to do next."

"Dame's right," said Howkel. "Never make plans when you're weary, and I'm weary. Been cuttin' hay the last eleven nights."

"There, that's so," the Dame said, nodding to her husband. "No more talk of roads tonight."

Glory and Bamber agreed, though Falija looked slightly mutinous. I reached out and petted her between the ears. Falija sighed and settled to her supper.

"There, now," said the Dame. "That's better. You're a dutiful Gibbekotkin, the more credit to you, but even the dutiful have to eat and rest." She turned to her own bowl, raising her spoon with a little moue of discomfort.

I saw that her arm was bruised. "What have you done to yourself there?" I asked. "That looks painful!"

"And so it is," said Howkel. "And it's gettin' no better, neither. It's a summer bruise, and it's been there a time now."

"Let me see," I said, taking the Dame's arm in my hands. Indeed, there was a darkness, like a bruise, except that on the green flesh it looked more like a crushed place, one that was not healing. "Tell me," I said, after some thought. "When you are ill, does your body get hot? Do you run a fever?"

"A fever? And what is a fever?" asked the Dame. "When our people are ill, they get cold."

"But this place on your arm is not cold. The tissue there is ruined. It needs to die and fall away, so the good tissue underneath can heal. Isn't that what usually happens?"

"Oh, aye, it does," said Howkel. "When Maniacal's toes were cut to pieces on the sharp rocks, they got cold and fell off, and the new ones grew. Thankful it was wintertime, we were."

I nodded. "But in summer, warm as it is, it would be hard for a bruised place to get cold enough to fall away. Well then, I would put ice on this. Is there any ice about?"

"Close enough," said Howkel. "And where did you learn such thinking out, ma'am?"

"My husband was a doctor," I said. "He always said, find out what the body does for itself and help it along."

"Think of that," said the Dame. "Just think of that, Howkel." And, with a smile of great sweetness, she reached up and kissed me on the cheek.

I Am M'urgi, with Fernwold on B'yurngrad

Once we were in Ferni's flier, I demanded to know what he meant when he said he was taking me somewhere safe.

"I overheard something," he said. "Perhaps meaningless, perhaps not. It made me believe you might be in danger."

"From whom?" I demanded.

He shrugged. "From someone who wants you dead, my love."

I laughed. "That's fairly indefinite."

"M'urgi. Listen to me. I was in a crowded place, waiting to take a ship from one place to another. Somewhere close to me a deep voice says, 'The word came down, all the way from the top. The orders are she's got to be killed, soon.' Second voice asks, 'Why some smoke-flavored old hag from the steppes . . .'"

"Old hag!" I interrupted angrily. "I am not an old hag!"

He said harshly. "I'm not finished! The first voice says, 'No hag, she's young yet.' Now, you tell me. Is there anyone else working here on B'yurngrad that answers that description? 'Smoke-flavored, steppes, young yet,' says you to me."

I couldn't answer. The words described me, and me only. "Who?" I said finally. "Who wants me dead?"

"I don't know. I couldn't find the speakers. I stayed there listening for a long time, no luck. I have no idea who or what they were. What enemies have you made while here?"

"Enemies made as whom? As the night flier, the shaman's girl? As the shaman herself after the old woman died? Since then, being a ghyrm-hunter? That last one we can answer. The ghyrm distributor probably wants all hunters off the job."

"There are a dozen hunters, at least. You're the only one fitting the description. Why only you?"

I shook my head at him. "I'm baffled, Ferni. If I've learned anything on this job, however, it's that a workman never knows how the work looks to people who see it from the outside. We carry ghyrm. That makes us devils to some. You saw how that oasthall emptied out when I was there."

"I imagined as much. That's why I said I was taking you someplace safer. Everyone around here knows who you are, what you are. They'll talk: 'Yes, the woman was here, she went off in that direction.' That's why I've gone five directions since taking off. If anybody's watching, we'll hope we lost them."

"And what is there, where we're going?"

"A lake. A forest. A waterfall. A little inn, where the Siblinghood sends people who need a long rest. A view over the grasslands. Horses."

"Horses?" I said doubtfully.

"Yes. The innkeeper keeps horses, for people to ride."

"That's new!"

"It is new, yes. Five or six years new. The Siblinghood brought in the original stock from Tercis, where they had too many. The grasslands are perfect for them. They actually eat plants the umoxen don't like, so they fit."

"Can I ride one?" I asked wonderingly.

"I should think so," he said, grinning at me.

I turned from him to look out the window of the flier. Below, the grasslands extended beyond the range of vision, a wave-rippled ocean of green, blue, silver, and almost yellow, with here and there a patch of vivid red and once in a while a copse of towering trees. I felt tears in my eyes and wondered why. It came to me after a while. Death threats or no death threats, I couldn't remember ever being this gloriously, miraculously happy.

I Am Margaret/on Fajnard

Glory, Bamber Joy, Falija, and I spent the night in the hayloft of the barn, where sheets and blankets had been laid atop the hay, and we awoke early to hear Howkel whistling as he milked Earthian goats down below. Now, where had they come from?

While combing hay out of her hair, Glory remarked, "One of the things Falija's folks said to me was that Falija would not be safe anywhere her people were known to be or known to visit. And Howkel says her people live here, so she's not safe here!"

"You haven't seen fit to mention this until now," I growled.

"I didn't remember it until now," Gloriana cried. "It never made any difference until now."

We told Howkel our dilemma at the breakfast table. He thought about it for some time before saying:

"There's a shortcut to the Thairy way-gate without going through Gibbekot country. Suppose I send a couple of the youngsters with you as guides. Good at sneakiness, youngsters. Never known one that wasn't."

"Send Maniacal and Mirabel," said the Dame. "They're sneaky, that's certain, and the longer the journey the better."

"Them's the oldest," Howkel confided. "My Dame's purely weary of wishin' they'd move on and set up on their own."

"Breakfast first," said the Dame. "Haycakes and syrup."

Midway through breakfast, Glory leaned toward me. "Did you know your face has turned a little green?"

"Did you know all your teeth were the color of grass?" I returned, without easing my pursuit of the last of the haycake around my plate. "Mighty peculiar-looking."

"You two stop it," muttered Bamber. "One of you'll say something, and the other one will pounce on it, and then no matter how high our mission, it'll all go to nonsense."

"Quite right," I agreed. "Your teeth are only slightly green, Gloriana."

"And your face hardly shows it except around your ears," Gloriana conceded.

Maniacal and Mirabel brought a wagon around to the front of the house, one seat in front and hay deeply piled in a short wagon bed behind. The three creatures pulling the wagon were leaner and taller than umoxen, with great, muscular hind legs.

"Gnar," said Maniacal. "Not as strong as umoxen for the long haul, but very fast when they need to be."

"You think they'll need to be?" asked Bamber John.

"We won't know 'til it happens, but if it does, you just burrow down in that hay and leave the rest to Mirabel and me."

We took the precaution of burying our packs in the hay to start with. Falija had said nothing all morning, and I didn't like the way she looked, her eyes unfocused and the fur on her face every which way.

"Did you have bad dreams, Falija?"

Falija nodded slowly. "I think I must have. I remember running as fast as we could away from something."

"That's a happy thought to start the day," I remarked, punching the hay to make a larger pillow. "Maniacal, where is this way-gate to Thairy?"

"First there's a long stretch of grass, then a bit of forest and a little climb. Pa Howkel told us how to find it. We won't be going near the Ghoss and Gibbekots, but we'll likely pass a few hayfolk farms. When we do, just hide 'til we get on by."

So the morning passed, us mostly lying on the hay, occasionally napping, sometimes burrowing while trying not to scratch or sneeze.

Noon came and went, as did a good part of the food Dame Howkel had packed for us.

Late afternoon had come when Mirabel said urgently, "Get down into the hay. Somebody coming."

We burrowed. Mirabel got into the wagon bed and carefully covered any parts we'd left showing. The wagon moved along, easily, not fast, then suddenly Maniacal let out a whoop and we began to clatter along the road at very high speed.

Mirabel leaned down and said, "Two humans in some kind of machine. Maniacal is heading for the woods."

"I'll bet it's Ned and Walter," mumbled Bamber Joy, around the wisps of hay that kept creeping into his mouth and nose. "Or somebody just like them. I need to see."

He tunneled through the hay until he was under the wagon seat, then pushed his head up under it where he could look out through a crack. "Not the car from Tercis," he cried. "Another one that smokes and snarls, but it's not catching up yet."

Time went by as we rushed and clattered.

"Now they're catching up to us," cried Mirabel.

"Look up there ahead," growled Maniacal. "What do you see across the road?"

"Oooh," she said. "Gizzardile. Oooh, Manny, that's the biggest one I ever saw!"

"Hold on tight," shouted Maniacal. "Go, gnar, go . . ."

Our speed increased, the rattling turned into a chattering hum, the vehicle behind us sped up as well as we flew down the ruts. I had tunneled up next to Bamber Joy, and we both saw the cylindrical something or other, like a mighty tree trunk, down across the road. No forest anywhere near, and the buggy was flying toward it, was going to hit it at full speed . . .

"Fly, gnar, fly," yelled Maniacal, and the buggy flew, or at least it leapt, following the trajectory of the three animals that took off as one in a long arc across the gizzardile, landing beyond it with a great swaying and crashing as though the wagon were falling apart.

Bamber and I quickly looked behind us. The pursuing vehicle was closing on the gizzardile, which suddenly and quite quickly, considering its bulk, reared its forward end and turned it to face the noisy machine. The fin that had lain along the creature's back rose into a huge fan, numerous legs stretched out on either side, and before the vehicle could stop, turn, or maneuver in any way, the gizzardile chunked its huge, lumpy lower part directly into its path, and when the machine struck, collapsed its higher parts on top with a great shriek of rending metal.

"Whoa, gnar," said Maniacal.

"They were after me," Falija remarked. "That must be what I dreamed about, but they didn't catch us after all!"

Maniacal was out of the wagon, unhitching the Gnar.

"Don't we still need them?" Bamber asked.

"When good creatures do a great good thing," said Maniacal, "we don't ask them to spend their strength doin' more when our own strength will suffice. So Pa Howkel has always told me. They jumped their weight, and ours, and the wagon's over that critter. That's a story for tellin' at the Haymeet, many a year from now . . ."

"Nobody'll believe it," remarked Mirabel.

"Not if you tell it, but they know I'm no tale maker. See yonder? Just above those trees? That's where we're going, and these good creatures can find their way home by theirselves while that gizzardile is occupied. Since gizzardiles eat most everything including rocks, it'll be a while."

"We won't make it before night," I said.

"No," said Mirabel, "but there's a little cave up there, above the lake, where Pa's camped out many a time. We can get there by full dark, and there's both late and early moons." He pointed high above us, where a half-moon was in bud, to the west, where a crescent sailed like a little boat toward the horizon, while far to the east an almost full moon blossomed over the hills.

"How'll you get your wagon back?" I asked. I had been thinking to myself that for a wagon that looked as rattletrap as this one did, it had held up extremely well: more to it, perhaps, than met the eye— just as with Pa Howkel.

Mirabel said offhandedly, "Pa'll bring an umox team to get the wagon when the gnar get home without it."

And with that, we shouldered our packs and made for the line of forest, which was now no great distance ahead. Behind the forest lay the mountains, slowly thrusting up to cover the last of the sunset yellow sky while rosy clouds gathered like bridesmaids, and a diamond star pulsed against the high blue, like a signal light someone had lit in a window.

"What star is that?" asked Bamber Joy.

Maniacal looked up at it, cocking his head. "That's the summer star. That's the star that shines on Thairy."

I Am M'urgi, with
Fernwold on B'yurngrad

The inn was very much as Ferni had described it. The rooms were very simple, paneled in smooth, aromatic wood. In our suite, I luxuriated in a hot, foamy bath that smelled of flowers and found myself becoming somewhat resentful toward the Siblinghood.

"They never mentioned this place. They never told me I was entitled to a vacation. They never suggested I might need a rest. I'm still digging soot out of the creases in my skin!"

"I can't see any," remarked Ferni from the other end of the tub. "Not anywhere. I'm looking very closely."

I flushed and submerged. When I came up again, I grinned at him. "Behave yourself, or I'll do a chant on you."

"What is that?" he asked.

"What is what?"

"I've never understood that shaman business. The chants, what you did with the girl at the oasthall. What they call night flying. All that."

I twisted my wet hair into a knot atop my head and let the water lap at my chin. "You really want to know?"

"I don't suppose I can *know*, but I'd like to understand."

I sat up a little. "All right. The first lesson the shaman taught me was belief. Before I could do anything I had to believe that here, around us, is an insubstantial entity that senses everything. It wraps around stars, it surrounds worlds, moons, comets, all the trash and dust that's out in space, encompasses all races of creatures no matter how small, is everywhere. It pushes things together to separate one thing from another; it forms boundaries. The shaman calls that entity Kuzh. We'd say 'the Holder.'"

"The Keeper?" murmured Ferni in a strange voice.

"The Keeper? Yes, that would convey the same meaning. The shaman taught me to believe by showing me that the existence of the ... 'Keeper' was the only explanation for what she could do. Once I'd really perceived what she could do, once I'd tried to think of anything else that would explain it, I believed, I learned to touch it, go into it, move inside it, not with my body, just with my senses. Kuzh is insubstantial, so bodies can't move in it, but senses can. Whatever senses you have, you can use them there to learn what's going on. The shaman and I used ours to prevent as much slaughter as possible among the tribes. We nudged them gradually toward something less violent. The shamans call it night flying because it's easiest to do when sensory stimulation is decreased, when it's dark. The Kuzh, the Keeper around you is not only sensing, but also reflecting the patterns of what's going on, sensing what each pattern will lead to and how long it will take. The closest times are the most accurate. That's the way we foretold and prevented massacres."

"How?" he asked.

"Sometimes just by whispering a word in someone's ear. Sometimes by asking the nearest settlements to make a raid just before war was to break out. Different ways."

"How long did it take you to learn to do that?"

I sighed. "It took me three years just to make the first contact. Another year to learn to lie on the night and go with it. Maybe two more years to pick up the sense of what was going on around me. The old woman said I was way too old to learn easily, a child of three or four is better at it. Still, she got four good years out of me. Enough for us to prove that some of the tribes were running ghyrm into the settlements."

"Did you find the source of the ghyrm?"

"We came close. All we had was the pictures they had in their minds. They went down into a darkness. Someone gave them the ghyrm, and they were paid in weapons. We tried again and again to follow them when they went wherever it was. We were never there at the right time."

He laved his arms. "Do you miss it? That work?"

I felt my brow furrow. "Well, Ferni, I was generally very dirty, very stinky, no baths out on the steppes, our clothing was mostly uncured hides, we slept itchy, we had bugs and what not. Do I miss it? Not the doing of it, no. The feeling of it, yes. That weightlessness. That was a nice feeling. But, so is this."

He grinned at me. "What do you want to do today?"

"Horses," I cried. "You promised me horses."

We rode, later on, down a forested valley where a bright, tumbling river spilled a lake into the grasslands at the foot of the hills. I experimented with my posture, the saddle, the animal, trying to figure out what was possible, what was comfortable, what was least painful. Ferni had picked up considerable skill, which he patiently passed on. By noon, we were well out into the grasses, the hills some way behind us. We stopped among a scattering of small trees by the river, tied the horses, and spread out our lunch.

"I'll never get back on that animal," I snarled. "You didn't tell me it hurt."

"Only the first few times. Walk around a bit. That'll help. Have some wine. That'll help even more!"

"Oh, I'm sure being sotted would enable me to ride like the wind, for all of two steps before I fell off!" He hadn't brought enough wine to made me insensible, but he was right, it did dull the pain.

I lay back on the grasses, head propped on one hand, admiring the velvety turf and the herd of gnar some little distance away, peacefully grazing while their young leapt and pretended to fight with their front feet. We watched them for a long, contented time.

"Are they native here?" Ferni asked drowsily.

"Umm," I replied, lying back on the blanket. "What? The gnar? Yes. They're native here, but they've been transplanted to several other grassland planets. The closest one I know of is Fajnard. Only on the highlands, though. They won't stay anywhere near the Frossians."

"They're kept for wool?"

"It's more hair than wool. In the winter they grow an undercoat that's warmer than any other natural fiber known. It's not as fine as umox hair, but it's hollow, and that makes it a marvelous, lightweight insulator. The herders pull it out in the spring with combs shaped like little rakes."

"Can they be ridden?" he asked sleepily.

"No. They're very good at pulling light wagons, but their body proportions are all wrong for carrying people as horses can, or as umoxen will, even though they're very slow."

The herd went leaping away, toward the hills, in great, ground-eating bounds, and I, half asleep, wondered what had spooked them. All was silent except for the horses' teeth, chomping grass, the twitter of some small creatures in the reeds along the water, the deep breathing of us two drowsers.

The tribesmen came out of the grasses fast and low. Four of them leapt upon Ferni and held him down, tying his hands behind him, his feet together, blindfolding him. Four of them seized me up, gagged me, wrapped me in a net, and ran off into the grasses. The horses jerked wildly at their reins, whinnying and screaming.

From the net that held me I thrust my mind back to the place Ferni was. He was pushing his face against the ground, shoving the blindfold away to find himself alone. "Stupid idiot," he raged at himself. "Promised her horses. Promised to keep her safe. Damn! Where did they come from? No tribesmen nearer than a three-day ride, they told me! No danger! Don't worry!"

While he railed at himself, he was working his hands as far apart as possible so he could sit on them, work his way back, move the hands forward, damn, damn, nearly dislocated a shoulder there, never mind, go ahead, dislocate the damned thing, get the hands in front, in front, pull up the knees, get his feet through. He was thinking he had done this before, but it had been a long, long time. Now the thongs were at mouth level and he chewed them, slobbering as much as possible to get them wet, stretching the wet leather, more, more, one loop between his teeth, up and over, another loop, up and over, now loosen the whole thing. Off!

I watched him as in a dream. His hands were numb. He had to wave them, yell at them before they'd stop pricking and work. Now.

Leave the clutter by the river to mark the place. Get on the horse and follow . . .

I saw him searching, read his face: Where? No sign. No sign at all. Not a trail through the grasses. He couldn't follow a trail if he wasn't high enough to see a trail!

I sensed his frustration, fury, grief. He mounted one horse and grabbed the other's reins to lead it as he raced back the way we had come to get help.

I Am Margaret/on Fajnard

Even though we had ridden in the wagon all day, we were tired, and the moonlight was not restful. Romantic as all get-out, probably, but not helpful, except as it kept us from stumbling, falling, or running headlong into one another. Even the young ones were weary, though the hayfolk young were more accustomed to the light and the terrain than we three from Tercis. Falija was by now resting on Bamber's shoulders like a fur scarf, head hanging, half asleep.

We had been walking for some time on a trail that ran along the side of a rocky hill—one of the Mountains of Mupple, Maniacal claimed—heading toward a comfortable cave, though what made a cave comfortable had not been explained. I was second in line. Ahead of me, Maniacal was pointing at something.

"There's a light there," I said stupidly. "Is there supposed to be a light there?"

Mirabel's voice came from behind us. "The Ghoss use it sometimes."

"But not the Frossians?" I asked hesitantly.

"Never the Frossians, no," said Maniacal. He moved slowly forward, the rest of us following, our eyes darting back and forth between the rough footing and the distant flicker of firelight, crossed by a walking shadow that went, then returned in the opposite direction.

"I'll go on ahead," said Maniacal, when we were only a

short distance from the cave opening. He edged away from us and went more rapidly, stopping a few paces short of the opening to creep forward slowly, extending his neck like a telescope to peer around the nearer stones.

"What's he doing?" whispered Glory. "How does he do that?"

"We all do it," said Mirabel. "It's how we keep track of where we are in the deep grasses, put our heads up when we need to. You bony people can't do it, and I've never figured out how you manage without."

"You don't have bones?" asked Grandma.

"Only a few," said Mirabel. "Here and there, and they do wander about."

Maniacal was returning. "It's a Ghoss," he called. "He's got another Ghoss there, sleeping, but he says come ahead."

We went on. Inside the sandy cave an elderly man stood to welcome us, bowing, introducing himself. "I'm Rei. The one sleeping over there is Mar-agern. Come in, sit down. I was just heating water for tea. I know you raiders can't go long without your tea, and I happen to have some." He stopped in some confusion as he got a good look at me. "Excuse me. You're not all hayfolk. Ma'am. Ah, well. Not Ghoss, then. Not you, not the young ones. Escaped bondspeople?"

"No," I said with some asperity. "I'm Margaret. This is my granddaughter, Gloriana, and her friend, Bamber Joy. And this is Falija."

Rei bowed deeply to Falija, still curled around Bamber's neck. "Gibbekotkin," he murmured. "Welcome. Do you come from the city?"

Bamber squatted to let Falija jump down. She sat on her haunches, eyes moving around the cave as though to penetrate its stone walls before she turned her gaze back to the man who had welcomed us. "We thank the Ghoss, Rei," she said. "These people came with me through a way-gate from the planet Tercis. We are bound for the way-gate that leads to Thairy. We were pursued, our lives threatened. A gizzardile intervened and saved us inadvertently. We are very weary and grateful for your help."

The Ghoss bowed again. "As our ancestors promised yours, we will do whatever we can do."

"A little rest would be most welcome," I said, trying to swallow a yawn.

We sat around the fire. Tea was poured and another pot heated and brewed. Maniacal distributed the food we had left, but we only nibbled at it, too tired to be hungry. The Ghoss did not question us, but he stared at me with particular intensity.

Finally, intercepting this gaze, Falija said, "We are on a quest, Ghoss Rei. There are creatures about who don't want us to make it. They were on Tercis, they are here on Fajnard, possibly they will be on Thairy. The quest is to walk the seven roads that are one road."

"A riddle?" suggested Rei.

"You could say that, yes," I said. Some color had returned to my face, and I felt both slightly strengthened and in need of going some-place private. I shifted uncomfortably.

"Around the corner, there," suggested Rei. "You'll find what you need."

Seeing my startled look, Mirabel said, "They're telepathic, the Ghoss. They can tell what you're thinking or needing."

"Ah," I said, at a loss for any real words and not at all sure I liked people being aware of when I needed to pee. Around the corner was a wooden seat over a crevice in the rock as well as a waist-level stone hollow constantly filled by a seep from above. I washed my face and hands, feeling somewhat refreshed.

When I returned to the others, I had to pass the sleeping person very closely, and I looked down, to avoid stepping on him, her. I looked down, and stood, looking down, not moving, not moving at all.

"Grandma?" cried Gloriana. "What is it?"

"It's me," I answered, eyes still fixed on the sleeping form. "For the love of heaven, Gloriana, it's me."

Gloriana came to stand beside me, gaping, moving about to get a better look. "She's . . . she's younger than you, Grandma."

"She's me, the way I looked in the mirror, not all that long ago." I turned to face Rei, demanding, "Who is she?"

"Mar-agern was a bondslave sent here to Fajnard," said Rei, glancing back and forth between us. "You're right. I saw the resem-blance when you came in. She came from Earth when she was about twenty-two."

"I came from Earth, when I was twenty-two."

"And your father's name was . . . ?"

"Harry Bain. And her mother's name was . . ."

"Louise Bain," said Rei.

"How did this happen?" I cried, looking from face to face. "How did this happen?"

"Shhh," said Rei. "We don't know how. Perhaps we know why . . . Gibbekot?"

"Her name?" I cried. "What's her name?"

"As I said, her name is Mar-agern," said Rei.

"Not quite close enough to be Margy," I laughed. "Or maybe it is? One of my play people. Margy. First Wilvia, then Margy. Is there to be a Naumi as well?"

"Sit down, Grandma," Glory urged. "You're very pale. This is all very weird and strange, and you're allergic to strange."

Bamber took one arm, Glory the other, and they sat me down near the fire, where I shook my head silently, slowly, hoping to negate the existence of everything in the neighborhood, perhaps myself included.

"Gibbekot?" asked Rei, again. "Do we know why?"

"Yes," whispered Falija. "Yes, of course. That is, perhaps, though as yet there are only two of her, and the story would demand at least seven . . ."

A low, continuous moan came from the sleeping woman. She rolled restlessly to one side, then the other, exposing the back of her head.

"What is that on the back of her head?" I demanded.

"That is a mother-mind," said Rei.

"Where did you get it?" demanded Falija harshly.

"I didn't," Rei replied. "The Gibbekot got it from the same place they got the ones they gave our ancestors. They grew them. With grown-up humans, the network just works its way up inside the bottom of the skull. The one on Mar-agern is almost absorbed. She'll wake within another few hours." He sighed deeply, tiredly. Evidently he had been under as much stress as we had.

Falija spoke to Glory and me. "It's as I told you. Nothing to be afraid of."

Rei said, "You said there was a story about seven?"

"There is a story about a man who spoke to a fish," said Falija, beginning the tale.

I lay down, all at once, before I simply collapsed. My eyes flickered. "Excuse me if I don't listen, Falija, but I've heard the story, and I am very tired."

"Sleep," said Gloriana. "It's okay. We'll keep an eye on things, won't we, Bamber, Maniacal?"

They spoke together. "Oh, yes." "We will."

I heard Falija's voice going on with the story, saw the light of the fire flickering on the cave wall, saw Maniacal and Mirabel curl up against the wall to sleep, later felt Gloriana and Bamber Joy lie down on either side of me, probably to keep me warm. Then I didn't see anything or feel anything for quite some time.

I Am M'urgi/on B'yurngrad

I woke to the terror of being blind and speechless, or, as I admonished myself after a moment's panic, blindfolded and gagged. Nothing wrong with my senses, just my surroundings. I was being carried in some kind of sling or net through grasses that rustled. I had seen tribesmen carrying butchered game this way, all the meat piled into the hide and slung on a pole between two of them. Were these tribesmen? Probably. The danger Ferni had warned me of? Probably not. If the goal had been to kill me, they could have done it at once, while I was sleeping.

So, what did they want?

I took a deep, deep breath and let it out slowly. Then another, and another yet. I was not in pain, which made it easier, though I had learned to do it even when in pain. The jostling didn't help, but I could overcome that. Stillness. Inside, the stillness. I straightened myself in the sling and brought my head forward, onto my chest. Now, now, now let the spirit find the knowing cloud, the being, the great register, the omnipresence, the all, now, now, now lie forward upon the cloud and look down . . .

Five of them. Two carrying, two running alongside to spell them when they were tired, one in front to lead them along the back trail through the grasses which led, led, led there, inside the forest, a temporary camp. Small huts covered in hides. A campfire circle with a spit above it. No women. One of the huts new, the scraped hides bright and clean, and a narrow bed and chair inside. They didn't use chairs, or beds. The furnishings were for me, as were the chains attached to a stout pole that ran up the middle of the hut, buried at the bottom, tied to the framework at the top. So. If I proved unwilling, they intended to keep me by force. For someone? For something?

Back, back to the five runners, skulls painted on their faces, death-and-honor tribesmen. Each face, carefully, carefully, not that one, nor that, nor either of these others. The one in front. Yes. Very possibly. He had changed a good deal in the intervening years. He was no longer a boy. Now he was a man, scarred from battle.

Could I find the time trail that led to him? I drifted, searching, there he was, there the woman who had tried to poison his father. There the woman was, slain, as the old shaman had foretold. There was the father, slain in his turn, and others, over and over, leaving only this one and a scatter of other youngsters. He took them. He wove them. He made them a tribe. They captured women. They fathered children. Here he was, planning this raid. The ghostwoman, he said to them. The ghostwoman who saved the life of my father. She is here, nearby. All the tribes know I want her, that I will pay for her. Someone has seen her. He will lead us to her, for gold.

Where did a tribesman get gold? I flew on the word, on the image, the warm gleam, the soft shine, searching, finding it at last, an ancient place, buried under a landslide, tunneled now by avid hunters, guarded now by members of the tribe . . . So. They had found some ancient, wonderful city here on B'yurngrad, where no city had ever been found, and they had burrowed into it like rats. He had paid someone to find me, and he himself had come to get me, and his motive was not murder.

I looked around at the landmarks, the mountains, where the stars stood, then fled back, back to my body, which had by now been carried near to the forest camp. The bodiless search had taken hours.

They entered the camp. I was untied, unblindfolded. I stood up arrogantly. "Bring me watah," I demanded. "I will go in mah own place." And I strode into the hut I had seen, finding it as I had seen it.

When they brought the water I sneered. "Wahm it. I will not wash myself in cold watah." And, when they returned with warm water, I said, "Go away. I am mos angry!"

Each time I was obeyed without question, but still there were five guards set around the perimeter of the hut, still there were half a dozen others a bit farther out, keeping watch. And he who had paid for me squatted by his campfire, watching the door of the hut as a starving man might watch the prey he needed to keep life within him. Something deep and terrible was happening, and every man here knew of it.

I stayed inside long enough to make it clear I did only what I willed to do, then came out of the hut and went to the fire. "Bring my chayah," I commanded.

Someone brought the chair. I sat down, looking down on him. "Sssso," I hissed. "You clevah boy, save yr dah, ya did. Then he go muck it all, fahget taboos. He get kill fah nothin. Now you here, now you lay hans on ghos-woman, make all tha ghos angry wit you. Whas in you head, runnah?"

He ducked his head, rolling it on his neck as though it hurt. "Don wan muck it all. Din take hohses. Din hahm man. Mean no hahm. Mean no blood. Need . . . need somebody hehp us."

It was the face I had seen years ago, determined yet unsure, concerned not to make a mistake, meaning no harm, threatening no blood, no theft of horses. Ah, well, only a matter of time until the tribes got their hands on horses. Then things would become interesting.

"Tell me!" I demanded.

"Cahn you see?" he cried.

"I tiahd," I exclaimed angrily. "I soah! Ya haul me lahk meat and spec me to see? Ya tell it, den I see."

He leaned over the fire, stirring it with the stick in his hand. "I got woman," he said. "Chil'ren, l'il ones. We all got women, chil'ren. We talk to tribes, here, there. They dyin'. Dis thing comes, kills 'em."

"Ghyrm," I breathed. "You speak of ghyrm!"

"Yesss . . ." Like the hiss of a serpent, eyes wild.

"Some tribes carry ghyrm! Your dah, he carry ghyrm!"

"All," he whispered. "All tribes carry, like spear, like arrow, not hurt dah one dat carry. Now . . . now it hurt dah ones dat carry . . ."

"Tuhned on you," I said. "Evil tuhns on da one who use it, no one evah tell you dat? You not lissen to dat?"

"You a huntah," he said in accusation. "They say, you a huntah, findah. You kill the things."

I stood, thinking furiously. Yes, I was a hunter, yes, I could kill the things, but if they were widespread among the tribes . . . then all of B'yurngrad was in danger. "Not alone," I cried. "I mus bring moah my people! Moah huntahs!"

"Nah," he said, face obdurately set. "They say ahl righ one huntah. No danja foah owr folk in one huntah."

I sat down. "Yoah name?"

"Dey call me Dahk Runnah."

"Dahk Runnah. Yah go to hunt meat, yah go alone?"

"Go wit men in tribe."

"I hunt ghyrm, I hunt wit folk, mah tribe. Alone, I cahn do no good."

"Iz lie!" he said angrily. "You go alone mahny times. Mahny times!"

"I go find alone," I said. "Suah. Find one, mebbe can kill if I have special knife. Moah dan one, no. If many, cannot kill alone."

"You find. We kill'm."

"Dahk Runnah, you no can kill'm. You think you kill'm, but they still alive, on you body, tiny, so tiny you no can see'm. I need special stuffs, special folk to kill'm wit."

"Nah," he said, scowling. "Jus you. Nobody moah."

"Tha mahn," I suggested. "The mahn, he a good huntah. Wit the mahn?"

He turned from me and stalked away. Several of his men gathered around him, talking urgently, throwing angry looks in my direction.

I took up a brand from the fire, gathered wood from the pile, returned to my hut to make a tiny fire in the circle of stones. I sat beside it. They would do as they would do. I could find the ghyrm for them, but I could not kill the creatures without sanctified instruments or the machines the Siblinghood had to offer.

There was one thing I could do. If I could still do it, out of practice as I was. If Ferni . . . ah, if Ferni was only receptive.

I Am Gretamara/on Chottem

The Gardener had asked me to accompany Sophia to the city of Bray, as otherwise the heiress would be without friends or confidantes. It became obvious that more than mere friendship was needed as soon as we arrived at Stentor d'Lorn's mansion. Even though workmen had been sent ahead, we knew it would take both of us to deal with the mess.

Battalions of men and women with shovels and buckets and washtubs were still laboring to erase what a few decades of leaking roofs and inattention had allowed to accumulate. The carpets, which had been thickly strewn with Cantardene charbic powder to keep them safe from vermin, were rolled against corridor walls. These had to be taken out of doors on a day the wind blew toward the sea and there well beaten before anyone could breathe in the same room with them. Many of the furnishings were simply falling apart. The walls were mapped with continents of mildew crossed by wandering tributaries of cracks. While the entire planet of Chottem was still relatively primitive so far as plumbing and sanitation went, the mansion had been built before even that low standard had been achieved.

Sophia and I took up residency in a small house at the back of the property that had been occupied by a watchman's family, a place to which we could retreat from the stench of sewers, the reek of paint, and the chatter of hammers.

There were also interruptions. Von Goldereau d'Lornschilde dropped by frequently, usually to be told we were not home. We heard it rumored that he had challenged Sophia's identity, on the grounds that Stentor's granddaughter should be older than Sophia appeared to be. Hearing of this, Sophia summoned an attorney and sent him to Von Goldereau with a message saying that friends of the Siblinghood were granted the favor of youth, as indeed, we were, and members of the Siblinghood would be glad to testify for us. She and I had aged mostly on the Gardener's time.

A day or two after we arrived, a strange old man came with a bunch of keys, which he said Stentor d'Lorn had put in his keeping with instructions they were to be given to his granddaughter and none other.

"There's a man been looking high and low for these," the old man said. "Name's Von Goldereau d'Lornschilde."

"He didn't know you had them?" I asked him.

"No. He looked among the mighty, never thought to look among us, the little folk."

"Why did d'Lorn leave them with you?" I asked.

"Oh, I owed him a favor, ma'am. He took my son, Fessol, his name is, when he was only six years old. Stentor d'Lorn took a liking to him and sent him to another world to be educated and made into a fine gentleman. Told me if I'd keep these keys until his granddaughter came to reclaim them, she'd see I got to go there, see my boy, how wonderful a life he has."

I shivered when I heard this, for no reason except that such an act of charity was out of character for the man who had brooked no opposition from anyone during his life, and who had killed his son-in-law out of hand—as was well known in Bray. Sophia, however, took the keys without comment, asking only for the oldster's name and where he might be found, that she might properly reward him when she learned where his grandson had gone.

A goodly number of cooks and butlers and other assorted functionaries were hired and let go again before the heiress had assembled a staff that could, in her opinion, acquit itself well in opening the house to guests.

"Anytime soon?" I asked in dismay.

"Not soon, no," said Sophia almost fretfully. "I want to be an influence for good on this world, and this house . . . it works against me! I'm not comfortable in it."

No more was I. Shadows swallowed the corners; sounds chittered along the ceilings; a foul smell which was not sewers came and went at intervals. The place displayed luxury without comfort, ostentation without art. I hated it. Each day saw the arrival of people paying calls, not only people from Bray but from all the cities up and down the shore. Some of them, who hinted to Sophia's butler that they had handled her grandfather's business (wink, nod, wink), she declined to speak with personally, leaving it to the servants to put them off with evasion or hauteur or whatever worked best.

Sophia learned of a man in Bray who located people, and she hired him to find any still living who had served the house in Stentor's time. When they were ferreted out, she spoke with them, giving them generous gifts in return for information. From one of the former gatekeepers, she learned where Benjamin Finesilver's bones had been hidden. She sent for them to be moved into the tomb of the d'Lornschildes, directly above the tomb that held Stentor himself, but she planned no vengeance on those who had followed her grandfather's orders. We had both learned from the Gardener that old vengeance is like old cake: still seeming sweet, but so dry that one invariably chokes on it.

Some days, I simply had to get away from the place, and since there was always marketing to do, I took the basket and strolled down into the town to spend a few hours among the sellers of eggs, fruit, vegetables, fish—many of them things I had eaten in Swylet—and in the little alleys where stilt walkers and fire-eaters, fortune-tellers, magicians and jugglers amused the populace. One I most enjoyed was a Trajian, long-armed and long-legged, with a furred little body and a face like a sloth, a visual cross, I thought, between that animal, a teddy bear, and a monkey. He always finished his act by putting out a little table and two chairs, then seating a doll in one of the chairs, a doll dressed as a crowned king. The Trajian juggled the table, the chairs, the king, who promptly came apart in the air, arms, legs, body, head, crown, all seven parts spinning off in different directions, only to be skillfully gathered on the fly and reassembled.

Each time I saw the performer, he looked directly at me and smiled. This confused me a little. Trajians, so the Gardener had told me, kept themselves at a distance from people of other races, for they were a people many times unjustly accused of everything from laying misfortune to the spread of dread diseases.

Knowing this for the nonsense it was, I smiled at him in return, and dropped a coin in his bowl each time I went. On the fourth or fifth such occasion, I turned from leaving my gift to confront a bulky man in the livery of Von Goldereau's house, obviously drunken and belligerent. "Yul bring bad down on us," he growled, laying his hand on my shoulder, to push me back. "Y've no right smilin' at the likes of that!"

"Oh, sir," cried the Trajian. "She was only being amused at the juggling . . ."

"And y'filth, y've no right speakin' to me at all," said the ruffian, flinging out one huge arm that caught the juggler across the face.

I heard his neck snap. I felt the juggler die. Everything became very still and very hot. "You," someone cried in a great voice that echoed down the street as though a cataract had shouted in a stony canyon, the reverberations continuing as in a monstrous bell. "You have brought down bad fortune upon yourself and your house. You will leave no child; you will gain no profit; you will taste no food. From this moment, your body will shrink into nothingness, for I, the Healer, take life from you to restore what you have unjustly taken!"

And I laid my hands upon him. For one instant he looked surprised, then horrified. His eyes rolled up into his head and he fell, gurgling, his face turning white. The crowd drew away from me as I knelt beside the juggler, putting my hands on him. I felt the life flow into him, the life I had taken from that other. I felt the bone knit. I felt the heart beat beneath my hands, like that of a bird.

He opened his eyes. He said, "You look so like her, so like sweet Queen Wilvia . . ." And then he fell into sleep. He had healed completely; I knew it to be so.

A female of his kind, dressed like a princess, came from the wagon with several other of her kind. "I am the wife for whom Yarov, Juggler to the Queen of the Ghoss, paid a great price," she said. I knew it was the way of Trajian women to introduce themselves so. I nodded respectfully to her, and her people picked the juggler up and took him away.

Only when I felt the pain in my throat did I realize that great voice had been my own. When I went through the marketplace on my way home, people stood aside and lowered their heads. One or two, I touched, for they were in pain, and the anger that had moved me was still strong enough in me to heal them. The Gardener had told me of this, this avenging fury, but I had not known I could feel it. I was not sure I ever wanted to feel it again, though I knew I would not be able to withstand it.

Gradually, the workmen at the mansion accomplished their tasks. Outbuildings filled up with leftover lumber, tools, ladders, and paint. One old stable held enough powdered charbic from Cantardene to mothproof ten mansions. In time each problem was solved, each bit of wreckage was removed or repaired, each group of workmen was paid and went away. The place became orderly, clean, and quiet, and for the first time, I thought we might have time to reflect upon why Sophia had returned to Bray, what we would do about the mansion, and what she might accomplish here. Sophia, however, had a remaining concern that she mentioned to me over breakfast:

"I've been considering this discomfort we feel. You know, we haven't even looked in the cellars."

I shuddered, thinking first of the effusive old man who had brought the keys. The cellars could not be in any better condition than the rest of the house and might be worse. Sophia ignored my shudder and went to get the keys, which were heavy and unnecessarily intricate. Or so we thought until we had penetrated past the second door, at which point we went back and quietly closed and locked the doors behind us in order to prevent inadvertent interruption.

"Where did he get these?" demanded Sophia, holding out a ruby the size of a pigeon's egg, the topmost from a keg of similar stones. "I've never seen jewels like these."

"There's a world's ransom here," I replied, wishing desperately that the Gardener were with us.

"Let's just look quickly, then close it all up," Sophia urged. "This isn't something we can deal with now."

Even our quick look disclosed endless stores of treasure, none of it in the least corrupted, not even the fabrics: cloth of gold embroidered with emeralds, cloth of silver dotted with sapphires, cloth of diamond in the original bolt, woven from crystalline thread as made only by the Pthas and never by any race since.

"An old city," I mused, on recognizing this latter fabric from a sample the Gardener had once shown me. "Someone has found a great treasure-house of ancient times."

Beyond the last door, triple-barred, triple-bolted, triple-locked, we came upon an unlit tunnel where a lantern was set upon a table next to a stoppered bottle of lamp oil and a cane with a protruding sword tip. This last, I picked up as I followed Sophia, who carried the newly filled and lit lantern. The tunnel had not been formed by men. It was part of a natural cave, with stalactites hanging from the ceiling.

"He found this place," I said with certainty. "He had the rest of the cellars dug around it, but this one he found!"

"Yes," I said sadly. "And he had the doors built, then closed in the men who built them." I followed her pointing finger to the cluster of desiccated flesh and protruding bones against the wall. Four men, or what had been men. They wore the shackles of bondsmen, and they had written their fate in their own blood on the floor beside them. *"He does not want anyone to know what is here."*

Turning aside from this pathetic message, we stopped momentarily, for the cavern split into a Y, each arm blocked by an iron grille before a viscid, quivering curtain. To the left, the curtain was pale, lit with rainbow gleams. To the right the curtain was obsidian, not quite opaque, with shadows moving in it. Scattered folds of yellowed paper and the dried corpses of weirdly shaped creatures had penetrated the grille and were stuck to the walls and the floor before the dark curtain, some of them outside the grille. Moved by an instinctive revulsion, I used the tip of the sword to flick the creatures through or into the curtain of light, only to see them flair and vanish into nothing. Meantime Sophia picked up one of the papers, unfolded it, and read:

"'Four thar of gems for each little human male.'" And another. "'A qualux of woven gold for half a dozen children, very young.'"

"What was he doing?" cried Sophia, a whispered cry, full of horror. She picked up the other papers and unfolded them, reading them out:

"'Why don't you answer! Five thar of gems for each little one. We need many!'

"'Why don't you answer!'

"'Why don't you answer!'

"'We don't have enough little human ones! We must have more! Answer or we will seek business with humans elsewhere on Chottem! We will send *them* to suck you dead.'"

I put my hand on Sophia's arm, silencing her. "Shh, look there!"

Sophia looked at the dark curtain where a deeper shadow was being cast by something passing there, a thing with several legs, at least four arms, and a limber body that writhed like a snake.

I took the papers from Sophia's hand, picked up the others that were scattered about, and said, "We are in danger here. We must send word to the Gardener! And we must relock all these doors and hide the keys, for what may come, indeed, what may already have come through this gate is something that must get no farther into the house."

We passed the old bones on the way out. I did not mention the message written in blood, which Sophia had not seen. Stentor had not merely left his workmen to starve. He had beaten them first. Both of us were pale and shivering when we returned to the upper floors of the mansion. "This is an evil house," said Sophia. "I thought so when I saw it, telling myself that it was only because it was dirty and unkept. Well, we have cleaned it and mended it and set it in order, and it remains evil. What am I to do?"

"For now, nothing," I said, though my aversion was as great as her own. "I agree, it is an evil place. Instead of moving into the mansion as we planned, you and I can continue living in the little house in the back garden. Let us hide these keys, and meantime I'll tell the Gardener what we've found."

That night I sat up very late writing a long letter describing what we had found below and enclosing the strange notes we had picked up from the floor. I knew that when she left us in Bray, she had planned to go on to many distant places, seeking information. I knew she could not keep close watch upon us at the same time. Still, I hoped she was within reach. I went to a back gate that opened upon the graveled alley used by tradesmen and collectors of trash. A horseman waited there, and I put the letter in his hand, whispering, "Quick as may be." He was her messenger. She had told me he would be there in case of emergency.

The next day Sophia told the housekeeper we would not be moving from the little house in the garden. The housekeeper bowed politely and said nothing. What difference did it make to her where the mistress slept or dined? If truth be told, the servants probably thought it spoke well of her, for all of them disliked being in the house of Stentor d'Lornschilde after dark.

I Am M'urgi/on B'yurngrad

When Ferni could not find my trail, he returned frantically to the inn where we had been staying and sent messages off in six directions asking for aid from the Siblinghood. He had returned his borrowed flier to the Order after we arrived at the inn, so he spent the rest of a frustrating day attempting to locate another one, meantime assuring himself that if the abductors had wanted me dead, they would have killed me where I slept at the riverside. He concluded, as I had done: They wanted me for something else; therefore, I was alive.

By the time he found an available flier, it was already dark. Since he would not be able to see the trail until morning, he ate a tasteless meal and lay down, requiring of himself the long discipline that would clear his mind and let him sleep. Not long into that sleep, a dream insinuated itself, a dream of me standing before him, taking his hands in mine, chanting. In the dream, he concentrated upon that chant, listened to it with all his attention.

"I am well," I sang. "I am here, not far away. They who hold me are tribesmen. They believe I alone can kill the many ghyrm among them. I have told them I need help, but they say no, so you must summon the help I need. Go to the Siblinghood. Tell them. Get from them all the things I will need, including a finder. Be sure you bring knives. Fly here at dawn tomorrow, bringing help. Now waken and remember!"

And with that he awoke, the whole thing clear in his mind: how I sounded, what the camp looked like and where it was located, what I needed, what he had to do! "Bless you, old shaman woman, wherever you are now," he muttered as he dressed himself. "You taught her well!" I was still there, watching, when he said it.

It was not long after midnight. We had not brought ghyrm-hunting supplies to the inn with us, but a Siblinghood outpost was only a short flight away. When he arrived there, however, it did him little good, for a very junior member was in charge who seemed to know little or nothing about where anyone in authority might be or when such a person might return. Ferni passed on the new ghyrm information to be added to that already in the file, then he requisitioned everything useful the more helpful supply officer would let him have, including a finder, though Ferni himself had not been certified to use one.

"Don't you even try to use it," the supply officer instructed sternly. "They do wicked things to the minds of those who are not inured to them. Leave the cover on the basket port. Land as near to her as you can get, put all the stuff out of the flier, then get out of there. Don't try to rescue her. Wait until we get set up to do that. I know M'urgi, and she can take care of herself. She knows the tribes as well or better than anyone else in the Siblinghood."

All this I saw, heard, knew of while lying on the bosom of the night. By dawn he had packed my personal belongings from the inn and was already hovering over the grasslands by the river. At first light, the shadow trail showed dark among the grasses, and he had not followed it far before he saw the smoke of our campfires. He hovered, waiting. I emerged from a hut, tribesmen gathered around me. I pointed upward at the flier, then down at the nearest clearing, and beckoned.

He put the flier down, took the supplies out, and laid them at the edge of the clearing. The last thing he moved was the basket with the finder in it, setting it carefully among the other tools of the ghyrm-hunter's trade. He returned to the flier, saw me come out of the trees among the tribesmen, saw me wave at him with a lifting motion, which he obeyed. As he turned the flier away, he saw the men carrying the supplies back toward their camp. He was wondering, I think, whether they would move the camp at once to keep him from finding it again. No doubt he knew I would lead him to them again if they did so.

On the ground, I supervised the arrangement of my supplies.

"In my own place," I demanded, pointing to the kit that held my personal things. Then at the basket, "That! Don touch that. I move it ovah on rocks, away from us. Don go near that!"

"I wahn see," said their leader, reaching for the clamps that held the lid. "I see firs, no hahm."

"Ssssss," I hissed. "You see, you die! I see, I die. You wahch!"

I opened the port on the basket. The tentacle came out, reaching, moving side to side with a sound like the slithering of snakes. The men backed off, muttering among themselves. The smell reached them, and they went farther away. After a long minute, I took a newly delivered knife from its sheath and held it toward the tentacle, which screamed an ear-shattering sound and retreated into its basket. I closed the port and turned, hand on the lid clamps of the basket. "Now you wan see?"

Though the leader shook his head, he was obviously not content. "You hab this why?" he demanded.

I smiled sweetly at him. "Is findah, Dahk Runnah. Is findah ob ouder ghyrm. You say I find, you kill'm. Ah don dink so. I dink when ah find, you *dry* kill'm, dey kill you."

"What we do?" he cried. "Mus do sompin!"

"We mus do sompin, yea, yea, sompin. But you wahn muck it? No? Den we dalk. We plahn. We dalkin' much by the fiah. Now you go, get yoah people. Bring dem heah. I look dem ober, see dey hab no ghyrm, show you how knife wuk, an we make plahn."

After more discussion, more argument, finally settled by Dark Runner, the tribesmen agreed to do as I asked, and two of them set out across the grasses to fetch the rest of the tribe. I, meantime, with a fine display of hauteur, told the ones remaining I was not to be disturbed, retired to my hut, rolled myself in the blankets provided there, reminded myself of a shaman's discipline, and fell instantly asleep.

Meantime Ferni—as I learned later—though less worried than formerly, was no less agitated, for he had run headlong into an uncommon and frustrating blockage in the normal operation of the Siblinghood. He had visited two other posts, saying he needed help, but the only people on duty were people who couldn't authorize it; the people who could authorize it were somewhere else, having a mysterious meeting with someone or something important; they would get back to him.

In a fury of stamping about and muttering, "Well, if that's the way they're going to be, the hell with them." His thoughts turned, as they frequently did, to Naumi. He would give up on the Siblinghood, for the moment at least, and go to Thairy for help. As Naumi had pointed out, he was only two days away, and Ferni knew I would be quite safe for two days, or for ten times that. Which did not mean he would put off rescuing me any longer than necessary, but which did mean he could take the time without feeling he had forsaken me.

By midafternoon, he was on his way. Half a day later he was at the transshipment point, where he rented a bed for a few hours and caught the earliest possible ship that would drop him at Point Zibit at noon, midnight, dawn, he didn't bother to find out which. He did, however, have a hope that not only Naumi would be there but also the rest of the talk-road crew. Ferni had a high opinion of their joint abilities, and just maybe, they could come up with something new about the ghyrm.

I Am Margaret and
Mar-agern on Fajnard

On Fajnard, when I, Margaret, woke in the morning, warm between Gloriana and Bamber Joy, I sat up to confront a younger self who was crouched at my feet, staring intently into my face.

"Margy?" I said.

"Mar-agern," said the other, in my—our voice. "Who're you?"

I looked around. Rci, the Ghoss, was rolled in blankets, sound asleep next to the wall. Maniacal and Mirabel had already gone, probably back to Howkel's house. Gloriana and Bamber still slept. Among all these sleepers, my other self had wakened and found herself duplicated. She was younger, thinner, and more muscular than I. Her skin was darkened by the sun, her hair bleached almost white and cut very short. Her hands were a laborer's hands, hard and somewhat gnarled.

"We," I said carefully, slowly, "are both Margaret. I don't know how, or why. We both left Earth at the same age, we both had the same parents. I assume we will both remember the same things, up until the time we left Earth."

The Mar-agern one of us thought. What thing might two of us have shared? Well, one at least this other would not have forgotten. "Who was my . . . our lover?"

"Bryan," I answered. "He volunteered to go to Tercis if I would marry him. I accepted his offer."

"I refused him," Mar-agern said. "I didn't think it was fair to him."

"Neither did I," I replied, "but I accepted and spent my life trying to make it up to him."

"I was shipped as a bondslave, here, to Fajnard. Among the Frossians."

"We speak Frossian," I said. "Fairly well."

"I speak it a good deal better than fairly well," said Mar-agern, her lips curving into a wry smile. "I'm also quite an expert on umoxen."

"I know nothing about them," I confessed. "You seem to be younger than I am."

"They told us about that," said Mar-agern. "It's the wormholes. Different ones take different amounts of time. Some even go back in time, getting there."

"Yes," I said. "Tercis is one of those."

We sat for a while, staring at one another, wondering.

Gloriana rolled over, and said, "Good morning, Grandma." Then, to Mar-agern, "You never were my grandma, so I'll just call you by your name. Good morning, Mar-agern."

"Mar-agern," said Bamber, sitting up and yawning. "The Gib-bekot gave you a mother-mind, did you know that?"

"Know what?" Mar-agern asked in surprise.

"You don't know yet?" came a voice from above—Falija. She had been curled up on a rock shelf some distance above our heads, and we had not seen her until that moment. "Well, there will be a book here, somewhere. Glory, I think it's over there in that pile of things by the wall."

Gloriana went to find it, brought it back, and handed it to me, and I looked Mar-agern in the face as I read the first page. "'Our word for insight is *Ghoss*.'"

While I read to Mar-agern, Bamber and Gloriana chopped kindling, raked the ashes from the coals, added splints of firewood, and blew the flames to life before hanging a pot of water on the spit above it. Rei, awakened by the noise, got up, folded up his blankets, went around the corner, and emerged moments later with his hair combed and his face washed. By the time the three of them had breakfast cooked, I had finished the first reading of the book, and Mar-agern was reading it again to herself, myself, on the ledge outside the cave entrance.

"Will it be as hard for her as it was for you?" Gloriana asked Falija.

"Probably not," Falija said, bounding from stone to stone down the wall. "She's spent a lot of time with the Ghoss, and they've got mother-memories, though theirs go back only to the time they received them from the Gentherans."

Outside, Mar-agern laid the book aside, put both arms around her knees, and rocked to and fro, making an unpleasant grating sound in her throat.

"On the other hand," said Falija from behind me, "I suppose it might be harder."

"Take her this," said Rei, handing Gloriana a mug of tea. "The Gibbekot who brought the mother-mind said it might help."

Gloriana took the tea to Mar-agern and coaxed her into drinking some of it before sitting beside her to talk about nothing in particular until Mar-agern stopped rocking and moaning. Falija came out, sat down on Mar-agern's other side, and said, in her own language, "You're doing very well. Much better than I did."

Mar-agern responded in the same language, "Really! I feel like a plether sat on me!"

Gloriana sniffed, saying, "Well, if you two are going to converse privately, I'll just have a bite more breakfast," as she returned to the cave.

I greeted her with a question. "I don't suppose I'm just dreaming, am I?"

"Sorry, Grandma. No. She's really you. And she isn't. She doesn't know me or anything about me, so she isn't Grandma. But she's like you, like a sister, maybe."

"Our . . . mission? Our quest? Is she part of it?"

"Falija thinks she has to be. Remember, she said something last night . . . that there had to be seven of you."

I felt myself turn pale, and I whispered, mostly to myself, "Seven. I can't believe it. Where could they be? Who would they be?" And even then, I knew who they would be. There had always been seven of me, of us.

"Maybe where we're going," Gloriana answered. "Where the way-gate goes, to Thairy."

"And the way-gate is where?"

"Rei says Maniacal told him where it was before they left early this morning. Not far from here."

I said nothing more, just put my nose in my cup of tea and kept it there, using the fragrant steam as a barrier between myself and whatever was going to happen next. Eventually, I said, "Gloriana, I thought you told me Falija's people sought you out by name. How did I get involved?"

Bamber Joy looked up from his pack. "Probably Gloriana was just the door that led to you. She'd be more willing to take on a pet cat than you would, Grandma. She'd be more open to strangeness than you would. If whoever set this up wanted to get to you, they could do it best by going through Gloriana."

"Falija didn't even ask me to come along," I said.

Gloriana grinned. "Falija is smart. She knew you'd offer. If you hadn't, she'd have made some reason you should. Something inside would have rung a bell or set off an alarm, and she'd have made sure you were with us. Are you scared or something?"

"Scared. Yes. Not frightened out of my wits, as I was yesterday, but quite apprehensive. Aren't you?"

Gloriana shook her head. "I don't see why! We escaped from Ned and Walter. We avoided the gizzardile. We met Howkel's people, and that was fun. So far nothing awful has happened."

I shook my head, drawing a deep breath. "Child, if someone set this up, all this weirdness and marvel, believe me, they weren't doing it just so we could meet the Howkel family, amusing though they may be! The reason has to be a big reason, and big reasons in my limited experience almost always mean very big risks. I remain apprehensive. Now, I'm going to wash my face, then I think we'd better be going. If my other half wants to go, that is. She may not, you know."

Indeed, Mar-agern did not.

"I know nothing about this," Mar-agern said. "Rei said we were going to Gibbekot country."

"I am Gibbekot," Falija said firmly. "I was sent to gather you people up and solve a great riddle. You wouldn't be here, right in our way, if you weren't meant to come with us!"

"I don't see that at all," Mar-agern said, with a shrug. "As a matter of fact, I can't think at all! My head is suddenly full of things I seem to know without ever having known them. It's very difficult, very strange."

Falija frowned for some time before saying, "Mar-agern. Let us sit out there on the ledge in the sun and talk. There are things you need to know, stories you need to hear. Then, when we have talked, you will be more comfortable with your situation. It really is a far better one than you were in just a few days ago, marked for death, as Rei says."

Rei, who had been outside for a while, came in to add his own point of view. "By all means talk with the Gibbekot, Mar-Mar, but the Ghoss say the Gibbekot here on Fajnard want you to go with the travelers. They have omens of consequentiality."

While Falija talked, Mar-agern simply sat on the ledge, umoxlike, head shaking as the umox seemed to do when they didn't like a situation. I knew how she felt, as though she, I, were being stretched in several directions at once.

I went out to put my arm about my other self, saying, "Surely it's better to move toward something than to run away from something."

Rei said, "She's right, Mar-Mar. The way-gate is only a short way. Take the things you need from here, and we'll go."

"You're coming with us?"

"No. There's a party of Frossians coming up the canyon where we walked. Some of our people are going to lead them astray. You should be on your way before I leave."

Though Mar-agern was still unconvinced and certainly unwilling, there was no more argument. We collected our belongings and set out upon a narrow path up the mountain, Rei in the lead, a coil of rope over his shoulder.

To me, Margaret, rope meant climbing or some other unpleasantness, and my already glum mood deepened considerably. When we reached a fork, Rei stood for a moment, recollecting what Maniacal had told him before choosing the route. This happened twice more, on increasingly faint trails, until we stood at a narrow cleft in a rock wall that we edged through one by one . . .

. . . and came out on a rock ledge edged by a line of stones. Near enough to wet us with spray, a waterfall plunged into a lovely pool among green mosses. Dead ahead was another rock cleft holding a black, wavering pool.

"We've been here," cried Glory. "We came in this way."

"And there's the way we go out," said Bamber, nodding to our right where a pale light pool glimmered at the back of a rocky recess. "I didn't see that the last time we were here."

"We never came this far across the ledge," said Falija. "We jumped down below." She turned to Rei, asking, "How did we get back here?"

"If you went down there," he replied, pointing below, "you must have taken the lowland road that leads in a long curve east and north to the hayfolk. When you left there, you took a road that went straight across the curve you'd made before, like the string of a bow."

He turned to Bamber, taking the coil of rope from his shoulder. "I'm told it's narrow in there. You'll need to remove your packs and drag them through. The Gibbekot say you'll need this rope at the other end, where the gate comes out in Thairy. They also say their people live on the heights in Thairy, but the people you need to connect with will be down by the sea."

He waited while we filed in, Gloriana first, then the rest of us.

I came out into a sandy cave, on Gloriana's heels. We stumbled just far forward enough to escape being knocked down as the others came through behind us. Birds murmured above our heads, drowsy sounds, as though settling for sleep, and the light on the cavern wall glowed red. Behind us, the way-gate we had just left was black and ominous. To our left, the tunnel curved around a corner, and there was another light-filled gate that went on to somewhere else. The two were really only a few steps apart, as they had been on Fajnard.

The cave entrance was the other way, a narrow slit facing west where a red fire of sun hung above a glistening sea. The cave entrance was midway up a sheer drop of stone that ended below us in a tree-edged clearing with a road running across it and upward to the right.

"Without wings, we won't get much farther," said Gloriana.

"'That's what the rope's for," Bamber Joy explained. "Though I don't know how the Gibbekot knew about it."

Falija said, "They probably use this way-gate all the time. We have people here on Thairy."

"Of course," I said, in a falsely pleased voice. "Isn't it nice to have one thing make some sense!"

"Tie the rope to that rock pillar," Falija directed. "We can lower Grandma and Mar-agern, then we'll knot the rope so Glory and Bamber can climb down."

"I do not need to be lowered," said Mar-agern, rather offended. "I can climb down the rope."

"Well then, you can help the children lower me," I said crisply. "I do need lowering."

When all of us but Falija had reached the clearing, she untied the rope and leapt from one invisible foothold to another, joining Bamber and Glory, who had already penetrated the thin line of trees at the edge of the clearing to look down another precipice to the sea.

"Town down there," cried Glory. "Looks like the road goes all the way down."

Falija was staring longingly at the upward road, as though trying to find some excuse to go in that direction. Her people, at least her kind of people, were up there, but I could tell she was being urged away from them just as she had been on Fajnard. With a tiny whine of frustration, she turned toward the downward road. I put my hand on the little person's shoulder. "You must be as confused as we are."

"It would be nice to rest," Falija said. "It would be nicer to talk to someone who really knows what's happening."

"Perhaps no one knows, and we have to figure it out for ourselves. At the moment, I'm thankful there's a town down there. Maybe we can sleep in beds tonight."

"If the people there are hospitable," said Mar-agern. "I haven't any money. We don't even know what's used for money here."

I exchanged glances with Gloriana, who felt for the money bag in the lining of her jacket, and said, "I'm sure we'll think of something."

The road rose to a shallow crest, and from there went steadily downward in an easy, curving, unwearying slope that turned sharply to the right at the bottom. From there it went only a short, straight distance toward a pair of open gates guarded by uniformed young men, stiff as broom handles. Nearby stood a cluster of older people, three men and two women, talking among themselves.

As we came closer we heard one of the women crying out, "Look there." She was pointing upward along the coast at a far-off speck against the now-crimson clouds. "That must be Ferni's flier! He'll be here very soon, Naumi."

"Now me?" I said. "Naumi? Wasn't that what we called . . ."

Mar-agern nodded. "I remember. It was indeed."

The two of us walked toward the group, I called out, "Naumi! Is that your name?"

The person I was hailing turned with a polite smile and froze, as though he were seeing a ghost. "My name is Naumi Rastarong." He paused, swallowed. "And yours and your sister's, ma'am?"

"Margaret," I said. "This is Mar-agern."

"Are we related in some way?" Naumi asked.

One of his friends came up beside him, and Naumi said, "Caspor, they look like family, don't they?"

Caspor said, "I could work up the odds on their not being, but the resemblance is astonishing. That dip in the upper lip, and the slant of the eyebrows!"

"And their noses," said another friend. "Even the same color eyes!"

Naumi said, "Jaker, let's introduce you four. Flek, Jaker, Caspor, Poul."

We all nodded somewhat distractedly at the two men and two women, and I asked, "Do you remember coming from Earth?"

Naumi cocked his head, obviously wondering at this. "No. As a matter of fact, my earliest memories start at about age twelve, when I survived some kind of accident and was put in the care of my foster father, here on Thairy."

"Age twelve," said Mar-agern. "When the proctor came."

"And nothing happened," I replied, "but I . . . that is, we always felt something had."

"Maybe something did happen," Falija offered, "and you just didn't know about it." She looked up to find five pairs of eyes staring at her as though she had grown another head. "Did I say something odd?" she asked.

Flek stammered, "It's just . . . we've never seen . . . we thought you were . . . I mean . . ."

"They thought you were somebody's pet," said Gloriana indignantly. "This is Falija, our guide. Her people are called the Gibbekot. A great many of them live up there, on the heights, or so she tells me."

"We thought that's where the Gentherans live," said Jaker. "And we've never seen any of them. We have no idea what they look like."

"Rather like me," said Falija. "Only larger." She turned toward Naumi. "Excuse me if I am impolite in not using your correct title, but you must be one of the people we're looking for."

"What people are those?" Naumi asked.

"The people who began life as Margaret Bain, who were split off from her in some way, at some time in her life, and who seem to be scattered across a sizable chunk of the galaxy. Margaret and Mar-agern were split at age twenty-two. You, Naumi, were evidently split off at twelve."

"But he's male!" Mar-agern snapped.

Falija said soothingly, "My mother-mind tells me that in all gendered races, one sex always shares some of the traits of the opposite sex. Perhaps he, Naumi, was split off from among the most male traits Margaret Bain possessed. Or maybe it really doesn't matter very much."

"This all seems very unlikely," I growled peevishly. "Just when I get used to something, the ground shifts."

A noise from above attracted our attention to the flier, which was approaching a landing pad not far from us. Naumi beckoned everyone to follow him, and we arrived just as a lean, dark-haired person came from the flier, threw his arms around Naumi, smiled across his shoulder at the others, and froze at the sight of Mar-agern, just as Naumi had done.

"Margy?" I thought he said.

"Mar-agern," she corrected him.

"But you . . . she . . . Naumi! Except for the hair, she looks exactly like M'urgi! They could be twins! What's going on?"

Naumi held up his hand, hushing him. "Ears are quivering over there at the guard post. Let's find somewhere less public. May I suggest the dorm common room? Plenty of room for the . . . ah . . .

people who have joined us. The reunion doesn't start for two more days, so there'll be no one there but us."

Chatting over his shoulder about the weather, the beauty of the sunset, how wonderful it was to see everyone, Naumi led our group past the guards at the gate. We went down a central road and turned right to enter one of the large buildings facing the side street. Inside, Naumi took us straight back through the building to a large room opening onto a central courtyard.

"All right," Naumi said. "Somebody tell me what's going on."

We looked at one another. Gloriana took a deep breath, and said, "This all started when Falija's parents left her with me . . ." She went on to describe briefly how that had happened. Falija, dutiful as ever, picked up the story from that point: her fostering on Tercis, her acquisition of the mother-mind, the threat on Tercis, our travels to Fajnard, where we had picked up Mar-agern, and our trip to Thairy. She said we had learned that the way-gates go one way in pairs, one coming in, one going out, and had verified that in the cave we had come in through.

"You came through that thing up on the cliff," Naumi said. "So that pool of light is a way-gate! I found it the first year I was here, but I'd never heard of way-gates, and it seemed a bit dangerous to try on my own. I'd almost forgotten about it!" He turned to Margaret. "But you called me by name. Both of you."

I said, "When I . . . that is, when we were a child, I, we invented imaginary people, roles to play, fantasies to act out. *Now me* was a warrior. I said to myself, 'I will be a queen,' and 'will be a' turned into 'Wilvia,' and there really is a Queen Wilvia, but we don't know where she is. Margy was our shaman . . ."

"That's M'urgi," cried Ferni. "The woman I'm in love with, the reason I came to Thairy! She's a shaman! She's been captured by tribesmen. They won't hurt her, at least not for a while, but . . ."

"Shhh," Naumi said. "Just a moment." He turned to me, I suppose because I was the eldest of the group. "I've found it isn't smart to believe or disbelieve too early in any situation, but one thing we need to know immediately: Are any of you in immediate danger? Are you being pursued? Is there an emergency of some kind?"

I turned to the others, who looked quite blank. Even Falija shook her head, no, not right now.

Naumi turned back to Ferni, took him by the upper arm, and sat him down. "Now. Everyone sit. Flek, will you and Poul get us something to drink? How about our visitors? Are you hungry? Well then, just something to drink while Ferni tells us whatever he has to tell us, because that does sound like an emergency."

Ferni, openly staring at me-Margaret and other-me-Mar-agern, began his story with the arrival of another Margaret on B'yurngrad. "Her name was Margaret," he said. "She was twenty-two. She was from Earth."

"So were we," Mar-agern and I said simultaneously.

Ferni went on with M'urgi's name change and education by the shaman. "I wasn't with her again, not for years," he said. He told of his search for her, of their ghyrm-hunting in the northlands. "I love her," he declared almost defiantly. "We love each other, and they took her! The tribes are being eaten by ghyrm, and they want her to kill them all, which she can't do by herself!"

"The Siblinghood won't help?" Naumi asked.

"I can't reach anyone above midmanagerial-not-allowed-to-decide-anything-unless-it's-in-the-book!" cried Ferni, pounding the table with one clenched fist. "Which makes me think there must be some great crisis going on somewhere. Someone may be available when I get back, two days from now, but I knew our old talk road was assembled here, and I thought we might come up with some answers."

"Talk road?" asked Falija.

Caspor laughed. "We used to call it that. When we had a problem, we'd talk about it, sometimes forever, and eventually we could almost always figure it out. Ghyrm infestations of tribesmen on another planet are a little outside our expertise, I'm afraid."

"Possibly not," said Flek. "The company has been working on a weapon."

"May I ask, what company?" I asked.

"My grandfather was Gorlan Flekkson Bray, originally from the city of Bray on Chottem. He didn't like some of the family ways, as I understand it, so he moved here, to Thairy, to start a company he later called Flexxon Armor. In Bray, he'd traded with the Omniont races for technological information. Here on Thairy, he recruited some very bright young people who developed their own refinements, and he began by manufacturing high-quality armor for the colonies . . ."

"Are the colonies under attack?" I demanded.

Flek shook her head. "Not yet. Everyone knows what the Mercans are like, though, and we're right in the middle of Mercan space! So, while we publicly supply armaments for the colony police and the frontier scouts, we're also developing and stockpiling very-high-tech arms and armament to help the colonies resist invasion. Gorlanstown, up the coast a way, is the only city large enough to furnish our work force. We have twenty different buildings there, under twenty different names, so that almost no one knows the full extent of what we do."

"Are you sure you should be telling us?" I asked.

Flek smiled, a surprisingly wicked smile. "I would tell Naumi anything. You either are or are not Naumi. If you betray us, you're not Naumi, and you're stupid, besides."

Glory choked back a giggle, but Mar-agern laughed until tears ran down her cheeks. "We're being tested, Margaret! What about the others who obviously aren't Naumi. Glory? Bamber Joy? Falija?"

Caspor said, "We've been told the Gentherans are completely honorable. If this young . . . Gibbekot is related to them, we may trust her honor. If these are your grandchildren, reared by you, then they, too, should be completely honorable."

I thought of explaining that neither of them was actually my grandchild, but let it go. It didn't matter. I trusted the boy at least as much as I trusted Gloriana. "You imply you have something to kill ghyrm."

Flek nodded. "We developed a metal that kills them, and we've been providing the Siblinghood with knives made from it. Recently, we've developed a machine that kills ghyrm in confined areas. The Siblinghood sent you one, Ferni, not long ago. Did it work well?"

"So I understand," he replied.

"That's good, because the first few models killed humans and a lot of other creatures as well. The problem was that the genetic code of the damned things is very similar to the genome that ninety-odd per-cent of all Earth mammals share, including humans."

"As though humans were the intended target?" Naumi asked.

"We've considered that possibility. The rest of the genome is a weird amalgam that no one has been able to identify! We've improved greatly on that model, however. What we have now is a small proto-type of a weapon that, when we enlarge it, can wipe ghyrm off whole worlds without killing people or umoxen or whatever. The prototype only covers fifty square jorub."

"Jorub?" I asked.

"Thairy measurement," said Caspor. "A jorub is ten taga, which is roughly three miles, old Earthian. Say four hundred fifty square miles. But how high?" he demanded of Flek.

Flek said, "The dimensions of the field, length, width, height are variable. Since ghyrm don't fly, the fifty-jorub figure has a low ceiling, to cover more ground. It would have to be set higher for mountain-ous terrain, of course. At this point we're sure it doesn't kill Earth animals or any creatures native to any of our colony worlds, but there's always the possibility it will kill some essential something that we aren't aware of. Eventually, if we can locate the place where the ghyrm are coming from, we plan to drop some really big machines on that location and wipe them out at the source. Anyhow, it seems rel-evant to our discussion."

Ferni said earnestly, "For my situation, it would be helpful if we could give the tribes a lot of those knives you mentioned. M'urgi and I both used them when we went ghyrm-hunting. We have to give the tribe something to make them let M'urgi go."

Caspor had been staring at the ceiling, his lips moving silently, and suddenly he demanded, "Where's the star map we used to have in here?"

Naumi looked up, puzzled. "Behind the screen, over there. It's a new one. The old one's display circuits were so worn, no one could read it. Why do you want a star map?"

"This way-gate business interests me. I'm wondering what the un-derlying logic of all this business may be. Margaret—if you'll excuse the familiarity, ma'am—came from Tercis to Fajnard. Then the group came from Fajnard to Thairy. They tell us the gates are one way, that each place has one gate coming in and one gate going out. It would be interesting to know where all the gates are . . ." He went to the screen, moved it aside, and stood before the map pedestal, mumbling to himself and switching it back and forth among view planes.

All of us newcomers were staring at Caspor wonderingly. Ferni said, "He'll do that for quite a while. Caspor has to figure everything out. If it doesn't have a logical, mathematical solution, he drives himself crazy."

"If he wants to know where the way-gate is that leads away from here," said Gloriana, "it's up in that same cave, just around another corner."

"There are two of them?" Naumi was astonished. "When I discovered it, I thought there was only one."

"You saw the outgoing one. The incoming ones are black," said Falija. "Don't try entering them from that direction."

"But I stepped inside the light . . ."

Falija said, "Yes. And then what?"

"I stepped back out."

"Then you never went all the way through. You were just inside the gate. If you'd gone on through, you couldn't have come back. Not the way you went."

Naumi furrowed his brow, staring at the ceiling as he tried to remember. "There was a dark recess to the left when I went in. The way in must have been in there . . ."

"We were discussing weapons," reminded Falija.

Flek nodded. "We have the next model of the machine in the final stages of assembly."

"Is it something you could do in a hurry?" asked Ferni. "I'm not worried about M'urgi, not really, but—"

"Well, I'm worried about her," I interrupted. "If she's one of us. It seems that seven of us may be necessary in order to do something important, and if M'urgi is one of the seven, she's probably irreplaceable." I thought about this for a moment, saying with surprise, "Any of us are!"

"Why seven?" demanded Caspor, from his position before the star map.

"It's a story," Falija responded. "About a fish and an angry man."

"Can you tell it briefly?" Caspor asked, turning toward her.

Falija said, "There's also a saying, and it's shorter. 'Who knows? The Keeper knows. Well then, ask the Keeper. Where do I find it. All alone, walk seven roads at once to find the Keeper.' The story repeats the phrase 'Seven roads are one road.'"

"What's a keeper?" asked Jaker.

"In the story, it was the little statue with a book in which everything in the whole universe was written," Falija said.

"The Holder," cried Ferni. "The . . . rememberer that fills the universe and senses everything that happens. M'urgi knows about that!"

"Ah," said Caspor, turning back to the map. "Seven. Seven directions. Now, how would that work out in pairs? Divided into our customary three hundred sixty degrees would be fifty-one-point-four-two-eight-five-seven-one and so on, more or less forever."

He punched keys on the map control and spun Tercis toward the top, another key and a line down from Tercis, slightly to the left. "Margaret came from Tercis to Fajnard," Caspor said. Another line, upward to the right, "Margaret and Mar-agern came from Fajnard to Thairy. If I come away from Tercis at the same angle . . ." One more line off at a weird angle. Caspor fiddled with the controls, spinning the line into a cone. "It ends up in the nowhere," he said.

"Let me try it," said Falija. She went to the map and stared at it for a moment before entering the next line. "I seem to recall that from there . . ." The line bounced back from nothingness and hit a star. "Chottem. Where my people are!"

"That's a colony world," said Margaret. "Where from there?"

"From Chottem . . . Cantardene."

"There's no colony on Cantardene! That's a Mercan world."

"We have people on Cantardene," said Naumi. "Bondspeople. The Margaret there may be a bondsperson."

"We have an import-export office on Cantardene," said Jaker. "That is, Poul-Jaker Import-Export does. There's a freeport area, Crossroads of the World, they call it. The bondservant market is there, and so is all the gossip twenty races can spread around. By wormhole, it's only a couple of days from here."

"We can send someone," said Poul. "That salesman of yours, Jaker! We could get him on the next ship out. You know who I mean, the one who seems to be able to talk anyone into anything, what's his name?"

"Stipps," said Jaker, grinning. "Stipps the Lips."

"I've met him," said Ferni. "On B'yurngrad somewhere. Do you have an export arm there?"

"We have an export arm everywhere," replied Jaker.

"Aha!" said Caspor as he spun the lines from Thairy and Cantardene. "They don't intersect anywhere. They come close at B'yurngrad. No, they don't. Yes, they do . . . didn't . . ."

"What?" blurted Naumi.

"I mean, let me play with it a while. I need to update the galactic shift . . ."

We turned our eyes away from the chart, unable to keep them away for long. Ferni said, "Flek, will you help me?"

"Ferni, I'll do everything possible. I'll see what knives we have in stock . . ."

"Can you lend us the prototype?" asked Naumi.

"If we can think of a good way to use it, sure. We can disassemble it so you can carry it. Jaker, you'd be welcome to go with me."

Jaker shook her head. "I'd just be in the way, Flek. I think Poul and I'd be more useful getting one or several spies into Cantardene and seeing if we can find the other person we're looking for. The K'Famir are among the universe's most despicable creatures; but they do business, and when creatures do business, they have to make deals, and you can't make a deal without betraying something of your nature. We're accustomed to snooping around to ascertain what people will buy or sell.

"I saw Stipps this morning, here on Thairy. He's one of those cocksure, egocentric people you love to hate, a very youthful arrogance for a person that age—and with only one eye, at that—but at least ninety percent of his opinion about himself usually pans out . . ."

"One eye?" asked Naumi. "How old?"

"Oh, middle years or more, and yes, one eye. Some kind of accident in his youth, he says. Why?"

"No reason, except that I knew, know someone like that, though I haven't seen him in years."

Jaker gave him a questioning look, but when he said nothing else, she continued. "If no one has any objections, we can get Stipps on the ship tonight, though . . . the task is a bit vague. Who are we looking for?"

"For me," said Mar-agern and I, as with one voice. "It would have to be a bondslave who looks very much like us," I continued. "Could be older or younger . . ."

"Younger," said Falija. "Somewhere around Naumi's age because they split off at the same time, and Cantardene isn't that far from Thairy."

I nodded. "She'll speak several of the local languages. Can't be too many women like that among slaves."

"What other skills will she have?"

Mar-agern and I looked at one another. "If she was only twelve?" I said at last, shaking my head.

Mar-agern said, "She would probably sew quite well. I did."

"Of course," I agreed. "She would sew well."

"Aha!" shouted Caspor. "Yes! Ferni, until this very moment that link didn't go to B'yurngrad! It's a new link."

"What?" "What do you mean," cried several voices.

"I mean, if we start on Tercis, it goes from Tercis to Fajnard, from Fajnard to Thairy, from Thairy to B'yurngrad, from B'yurngrad to Cantardene, from Cantardene to Chottem, from Chottem to that point out in nowhere . . ."

"I know what's there," said Falija. "My people found it ages ago."

". . . and from nowhere back to Tercis. One way. The whole way. Seven roads is one road, but it's only been one road since the last automatic update on galactic shift! B'yurngrad wasn't in position until very, very recently."

"How long does it stay in position?" I asked.

Caspor turned back to the map, whispering to himself, "There has to be some stretchiness in the connection, something that holds on for a while . . ."

Falija said into the silence, "This means the configuration is not a permanent one. We know some parts of it have been in use for some time. The one from Tercis to Fajnard and Fajnard to Thairy, for instance. Howkel knew where those roads ended up, so people came and went through them. Other points have come into contact more recently. And this last link . . . has only very temporarily completed the one road."

Caspor had been playing with the star guide, rotating the strangely angled image. Now it bloomed on the screen as a seven-pointed star. "From this point of view, it's a septagram, but all the end points are in motion. I postulate that once the connection is made, there's enough stretchiness to keep it in contact for a while, probably not very long. In a few days, the whole thing should fall apart."

Falija said, "So the seven roads are one road now. Seven Margarets on seven planets with one road among them . . ."

"And everything dependent upon time," said Ferni. "I wonder if that's what has the Siblinghood in a furor . . ."

Flek, Jaker, and Poul had risen, and they were gone almost before those of us remaining had digested what had just happened.

"I'm suddenly hungry," Mar-agern said. "Would it be possible to have something to eat?"

"Certainly," Naumi replied. "Especially if, during supper, we can hear more about this mother-mind business."

The eight of us, including Falija, dined alone in a small dining room at the officers' mess, an exceptionally good dinner, as the academy cooks were trying out the menus they had selected for the reunion. As we ate, we decided what else needed to be done before we could go to B'yurngrad. When we had freed M'urgi from her captors, we would continue through the B'yurngrad way-gate to Cantardene (assuming Caspor's map of the way-gates was accurate) to find another of us, if and only if Jaker's one-eyed egotist hadn't found her first.

"The gates on Cantardene may or may not be close together," I remarked. "The ones here and on Fajnard were. I never saw the one that enters Tercis . . ."

"I did," said Falija. "It was very near the one we used, hidden back in a cleft in the rock where most of them seem to be. It makes sense that each pair would be close together."

I murmured, "I should mention that we left Tercis because a couple of pseudohumans were chasing us. Or trying to. On Fajnard, they were definitely chasing us."

"Robots," said Bamber Joy, who, while eating enormously, had said very little up until then. "Acted like robots, talked like robots. Might have come from some technological Walled-Off on Tercis."

"What Walled-Off did you come from?" Ferni asked curiously.

"Rueful," I answered. "The name says it all, and it's too long a story for tonight."

"Not a high-tech place, though?" asked Naumi.

I shook my head. "No, Naumi, not a high-tech place. We had electricity, and that was about the extent of it. No powered vehicles except for those from Tercis Central we occasionally saw, plus the one Ned and Walter drove."

"Let's leave it until morning," Naumi said. "Our minds will go on worrying at it overnight, and they may give us a head start after we've slept."

We finished our meal and trooped back to the cadet house, where Mar-agern and I were given rooms down the hall. Falija, Bamber, and Glory took their pick of bunks in a nearby dormitory.

I returned to the common room, needing to sit quietly for a time before attempting sleep, but I found Naumi, Ferni, and Caspor still there. When I came in, Naumi rose, went to a low cupboard along the wall, and took out a bottle.

"Caspor? Ferni? Margaret? Yes? Me, too." He poured, distributed, and sat down opposite us, turning the glass idly in his hand. "Have any of you ever hear of a planet called Hell?"

"Yes," I said. "We learned of it in school, back on Earth, and Falija mentioned it to me just a few moments ago. The native race has almost gone extinct several times. By now, they probably are."

"That seventh star-point, hanging out there in the nowhere. That's how someone described that planet, Hell, to me."

"That's what Falija said. That's a seventh planet."

"We're a long way from walking road number seven," said Caspor. "Right now I'm a good deal more worried about a place like Cantardene in the known-where than anyplace in the nowhere. And there's always the possibility I'm totally wrong about this whole thing."

Naumi emptied his glass, yawned, rose, and bid us good night, concluding, "You're usually right, Caspor. I don't see we have any choice but taking a chance on it."

They went off to bed. I sat there for some time, thinking of that seven-pointed star, wondering about Hell, and what one of us could be doing on it, out in the nowhere.

I Am Gretamara/on Chottem

The Gardener arrived in Bray late in the evening. She found Sophia and me sitting on the terrace beneath the tree. As we rose to greet her, she said, "You've found out what was rotten here on Chottem!"

Sophia said, "Gardener, you knew something was wrong!"

"I'd smelled it, Sophia. This is too recently settled a planet to permit any legitimate accumulation of great wealth, not in one lifetime, not in several, yet Stentor was a rich man, and Von Goldereau grows richer by the hour."

"Slaves," I said. "Men grow rich selling slaves."

"Yes, selling slaves, including children, has always been a quick way to riches."

I said, "The children don't come from this world, Gardener. They have to come from somewhere else."

"An old man brought me the keys to the cellars," said Sophia. "He said he'd given his grandson to my grandfather to be sent to another world to be educated as a gentleman. I'm afraid this was a cruel and vicious joke. What world needs human children to educate and make gentlemen?"

"There is no such world. There is a world, however, where children are surplus, and another where children are bought and sold."

"Earth," I said. "And Cantardene."

Gardener nodded. "Yes. Anyone needing a guaranteed source of children would deal with Earth."

"Would any parent sell . . . ?" I breathed.

"Earthians have sold their children for thousands of years," said the Gardener. "Surplus daughters have been sold as prostitutes, surplus sons to the army. Among the sterile castes of K'Famir, human pets are common, but that does not account for the numbers necessary to have amassed this fortune."

I was gripped by the memory of my own feelings when I had been ripped away from my home. Through tears, I said, "With riches like those in the cellars, Stentor must have brought enormous numbers from Earth. But how? On what ships?"

"Omniont or Mercan captains wouldn't transport cargoes to Chottem that would sell for more on Cantardene," mused Sophia.

"True," Gardener agreed. "But the Lorn and Bray families were wealthy on Earth, and they bought ships to bring settlers from Earth. The wealth in these cellars could have purchased an armada!"

I thought out loud. "Stentor could have claimed the children were to be colonists, but where did he keep them?"

Sophia gestured widely. "Manland is vast, and mostly uninhabited. People have come here since we arrived, winking and nodding to say that they did business with him, Von Goldereau among them. Perhaps he knows."

"We know none were sent through these cellars since Stentor died," I said. "The notes we read make that clear. If Von Goldereau is in the same trade, he has another route."

"You left none of the dead creatures down there?" the Gardener asked. "I would like to have seen one."

"I left none, but I can describe them for you," I offered. "The size of my two hands, clenched together, with ten or eleven arms or legs or tentacles . . ."

"Ghyrm," said the Gardener. "Well, that's what I thought they must be. When Stentor did not reply, they were angered, and they sent ghyrm through the gate to destroy him. He was too wily to be taken so. Tomorrow we will go down there, Sophia, and have a look at this place, this doorway. Whoever is buying these children has access both to great wealth and to ghyrm, and I need to send word of that to my friends. Also, if your cellar can spare some of its riches, we may use some of it to pay for what we must accomplish next."

"I have never known you to buy anything," I cried, astonished.

The Gardener replied, "Warriors like to be paid, even those of the Siblinghood, who are choosy about what they fight for. We will have need of more than a few of them."

"Would my grandfather have approved of this expenditure?" Sophia asked with a sly smile.

"Almost certainly not." The Gardener grinned.

"Then you may use as much as you can, with my blessing," said the heiress.

I Am Ongamar/on Cantardene

In House Mouselline, I, Miss Ongamar, pinned and basted, seamed and embroidered, and each day my escape plans ripened. Those plans, almost a year in the making, were now complete. I had pulled together all the notes I had made, put them in order, and transcribed them all in minuscule script on the inside of my Hrassian robes. I had recently stolen money from House Mouselline, not a difficult task, since Lady Ephedra trusted Miss Ongamar to tally each day's receipts and make up the transfer document for House Mouselline's banker. These accounts would be audited, of course, but I had begun after the last audit and still had time to spare.

Disguised as a Hrass and using the stolen money, I had purchased a go-pass on an outgoing ship that was to leave during the anniversary celebration of the Great Leader's accession to power, tomorrow. House Mouselline would be closed, today was my last day, so I took my self-allotted share from the cash box and tucked it under my padding, totaled up the transfer document and laid it atop the box, then began tidying the little cubby where I worked, paying no attention to the clamor in the showroom, until I heard my own name.

"Miss Ongamar, yes. If you don't mind." I was stunned by the voice, a human voice, male, very firm, a little amused.

"This shop is only for the *tamistachi,* the elite of

K'Famir," shrieked Lady Ephedra. "Dirty human slaves are not welcome."

The man laughed, a deep, truly amused chuckle. "Ah, but Lady
Ephedra, I am not a dirty human slave, I am a diplomat from the
Dominion. Here, my diplomatic pass. Here's identification, see, my
likeness without a doubt, resembling no one else."

"It doesn't matter, it doesn't matter, someone may see you here,
someone may smell you here . . ."

"Then it would be wise to let me see Miss Ongamar so that I may
go away the sooner, would it not?"

I heard the scuttling feet and stood with my back to the wall. The
curtain that enclosed my cubby was drawn aside with a rattle of rings,
and Lady Ephedra pointed toward me with both left arms. "She is
here! See her and go!"

The man stood politely aside while the Lady departed, then slipped
into the cubby, looked me over from head to toe with one eye and one
eye patch, whispering as he did so:

"Gather up what you need and come with me."

"And who are you," I grated, halfway between anger and terror. I
had needed only one more day! If anything was guaranteed to make
the Lady Ephedra my enemy, this was it.

"I am sometimes called Stipps, sometimes Mr. Weathereye," he
said, bowing slightly. "I often work with the Dominion and the Siblinghood, which group tells me your term as a bondservant was actually fulfilled some time ago. I have the documents here, as approved
by the K'Famir official for this sector, and if you will be kind enough
to take me to your living quarters, we will discuss your future plans."

I dithered. If . . . if what he said was true, then I needn't fear the
retribution that Lady Ephedra would exact. On the other hand, if it
wasn't true, I was in trouble up to my eyebrows. On the one hand, the
man seemed very sure, but on the other hand, people were often very
sure about things that had no truth to them whatsoever . . .

He leaned forward. "Please, Margaret. Just release your hold on
the back of that chair and come with me."

"Ongamar," I corrected him. "Miss Ongamar."

"Yes, Margaret. I know."

Somehow, he managed to convince me. Somehow he managed to

dissuade Lady Ephedra from making a fuss as we went out of the building to the street and down the narrow way to my rooms. When I reached out to put my key in the door, he whispered, "Where is it?"

My throat froze. I shivered in terror, trying to speak.

"Point," he said in my ear. "Just point."

I did so. Mr. Weathereye said, "Ella May?"

"Here," said a female voice, the person herself coming through the alley gate, a sturdy woman with a case in one hand. We went in. The woman opened the case, empty except for a small set of implements, which she removed before she went to the closed closet door.

"It's in here?"

I nodded. The pair went in. I heard a scuffle, then a scream so shrill it made my ears hurt, then a panting sound, another scream and silence. The woman came out, wiping a peculiarly shaped knife on a piece of glowing fabric.

"Now," Mr. Weathereye said cheerfully to me. "Do you have anything here you want to take with you?"

I begged, "Where are we going?"

"Off Cantardene, my dear. My claim of signed release documents was a false one, for which I apologize. By this time, Lady Ephedra will have summoned the K'Famir, who will shortly assault this dwelling with the aim of killing you. We suggest you quickly put all necessities into this case, and we'll go."

I was jolted into movement. I had already set aside a folded change of clothing and shoes. My Hrass robes and disguise lay ready, and if this man could not do what he told me he could do, I might still use these to escape. I saw his eyebrows rise when I put the disguise into the case, filling it completely. Ella May dropped the implements atop the Hrassian false nose, and we went out the door.

The gate through the wall was open. In the alley outside a dark, smooth vehicle hummed quietly. Its doors opened, Ella May climbed inside and extended a hand to help me inside, where I collapsed onto the seat with an abrupt sense of mixed elation and horror. Either I would wake up and be back in Lady Ephedra's fitting room, or I had escaped. I had no intention of finding out which. If this was to be a temporary ecstasy, I would not abbreviate it.

The vehicle rose soundlessly except for an almost subliminal hum.

Mr. Weathereye touched the door and it became transparent. We looked down on K'Famir wearing the straps and weapons of police massed at the street opening of my little alley, then pouring down it in a flood, blocking both door and alley as a dozen or so of them rushed into my dwelling.

"Why?" I cried. "Why do they want to kill me?"

An old woman seated in front next to Ella May turned and said, "The orders came from the palace of the K'Famir Chief Planner. Next to the Great Leader, that's as high as K'Famir go. Some long time ago, he gave a Thongal spy a few ghyrm to be fastened upon certain human bondslaves on Cantardene to see if these bondslaves were part of a conspiracy. You were one of them. Lately, the Chief Planner learned that the Siblinghood had been looking for you, watching for you. This was taken as proof you were part of a conspiracy, so he ordered that you be killed now, tonight, instead of later, which Lady Mouselline preferred."

"Why?" I whispered. "Why would he even know about me?"

"Perhaps he doesn't. He probably takes take his orders from someone else," said Mr. Weathereye. "We don't really know what creature may be at the top, but if it isn't K'Famir, then it's Quaatar or Frossian."

"Or all three," said the old woman. She turned toward me once more. "I'm Lady Badness. We had already planned to come for you. Such badness here among the K'Famir, always such badness. Lady Mouselline always has her fitters killed, but she has delayed your execution several times, and we took advantage of that, not wanting to . . . betray ourselves beforetime. When we learned that the Chief Planner's office wasn't going to wait any longer, we moved quickly, as we are moving to find out who the creature at the top of this evil pyramid may be."

"Who told you that they wanted me killed?" I cried.

"Someone who listens for us," Lady Badness replied. "We have people who listen for us. The K'Famir walk in the Bak-Zandig-g'Shadup, their clothing brushes against one of our listeners, they walk away, but now their clothing listens to what they say and tells us about it."

"I guess I'm one of your listeners, too," I said. "That's what I did, there in the fitting room. I listened."

Below us, the K'Famir were coming out of the house. One of them waved something to another.

"What's that thing he's waving?" asked Ella May.

I looked down, uncertain. Suddenly the image magnified, and I saw what it was.

"Oh, no," I cried. "My go-pass. I was going to leave Cantardene tomorrow . . ."

"Will they know the pass was sold to you personally?" Lady Badness asked sharply.

I shook my head. "I bought it in the guise of a Hrass, for they're always coming through Bak-Zandig-g'Shadup . . ."

"You left most of your belongings back there," said Mr. Weathereye. "They may assume you plan to return. In any case, unless they've recently had a great advance in technology, they cannot see this flier, even if they are looking directly at it."

This rang an alarm in my mind, but for the moment I could not think why. "Where are we going?"

"We have a place here on Cantardene, a very safe place, we hope, and just until we can figure out a way to get back to . . . where do we want to get back to?" he asked the old woman.

"Thairy, I believe. That's where we started from . . ."

"But the others were going to B'yurngrad . . ."

". . . or B'yurngrad. I imagine either would do."

I murmured, "What do you do there, or here? I mean, what is your work?"

The man laughed. "Rescuing maidens. Not without self-interest, you understand. Since the K'Famir kill anyone they suspect of knowing something touchy about the K'Famir, and since you were scheduled for killing, we assume you have something that will prove to be very useful to us."

"Oh," gasped I with a spurt of pure joy. "Oh, after all these years, I do have something for you!"

Their ship sped across the pleasure quarter to the outskirts of the city, passing above Beelshi. I shuddered.

"What is it?" asked Mr. Weathereye.

"I saw them . . ." I began, stopping, gulping, my throat blocked by swallowed tears.

"Tell us," Lady Badness said firmly.

"I don't want to talk about it. I wrote it all down."

"Which is why you must! We haven't time for documents."

I started haltingly, finally letting it all spew out: the little creatures, the little boy, the creation of the ghyrm, the pools of light and dark I had seen in the mausoleum, the strange machine. Gasping, my face wet, I concluded, "The K'Famir worship the Eater of the Dead. Torturing living things turns them into what you killed back there."

Ella May cursed under her breath. "Lady Badness! Look there, ahead. They've found our ship!"

"How could they?" demanded Lady Badness. "It was shielded. No one comes out here!"

Below us the K'Famir swarmed over the ship like ants.

"They can't get into it," said Weathereye.

"Unfortunately, neither can we," said the old woman.

"They have shield detectors," I said, coming out of the spell of my narrative to realize what was going on. "One of the customers at House Mouselline was talking about its patron being honored for inventing it. The K'Famira laughed a great deal. He hadn't invented it, only bought it from the Omnionts."

"Now the woman remembers!" grated Weathereye. "We don't dare go down there. If we do the correct thing, we blow the ship right now and let them think we're in it."

"Too late," cried the pilot. "They've detected us!"

"Do the correct thing, then," cried Weathereye. "At least take some of them with it."

The ship below us went up in an enormous billow of smoke and fire that threw some hundreds of the uniformed K'Famir through the air like windblown leaves. "That should distract them for a time," growled Ella May.

"How does it work?" Weathereye demanded. "Their sensor. Does it detect the veiling system, or does it penetrate the system to detect the ship?"

I gaped, trying to remember what else they had said. "It detects the system," I said at last.

"Turn the system off in this ship, Ella May," Weathereye ordered. "Get down as close to the ground as you can. Night is coming. Set us down in the shadows somewhere, among these hillocks. We're trapped here now. Have to figure out something . . ."

"The gates," said Lady Badness. "She told us about the gates on the Hill of Beelshi."

"She didn't tell us where the hell they go," snapped Weathereye.

"They don't both go," the old woman snarled in return. "One goes, one comes. Remember!"

"What I remember is the genetic work the Siblinghood has done on the ghyrm," Ella May said as she searched for a place to set down. "And what you told me of the armaments research they're doing on Thairy. Whatever they came up with to kill ghyrm also killed humans. It finally makes sense!"

"It's true the closest tissue match to ghyrm is human," said Lady Badness, turning toward me. "Weathereye and I belong to a small group of interested bystanders, well, not always just bystanders, obviously, since here we are, not just standing."

"What do you mean, the ghyrm are human?" I cried.

"No, no, dear. Not human. Humans are the closest genetic match. What you saw there on the Hill of Beelshi makes it clear the ghyrm are manufactured from humans."

"But the little creatures I saw weren't human. I could hold one of them in my hands!

"They must have once been human, genetically speaking. The human genetic dictionary contains many words, perhaps whole paragraphs, that are not usually expressed. Under certain conditions, however, the genetic vocabulary changes. If the environment is impoverished, much of what is thought of as human is simply repressed, letting simple, earlier processes take over. Language is reduced, then lost. Argument is replaced with violence. Symbols and repetitive chants replace art and music. Minds are reduced in complexity, reactions are simplified. Reproduction may be limited to certain castes. So with the little ones you saw. Genetically, they must still be human, however. Torture simply removes the remnants of humanity— pain does that, you know. It destroys the higher centers of the mind, leaving only the screaming hunger that lies at the center of all ancient life."

"Leaving, also, genetics sufficiently like yours that your immune system does not react to them," said Weathereye. "Your bodies do not reject them, as they would anything foreign. Which means they can take their time to feed on you quite nicely."

"You say, 'genetics like ours,'" said I. "Your genetics aren't human?"

"Like, but unlike." Lady Badness laughed. "We're mere meddlers, my dear. Doing what we can for those we depend upon."

"There," said Ella Mae, indicating a fold of land now dark in shadow. The ship descended soundlessly into its depths.

I offered tentatively. "We are not far from the outskirts of the city, and we're on the Beelshi side. I can lead you to the mausoleum and the gates."

"I would feel better about that if I knew where the gates go," said Weathereye. "I should have asked. Still, since we have no way to get you and Ella May off this planet otherwise . . ."

"I have my own disguise," I said. "I don't have enough for all of us . . ."

"Quite all right, my dear," said Lady Badness. "Take your shape, and we two will copy you. We're quite good at that. We make our living at it, one might say."

I opened the case and took out my Hrassian garb, the nose, the paint, the wig, the dirty robes, the little mirror that let me see myself as I changed. "Now," I murmured as I worked, "the Hrass keep a solid wall to their backs whenever possible. Crossing open ground, they hurry, frequently glancing behind them. They mutter constantly. I think the real Hrass utter prayers, but I have had good experience with the phrase 'Old rhinoceros my brother will you have some bread and butter.' This phrase has in it many of the Hrass phonemes, and it avoids sounds they do not make. Please remember to start the phrase at different intervals and do not say it in unison." I stopped, for all three of them were grinning at me.

"You were on your way to becoming a translator, I believe," said Weathereye. "A woman who spoke many tongues."

I blushed. I had been going on and on, sounding like my own didactibot! "That was long ago," I said. "Some days it is hard to remember. I apologize for seeming imperious. You probably know all this far better than I . . ."

"Not at all," said Lady Badness. "We know little or nothing about the Hrass. We are human followers, our fates inextricably interwoven with your own."

"Do I set the destruct?" Ella May asked.

"I should think so," said Lady Badness rather sadly. "If they find it, we can't get it back."

I said, "We can work our way up the hill among the tombs, those big pottery jars that contain the bones of the dead. That is, I suppose they are bones by now. There's been no room on Beelshi for new ones for a very long time, or so I've heard. They chain the door to the room, so we'll need something . . ."

"I have the proper tool," said Ella May. She turned with a grin, displaying a small tool clasped in one hand. "Are we ready?"

"Just have to fix my nose," I commented, doing so and with quick strokes of my fingers blending the paint around the edges. "I can see you're amused by this, but I can't tell why. Beelshi is terrible and full of pain. I don't like going back there."

"We are not amused, dear lady," said Mr. Weathereye. "We are simply delighted with you, which is quite another thing. Your resourcefulness, your determination, both do you credit."

The four of us left the ship with me leading. When I looked back, it seemed to me two Hrass followed me, muttering, scurrying, glancing around quite as authentically as I could have desired. Ella May stayed between them, making do with a long cape and a scuttling walk. The Hill of Beelshi was to our left, across a well-traveled road and an open area of fields that might be fenced. If so, I would rely upon whatever tool the young woman carried to get us through.

We waited for the road to clear, then scurried across it without incident.

"Who is Ella May?" I panted to Lady Badness.

"She's a member of the Siblinghood of Silence. Have you heard of that?"

"I don't think so, no. What do I call her, Sibling?"

"That's considered quite proper, yes. But she would probably prefer to be called simply Ella May, since you're probably related to one another."

I had time for only one astonished look at the elderly person before resuming my scuttle. Beyond the road were fences, quite a number of them, but Ella May had only to touch them with the tool, whatever it was, and a sizable hole appeared.

We approached Beelshi on the side opposite the one I had climbed before. There were no guards. Presumably, all the guards were out hunting for Miss Ongamar, which thought offered fleeting amusement. Once among the funerary jars, I paused, allowing us all a brief rest. The distance had not been far, the terrain not challenging, but the skittering mannerisms took both concentration and energy. We worked our way upward, pausing outside the upper ring of temples and mausolea while I located the building I had spied from before.

When I pointed it out, Ella May whispered, "Since there's no one here, I suggest we go straight across. It's quickest."

I hesitated, my agitation no doubt plain on my face.

"What?" demanded Mr. Weathereye.

"You see that tall stone, the one that looks like a person hunched over the stone of sacrifice. I've seen its eyes. I got the strong impression that it could see."

"And you think it might utter an alarm?"

"I don't know. If I were here alone, however, I would work around behind it to the place I want to be, then go in very quickly, closing the door tightly behind me."

"I see no reason to doubt your counsel," Mr. Weathereye murmured. "Let us do so."

We were stopped in our tracks by a cacophony of shouts from the foot of the hill behind us. Ella May slipped away to a vantage point and returned almost immediately. "They have mechanical scent detectors down there, they've picked up our trail. I suggest, watching stone or no watching stone, we run for it!"

We did so, rushing across the rough pavement like so many cockroaches, I thought, harkening back to what vermin were left on Earth. Humans and cockroaches. As we crossed before the tall stone, I glanced up to see the red glare of its eyes fastened on me. The creased rock ridges of the mouth opened to emit a huge, stony voice. No one needed a translation, though I made one automatically. "Here, here, here it is!"

Within moments we were up the steps of the mausoleum, Ella May applied her tool to the chain, we pulled the door open, closed it firmly behind us and bolted it with the three huge bolts that were obviously well and frequently used, for they bore no rust and slid into their sockets with a satisfying thwack.

Ella May was facing the shimmering pool of light. She went toward it, thrust her hand in, drew it out again, then tried the same with the black pool, only to leap back with a choked oath.

"Way-gates," said Ella May. "One comes in, one goes out, and the black one is obviously the one that comes in."

The other gate, the shimmering one, had great stacks of empty cages beside it, along with heaped kegs of treasure.

"Read the meaning of this," demanded Weathereye of his female companion, gesturing at their surroundings.

"It says trade," said Lady Badness. "Treasure sent through this gate, creatures returned through this gate. What Miss Ongamar has seen is the key: The K'Famir were paying for human beings to be sent through this gate."

"Were paying?"

"Look at the dust, heavy years of dust. Nothing has come through here for a considerable time."

"But they used this one gate, both ways?"

Ella May said, "Nothing is stacked conveniently next to the other one, and that machine with wheels is an odd thing to find here . . ." She went to look it over more closely. "Phase transformer! Look at the size of it. It has to be salvage, because no one has used anything like this for years."

"Used it to do what?" Lady Badness demanded.

Ella May nodded. "The fields of these gates are obviously one-way. This thing, if started up inside it, or in contact with it, is probably designed to reverse it."

We turned toward the door as it clattered with a hammering of spearpoints.

"The K'Famir police don't carry energy weapons," said I. "But it won't take long to get them from the armory."

Ella May said, "I suggest we push this machine into that light pool and turn it on. It seems to have its own energy source."

"Don't push it all the way in," I cried. "Push in the front end, but leave the end with the controls out, so we can see what happens."

"An excellent suggestion, my dear," said Mr. Weathereye, applying his shoulder to the machine, which seemed reluctant to move in any particular direction. The clatter outside grew louder, and there were coordinated calls.

"They're bringing up something to batter the door down," I translated. "We have to make it move."

We managed to get it turned around, though it seemed to me that only Ella May and I exerted any real force upon it. With a last, desperate shove, we thrust the end of it through the glowing gate. When Ella May pushed the button, the shimmering pool turned abruptly black as air smelling of dust and damp rushed around us. When she pushed the button again, it reversed.

"So they were trading with one source," mused Mr. Weathereye. "I wonder where the black one goes."

I had gone to peer through the crack along the hinge side of the great door. "They're in the plaza. They're bringing up some huge . . . looks like a log?"

"Battering ram," said Ella May. "We don't have much time. I suggest we go through there"—pointing at the shining gate—"and take the machine with us."

"When we get to the other end, we use it to seal it off behind us," said Lady Badness.

"Exactly," said Ella May.

"This road, rather than the other one?" I asked.

Ella May shook her head. "We don't have time to move it to the other one. This one smells fairly clean."

From outside came a chant, "Hrnah, cush, hrnah, cush." The battering ram had arrived and was thundering against the door. The metal shrieked as it bulged inward in a huge, swollen carbuncle. Crates toppled in a cloud of dust. Ella May and I thrust the machine ahead of us.

Voices outside built to a bellowed unison: "Hrnah, cush, hrnah, cush!"

The door screamed, the hinges popped, long metal screws flew across the room, one striping my cheek with blood. Over my shoulder I could see the bolts bending slowly, a little more with each crashing blow. We pushed, grunting, sweating, the others swearing words I had never heard before, thrusting through the shining disk only moments before the great metal doors came off their hinges.

The heavy machine was moving more easily, as though downhill, and I glimpsed the room behind us as it filled with K'Famir who were obviously unfamiliar with the gate. Some of them approached it cautiously, some searched behind the crates, some approached the other gate and were shocked by it, as Ella May had been. We were still pushing when the machine reached the end of the way we were in and protruded into somewhere else. Several of the K'Famir tried reaching into the light gate, discovered it did not hurt them, walked boldly through and began to pursue, spears waving.

"Turn it around," I cried, shoving at the nearest exposed surface of the device with all my strength. The bulky device was now moving fast enough that the momentum carried it around and let it come to rest with the four of us in the clear while the front of it remained inside the gate. I was nearest to the control and I slammed my fist down on it, holding it down. From inside the gate we heard the high, ululating screeches of K'Famir voices just as we, ourselves, were thrust hard against the machine by a gust of air that came from behind us. It rushed away into the opening, then stopped.

"It's closed," said Lady Badness. "I hope whoever was in there was blown out. Now it's black at their end, just like the other one. They can't use either gate, unless they have another machine."

"Were the soldiers pushed back?" I whispered.

"The sounds of pain receded," said Mr. Weathereye. "I think it likely they were more than merely pushed. Flung, perhaps."

"It's dark in here," I said. "The only light is from the pool . . ."

"I have a light," said Ella May, turning it on. We looked around ourselves, trapped in a short tunnel, blocked at one end by the shimmering gate and at the other by a locked iron grille. Beyond the grille was a huge, heavy door.

Ella May asked, "Shall I see if I can cut through the grille?"

Weathereye shook his head. He sat down and leaned against the wall. "There's no hurry," he said. "We're not trapped. Cantardene can't follow us. While we have a moment, I'd like to sit here quietly while Miss Ongamar tells us what she has learned over the last decades she spent there."

To their manifest amusement, I took off my Hrassian nose, turned my outer garment inside out, and began at the left side hem to read them everything I knew about the K'Famir.

I Am Gretamara and Ongamar/on Chottem

When the Gardener joined Sophia and me as we breakfasted under the flowering tree, she seemed distracted. While we ate, she merely sat, eyes half shut, obviously troubled.

"Gardener," Gretamara said at last. "Something's wrong?"

"Something's happened, but I can't locate it. I knew something was going to happen, but I don't know what!"

Gretamara looked up, suddenly alert. "It's the cellars, Gardener. Sophia and I had the same oppressive feelings about the house, and they came from the cellars. This morning I had the feeling that a wind had swept through them . . ."

"But it was not something dreadful," the Gardener remarked. "Perhaps that's why I'm confused about it. If it had been dreadful, I would have thought of the cellars, but this . . ."

"Let's go look," I said, rising from my chair. "We'll stay behind the iron grilles, just in case."

We made our way down the many stairs, beyond the first, second and third doors, coming at last to that final door, triple-locked, triple-bolted, triple-barred. As we approached it, the Gardener held up her hand, tilting her head. "I hear a voice!"

We laid our ears against the crack where the door met

the jamb to hear a voice murmuring, or perhaps reciting something, for it went on and on, uninterrupted.

"It sounds like you, Gretamara," said Sophia.

The Gardener stood tall, eyes gleaming, her teeth showing between her lips in what I thought could be either a grim smile or a snarl. "Of course!" she said. "Unlock it!"

Sophia did as she was bade. The first bolt drawn silenced the voice beyond the gate. Moving the second bolt caused an eruption of noise, as if something on wheels were being moved. The third bolt and bar met only silence, as did the rusty squeal as the door was cracked open.

The Gardener spoke through the crack. "Is there someone there who has a name and a number?"

After a long moment, a male voice responded, "Is that you, Gardener?"

"What name and number have you, Weathereye?"

"I have Ongamar, and she is number four. What number have you?"

"I have Gretamara, and she is number three," said the Gardener, pulling the door wide open. Inside, facing us, were an old man with an eye patch and three women: one quite old; one middling young, stocky and healthy looking; the other smaller, thinner, more sallow and bent, but bearing a definite resemblance to me.

"Lady Badness!" cried the Gardener. "Weathereye! What brings you by this route?"

"We accompanied those for whom it was the only route," said the old woman. "You know Ella May, of the Siblinghood, and this is Miss Ongamar. You must hear what she's been telling us!"

"Who are they?" asked Sophia in wonderment.

"Old friends and a new one!" said the Gardener, as she signaled Sophia to unlock the iron grille. "One devoutly wished for! What is that machine you've brought?"

"A device for changing the direction of the way-gates," said Ella May, bowing to the Gardener and receiving in return a kiss on her cheek. "We believe there was a thriving trade going on through this gate, with goods passing in both directions. The machine made it possible."

The other woman was standing very still, her feet apart as though to brace against shock, as she stared into my face. "Who are you?" she asked at last.

"I . . . was Margaret," I said. "Now I'm Gretamara. And you?"

"I was Margaret. On Cantardene they called me Ongamar."

"When did you . . . when did you become someone else?"

"I was twelve."

"So was I, twelve."

"You're little more than that now?"

"I'm a lot older, really. I just haven't . . . aged much. We were split when the proctor came, weren't we?"

"Yes."

"Why?" we both said at once. "Why?"

"Because," said the Gardener. "It was necessary, for a very good reason, and it actually happened some time before that." She turned to Weathereye. "Was she in some kind of danger?"

"Oh, a very definite kind," he said. "Someone has found out too much and is trying to kill any or all of them."

"How?" the Gardener whispered. "How could anyone have possibly . . . ?"

"How could anyone have possibly what?" cried Sophia. "Gardener, what's going on?"

"Shhh," she replied. "Not here." She unlocked the grille, beckoned the others through it, relocked first it, then the heavy doors, and led us out the cellars, locking each of the doors behind us.

As we reached the ground level, Lady Badness said, "For all we know, there may be listeners down there. After all, the other end's in Cantardene."

"Which is a pesthole," remarked the Gardener. "If anything found out, I'd guess it was something from there . . ."

Miss Ongamar said, "The stone. The standing stone. They call it Whirling Cloud of Darkness-Eater of the Dead."

Sophia and I exchanged a horrified look. I murmured, "We saw it, didn't we, Gardener?"

Gardener said, "I took them to the Gathering, Weathereye."

Ongamar said, "The stone called out, 'It's here.' It meant me, didn't it?"

"Probably," said Mr. Weathereye. "As I said, the order to kill you came from the very top levels of Cantardene."

"The very top levels were present when they made the ghyrm," Ongamar said. "Anything any of them knew, that stone knew. What is that stone?"

"Ah," Lady Badness murmured. "What a good question. What would you say, Weathereye? Not merely K'Famirish, is it? Something of the slaughterhouse added? The torture chamber? The mass grave? One, or more, of the ancients in the Gathering?"

"Quite possibly," said Mr. Weathereye crisply.

"Quite possibly what?" cried Sophia, stamping her foot.

"Quite possibly an amalgamation of K'Famir and Frossian gods along with something a good deal older," the Gardener answered crisply. "You and Gretamara were there, Sophia. You saw the Quaatar."

"You said they couldn't do anything . . . by themselves," I cried.

"They can't," said Lady Badness. "Just as a battery can't do anything by itself. Attach a wire to it, however, and current flows. We gods are like that. We accumulate energy, feelings, emotions, needs, wants, hopes, dreams, hatreds, everything. Normally, most of it cancels out: Love balances hate, hope balances despair, joy balances sorrow. If you get a god that's only one thing, however, only pain, only hate, only death, with nothing to balance it, then it accumulates. Attach a mortal to it, and you've got a lynching, a crusade, a clinic bombing, a jihad, an inquisition, an assassination. Those three, Dweller, Drinker, Darkness . . . they've set up a hate-and-horror generator! I would like to know how they found out about our plan, though. I thought we'd done an excellent job of hiding our traces."

"Did the plan have anything to do with me?" asked Ongamar, tears gathering in her eyes. "If it did, they've found out from the ghyrm. I saw the ghyrm being created, and one of them has been feeding on me for years, using me to spy out horrors. I tried to keep some things to myself, but it knew me. It knew all about me . . ." She looked imploringly at the Gardener. "I know it doesn't keep information to itself, I know it doesn't. That . . . that stone probably knows everything the ghyrm does, everything *every* ghyrm does . . ."

"But what does it know?" the Gardener asked. "That you are Earthian? Everyone knew that. That you are female, sick of the place? Obviously."

"I saw them being created. I don't think the ghyrm learned that from me, but I can't be sure."

"Ah," said the Gardener. "Well. Would it know there are more than one of you? You didn't know that yourself . . . unless . . ."

"Of course," said Mr. Weathereye, scowling. "Unless another one of the seven is also in contact with a ghyrm! Well, I was sent to Cantardene to find someone who had been Margaret. Aha. Yes. And why was I sent? Because there were already three Margarets on Thairy and another one on B'yurngrad who was in danger, and the one on B'yurngrad is a member of your Siblinghood, Ella May, and she's a ghyrm-hunter, like you, who usually carries and feeds a finder. Which is, as we all know, simply another ghyrm.

"So, if we have one Margaret on Cantardene, known to a ghyrm, and another Margaret on B'yurngrad, also known to a ghyrm, and if those devils in The Gathering know everything the ghyrm know, then it would not take them long to figure out there was at least one more Margaret than there should be . . ."

"They identify us?" Ongamar asked. "Individually?"

"Oh, I imagine they can," said Lady Badness. "At least the ones they don't kill."

"There are such things as identical twins, or even triplets," I said indignantly. "Don't they know that?"

"Of course there are," said the Gardener. "But if a monster is several million years old and has survived enough extinction episodes to become completely paranoid, one is not averse to killing a few twins to eliminate a possible threat."

"Several million years old!" whispered Ongamar. "Who?"

"This is not the place nor the time," said the Gardener. "We must move very quickly before they know we've been warned . . ."

"Where are we?" asked Ongamar

"On Chottem. Weathereye, you say there are three already assembled on Thairy? What are they doing?"

"Going to B'yurngrad to pick up a fourth one," he replied, with satisfaction.

"Two here, four there, leaving only one, and we know where she is. So, Weathereye will take Ongamar to B'yurngrad, where she'll tell them about ghyrm. Then they find transport . . . Not a way-gate. No! The way-gate's reversed. We can't leave it that way!"

Weathereye frowned, eyes suddenly widening. "Of course! We need to change the gate so it goes from Chottem to Cantardene, the way it was, then we have to hide the machine."

"There will be guards posted at the far end, on Cantardene," said Ella May. "If you turn it around, they'll come through."

"Do you have charbic?" asked Ongamar. "They grow it on Cantardene for export to Chottem. Charbic is lethal to the K'Famir, so they use slaves to work the fields."

"Charbic?" mused the Gardener.

"Sometimes called mothbane," I said. "The carpets here were adrift with it when we arrived."

"So they were," cried Sophia. "There are still sacks of the stuff filling up one of the stables."

"Ah, very well," said Mr. Weathereye. "Do you have stout retainers, Sophia? Stout enough to lug the stuff down below."

"I don't want them to see . . ." Sophia said.

"They won't see," said the Gardener. "Lady Badness can arrange that your men see nothing but floors and walls." She stood, beckoning to me. "Gretamara and I will go just before the way is locked. Weathereye will precede us, with Ongamar and Ella May, continuing through the way-gates to Thairy, then on to B'yurngrad if that is where the others have gone."

"You're leaving me here alone?" asked Sophia in panic.

"I'll stay with you," said Lady Badness. "I'm really quite useful. Don't worry."

The Gardener stayed above while the rest of us returned below, and into the right-hand branch of the tunnel.

"If the K'Famir get through the grille, they'll go through this gate, too," whispered Sophia.

"It will do them no good," said Lady Badness with a peculiar, almost anticipatory smile.

"We're off, then," said Weathereye, patting Sophia's shoulder.

"There are four gates between us and Thairy, but it will take us very little time." He bowed the women through, then followed.

Sophia took a deep, shuddering breath.

"You feel adrift," said Lady Badness, patting her hand.

"Gardener has been . . . my mother, my family," said Sophia. "I know all about my real mother. I know what kind of family she had. I think the Gardener is a lot harder to live up to."

"She is only what our source is, and you're part of that."

Sophia was not cheered by this, as it seemed only to deepen her responsibility, but she resolutely sent for men to fetch sack after sack of powdered charbic root, then led them below to dump them just inside the gate.

"All kinds of vermin come through here," Sophia said loudly, with a convincing shudder. "The charbic root will kill them, and we'll shut this entry down."

"Entry, ma'am?" asked the most forward of the men.

"A way my grandfather used to get down to the harbor," she said. "He bought it from the Omnionts, but it lets rats in."

When everything was prepared, the four strongest were told to stay by the machine while she pushed the button. Then they pulled the bulky thing back through the grille door, the sound of shrieking wheels covering the faint, distant howls that Sophia heard. She locked the grille and the gates behind her, then pointed out a dusty corner where the machine could be hidden under a pile of old sacking.

I watched them as they crossed each of the cellars, looking around with great curiosity. Everyone had heard the rumors of Stentor's great hoard, but all I saw, all they saw was stone, dust, and cobwebs, with not so much as a scatter of coins on the floors. None of them noticed the old woman sitting quietly in a corner. When they had finished, Sophia thanked them for a job well done, paid them exorbitantly, and told them to take the day off.

"Now what are we to do?" Sophia asked Lady Badness.

Lady Badness turned toward me and asked, "Are you and the Gardener ready to go?"

"We are," said the Gardener, coming down the stairs.

"It will be frightening, just waiting to see what happens," said Sophia.

"We will stay busy," said Lady Badness with a somewhat-gloating look. "Since the K'Famir may actually try to come through the way-gate, you and I, Sophia, must be ready with a proper welcome."

The doors and the grille were unlocked only long enough to let the Gardener and me into the tunnel. We heard them being locked again, behind us.

We emerged from the way-gate into darkness. Light bloomed slowly around us. We were in a cube, a gate in the wall behind us, another in the wall ahead, an uninterrupted wall to either side, a ceiling, a floor.

"Do you have a name and a number?" whispered a mechanical voice.

"The name is Wilvia, the number is two," said Gardener.

The wall to our left slid open, making a slender opening. We squeezed through and it shut behind us.

"It's a Gentheran survey ship," remarked the Gardener. "It's been buried here for a very long time."

We moved down the dimly lit passageway and came to a viewscreen that looked across a clearing into a forest. Through the trees we saw a shoreline and an expanse of water. Along the shoreline was a village swarming with very small people, somewhat humanlike in appearance.

"Where are we?" I asked.

"At the far end of nowhere," replied the Gardener. "A place that interests no one, a place visited only by accident. The Frossians were determined to kill Wilvia, Queen of the Ghoss, so we kept moving her about in order to keep her safe."

"When we were children," I said, "we invented Queen Wilvia, and Naumi the Warrior, and all the others. There was a spy, too. I suppose Ongamar was the spy. I wonder if they found a warrior . . ."

A door opened at our approach to disclose a courtyard garden with flowering trees grouped around a burbling fountain. Cushioned chairs were set around it, one of them holding a slender, careworn woman, who rose, startled by our arrival. She wore a simple white robe and a diadem. The glowing gem at the center of her forehead was her only adornment.

"Gardener," she said, but she was not looking at the Gardener. Her eyes were fixed on me.

"Wilvia," the Gardener cried. "You're pale, tired. Why are you all alone? Where are your companions?"

"They had to go," she gestured, her eyes still fixed upon Gretamara. "A long, long time ago. Who . . . how . . . ?"

The Gardener motioned to me to be seated, remaining standing herself to observe the two of us. "You recognize yourselves?"

"Myself?" Wilvia stood. "She's younger than I."

I shook my head. "I've been living with the Gardener since I was twelve. People who live there don't age very fast. One named Ongamar has been a bondslave on Cantardene since she was twelve, and bondslaves do age. There are four more of us."

"As I told you," the Gardener said to Wilvia.

"I know you told me!" Wilvia took a step away, her cheeks burning with quick, hectic color, her eyes shifting restlessly, her voice shrill. "Being told is one thing. Confronting oneself, after all these years . . . Oh, Gardener. When I saw you, I thought it might be my children! Or Joziré!"

"You know your children are well, for you and your friends left each of them in a safe place, did you not?"

"Yes," she whispered. "My friends and I . . ."

"But where are your companions? They should be here."

"Gone," said Wilvia, taking a deep breath. "They had to go to Tercis to take their child. They weren't supposed to be gone for very long, but when they started back, they realized they were being followed. They sent a message here, to the ship, to let me know why they hadn't returned."

"I need to see," said Gardener, moving through the garden. I rose to follow her, but Wilvia stayed where she was.

"Gardener, there's something wrong with her," I said, as we went from the garden into another ship corridor.

"Isolation is wrong with her," the Gardener said angrily. "Isolation, and grief. Her children were taken away for safekeeping, her husband also, a pair of Gibbekot were her only companions. We didn't mean for her ever to be left alone!"

A door opened, and we went through into a control room. The Gardener turned to the right, to the communications room. "Access message from Prrr Prrrpm and Mwrrr Lrrrpa."

"Message accessed." Two faces appeared on the screen.

The Gardener said. "Prrr Prrrpm and Mwrrr Lrrrpa. Message!"

The larger Gibbekot said, "Wilvia, we can't come back to you just now. We have placed Falija in foster care, as planned. As we were leaving Tercis, we detected someone following us, which means we have to lead the followers away. We knew it was a risk. Have patience. We will return to you as soon as possible . . ."

The screen went blank. We returned to Wilvia.

"You've been alone since they left?" cried the Gardener.

"Alone, yes. I know it seems longer than it really has been. I still have books to read. There's plenty of food. Sometimes I spend days just watching them, out there, wondering at them. They've been almost wiped out over and over, but they don't remember a thing . . ."

"And no one has come here at all?"

"Sometimes in the nights, I've wakened, thinking I've heard the gate. It makes a kind of liquid sound, you know, like water, flowing, but nothing happened except for the sound. I'm sure you're right, that no one knows the ship is here." She sat down again, closing her eyes and trembling. "Tell me it's time to go?"

I got up and sat beside her, putting my arm around the queen. "You will not be left here alone again," I said, staring directly at the Gardener as I said so.

"Quite true," said the Gardener. "If the two of you will give me just a day or to so I can make sure everything is . . ."

"No," said Wilvia. "Enough, Gardener. Years in the first place I was taken, years in the second and third. Almost a year, maybe more, in this place. I am beginning to think I have died and am only imagining being alive! I'll go where you go, or I'll go through the way-gate to Tercis."

The Gardener sighed. "No doubt that will do as well, though by this time the way-gates may be swarming with K'Famir."

"We can be sure there's no one in the gate-room," said Wilvia. "You put a sensor in there."

"And you left Lady Badness behind on Chottem," I said. "I doubt she's let anyone come through."

"Lady Badness?" asked Wilvia.

"Lady Nepenthe, Mistress of Forgetfulness," said the Gardener, with a twisted smile. "A talent we share. Mankind gave us that talent, they wanted us to have it because they needed it themselves. I have used it regularly on the villagers in Swylet. Lady Badness will have used it on the men in the cellar who saw all that treasure and forgot it even while they were looking at it. But it's a human thing, and it's not likely to work on K'Famir, though . . . who knows? Very well, we'll go to Tercis, and you two will wait for me there while I go to B'yurngrad by other ways."

Wilvia stood, shaking her long garments down around her. She stood proudly erect as though stretching herself upward.

"Don't you need belongings of some kind?" I asked.

"I need nothing," she said, with a smile that trembled into tears, "save to leave this dreadful place."

She followed us back the way we had come. The door opened on an empty room. The door slid open. We moved quickly to the shining gate and went away.

We Margarets Assemble/
on B'yurngrad

I, Naumi, was at the academy when Jaker commed me from the office of Poul-Jaker's import-export company, to say their sales rep Stipps had returned with the bond-slave they wanted. Her name, he said, was Ongamar. She did speak several languages, and sewing had indeed been her livelihood. Though he had been directed only to find her, matters on Cantardene were extremely volatile, and since her life was at risk, he had taken the liberty, which he hoped would be forgiven, of rescuing the poor woman.

"Where is she?" I demanded, after a moment's awed appreciation of this folderol.

"He brought her here," said Jaker. "But we can be with you shortly. It seems appropriate to let her rejoin her . . . other family members."

I set out to report this development to everyone else, wherever they were, just getting out of bed or bathing or having breakfast, and in a very short time they commed from the gate to tell me we had visitors. When I arrived there, so-called Stipps bowed, saying:

"You're looking well, Naumi."

"Thank you, sir," I replied. "I rather expected to see you. Just at the moment we're very busy. Is this the lady?"

"Ongamar. She has important information about the ghyrm. I know you're very busy, but do you feel it would be worth your while for the two of you to find out precisely what our enemies are up to just now? I know the Gardener and Lady Badness have been otherwise occupied. It would only take us a moment."

I laughed, not from amusement. "If the lady is willing, I am willing, Mr. Weathereye. Flek, Jaker, will you be host for me? See that everyone has breakfast, and we'll be back shortly."

"You *know* him," said Jaker. "What did you call him?"

"A nickname. From my youth. I'll tell you all about it when we return . . ."

Ongamar was small and somewhat bent, as though by habit, but her eyes snapped as she looked at me. I hustled the other two past the gate guards and returned. Mr. Weathereye took us each by the hand and we . . . traveled somewhere.

We very gradually coalesced not far from a trio of towering . . . what? Smoke. Fire. Sullen darkness lit with livid flame. Dweller, Mr. Weathereye told us without words. Drinker. Darkness. They were immense, and we were nothing, a huddled, small, muttering form. Ongamar and I knew that humans spoke many languages: dead ones, live ones, artificial ones, extraterrestrial ones. Mr. Weathereye had a wide variety of mutters to pick from, and esoteric nonsense in several tongues slipped from his mouth.

"What is it saying?" demanded Drinker of Blood.

"Just babble," replied Dweller in Pain. "Some prelinguistic source has been carried into space by a more advanced race, and their Members have ended up here. Ignore it. You were telling us about Cantardene . . ."

Darkness replied, "We found the copy! The one to be killed. It got away through a trade duct! I howled for the source to come, but the copy got away and took our machine with it!"

"It doesn't matter, does it?" said Dweller.

"What do you mean, it doesn't?"

"You don't need the machine because you don't need the duct. You're getting the raw material directly from Earth through Chottem, aren't you? That supplier, what's his label?"

Darkness snarled, "D'Lornschilde. And he overcharges us."

Dweller continued. "That doesn't matter either. When our people conquer Chottem, as we will, we'll get it all back."

After a pause, Darkness muttered, "I suppose you'll say it doesn't matter that the copies are named Mar Gar Et. A ghyrm told us about the Mar Gar Et on Cantardene, one coded On Ga Mar. The ghyrm said there was another Mar Gar Et on B'yurngrad, one coded Mar a Gi. They're copies, and copies are dangerous."

"That is dangerous," admitted Dweller.

"Why? Why dangerous?" asked Drinker.

"Dangerous because of ancient oracle!" cried Dweller in Pain. "All Quaatar know when seven roads are walked at once, Quaatar end. Frossians too, most likely. And K'Famir. This oracle goes far, far back in history of great Quaatar race."

Darkness nodded ponderously. "This is why we look for copies. We found more! One Mar Gar Et in Fajnard. One Mar Gar Et on Tercis, where Gentherans were seen! That's four."

"Four can't do anything," said Dweller.

Darkness said sulkily, "The Mar Gar Et that got away on Cantardene knows about ghyrm. If she talks to Gentherans, she'll tell!"

Dweller laughed, a fume of smoke and licking blue flame. "Even if she tells Gentherans everything, I say, again, again, it doesn't matter! Five copies, six copies, doesn't matter. It's too late to help the humans, because very soon there will not be any humans. There are enough ghyrm piled up on Cantardene that we can start dropping them on Earth right after we test them on B'yurngrad."

Our substance became rigid and manifested a foggy mass rather like a huge ear.

"B'yurngrad is our test. We will drop enough ghyrm to kill every human there. If one of your Mar Gar Ets is on B'yurngrad, there will be one less copy. When B'yurngrad is dead, we scoop up the ghyrm and take them to Earth."

Our muttering little form eased away, losing shape, losing substance, becoming nothing. Ongamar and I felt solid soil beneath our feet, looked up to see the sky, the building where we were all staying at the academy.

"You will be going to B'yurngrad almost immediately," said Mr. Weathereye in a strange, far-off voice. "Perhaps I will see you there."

"Where did he go?" asked Ongamar in a strangled voice.

"God knows," I said, then surprised myself with a blat of nervous laughter. The episode had been ridiculous, but I was sweating, my teeth were clenched, my stomach felt as though I had swallowed an anvil. Ongamar was gray, shuddering, tottering. I took her arm to support her, and she leaned as though to hold me up. Perhaps I needed it. So propped, we entered the building and found the common room where Flek and Jaker were with Mar-agern and Margaret. Gloriana, Falija, and Bamber Joy arrived almost immediately. Margaret provided us with cups of strong coffee—from the new coffee plantations on the Southern Isles—and we made halting conversation while we waited for Ferni. When he arrived, I introduced Ongamar, adding, "Mr. Weathereye says she has vital information."

"He thinks so," Ongamar said. "I have seen ghyrm being made, and he thinks I should tell you about it."

Then she told us a story. It was obviously one she had told before, for she told it without hesitation, almost matter-of-factly, while giving us far greater detail than I, for one, felt was necessary. Several of us had to leave the group to stand breathing deeply in the open window.

"That's why the genetic match," cried Flek. "They're made from human beings."

"Assuming the little creatures I saw were a kind of human, yes," Ongamar agreed.

"At least the ghyrm bodies are," said Ferni.

"Is there anything to them but bodies?" Caspor asked.

Flek said, "Something, yes. Something that processes information, remembers, reports. Not a brain, exactly. More of a computer with only one program."

"So if the flesh is mostly human," said Jaker, "where does it get its motivation? That has to come from somewhere else."

I asked, "Ongamar, did you ever detect anything from your parasite that felt human?"

She considered. "Not really, no. If I delayed giving it what it wanted, it punished me. I suppose humans might have that reaction, but the ghyrm was that way all the time. It wanted blood and pain, only that. It didn't eat, smell, touch, or look at anything else. It wasn't interested in anything else. If it had been human, surely it would have . . . wanted some variety, wouldn't it?"

We spoke of this for some time. I did not want to discuss the other thing. I did not want to think about the other thing, but finally we ran out of anything more to say about the ghyrm, and I could not hesitate any longer. I told them what the cabal planned to do, first on B'yurngrad, then on Earth. "When they have killed every human on B'yurngrad, the Mercans will scoop the ghyrm up and repeat the process on Earth itself."

There was a long, deadly silence before Flek cried, "But that's ludicrous. This cabal—it sounds like monsters out of a fairy story! Shadowy beings of total terror. Surely they have families, children that they care about. No living thing could be that . . . that uncaring. That bloodthirsty."

"You would not say that if you had been there," said Ongamar harshly. "If there was anything but cruelty inside the K'Famir on Beelshi, it didn't show. And they don't care about their own families. Their women are for amusement or breeding; their daughters are for sale or disposal; their sons are turned into copies of their fathers. Living creatures are valued only for their usefulness, and if they aren't useful for anything else, they become useful for the young males to use in perfecting their skills of torture in their malehood schools."

"But we don't understand why," I said, sounding plaintive even to myself. "We feel we need to understand why."

Margaret responded. "Naumi, I strongly suspect they don't need a why. When one considers violence and cruelty, the whys seem to get lost. During my studies on Earth, I had to watch accounts of human history, and I can't count how many times I saw and heard some human cry out, 'But why do they want to kill us?' People of one color killing another. People of one religion killing those who followed another. People of one language killing those who spoke another. Sometimes just people rioting, killing anyone, because they couldn't stand the lives they had . . ."

"We don't do that," cried Flek, obviously distressed.

Margaret said, "You personally may not, but humans do. The only difference between the human race and the Quaatar is that humans in general believe those who do so, do so in error, and they urge penitence. When I studied the Quaatar language, I learned they believe avoidance and regret are signs of weakness. You can't convince them they're wrong because right and wrong aren't part of their vocabulary. Male Frossian and K'Famir are like that, but so are some humans."

A silence fell. My old friends gathered around me.

"Remember Grangel," said Caspor. "He was sort of Frossian."

"He was," said Flek, beginning a chain of reminiscences. I knew what she was doing. Trying to talk us into calm.

I said to the others, those still strange to us, "Why don't you go on over to the commissary and get something to eat? Ongamar looks like she could use both food and a lot of sleep."

Margaret and Mar-agern chivvied them out. Though Glory and Bamber Joy looked rebellious, they were too well mannered to object. The six of us continued talking. The others returned and scattered in various directions to take naps. Later that afternoon, when Ongamar and Margaret came back into the common room, they found me sitting there alone.

"Was your discussion valuable?" Margaret asked.

"Possibly," I said, feeling a quick, almost furtive smile cross my face. "Our old talk road has yielded a plan, and Flek has made certain adjustments to her machinery. There's one rather large detail to be sorted out yet, and given that uncertainty, one hesitates to say how valuable the discussion may have been. We'll be ready shortly, however. You need to tell your people to prepare. We're leaving for B'yurngrad!"

Those of us who assembled at the way-gate to B'yurngrad included Ferni and Ongamar, all those who had arrived through the gate from Fajnard, plus Caspor and Flek to see us off. Some of us had climbed and some of us had been hoisted; all seemed to have greeted the experience with grim resolution rather than any sense of adventure, except perhaps for Ferni. Ferni was the perennial adventurer, and I could tell that M'urgi was very much on his mind. Ferni, Mar-agern, and I carried armor, knives, and the components of the newly calibrated anti-ghyrm machine, as well as weapons ready for use. The others bore lighter packs of supplies, and Falija rode on Bamber's shoulders.

Caspor said for the sixth time, "You understand, we have no idea where on B'yurngrad the way-gate will come out?"

I gritted my teeth. "Caspor, we know. We intend to use the gate to get on planet, then we'll contact the Siblinghood and have them pick us up."

"If they're reachable," said Ferni in a surly voice. "Which they were not when I left there."

"You can always go back by ship, the way you came," I suggested through still-gritted teeth. There was entirely too much repetition going on. I have never liked repetition.

Ferni growled, "There's a two-day difference. Even if we can't reach the Siblinghood, we ought to be able to . . ."

"Stop arguing," said Flek. "You could emerge in wilderness somewhere, which is why you're all wearing locators, so the ships with the heavier machines will be able to find you."

"Let's get on with it," snapped Margaret. "You're saying the same things over and over, and we've already waited extra time for them to recalibrate this equipment . . ."

I threw her a grateful glance. She winked at me. I thought how odd it was to wink at oneself.

"Keep in mind the machines aren't thoroughly tested," said Flek. "The running time on the prototype is short. With these new settings, it'll burn itself out even sooner . . ."

"Right," I said, almost shouting. "We know, Flek. We know there's a risk, but Margaret's right, we've talked it to death."

Checking our weapons, Ferni and I went first through the gate, while Mar-agern, cradling her weapon somewhat apprehensively, brought up the rear.

We emerged between huge stones into a rock-walled, grass-carpeted corridor that was open to the air above us. A few paces away, the corridor split into two. The right turn brought us to the sister gate, the pale one that would lead, if Caspor was correct, directly to Cantardene.

"Well," said Margaret, "I guess we don't have to use that one. Ongamar's already been rescued."

"Oh, yes, indeed," said Ongamar.

I pointed in the other direction. "That way."

We squeezed through the very narrow opening to the left and

came out between the boles of two huge trees at one edge of a small, sun-stippled glade. On its far side, a narrow opening showed us grasslands freckled with hide-covered tents, smoke skeining above them into a calm and cloudless sky. In the opening between glade and grassland, facing us, a woman sat enthroned, with a considerable company of armed tribesmen squatting at either side.

"That's M'urgi," said Ferni unnecessarily.

"How did she manage to be right here?" I marveled.

Ferni shifted the weight of his pack. "She probably went night walking, saw us coming out here, decided to meet us."

"Night walking?" asked Margaret.

"You know. It's an out-of-body thing."

"I don't know, but it doesn't matter." She leaned to one side, depositing her pack on the ground. "Naumi should wait, I think, but Mar-agern, Ongamar, we three should introduce ourselves."

Ongamar chirped, "Might as well."

"No time like the present," said Mar-agern, dropping her load and weapon.

The three women walked toward the enthroned M'urgi, who was staring at them in total astonishment. The rest of us followed, getting just close enough to hear what went on. For a moment M'urgi looked past the women at me, then at Ferni, then back at them, standing up and moving toward them as they neared, gaze moving steadily among them.

"Who?" she asked.

Ongamar said, as we had rehearsed: "We were twelve years old. The proctor found out I wasn't a two-three-four . . ."

"He said our family was fine," grated M'urgi.

Mar-agern cleared her throat. "We weren't fine, though I didn't know it until I was twenty-two. We were supposed to be headed to Omniont space . . ."

"They asked for people who knew Mercan languages," said M'urgi. "I paid no attention to it."

"I paid attention," said Mar-agern. "I offered my talents, for what they were worth. I ended up a bondslave on Fajnard."

"Ah," breathed M'urgi, turning to Margaret. "And you?"

"I said yes to Bryan," she said flatly.

After a moment of wide-eyed silence, M'urgi asked, "Where was it he was going? Tercis, wasn't it?"

"Tercis," Margaret agreed. "A Walled-Off called Rueful. I've been there ever since."

M'urgi shifted her weight. "How about him, back there? He looks like . . ."

"Naumi's one of us," said Mar-agern. "He got split off when Ongamar did. He had his sex changed somewhere along the line. He grew up on Thairy. We thought he should wait while we introduced ourselves since he's a little less believable and has gaps in his memory."

"So there's five of us?"

Margaret took a deep breath. "Actually, there have to be two more, seven altogether."

"Seven. How interesting. Lately, I've been dreaming of that number. Those dreams reminded me of one I had years ago of meeting myself here, at this place." She paused, swallowed deeply, managing a casual tone. "I see Ferni's with you."

"He came to Thairy to get help finding you."

M'urgi glanced at the packs the others carried. "What've you brought?"

Mar-agern replied. "Stuff to kill ghyrm. As many knives as we can carry. We have a prototype ghyrm eradicator, and there are bigger ones coming that they can't fit through the way-gate. The Sibling-hood should be bringing them by ship."

"I hope it's enough," said M'urgi, with a grim smile. "This morning, a friend of yours arrived to tell us the enemy has declared war."

"Friend?"

"An old guy, Weathereye. He brought a member of the Sibling-hood with him, Sister Ella May. She knows Margaret, and he knows Naumi, or so they say. Let's go sit down in my tent and find out where we are."

M'urgi sent two young men running to pick up the packs Margaret and Mar-agern had carried as the others came forward, Falija lying across Bamber's shoulder.

There was a stir among the tribesmen.

"What is that animal?" M'urgi muttered.

"Not an animal. Gibbekot," said Margaret.

Mar-agern said, "Tell them it's . . . it brings good luck."

M'urgi turned and spoke to the tribesmen. Margaret and Mar-agern identified the speech as an intelligible dialect of Earthian with certain consonants blurred or missing: final l's that sounded like w's. R's that disappeared.

"Gibb ah cot," she said. "Come to hep us kill ghyrm."

I saw Mr. Weathereye standing to one side, a woman beside him. I went to meet him. "Mr. Weathereye. And you must be Ella May. You got here ahead of us."

"Ah, well, my boy. Difficult times almost always produce unexpected encounters."

"Turns out there's more to me than meets your eye, Mr. Weathereye. Or less, perhaps. Did you know I wasn't meant to be a man at all?"

"You sound angry about that."

I hesitated. I was angry about that. Anger was sometimes useful, but might not be at the moment. "Yes," I admitted. "Why?"

"Camouflage," said Mr. Weathereye. "If the human race is to survive, we needed seven of you with a broad variety of experiences. Some were enslaved, some were sovereign, some labored, some thought, some were hidden, some were put in unexpected places, some were left out in plain sight to see if anyone showed undue interest. You were camouflaged."

"If the human race is to survive," I said. "All that, dependent on making a man of me?"

"A man of you; a shaman of M'urgi; a spy of Ongamar. You'll have to decide for yourself whether it was worth it." Weathereye sighed. "Since we and the Gentherans have another agenda for humanity, we think it was worth it, yes. We're opposed to your being wiped out. We hope to restore humanity to itself."

"And how we are to do that?"

"You know how, Naumi. The Siblinghood told you how."

"By finding someone who knows everything. Perhaps by walking seven roads that are one road, all at the same time."

"Exactly. And by doing so, regain something humanity lost a long time ago. Something the Gentherans say you once had that was stolen from you."

"By whom?"

"The Gentherans believe it was done by the Quaatar, but they admit they're extrapolating."

Over Mr. Weathereye's shoulder, I saw my companions entering one of the tents. I said, "Later," in a significant tone, and went to the tent where people were seating themselves around the barely smoldering fire with M'urgi. Our small group was surrounded and outnumbered by a silent circle of squatting tribesmen, obviously alert to every word that was being said. Mr. Weathereye and Ella May came to stand inside the tent flap.

M'urgi dipped her hand into an open jar, threw a handful of something onto the fire, and said through the resultant fragrant smoke, "Mr. Weathereye spoke to us before you came. He says that K'Famir, Frossian, and Quaatar ships are about to attempt eradication of the human race, starting here on B'yurngrad. He says it is not a reasonable enmity but merely an old grudge the Quaatar have against humans, one so old they've forgotten the reason for it."

"What are they going to do?" asked Margaret.

"They're going to drop ghyrm all over the planet."

"No," I said flatly. "They must not be allowed to do that. A few days from now, it might not matter, but right now, it's absolutely necessary that they drop the whole load, whatever that amounts to, on top of us, right here!"

"Why?" cried M'urgi, eyes wide with shock.

Ferni answered. "We brought a prototype machine with us, M'urgi: first one out of the factory. They're sending larger ones, but right now, this is all we've got. According to Flek—the armaments person—this one will cover about thirty square jorub, not much compared to the surface of a planet."

"No, but it's still a considerable area," said M'urgi. "Enormously larger than our encampment. You want them to drop the whole load here because we can destroy the whole load if they do?"

"Exactly!"

"How do you propose to get them to do that?"

Stubbornly, I repeated myself. "I don't know how, but somehow it has to happen. We're hoping they bring along many high-ranking members of their societies to watch us being slaughtered. We have to figure out how to make them do that."

Silence. Furtive looks, one to another.

"You mentioned the Quaatar?" Mar-agern murmured, staring at Margaret. "What was it we learned about the Quaatar, Margaret?"

Margaret rubbed her forehead, thinking. "They believe themselves and their language to be sacred. They consider it blasphemy for any non-Quaatar to speak their language. Also, all other races are considered to be food sources."

M'urgi asked, "Who would be doing the actually ghyrm-dropping? Themselves, or would they hire someone?"

Mr. Weathereye said, "There's no way of knowing who they plan to do the actual task of pushing the things out of the ships, but my guess is that most high-ranking Quaatar, Frossians, and K'Famir will want to see it."

"Yes, my friends and I thought that likely," I said. "Torturers like to watch; it's no fun if they can't see and hear what's happening."

"We know where they make the ghyrm," said Ella May. "On Cantardene. Should we ask the armorers to get one of the big machines onto Cantardene? And on Earth, just in case? And on every colony planet?"

"The big machines are later," I said. "I'm talking about now. Within the next few days, right, Weathereye?"

"They have to go to Cantardene, load, and return here. Within the next three or four days, yes."

A silence fell, broken by Falija, who yawned widely, licked her fangs, and said, "If the trick is to get all the high-ups on board, you'll need to insult them."

The tribesmen started, stared at Falija, then shouted, some of them half standing.

"Sit down," barked M'urgi. "Ah say dis is good luck. You heah? Dis is voice of good luck. You heah me!"

"What do you mean, insult them?" asked Margaret, when the tribesmen had subsided into sulky, shoulder-humped silence.

"Say something nasty to them in their own language," said Falija. "Margaret is right. It's blasphemy for another race to use the sacred Quaatar language; the K'Famir have a ritual language as well; and Mar-agern says she suffered the penalty for speaking Frossian to a

Frossian. Insult them in their own languages. It will make them very, very angry."

"She's right," cried Mar-agern. "Remember, Margaret, we studied Quaatar! I—we were almost the only ones who did, but we learned to read it and speak it!"

"I remember," said M'urgi. "Though it seems another life ago. What do we say to them, and how? Does anyone even know where they may be found?"

"On their home planets," offered Ella May.

"Too far, tactically impossible," I said.

No one said anything. I ground my teeth and told myself to be patient. "Think about it. We'll come back to it very soon."

Mar-agern turned to M'urgi. "There's a real mob outside."

M'urgi nodded, tiredly. "One tribe came, two others followed, four followed them. It turned into a horde. They're still arriving. Every group has one or two ghyrm-eaten ones. I've been killing ghyrm for days, but I had only one knife . . ."

"Open the packs," Ferni said. "There are a hundred knives. Give the knives to whoever can best use them."

"Everyone's getting off the subject," Margaret complained loudly. "What blasphemous message could we impart? Falija? Weathereye?"

Mr. Weathereye pursed his lips. "It doesn't need to be subtle. Something along the lines of 'The holy Quaatar people are a crock of shit' would probably do."

Margaret made a face. "I don't remember learning a word for excrement . . ."

Falija said, "*Umfa!,* with a click at the end. That's the Quaatar word for shit. It was in my mother-mind. Gentherans use it all the time, whenever they're talking about the Quaatar."

"While you're deciding that, I'll distribute those knives," said M'urgi, rising and leaving the tent. The tribesmen followed her, and Ferni followed them. I watched through the tent opening as the sheathed knives were distributed, carefully, with many warnings.

Ella May came over to me, saying, "It's possible the Quaatar have some kind of sensors planted here. If not them, then one of the others in the cabal. They've been looking for Margarets. They might have some kind of spy eye around nearby, something they would pick up an insult through . . ."

I turned, alerted by this new possibility. "There's detection gear in the red pack. Use it if you like."

"We two can work on the message," said Mar-agern to Margaret.

"Short, simple, and insulting," said Falija.

"I don't know any way to be useful," Gloriana whispered to Bamber Joy. "Do you?"

"Sure," he grinned. "Keep out of the way, don't whine, and be available if anyone needs a hand. I think we might also eat something, because breakfast was skimpy this morning, and we're growing . . . people."

Gloriana retrieved her pack from outside, and retreated with Falija and Bamber John to a back corner of the tent, where they made themselves comfortable on folded blankets while eating food they'd brought from Thairy. Nearby, Margaret and Mar-agern scribbled and crossed out and once, surprisingly, giggled.

"The blankets smell like hay," Gloriana said half sleepily. "Like the Howkel kitchen. It would be really nice to be finished with this and not have to worry if there's anything you didn't do or haven't done right."

"I think we're all going to be finished very soon," Bamber Joy said. "It feels like everything is coming to a close. It's a kind of sad, autumny feel, like when the last leaves come down, and you know that's it. No more life until spring."

Gloriana started to say something, then caught herself. I knew she had been wondering if spring would come, this time, even though all three of them sounded quite relaxed and sleepy about the whole thing. They were young. They hadn't had that many hard times, but I wasn't at all sure we were ready for the storm that was coming. There were too many ifs: if the machine worked; if the Quaatar people got angry enough; if they dropped the ghyrm only here instead of all over the planet; if the Siblinghood really got the big machines to them in time . . .

Margaret came over and sat down beside me. "Naumi," she said. "I want to thank you."

"For what?" I sat up, astonished.

She frowned, shook her head. "Confession, Naumi. I once let someone do something for me that was against his own best interest. I've spent my life since trying to atone for that. I've been ashamed. Rueful. All my life." She looked up, shook her head. "There've been joyful moments, sure, but in the main, rueful says it.

"And then I met Mar-agern. She's me. She's lived a totally different life, but she's me. And M'urgi, and Ongamar, and you. They're your lives, but they're mine, too. I . . . isn't it weird we all think of as ourselves as me . . . Well, Margaret's identity has not been as unworthy as I always rued it being. And I have you and the others to thank for it."

I took her hand. It was my hand. I knew that hand.

"You're welcome," I said.

I Am Gretamara/on Tercis

On Tercis, the Gardener preceded Wilvia and me, Greta-mara, out of the way-gate and onto a sloping forest floor. Gardener led us slowly downward, stopping momentarily to say, "The outgoing sister to the gate we just used is up there, between those two rocks." She pointed to her left toward another group of stones. "It goes to Fajnard."

"Where are we going?" asked Wilvia.

"Down the hill to the home of Margaret Mackey."

The way was not long. We arrived before a small house, set among the trees, the far side of it looking out across a rocky shelf into great distances of valley and hills. The door of the house was broken.

"Beasts," snarled the Gardener. "Let's see what dam-age they have done!"

I thought it looked even worse than the great house in Bray had looked. Inside, belongings were strewn about, cupboards were open, doors half off their hinges, the bed ripped apart. "What were they looking for?"

"Nothing. They didn't find the woman they were look-ing for, or the Gibbekot they thought would lead them to her. They destroyed out of the spite that was built into them by their designers. It is an old viciousness not un-known to humans: 'If you can't prevail, destroy.'"

"We can set it in order," I said firmly. "Will we be stay-ing here?"

"Only briefly," said the Gardener, looking through the stores in the tiny kitchen. "There is food here enough for several days. Show no light at night. Margaret's daughter lives just down the hill, but the house is empty now, for the families who lived on outlying farms are staying in Crossroads to be safer. The hunters went through the valley like a scythe, and they badly frightened the people here."

Wilvia asked, "Margaret's family? Do they know she is gone?"

"They know she and two children went off into the woods before the happening. They are concerned, but not terribly worried. Perhaps Margaret will be back before they have time to be anxious."

"And we?" I asked.

"For the moment, you stay here. Wilvia, if anyone comes near, take off your diadem. If anyone approaches, say you are Margaret's cousin. You arrived after the damage was done, and you have your daughter staying with you to help. Meantime, I must make sure that several other people arrive here very shortly. The Gentherans expect it of me, and of themselves."

I went outside with her and stood on the rocky shelf that overlooked the valley. Only peace. Far down the road, a buggy. Someone going home to a farm to feed the animals and to be sure they had water. There was no sign that the hunters were still here.

The Gardener read my thoughts. "Likely they are assembling near B'yurngrad, where all the other Margarets are together, making an easy target. Farewell, but only briefly, Gretamara." She walked into the woods, dissolving herself onto a shining road that led to B'yurngrad.

I Am Naumi/on B'yurngrad

After I, Naumi, had done everything possible to help any-one needing help, I lay down in M'urgi's tent and closed my eyes. The world seemed to be spinning, and I could not convince myself it wasn't, or that time wouldn't stop, or that we all wouldn't die . . .

Falija, who had been lying between Bamber Joy and Gloriana, suddenly sat up and made a loud, spitting noise of annoyance.

"What?" demanded Gloriana loudly.

I opened my eyes and listened.

"We don't need to insult the Quaatar directly," said Falija. "We just need to let the Quaatar think they've been insulted."

Bamber Joy yawned. "Is it any easier to do that than to actually insult them?"

"Of course," said Falija. "All anyone has to do is go somewhere frequented by K'Famir or Frossians—or Quaatar, though that's harder, because they don't usually associate with other races—and tell someone, loudly, that he or she was recently on B'yurngrad and there was a great meeting of Earthians and Gentherans who were insulting the Quaatar in Quaatarian. We can throw in the Frossians and the K'Famir at the same time. We need someone who isn't either Earthian or Quaatarian to do it, of course . . ."

"I'll go get Grandma," said Gloriana.

I sat up, still tired, but interested. Margaret returned with Gloriana and Mr. Weathereye. One might have known!

"Interesting," he murmured. "We need only let them overhear someone saying that Gentherans and Earthians on B'yurngrad are assembled in one place insulting the Quaatar."

"The person saying it can't be human," insisted Falija.

"How about someone like a K'Vasti?" asked Mr. Weathereye, with a peculiar smile. "Who heard it from a Hrass? Thank you, Falija. That is completely doable."

They told me later the place they picked was Gilfras Station, the same nonplanetary transshipment point that Ferni and I had used as a rendezvous not long before. K'Famir and Frossians were numerous there, as were a dozen other races, including the inevitable Hrass, huddled in small groups in corners, trying to be inconspicuous. One of them, however, was accompanied at his table by a loud, drunken K'Vasti, who shouted, "What do you mean, all the Gentherans were talking Quaatar. Nobody talks Quaatar."

The Hrass murmured unintelligibly.

The K'Vasti bellowed, "Called the Quaatar *umfa!* I don't understand that."

The Hrass murmured, gesturing.

The K'Vasti brayed with laughter. "Oh, that's a good one. Gentherans and Earthians, having a contest on B'yurngrad to see who can write the most insulting poems about the Quaatar in Quaatarian!"

The Hrassian leaned forward, saying something urgent.

"Not only the Quaatar? Insults in Frossian and K'Famir as well. Ha. Where's this contest being held?"

The Hrass murmured, swinging its nose in what might be presumed to be laughter.

"At a tribal camp northwest of Black Mountain? Out in the wilderness. Guess they figured nobody would hear them out there . . . Whoops . . ." Abruptly the K'vasti rose to his feet and staggered off toward the toilets. While all eyes followed him, the Hrass, as was customary in his race, quietly slipped away. Seemingly the K'vasti had had far too much to drink, for he, too, did not return.

• • •

M'urgi and I sat wearily at the foot of a tree, looking off across the campgrounds when Mr. Weathereye returned in the company of a Hrass, who promptly took off her nose and emerged as Ongamar. "It's done," he said. "We put on the performance. I played the K'vasti. Ongamar played the Hrass. We were both totally believable in the roles."

"I've recruited bellowers to shout insults, just in case the insulted need convincing," said M'urgi in a weary voice. "What do we do now?"

"We wait," I said. I glared at Weathereye, who from my point of view had a lot to answer for. "You did say the word would travel rapidly?"

"You may rely on it, my boy," said Mr. Weathereye. "It's taken us almost a day to get back, so we did our little playlet that long ago. In half a day, the word was widespread among K'Famir and Frossians, and the first of them to hear of it would have been in touch with at least one Quaatar, if for no other reason than to enjoy Quaatar agitation. The moment even one Quaatar knew, all the Quaatar would know." Weathereye shifted a bit uncomfortably. "I do hope we're ready?"

"The machine's in the center of the camp, and we've checked the new calibrations," said M'urgi. "One of us is always beside it, an hour at a time so we don't risk falling asleep."

"I sent word to the Siblinghood," I said. "Told them we knew the origin of the ghyrm. The K'Famir have been ordering a lot of big weapons from Omniont space, and the Siblings intend to substitute our machines, remotely controlled, for several of theirs."

"How long will it take?"

"Some time. The machine isn't even finished yet," I replied, searching the skies above them. "What do you think they're doing right now?"

"The K'Famir, the Frossians, and the Quaatar? I think they're working themselves up into a killing rage," said Weathereye. "I think they have an interesting synergy going between themselves and their gods. They planned originally to test their ghyrm-drop quietly, without fanfare, hoping nobody much would notice until B'yurngrad was uninhabited, but if they're sufficiently insulted, they won't care who notices."

"It's a pity we have to have all this destruction," said M'urgi.

Weathereye nodded. "Oh, my dear lady, I do agree. From my own personal point of view, however, I'd prefer that humans not go extinct, and I know of no peaceful way to prevent it. That possibility is really a question for races like the Gentherans, who love complex ethical issues. When is it justified to kill or destroy? In self-defense, or never? I, of course, can only think what humans think, and I think we're justified in getting rid of ghyrm along with certain bacteria and viruses."

"Look there," said Naumi, pointing toward the sky. "There, a little east of south, fairly low. That's a ship."

"Go warn Mar-agern," said Mr. Weathereye. "And the tribes."

"There are lookouts," M'urgi said, not moving.

A mournful horn sounded from a nearby rise, a sound echoed almost immediately by dozens of others, from all directions. M'urgi sat up straight and closed her eyes. I knew she was sending herself to the place Mar-agern sat next to the machine, finger on the start button.

M'urgi sighed, relaxed, came back to herself. "Everyone's alert," she reported. "Mar-agern's ready."

M'urgi and I rose. The ship came toward us, four others descending into view behind, followed in turn by four more.

"They're huge," I breathed. "I've never seen anything that size! If they're full of cargo . . . full of ghyrm . . . no way we're going to be able to . . ."

"Nine of their biggest ones," said Mr. Weathereye in a faraway voice. "The ones they use for cargo shipments."

"Our people will need our help," I said, starting away down the hill, M'urgi trailing behind me, only to stop as we saw a red-robed women approaching.

"Naumi," she said. "M'urgi. What have you set up here? A trap?"

I had the very strong impression I had seen her somewhere before. "The dragonfly I dreamed about," I said abruptly to M'urgi. "The dragonfly. She was the pilot!"

"So I was," said the Gardener. "I bring you greetings from Gretamara, and Wilvia. They await you in Tercis. I ask again, what have you here? A trap?"

"We calculated it would be a trap," I confessed, suddenly convinced that I ought to tell her everything that was going on, without reservation. "We have a machine to kill ghyrm, and we thought if we could get them all dumped on top of us, we could wipe them out here. But look at those ships? If they're stuffed full of ghyrm, it will take too long . . . and the power source is limited. If they pour those things out, hour after hour, there won't be time. There's not even time to get word to the Siblinghood."

She looked up at the huge ships, her eyes veiled. "One never foresees everything," she said. "One can only do the best one can, with what one has to work with." She spoke over my shoulder, to Weathereye. "I came to tell you that the Gentherans have found the place on Chottem where a man named d'Lornschilde has been keeping the human children from which the ghyrm are made. They are being transshipped to colony planets as we speak. Also, they have found the ships he used to bring them to Chottem, and those are being destroyed."

M'urgi said, "Yesterday, I would have considered that to be good news! Before I saw that armada overhead . . ."

"Your plan must proceed," Gardener said to me. "I am told you did well as a tactician. I have faith in your plan."

"M'urgi, Naumi," said Mr. Weathereye. "You haven't met the Gardener. She is the one who has kept Wilvia safe, and she is a friend of Earthians and Gentherans. She has been in this business from the beginning."

"Then you know about the seven roads," I said.

"I do," she replied. "Which we'll soon be walking."

"Provided all goes well." M'urgi grimaced.

"Well or ill, still we must walk," said the Gardener. "It took us over a thousand years to find a sevenfold road that would exist for a little while in the now, the here! It took two hundred years to arrange the emergence of the walkers and another lifetime to prepare them. We have only hours to accomplish what it has taken over a millennium to arrange. Even if this world ends, we must walk."

The horns moaned again, more loudly. "Where did they get those horns?" I cried. "They sound like the end of the world."

"They're from old umoxen," M'urgi said. "The tribes find the bones and horns on the prairies, where an umox has died. The older the animal was when it died, the longer the horn and the more mournful the sounds are. Look! They're dropping cargo."

The ships were sowing seeds into the sky, dark specks that drifted downward. At the center of the encampment, something hummed briefly, faded to a drone, then to a hissing sound, like waves on a shore. Out on the prairie, tribesmen danced, waving their spears and insulting the Quaatar at the top of their lungs.

Thousands of the specks were drifting toward them, becoming visible as circles of pale tissue supported by radiating arms, the whole almost transparent, floating downward like tiny parachutes. Looking straight up, we could see the ghyrm dwindling into the distance. As the falling creatures passed an invisible line, the tissue darkened, the arms curled. When they were close enough to be seen in detail, the arms were shriveled, the disks of pale tissue were darkening. The last few dozen feet, the things crumpled and fell, littering the ground around us, unmistakably dead.

Out on the prairie, the tribesmen went on shouting, and I cursed my own stupidity!

"Tell some of them to pretend to die," I shouted. "I didn't think of it until just now. The Quaatar will stop dropping the ghyrm unless they can see some of us dying!"

M'urgi ran down the hill, spoke urgently to one of her messengers, who sped off. I, watching from the hill behind her, saw the message relayed to others who fled away in their turn, a spiderweb of messengers, radiating off into the chaos of the camps. A few men near the hill began to stagger, clutching first their throats, then their bellies, falling and writhing with arched backs and histrionic faces. A few more, not too many, then others, while some of the first played dead.

The ships turned in a wide swoop that brought them lower, and lower still. The sun faded behind the rain of ghyrm. I looked down to find I cast no shadow. Well, if I could not see the sun, likely the creatures in those ships couldn't see what was happening on the ground! I tried to estimate how many ghyrm were being dropped. Millions. Millions. "How many could they have had?" I cried to Mr. Weathereye. "Each of those, a human life?"

"Shipload after shipload of Earthian children, year after year," said the Gardener from behind me. "Plus we understand they've learned to clone them. We can't stay to see the end of this, however. It's time for you and the others to go. Round them up quickly. We go to Cantardene, then to Chottem, swiftly through a gate on Hell, and so to Tercis, where the others are waiting. It will take us less than an hour."

"Who?" I asked. "Who's going?"

"Everyone who came with you from Thairy, plus M'urgi," said Weathereye. "It's time. What we do, we must do now, while the road is open and the enemy fully occupied here."

We were fetched variously: M'urgi, reluctantly, from her station amid the battle, where she had been whispering orders to tribesmen; Mar-agern from her post outside the tent, weapon at the ready; Margaret from her seat by the fire in the tent where Bamber Joy, Falija, and Gloriana lay asleep. I found Ferni in the thick of the shouting, and dragged him away as he protested. Meantime Mr. Weathereye found Ella May and gave her certain instructions.

"No time for you to pack anything," the Gardener told M'urgi, who was reaching for her kit. "Bring weapons only." We joined the others, who were moving quietly through the clearing. One by one, we squeezed between the two big trees and lined up outside the shining gate, all of us keyed up, nervous, frightened, each of us trying desperately not to show it.

"The first stop is Cantardene," said the Gardener. "We may find no one at the Cantardene gate. Their ruling class is in those ships above. In case they've left a guard, Naumi, Ferni, and M'urgi should go first, armed and ready, the rest to follow."

We came out in the mausoleum on Cantardene, empty of any living thing. I heard voices from outside and went to look out over the slanting bulk of the huge door that rested on one corner and one hinge. Outside in the plaza, a few soldiers knelt at a gambling game beside the stone of sacrifice.

The Gardener came up beside me, pointed to the tall stone, and said, "That is empty, too. Whirling Cloud of Darkness-Eater of the Dead is elsewhere. Now the next gate. Cover your faces and walk slowly, for the floor is covered with charbic root."

We waded through the layer of powder, lifting our feet high and holding kerchiefs over our faces. We emerged into darkness. The Gardener said we were in the cellars of Bray, and only the light from the farther gate illuminated our way. Iron grilles were fastened, but the weapon Mar-agern carried broke the locks. The next way-gate took us to a steel room. We walked on a steel floor that rumbled to our footsteps, through the opposite gate and out behind a tangle of vines opening into a forest. Down the slope was a snug little house with smoke coming from its chimney.

"Home," said Margaret, her voice breaking. "Gloriana, Bamber Joy, it's home."

We Margarets Walk

I, Margaret, led the way down the hill, the others in a straggling line behind me. As we approached the house, I saw shattered fragments of my door piled to one side of the porch and a blanket hung where my door should have been. I shivered. The apple tree at the corner of the house was bare. Winter had come while I was away.

Gloriana pushed the blanket aside and called into the house. "It's me, Gloriana."

A glad outcry from inside startled us all. "Gloriana, is Bamber Joy with you?"

Bamber Joy cried, "Mother!" and thrust past Gloriana.

When Gloriana and I entered, we found the boy on his knees beside the couch, his head pressed to the woman's breast. Gloriana shifted from foot to foot nearby as the woman reached a hand toward her.

"Gloriana," she cried. "Oh, sweet, dear girl-child! Oh, poor thing, you haven't any idea who I am, do you? And you both look so much like Joziré, and so tall!" She turned to me, tears covering her face. "Are you the one of us who cared for them?"

"I'm Margaret," I faltered, momentarily witless with surprise. "I . . . I thought Gloriana was my granddaughter . . . adopted, that is . . . Bamber Joy, well, he was left with Abe Johnson . . ." My voice trailed off, and I simply stared. So Wilvia was Gloriana's mother. Which meant that I myself was Gloriana's mother?

"I had to leave them both," she said, tears still flowing down her face. "The Gentherans thought the children would be safer if separated, from one another and from me. The Thongal were paid by the Quaatar to wipe out the royal house, so they had to be hidden . . ."

"Then you're Wilvia," said Gloriana. "And you're my real mother? Which means Bamber Joy is my brother, and my grandmother was my real mother, sort of. And her daughter was my foster mother, sort of . . ." She turned to me. "Grandma, I thought it couldn't get any more confusing!" She stopped, seeing Gretamara for the first time. "Another Margaret?" she croaked. "That's all seven of you, isn't it?"

The new one introduced herself, and I saw Gloriana put on the concentrated expression she wore when she was determined to get something right. She was memorizing them, us. I did as she did, looking at each of us in turn. Gretamara was twentyish, very gentle-looking; Mar-agern and M'urgi looked to be in their early or mid thirties, both brown from the sun and very muscular.

Wilvia couldn't be mistaken for anyone else, not with that diadem, a little older yet. Naumi was about that same age, with wide shoulders and a strong jaw, and a deeply curved mouth. Then Ongamar, smaller and thinner than the others, appearing only slightly younger than I was myself. Some forty years' apparent difference between oldest and youngest (though one really shouldn't count Gretamara), and one of us male . . .

A shadow on the glass caught my eye. Through the window I saw Ferni standing in deep shadow on the porch, unseen by the others and wearing an expression I could not read. His eyes kept going from Wilvia to M'urgi and back again, like an avid cat watching two birds, unable to decide between them.

I turned to the Gardener, and demanded, "How did you do it? You are the one who did it, aren't you?"

She patted me on the shoulder. "The Gentherans did it, Margaret. As to how? Well, I can hypothesize: Say they picked a woman who had twins in the family. Twins in both families, as a matter of fact, father and mother. Suppose they encouraged the original fertilized egg to split, making two, and then again making four, and then again, making eight . . ."

"But there are only seven of her!" Gloriana said.

"One died," I said. "My mother had twins, on Mars. I was one. The other died. What, was she supposed to be a spare?"

The Gardener shook her head at me, and I flushed. "And, I suppose you're saying the other six were taken away, somewhere."

Falija said, "Where they could have grown up just as you did, Grandma, in mirror worlds that reflected everything in your world, each of them thinking she was Margaret, until one was nine, until three more were twelve, until the last three were twenty-two."

"How?" demanded Gloriana.

Gretamara answered. "It may have been in the same way I grew up, Gloriana. In a place that exists but is not real. In a world that may be observed and interacted with, but is not actual. A virtual world, as Earthians would call it, that ended for each of us when we entered a real one. In the end, there were seven real worlds: I was on Chottem; Naumi was on Thairy; Ongamar was on Cantardene; Mar-agern was on Fajnard; M'urgi was on B'yurngrad; and Margaret was on Tercis."

"And Wilvia?" Gloriana asked.

"Here and there," Wilvia herself said. "B'yurngrad first, then Fajnard, then other places, and finally, I was in Hell."

"That is one of the ways it could have happened," the Gardener said. "The how is less important than the why. It was done to save your people."

"Because we owe them a debt," said Falija very solemnly. "From long, long ago. Because humans don't have racial memories, and they need them very badly. And there's only one place in the universe where man's history can be found, and that's with the Keeper."

Mr. Weathereye, who had been leaning in the doorway, said, "We are told the Keeper is an observer, not a creator. It is eternal and omniscient but generally uninvolved; one who hates being bothered but enjoys puzzles and riddles. The last people to bother it were the Pthas, who came to the Keeper with a request. The Keeper honored their request, but then it put itself in a place where no one could bother it again unless one person could walk seven roads at once. It sounds childish in the saying, like a nursery rhyme. Just as nursery rhymes mean far more than the children who chant them know, this meant far more than it said. It was anything but childish in the doing.

"Twice before, the Siblinghood had found seven way-gates that made one road. Stars and their planets move, you know; they don't stay in the same relative positions forever. Consider the movements of billions of stars in a galaxy. Consider how difficult to find seven of them, well in advance, mind you, that will make the one configuration. The First Order of the Siblinghood tried, and most of them died in the attempt. The Second Order tried and was forestalled. Now, this hour, the Third Order of the Siblinghood makes the attempt once more. Here are the seven walkers who are one, and before this hour passes, they must walk the roads, find the Keeper, and ask it to give humans back the racial memory the Quaatar took from them when they were barely human."

"Now?" said Wilvia in weary but dignified disbelief.

"Now, while the vile races are preoccupied elsewhere," said the Gardener. "Before that machine runs out of power and they start thinking again about finding and killing you. We must not take an extra moment. Come now, just you seven and Falija. We must go back up the mountain to the way-gate into Fajnard. Mr. Weathereye is no doubt needed on B'yurngrad, and the rest of you must stay here."

We moved, though unwillingly. Wilvia and I seemed least disposed to go, I imagine for identical reasons. Each of us felt we had just returned home, to those who mattered most to us. As we went, I noticed Ferni still standing at the corner of the house behind us, staring after us as though his whole life were being torn away.

The Gardener walked among us. "I have something to tell you. Some of you may not return from this effort. If a choice were to be made among you, Margaret, how would you feel about that?"

I looked at her with disbelief. "You mean, some of us may end up dead."

"It's possible."

I laughed, shaking my head. "If you had asked me that a week ago, Gardener, I'd have said fine, so long as I don't have to go on ruing all the mistakes I've made."

"And now?"

"When I saw Wilvia's children and realized they weren't cursed, as mine had been, when I saw the others . . . I don't have to rue my life. Together, Margaret has not done badly."

"So you're no longer willing to die, to escape your regrets?"

"If you have to choose one to live, choose someone younger."

"And you, Ongamar?" the Gardener asked.

Ongamar whispered. "Oh, I've looked forward to forgetting what I've seen for such a long time . . . don't choose me to live, Gardener."

"And you, Mar-agern?"

"I have no thoughts on the matter. I've never thought of doing away with myself, but if a choice had to be made, I wouldn't be afraid . . ."

"And you, Naumi?"

He turned to stare at her. "I have wanted only a few things in my life, only one of them greatly. Since that is not to be, further life seems rather barren. There are others here who will live more happily than I."

"And you, Wilvia?"

Wilvia smiled. "My dearest wish . . . one of them, at least, has been granted. My husband and children were, are far more important to me than my own life. If Joziré were still alive, he'd have returned to me! And if he is truly gone, and I can save my children by letting them go, then I will let them go."

The Gardener whispered, "And you, my child, Gretamara?"

She looked up, far up, where the stars reached their light across the universe. "My life has always been in your hands, Gardener. I'm content to leave it there."

"And lastly, you, M'urgi?"

She replied truculently, "Well, don't expect me to march off to battle singing hymns of martyrdom! A few years ago, when life was smoke and dirt and desperate interventions that didn't work a lot of the time, I'd have been more willing. But lately? I have something to live for. I saw Ferni's face back there. He's waiting to see what happens . . ." She stopped, looked up, tears glinting at the corner of her eyes. "Even so, well, even so, if my death helps the human race . . . the shaman taught me to die."

We had arrived at the way-gate and the Gardener lined us up

while glancing at the horizon where the first faint light was show-ing. "We don't know how the Keeper will respond. It may refuse us. It may grant your request but take your lives in payment. Noth-ing of the little we have learned of the Keeper tells us it will do this, but it is a possibility. It may let all of you live, which is also a possibility, and if that is so, when this is over, we will have much to rejoice over."

I, Margaret, heard a sigh from someone, a deep breath from an-other, the slight shifting of our feet, but nothing more.

"Very well, one at a time: you, Margaret, go seven roads, and stop just inside the way-gate we just arrived through, up the hill, here on Tercis." She pointed up the hill, toward the black pool hidden in the forest. "You, Wilvia: six roads, stopping on the world where we found you, just inside the gate. You, Gretamara: five roads, stopping at Chot-tem, and you, Ongamar: four roads to Cantardene . . ."

"The K'Famir . . ." Ongamar said between clenched teeth.

Weathereye patted her shoulder. "The Siblinghood has warriors between every pair of gates. They will not stand aside for any but you seven."

Gardener continued. "M'urgi goes three roads to B'yurngrad; Naumi, two roads to Thairy; Mar-agern, one road to Fajnard, each of you stopping *inside* the gate. As the Third Order discovered, as Nau-mi's friend Caspor discovered, when the roads among these gates are shown in a particular two-dimensional plane, they make a seven-pointed star with a seven-sided space at its center. On star maps, that space is light-years in width and empty. We have reason to believe the interaction of the way-gates around it make the space much smaller than it looks.

"When you are each in your assigned gate, the center of that space will be to your left. I have seven timepieces here, to hang around your necks. When your timepiece says zero, you turn and walk to your left, through the side of the way-gate."

"And what will happen?" I, Gretamara, asked.

"I don't know," said the Gardener, extending her arms in a gesture of relinquishment. "Those of us who planned this and brought it to fruition believe someone will await you there, but this is a blind road with an unknown end."

Voices murmured a response. The Gardener put the timepieces around our necks. Gretamara reached up to kiss the Gardener's cheek. Ongamar pulled herself erect, and said, "I walk for an end to pain and an end to Cantardene."

M'urgi cried, "If I don't return, give my love to Ferni . . ."

Naumi murmured, "Same message, to the same recipient."

"Enough poignancy," said Mar-agern. "This new brain of mine is equipped with all sorts of hope. Farewell for now."

We went into the pool, I first, since I had the farthest to go. Light and dark, light and dark, counting, being sure I went six gates. Behind me always a quivering surface, shimmering with something that was not light. It might as well have been the sound of dry leaves rubbing together, or the feel of a draft under a door, the smell of old ice, the rasp of a file on the skin of my hand, any sensation or none. At last, the exit to Tercis was ahead of me.

I turned to my left and checked the timepiece the Gardener had hung around my neck. The others would all be in place by now, all of them waiting for zero. I concentrated on breathing quietly until zero came. When it arrived, I stepped through the wall of the way-gate, then stepped again, the scintillating specks that pulsed around me fading with each step: fading, fading, gone. Ahead was nothingness, and I walked into it, wondering desperately if I would be able to keep a straight line.

After what seemed a considerable time, I heard someone calling "Margaret?" into the silence of the place. Naumi's voice, deeper than the others'. "Ongamar?" he called.

A sound, perhaps an answering voice. I started to go toward it, then stopped. Better just go on walking. After a while, he tried again, off to my left. "Margaret?"

"Over here," I called. "Should I come toward you?"

"No!" he said. "Not until we're all within sight of one another."

Calls came from left and right and we walked. The sounds came nearer. The nothing below our feet became something. A surface. I saw Gretamara emerging from a dark fog to my left, and beyond her, M'urgi. On my right, Naumi appeared, then Ongamar. Between M'urgi and Ongamar, two shadows came toward us, emerging as Mar-agern and Wilvia.

"Keep walking until we can touch one another," Naumi called.

We walked for what seemed a very long time. We could see one another, but the distance stayed the same. The floor seemed to roll away beneath us like a treadmill that welled up from some point in the center of their circle and flowed out continuously, keeping us in the same place.

M'urgi called, "Stand still a minute."

We did so, watching her. She stood very straight, concentrating, and a trail of light shot upward from her forehead, high above us all. I thought of her leaning upon the substance that fills the universe, which separates matter and transmits light and knows and remembers everything.

"Shut your eyes," M'urgi called. "Hold out your hands. We're right next to one another."

I reached out my hands, grasping at others I felt on either side, the three of us tugging and sidling as we connected with the rest.

"Now," cried M'urgi. "Open your eyes but hold on tight."

We stood in a circle only a few steps across. In the center, suspended in space, I saw a little creature, legs crossed, a book on its lap. Across the pages words ran endlessly from right to left, left to right, top to bottom, bottom to top, interweaving with one another.

At the same time I saw this, I saw what the others saw, just as I had used to sense as they did when they were part of me. M'urgi saw a pillar of fire, words of smoke pouring up through it. Naumi saw a tree, its roots extending into the depths beneath us, its higher branches beyond his sight above, and every leaf a journal. Wilvia saw a dragon with jeweled scales, each one engraved with a history. Ongamar saw a stone pillar reaching from the beginning to the end of the universe, with little beings swarming all over it, carving words. Mar-agern saw herds of creatures in a meadow, each of them reciting the story of a people. Gretamara saw an anthill, each ant carrying a grain of sand on which was engraved the chronicle of a living race.

I was the eldest. I swallowed deeply, and asked, "Are you the Keeper?"

It looked up from its book, out of the flame, out of the leaves, the dragon's eyes, the words on the stone, the meadow creatures, the anthill. "Think of it!" it said wonderingly. "One road is seven roads, walked simultaneously by one creature. How did you manage that?"

Wilvia smiled at the dragon charmingly. "Only through great sacrifice, Keeper."

"Patience," said M'urgi.

"Labor," said Mar-agern.

"And torment," Ongamar offered.

Naumi shook his head. "Only by doing our duty, but the how is not as important as the why, Keeper—"

"—which is to heal our people," interrupted Gretamara.

The little man hummed, the ants hummed, the tree hummed. "I have not been near creatures in a very long time. The rule is, one must have a bell and a gate, but I thought I'd made both very difficult indeed. Yet here you are. What have I to do with you? Who are you?"

"The human race," I said.

M'urgi added, "You have our history in your smoke."

"Oh, yes," it said, peering at us with myriad eyes. "You're not very old, and you're quite ignorant."

"We are imperfect," said Gretamara to the ants, who had flown together in a swarm before her. "We are lacking. We have no memory of what we were, and thus no reach toward what we may become. We desperately need to know our past, but in all the universe only the Keeper has the racial memory of mankind."

"That is true. I have the histories of every race, every kind, all the move-about, reproduce creatures, and also those of others that have lived without moving or creating. I have the secret lives of stones and the memories of stars. I have the initial impetus, the births of all galaxies, the deaths of a good many. I have millions of years of some races and a few moments of others. Their souls are here."

"Their souls?" faltered Ongamar. "Of every creature?"

"Is each of you a creature?" asked Keeper.

"That's a trick question," Naumi said quickly. "We couldn't have found you if we each were a separate creature. No, all of us are one creature."

"I know that," said Keeper. "All of you are human, and billions more are human, and all humans are one creature, sharing one soul. Yes. And one for birds, and one for the dinosaur . . ."

"One soul for the dinosaur?" asked Mar-agern. "Then one soul for the umoxen, as well?"

"Oh, an enormous, ramified soul for umox, going back to the very beginning of life on its planet. Umox arose from a star race that went before, as the soul of Bird arose from the soul of Dinosaur. The soul of the scurrying lizard inhabits every warm-blooded winged thing, the soul of the brachiating gibberer inhabits the soul of man, and the soul of great singers and sages inhabits the soul of umox and chitter-lain . . . Oh, yes. Keeper has seen this. Keeper has perceived it."

"But no . . . no soul for each of us?" asked Margaret.

The man turned his head, the tree turned a twig toward her, each leaf an eye that seemed to look into her heart.

"Each of you?" the Keeper asked. "One brief life of limited experience, barely informed? Full of false starts, marred by misinformation, rife with regret? Much given to embarrassment and sorrow, lit here and there, if you are lucky, with delight. Do you really want to spend an eternity being only that? What of the lives you've lived within your minds, and what of your other selves in other worlds? Each time you make a choice, your universe splits. One of you does one thing, one of you does the other. One of you goes on to fulfillment and joy, the other is mired in pain and anxiety, each in a separate world, but they are all you . . .

"All the fragments, all the sundered parts come here, melded then into a single me-ness with all possibilities realized, all pains endured, all joys delighted in, one mind containing all that it was and could have been or hoped to be or imagined itself to have been!

"You need not go back to fix it, Margaret. In some world, you did fix it! You need not go back to unsay it, Mar-agern. In some world, it was unsaid. Ongamar, in some life it was untouched. And when you are assembled, you will know it, in that everlasting instant . . ." Keeper paused, stared, as if dreaming.

"An everlasting instant?" whispered Naumi.

"That instant when the whole being that is you is aware of itself as a whole and dances together upon the green meadows of eternity in a dance that seems endless . . ."

"Only that instant?" asked Wilvia longingly.

"Long enough for you to *know*! Once you know, you know. Once you are complete, you are complete forever. And all that, every moment of every day of every lifetime, makes only one leaflet growing on the sprig of humanity. Still, that leaflet is one I keep forever . . ."

Everything became very still. All movement stopped. The Keeper swelled in size: "The Gentherans sent you here, did they not?"

"The Gentherans are our friends," said Gretamara.

"Keeper knows that. You are here because of them, and because my daughter, the Gardener, has espoused your cause. You are here because she and her friends conspired so that nature's laws might be broken without disobeying me. Ah, she is clever, my daughter. Wily, too. And now she sends you here, telling you what?"

"Telling us nothing," said Wilvia in her most queenly voice. "Except that we may die in the attempt. We have agreed to that, even if this plea is fruitless. It is a chance we took to benefit our people."

Keeper seemed to ponder this before replying. "Who is to say the memory of all mankind would work for you as you believe it will? What do other races think? Perhaps they would prefer you fade and die, becoming only a footnote in my journal. Who would speak for you?"

"We would," said someone outside the circle. Margaret looked over her shoulder. "Falija," she murmured.

"Falija," the little person affirmed. "Together with a number of our people, Keeper." She murmured their names as they came into view, a great many of them, gathering into a ring around the seven. "My parents, their Gibbekot and Gentheran friends, their friends of other races who have found humans to be worth the saving."

Naumi tried to see into the fog, but saw only shapes there. He heard a chittering, a birdsong, a bray that was half cow, half horse, the chatter of people.

Falija said, "My people have watched the human struggle for thousands of years. Without the means to be good, still they struggle to be so. Seeing such a struggle, any ethical and powerful race would do what could be done to ease it. Such a powerful race would say, 'Other races have a racial memory, can we not provide man with one of his own?'

"We could try. Still, no matter how much truth it might contain, the whole would be a lie. Should we ask a race to gamble its future on the basis of a lie? Only Keeper records only truth."

"True," said Keeper.

Falija went on, "In the great history of the Pthas we read of the delegation they sent to the Keeper. They found you, they spoke to you, you spoke to them. They asked a boon, you granted it. Will you do as much for Genthera?"

Keeper seemed to look elsewhere, into infinite distances. "Keeper might not will to do it for Humans, who are silly infants, meriting very little. Keeper might not do it for the Gibbekot or their Gentheran kin, for even they are not yet fully grown."

A sigh breathed through the circle, the tiniest moan.

"But," said Keeper, "Keeper would do it for umoxen, whose soul is far older than Genthera." He stared at Mar-agern, and Mar-agern returned the stare, astonished.

Keeper turned to M'urgi. "M'urgi, Keeper would do it for chitter-lain, whose ancestors moved among the stars a billion years ago. Ongamar, Keeper might do it for the humble Hrass. Naumi, Keeper might do it for the gammerfree, and Margaret, for the hayfolk Dame. And you, Wilvia and Gretamara, Keeper might do it for a Trajian juggler upon whom one took pity and the other avenged. Yes, all of them are older, and far wiser, than mankind.

"You were kind to their people," said Keeper, focusing on each of us in turn. "There will be a price to pay, of course, but Keeper is fond of their people, and so would be kind to your people."

Into the wordless and shocked silence, Wilvia spoke. "We thank you, Keeper."

The beings who had surrounded us had vanished, drawn backwards into the great wind that came all at once, loosening the grip of our seven pairs of hands and wrenching us apart. I, Margaret, felt them blown away into the howl of a black storm, bodies incapable of movement, wills paralyzed, minds in confusion, scraps of perception driven into an unimaginable otherwhere, each of us holding, only briefly, the same clear, perfectly accepted thought.

Well, this is death, but we have done what was to be done.

And yet I was still somewhere, with the Keeper, now in a shape I have tried since to remember and cannot. It spoke into my ear: "Don't forget what your father told your mother, Margaret. About what he was trying to do on Mars . . ."

"Father never really knew what would happen," I cried.

"No. The Scientist does not know the result until it happens. You are part of its workings. I am the record it keeps of what succeeds and will be used again and what fails and will be excluded forever . . ."

And then, only silence.

On the world called Shore by the people who lived there, and Hell by those who didn't, the people woke one morning with a strangeness in them. None of them rose from their beds. They just lay there very quietly, thinking.

"Did you know we were humans once?" said one to his mate.

"I didn't know it before," she said. "We were humans when we came here on the moon. Except it wasn't a moon. It was a starship, a Quaatar starship."

"Do you think we are human now?" he asked.

"I don't know," she said. "If we're not, why do we remember being? I remember we gave up living in trees . . ."

"I remember we killed Earth," he said.

"I remember we were going up the river soon to cut trees to make a new town and build many boats . . ."

"I remember we have to make room for more . . ."

Outside the house, some of the people were moving about. The town leader came out of her house and sat down on her stool, by the door. Each day the leader did this and the people came with their questions.

They gathered now.

The leader did not wait for questions. "Mika, Dao, Tinka. We have made a nasty at the creek. It smells bad. Nothing grows there. Dig a pit inside the forest, put all the nasty into the pit, and cover it with earth. In time it will feed trees. Choun, Bila, Fet, consult your minds and make a plan so no more nasty happens, then come tell me." The leader fell silent.

"Today we plan to go upriver and make a new town," said one of them. "We will cut trees to make room for more?"

"Not today," said the leader. "Today we count people. Today we count how many trees each person uses every year. Today we count fishes for each person, mollusks for each person, freshwater for drinking. Today we begin to learn how many people can live on this world without ruining it."

"What shall the rest of us do?" someone asked helplessly.

"Today," the leader said, *"you all stop making room for more and take time to remember."*

On Tercis, the Gardener waited, her head bowed. Falija had gone. Time stretched thin, the sound of its tenuity becoming intolerably shrill. No one returned. At last, with a shuddering sigh, the Gardener entered the way-gate before her.

On Fajnard, she found the Siblings guarding the way-gate. "All quiet, ma'am," they reported.

"Come with me," she said.

On Thairy there were other Siblings to join the group, and again on B'yurngrad, Cantardene, and Chottem. They stepped into the last gate but one and emerged into the buried starship on the planet called Hell. A naked woman lay on the metal floor, faceup, hands folded upon her breast. Gardener squatted beside the body, laying her long hands on the woman's face and neck.

"Who is it?" whispered one of the Siblings.

Gardener shook her head. "I don't know. I've never seen her before, but whoever she is, she's alive."

One of the strong Sibling warriors, Sister Ella May Judson, stepped forward to throw her cape across the person before lifting her in her arms. Together they went through the last gate, back to Tercis.

"Will you stay here, Gardener?" Ella May asked. "I was born in this place, and there is a house nearby you can use."

The Gardener said, "We've already been to the house, Ella May, and people are waiting for us there. Carry her for me if you will."

Ella May murmured, "It is Margaret's house, my Grandmother's house. I will stay with you, Gardener. You will need someone to fetch and carry, and I know Rueful."

"That would be a kindness. Thank you, Ella May." She turned to the other Siblings. "The rest of you may return to your own places, with my thanks."

Ella May carried the woman's body down through the woods, and from below them, someone called, "They're coming."

Bamber Joy and Gloriana were awaiting them on the porch, as was

Ferni, sitting on the step, staring at Ella May and her burden, his face wet with tears.

Gloriana cried, "Is that you, Ella May! Who's that you're carrying?"

The Gardener replied, "Gloriana, we don't know."

Ella May laid the quiet body on the couch.

Bamber looked at the face somberly. "Not our mother, Glory. Not Grandma, either."

"I think . . . I think it does look a little like Queen Wilvia," Glory said. "And a little like Grandma, too. From those pictures we have of her, when she was a lot younger."

Ferni had come in from outside. Now he spoke in a lost, weary voice. "Is there something of M'urgi there. Something of Naumi?"

"Both, I think," said Glory. "Did the Keeper put her back together?" She turned to the Gardener. "Is that what happened? You never mentioned that!"

"No," the Gardener confessed, with a low, self-mocking laugh. "With all our thought, all our planning, we never thought of that. We recited the old stories, over and over, 'Seven makes one, seven makes one,' each time thinking of the road, never considering the walkers."

She knelt by the couch, searching the face before her for Gretamara. This woman was older than Gretamara, though much younger than Margaret. She had lines of pain in her face, as Ongamar had had, though not as deep. Her hands were hard and strong, as Mar-agern's had been. The mouth . . . Naumi's mouth, and M'urgi's. The skin was not as dark as Mar-agern's, but darker than Gretamara's. The hair was longer than Mar-agern's, shorter than Wilvia's, but she had Wilvia's eyes . . . which had just opened.

"You're awake," cried Glory.

The woman turned her head. "Gloriana," she whispered. "And Bamber Joy. My . . . our children."

"Gretamara," said the Gardener.

"Gardener," she said.

"Grandma," said Ella May, with certainty.

"Why . . . Ella May. How strong and well you look, my dear."

"Naumi?" said Ferni. "Naumi?"

"Oh, damn, Ferni. Yes, I'm here!"

"M'urgi? Wilvia?" he whispered.

But her eyelids had closed, and she slept.

"Well," said the Gardener, rising to her feet. "I wonder if Keeper did anything besides reuniting Margaret."

"Oh," cried Glory. "You don't know. Well then, you must not be . . ."

"Not be what, child?"

"Human," said Bamber Joy. "You must not be human, or you would know!"

"Just tell me what it is I should know!"

Bamber Joy said, "Just a few moments ago. Something happened. We all know things now. Things we never really knew before."

"It worked!" the Gardener said, marveling. "It really worked? I hadn't stopped to consult my source." She closed her eyes, after a moment opening them once more to beam at them.

Gloriana smiled at her, a bit tremulously. "It really did, Gardener. And we're all just the way Falija was when she got her mother-mind. We're all itchy and uncomfortable, because our heads are too full, and it's like trying to find our way around a strange house that has too many rooms with too many doors in it."

Ferni said, "Forgive me, Gardener, but is it true? You're not human?"

"Oh, Fernwold, of course not!" she said with some acerbity. "I am not human, and my colleagues are not human. We wonder at ourselves, coalesced, as we are, out of human hope and need and pain. We see, we speak, we are seen, we are heard, yet every thought, sight, word has been created for us by others. We have no creativity; we have no imagination; and yet we seem both creative and imaginative because we have such a vast grab bag of ideas and dreams to draw from. Each thought, plan, idea, notion is like a piece in an enormous jigsaw puzzle. At the end of time, they will all fit together to make a picture of mankind we have no conception of . . ." She stood up.

"In the meantime, we seem to have power, if it is only the power to take an idea from one mind and plant it in another, as a bird takes a fruit from a far, lone tree and lets fall a seed in quite another place. Old gods sometimes do that in their retirement. They become galactic social workers, self-appointed do-gooders."

Falija said from the doorway, "But that's only a lesser part of the truth, Gardener, because you can do things the other gods can't do. They can't move a material thing, but you can and do. You're Pthas, aren't you?"

Gardener looked up, for a moment seeming larger and older than she had ever looked before. "Why, how very perceptive of you, Gibbekotkin! Yes. I am Pthas. As is Weathereye, and Lady Badness, and a few more. The boon we asked of the Keeper just before most of us left this galaxy to go on to another, was that some of us be allowed to stay on, to take a new form and help others who need help. We had long contended against vile races, vile ideas, and we thought our experience would be valuable. The vile races we contended against are long gone. The vile ideas seem to be immortal."

Falija said, "The Keeper called you its daughter. And being Pthas would explain a lot of things, like how you knew about the Keeper. The Gentherans will be interested in that!"

Ferni had been sitting quietly in the corner, his eyes fixed on the woman they had brought from the gate, who was now struggling to sit up, staring wildly at him, and whispering, "Is that you, Joziré?"

"Yes he is," said the Gardener. "Though he still does not know it. Lady Nepenthe has moved in and out of his life several times, but there will be time to talk of that later."

Ferni almost growled, then stood very tall and demanded, "One thing will not wait until later! What's happened on B'yurngrad?"

Gardener was startled. "I don't know. Mr. Weathereye went back to see the end . . ."

"I did see it," said Mr. Weathereye.

They turned to see him leaning in the doorway. "The three races continued dropping ghyrm," he rumbled. "More and more of them at a time. They had unlimited numbers of them aboard, and the persons on the ships were drunk with destruction. It seems Naumi and his talk road had had what Caspor calls 'a hunch.' They had changed the calibration of the instrument so that it covered less surface area but reached much, much higher. The ships came lower and lower, so they could watch the carnage below them, oh, so well acted by the tribesmen, who writhed and twisted and screamed, then crawled away, recovering only to die again. They have a talent for dramatics, those men, born, I should think, from many generations of braggadocio around the campfires . . ."

"What happened?" shouted Ferni.

"We watched the ships drop down, watched the gauge on the fuel cell of the machine, dropping as the ships did, almost reaching zero, and just as the machine approached the end of its power, the ships themselves dropped within range of it, and every ghyrm still on the ships died."

He heaved a great sigh. ". . . and not only the ghyrm."

"Not the tribes? The umoxen," we Margarets cried.

"Quite safe, lady. Not so, however, the K'Famir, the Frossians, the Quaatar on board the ships, for they died as their creatures died. You will remember the size of those ships? They were the ones the trading races use to carry huge cargoes plus huge numbers of crew and their families, and they were full to bursting with Frossians, K'Famir, and Quaatar who wanted to see us die. There might have been a million of them on those ships, the entire ruling class of three starfaring races. We had no idea they would do that . . ."

"We did," said I from my place on the couch. "Naumi did."

The Gardener peered at Weathereye. "But Ongamar thought they made the creatures out of human children!"

"They made them out of human pain," I said. "But it was themselves they put into the making! The tissue, the flesh, was most closely matched to human, in order to be able to attach to it, feed on it, but it wasn't the flesh that mattered! It was the bloodlust that moved them, and whatever will kill the ghyrm will kill those who made them as well." I lay back; my eyes closed; I heard them go on talking.

Gardener asked, "What has the Siblinghood done? They haven't started a war?"

Weathereye shook his head. "They had planned to ship a machine to Cantardene. Then the change happened, you know, the mother-mind thing. Everyone was very confused. When the confusion grew a little less, and when they saw what had happened on B'yurngrad, they decided not to do it. They've put the machines in storage."

The Gardener nodded. "Something in their history has moved them to patience. Wise leaders do not go to war with enemies, not even evil enemies, unless they have thought it through to the end."

Time went by on Tercis.

Gloriana and Bamber Joy went to Maybelle, Jimmy Joe, and Jeff, to tell them, and only them, what had happened. It took more than one telling, over considerable time, and once again Gloriana was accused of telling fairy tales. Despairing, Gloriana took Maybelle to visit the Margarets. Maybelle had tea with them, her, and they talked for hours. When Maybelle left, she still appeared confused and a bit teary, but she looked happier than when she had arrived.

Subsequently, in the Ruehouse in Crossroads, Pastor Grievy held a memorial service for Margaret Mackey, lost in the river while escaping from the bad men during the recent unpleasantness in The Valley. Gloriana and Bamber Joy had been unable to save her; but it gave them solace, they said, to dedicate the stone that was set in the cemetery, next to Dr. Mackey's, in her memory.

"And it's true, sort of," said Gloriana. "Our grandma is really gone."

The Allocation people on Tercis, following the acquisition of mother-mind and after lengthy consultation with the Gentherans, changed many of their assignment procedures. Most of those on Tercis had reacted to the acquisition of mother-memory with significant and positive personality changes, but some had proven to have a mental defect that made them impervious to history. Among the latter were Billy Ray and Mayleen, who together with Benny Paul, Janine Ruth, and Sue Elaine were moved to a new Walled-Off, created especially, as Jimmy Joe put it, "For them as are pigheaded, mule-stubborn, and thick as a post!" Jeff's brother, Til, was assigned to the same Walled-Off, with the understanding that he might receive, from time to time, a chance at reassignment. Trish was moved to a small Walled-Off created especially for people like her, where she could be contented and cared for.

Maybelle and Jimmy Joe agreed to foster Orvie John and little Emmaline while keeping their fingers crossed.

Ferni stayed on Tercis, spending much of his time with Margaret, though he didn't call her that. Or M'urgi. Or anything except you, or lady, or very occasionally, dear one.

Lady Badness dropped by one day and ran her hands over his head while the Margarets looked on.

"Who are you and where did you live your first twelve years?" she asked him in a chuckling voice.

"My name is Prince Joziré. I lived on Fajnard with my mother, the queen. We had to go into hiding. The Gardener took me, and also a girl named Wilvia. We went to B'yurngrad, to school . . ."

"And then where did you go?"

"To the academy, on Thairy. I forgot about Wilvia. Oh, how could I have . . ."

"Don't worry about it. How long were you there?"

"I was there for four years. I met my best friend there. His name was Naumi . . ."

"And then?"

"Then . . . I went to work for the Siblinghood, on B'yurngrad. That's where I met M'urgi . . . But they wouldn't let me stay there, I forgot about M'urgi, I forgot Naumi, I remembered my mother, and I remembered Wilvia, and we were married. We ruled the Ghoss together, for five years. We were expecting our first child, then the Thongal invaded at the behest of the Quaatar . . ."

"And then, after that?"

"I forgot about being the King of the Ghoss. I forgot Wilvia. I was taken into the Siblinghood, I went here and there, I found M'urgi again, and Naumi . . ."

I, Margaret, was crying very quietly while all this went on. After Lady Badness left, Ferni and I spent a great deal of time together.

Time went by on Cantardene.

Though bondslaves were still being imported onto the planet from Earth, the rituals atop Beelshi were no longer conducted, not there, not on any similar site elsewhere on the planet. No one was left alive who knew the procedures, the incantations, the purpose. The standing stones that had existed in all the sacred places began to fall to pieces. Beelshi itself was rumored to be a place of ill fortune, and no one went near the hill . . .

Except, that is, for Mr. Weathereye, who spent some time spying on a few surviving and exceptionally wealthy K'Famir. This surveillance eventually led him to the buried city of the Pthas. A short time later, Gentherans began arriving through the gate in the darkness of moonless nights, traveling to the buried city and taking away everything that could be taken—including all the K'Famir who had known where the place was—and burying the rest beyond finding again by any save themselves. After their final visit, they built an impenetrable wall inside the mausoleum, covering the door and joining the incoming to the outgoing gate for the lengthy time Caspor said this link of the one road would stay in place.

Time went by on B'yurngrad. The Siblinghood moved among the tribes in great numbers, pointing out the historical connections among death-and-honor religions. Those capable of understanding were let alone; those few who could not be reached went to the newly constructed Death-and-Honor Walled-Off on Tercis. Since Death-and-Honor religions were male inventions, almost entirely, so was the population male, almost entirely. So much had been learned from Tercis. For those impervious to history, only sterilization and quarantine are efficacious.

Inevitably, those among the tribes who knew the location of the great treasure hoard talked about it to someone who passed the knowledge on. This great trove, as well, was added to the wealth of the Siblinghood.

Time went by on Chottem.

Sophia summoned the people of Bray to a meeting and told them what d'Lornschilde had done. He was arrested, tried, and sentenced to be deprived of his tongue and sold into bondage in the mines of Cantardene. Saving aside some treasure to implement her own good works, Sophia added the balance of the riches of the House of Lorn to the wealth of the Siblinghood. Subsequently, Sophia met a very likeable young man of nonaristocratic family whose wooing she gently encouraged. When the leading families of Bray and Lorn looked askance, she did not seem to notice.

Time went by on Fajnard.

The Frossian underlings were touched by the same wave of ill fortune that had taken their leaders. The planet no longer appealed to them. The world was too slow, too uncertain, the umoxen were increasingly reluctant to be herded. One day, as if by prior agreement, the Frossians began leaving Fajnard, waves of them. On the day the last of them departed, the Ghoss returned to the lowlands, and the umox hum could be heard to the outer edges of the atmosphere.

Very soon thereafter, on the heights of Fajnard, a great reception was held for the King and Queen of the Ghoss, long separated from their people, now returned as though from the dead, both somewhat changed, but recognizable. As the couple waited for the fanfare that would summon them to the high dais of the Council Hall, the queen turned to her spouse, rearranged the lace collar that fell in delicate folds at the throat of his velvet jacket, and said, continuing a previous conversation, ". . . I don't think my adoration of you is at all strange. Three-sevenths of me loved you to distraction already."

"True," he said, eyes fixed, for some reason, on the curls of hair around the queen's ears. "Obviously, your very best parts."

The queen smiled and blushed.

Trumpets sounded in the Council Hall. Footsteps clattered far away, down the hallway. Ferni looked into nothingness and the queen followed his eyes, wondering what he was hoping to find there. Answers?

"I was thinking about that fleet of ships above B'yurngrad. When those aboard died, the ships went into automatic orbit, the Gentherans boarded them and sent them into the sun. Everyone on Quaatar, Cantardene, and among the Frossian worlds knew what they had set out to do, but none of them knew what happened. The Gentherans won't tell them. So far as the vile races are concerned, everyone who set out to kill off humanity simply vanished. When asked about it by inquisitive members of other races, those in the Siblinghood merely say, 'Well, of course. What did they expect?'"

The queen smiled. "So, we have become nemesis. Not a bad thing, on the whole. And all Flex's armaments? Where are they now?"

"Stored. Carefully stored. Now we all remember what armaments lead to. As the Gardener said, beginning a war is easy. Any fool could do it and frequently did, but all of us now remember the kind of messes that came after. Instead of going to war, everyone is waiting to see what the vile races will do. Mr. Weathereye says it's possible they'll just dwindle away."

The queen turned to catch a glimpse of herself in the tall, gold-framed mirrors that lined the wall. Light splintered in the jewels of her diadem, swept in glowing rays across her silken robes, became trapped in the incredible cape crafted from cloth of diamond, Sophia's gift from the cellars of Lorn. She was Queen of the Ghoss. "Will we rule perfectly, Joziré? Will our people work together in perfection and joy?"

"Madam," he said, taking my face between his hands, "we will do our damnedest!"

He started the kiss, but I refused to let it end. Holding Joziré wiped out all recollection of old regrets, pains, and sorrows. I could not be grateful enough for several lives' worth of experience cased in one body still capable of this particular delight ... And even these to be joined at the end, as the Keeper had told me.

The trumpets sounded again. We two stepped away from one another, faces flushed, fingers clinging, as ponderously, ceremoniously, the doors swung open. In the vaulted room beyond were the Gibbekot, the Gentherans, the Ghoss. Near the dais sat Falija, together with the Crown Prince and Crown Princess, Bamber Joy and Gloriana, who looked both determined and slightly embarrassed in their diadems and court dress. In the front row, by special invitation, were Maybelle, Jimmy Joe, Jeff, Ella May, and Sophia, with the young man she had decided to marry. Among the onlookers was a Trajian juggler with his wife; upon the rafters a flutter of chitterlain; in a corner, beside Howkel and his family, a scuttle of gammerfree. Peering through the wide-flung doors of the terrace, ranks of umoxen stood shoulder to shoulder, while upon the dais stood the Gardener, Mr. Weathereye, and Lady Badness.

Everyone present was there for the same reason. We were a cluster of organisms, experimentally working together to bring joy to Fajnard, hoping such joy could be become contagious and infect others beyond Fajnard, and perhaps, someday, spread to the middle of things and the edges of things. If not in this great experiment, then perhaps in the next one, or in the one after that . . .

The wide aisle to the dais was laid in soft, scarlet carpet. Upon the dais were two tall thrones. Smiling at one another and all those assembled, we rested our hand upon the hand of our love, and stepped forward into our lives.

SPEAK
AMERIC

*How
and Y

A Visu

SPEAKING AMERICAN*

*How Y'all, Youse, and You Guys Talk

A Visual Guide

JOSH KATZ

Houghton Mifflin Harcourt
Boston   New York   2016

For information about permission to reproduce selections from
this book, write to trade.permissions@hmhco.com or to
Permissions, Houghton Mifflin Harcourt Publishing Company,
3 Park Avenue, 19th Floor, New York, New York 10016.

www.hmhco.com

Library of Congress Cataloging-in-Publication Data is available.
ISBN 978-0-544-70339-1

The maps on pages 4–43, 52–87, 94–119, 127–165, and 173–193 draw on data collected in
response to surveys that included questions appearing in the Harvard Dialect Survey, by Bert
Vaux and Scott Golder (Harvard University Linguistics Department, 2003), among the topics
surveyed. The examples of terms for rain while the sun is shining are drawn from responses
compiled in Vaux's 1998 "Sunshower Summary."

All maps courtesy of the author

Book design by Stoltze Design

Printed in China
SCP 10 9 8 7 6 5 4 3 2 1

* To my mom, who always encouraged me to ask questions, and my dad, whose funny accent inspired my curiosity about language.

CONTENTS

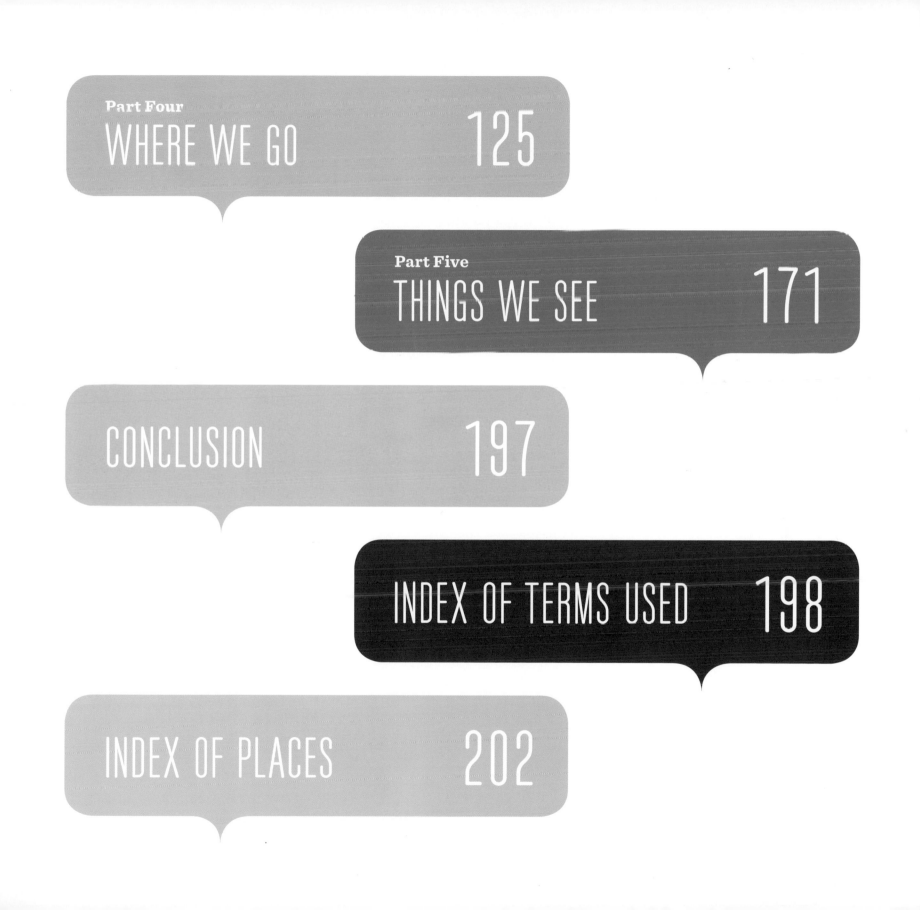

AUTHOR'S NOTE AND INTRODUCTION

Drawing on work from the *Dictionary of American Regional English*, the Harvard Dialect Survey, and suggestions from friends and family, in the fall of 2013 I set out to develop an online survey to gather data on how Americans talk. The maps that follow are a product of that survey—which collected more than 350,000 unique responses. Enjoy.

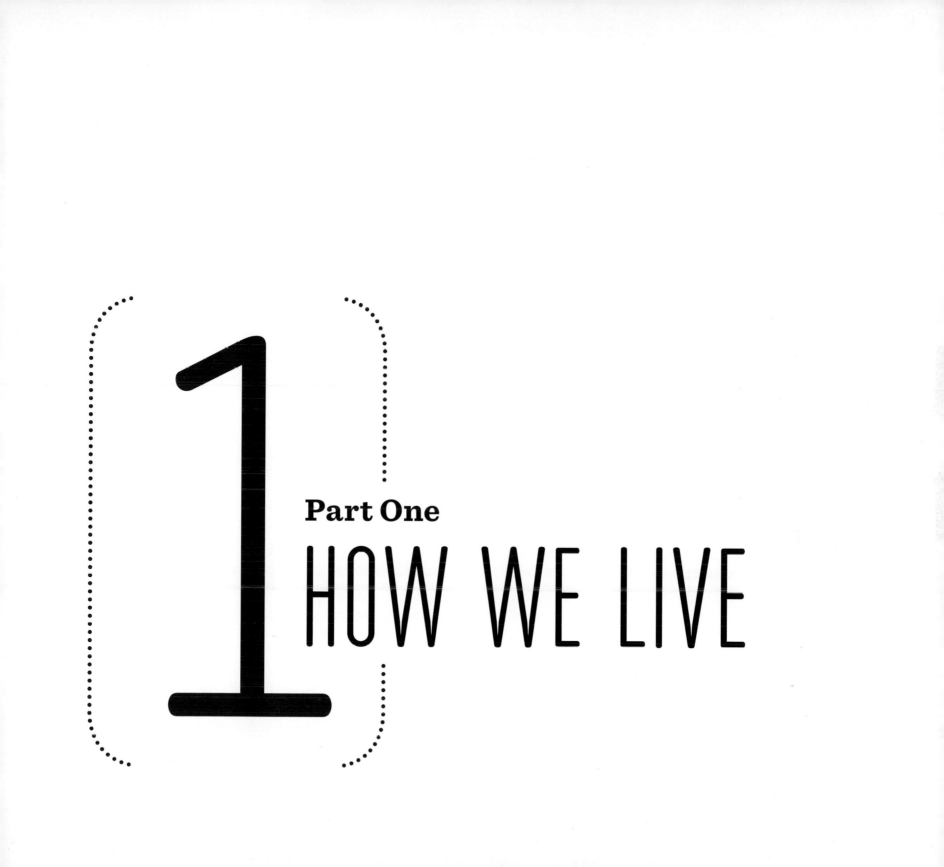

Part One
HOW WE LIVE

WHAT WE CALL

THE SHOES WE
WEAR TO THE GYM

It used to be that if you wanted something to wear on your feet, your only option was expensive handcrafted leather. But in the late nineteenth century, the assembly-line efficiency of the Industrial Revolution and the advent of new materials like vulcanized rubber gave rise to new, cheap, mass-produced footwear. Typically, it had canvas uppers and soft rubber soles.

What to call this newfangled footwear? People quickly began using them to play tennis, so why not *tennis shoes*? Makes sense. That was good enough for most of the country, but in Boston, for reasons lost to history, people thought: *Hey, I can really sneak around in these things; let's call them* sneakers. And from the shoes' rubber, or gum, soles, we also got the word *gumshoe,* which didn't take hold as a name for the shoe but came to be associated with skulking about. Now it's common slang for a detective.

TENNIS SHOES

As with many of the words in this book, no one can quite agree on who invented the term *sneakers* first, but it's been around since at least 1887, when the *Boston Journal of Education* wryly observed, "It is only the harassed schoolmaster who can fully appreciate the pertinency of the name." A few years later, an ad for the Boston-based department store Jordan Marsh was published, hawking its *sneakers* for 50 cents a pop. By the early twentieth century, *sneakers* had gone mainstream.

Perhaps surprisingly, given the word's dominance in popular media, the common use of *sneakers* fades rapidly today once you're outside the Northeast. What's more, *tennis shoes* shows no sign of abating, with teenagers using the word just as often as those in their sixties and older.

Other popular names include *gym shoes* (Chicago and Cincinnati), *running shoes* (parts of California), or just plain old *shoes* (Hawaii).

CHICAGO and **CINCINNATI** are the two places where majorities would instead don *gym shoes*.

SNEAKERS

Out in the mountains between **PHILADELPHIA** and **PITTSBURGH**, *sneakers* suddenly gives way to *tennis shoes*.

ATLANTA and **RALEIGH**, while still firmly in *tennis shoes* territory, are more partial to *sneakers* than the surrounding region. This dynamic is common, with many urban centers showing slightly different language patterns than their exurbs.

WHAT WE CALL

A SALE OF ASSORTED HOUSEHOLD ITEMS

Most of the country is split between *garage sale* and *yard sale*, with *garage sale* reaching its peak out in **OKLAHOMA** and **KANSAS** and *yard sale* peaking in eastern **NEW ENGLAND** and **NORTH CAROLINA**.

RUMMAGE SALE

TAG SALE

GARAGE SALE

YARD SALE

MANHATTAN

QUEENS

BROOKLYN

TRENTON

NEW HAVEN

The *tag sale* is unique to **CONNECTICUT** and western **MASSACHUSETTS**.

LONG ISLAND

The **NEW YORK TRI-STATE AREA** changes from *tag sales* in **CONNECTICUT** to *garage sales* in **NORTH JERSEY** to *yard sales* in **SOUTH JERSEY** and **PHILADELPHIA**.

As you drive along the turnpike into **SOUTH JERSEY**, *garage sales* transition abruptly into *yard sales*.

HARTFORD

NEW HAVEN

TAG SALE: WELCOME TO CONNECTICUT

The *tag sale* is unique to Connecticut and western Massachusetts. It's almost never encountered west of the Hudson and is rarely heard within New York City. It's one of the few dialectology tidbits that Connecticut can call its own—not from wider New England and not from New York.

The origin of the term is fairly straightforward. "You aren't selling your garage, are you?" as one commentator put it during an online debate over language use. "You aren't selling your yard. It's a tag sale. You sell the things that are tagged." To which someone might reply that you aren't selling the tags either, but as a general rule, it's best to avoid wading into the comments.

While Merriam-Webster says the first known use of *tag sale* occurred in 1929, an earlier sense of *tag sale* developed around the beginning of the twentieth century. At that time, a *tag sale* was a specific kind of fundraising effort in which your donation came in the purchase of a tag to show that you'd donated.

PERCENT SAYING *TAG SALE*

| 0 | 10 | 20 | 30 | 40 | >50% |

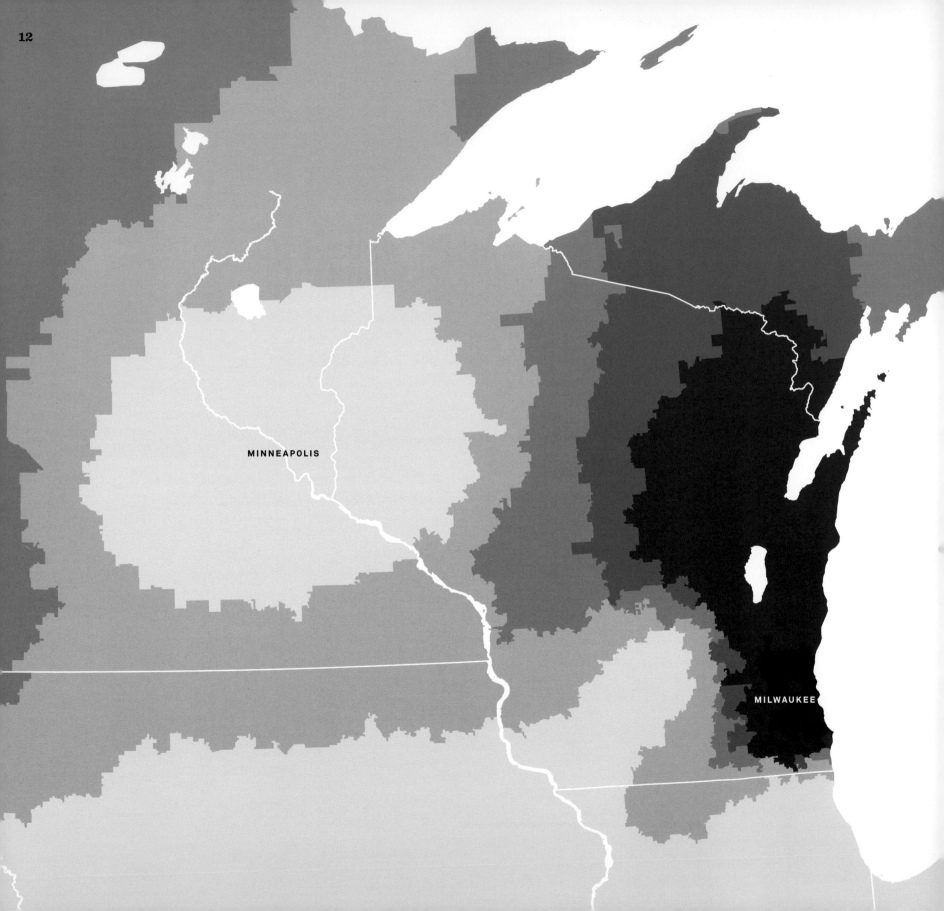

MINNEAPOLIS

MILWAUKEE

RUMMAGE SALE

The residents of southeast Wisconsin see the whole *yard sale* vs. *garage sale* dispute as a moot point. To them, the event is most certainly a *rummage sale*. Which seems like poor branding: *rummage sale* can evoke a big pile of junk and might just sound to a non-Wisconsinite like a random-stuff-I-found in my-attic sale. But it works for Wisconsin.

The term can be traced all the way back to the sixteenth century, when *rummage* entered English from the French *arrumage,* meaning arrangement of cargo. The word originally referred specifically to arranging cargo on a ship, hence the term *rummage sale* cropped up in the early 1800s to mean a sale of unclaimed goods at the docks.

PERCENT SAYING *RUMMAGE SALE*

| 0 | 10 | 20 | 30 | 40 | >50% |

HUGE STOOP SALE
/83 AMITY

STOOP SALE:
THE HISTORY OF A NEW YORK INSTITUTION

New York has much to offer: world-class food, art, and nightlife, but when it comes to front yards, not so much. Nor, for that matter, are garages commonly encountered in a city where space is at a premium and a second bedroom is a luxury item. But New York does have an abundance of stoops—those staircases leading up from the street to the entrances of row houses and brownstones.

In the eighteenth century, the influence of the Dutch over their former colony remained strong, and the Dutch word *stoep*—meaning a flight of stairs, though also used in the sense of a small porch with seats or benches—had entered the American lexicon as *stoop* by 1755.

Some argue that the ubiquity of stoops in New York is itself a byproduct of the Dutch proclivity for building elevated houses; others, that the stoop functioned to separate the formal entryway to the home from the entrance to the kitchen and other service offices, which were usually kept just below street level.

Regardless, the stoop plays a central role in city life—it is a meeting place, an observation deck, a buffer between the home and the commotion of the streets. And it provides prime real estate for the aptly named *stoop sale,* a term confined almost entirely to New York City.

MANHATTAN

JERSEY CITY

QUEENS

BROOKLYN

PERCENT SAYING *STOOP SALE*

0   2   4   6   8   >10%

16

AMERICANS ARE DIVIDED OVER LAWN CARE

PERCENT SAYING

0   10   20   30   40   50   75%

MOW THE LAWN 70%

CUT THE GRASS 20%

MOW THE GRASS 9%

FRYING PAN

OUT OF THE FRYING PAN, INTO THE SKILLET

Almost three-quarters of people from **LITTLE ROCK**, **ARKANSAS**, say *skillet*—the highest concentration in the country. With 73 percent of its residents using *skillet*, it's the place you're most likely to hear it, while only 10 percent of people in and around **NEW YORK** and **NORTH JERSEY** use the term.

PAPER THAT HAS ALREADY BEEN WRITTEN ON

The residents of **DES MOINES** are champions of fine semantic distinctions. Nearly 40 percent of them contend that *scrap paper* be reserved for paper that's no longer usable, while *scratch paper* can still be used for, say, note-taking or solving a tricky math problem. (As an aside, the proper demonym for Des Moines remains, as of this writing, an unsettled question: Des Moinesians? Des Moineseres? Des Moineserians? The world wants to know.)

SCRATCH PAPER

SCRAP PAPER

WHERE WE THROW OUR TRASH

Since the 1950s, *trash can* has become increasingly common in American speech. Two in three people born in the 1990s would say *trash can* over *garbage can*.

PERCENT SAYING, BY BIRTH YEAR

67% *TRASH CAN*

60%

40

20

16% *GARBAGE CAN*

14% *TRASH CAN* AND *GARBAGE CAN* REFER TO DIFFERENT THINGS

1950   Birth Year   1995

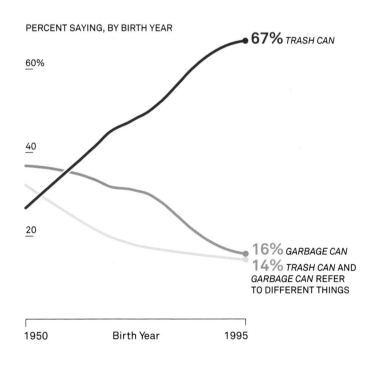

GARBAGE CAN

TRASH CAN

BLESS YOU 73%

PERCENT SAYING

0 10 20 30 40 50 75%

PERCENT SAYING

	BLESS YOU	GESUNDHEIT	NOTHING
WOMEN	83%	13	4
MEN	73	17	9

GESUNDHEIT 18%

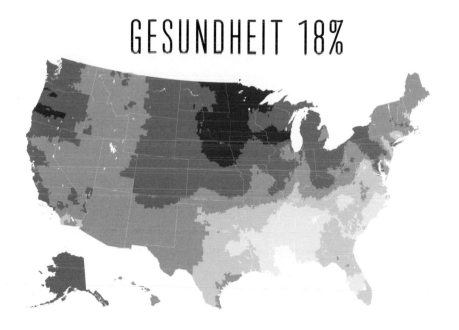

NOTHING 6%

A QUESTION OF ETIQUETTE

The practice of offering a comment after a sneeze is almost universal. It extends across a wide range of cultures and languages, from Hindi to Czech to Hebrew. In the Western world, it appears in ancient writings as far back as A.D. 77.

The adoption of the German *gesundheit* (health) began in the early twentieth century amidst an influx of German- and Yiddish-speaking immigrants. It became especially common in Wisconsin and Minnesota, home to large German populations. But its popularity has waned over time—you're now far more likely to hear some variation of *bless you,* even in the upper Midwest.

The post-sneeze remark is also one of the few areas of terminology where gender differences exist, with men slightly more likely to say *gesundheit* than women—and more than twice as likely to say nothing at all.

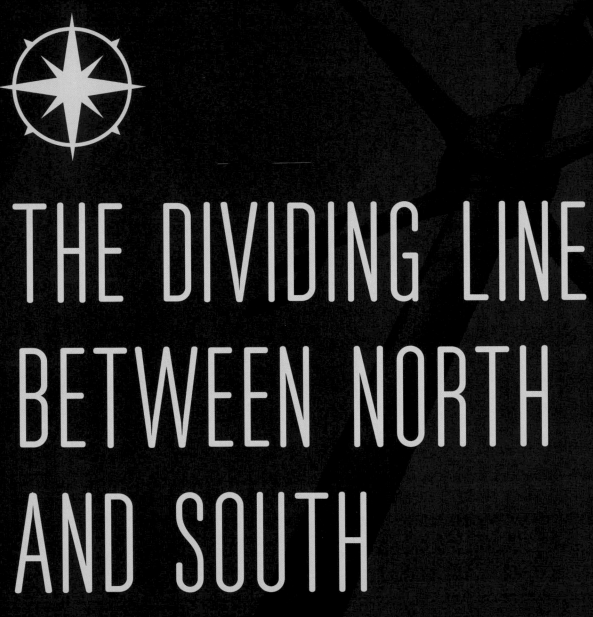

THE DIVIDING LINE BETWEEN NORTH AND SOUTH

Almost 30 percent of people in **PITTSBURGH** and its surroundings would say *yins*.

YOU GUYS

Y'ALL

In **KENTUCKY** it's *you all*.

Nineteenth-century migration in the United States was primarily a tale of westward expansion. As settlers moved west, they carried their culture—and their language—with them. Thus the divisions seen on the East Coast perpetuated themselves westward, as people from different parts of the East moved to different parts of the West. A linguistic fault line runs from Texas up through Arkansas, then tracks the Ohio River along the northern border of Kentucky toward the Mason-Dixon Line.

One of the clearest expressions of this fault line is the boundary between where they say *you guys* and where they say *y'all*.

YOU GUYS 50%

Y'ALL 28%

YOU ALL 10%

YOU 10%

YINS <1%

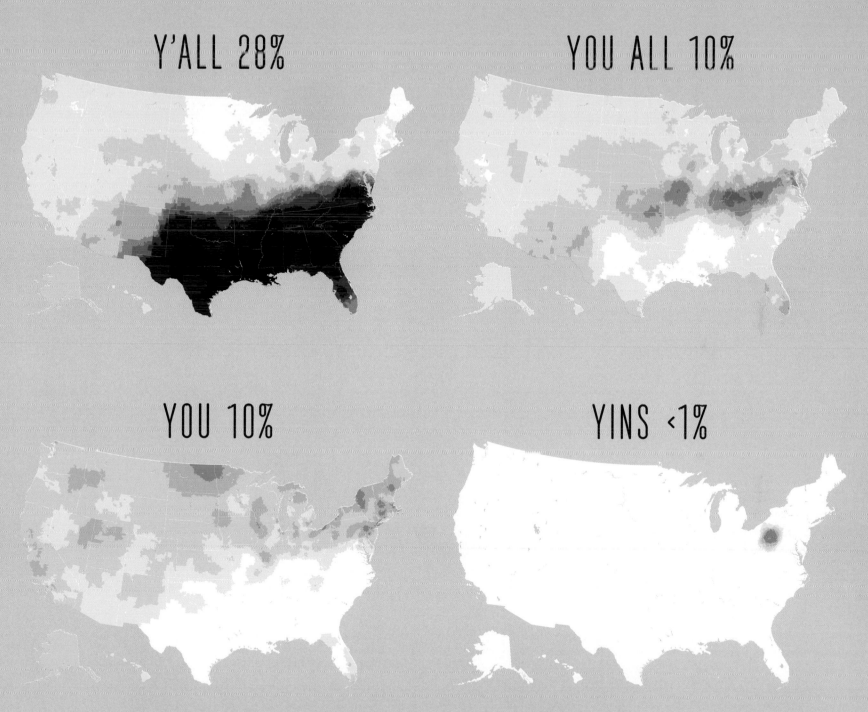

PERCENT SAYING

0   10   20   30   40   50   75%

YOUS/YOUSE

PERCENT SAYING

| 0 | 5 | 10 | 15 | 20 | >25% |

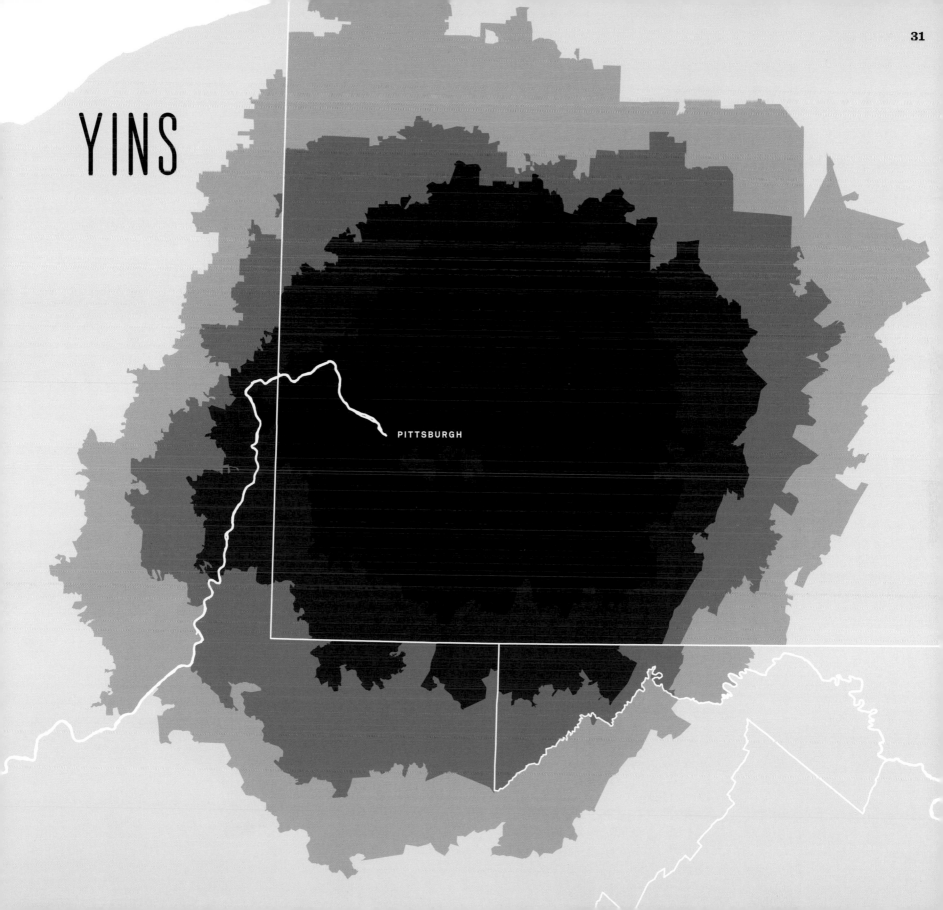

YINS

PITTSBURGH

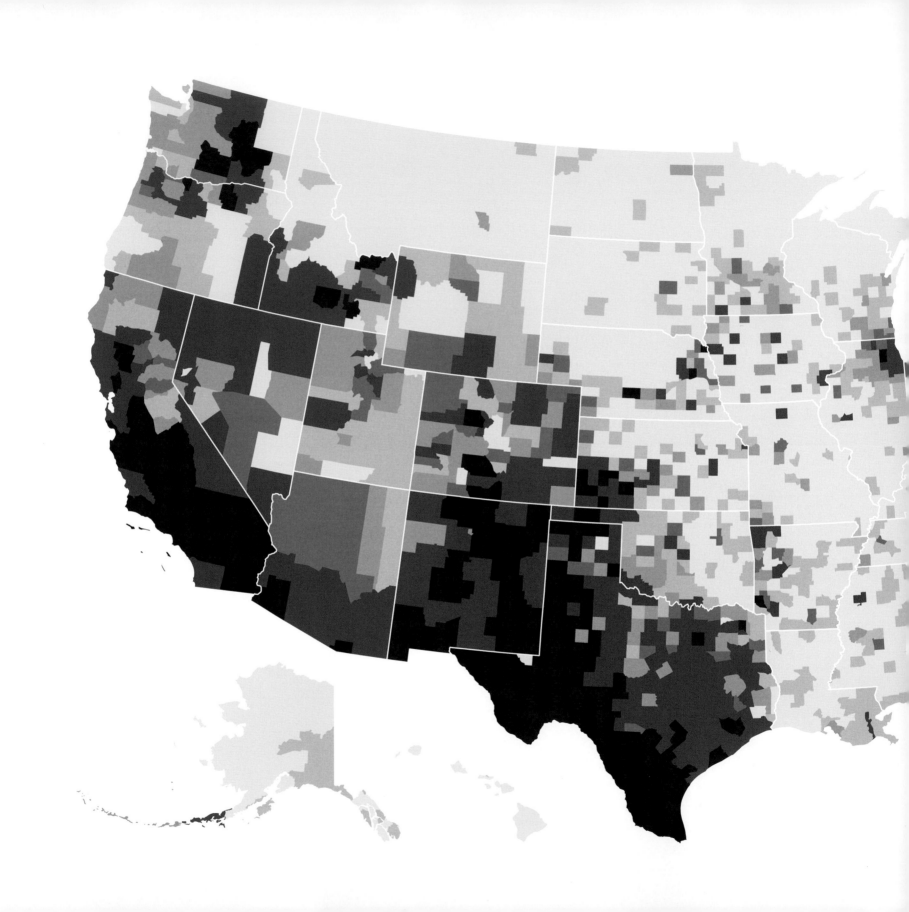

SPEAKING AMERICAN DOESN'T ALWAYS MEAN SPEAKING ENGLISH

Although this book focuses on the many ways of speaking English in America, it would be incomplete without noting that to speak American is not necessarily to speak English. By last count, more than 60 million Americans speak a language other than English in their homes. For more than half of these homes, the language is Spanish.

The distribution of Spanish speakers is of course a function of geography. There are many counties in the Southwest where a majority of households speak Spanish. In Starr County, Texas, a whopping 94 percent of people speak Spanish at home.

PERCENT SPEAKING SPANISH AT HOME

0   10   25   50%

THREE FORTY-FIVE 51%

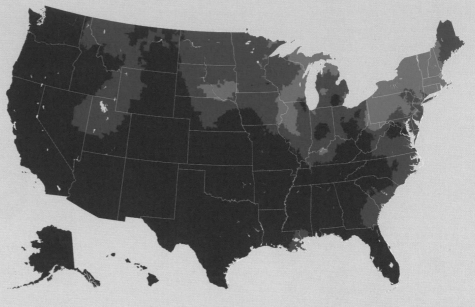

HOW WOULD YOU SAY 3:45?

QUARTER TO FOUR 34%

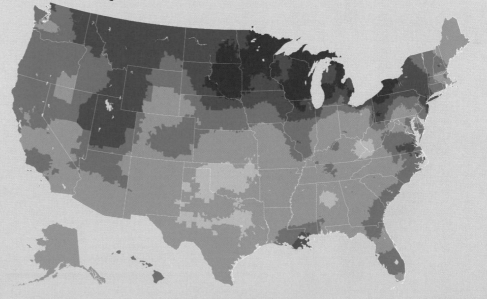

QUARTER TILL FOUR 8%

QUARTER OF FOUR 6%

PERCENT SAYING

0   10   20   30   40   50   75%

ON THE NIGHT
BEFORE HALLOWEEN

From its earliest beginnings, stemming from the Celtic festival of Samhain, Halloween has been associated with mischief.

Lisa Morton, a historian of Halloween, writes that in the 1920s, mischief began to take on a more sinister quality, as arson and vandalism joined more innocent pranks like rapping on neighbors' windows, jamming doorbells, or occassionally tipping over an outhouse. As Halloween became more popular after World War II and developed into a full-fledged national holiday, civil society made a concerted effort to avoid the darker parts of the holiday. They emphasized costume parties, parades, and contests for the best costumes and window decorations.

Around this time, trick-or-treat began to spread throughout the country. It was a way of acknowledging the destructive potential of the festival and, in the process, sublimating it. The efforts worked. In the 1950s and '60s, Halloween was transformed from a destructive night of anarchic vandalism into a night that was, writes historian Nicholas Rogers, "consumer-oriented and infantile" and "a boon for food manufacturers and retailers." By the 1960s, Halloween in the United States had been largely tamed.

But the reformers did not eliminate the pranking. Some of it remained, and other parts of it moved to the night before—October 30, which acquired one of several different names, depending on geography: *Devil's Night* in Michigan and Pittsburgh, *Mischief Night* in South Jersey and Philadelphia, or *Goosey Night* in a tiny sliver of North Jersey. Just as trick-or-treat was turning Halloween into a family-friendly night of consumption, the first written references to the night before Halloween as a night of vandalism and pranking began to emerge.

38

MISCHIEF NIGHT 8%

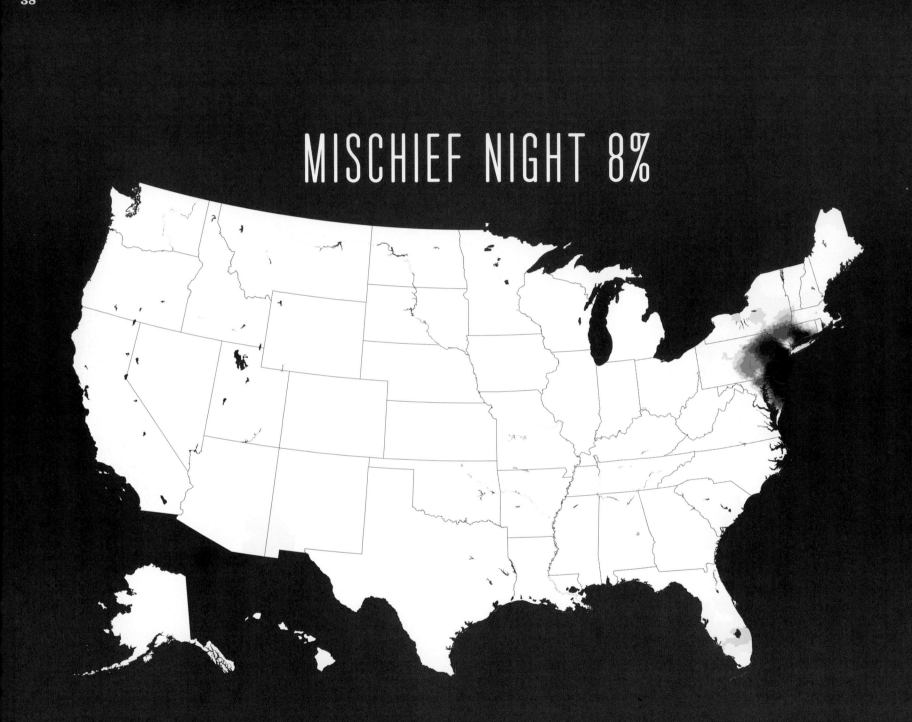

PERCENT SAYING

0   10   20   30   40   50   75%

DEVIL'S NIGHT 7%

MISCHIEF NIGHT

PERCENT SAYING

0   10   20   30   40   50   75%

GATE NIGHT

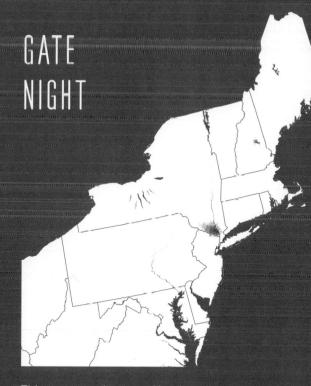

This name can be traced back to the practice of dismantling the gates of nearby houses, removing them from their hinges (and sometimes placing them in the middle of the town square or up in a tree).

CABBAGE NIGHT

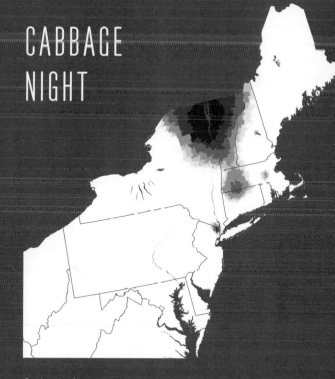

On both the **NEW YORK** and **VERMONT** sides of Lake Champlain, the holiday is often called *Cabbage Night*, a reference to the tradition of raiding nearby cabbage patches, uprooting the vegetables, and hurling them at neighbors' front doors.

GOOSEY NIGHT

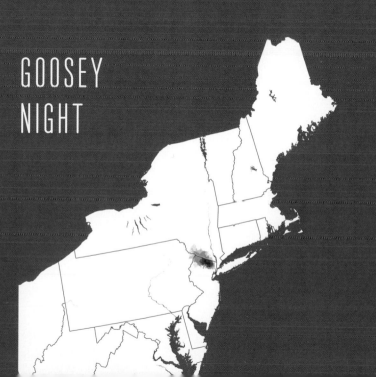

DEVIL'S NIGHT

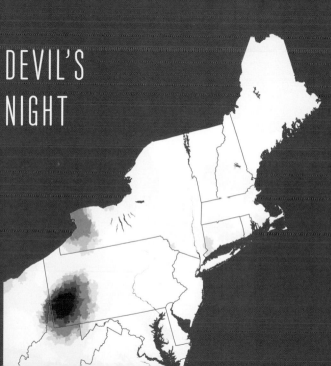

PROBABLY EASIER
TO JUST POINT
ACROSS THE STREET

About 80 percent of the country would describe something across the street from them diagonally as either *kitty-corner* or *catty-corner,* with the dividing line between the two running east to west across the United States.

Around 93 percent of people from **GREEN BAY**, **WISCONSIN**, say *kitty-corner.*

In scattered sections in and around **NEW YORK CITY** (and also in southern **FLORIDA**), people find both *kitty-corner* and *catty-corner* to be bizarre, so they just say *diagonal.*

KITTY-CORNER

CATTY-CORNER

Roughly 75 percent of people from central **TEXAS** say *catty-corner.*

OHIO

From the outside, Ohio might seem like the kind of state that would have a generic sort of Midwestern dialect, but in reality it's composed of several distinct speech regions, divided between Cleveland in the northeast and Cincinnati in the southwest.

In Cincinnati, 60 percent of people say *gym shoes,* but few call them that in Cleveland, where it's almost always either *tennis shoes* (68 percent) or *sneakers* (28 percent). In Cincinnati, more than 80 percent of people call a woodlouse a *pillbug* or a *roly-poly;* in Cleveland, you're more likely to hear *potato bug.* Cleveland has the *freeway;* Cincinnati, the *expressway.* Cincinnati has *roundabouts.* Cleveland has *traffic circles.*

In Cleveland, on the southern shore of Lake Erie, the strip between the sidewalk and the road is the *tree lawn,* or, elsewhere, the *berm.*

WISCONSIN

If you're from Wi-*scon*-sin (not Wis-*con*-sin, as the outsiders would say), throw some *pop* into a *bag* (pronounced *bayg*) and head over to the *covered-dish* (potluck). Bring some *bars* along for dessert and remember to turn left at the *stop-and-go light.*

Here, a water fountain is a *bubbler,* the strip of grass between the sidewalk and the road is the *terrace,* and, as we've seen, it's neither a *garage sale* nor a *yard sale,* but a *rummage sale.*

As for those cheeseheads, as recently as thirty years ago the term was considered an insult ("a stupid, lazy person" in the 1985 edition of the *Dictionary of American Regional English*). But that was before Milwaukee resident Ralph Bruno created the first cheesehead hat in 1987, as Joseph Kapler Jr. reported in the *Wisconsin Magazine of History:* "'I just wanted to take something negative and turn it into a positive,' Bruno [said]. 'The cheesehead was a way to show my pride in Wisconsin and at the same time have fun with an insult.'"

When the hat found its way onto the heads of Green Bay Packers fans—and the Packers found their way back onto the national stage in the 1990s—the term quickly wormed its way into the American consciousness. By the late 1990s, *cheesehead* had become just another word for a Wisconsinite.

The Cornhusker State is a place where spinning your car in circles is *doing cookies*, *creek* often sounds like *crik,* and you'd carry your *pop* home in a *sack.* The grass between the sidewalk and the road is the *parking,* and you might drive to the store to pick up some *pickles*— not cucumbers preserved in brine, but *pickle cards:* pull-tab lottery cards (cousins of the *scratch-offs* you might find elsewhere).

Gambling in America is a state-regulated industry, which is why this term, similar to some of the words for roads or drive-through liquor stores, tends to stop abruptly at the state line. And the terms of use in Nebraska are explicitly set forth in the Nebraska Pickle Card Lottery Act (a real law), which specifies, among other things, that:

> A pickle card shall mean any disposable card, board, or ticket which accords a person an opportunity to win a cash prize by opening, pulling, detaching, or otherwise removing one or more tabs from the card, board, or ticket to reveal a set of numbers, letters, symbols, or configurations, or any combination thereof.

According to the Nebraska Charitable Gaming Division, the term derives from when the cards were illegal, and bartenders would store them "in large empty 'pickle jars' which could easily be skirted out of sight."

HOW TO PRETEND YOU'RE FROM
NEBRASKA

HOW TO PRETEND YOU'RE FROM
MICHIGAN

Of everyone nationwide who says *Devil's Night, fireflies,* and *pop,* 85 percent of them come from Michigan. Another way to think of it: if you meet a random American who uses these three terms, there's an 85 percent chance that you're talking to someone from Michigan.

Michiganders often distinguish between the Lower and Upper Peninsulas of their state. Linguistically, however, the state is one. The denizens of the Upper Peninsula (*yoopers*), while having their own linguistic quirks, are still closer in dialect to mainland Michigan than anywhere else. The Mackinac Bridge, which connects the two peninsulas, is not much of a dividing line. Only once you cross through the Hiawatha National Forest and emerge on the other side do the people begin to speak more like their neighbors in Wisconsin.

HOW TO PRETEND YOU'RE FROM
PHILADELPHIA

Philadelphia is only a couple of hours away from New York, but the speech in the two cities is sharply different—which may well be a reflection of the cities' ages. They were both urban centers long before cars and trains brought them closer together. In addition to its distinct accent, in Philadelphia you'll find *pillbugs, jimmies* on ice cream, *hoagies* (not *subs*), and *Mischief Night,* the night before Halloween. You might hear the word *jawn* as a stand-in for just about anything (similar in some respects to the use of *da kine* in Hawaii), and, during the summer, you don't go *to the beach,* you go *down the shore.*

Philadelphia is also, along with New York and Boston, one of the places you're least likely to encounter someone who pronounces *Mary, merry,* and *marry* the same. If all three words are pronounced differently or if *Mary* and *merry* sound the same but *marry* is distinct, you're most likely from around this area.

Philadelphia speech fades sharply as you move west over the Alleghenies into the area affectionately (or not) referred to as Pennsyltucky, before the Pittsburgh dialect begins to take over. But the Philadelphia influence can definitely be heard as you head east into New Jersey, a state that doesn't really have a dialect of its own but is rather sharply divided between Philadelphia-influ-

enced South Jersey and New York–influenced North Jersey. The line between the two stretches diagonally from northwest to southeast, running just north of Trenton, along the northern boundary of Burlington County, down toward Atlantic City.

If you find yourself in this region, be sure to stop for a *cheesesteak,* a sandwich on a long roll laden with chopped steak and topped with cheese—sometimes American or provolone, but often Cheez Whiz (or just *wiz*), a gooey orange cheese-like substance. What elsewhere might be called *Italian ice* here is simply *water ice,* which, when said with a Philadelphia accent, usually sounds closer to *wooderice.*

HOW TO PRETEND YOU'RE FROM
PITTSBURGH

Because the modern age has erased many of the local boundaries that once existed—with the spread of chain restaurants, cable television, and, of course, the web— many people yearn to recover a sense of belonging and of place. That's why they often turn to their local dialects as a source of pride. Perhaps nowhere else exemplifies this as much as Pittsburgh, a city that, like Boston and Philadelphia, is proud of its distinctive speech.

When I published an initial round of dialect maps online in 2013, they left out Pittsburgh's distinctive *yins*. It felt as if the entire city of Pittsburgh let me know about it.

The language in Pittsburgh still bears marks of the Scots-Irish immigrants who settled in the western foothills of the Alleghenies. Unlike in Philadelphia, on the other side of the Alleghenies, here *cot* and *caught* are pronounced the same. (To learn how this happens, see page 102.) As in Philadelphia, you'd get a *hoagie* here, but perhaps you'd tie it up with a *gumband* instead of a *rubber band*. A faucet is a *spicket*, a traffic light is a *redlight*, a chipmunk is a *ground squirrel*, and you might hear someone refer to *onion snow*—a late spring snowfall.

Part Two

2 WHAT WE EAT

WHAT WE CALL

A SANDWICH ON A LONG ROLL WITH MEATS AND CHEESES

The Hoagie:
Four Origin Stories, All Likely False

About 82 percent of the country calls a long sandwich with an assortment of meats and cheeses a *sub,* but in the area around Philadelphia and South Jersey, this sandwich is always a *hoagie.* While the true origins of the term have yet to be conclusively established, many theories have been suggested over the years. Here are four.

- The hoagie was originated by Al de Palma in the 1930s. Failing to find work as a musician following the Great Depression, de Palma opened a sandwich shop in 1936 and dubbed his sandwiches *hoggies*—a reference to the fact that you'd have to be a hog to eat one. Over time (due to the Philadelphia accent, de Palma insisted), *hoggies* came to sound like *hoagies.*

- During World War I, the American government contracted with American International Shipbuilding to build the largest shipyard in the world, located at the southern end of Philadelphia, on the shores of the Delaware River, in an area called Hog Island. The Italian immigrants—allegedly known as *hoggies*—who worked in the navy yard building ships for the war effort would bring sandwiches loaded with meat, cheese, lettuce, tomatoes, peppers, and oil on a long submarine roll: the hoggie sandwich. At some point, *sandwich* was dropped, the short o sound became a long o, and the *hoagie* was born. (It's worth noting that the shipbuilding facilities at Hog Island had shut down some fifteen years before the first appearance of the word *hoggie* in 1936.)

- Howard Robboy, a sociology professor at the College of New Jersey and an expert in the history of the hoagie (yes, people do study such things), offered another explanation

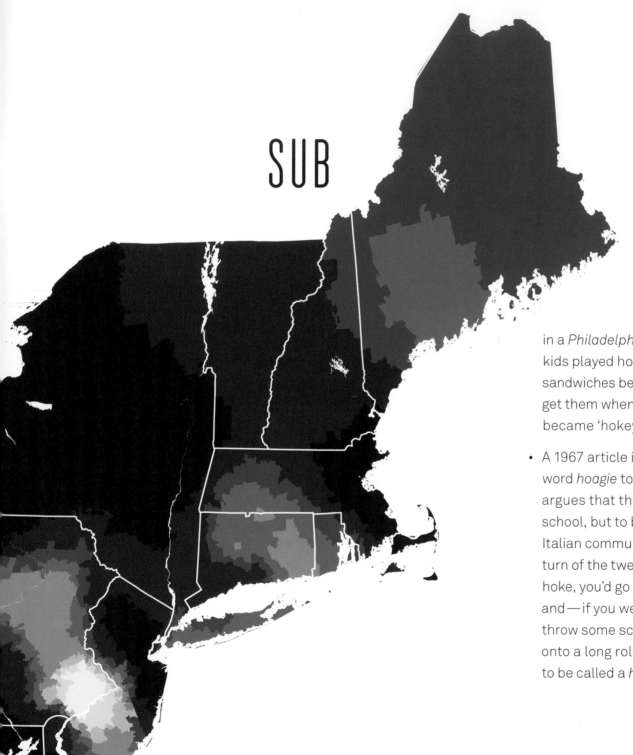

SUB

in a *Philadelphia Inquirer* article in 2003: "When kids played hooky from school, they'd buy the sandwiches because they didn't cost much. They'd get them when they were 'on the hoke.' That became 'hokey,' and 'hokey' became 'hoagie.'"

- A 1967 article in *American Speech* also traces the word *hoagie* to the expression *on the hoke,* but argues that the phrase referred not to skipping school, but to being poor. It's said that in the Italian communities of South Philadelphia at the turn of the twentieth century, if you were on the hoke, you'd go begging from store to store, and—if you were lucky—a deli owner would throw some scraps of leftover meat and cheese onto a long roll, giving you a sandwich that came to be called a *hokie*.

PERCENT SAYING

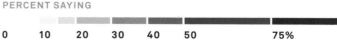

0   10   20   30   40   50   75%

HOAGIE

HERO

WEDGE

GRINDER

ITALIAN SANDWICH

PANCAKES

Turns out, almost no one says *flapjacks* anymore.

WE ALL AGREE THEY'RE CALLED *PANCAKES*, BUT HOW DO WE DESCRIBE WHAT WE'RE POURING OVER THEM?

Americans are split fairly evenly on the question of whether syrup is pronounced *sir-up* or *seer-up*, with a less stark geographical divide than for many of the other language splits in this book. A slight majority goes to *sir-up* (53 percent). The long e *seer-up* is rarer (36 percent), concentrated in southern New England and the Mid-Atlantic states, most strongly in Pennsylvania, just north of Philadelphia.

SEER-UP

SIR-UP

SEER-UP

CARBONATION WITH AN IDENTITY CRISIS

Sometimes the boundaries between terms are fuzzier. In **OKLAHOMA**, *soda, pop,* and *coke* all mix together. Contrast this with the sharp boundary dividing **MILWAUKEE** *soda* territory from the *pop* country of northern **ILLINOIS**.

POP

SODA

COKE

60

SODA 59%

POP 18%

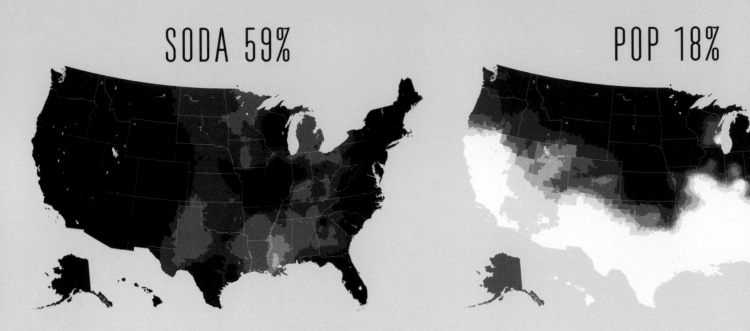

COKE 17%

SOFT DRINK 6%

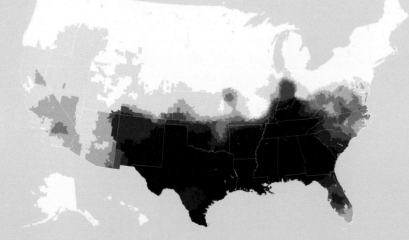

PERCENT SAYING

0   10   20   30   40   50   75%

COCOLA

PERCENT SAYING *COCOLA*

0   10   20   30   40   50   75%

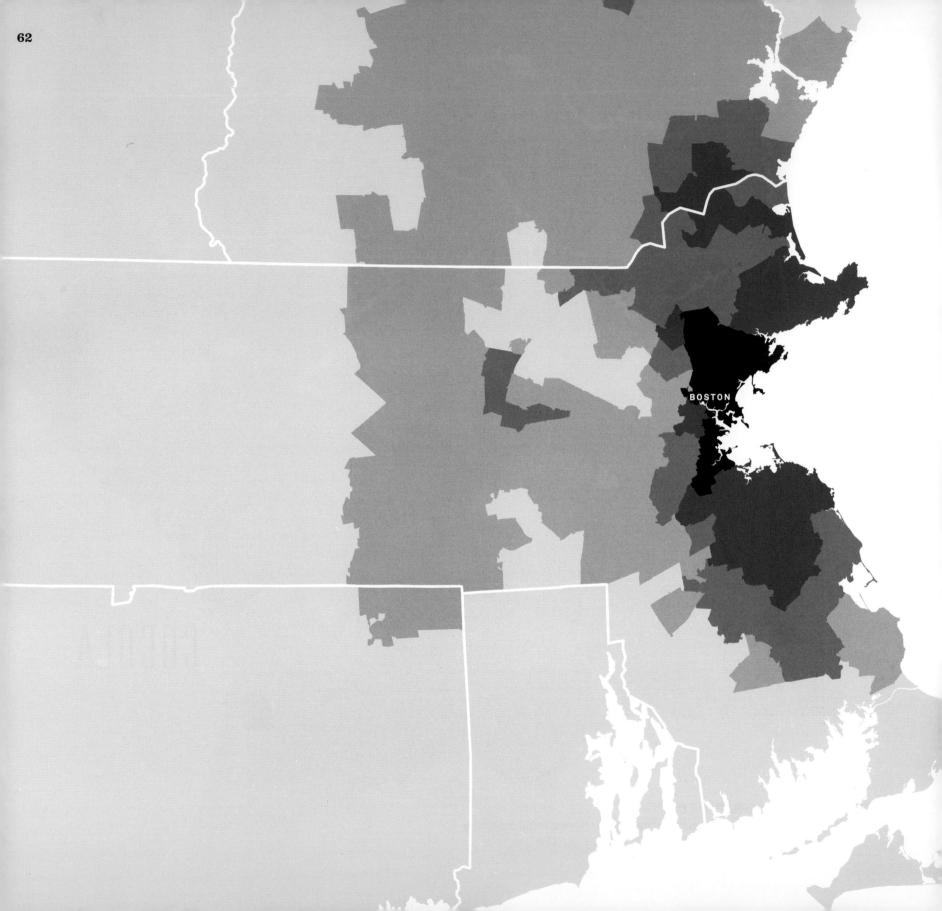

BOSTON

TONIC

Previously a common phrase in the Boston area, the use of *tonic* as the general word for a soft drink is on the decline.

While over 30 percent of Massachusetts residents born in the 1940s say *tonic,* almost none of the younger generation does: over 95 percent of those under the age of twenty-five say *soda.*

PERCENT SAYING *TONIC*

| 0 | 5 | 10 | 15 | 20 | >25% |

WHAT DO YOU CALL THIS?

The country can't quite get on the same page regarding how to pronounce the name of this vegetable. While the majority pronounces it *kaw-lih-flower*, a little over one in four people say *kaw-lee-flower*, most of whom are concentrated in the **NORTHEAST**.

KAW-LEE-FLOWER

KAW-LIH-FLOWER

WHAT DO YOU CALL THESE?

SCALLIONS

GREEN ONIONS

SCALLIONS

PLEASE BE MORE SPECIFIC ABOUT THIS PILE OF SHREDDED VEGETABLES

The *stoop sale* was far from the only contribution the Dutch settlers of New Amsterdam made to American English: *cookies* (from *koekjes,* meaning little cakes), *waffles* (*wafels*), *boss* (*baas,* meaning master), and perhaps even *Yankee* all derive from Dutch. So does the blend of shredded cabbage that the Dutch called *koolsla*—a combination of *kool* (cabbage) and *sla* (salad).

The anglicized *cold slaw* appears in written works as early as 1794, with the spelling *coleslaw* (or *cole-slaw*) developing in the mid-1800s. These days, in parts of the southern United States, the *cole* is often dropped, and the food is referred to just as *slaw*. The shortened form is most common in North Carolina, where more than 90 percent of people use it. It is least common in parts of California, where more than two-thirds of people stick with the full *coleslaw*.

The Great Cole Divide has as much an **EAST/WEST** division as a **NORTH/SOUTH** one. Resistance to the use of *slaw* as shorthand for *coleslaw* increases in the western part of the country, peaking in **HAWAII**, where 70 percent would not do so, including 16 percent who had never before heard of such a crazy idea.

WHERE THEY DON'T CALL COLESLAW *SLAW*

As for the **NORTH/SOUTH** divide, it mirrors many of the language divisions seen so far, with one exception: here the *slaw*-only group has pushed well north of *y'all* territory into **MISSOURI**, **INDIANA**, and southern **ILLINOIS**.

WHERE THEY DO

WHAT DO YOU EAT WHEN YOU DON'T FEEL LIKE COOKING?

CARRY-OUT 24%

PERCENT SAYING

0   10   20   30   40   50   75%

TAKEOUT 72%

In most of the United States it's *takeout*, but in a swath of the **MIDDLE OF THE COUNTRY**—plus **WASHINGTON**, **D.C.**, and **DETROIT**—it's *carry-out*.

TAKEOUT

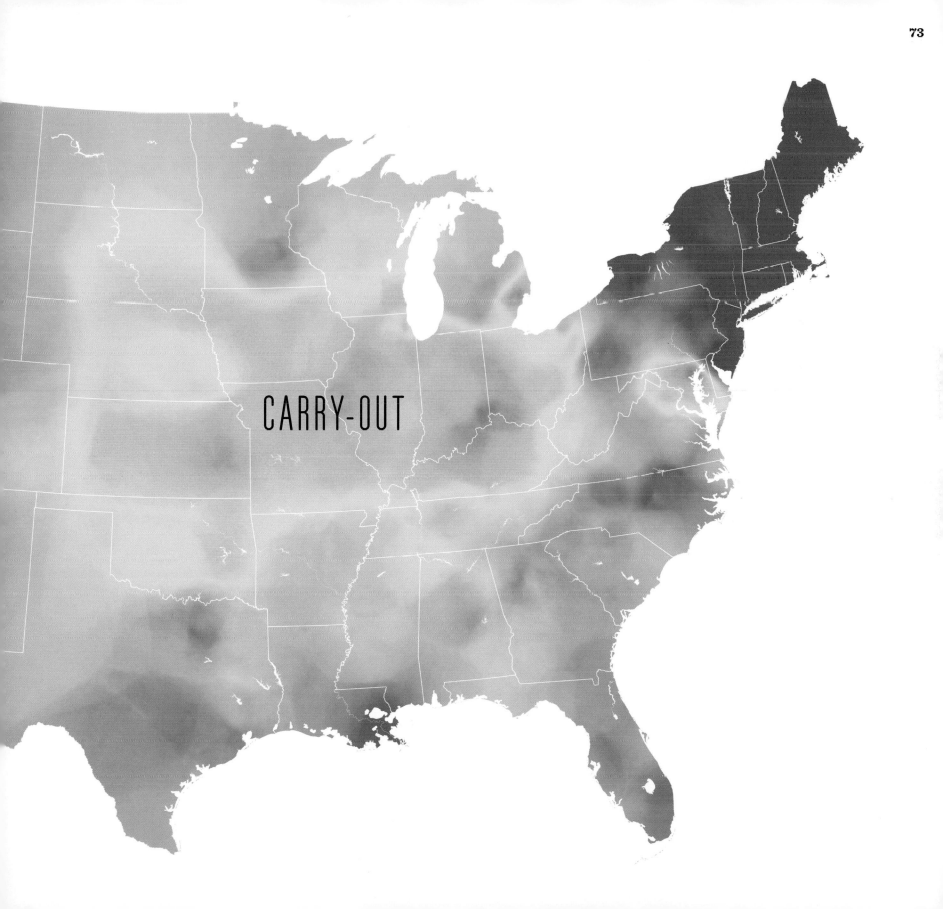

CARRY-OUT

WHAT DO YOU CALL THIS?

APE-RICOT

APP-RICOT

DRINKING FOUNTAIN

WHAT WE DRINK FROM AT SCHOOL

BUBBLER

BUBBLER

WATER FOUNTAIN

BUBBLER

No one quite knows why people in Milwaukee drink out of *bubblers*. Even fewer know why denizens of Rhode Island share this quirk.

In 1859, the first public drinking fountains were installed in New York and London. Crowds gathered to witness their unveiling. A reporter for the *New York Times* hoped that "public drinking fountains in this City will soon be so numerous that they will cease to be the subject of remark." Each early fountain came with a cast-iron cup, attached to the fountain body by a long chain, and people would drink from the communal cup.

As the fountains spread across the country, they acquired a different name in a few places: *bubblers,* presumably in reference to how the water would bubble up from the fountain. In eastern Wisconsin and parts of southern New England, the name stuck and remains common today.

PERCENT SAYING *BUBBLER*

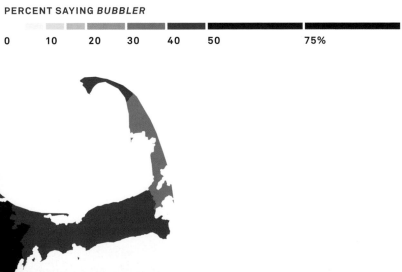

0   10   20   30   40   50   75%

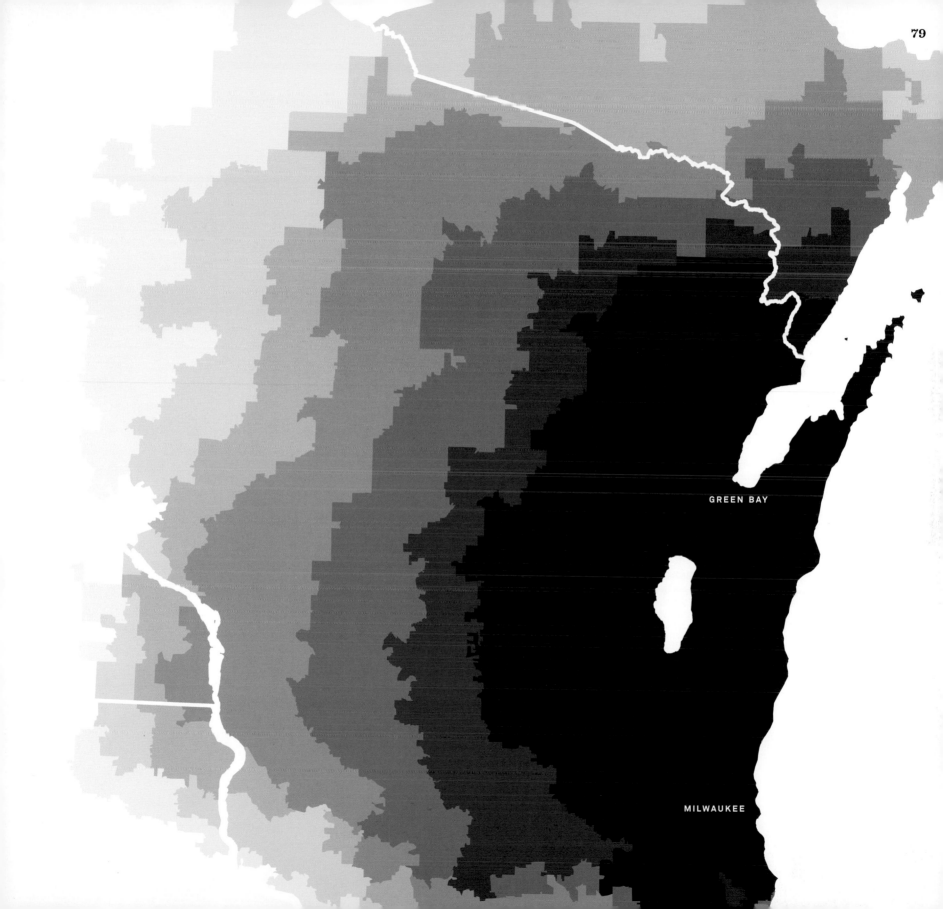

GREEN BAY

MILWAUKEE

HOW DO YOU SAY *PECAN*?

PERCENT SAYING

0   10   20   30   40   50   75%

PIH-*KAHN* 39%

81

PEE-*KAHN* 16%

PEE-KAN 12%

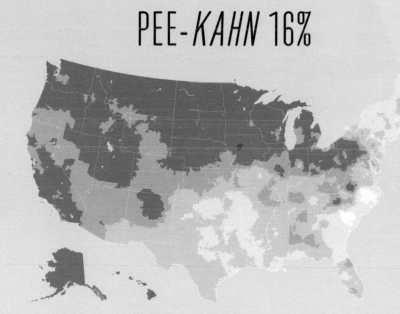

PEE-KAHN 9%

PEE-*KAN* 9%

CAN YOU USE *FROSTING* AND *ICING* INTERCHANGEABLY?

For what it's worth, the *Associated Press Stylebook*—a veritable bible in many newsrooms—somewhat pedantically insists that *frosting* is the term to use for cupcake and cake topping, while *icing* should be reserved for the sugar decorations applied to cookies.

NO YOU CAN'T

THE GREAT DEBATE: *SPRINKLES VS. JIMMIES*

PERCENT SAYING

0   10   20   30   40   50   75%

For almost the entire country, the hard bits of sugar on sundaes or cupcakes are *sprinkles,* but in South Jersey, eastern New England and, to a lesser extent, Pittsburgh and Milwaukee, they are often called *jimmies*. Especially around Boston, many argue that *jimmies* refers specifically to the chocolate version, while the other varities are indeed *sprinkles*.

According to the candy company Just Born (maker of Peeps), *jimmies* can be traced back to its original Brooklyn, New York, store, which opened in 1923, and the employee who first made them. He was Jimmy Bartholomew, and chocolate was long the only variety of sprinkle that he made and that Just Born sold. There is no credible evidence to corroborate this story, alas.

SPRINKLES

Another legend holds that *jimmies* comes from the Jimmy Fund, a well-known Boston charity for cancer research that the Boston Red Sox have long supported. The charity was itself named after a young cancer patient… named Einar Gustafson, who was first introduced on the radio as Jimmy in order to protect his privacy. The claim is that a local ice cream store charged extra for ice cream with sprinkles on it and would then donate the money from the sale of the *jimmies* to the Jimmy Fund.

A persistent myth suggests that the word *jimmies* carries racist connotations, but, while the true origins of the word remain unclear, all research on the topic to date has failed to turn up any evidence of a racist past.

A more prosaic, and more plausible, story comes from language columnist Ben Zimmer, who notes that the word's origins can probably be traced to *jim-jams*, a term for small articles or knickknacks that has been around since the mid-sixteenth century.

JIMMIES

JIMMIES ARE
CHOCOLATE SPRINKLES

HAWAII

Nowhere in the United States is as linguistically diverse as Hawaii. Waves of Chinese-, Portuguese-, Japanese-, and English-speaking immigrants have all left their mark on the linguistics of the archipelago. It's the only state where the second most common language after English is not a European language. It is instead Tagalog, a language native to the Philippines. The U.S. Census Bureau estimates that fully a quarter of the Hawaiian population speaks a language other than English at home.

For a few thousand people, that language is Hawaiian, a Polynesian language spoken on the islands long before the arrival of English settlers in 1778. The use of Hawaiian decreased following English colonization of the islands, to the point at which it was almost lost entirely. But in the past several decades Hawaiian speakers have made a concerted effort to preserve and promote the language. Some schools offer immersion courses, many children learn Hawaiian as a second language, and it is now one of the official state languages of Hawaii (the other is English). But with so few native speakers of it, UNESCO still considers the language "critically endangered"—the highest degree of language endangerment, just short of extinction.

You're more likely to hear the locals speaking another language: Hawaii Pidgin English, which about half the population speaks to varying degrees. The language evolved out of a blend of Chinese, Japanese, English, and Hawaiian, and it continues to develop today. A translation of the Bible, by linguistics professor Joseph Grimes, gives a sense of how the language sounds. The translation, called *Da Jesus Book*, begins:

> Da time wen eryting had start, God wen make da sky an da world. Da world come so no mo notting inside, no mo shape notting. On top da wild ocean dat cova eryting, neva had light notting. Ony had God Spirit dea, moving aroun ova da watta.

The line between Pidgin and English is not always clear, as the English spoken in Hawaii is itself quite different from the English you'd hear on the *mainland*.

If you've done your work you're *pau hana* (or just *pau* for short), good food is *grinds,* and *da kine* is used for, well, just about anything. In Hawaii, flip-flops are *slippers,* goose bumps are *chicken skin,* and someone of European ancestry (or someone from the *mainland*) is a *haole.* Perhaps surprisingly, many subtleties of Hawaiian English are closer to the English spoken in England than that spoken in America. In Hawaii, for example, people are more likely to refer to a trash can as a *rubbish bin* than anywhere else in the United States.

ALASKA

When those from the *outside*—that is, the *Lower 48* states—first make their way to Alaska, they're known as *cheechakos*. Once they've been there a while, they're called *sourdoughs*.

Hooch, a word for illegally made or low-quality liquor, was introduced to the contiguous United States by miners returning from the Klondike gold rush in the late 1890s. It's a shortening of the Tlingit *hoochinoo,* an alcoholic drink made from rum and molasses. And if you're going to go out into *the bush,* watch out for the *williwaw* and *taku* winds and grab some food from the *cache* (a small food-storage cabin elevated high off the ground to keep bears out). And while we're on the subject, you'd do well to bring some *bear insurance* along with you—that is, a gun or two.

Alaska is home to the highest percentage of people—roughly one in twenty—who speak a Native North American language other than Navajo in the home. These languages include Yupik, Aleut, and Inupiat.

The debate over whether Native Alaskan languages really do have dozens of words for snow (which, of course, English has as well: *snow, sleet, flurries, slush, hail*) is a tricky one. Linguists seemed to debunk the hypothesis in the mid-'80s, but since then it has made something of a comeback. Some examples:

- *Piegnartoq* (good snow for driving your sled)

- *Qissuqaqtuq* (snow that has frozen overnight, becoming good for travel)

- *Apputtattuq* (snow that accumulates on newly formed ice and causes its thinning)

- *Aqilokoq* (softly falling snow)

HOW TO PRETEND YOU'RE FROM
THE PACIFIC NORTHWEST

A general feature of American dialects is that as you move south and west, farther from the original linguistic centers of colonial America, differences in speech patterns become more subtle. It's as true of the Pacific Northwest as it is of California.

The Pacific Northwest is notable for some of its odd juxtapositions: it's one of the smattering of places where *potato bug* is a common word for the woodlouse. In California you're more likely to hear *roly-poly, pillbug,* or *sow bug.* If you meet a random American who knows about *potato bugs,* knows that spinning a car in circles is *doing cookies,* and calls a mountain lion a *cougar,* there's more than an 80 percent chance that they're from Washington or Oregon.

Distinguishing among Washington, Oregon, and Northern California is a task all its own. One easy tip: in Washington you go *to the ocean,* while in Oregon you go *to the coast.* Meanwhile, in California you go *to the beach,* and way off in South Jersey you go *down the shore.* And Oregon is *doing cookies* territory, while Washington is definitely not.

HOW TO PRETEND YOU'RE FROM
COLORADO

Welcome to Colo-*rad*-oh (it's often pronounced *rad,* like *bad,* not *rahd,* like *rod*). Note too that the town north of Denver is pronounced *lewis-ville,* not *louie-ville,* as it is in Kentucky. Many towns have Spanish names, but few retain their Spanish pronunciations. Thus, Buena Vista is *byoo-nuh vista* (*byoo-nee* for short), Salida is *suh-lye-duh,* and Arriba is *air-uh-buh.*

If you're wondering why there are so many *parks* in Colorado town names, it derives from the French-Canadian fur trappers who settled the area in the nineteenth century. They called mountain valleys *parks* or, as in neighboring states like Wyoming, *holes* (as in Jackson Hole).

HOW TO PRETEND YOU'RE FROM
CALIFORNIA

Once you get *out west*, there aren't as many regional vocabulary quirks as *back east*. No one thing identifies someone as definitively Californian, but there are some clues: In California you find *freeways* and *big rigs*. You stop for some water at the *drinking fountain*.

Like many of the things in this book, the story of California's language is a story about two things: migration and media.

By nature, when two people with different accents converse, they unconsciously shift their speech patterns toward each other — almost averaging out their own speech patterns, in a way. So, for much of the early twentieth century, California speech sounded like a mishmash of dialects from everywhere else. California was a giant blender of the rest of the country's speech: the general American dialect.

In the mid-twentieth century, though, national radio began to replace local radio for the first time. The voices in Americans' living rooms were, by and large, the voices of those in America's media and entertainment hub: Californians.

National media in the twentieth century and the Internet in the twenty-first do not remove geographical quirks or obliterate local speech patterns, but they do allow for linguistic innovation to spread far more rapidly and far more extensively than ever before.

In addition, migration into Southern California and the region's position at the heart of American media and entertainment production mean that many speech patterns that start in California are quick to catch on in the rest of the country. Surfer speak, valley girl, etc., all began as niche dialects in Los Angeles. Forty years ago, words like *dude, cool,* and *gnarly* weren't widely known. But when surfer culture developed in the 1970s and valley girl speech began to take shape in the 1980s, those ways of speaking quickly caught on elsewhere, thanks to national media.

Part Three

HOW WE SOUND

WHAT WE WEAR
TO SLEEP

PUH-JAH-MUHZ

HOW WE SAY
AUNT

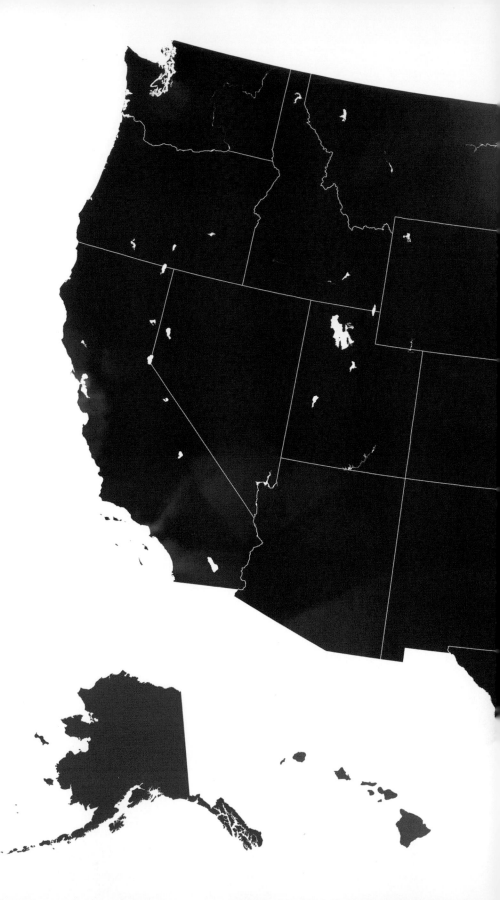

TO SOUND LIKE *AHNT*

TO SOUND LIKE *ANT*

DO YOU PRONOUNCE THE *T* IN *OFTEN*?

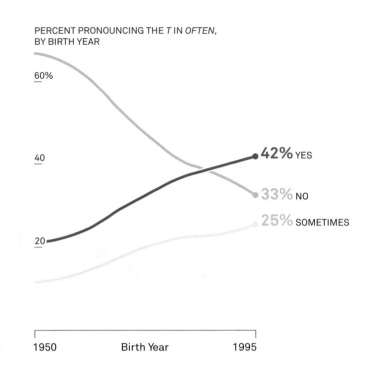

PERCENT PRONOUNCING THE *T* IN *OFTEN*,
BY BIRTH YEAR

60%

40

42% YES

33% NO

25% SOMETIMES

20

1950   Birth Year   1995

Despite the appearance of both pronunciations in most dictionaries, strict prescriptivists and pedants maintain that the only acceptable pronunciation for *often* is with a silent *t*.

The audible *t* pronunciation is not a recent invention, but rather a return to the original pronunciation of the word, harking back to when *often* first entered the English language as a modification of *oft*.

According to the *American Heritage Dictionary,* the audible *t* sound began to recede in the sixteenth and seventeenth centuries, as part of a broader trend of dropping consonants to make language easier to articulate.

The silent *t* version was the accepted pronunciation until the nineteenth century, when more people began to learn how to read. In an example of what linguists call a *spelling pronunciation,* people gradually began to pronounce the word as it's spelled, with the *t* and all. It's unclear why spelling

pronunciations develop for some words and not others: note, words like *soften* and *listen* both retain their silent *t*.

These days, the pronunciation of *often* doesn't have a particularly striking geographic pattern. The use of the audible *t* is most common in Florida, where roughly half the population pronounces it, and least common in Minneapolis, Boston, and New York, where less than 20 percent does.

But there is a noticeable effect of age. Two-thirds of those born in the 1950s pronounce *often* with a silent *t,* compared to only one-third of those born in the 1990s. If the trend continues, it would appear that the silent *t* pronunciation is on its way out.

NO 48%

YES 33%

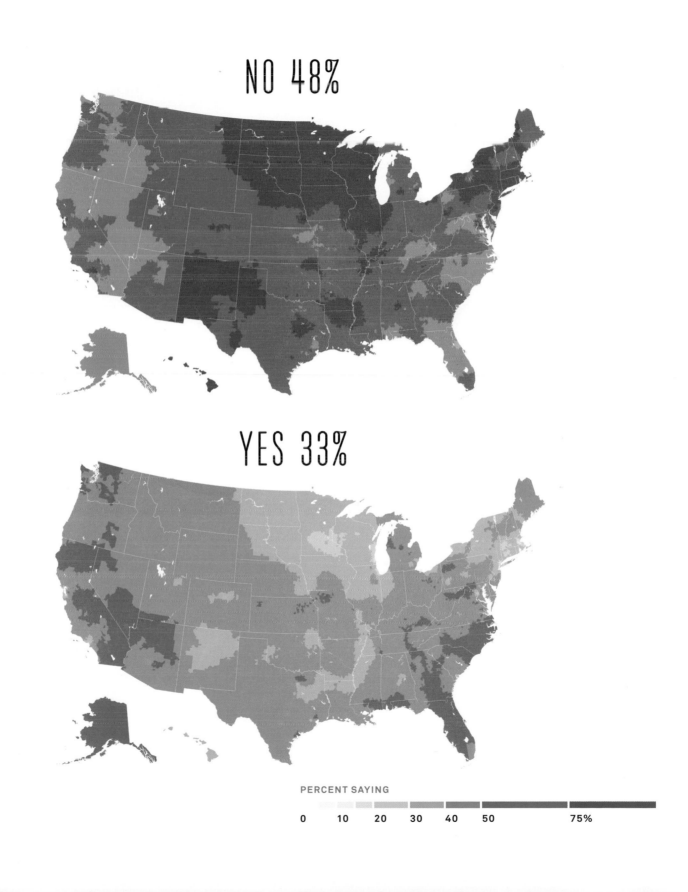

PERCENT SAYING

0   10   20   30   40   50   75%

WHEN TWO VOWELS
BECOME ONE

COT AND CAUGHT
SOUND THE SAME

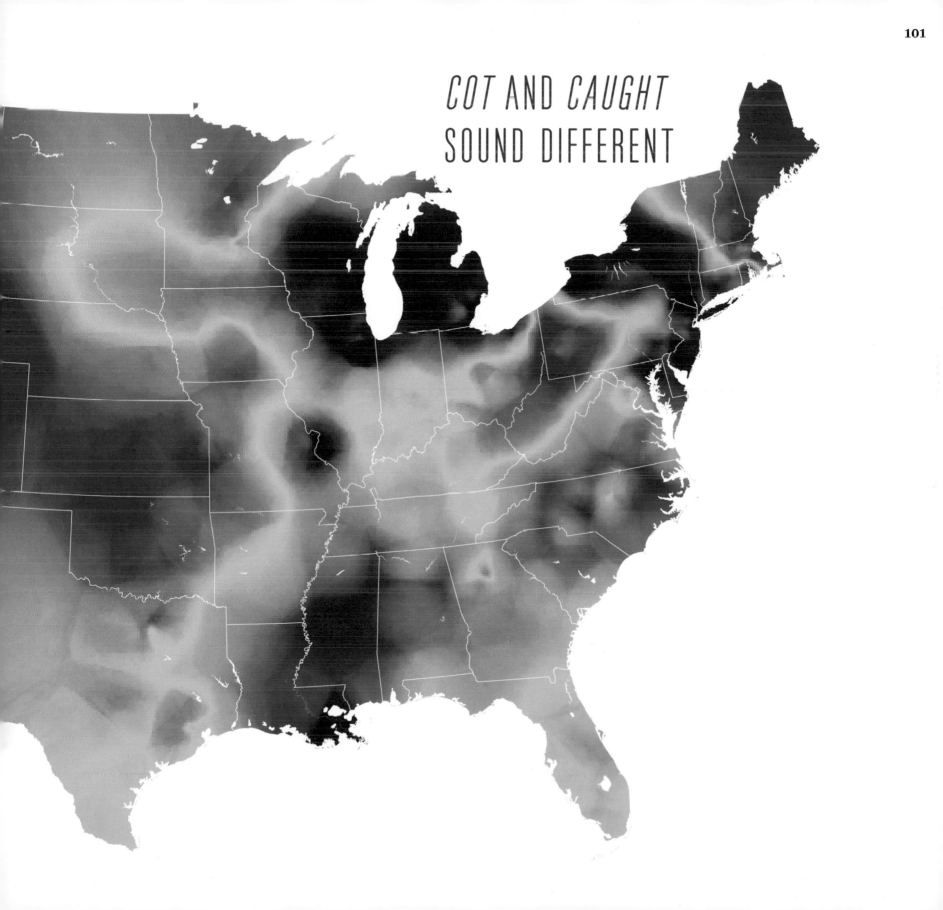

COT AND *CAUGHT* SOUND DIFFERENT

Linguists call it a *phonemic merger:* two sounds, previously distinct, suddenly begin to slide into each other. Over time, the once separate vowel sounds become one: in this case, the short o sound in words like *stock, pod,* and *cot,* and the *aw* sound in words like *stalk, pawed,* and *caught*.

While we can't take a survey of 1940s American-English speakers, we can do the next best thing and see what people born in the 1940s are saying now. This lets us see the vowel merger in action, as the blue (merged) areas gradually eat away at the red (unmerged) areas among younger speakers.

Holdouts remain, and majorities in Michigan, New Jersey, New York, and Chicago continue to pronounce the words differently, but it may be a matter of time before the two sounds merge completely and American English loses a vowel sound.

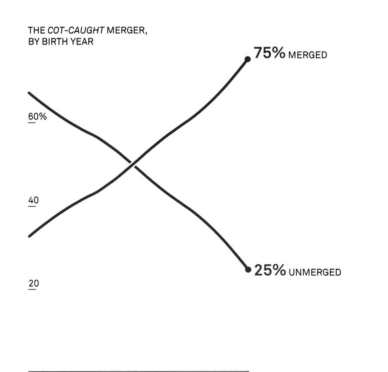

THE *COT-CAUGHT* MERGER, BY BIRTH YEAR

75% MERGED

60%

40

25% UNMERGED

20

1950   Birth Year   1995

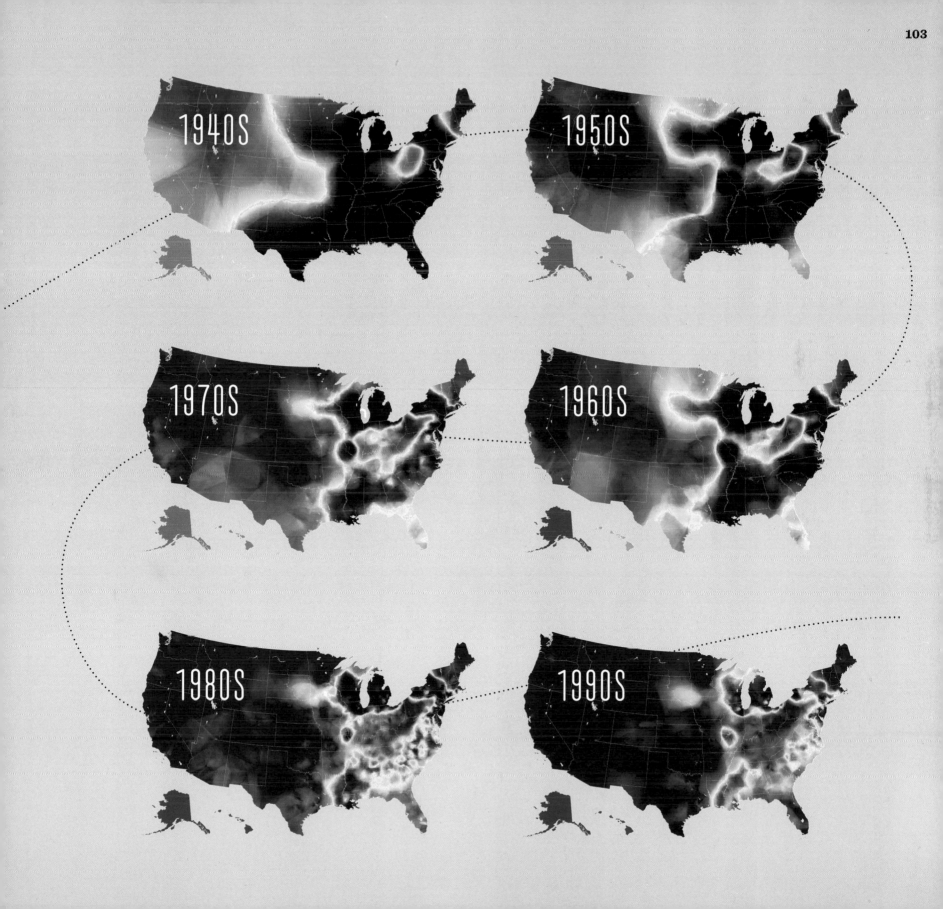

1940S

1950S

1970S

1960S

1980S

1990S

WHAT DO YOU CALL THESE?

Crayola, the marquee crayon brand from the largest crayon manufacturer in the United States, takes no official stance on the pronunciation of *crayons,* instead deferring to the dictionary, which states that "the proper way" to pronounce *crayons* is with two syllables.

KRANS

KREY-AWNS

KREY-AHNS

KREY-AWNS 42%

KREY-AHNS 39%

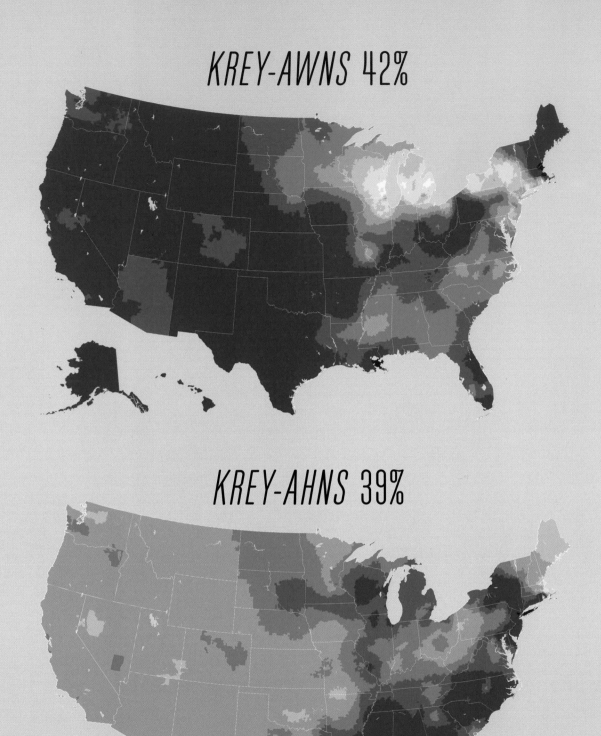

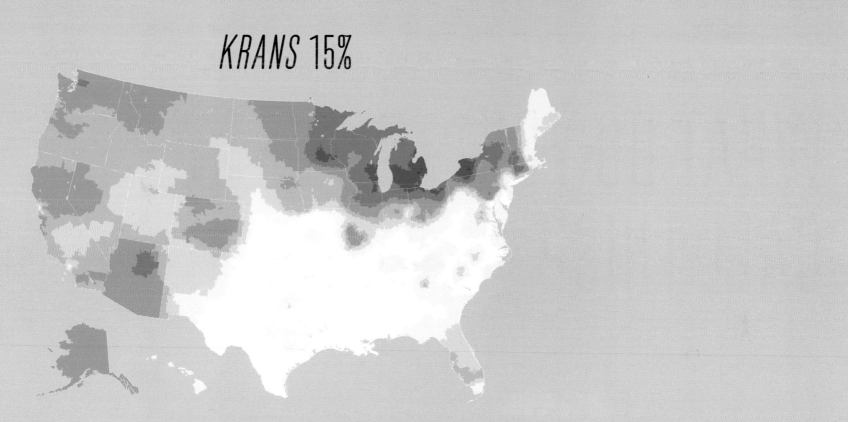

KRANS 15%

KROWNS 2%

PERCENT SAYING

0   10   20   30   40   50   75%

WHAT DO YOU CALL THIS?

Though about 80 percent of the population born in 1950 pronounces the word *quarter* as though it is spelled as *kor-ter*, that pronunciation is increasingly rare. Over two-thirds of those born in the 1990s instead pronounce the word as *kwor-ter*.

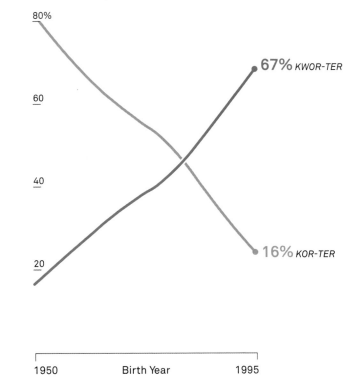

PERCENT USING, BY BIRTH YEAR

80%

60

67% *KWOR-TER*

40

20

16% *KOR-TER*

1950   Birth Year   1995

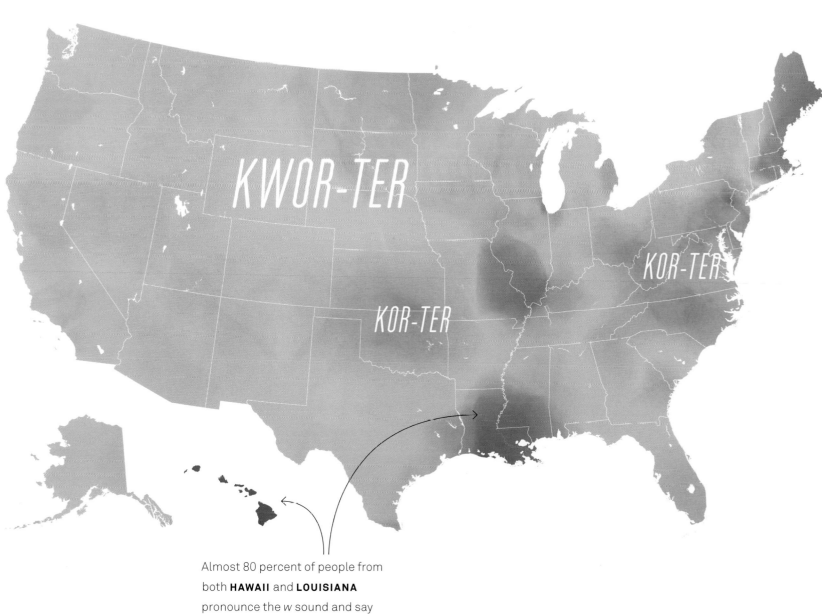

KWOR-TER

KOR-TER

KOR-TER

Almost 80 percent of people from
both **HAWAII** and **LOUISIANA**
pronounce the *w* sound and say
kwor-ter, making for an odd
geographic pairing.

110

PERCENT SAYING

0   10   20   30   40   50   75%

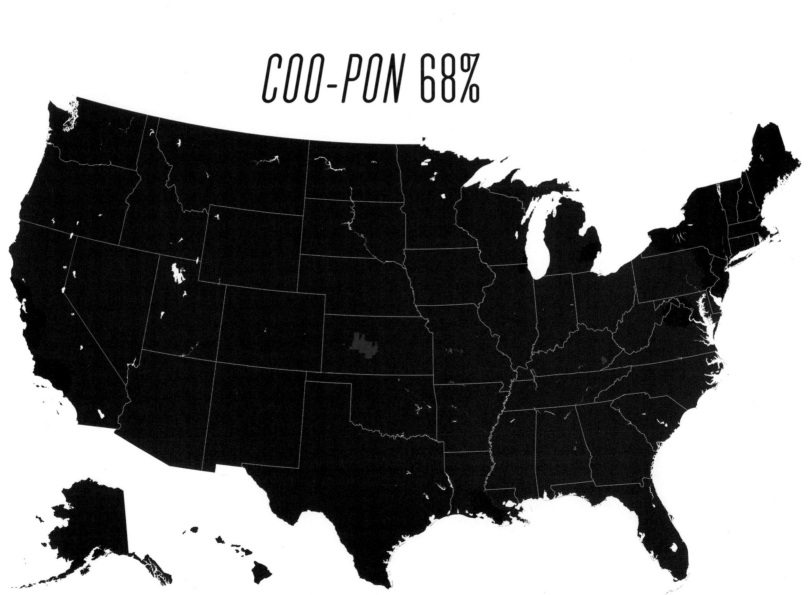

COO-PON 68%

WHAT WE USE
TO SAVE MONEY

CYOO-PON 31%

WHO TO CALL WHEN YOU GET ARRESTED

LOY-ER

112

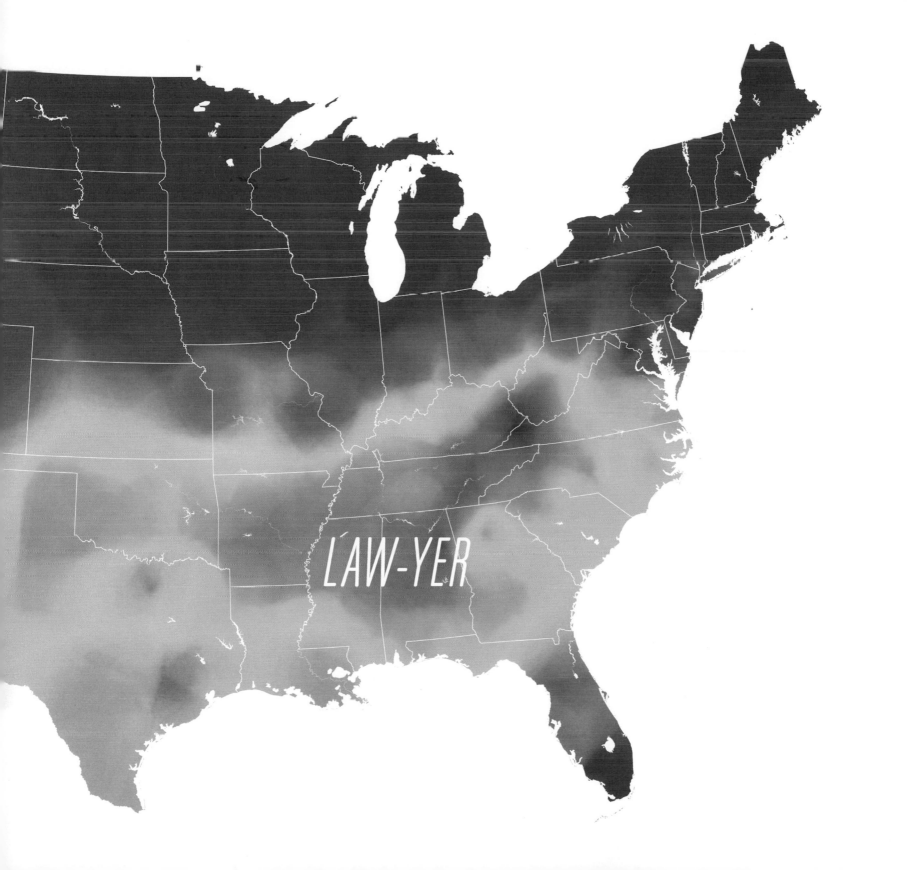

LAW-YER

DO YOU PRONOUNCE THE FIRST *D* IN *CANDIDATE?*

PERCENT SAYING

0 10 20 30 40 50 75%

YES 46%

SOMETIMES 30%

NO 23%

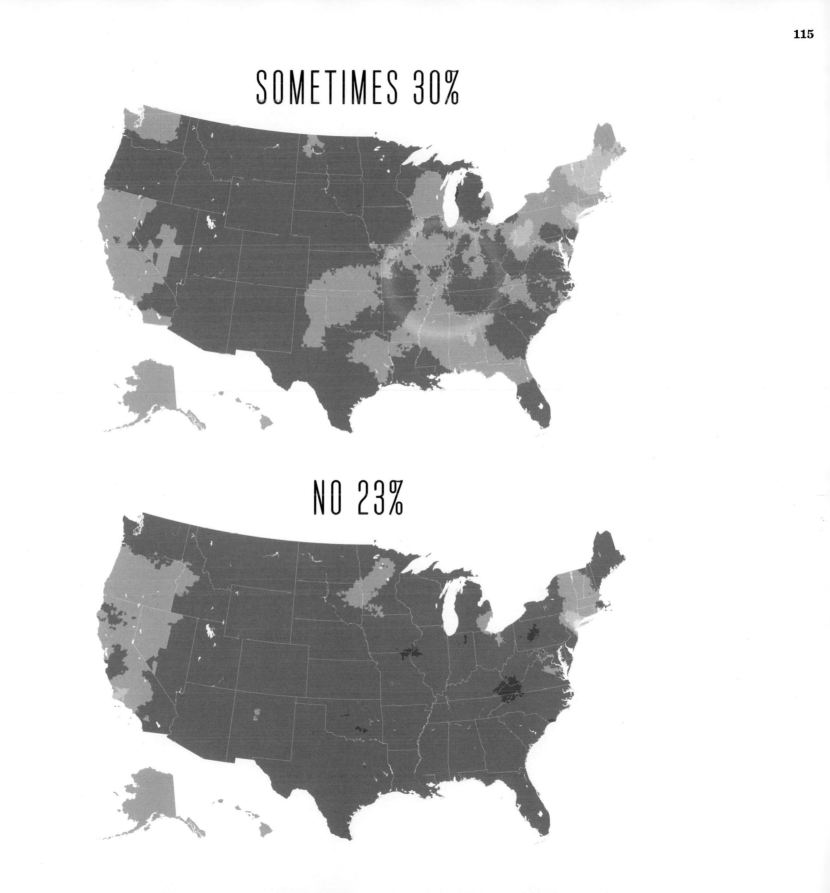

EITHER 24%

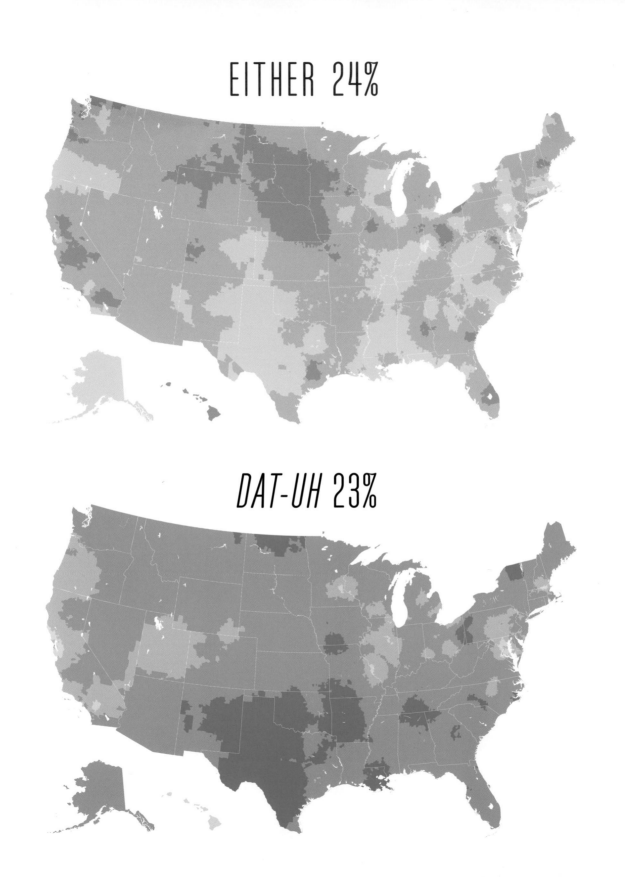

DAT-UH 23%

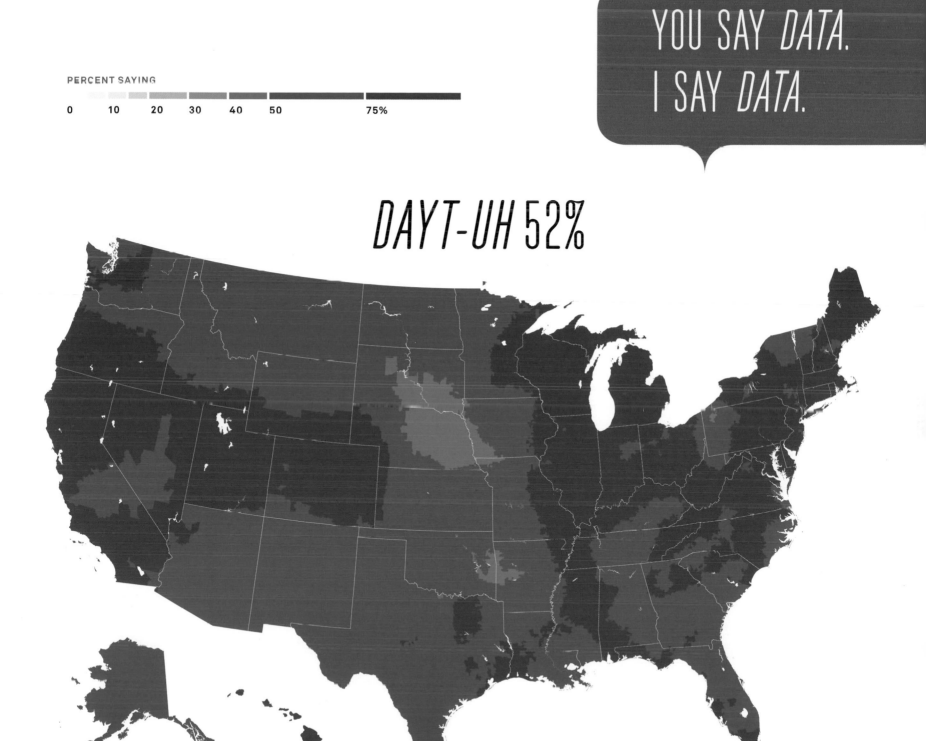

PERCENT SAYING

0   10   20   30   40   50   75%

YOU SAY *DATA.*
I SAY *DATA.*

DAYT-UH 52%

HOW WE
SAY *BEEN*

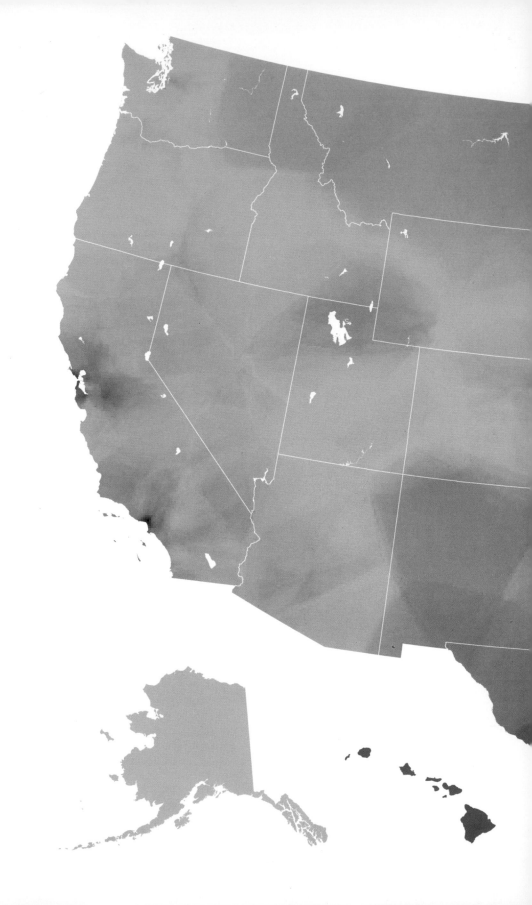

BEEN SOUNDS LIKE BEN

BEEN SOUNDS LIKE BIN

HOW TO PRETEND YOU'RE FROM
BOSTON

As one of the original linguistic centers of the thirteen colonies, Boston has always had its own distinct way of speaking. The phrase "Park your car in Harvard Yard"—or, for the Bostonian, *"Pahk ya cah in Havad Yahd"*—has become the standard cliché to test for a Boston accent. But the prevalence of that accent, particularly the Boston Brahmin accent of the old Boston upper class, has lessened over time. While the dropped *r* for which Boston has long been known is not as widespread as it once was, New England has an entire vocabulary of its own.

Here, you might *hosey* (claim) the front seat of the car on the way to the town *common*. What elsewhere would be a *milk shake* roughly half the people in New England call a *frappe* (in Rhode Island it's a *cabinet*), and almost 8 percent of people call soda *tonic*. You might hear a shopping cart called a *carriage* and, especially in Vermont, a mountain lion called a *catamount*. And, as we've seen, Rhode Island is one of the few places outside of Wisconsin where you're likely to hear a water fountain called a *bubbler,* with or without the *r.*

HOW TO PRETEND YOU'RE FROM
WESTERN NEW ENGLAND

Western New England, the region squeezed between the linguistic centers of Boston to the east and New York to the west, has developed its own way of speaking that is distinct from both. Here you'll find *tag sales* and *grinders,* and you get your water from a *drinking fountain* rather than a *water fountain* (or a *bubbler,* as you would in Rhode Island to the east). In Connecticut, the night before Halloween is *Mischief Night;* in Vermont it's *Cabbage Night.*

HOW TO PRETEND YOU'RE FROM
BALTIMORE

Dialect-wise, Maryland is an odd state. It lies south of the Mason-Dixon Line, but in style is a northeastern city, part of the megalopolis stretching from Washington, D.C., up to Boston.

Where New York has *stoops,* Baltimore (pronounced *Bawlmer*) has *front steps*. While you're there, head *down the ocean* and pick up some *carry-out: coddies* (deep-fried potato cakes flavored with salt cod), a *chicken box* (carry-out consisting of a box of fried chicken and french fries), *half-and-half* (a drink of half sweet tea, half lemonade), a *snoball* (shaved ice doused in a sweet syrup, served in a Styrofoam cup), and *lake trout* (battered and fried whiting, usually served with white bread and hot sauce). Then wash it all down with a six-pack of *Natty Boh.* (That's National Bohemian beer, formerly brewed in Baltimore, now owned by Pabst Brewing Company in Los Angeles. Incidentally, Pabst was the first American brewer to sell cans of beer in six-packs.)

And Baltimore's probably the last place in the country you might still see *arabbers* (pronounced *ay-rabber,* the first syllable rhyming with *day*) on the streets—men selling produce from horse-drawn carts.

Arabbing was once plentiful in the city but has been in decline since around World War II. While today only a handful of arabbers remain on the streets of Baltimore, the practice has a history stretching back to the years immediately after the Civil War. Maryland was a border state during the war—a slave state that fought for the North—hence it was not covered by the Emancipation Proclamation. After slavery was abolished in Maryland in 1864, arabbing was one of the few jobs available for black men, and it developed into a tradition, a business that was often passed down from fathers to sons.

HOW TO PRETEND YOU'RE FROM
NEW YORK

One of the most distinct dialects in the public imagination is that of New York—or, that is, *Noo Yawk.* Among other things, the stereotypical New York accent often drops the *h* in *huge* in favor of a *y,* so the word sounds like *yuge.* Like accents in Boston and parts of the Deep South, it is nonrhotic—dropping the *r* sound unless it is followed by a vowel, so that *butter* becomes *buttah* and *card* becomes *cahd.* For a long time, people considered this to be a mark of refinement. Think Franklin Delano Roosevelt. But over time, as with many strong accent markers, Americans began to associate nonrhotic speech with the working class, and it began to fade away.

But while accent becomes a marker of class, broader dialect signals, particularly those involving word choice, are generally more subtle. Regional words for common nouns are typically less tied to education and economic levels and are not consciously suppressed (of course there are exceptions to this rule, as anyone who has ordered a *pop* in the Northeast can tell you).

For one thing, New Yorkers almost always wait *on line,* not *in line.* When you get to the head of the line, the cashier may ask for the *following guest* to step down, a relatively new development that's taken hold only over the past twenty years or so. Around New York, especially in the outer boroughs and Long Island, you might order a *hero* rather than a *sub* and then take it back to your *walk-up* (an apartment in a building that doesn't have an elevator).

Of course, all of this really applies to New York City, Long Island, and the northern half of New Jersey. The rest of New York—that is, *upstate*—is an entirely different story. The eastern portion of the state is, linguistically, more a part of Connecticut, Vermont, and western New England. The western part—Buffalo, Rochester, and Syracuse—is its own dialect region.

As you drive west along the New York State Thruway and into upstate New York, you're actually passing from the northeastern coastal dialect regions into a wholly different place, linguistically: the region linguists refer to as the Inland North—a stretch of counties running along the southern shores of the Great Lakes, from Buffalo to Cleveland, through southern Michigan to northern Illinois and Milwaukee.

It's here you find a vowel pattern that linguist William Labov dubbed the Northern Cities Shift, a series of changes in vowel sounds that researchers first noted in the 1960s. Linguists often think of vowels in terms of the position of the speaker's tongue. You probably don't think about this much while you're speaking, but the different vowel sounds come about largely from having your tongue in various positions in your mouth.

Suppose that you and everyone you speak to start to change the way you pronounce a vowel. Say that your short *a* starts becoming "raised" and "fronted" (meaning that your tongue is higher and more forward in your mouth) so that *cat* starts to sound more like *kit*. But before your tongue gets too far, it ends up back where it started, turning the vowel into a diphthong (a syllable with two vowel sounds): *kyat*. As the short *a* changes position, pretty soon it's running into the space where the short *i* sound usually is. Sometimes when this happens, the sounds merge. But if the two sounds are to remain distinct, the short *i* has to go somewhere else, which it does, moving toward a short *u*, making *bit* sound like *but*. Then the short *u* moves toward the *aw* sound in words like *straw*.

This picture of the Northern Cities Shift is, of course, an oversimplified description. Rather than the dynamic described above where one vowel "pushes" another out of the way, linguists generally believe that the process is more akin to a "pull," where vowels move to occupy the space vacated by other shifted vowels.

Only some of these shifts have occurred throughout the Inland North, but you can hear examples of each to some extent in various combinations throughout the region.

HOW TO PRETEND YOU'RE FROM
CHICAGO

Lace up your *gym shoes* and head to Chicago, where you don't ride the subway but the *L,* the elevated rapid transit system whose tracks crisscross the city (analogous to the *T* in Boston). Even the sections of track that are underground are still referred to as the *L,* which you might take to avoid the *gapers' block* or *gapers' delay* (a traffic jam caused by drivers staring at an accident) on the *expressway*.

Overall, if you say *gapers' block, expressway,* and *gym shoes,* there's a greater than 95 percent chance you're from the Chicago area.

4

Part Four

WHERE WE GO

WHAT WE CALL

A FREIGHT TRUCK

Elsewhere in the English-speaking world, you might find a *transport truck* (Canada) or an *articulated lorry* (Ireland and the United Kingdom), but in the United States, depending on where you are, you're likely to see a *semi* (or *semi truck*), a *tractor-trailer,* or an *eighteen-wheeler.*

TRACTOR-TRAILER

SEMI/SEMI-TRUCK

EIGHTEEN-WHEELER

128

Not particularly common
anywhere, but almost unheard-
of outside of **CALIFORNIA**, a *rig* or
big rig is most common around
SACRAMENTO, **SAN FRANCISCO**,
and parts of **LOS ANGELES**.

RIG/BIG RIG

PERCENT SAYING *RIG/BIG RIG*

0	5	10	15	20	>25%

WHAT WE SAY WHEN WE WANT OUR FRIENDS TO JOIN US

People are most likely to ask "You coming with?" in Minnesota and Chicago, but language divisions are not only geographic.

Regardless of where you live, the younger you are, the more likely you are to ask "You coming with?" as a complete sentence. Fewer than 20 percent of Americans born in 1950 do so, compared to half of those born in 1995 or later.

**PERCENT ASKING "YOU COMING WITH?",
BY BIRTH YEAR**

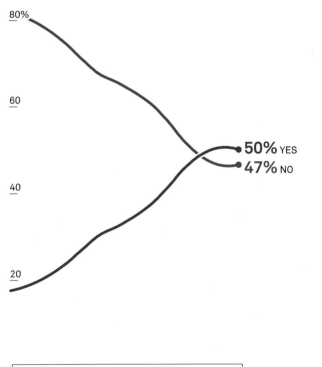

80%

60

50% YES
47% NO

40

20

1950   Birth Year   1995

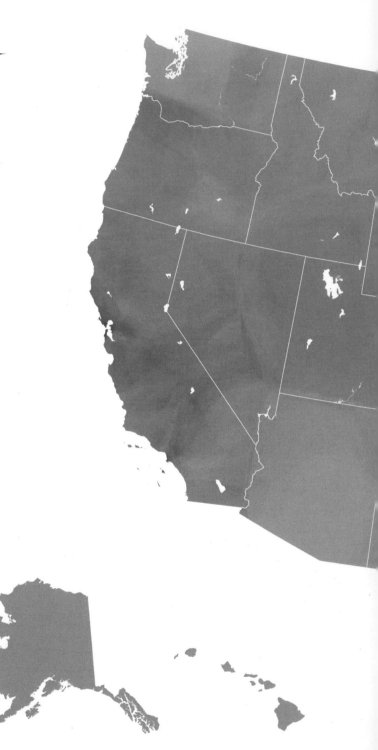

WHERE THEY ASK "YOU COMING WITH?"

WHERE THEY DON'T

HOW WE SAY *ROUTE*

LIKE *ROUT* 38%

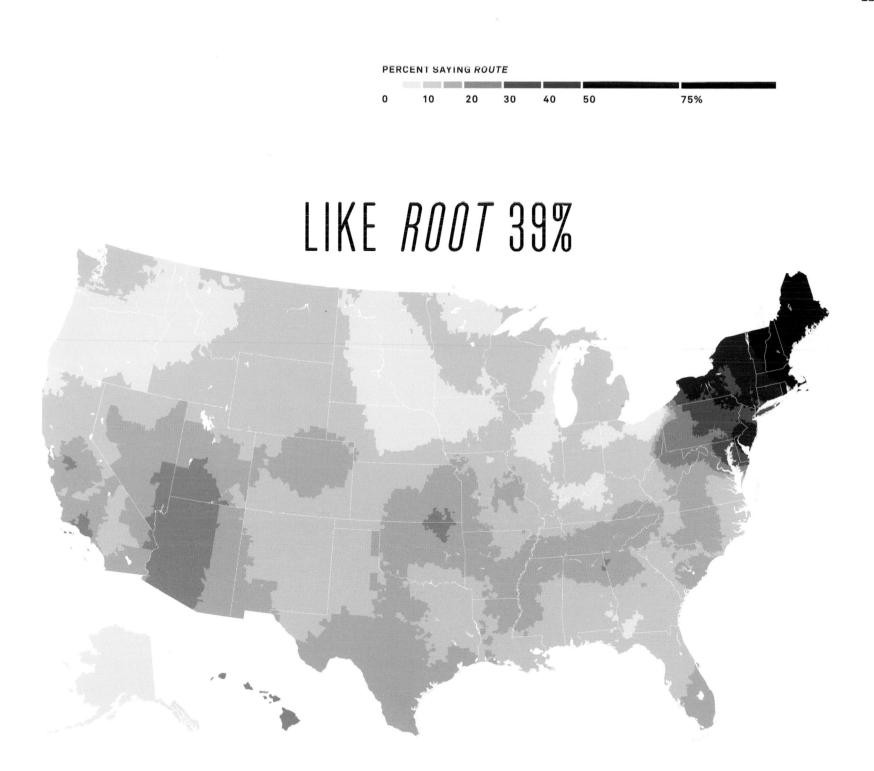

LIKE *ROOT* 39%

WHAT WE DRIVE ON

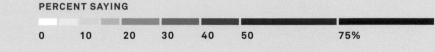

PERCENT SAYING

0 10 20 30 40 50 75%

HIGHWAY 56%

FREEWAY 31%

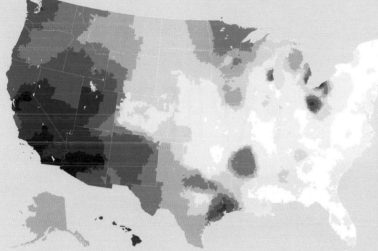

EXPRESSWAY 4%

THRUWAY <1%

A very clear dividing line between **BUFFALO** and **ROCHESTER**, **NEW YORK**, emerges once you start asking people about their generic word for *highway*. In **BUFFALO**, whose suburbs the New York State Thruway cuts through on its way south, over a third of people use *thruway* as their generic term, the highest percentage in the country by far. Nowhere else in the United States has a percentage higher than 10.

EXPRESSWAY

ROCHESTER

THRUWAY

BUFFALO

In **ROCHESTER**, on the other hand,
with its Eastern and Western
Expressways, you're more likely
to encounter expressway than
anywhere else in the country
outside of **CHICAGO**, **ILLINOIS**,
and **FLINT**, **MICHIGAN**.

FRONTAGE ROAD 31%

SERVICE ROAD 26%

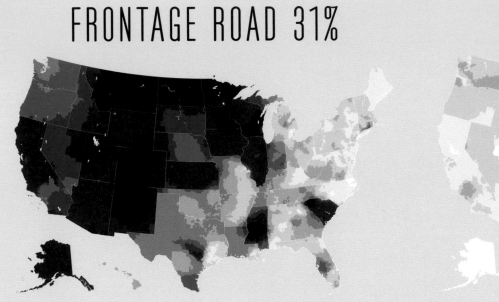

ACCESS ROAD 20%

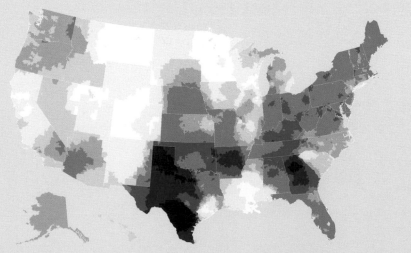

NO WORD FOR THIS 18%

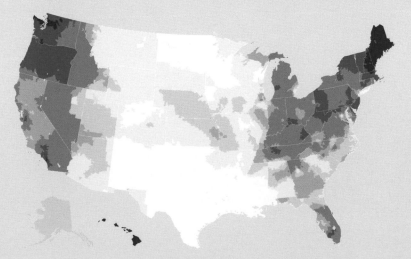

FEEDER ROAD 3%

OUTER ROAD <1%

WHAT WE CALL THE LITTLE ROAD THAT RUNS ALONGSIDE THE HIGHWAY

PERCENT SAYING

0   10   20   30   40   50   75%

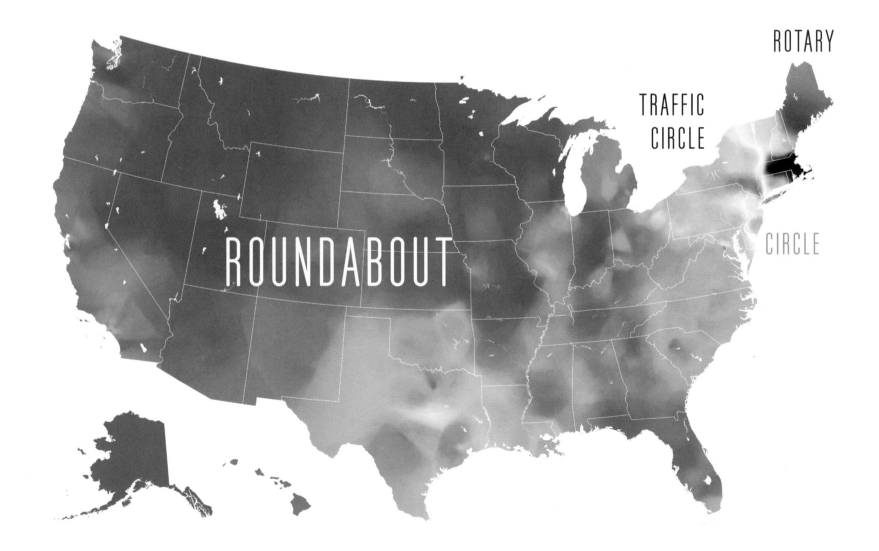

HOW WE DRIVE
IN CIRCLES

ROTARY

TRAFFIC
CIRCLE

ROUNDABOUT

CIRCLE

The use of *roundabout* has spread throughout the country over the course of the past century.

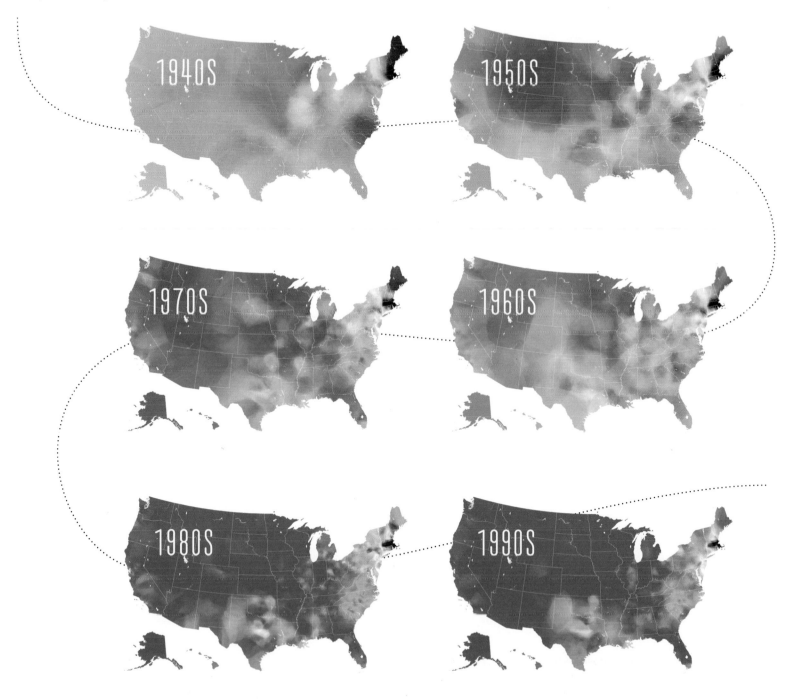

ROUNDABOUT 55%

TRAFFIC CIRCLE 29%

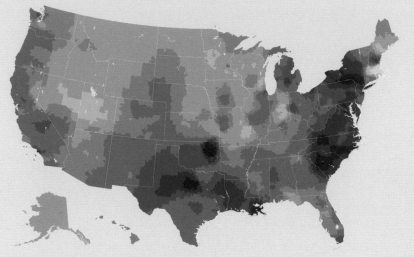

ROTARY 7%

CIRCLE 5%

PERCENT SAYING

0   5   10   15   20   >25%

Some of the final holdouts against *roundabout* are in the **NORTHEAST**. **MASSACHUSETTS** and **MAINE** have their *rotaries,* and **NEW YORK**, eastern **NEW HAMPSHIRE**, and elsewhere have their *traffic circles*. In **SOUTH JERSEY**, on the other hand, the word *traffic* is implied, and it's simply called a *circle*.

TRAFFIC CIRCLE

ROTARY

ROUNDABOUT

CIRCLE

WHAT WE CALL

THE STRIP OF GRASS BETWEEN THE SIDE-WALK AND THE ROAD

Perhaps no term is as regionally distinct as Clevelanders' word for the strip of grass between the sidewalk and the road.

Almost three-quarters of the country has no word for it at all. But in Cleveland and to some extent in nearby cities like Akron, Ohio, and Erie, Pennsylvania, it's the *tree lawn*.

Other terms for this little grassy bit are scattered around— *berm, parking, verge, devil's strip, terrace.* For my part, I've always called it the *country strip.* But Cleveland is the only place where a majority has a word for the thing at all.

PERCENT SAYING *TREE LAWN*

0   10   20   30   40   >50%

TREE LAWN

CLEVELAND

Perhaps people only acquire this knowledge in their
later years or perhaps the term is on the decline, but the
younger you are, the less likely you are to have a word
for the strip of grass that those from Cleveland usually
call the *tree lawn*.

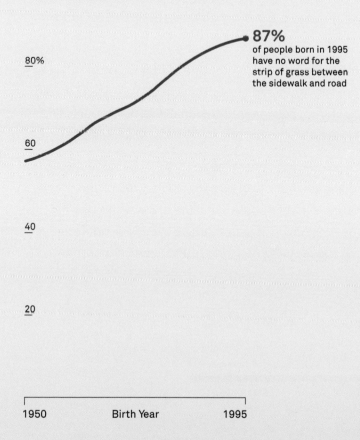

87%
of people born in 1995
have no word for the
strip of grass between
the sidewalk and road

80%

60

40

20

1950   Birth Year   1995

WHAT WE CALL THAT STRIP OF GRASS IN THE MIDDLE OF THE ROAD

Historians say that the history of *neutral ground* goes all the way back to 1803 and the Louisiana Purchase. At that time, a massive influx of English-speaking migrants descended on New Orleans, joining the French and Spanish inhabitants of the city. The newcomers settled upriver, on the other side of a long strip of land intended to become a canal.

Real tension existed between the two groups—fights were common, intermarriage was not. But envoys from the French and Spanish sections of New Orleans would meet at this *neutral ground* to conduct business. The canal was never built, and the land instead became Canal Street, a major thoroughfare with a median.

But the name *neutral ground* stuck, and it continues to this day to serve as the term for a grass strip running down the middle of a road. While widespread in New Orleans itself, with more than 90 percent of people using the phrase, the use of *neutral ground* fades sharply as you leave the city limits. Even in Baton Rouge, only 80 miles away, the share of those using *neutral ground* is only 45 percent.

PERCENT SAYING

| 0 | 10 | 20 | 30 | 40 | 50 | | 75% |

BOULEVARD

NEUTRAL GROUND

WHAT WE CALL

A DRIVE-THROUGH LIQUOR STORE

For years before the first McDonald's drive-thru opened in 1975, Americans had been buying liquor from their cars at drive-through liquor stores. They're unknown in much of the country but go by a variety of names in Texas and pockets of the Deep South.

If you're looking to buy beer without leaving the comfort of your vehicle, in and around Dallas, throughout Mississippi, and in Tallahassee, you'd head to a *beer barn*.

But in the expanse of country west of San Antonio, you'd head to a *beverage barn* instead, as you would in Tampa, Florida.

Though if you're going to come up with a name for a drive-through liquor store, *party barn* is pretty good. So well done, Corpus Christi.

NO WORD FOR THIS 77%

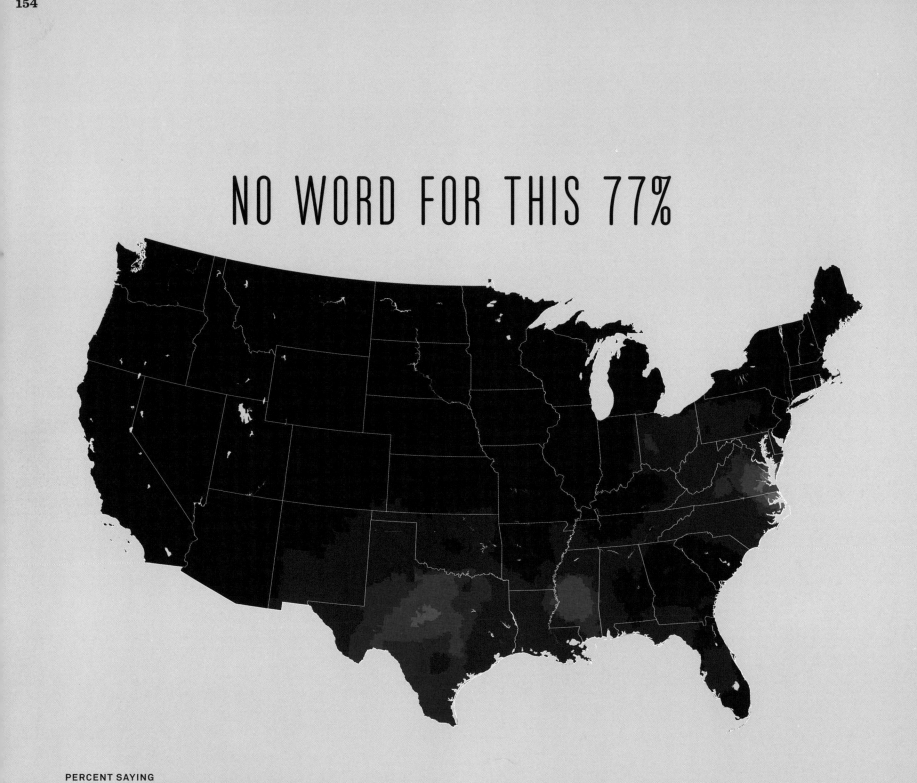

PERCENT SAYING

0   10   20   30   40   50   75%

BEER BARN 6%

BREW THRU 6%

PARTY BARN 1%

BEVERAGE BARN 1%

TRANSIT NETWORK TRICKERY

LIGHT RAIL

TROLLEY

STREETCAR

157

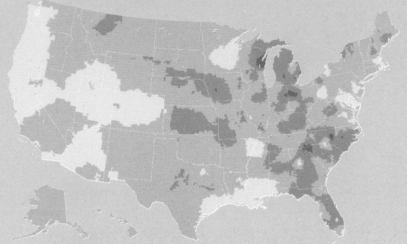

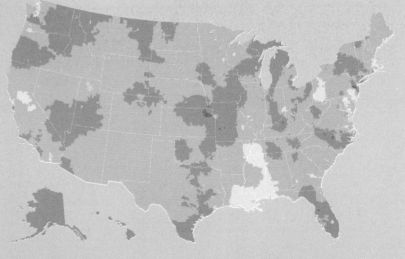

METRO 3%

NO WORD FOR THIS 3%

TRAM 9%

LIGHT RAIL 12%

PERCENT SAYING

0   10   20   30   40   50   75%

158

CABLE CAR 4%

TRAIN 6%

STREETCAR 24%

TROLLEY 34%

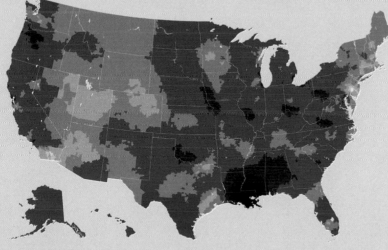

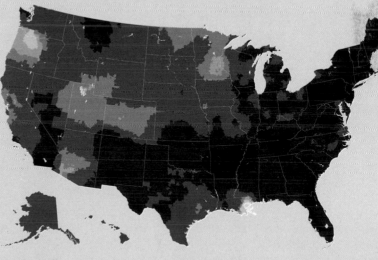

SACRAMENTO

SAN FRANCISCO

SAN JOSE

A STREETCAR NAMED *LIGHT RAIL*

In 1888, Frank J. Sprague's streetcar design, which used a trolley wheel, or *troller,* to feed electricity from overhead wires to the streetcar engine, revolutionized urban travel. Within a year, Sprague's *trolley car* was in place in more than 150 railway systems in the United States. The change ushered in the modern American city. People no longer had to live within a short distance of their jobs. Suddenly, communities began to spring up 15 or 20 miles from the center of the city.

The rise of the automobile in the 1940s and '50s sent many streetcars into retirement, and almost all of the original lines closed. But in recent years the light rail has undergone something of a renaissance, with many cities building new rail lines. It has become popular again as urban living has become more popular.

What people call the light rail car is often a product of the name of their city's light rail network. San Diego has *trolleys* (from the San Diego Trolley, the first of the second wave of light rail lines, which began service in 1981). Sacramento and San Jose have *light rails.* San Francisco, less than 100 miles away, has *streetcars.*

These terms also vary across the country, with little geographic cohesion. Philadelphia and Memphis have *trolleys.* On Team Light Rail: Denver, Minneapolis, and Phoenix. On Team Streetcar: New Orleans and Cincinnati. And with the Portland Streetcar system joining the city's MAX Light Rail in 2001, that city now shows an almost even split.

Some rail enthusiasts argue that there are semantic distinctions among the terms, with *light rail* denoting a faster, higher-capacity service with longer distances between stations. But that notion doesn't always match reality. San Diego's *trolleys,* to take just one example, move as fast as Sacramento's *light rail,* with stations spread farther apart.

WHERE WE SHOP

GROH-SERY STORE

GROH-SHERY STORE

GROH-SERY STORE

In and around Boston, New York, and Philadelphia, you're more likely to hear *groh sery store*. But in much of the country, the (once non-standard) *groh-shery store* pronunciation dominates. What's more, the pronunciation with the *sh* sound is on the rise: nearly two-thirds of Americans born in 1995 or later use it, suggesting the alternate pronunciation could one day become the norm.

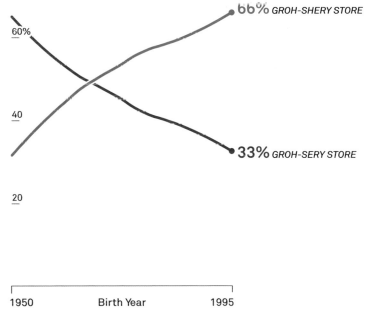

GROCERY STORE PRONUNCIATION,
BY BIRTH YEAR

66% *GROH-SHERY STORE*

60%

40

33% *GROH-SERY STORE*

20

1950   Birth Year   1995

WHAT WE PUT OUR STUFF IN WHILE WE SHOP

In 1937, Sylvan Goldman devised a way that customers at his Humpty Dumpty supermarket in Oklahoma City could hold more groceries. What you might call a *carriage* in Massachusetts or a *grocery cart* in Nebraska is most commonly known as a *shopping cart*. In Alabama, however, more than 40 percent of people call it a *buggy*.

Goldman's cart wasn't an immediate success. It reminded many women of a baby carriage, and some men felt it insulted their masculinity, writes Ellen Ruppel Shell in her book *Cheap: The High Cost of Discount Culture*. Others feared that the soiled diapers of babies sitting in the front of the carts would make the carts unsanitary. Goldman persisted, however, handing people the carts as they entered and even hiring people to push loaded carts back and forth in front of his store as a demonstration. Eventually, the cart became a staple of the American retail experience, making Goldman a millionaire in the process.

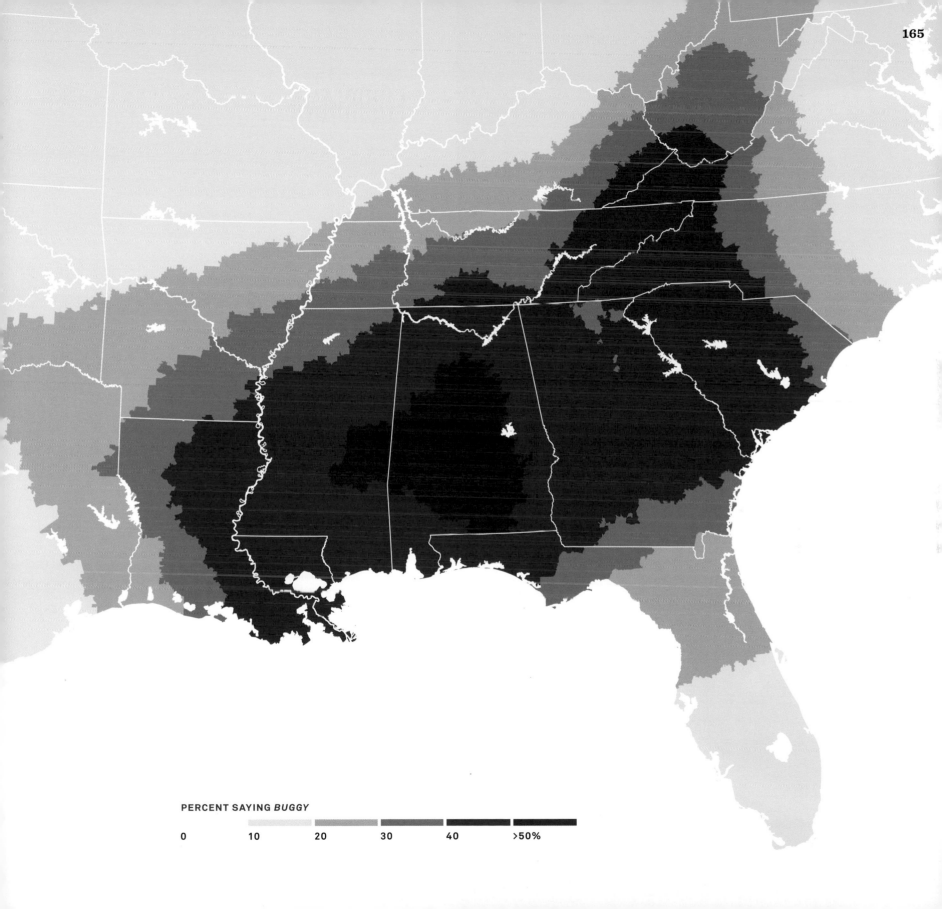

PERCENT SAYING *BUGGY*

0   10   20   30   40   >50%

LOUISIANA

The distinct cultures and influences of New Orleans—French, Spanish, creole—blend together to make English sound different here than it does pretty much anywhere else in the country. The influence of French—more specifically, Cajun French—is everywhere. In some parishes, more than a quarter of the population speaks French at home.

Many of their dialect words come from their local foods: *gumbo* and *jambalaya,* and *po'boys* and *beignets,* of course, as well as *daube glace* (a chilled, jellied beef or veal stew, usually served as an appetizer with sliced French bread).

The distinct patois of New Orleans is not all about food, though. There's also *neutral ground, crawfish* (not *crawdads* or *crayfish*), and *doodlebugs*. Louisiana doesn't have *Mischief Night,* but if it did, you might go *rolling* (covering houses in toilet paper). The state is the one place where people refer to the end of a loaf of bread as the *nose* and where *aunt* might sound like *ain't*.

A *lagniappe* (pronounced *lan-yap*) is a small gift that often accomanies a purchase. It's a word with definitive creole origins: From the indigenous Quechua language of South America, Spanish colonizers got *la ñapa* (meaning extra or bonus). After several centuries of mixing with French, *la ñapa* transmogrified into *lagniappe*. It is, as Mark Twain wrote in *Life on the Mississippi,* "one excellent word—a word worth traveling to New Orleans to get."

HOW TO PRETEND YOU'RE FROM
THE DEEP SOUTH

Dialect-wise, the deepest part of the Deep South comprises Alabama, Mississippi, western Tennessee, and the eastern half of Arkansas.

Around here, you might toss some *cocola* (soda) into your *buggy* (shopping cart) and then stop off for some *flapjacks* (pancakes). Less than 2 percent of people in the Deep South still use the word *flapjacks,* but of all those in America who say *flapjacks* instead of *pancakes,* almost a quarter of them are from around here. Residents of the region are also fond of *Lane cake,* a buttery layer cake with white frosting and a large helping of bourbon.

You might be from the Deep South if you:

- call covering someone's house in toilet paper *rolling,*
- say *eighteen-wheeler,* and
- use one of the more colorful expressions for when it rains while the sun is shining, like *monkey's wedding, the wolf giving birth,* or *the devil beating his wife.*

HOW TO PRETEND YOU'RE FROM
GEORGIA

Georgia speech can be tough to distinguish from the words alone, particularly because the dialect of Atlanta is so different from that of the surrounding countryside. In many respects, speech in Atlanta bears more resemblance to that of Raleigh, North Carolina. Both cities show more of a northern tilt, thanks in large part to the influx of notherners over the years.

Of course, Georgia has its own particular food terms: *chicken mull* (a creamy chicken stew, various versions of which can be found scattered around Georgia and North Carolina) and *egg bread* (cornbread made with eggs) among them. And don't forget *crip course* (an easy class), *access road,* and *buggy* (shopping cart); if you hear those three together, there's a 50 percent chance you're talking to someone from Georgia.

HOW TO PRETEND YOU'RE FROM
SOUTH CAROLINA

Charleston, South Carolina, was a major city in colonial times—one of the original six linguistic centers of the United States.

South Carolina is also home to the endangered language of Gullah, which can still be heard out in the Lowcountry and Sea Islands of South Carolina and Georgia. It developed among West African slaves working the coastal plantations, a combination of English and West African languages like Fula and Mende that became a distinct creole. The islands' geographic isolation allowed the community to develop a way of speaking distinct enough from everyday American English to become its own language. While the population of Gullah speakers numbers around 250,000, most do not speak it as their first language. The most recent census puts the number of people speaking Gullah at home at fewer than one thousand. About one-third of all Gullah speakers live in South Carolina, and the other two-thirds live in New York.

There are not *garage sales* here, only *yard sales.* People don't say *semi* or *frontage road.* It's distinctly *y'all* territory, and it remains one of the places you're most likely to hear someone say they *might could* do something (a construction known as a *double modal*).

As is the case with Georgia, North Carolina is linguistically divided between a more northern-influenced urban area (the Research Triangle) and a surrounding countryside. There's the Outer Banks, the middle section around Raleigh and Chapel Hill (the Research Triangle), and in the western portion of the state, which more closely resembles eastern Tennessee than central North Carolina, you'll find that the dialect has an Appalachian tinge. As you move east, toward the Outer Banks, you're more likely to find someone familiar with the local *brew thru.*

Just to the southeast of the Research Triangle is where you're most likely to hear someone call an easy class a *crip course.* In addition, if you hear someone say *tractor-trailer* and use *granddaddy* for the long-legged spidery-looking thing that I'd call a *daddy longlegs,* there's a 50-50 chance you're talking to someone from North Carolina.

HOW TO PRETEND YOU'RE FROM
NORTH CAROLINA

HOW TO PRETEND YOU'RE FROM

FLORIDA

Florida is really more like two linguistic states, with the dividing line between north and south running from Port St. Lucie on the Atlantic coast roughly southwest through Lake Okeechobee (a name derived from the Hitchiti words for *big* and *water*) to Fort Myers and the Gulf of Mexico. An old cliché about Florida holds that "the farther north you go, the farther south you get," and it applies to speech too. The northern region speaks something closer to a southern dialect while the southern region speaks something closer to a northern dialect. Southern Florida is also notable for the influence of Spanish immigrants. Over 90 percent of people in Hialeah, just west of Miami, speak Spanish in the home.

Florida's speech divide follows the more subtle aspects of the entire country's northern and southern dialects. Of the Floridians who use the word *supper,* call the bug that curls up into a little ball when touched a *roly-poly,* and don't use the word *sunshower,* 80 percent of them are from northern rather than southern Florida.

But enough coherence still exists between the two halves of the state to give Floridian speech its own character. The biggest unifier is *panther.* Half of those who say *panther* instead of *mountain lion* are from Florida, as are 75 percent of those who, in addition to saying *panther,* use *scallion* over *green onion* (usually restricted more to the northeastern states) and know about drive-through liquor stores but don't have a special word for them.

Part Five

5 THINGS WE SEE

WHAT WE CALL

THE INSECTS THAT GLOW AT NIGHT

Judging people by their speech is nothing new. In the 1800s, British writers scorned their American counterparts for their peculiar habits, such as calling a wide variety of different insects *bugs:* thus we had May bugs, June bugs, and, of course, *lightning bugs*.

The term *lightning bug,* well known in America since at least 1778, was never universally adopted in the country, and even today its use offers one of the few examples of a sharp divide among the boroughs of New York City. Manhattanites tend to eschew the Americanism in favor of the more British *firefly,* while the denizens of Staten Island take their cue from New Jersey and stick with *lightning bug*.

Yet some evidence suggests that *lightning bug*'s days may be numbered: Though it is twice as popular as *firefly* among speakers born in the 1950s, for those born in the 1990s the ratio is flipped.

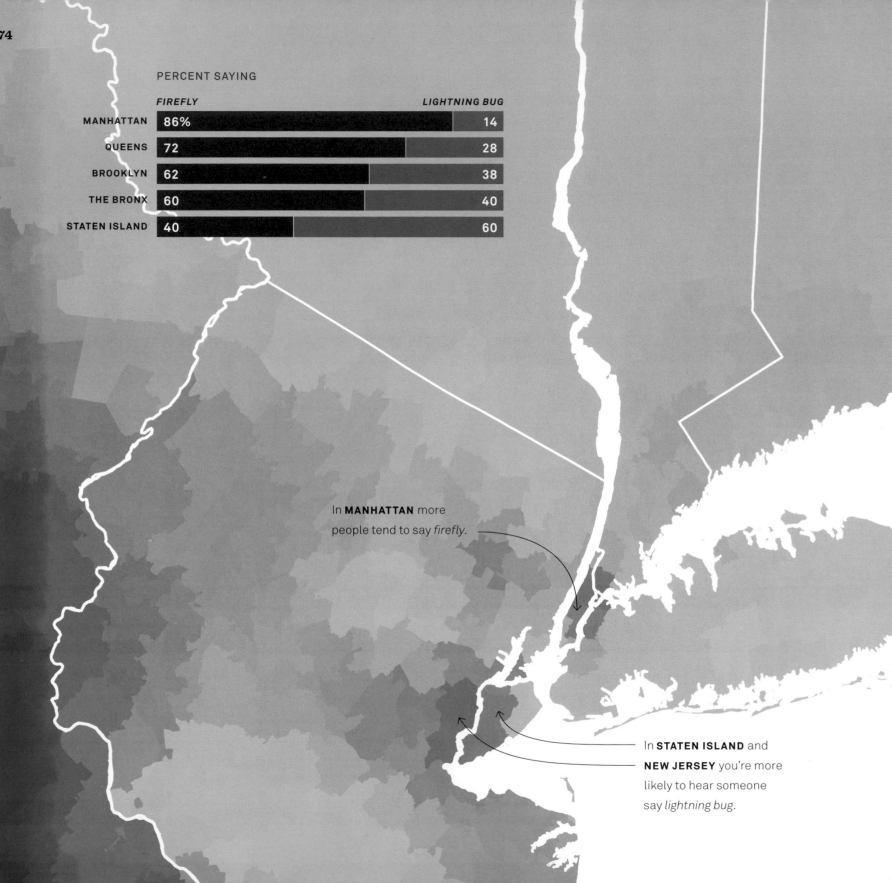

PERCENT SAYING

	FIREFLY		*LIGHTNING BUG*
MANHATTAN	86%		14
QUEENS	72		28
BROOKLYN	62		38
THE BRONX	60		40
STATEN ISLAND	40		60

In **MANHATTAN** more people tend to say *firefly*.

In **STATEN ISLAND** and **NEW JERSEY** you're more likely to hear someone say *lightning bug*.

NO MORE LIGHTNING BUGS?
Over the past century, the part
of the country where speakers
are more likely to say *firefly* has
expanded.

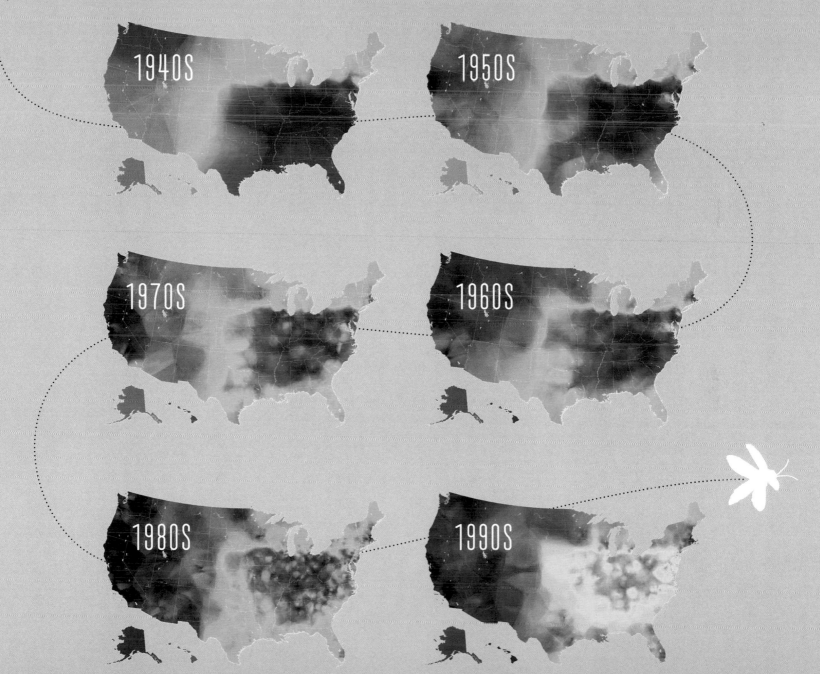

A PHIL BY ANY OTHER NAME WOULD BE AS ACCURATE

Most of the country prefers *groundhog*, particularly the Appalachian region around West Virginia and western Pennsylvania, home to the country's largest Groundhog Day celebration and most famous groundhog: Punxsutawney Phil.

Groundhog Day, celebrated on February 2, derives from the ancient Christian tradition of Candlemas Day. The Pennsylvania Dutch, seventeenth- and eighteenth-century German immigrants who came to Pennsylvania speaking *Deutsch*, brought the tradition to the United States.

Despite the ubiquity of the holiday, people in New York, New England, and parts of the upper Midwest more often call this animal a *woodchuck*.

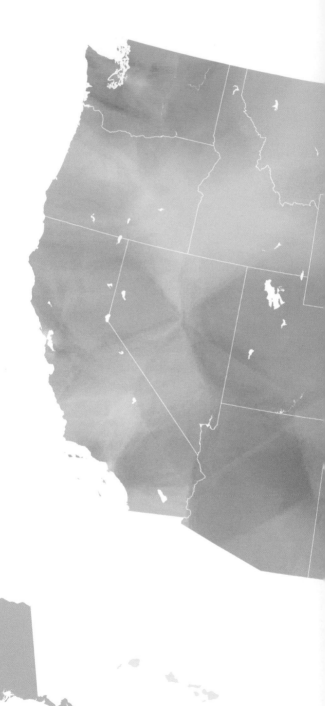

WHAT DO YOU CALL THIS?

Unlike the rest of the Pacific Northwest, **SEATTLE** and the surrounding area prefer *crawfish*.

CRAYFISH

CRAWDAD

CRAWFISH

The capital for *crawfish* is, of course, the capital of Louisiana, **BATON ROUGE**. The word is more popular there (chosen by over 97 percent) than in any other city in the United States.

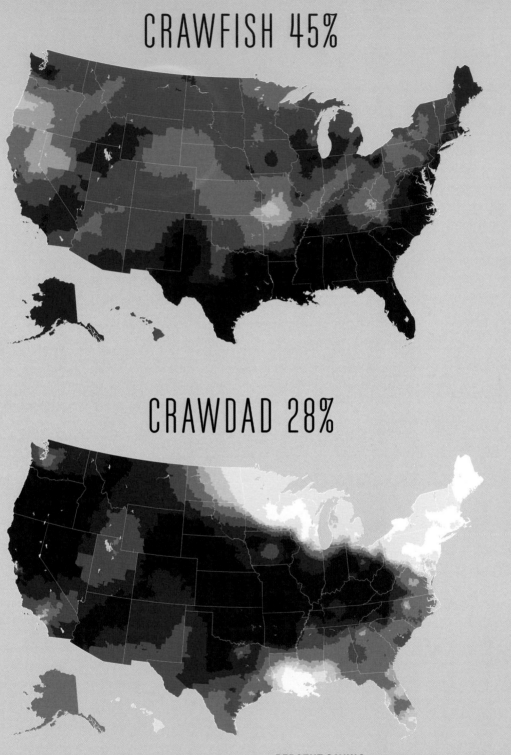

CRAWFISH 45%

CRAWDAD 28%

PERCENT SAYING

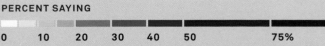

0   10   20   30   40   50   75%

CRAYFISH 23%

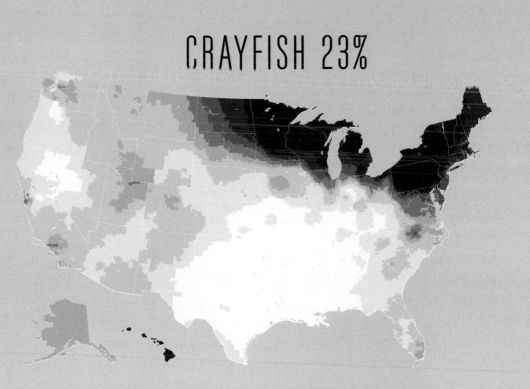

NO WORD FOR THIS 2%

WE DON'T EVEN KNOW

WHAT THIS BUG IS, NEVER MIND WHAT TO CALL IT

The little critter (the woodlouse) isn't technically an insect—surprisingly, it's a crustacean. It is commonly found in the damp, dark spaces underneath rocks and logs, and its most noticeable characteristic is its tendency to curl up into a little ball when disturbed. Hence the name *roly-poly*.

But while *roly-poly* is the most popular name for the bug, er, crustacean, almost half the country prefers another word, with great geographic variation in people's choices. *Pillbug* is the most common response in Cincinnati, and *doodlebug* in New Orleans. In New England, many people have no word for it at all.

And in a seemingly random smattering of places around the country—including western New York, Utah, the Pacific Northwest, and, to a somewhat lesser extent, Pittsburgh, Milwaukee, and Washington, D.C.—you find instead the term *potato bug*. No one I talked to could offer a solid explanation for this odd geographic grouping. For the time being, the mystery of *potato bug* endures.

Once confounding factor to keep in mind: *potato bug* is often applied to at least three different insects—not only the woodlouse but the Jerusalem cricket and the potato beetle as well.

ROLY-POLY 54%

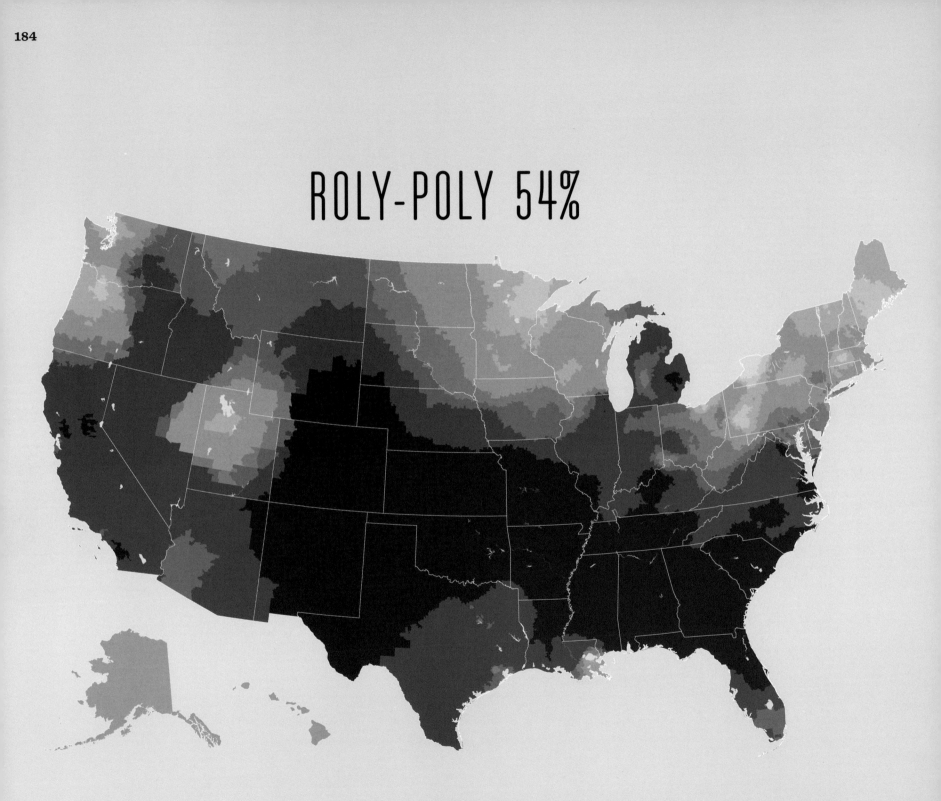

PERCENT SAYING

0   10   20   30   40   50   75%

PILLBUG 13%

NO WORD FOR THIS 11%

POTATO BUG 10%

DOODLEBUG 3%

CENTIPEDE 3%

FOUR WORDS.
ONE CAT.

You may have heard people talk about *mountain lions, cougars, catamounts,* and *panthers* without realizing that they're talking about the same animal.

Panther is distinctly Floridian. It is one of the few quirks of both the northern and southern Florida dialects, and its use falls sharply at the state line. Within Florida, usage tops 40 percent, but Mobile, Alabama, just west of the Florida Panhandle, is the only place outside the state where more than 10 percent of people use the word.

The rarest name of the four is *catamount*. It's not the most common term anywhere in the country, but it reaches its peak popularity around Burlington, Vermont, where more than 20 percent of people choose the word. The high for every region outside of Vermont is 3 percent. No wonder the University of Vermont, which is in Burlington, calls its teams the Catamounts.

While *panther* and *cougar* are two of the more common team nicknames in sports, *catamount* has yet to catch on to the same extent. The only other *catamounts* I could find are at Western Carolina University, in Cullowhee, North Carolina.

MOUNTAIN LION 75%

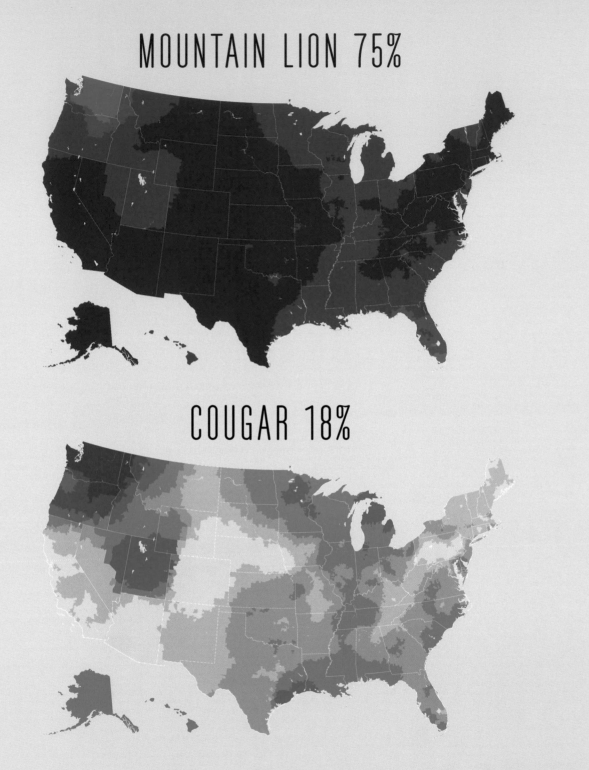

COUGAR 18%

PERCENT SAYING

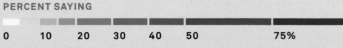

0   10   20   30   40   50   75%

CATAMOUNT <1%

PANTHER 4%

WHAT WE CALL IT WHEN

IT'S RAINING WHILE THE SUN IS SHINING

SUNSHOWER

NO WORD FOR THIS

THE DEVIL BEATING HIS WIFE

SUNSHOWER

THE DEVIL BEATING HIS WIFE

I'm a northerner, and nothing surprised me more in my research than the evocative phrase *the devil beating his wife* for the mixture of sun and rain that I've known all my life as a *sunshower*.

The mix of sun and rain is sufficiently odd that it brings out folk expressions in a staggering number of languages. Many involve the wedding or birth of various animals—*fox's wedding* (Japanese), *the wolf is having a baby* (Armenian), *the leopard is giving birth* (Luganda), or *a wedding for monkeys* (Zulu). References to *the devil beating his wife* are found in Dutch and Hungarian. In Bulgarian and Turkish, *the devil is getting married*.

Jonathon Green, author of the authoritative *Green's Dictionary of Slang,* traces the expression back to the French idiom *le diable bat sa femme et marie sa fille* (the devil beats his wife and marries his daughter), an expression that has been reported to have taken hold in the south of France.

Regardless of its provenance, the phrase is still widely used in the Deep South. Over half of respondents in and around Mississippi and Alabama use it.

In **HAWAII**, the same phenomenon is often known as *liquid sun*.

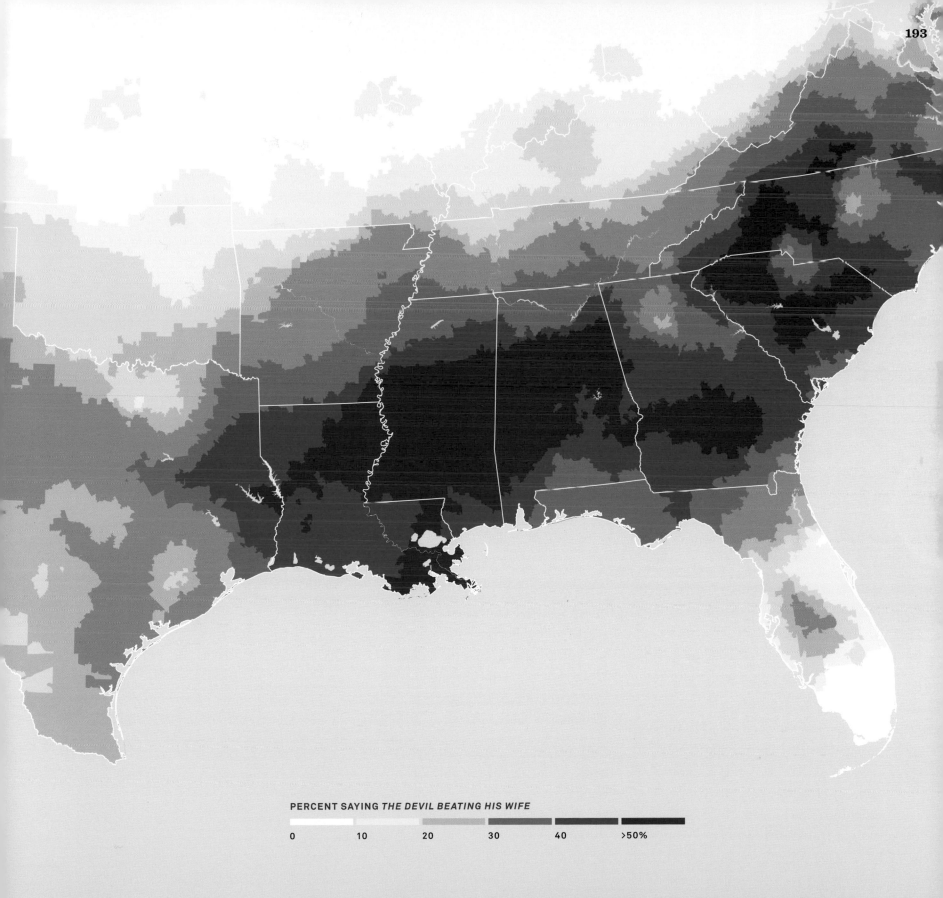

PERCENT SAYING *THE DEVIL BEATING HIS WIFE*

0   10   20   30   40   >50%

HOW TO PRETEND YOU'RE FROM
MISSOURI

Missouri is divided culturally between Kansas City in the west and St. Louis in the east. And it isn't only a difference in barbecue styles or baseball-team affections that signal you've crossed the dividing line.

The strongest linguistic dividing line is our good friend *cot* vs. *caught*. In St. Louis, the vowels are still distinct among almost 90 percent of the population. In Kansas City, less than 25 percent of residents still pronounce *cot*

differently than *caught*. The two metro areas have been different in this respect for some time. But while Kansas City used to be the outlier, St. Louis now is. It's the only place in the region where the unmerged outnumber the merged.

One of St. Louis's other strongest distinctions, relative to the rest of the region, is the persistence of *soda*. *Pop* territory lies to the north in Iowa and to the west in Kansas, and Arkansas and

Tennessee are *coke* country. Start traveling farther east, into Indiana, and you're also likely to hear more people say something other than *soda* (*coke* in Evansville, *pop* in Fort Wayne). But not so in St. Louis, where 93 percent of people say *soda* — the second-highest concentration anywhere outside the Northeast. Milwaukee is at 94 percent.

The last St. Louis tick is Missouri's word for the small roads that run parallel to highways. What do you call them? If you say *frontage roads,* there's about an 80 percent chance that you're from the Kansas City portion of the state instead of the St. Louis portion, where it's more likely that you say *service roads* or *outer roads.*

If you find yourself in a room full of Missourians and want to figure out whether you're talking to someone from Kansas City or St. Louis—without being so forward as to ask—just watch for whether they

- say *soda,*

- don't call those small roads *frontage roads,* and

- pronounce *cot* and *caught* differently.

If they meet all three criteria, there's a 95 percent chance you're talking to someone from St. Louis.

HOW TO PRETEND YOU'RE FROM
OKLAHOMA

Head on down to the *beer barn* and bring the brews back to your house in a *sack*. In Oklahoma the first syllable of *lawyer* sounds like *law* and the last syllable of *Texas* sounds like it's spelled with a *z*. Use a *tea towel* to dry your dishes, and head down to the *creek* to catch some *crawdads*. This speech region bleeds over into the Texas Panhandle to the west and parts of Arkansas to the east.

HOW TO PRETEND YOU'RE FROM
KENTUCKY

Where *crayon* sounds like *krown*, highways are *expressways,* and *you all* might order a *soft drink* or a *coke* with your *carry-out*. Try some *Kentucky oysters* (chitterlings, pronounced *chit-lins*), if you have the stomach for them (they're made from the small intestines of freshly slaughtered pigs). If not, perhaps stick with the *Kentucky jam cake* instead—a layer cake with jam blended into the batter, often served with caramel *icing* (not *frosting*).